NIGHTFALL IN THE FOREST OF BROKEN DREAMS

A TALE OF MAGIC & LIES

THE NIGHTFALL SERIES BOOK 2

LOREN TUXFORD

Cover, map & text by Loren Tuxford
Character Portrait Illustration by Erika Mae Saguran

ISBN: 978-0-6486367-2-4 (eBook)
ISBN: 978-0-6486367-3-1 (Paperback)

A catalogue record for this book is available from the National Library of Australia.

www.lorentuxford.com

by Loren Tuxford

The Nightfall Series:
Nightfall in the Forest of Betrayal
Nightfall in the Forest of Broken Dreams
Nightfall in the Forest of Destiny
Nightfall in the Forest of Burning Hearts (2026)

Content Warning

The Nightfall Series is an epic fantasy tale featuring multiple POVs. It contains mature themes such as mild violence, coarse language, and romance (MF in Book 1, MF & MM from Book 2 onward).

Dedication

For little Loren.
The monsters weren't under the bed,
they were among the trees, full of mirth.

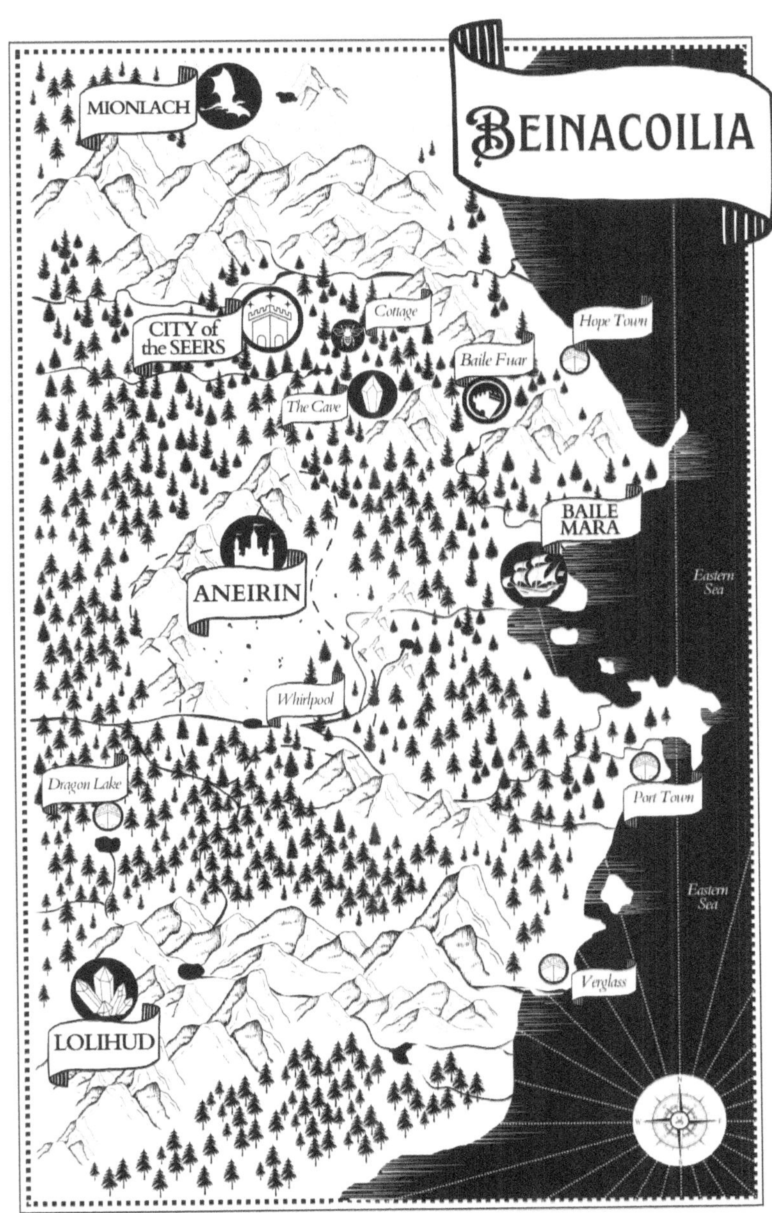

MIONLACH
BEINACOILIA
CITY of the SEERS
Cottage
Hope Town
Baile Fuar
The Cave
BAILE MARA
ANEIRIN
Eastern Sea
Whirlpool
Dragon Lake
Port Town
Eastern Sea
Verglass
LOLIHUD

Contents

PROLOGUE

Seedlings

"A seedling is the shoot of a new seed as it first reaches above the ground. As the young tree reaches for the light, it is an act of infinite creation and wonder. However, it is at this point that a tree is at most risk of damage."

Taken from 'Plant Lore for the Continent of Beinacoilia' by Hypatia Carter, commissioned for the Library of Seers.

Added underneath in an expressive scrawl:

'My dear wife, we never wanted children, but our boys are a delight, and cause for much study. May we be upstanding in their care, in the same way that you tend those blasted crystals and seeds.

x Illarion'

Rhydian

Year 367

Aneirin Castle

The weeping child crouched alone in the forest.

Warm night air caressed his face and tasted of green ferns and wet rocks. Above, there were no stars to be seen through the giant trees. Nearby, just audible over the sighs and whispers of dark green leaves, was the bubble and echoes of a river. And amongst the symphony of the nighttime forest was the sound of something big moving in his direction.

The little boy wasn't afraid, but he was sad. He remembered the librarian telling him of a dark night falling upon his family's kingdom, and the people who lived within.

Wiping his face with damp hands, the boy felt the earth under his bare feet shift with a heavy weight as the big creature moved past him through the trees. The creature stopped and paused. Around them, the forest noises quietened. The little boy held his breath.

A soft, muffled sound came from the creature. The child let out a slow breath but stayed where he was in the shadows. The creature was digging.

As the boy wiped his face again, he inhaled. There was a fresh scent, something metallic and hot. Words shifted inside his heart and mind; something broke free of the fog inside of him. The gloom of the forest shifted, and the boy gasped.

The creature was a dragon.

The boy blinked away his tears, his vision clearing with each movement of wet eyelashes. Before him, the dragon was impossibly large, its scales a shimmering ripple of radiance that shifted and changed to colours the boy could not name. It was like rainbows had come together to animate a creature made of glass and shifting lights.

Dragon, the boy mouthed silently. And with the word came a heart-wrenching pang of guilt. The boy winced. He didn't understand why.

Despite the deep shadows of the night above, the forest was growing lighter. A soft mist was forming where the figure was digging. He took a tentative step forward.

The little boy jerked his hands to his mouth to muffle a shout of surprise.

Like a popping cork from some unearthly bottle of mead, a column of green light burst forth from the ground at the dragon's claws. The bright column, like crystallised light, seared up out of the earth, through the canopy above towards the midnight sky. The boy's gasp turned to a sigh of wonder. He could see shapes within the light, like the treasure from his favourite stories: jewels and emeralds and fairies and stars and gold.

As the light shone brighter and brighter, the shining dragon paused its digging. With its great claws dripping dirt, it turned to the little boy, and the earth shuddered as it reared up on its hind legs. Its great size was revealed to the child, and the boy trembled in awe. In a slow pageant of strange shapes, shadows and reflections, the glowing green column of light silhouetted the beautiful, rainbow-filled creature. The boy tilted his head up, up, and up, to meet a pair of large metallic eyes.

'Go back.'

The voice rang like a bronze gong in the little boy's mind.

The child felt dizzy as his eyes struggled to make sense of the shapes in the column of light, and the great shining gaze of the dragon upon him. Light was expanding and glittering in an iridescent green fog of rippling energy. The earth trembled.

'Go back. The sun has risen. The son must live. Go back.'

The voice sounded again, this time echoing in the child's bones.

The child stepped back in alarm, coming up against something behind him. He cried out, but then another voice, a woman's voice, drifted past him from behind.

'Go back, Rhydian.'

Her voice was a soft whisper in his ear compared to the dragon's startling words. The words wavered around him like moth wings fluttering, not quite landing on his skin.

'Rhydian, she is coming.'

Firm hands clasped his shoulders, and the chilled touch caused a fission of shock to ripple down his spine. Accompanied by the scent of dried flowers and strange spices, the woman bent her head close to his, luminous pearlescent hair falling like a curtain around them.

'Go back, Rhydian. She is coming.'

The child sunk to his knees in the soft moss.

'I can't leave,' he sobbed, clawing at the rumbling ground, tears dropping onto the lush forest floor. 'I must stay, I must make amends...' What for? The little boy didn't know. He only knew that he must.

'You can if you go back,' the feminine voice called from somewhere amongst the trees. 'Please child, go back.'

With sticky, dirty hands, the boy continued to dig, searching for the same green light that was pulsing behind the looming dragon. But as much as the child scrabbled at the earth, no light burst forth for him. Crying out in frustration, he pressed his face into the trembling earth, a roaring in his ears. It felt like his mind was coming apart.

Behind the great shimmering dragon, the emerald column of light suddenly fractured into glowing green embers, spiralling about on a violent wind. The boy's consciousness faded even as the light expanded, like a green sun through the nighttime forest.

Words spoken in the endless light made it to him before his mind collapsed upon itself. The little boy wasn't sure if it was the woman or the dragon.

'You must find a way to stop her, and him too.'

Pain choked him, and his throat felt strange, hot and cold all at once.

Who? he tried to say, but his voice wouldn't come. The pain in his throat grew worse as the surrounding forest faded. Right before the blackness enveloped him completely, the woman's ethereal voice came again before the world went dark.

'Go back...'

PART ONE

Maturity

"After many seasons, a tree will find its place in the forest. Its roots will touch the roots of others, in the depths of the life giving soil. And finally, it will bud, and bloom. And seeds will fall. Like a single shooting star among the billions across the heavens, perhaps a seed may find itself carried across the forest, and find a safe space for nurturing and growth."

Taken from 'Plant Lore for the Continent of Beinacoilia' by Hypatia Carter, commissioned for the Library of Seers.

Added underneath in an expressive scrawl:

'My dear wife, no matter what happens, I am with you, with our boys. Our motives were true. Even if our actions were questionable. All my love,

x Illarion'

1

Rhydian

Year 367

Aneirin Castle

Rhydian drifted towards consciousness, into shimmering light and pain.

Gasping in agony, his eyes opened. Even in the gloom, Rhydian could see there was a tiny metallic dragon clasped to his bare chest, minute claws digging into his flesh. Flare's small scaly face pressed to Rhydian's nose; despite being out of focus, he could see that the dragon's purple snout was covered in fresh blood.

Rhydian tried to move. He found that he couldn't.

"Rhydian! Get up!" Flare wailed, frustration and fear in his shining eyes.

Rhydian tried to answer that he would very much like to.

He passed out again instead.

The room was still. A single candle, its flame a strange blue, was burning on a side table nearby.

Rhydian came to once more. He blinked, eyelids dragging over dry eyes, wondering at the candle flame's odd colour.

He was slouched in his favourite wooden chair, lungs wheezing with shallow breaths. His heart was shuddering out a sickly rhythm within, and his flesh was clammy.

Barely able to turn his head towards the bed, Rhydian's gaze met a tiny pair of eyes. Blue flames were reflected in each, two tiny points of light. Childish images drawn on forgotten castle walls came back to him.

A dragon.

Aurelia.

The dagger.

"The dagger," Rhydian choked out, coughing out a small spray of blood. His neck felt like it was on fire. "Shit."

On the bed, Flare swallowed. With the dry rustle of leathery wings, the dragon lifted into the air and glided across the room. He landed on Rhydian's chest, and his tiny pincer claws caught at Rhydian's skin. The blood on the dragon's snout looked dry now, brownish purple in the blue light of the candle.

"Flare," Rhydian wheezed, trembling, "sharp..."

"Rhydian! Don't close your eyes! I can't face h-him without you! We need-"

Rhydian gasped as Flare's claws jerked in time with his speech.

"Slow d-down," said Rhydian, trying to swat the dragon away. His arms had yet to obey him, however.

There was a sigh of frustration. But Flare's claws stopped their painful twitching.

"You can do this," Flare muttered to himself. "It's only a little magic."

Where the dragon's claws met Rhydian's aching chest, there was heat, pulsing in time with the dragon's breath. With his eyes closed, Rhydian could feel the heat spread, and his skin tingled as it rushed to his extremities. Eventually, the waves of healing faded, and no longer icy, Rhydian sighed with relief. Able to shift his head a little, he glanced down at himself.

Tears gathered in his eyes as he beheld blood drying to a sticky mess over his chest, arms and thighs. It had even splashed over his chair and onto the stones below.

Flare's hot puff of breath in Rhydian's face tore his eyes from the grisly scene.

"Your flesh was fighting me," Flare panted, "but now the sun has set, it was easier done."

"What?" Rhydian wheezed.

"Ah... no matter. What I need you to do is get up. *Now.*"

They stared at each other, Flare's breathing short and quick, Rhydian's a struggling, painful sound.

"What happened? I thought I wouldn't die... my father... Aurelia-"

A racking cough cut Rhydian's words off. The spray of purple red droplets had only one place to go, which explained the blood on the dragon's snout. Some wild burst of hysteria made him want to laugh at Flare's expression. Instead, his lungs twisted in a painful spasm.

Flare dug his clawed feet deeper into Rhydian's chest, and the pain forced Rhydian's eyes wide open. He nodded in understanding, his limbs tingling, feeling and a vague strength coming back to his extremities.

Rhydian pushed away from the chair with shaking hands, intending to stand. He slipped forward off the chair instead.

"Ah, shit," he gasped, falling.

His legs were unable to support his weight and his knees gave way, leaving him kneeling on the floor. Rhydian cursed in pain as his barely working hands flailed out and connected with the bloody floor. Flare flapped madly away to avoid being crushed.

Coughing, Rhydian pushed himself upright. On his knees, he sagged back against the leg of the chair. Below him, the floor was red, sticky. The metallic smell made him gag.

"If you're up, then get up," Flare called from above. The dragon swooped overhead and dropped something into Rhydian's head. "I need your help to find her!"

His sluggish mind worked hard to process Flare's words. Dragging the item off his head, he realised it was a shirt. He was weak and bloody, but the healing of earlier was helping the strength to bloom in his arms and legs. He hung his head, letting feeling and energy return while he caught his breath. By the strange blue candle, he could just make out a crystalline green shape on the stones beside him.

It was the dagger, lying innocently in a pool of his blood.

Looking at it made him want to throw up. He swallowed and peered down at the shirt that the dragon had dropped onto him.

"Get up, get dressed and come. *Now.*"

It was painful, but Rhydian managed to slip first one arm and then the other into the dark shirt. He hissed when he stretched his arms to pull it down over his head and shoulders. Rhydian cursed as Flare dropped pants onto the sticky floor. He snatched them up with a trembling hand and stood with small, careful movements.

As feeling returned, he was sore all over. But the pain helped clear his mind. After he was clothed, Rhydian ran a hand through his sweaty hair. The room was cool, but the effort left him feeling like he'd run up his tower stairs.

"Aurelia," Rhydian said quietly, "she went through with it." Trembling fingers traced the sharp ache over his throat. "And I let her."

As if the words were a spell, all at once, the last of the fog in his mind cleared away. Not just from what Aurelia had done, but the fog that had been laid upon him by his father.

Where was his father now?

Did he know what Rhydian had done, some wild attempt to break his father's magic open and allow light to shine over his family's lies?

Earlier, Rhydian had waited, his anxiety growing as the hours passed. But finally, as if his concern had summoned her, Aurelia had slipped into his chamber. They'd made love. He'd said a prayer to the gods who maybe never listened and closed his eyes, willing the magic binding over his people to break.

Aurelia had slit his throat.

And Rhydian had let her.

But had it worked? Had it broken the dark hold that magic had over his people and hers?

Was it enough?

"Rhydian! Open your eyes!"

Tiny claws grabbed Rhydian's shirt collar, and he was face to face with the dragon. Rhydian realised he was slumped in the chair once more. He had blacked out again.

"I have healed you. You must now help me! We need to go after Aurelia, and Fox likes you more than me. So let's go!" Flare hissed, his snout stuck right against Rhydian's face, with only drying blood between them.

"Aurelia," Rhydian murmured.

Rhydian touched his neck, feeling oddly calm. Blinking at Flare, the purple dragon's features blurred with that of the fading memory of his dream. There had been another dragon, indescribably beautiful. The dragon had... had what? Rhydian shook his head. The room spun.

Aurelia, where are you?

"We're going to help her?" Rhydian mumbled. "Not hurt her? I know she didn't do this for-"

"Yes! You need to help me find her before she does it to herself. Fox is unconscious, Aurelia has gone while I was... If Aurelia is hurt, Fox will," the dragon sobbed. "This wasn't supposed to happen." Flare pressed his face even closer. "Now, get up!"

At the dragon's frantic hiss, something dark broke across Rhydian's vision. There was a ringing in his ears. Rhydian's hands whipped up, clasping the tiny reptile, crushing leathery wings to the scaled body. Flare squeaked in shock, purple eyes wide.

Neither of them moved. Rhydian's heart thundered in his chest, and the blue candle dimmed. Slowly, the dark haze lifted.

"Rhydian?" said Flare, his eyes wide with shock.

Rhydian stared at Flare and thought of the power within the unassuming creature, the magic that could expand and shift. And manipulate. He also thought of dragon bones amongst the solemn, giant trees.

He opened his hands.

Eyes wide, Flare unhooked his claws delicately from Rhydian's collar and ruffled his wings. Neither of them spoke.

The blue flame of the candle glowed brighter.

"I'm sorry," Rhydian managed. "I don't know what came over me, Flare." Rhydian cleared his throat. "Please. Tell me what to do."

2

Flare

Year 367

Aneirin Castle

"Poke him with your boot!"

At the top of the steps leading down into the courtyard, Rhydian's trembling hand grabbed one of the great doors for support. He turned to stare at the dragon, peering out from inside Rhydian's hood.

"Poke *Fox* with my f-fucking *boot*?" Rhydian wheezed, incredulous.

Fox was unconscious near the top of the steps, sprawled out on his side, legs half folded awkwardly beneath him. Fox's black cloak was draped like a shadowy puddle underneath him. His inky black hair was a wild mess around his face, his lips covered in blood still trickling from his nose.

"Flare, t-tell me honestly," Rhydian panted, clutching his throat. "Do you think you could bring me b-back from *that* certain death?"

Flare peered past the edge of Rhydian's hood. Even unconscious, Fox had a menacing aura around him like a gloomy shroud.

"Hm. Perhaps not."

Fox was volatile at the best of times. But an unconscious Fox? Flare didn't know what to expect. What he did know was that they had to keep moving.

"Aurelia's scent is fresh, and we need to find her. You, ah, we need to wake him up."

Rhydian tried to say something, but his wheeze turned into more coughing instead. He was upright, but the prince was clearly not yet fully recovered. Flare winced, feeling like he had already spared enough of his power, in sealing the wound on the prince's neck. The curse was breaking apart. That was true. Enough blood had been spilt across the castle stones for the years-old binding to break open. But Flare dared not leave Aurelia alone after such a task. And he refused to think about what Fox would do to him if Aurelia was harmed in any way.

She'd disappeared by the time he'd returned to the prince's chamber, after leaving them alone for privacy. He'd returned too late to be there for her when she'd needed him most. Another error of his own making. Flare cursed under his breath.

Tasting the air, Flare detected the bitter tang of the broken curse and the fading scent of a familiar floral aroma. "I can track Aurelia if she's not far. We need to *move*."

Rhydian glanced around. Taking a rasping breath, the prince dropped his hand from the doorway.

"Fuck it."

Gingerly, Rhydian stuck out the toe of his boot and nudged Fox's limp hand. Flare shrunk deeper into the folds of Rhydian's cloak.

Nothing happened. The unconscious man didn't move.

Rhydian's sigh turned into another deep, racking cough. Flare was about to suggest something even more drastic, but he paused at the sound of approaching horses, hooves clopping over the cobbles from the shadows. Flare stuck his head back out of Rhydian's hood as the prince turned, still wheezing.

It was Jessikah. She was leading three horses by their bridles, two browns and a grey. Stumbling a little as she walked, Jessikah looked as sullen and miserable as Flare had ever seen. A bloodied smear under her nose, and across her cheek, had dried into a grisly parody of a smile.

"Jessikah? What happened?" Flare hissed in vain. Jessikah had been mute ever since he had first met her.

Jessikah brought the horses to the bottom of the steps. She stared at Fox, eyes narrowed, filled with such an intensity that when her gaze travelled up to Rhydian and Flare, the little dragon flinched. Wiping her nose with the hem of her tunic, she shrugged, a cruel smile twisting her lips. Flare shifted his wings. He turned away from Jessikah's yellow eyed smirk to whisper into the prince's ear.

"Rhydian, perhaps-"

A vicious snarl cut off his words. Rhydian was jerked backwards.

With a startled flap, Flare launched into the air, twisting clear. He glanced back in time to see the prince get slammed against the wall beside the open doors.

Fox was awake.

Landing on an ornately carved part of the castle wall above, Flare hopped from claw to claw. Fox had a white hand wrapped around Rhydian's throat, while the prince clawed desperately, his boots dangling madly above the steps. The prince was trying to speak, his face turning red.

"Auurrnnggg..."

"What did you do?" Fox hissed, his face centimetres from the prince.

"Rrrelllnngg..." Rhydian choked again.

"What happened?" Fox snarled, jerking the struggling man.

Rhydian's hands were less frantic against Fox's deadly grip. His face was turning a darker shade of red.

Flare took a breath. "Fox!"

Fox stiffened. He turned to glare up at Flare. The man was swaying slightly, but his gaze was full of violence. Flare's stomach lurched, and he swallowed.

"Fox! Please. The prince did nothing wrong!"

Fox's eyes narrowed to black slits. In his grip, Rhydian struggled wildly. Fox ignored him.

Flare flapped his wings. "Aurelia is gone!"

"Auuurrr..." moaned Rhydian, clearly desperate for air.

Fox turned back to the prince and stared at the slowly suffocating man for a moment. Eventually, his grip relaxed around Rhydian's throat. The prince's great wheezing inhalations showed how close the prince had been to asphyxiation. The prince slid down the wall and Rhydian's boots made contact with the top step. Fox's hand twitched around Rhydian's neck. The prince's hands stayed firmly wrapped around Fox's wrists.

The bloody mess of Fox's face twisted into a scowl.

"Where is she?" Fox snapped. He jerked Rhydian against the wall.

"F-fuck," the prince coughed, "you."

Flare held his breath, but Fox only blinked. With a twitch, he released the prince and stepped back onto the step below. Rhydian stayed where he was, rubbing his throat and breathing deeply. Surprising Flare, instead of retreating to safety, Rhydian stepped down. He grabbed the dark material of Fox's shirt.

"I'm trying to help her," Rhydian gasped directly into Fox's white face.

He opened his mouth to speak further, but Rhydian's legs gave out. He overbalanced, sliding down Fox's front. Rhydian fell to his knees, hands grasping Fox's thighs, gasping for air. A surprised squeak escaped Flare as Fox sunk down to his own knees. He caught the prince, hands steadying Rhydian's shoulders.

Flare glided down to land on the step. Fox's head was bent towards the prince.

"I'm sorry," Fox murmured, sounding pained. "After what she had to do, I didn't realise you were helping her. I didn't think you'd actually go through with this."

"I don't care what you think," Rhydian snapped with a dry rasp. "I accepted what was going to happen. It's done. Now help us help her."

Flinty black and gold eyes met Flare's over the prince's shoulder. With a twist of his lips, Fox broke their stare. The man's black hair was a wild tangle, as his gaze found Jessikah with the horses below them. She shrank back; the horses shifting uneasily around her.

Fox nodded, straightened up with his usual scowl across his bloody face, and offered the prince his hand.

"Let's go."

Don't move, don't move, don't move, Flare repeated to himself. He was trying to concentrate on any thread of Aurelia's faint Elven magic, or her floral aroma.

The dragon was back inside the folds of Rhydian's hood, who was on the grey horse. Flare's wide eyes were glued to the pair of arms reaching around the prince below, white hands holding the reins.

Flare winced. Fox's cool breath was only centimetres from where Flare was shuddering, and his wings twitched with each cold passage of air.

Like a barely restrained deadly storm, Fox was on the same horse as Rhydian. He sat behind the prince, arms around the still recovering young man, keeping Rhydian upright as they trotted down the steep roads. Rhydian's mad dash down the tower hadn't opened up the gash in his neck, but had left the prince reeling. And being near strangled by Fox hadn't helped. His coughing had slowed, although his voice was still hoarse.

They had left the courtyard, following the trace of Aurelia's scent on the air, making their cautious way down the steep switchback roads of the city. Despite their haste, it seemed prudent to leave without too much noise, and quicken their pace once outside the city walls. Jessikah was riding ahead on the tallest brown horse and leading the spare. As they passed each set of gates in the walls, Fox shifted uncomfortably. The prince remained silent as they rode by, the telltale drops of blood evidence of what had happened.

"Your guards," Fox said, grimly, "I expect most will wake up." He paused. "At some point."

The prince said nothing.

"It shouldn't have happened like this," Fox offered.

The prince cleared his throat.

"They were all good men and women," he rasped. "This wasn't their fault."

"I know," Fox murmured.

Flare watched pale hands tightened on the reins.

It was just before the dawn, but many houses had the telltale illuminated crack of light behind closed shutters. Candles and lanterns had been lit; all would have heard the roll of thunder cracking across the land as royal blood spread over the floor in the castle. But no one was on the streets, apart from the occasional alley cat that hissed at the riders as they made their way past.

Jessikah looked back, and Flare could feel Fox behind them jerk his chin at the woman. Now that they were approaching the last gate, she increased their pace, and the prince used his knees to encourage their mount to follow. Eventually, Rhydian broke the noise of the horse's hooves on the cobbled streets.

"Is the curse fully lifted?" the prince croaked over the noise of the horse's hooves on the road.

A wet sniff came from behind. One of Fox's hands disappeared from the reins for a moment, only to return with fresh blood on the back of it.

"I feel like I can breathe now. But," Fox muttered, his bitter voice caressing Flare like a glacial breeze, "Ask the dragon."

"What?" Flare squawked.

What did Fox know?

Was Fox implying he knew something of what had happened all those years ago?

He had to exercise all his self-control to not fly screaming off into the night at the thought.

"You heard me, lizard."

"Um." Flare was thinking frantically. "Not fully. But the magic is breaking."

"How would Flare know?" interrupted Rhydian, coughing again as they reached the lowest gate, with the open farmland beyond.

Their horse's hooves rang loudly in the night. Jessikah and the spare horse continued ahead of them. As Fox spoke again; Aurelia's scent grew stronger.

"Your father might be a powerful magic user, princeling, but this curse was something else. One can assume another great magic user, say, a dragon perhaps, must have helped."

Flare bit his tongue.

"Flare?" The prince paused. "Wait, how did Aurelia get past you, Fox?"

There was silence. A pale hand twitched on the reins. There was silence apart from the horses and the jingle of tack as the farmlands of Aneirin sped by.

"Fox?" Rhydian prodded.

Fox cleared his throat.

"She fucking knocked me out."

A rasping sound from the prince startled Flare. Rhydian was laughing.

"Fuck you," Fox said, unamused.

"I'm s-sorry," Rhydian wheezed, trying to be heard over the thud of their horse's hooves. "I'd liked to have seen that."

"Hilarious," Fox muttered. "And how about you, Flare? How did Aurelia get past *you?*"

Flare, trying to sound calm, dug his claws into the prince's cloak. "I left to... um, give them privacy. I went to the library... I returned after..."

"You can say it," Rhydian sighed with a croak. "After we made love. After she..." Rhydian shivered, and one of his hands reached up to his throat. "After she broke the curse with that blasted dagger."

Flare stared straight ahead at the dark countryside opening up before them, at the form of Jessikah ahead of them. Even with their horse's hooves loud on the packed dirt road, it was eerie.

Flare cleared his throat, his voice barely a whisper from the prince's hood. "I should have been there for her. I'm sorry."

"If she's not alright," Fox's voice was full of deadly promise, "you fucking will be."

Flare didn't respond.

He *would* be sorry if Aurelia hurt herself, lost to despair. How could she have known that Rhydian would come back from what she had done? Flare hadn't. But when he had returned to find Aurelia gone, the scent of her terror in the air, Flare had realised he had to try. It had pained him to leak his magic away, with no chance of crystals to refuel himself nearby.

Her task was supposed to be straightforward. But it hadn't worked out that way. Aurelia had trained her whole life to undo the curse so the Elder One, once a queen, could reclaim what was taken from her all those years ago. The Elves would attack and overthrow the king before he made a move of his own. Flare grimaced. It had been guilt that had kept him close to the queen while she planned.

It wasn't over yet though, even with the prince's blood spilt over the stones.

Thinking of the battle to come, Flare wondered if it ever would be.

Flare stuck his head further out of Rhydian's hood. They were halfway between Aneirin City and the forest.

Before them, the road stretched on ahead, to the dark line of the immense trees and the churning river, where Aurelia's floral scent led. The open farmlands around them spread out on either side of the road, with various crops at different stages of their life cycles. Forgetting himself, Flare twisted back to examine the vista behind. Behind them, under the gloomy sky, the castle loomed like part of the mountains. And right before him, Fox's smoldering gaze was narrowed maliciously at Flare.

The dragon jolted with a squeak. Fox's eyes narrowed until two flinty slits glared at him, centimetres from his trembling form.

Flare whipped his head back around to Rhydian.

"We're close! I'm taking to the air now!" he gushed, then took off for the relative safety of the sky. He could feel Fox's cold eyes on him even then.

Swallowing, Flare tried to concentrate on Aurelia's scent as the horses below passed through wide expanses of grain fields. The crops spread out, undulating like a black sea. Thankfully, the air outside of the city had lost the bitter tang of the broken curse as the binding magic was coming undone.

Soon, though, Flare was tiring as he flew. Expending his magic to help Rhydian had drained his emotional, physical, and magical reserves. There were no crystal mines here that he knew of, and no elves to dig them out of the earth for him. He pushed his weariness away and concentrated on the ground below.

"There are no tracks in the fields. She must still be on the road," Flare called down.

Aurelia, where are you?

Please, whatever you think you need to do in penance, just don't!

The Elder one would know what had happened, Flare was sure of it. Would she care that Aurelia had completed her task at the expense of Aurelia's own pure heart? And where was the king? Surely he had felt and heard the curse come undone?

"Stay with me, princeling," Fox demanded below.

Flare glanced down. Rhydian had slumped forward. The horse under them danced a few uncertain steps out of its steady rhythm as the prince straightened up.

"Sorry," the prince mumbled. "I've had better days."

"You're alive, aren't you?" Fox snapped. Rhydian turned awkwardly to stare at Fox.

"What's wrong with you?" rasped the prince.

"What?"

Even seen from above, Flare could see Fox's expression was clearly one of incomprehension.

"I'm alive, yes," Rhydian croaked. "But barely, because you *choked* me after Aurelia..." Rhydian's voice faded into a dry cough, and his hand went to his throat.

"Oh." Fox's expression cleared. "You're right. Here."

Flare flew back across the road, eyes peeled for Aurelia. As he passed over the horses again, one of Fox's pale hands moved from the reins to Rhydian's chest. In the fading darkness below, a soft blue glow came to life under Fox's hand, accompanied by his cool voice.

"Better?"

"Yes." Rhydian cleared this throat. "Thank you."

The prince's voice was still dry, but it was stronger. Flare's eyes widened. As he flew down low again, he got a better look at Fox's face. His black eyes were sweeping the road, the fields, and the ditches as they passed. The man seemed unaffected by healing the prince.

"Tell me something Rhydian," Fox murmured, barely loud enough for Flare to catch as he swooped low again. A long finger tapped the side of Rhydian's head. "The fog. Is it gone?"

"I think so," the prince's reply was faint. "When I was out cold, I had a dream."

"Keep up!" Fox called to Jessikah, whose horse had slowed its pace. Then to the prince, "A dream?"

"Before Flare revived me. There was a woman and a dragon."

"A dragon? Is that so?" Fox watched as Flare passed above their heads again. His expression was unreadable. "What colour was it?"

Flare nearly fell out of the sky.

Of all the questions to ask, how would Fox know to ask that?

Flare flew high, getting away from the angry gold sparks in Fox's eyes. The man's gaze followed Flare through the sky. Unfortunately, Flare missed the prince's answer. But Fox's earlier remarks came to Flare's mind about the king requiring powerful help. A bleak shiver rippled along his scales.

It wasn't until they were close to the forest that Flare dared enough to fly lower, his wings aching, his head spinning with worry.

Fox glared at the dragon for a moment, then lowered his gaze. "You are the child of a magical king, princeling," Fox was saying. "You could find out for yourself." He nosed the back of the prince's hood. "If you want."

Dammit! What had they been discussing?

The prince's voice was faint. "All I want right now is Aurelia, safe and in my arms."

As the dawn sky lightened further into radiant streaks of pale light, the breeze shifted. Flare gave a cry of triumph.

"She's close!"

"Can you tell what direction?" Rhydian called.

"What else is here?" Fox asked as he glanced around. "Besides the farms?"

"Nothing," the prince replied. "Just the meadow with the stone circle, the river, and then the forest."

Fox sat up straighter. He seemed to be lost in thought, and he tilted his head, listening just as the horse beneath them called out with a shrill whinny.

There was an answer ahead, from a horse trotting towards them out of the gloom. There was no rider upon its back. Rhydian made a strangled noise, and they sped past the grey beast while it blinked at them in confusion, watching them go. Full of dread, with a sorry flap of wings, Flare landed back on Rhydian's shoulder. He kept his wings tight to avoid any contact with Fox.

"Why doesn't she need the horse?" Flare hated the panic in his voice.

Fox hissed as another noise greeted them. A low, rumbling hum.

"What is it, Fox?" Rhydian asked, twisting. Flare had to duck out of his way.

"The river," Fox murmured.

"What?" Flare squeaked.

"Aurelia can swim. But that won't matter if the current is strong."

"Fuck," Rhydian's voice was full of shock. "The whirlpool. *Shit*! Hurry!"

Flare trembling; held on tighter as Fox kicked his heels into the horse's flanks and their fast trot quickened into a gallop. The river wasn't far ahead.

"Flare," Rhydian bit out. Fox's arms were tight around him to stop him from being bucked off the straining horse. "You saved my life."

Flare remained silent, concentrating on following the scent. Dreading that it was getting stronger the closer the river became.

"I thought you didn't like me," the prince continued.

The tiny dragon shook his head, impatient. "I'm not sure I do."

"You saved my life," the prince's voice was soft. "I owe you."

Flare had saved Rhydian's life. Not just for the guilt he felt about the curse, but for the sake of Aurelia.

"Just help Aurelia for me," Flare hissed. "This isn't her fault, she shouldn't be caught up in this."

"I will," gasped Rhydian. "I promise."

Fox's voice had a chilling quality to it, mirroring the coldness of the dark seas of grain and grasses speeding by. "I wonder whose fault it was."

Flare's eyes sprung open. Not only at the dark promise under Fox's words, but at the scent. It was strong, fresh. Around them, the fields had given way to the meadows, and the dark ring of stones was just visible off to their right. The river and the bridge were ahead, the distance closing rapidly as their horses raced on.

Fox cursed.

A lone figure, wrapped in a cloak, was on the bridge. They were sitting on the rail, boots dangling a few metres over the downstream current. Not far away was the whirlpool, a dark abyss. The rumbling here was loud.

"Aurelia!" Rhydian shouted, his voice cracking on her name. "Wait!"

Like a dark flower dropping from a dying tree, the figure separated from the bridge, falling. With barely a splash, the churning waters pulled the figure down, swift and deep.

Fox jerked their foaming horse to the left, following the dark current downstream, passing Jessikah's horse. As their horses finally skidded to a stop near the churning surface of the whirlpool, Rhydian slid from the horse, out of Fox's grasp. Flare hissed and flew upwards while Fox cursed, but Rhydian's terror for Aurelia had overcome his failing strength.

As Fox landed with a stumbling thud on the rocky ground, Rhydian had already plunged off the rocky bank into the violent water.

Astonished, Flare landed on the wet rocks, eyes wide. He turned to the shocked face of Fox.

"Why would he do that?" Flare cried. "He can't swim!"

"He can't swim?" Fox looked at Flare blankly. His pale face had whitened further. "And he just jumped in after her, after she slit his throat?" Fox shook his head, even as his mouth tightened in anger. "Bloody hell, it must be love after all."

Flare flapped hard, rising off his rock, landing on a boulder further out. "He can't swim! Help them!" he wailed.

"I am going to," Fox bit out. Stomping to the edge of the churning waters, he dropped his cloak, his sword belt and kicked off his boots.

"Keep watch," Fox hissed behind him, making his way quickly over the mossy rocks.

"For what?!" cried Flare.

"The king, you fucking idiot," came the snarled reply.

However, even as furious as Fox sounded, Flare could hear the fear beneath.

His wings aching, and his heart breaking in fear, Flare watched Fox leap off a boulder. His body arched as he dived deep into the deadly waters. The sun had not quite risen, and the river was a gloomy, milky grey. As Fox swam for the whirlpool, a sharp pang of guilt crossed through Flare's fear for Aurelia. Despite their mutual dislike, Fox was now another person at risk of injury or death, since Flare had been trying to undo the curse.

Flare was hopping from foot to foot in agitation, but suddenly he froze. Something was happening. His scales were prickling with the sense of... What? He looked up. The sun was breaking over the horizon in the east.

"The sun," Flare breathed, his eyes back on the river, watching the dark waters close over Fox.

As the man disappeared beneath the surface, a blinding light bloomed like an exploding star under the churning waters. And in the centre of the whirlpool, the river was lit from within. A powerful golden glow grew from a bright spark and then expanded rapidly outwards to span the entire width of the river. With a sound like shattering glass, the light burst up from the surface in achingly beautiful streamers of light. The golden streamers raced upwards to the sky, the world around them going quiet, only lasting for a few seconds before they faded into wisps of a pale mist.

Then the mist was gone, and slowly the noise of the river returned.

Dumbfounded, Flare stared at the water.

Just who was Fox, really? The possibilities of who he could be behind his icy façade, were too horrific for Flare's dragon brain to contemplate at that moment.

Shocked, Flare turned, meeting Jessikah's wide-eyed stare.

Dismounted on the bank, she gripped the reins tightly in her hand. Jessikah was shaking her head, mouth hanging open, looking like she would have cursed if she could talk.

Flare made do for them both.

"Holy hells," squeaked the dragon.

3

Aurelia

Year 367

The River, Aneirin Farmlands

A thousand memories and sensations flashed through Aurelia's mind, full of joy, determination, and pain.

Guilt.

No.

I didn't go through with it, did I?

The dagger. The prince.

No. He wasn't dead.

Yes.

Yes, I did.

I chose!

I chose for my people... I chose...

The dark waters closed above her head, and the current dragged her downstream, the whirlpool embracing her with liquid violence.

Rhydian's name was a gasp of bubbles from her blue lips, snatched away by the churning around her.

Rhydian.

Aurelia let herself go limp, letting the waters and memories carry her under.

A small child, barely walking, making painted shapes on the shimmering rock of her bedchamber walls. Swirls of purple, green, and blue paint. Spirals and stick figures, brave warriors and winged beasts and trees. Always trees. Stylised stick and blob shapes of trees. Forests of trees. Valleys, mountains and plains. Being summoned to the Elder One's private chambers, where promises of glory and triumph awaited. Strange, glittering eyes of the inky-haired man, wrapped in shadowy clothes like veiled, black mists.

Watching.

A young girl, running by herself through the caves. Counting the shapes and patterns of the marble slabs that made up the great chamber floors. Creating games and challenges to cross without falling into make-believe abyss and voids. Coming across the Shadow Man, her fingers stained with the ink destined for his icy skin. His fierce expression, softening at seeing her. His dark eyes.

Watching.

A young woman, exploring deep caves and icy outcrops. Letting the snow and the wind blow around her, freezing her lungs. The smile of victory on her face when she always felt the shadowy figure approach through icy, shifting winds, his presence cool and warm to her, all at once. His face amused. Watching.

A young woman, training. Forest lore, weapons, strength and endurance. Groups of other Elves of the caves, vying for glory. Training in dark caves full of strange bugs and bacteria that glowed and painted their pale faces with sickly washes of green and blue. The man that directed their efforts, arms crossed. Black and gold eyes on her.

Watching.

A woman determined to get what she felt was owed. Knowing her training had taken her as far as it could. Being chosen to carry out the spearhead of their campaign to take out the threat from the dark kingdom in the north. Sinking into glowing waters, the feel of a cool body behind her, taking her, holding her in powerful arms. The icy voice sending shivers through her body, her mind. His dark eyes.

Watching.

Always watching over her.

Something touched her face.

Aurelia jerked under the cold water, opening her eyes. A figure was sinking with her, trying desperately to reach her.

No.

She wanted to sink alone.

She wanted to get away from the horror of the blood, the sacrifice above. The waters here, while turbulent, would soothe her with the images of the past where all was known.

Aurelia clenched her eyes shut, and as something touched her again, she tried to fight the figure off.

Warm hands grabbed at her, and bubbles escaped her mouth. She wanted the stillness of the caves, the glowing pools. To feel icy arms around her again. Holding her. Letting her go. To sink in peace. Before the guilt burnt her up.

Let me go!

Her mouth filled with more water. She tried to fight the warm grip on her arms, but a hand caught her neck. Something else jerked at her hair. The waters spun them around and the noise of bubbles in her ears was as disorientating as the shifting currents that reached arms out, begging to sink her deeper.

Her hand flailed and connected with something.

The figure stilled. The warm grip on her neck was failing.

Warm hands.

Warm hands.

Her eyes snapped open.

The grip on her hair let go.

And then the sun came out.

Right under the water, a sun rose. Yellow, golden, blinding.

The bright light illuminated the blue on blue eyes of the figure before her. Eyes with life fading, even as the light grew brighter still.

In shock, Aurelia tried to yell, swallowing more cold water.

Rhydian!

This wasn't a hallucination. Was it? She'd never think of him with the life fading from his eyes. She had seen that already and would never forget it.

He was alive?

Or was this death's last cruel twist for her? A punishment?

Or was he right here, drowning to save her? *Her,* of all people? With the sun coming from nowhere and everywhere all at once around them.

The warm hand on her neck jerked again. His hair whirled around his face. But his eyes, with their pain and shock and sorrow, were dimming before her. Then his hand at her neck weakened still.

And finally, he let her slip away.

Bubbles escaped his mouth, his nose. He was drowning. Just like her. Aurelia reached out, hands clawed and grasping, water burning her lungs. The waters caught them, spinning them around, separating them further.

The light vanished.

All was dark.

Screaming underwater, Aurelia choked as the river rushed into her mouth.

Rhydian!

The water choked her further. The dark became darker still. Her eyes were stinging, her head throbbing, limbs straining against the press of waters, above, below, all around.

There was only water now. In her eyes, her ears, her mouth and lungs.

As her body started to spasm, the bubbles of her sodden cry rose to the surface as she sank. Until something else reached out from the watery void. It grabbed her floating hand, and Aurelia was enveloped with ice and snow. All at once, with a cruel jerk, she was rising.

Her hand was grasped by flesh colder than the turbulent, icy river water that even now tried to pull her down.

An *icy* hand.

Belonging to her Shadow Man, he who was always watching.

As her vision dimmed, Aurelia's frantic thoughts were on the two men who had *seen* her, who had wanted her to choose freely.

So she chose.

Fox!

She tried to yell, but water clogged her lungs.

Not me!

Save him, save Rhydian!

4

Fox

Year 367

The River, Aneirin Farmlands

The sun had crested the eastern horizon, but stars were still visible, shining against the last of the night sky. The lights seem to whisper secrets directly to his heart.

Not so cold, are you?

Lying on his back, panting, Fox shut his eyes to the stars. For some reason, the sky looked as golden as it appeared much further to the north. Was he hallucinating? Or was he so full of desperate, aching relief that the world had changed? The unfolding crest of rising emotions within him threatened to break free in a wave of absolute fury.

Water streamed off his face, dropping from his hair onto the rocks and pebbles underneath him. Blowing the droplets away from his mouth, irritated by a new tingling sensation across his skin, Fox grimaced. In the water that was streaming off of him, there was some remnant of the light, some remnant of the power, which had bloomed around the three of them while underwater. The sensation was like tiny bubbles popping and releasing over his skin. It was adding to the emotions riling up his guts. The knowledge that he should have prevented this, that he should have stepped in sooner, was shattering his control.

Calm down, Fox hissed to himself, *calm the fuck down.*

Yes, he was half drowned, something he didn't think was possible. But rescuing two idiots from the swirling waters had left what felt like half the river inside his lungs.

But at least Aurelia was safe. And so was her prince.

For now.

Rage choked his lungs, and he opened his eyes. He stared at the shining stars and the glittering gold of the dawn sky, with the river churning and humming beside him.

Was it worth this? Helping the Elder One out in her revenge? For it to come to this?

For not the first time if he was being honest, Fox didn't know. All he knew was rage, and beneath that, like a shard of ice in his heart, was the bone chilling fear of nearly losing his only friend. By her own hand.

The unwelcome feelings rose higher within him, but a wet cough beside him interrupted his spiralling thoughts.

It was Aurelia, sounding like she was spitting out half the river. Turning his head, Aurelia was on her hands and knees, retching over the rocks. Her green eyes met his for a moment, and then she hung her head, her wet hair covering her expression. But he'd seen it. She was ashamed.

And so she should be!

Unable to help himself, his heart pounding, Fox pushed himself up. His usual chill had been extinguished as his rage choked his throat like fiery sparks.

"For fuck's sake, Aurelia!" Fox yelled. "What the fuck was that?"

Aurelia opened her mouth, but Fox didn't let her drop a single syllable. Jerking himself to his knees, he slid over the wet rocks and grabbed her shoulders. He hauled her upright to her knees, so he could shout directly into her face.

"Don't *ever* fucking do that to me again!" Fox yelled, even louder.

He was full of too many feelings, *unwanted* feelings, so that he was trembling. As she winced, Fox glanced down, realising his fucking hands were icing up, adding to the chill that was turning her lips blue.

Fighting to catch his breath, Fox tried to summon the control that was clearly required to deal with this rage, this intoxicating fear, that was pulsing through him. Aurelia simply stared at him. As the ice slowly receded from his hands, she shook her head. It finally dawned on him that she was trembling, too. His rage instantly disappeared like steam in the snow.

"Oh Aurelia, don't," Fox whispered, gathering her close to him, her wet garments squelching as he hugged her tightly. In all likelihood, he was chilling her further, but he was unable to let her go. "Please don't do that again. Not that, *never* that."

She shuddered, and her forehead moved against him. She felt like a cold, damp animal trapped against a snowdrift.

"I'm s-sorry." Her words were a soft mumble against his chest. "I... it *hurts*."

"I know, Little Thing," Fox murmured against her wet hair, and then pulled back, blinking frost away from his lashes. "I know."

Shifting his legs to sit down, his legs straight out before him, he settled her between his thighs. Raising his gaze from her trembling form, Fox met the eyes of the prince.

Rhydian, kneeling not far away, was watching with wide eyes. At Fox's glare, the prince sniffed and looked down, watching river water stream from his clothes onto the shore beneath. Flare was nowhere to be seen. Jessikah was crouched nearby with the horses. Fox didn't think he could walk, or even crawl, anywhere just now.

Against Fox, Aurelia choked back a sob. He rubbed her back, attempting to soothe. It would never be enough, though he would try.

"Hey," Fox said, and kissed her wet hair. "Hush. I've got you now."

Her shaking only increased, and Fox wasn't sure what to do. "Hey," he murmured, "guess what?"

She mumbled something.

"Touching you like this, when you're this cold and miserable," he murmured. "It's like touching *myself*."

A sobbed snort was his only reply. Rhydian raised his head from behind her, his gaze disbelieving. The prince's lips moved silently, but clearly enunciating his words, which looked a lot like *thank you for saving my life, but you are an idiot*.

Fox ignored him and tried again.

"This isn't your fault," Fox said, quietly. "I'll do better next time, better prepare you, or step in and you won't ever have to-"

Aurelia pulled back, her damp cheeks catching the growing light of the dawn sky. But her green eyes were dull.

"What?" She sniffed. "*No*. I chose this! This was *my* choice..."

"Perhaps. But I should have been with you from the start to get this done..." Fox's voice faded away, his eyes back on the prince's. This time, Rhydian's gaze was cool, something different shining in his blue ringed eyes.

Aurelia coughed, trembling further, and the prince's blue eyes dropped to her shivering back. Fox wiped wet hair out of his face, pressing a hand to her back. Her lungs felt clear. Over her shoulder, blue eyes met his. Fox kissed Aurelia's wet hair again, his eyes on the prince, and raised his eyebrows. The prince nodded, shuffled closer, and held out his arms.

Turning Aurelia gently, Fox manoeuvred her to the prince. Rhydian's warm arms wrapped around her, and Fox could see the prince's face relax. His undying, unfathomable love was clearly written across his face. Aurelia stiffened at first, but as Fox unwound her hands gently from his sodden shirt, she relaxed back into the warmth against her. Her green eyes stared out at him, expressionless.

Turning away, Fox forced himself to stand up, wringing out the bottom of his shirt. Ignoring his shaking hands, Fox wiped dripping hair off his face once more. His gaze landed on the compact figure of Jessikah.

"Give them your cloak," he snapped at her. She stiffened. "Fetch mine."

With pursed lips, she dropped the reins of the restless horses and set to. Aurelia tried to get up, but Rhydian held her close, as she was still shivering. Jessikah stomped over and dropped her thin cloak around the prince and Aurelia. Rhydian murmured his thanks, all the while throwing Fox a dark look.

Fox shrugged off Rhydian's disapproval and looked up. Above them, the shimmering sky was growing steadily brighter, the honey gold bright and full of promise. Stars were winking out, one by lonely one. As much as Fox wanted Aurelia to warm up, they couldn't risk a fire. Guards would spot it from the castle walls easily, despite the distance.

Jessikah approached him cautiously, his great black cloak clasped in her small hands. Holding her yellow gaze, Fox stripped off his soaked black shirt. Behind him, Rhydian gasped as he caught the barest glimpse of Fox's tattoo. Even in the dim light of pre-dawn, it would be vivid and grotesque.

Fox smiled to himself as his cloak was shoved around his naked torso by small, shaking hands. She'd got it tangled around his neck somehow and there was a rough jerk against his throat, but at last the cloak settled around him. He raised an eyebrow at Jessikah as she stepped back, eyes wide, her hands clenched against her chest. There was blood still crusting under her nose from the effects of the curse; she hadn't washed it off yet.

Fox stepped towards the small woman, trying to gauge her unreadable expression. There was something there, but Aurelia's racking cough behind him pulled him up short. He narrowed his eyes at Jessikah before making his way back to the huddled figures on the bank beside him.

With his lips against Aurelia's wet hair, the prince's blue eyes met Fox's as he crouched down before them. Fox reached out and rested one hand on Aurelia's bent knee; his other clasped the prince's ankle.

The prince's eyes darkened and Fox smiled faintly.

"Thank you for saving me, for saving us," Rhydian said quietly, before clearing his throat. "Uh, that light, was that you?"

Fox raised his gaze from Rhydian and appraised the river to his left. The eastern horizon was a grim mix of night sky with the barest hint of the gold skies that shimmered within his mind.

"No. That wasn't me. But dawn is breaking," Fox murmured as he shook his head. Feeling water slide down his neck and face, he licked the water from his lips. Rhydian swallowed and shut his eyes. "I think the light was you, my prince."

The prince's eyes snapped open.

"The light?" Aurelia croaked. "Rhydian?"

"Yes," Fox said, his hand tightening on Aurelia's knee, simultaneously poking the prince's ankle with an icy finger. "There is a certain kind of symmetry. I suspect the curse had something to do with the dagger, a sacrifice, and the night sky. The dawn light, breaking the dark, might have been the last piece of it coming undone."

Aurelia nodded against Rhydian's chest, her hands clasped limply in her lap. Rhydian tried to speak, but coughed instead. The bruising on his throat was an angry dark mark in the dawn light. One of the prince's hands left Aurelia's back, and he rubbed his throat, blue eyes unfocused.

Aurelia looked up, and horror dawned on her face as she glimpsed his throat. "Rhydian…"

"Hush." Rhydian dropped his hand back to Aurelia's back, drawing her tightly to him. His eyes were glued to Fox's. "Flare healed me. *This* mark wasn't you."

Aurelia, her face pinched with worry, pulled away from Rhydian, following the direction of his gaze. Her wide eyes met Fox's.

Fox shrugged.

"Fox? What did you do to him?!" Aurelia rasped, her green eyes flinty.

Fox sat back on his heels and simply looked at her, eyebrows raised.

Aurelia looked indignant for a moment, before guilt flashed across her face. Her mouth formed an O. She bit her bottom lip and rested back against Rhydian, the man whom *she* had sliced open only a short while ago.

Fox looked up and around for Flare, but the purple little shit was nowhere to be seen.

"Is that how you are... here?" Aurelia asked tentatively, her hands twisting together.

"Yes, Flare healed me." Rhydian replied, his voice low.

"Oh."

"*Oh* indeed," snapped Fox. "I'm impressed with him using his preciously hoarded magic on you, princeling."

"None more than me," Rhydian admitted, wincing. "I know you don't like Flare, but considering the current circumstances, you should go easy on him-"

"*Go easy on him*?" Fox repeated, his voice dangerously low.

"Shut up, both of you!" Aurelia snapped, sounding angry and weary all at once. "You're both being ridiculous. This is *all* ridiculous. The Elder One, Rhydian, she's...." As the two men turned their faces to her in astonishment, her cheeks lost some of their pallor as she flushed. "I'm sorry. I...this is too much. I..."

"Hush," the prince murmured into her hair, his eyes avoiding Fox's fiery gaze. "It's over-"

"All of this is *not* over," Aurelia interrupted, sounding stronger now she was angry. "And you! You jumped in, not being able to swim! I thought I was hallucinating, you idiot...!"

Rhydian wiped her damp cheeks with his hand, wiping away her tears with a tenderness that had Fox's rage leech away, if only slightly.

"You're both idiots," Fox said coldly. "You both made choices freely. Which is exactly what needed to happen. You're both alive. So here we all are, half drowned, but alive. Now what? What's it going to be, Aurelia?"

"It's okay," Rhydian murmured to Aurelia, ignoring Fox, who flung up his hands impatiently. "I chose to be the sacrifice in order for this curse to be broken, and I chose to save you, too. My father will answer for this."

Aurelia shook her face against his chest.

"But it wasn't just the king..." her voice trailed into silence.

Fox met Rhydian's gaze over Aurelia's dark head. The prince stared steadily back, a muscle tensing in his jaw.

He knows, Fox thought. *He knows who else is involved here.*

Rhydian continued, something hardening in his blue eyes. "Someone needed to pay a price. And I suspect that you know all about that, Fox."

It took a moment to realise what Rhydian had said. Fox stared at the prince, fascinated by the new light in the prince's eyes.

"Do you?" The smile spreading across Fox's face didn't meet his eyes.

Rhydian held his gaze, and this time Fox looked away.

"Like I said, now what?" Fox said with an unaffected sniff.

Behind them, the whirlpool churned endlessly, and the sky was brightening from grey into a vast expanse of rich purple and burnished gold.

"Where's Flare?" asked Rhydian.

The prince turned around, and shaking out his wet hair while he searched. Some of the droplets caught Fox across the face, and Rhydian's lips twisted in a satisfied smile. Fox stared at him a moment, a muscle twitching in his jaw.

"I was wondering the same. But I suspect he is on lookout duty." Fox eventually answered, jerking his chin upwards. "Your father must know the curse is broken."

"That's good. We'll work out how to get you out of here safely, then, okay?" Rhydian asked, and then frowned. "Aurelia?"

Instead of answering, Aurelia dropped her head into her hands. She was clearly overcome with the events of the past few hours, and the past few days. Rhydian's expression turned immediately to concern, and he pressed his face to the top of her head, murmuring softy.

Standing up with a groan, Fox examined their location. Jessikah was wringing out his shirt. After watching for a moment, Fox touched his bare chest, feeling around under his cloak. He froze.

The gold chain, with its gold charm and topaz jewel, was lost. Gone forever.

Fox bit his lip, his dark gaze rising to take in the deadly waters offshore. The whirlpool hummed an endless song of depths, currents and of lost things.

Gone just like Owaen, who Fox had stolen the chain from, before stealing the man's life as well.

Fox watched Rhydian lead Aurelia to the horses. Her eyes were red, and she was moving stiffly. The prince wasn't looking too great either, but was doing better than his lover.

Arms crossed over his bare chest, Fox strode towards them. Perhaps the prince was feeling more certain of himself now that the curse was breaking apart.

Meanwhile, Fox's skin prickled only slightly now. The curse was indeed loosening its hold on the land.

"Ah, shit, my head hurts," Rhydian was muttering.

As he reached them, Fox snorted. "Is that all?"

"Don't," Aurelia whispered, looking sickened as Rhydian scowled at Fox. "Just don't."

Fox touched her arm, squeezing gently in a reluctant, wordless apology. He turned to Rhydian. "Do you have the dagger?"

Rhydian's mouth tightened. "Yes."

"Give it to her."

Rhydian glanced down at Aurelia. She was resting her head against the side of the horse, breathing slowly. Her damp hair was soaking into the horse's glossy coat.

"You can't take it back there," Fox said.

"What?" Aurelia raised her head, a frown marring her forehead.

"He can't take it back to his father," Fox explained impatiently.

"But he's not going back," Aurelia croaked, eyes wide. "He's coming with us."

The prince sighed.

"You can't," Aurelia whispered, trembling, her gaze shifting back and forth between Fox and Rhydian.

"You have to go," Rhydian murmured, turning her towards him. "And I have to go. We've both come so far. You were right, it's not over." He kissed her hair as his arms wrapped around her once more. "Both of us need to be with our people, to try to change what is to come."

"Don't do this to me," she whispered. "Don't be stupid. *Please.*"

"You say the curse is broken, my love," Rhydian said quietly. "So the people of Aneirin will be like I am, but without guidance. Lost, they were bound up in this too. I can't leave my people to... to deal with my father alone."

Aurelia shook her head. Rhydian kissed her hair and continued to speak quietly, trying to soothe her.

"You did what you needed. We both did. Now we owe it to ourselves and our people to reduce the damage that my father, my whole family, has caused."

The flap of tiny wings interrupted them. For a moment, Fox was relieved. Flare was a scaly little shit, but the heartbreak on Aurelia's face was more than Fox could bear.

"There is a party of guards sweeping the farmlands," Flare called, his voice weary. Fox narrowed his eyes, following the path of the purple beast as he circled above their heads. It was time to go.

Rhydian reached down to his belt and retrieved the green dagger. Even though Aurelia tried to refuse, he pressed it to her shaking hand.

"Take it," Fox snapped. "We have to go." Her hurt eyes swung his way.

"You *must* take it," Rhydian urged.

As Aurelia's trembling hand closed over the hilt of the dagger, her expression seemed to fade back into the shock from earlier.

"This isn't over yet," Rhydian murmured. Numbly, Aurelia let him lift her up, settling her onto the horse. The dragon hovered overhead, circling in a slow glide.

Fox stepped closer to Rhydian as he turned from the horse, one hand on Aurelia's wet pant leg. Aurelia was staring straight ahead, across the river to the forest. Her face was expressionless, dull.

"Be smart now, princeling," Fox said. "Use whatever you can to survive this mess for her and your beloved people."

"What does that mean?" Rhydian asked, eyeing Fox up and down, his hand refusing the let go of Aurelia. The prince looked calm, but it sounded like he was trying not to cry.

Fox let out an exasperated puff of air and glanced up. Flare had disappeared again.

"I mean, you need to cut the head off the fucking dragon," Fox finally replied, and jabbed Rhydian in the chest with a pale finger. Rhydian's eyes widened with horrified understanding.

With nothing left to say, Fox swung himself up behind Aurelia, adjusting his sword belt and cloak. Jessikah had mounted her horse beside them. Eyeing Fox warily, she held up the spare reins in question.

"Keep it," Fox muttered. "We'll need it to for the army. There's still going to be a war, it seems." Her sullen eyes looked away, and she turned the horse, heading for the bridge. Tightening his arms around Aurelia, Fox turned his horse to follow. Flare would have to catch up. Aurelia was still trembling in Fox's embrace.

As they approached the crossing, Fox realised that not even an hour had passed, when Fox had been riding with the prince towards Aurelia. Now he was riding with Aurelia, away from the prince. This game was like the whirlpool they were leaving behind, endlessly gurgling and humming beside them as their horses stepped onto the bridge. Spinning them all around, in the name of revenge, betrayal, triumph, and loss.

He was tired and cold.

Was there no end?

Rhydian's voice called out behind them, thick with emotion.

"Aurelia."

Aurelia stiffened, refusing to turn around. Her head was down, and Fox realised she was staring at the dagger, clasped in her trembling hands.

Fox stopped their horse on the bridge, twisting back to stare. He braced himself with one hand on his horse's rump, the other still clasped around Aurelia.

Rhydian had followed them to the bridge; he was standing in the middle of the dirt road. One of the prince's hands was pressed to his lips, and as Fox watched, Rhydian dropped it to his throat. Fox couldn't put a name to the expression in Rhydian's eyes. It was wild, dark, and fierce.

"Thank you for freeing my people from this curse. I know what it cost you," Rhydian called loudly, over the noise of the river. "I love you, Aurelia."

Aurelia spoke coldly to the forest ahead of them, not looking back.

"I... I hate you."

Somehow, the prince had heard her over the angry hum of the river. Fox winced at how her cruel words would be received. But to Fox's surprise, Rhydian's face softened.

"No, you don't," Rhydian called back, his hand dropping from his throat to his chest. "You just hate yourself right now."

Against Fox, Aurelia seemed to stop breathing. Then she yanked the reins from Fox and urged the horse to walk on. Behind them, Rhydian's voice rang out once more.

"I'll love you for the both of us. I always will."

The prince's shining gaze slid to Fox, daring him to comment. Fox held Rhydian's gaze for a moment, nodded once, before turning away to wrap both arms around Aurelia's stiff form. Their horse continued across the bridge, towards the line of giant trees, their expansive moss-covered trunks and branches reaching out for the morning light.

Was there no end to this mess?

And if there was, how in the hell's were they to get there?

Fox brushed his lips across Aurelia's damp hair, not knowing how he could help her.

The thought twisted through Fox like a cold stab of fear, as if Aurelia had used the dagger on him instead.

5

Gavin

Year 367

Elven Camp, South of Aneirin

"Let me through."

"The Elder One is not to be disturbed."

"I am one of her *commanding* officers. I repeat, *let me through*."

"The Elder One is not to be disturbed."

Gavin frowned at the guard, but she avoided his eyes, staring out into the Elven camp through the vast spread of dark trees.

"I *will* see her."

"The Elder One is not to be disturbed," repeated the guard. The Elven warrior shifted on her feet, her red spear still blocking the tent's entrance flap.

Eyes narrowing, Gavin shook his head. The guard's expression was a mixture of distaste and unease, still not meeting his eyes.

"For hell's sake," Gavin spat, intending to push his way in. But an irritated voice called from within.

"For hell's sake indeed," the Elder One's voice snapped, sounding different. "Send the little brother in before he wakes the entire camp. My army," a harsh laugh turned into a soft purr, "needs their rest for what is to come."

A hot flush of shame rushed up Gavin's spine.

Little brother?

I'm one of your bloody commanders.

The guard's eyes widened at Gavin's expression, the flickering light of the small charcoal brazier showing her hand tightening on her spear. But she finally stepped aside; spear tilted upright, no longer blocking the entrance. Bronze armour creaked as she moved, letting out a quiet breath.

Without glancing at her, Gavin stalked past. He yanked the heavy flap out of his way, stepped inside, and froze to a complete stop.

The Elder One stood right in front of him, their drastically altered face mere centimetres away.

Gavin had heard the whispers that night, but hadn't believed them.

He had been settled on top of his bedroll. He was wide-awake; staring at the crowded trees, peering from great heights down onto the Elven army camped below.

What were they marching towards? Had that bitch Aurelia finally done what she was supposed to? Were they marching through the forest towards victory? As Gavin tasted blood in his mouth from biting the inside of his cheek, voices murmured in the dark nearby.

Aurelia. She had done it!

But somehow, the prince had *survived*.

What the hells did that even mean? How could the prince, sacrificed instead of the king, have survived?

Fox had to be behind this. Gavin clenched his teeth. What the hell had Fox, or the man who looked like his brother, done with Aurelia and that bloody dragon?

And more importantly, how did others in the camp know before Gavin had?

He'd sat up from his bedroll, glaring at the Elves around the campfires close by. Whispers had fallen silent. Ever since Fox had shamed him before witnesses in the great hall back at the caves, Gavin was an outsider.

No one wanted to associate with the brother who had fallen out of favour with the *oh-so-powerful* Fox.

Gavin shut his eyes, and fresh blood coated his teeth.

Bastards.

Gavin had jumped to his feet, grabbing his weapons belt, cursing as he buckled it on. He had hurried through the camp, dodging legs, heads and weapons crowded for space amongst the trees. All were pretending to sleep. But he knew they saw his flaming cheeks as he stumbled furiously toward the Elder One's tent.

"Hey! Watch out you..." the soldier's sleepy voice cut off as Gavin had stepped right over the embers of a campfire. The man had seen who it was and had wisely shut his mouth.

As Gavin stalked beyond their dim fire, he'd finally made it to the Elder One's tent.

This tent was the only one to be raised. There was simply not enough room amongst the dark trees, watching ominously as the army crept its way forward north. So the army slept on the ground, and the Elder had their tent. It was a large rectangular contraption of thick canvas, stretched over thin but sturdy poles. Very little light spilled out of the corners and seams.

An armoured, sleepy guard had stood with a red spear at the door. A small bronze brazier let a little light scatter across the small, uneven clearing where the tent was pitched.

Gavin had paused a few metres away, next to a tree that smelled faintly of the pine trees of home. But in the warmer climate, this tree was subtly sweeter.

His heart had beaten a wild rhythm. His breathing had been shallow, the whispers that had fallen silent on his stomp through the camp starting up behind him.

Aurelia. The hero.

Aurelia. The curse was broken, and they could cross its once impenetrable barrier.

Aurelia. Who had killed a man, a man so deep into dark arts he had risen from the dead.

Aurelia.

Gavin had turned his head and spat onto the fallen needles below.

And then he'd stormed out into the flickering light, intending to be admitted immediately.

"E-Elder One?" Gavin choked out in shock.

The inside of the tent blazed with candles. He could see *her* face clearly.

Her.

The Elder One was a woman, Gavin realised. Something had happened.

The curse? Was it breaking? No one had told him!

The woman's cruel smile turned triumphant, clearly enjoying his reaction. She stood just inside the tent flap; green eyes burning, lips flushed a soft pink, and her once colourless hair now contained dark, shining streaks. The wrinkles had faded to what looked like fine scars, crossing her face in thin, shimmering lines.

The Elder One, normally a bent figure of stooped shoulder, colourless and wrinkled, was now a woman in the prime of life.

Gavin swallowed.

Her smile grew wider.

He cleared his throat.

"Elder One, what... I mean, are you... well?"

Green eyes narrowed, but smiling all the while, she waved a lithe arm for him to enter. Her red velvet robes rustled quietly as she stepped aside. A small green pendant on a metal chain flashed from the fabric over her breasts, mimicking the sparks that danced in her strange gaze.

Gavin wasn't sure what to think. The first thing that came to mind was the luxury inside the tent, explained the extra packhorses.

The interior was lushly furnished with rugs and cushions in bright colours. Little tables held bowls of fruit and pitchers of wine. A small but elaborate trundle bed was set up to the right, and all flat surfaces held burning candles, hundreds of them. The inside of the tent was hot and stifling.

Gavin's gaze returned to the tent wall opposite, and he started with a soft gasp. There was another figure there he hadn't noticed at first. His hand tightened on his belt.

The Elder One laughed softly and moved beside him. She sat down on an ornately carved chair, carefully arranging the red velvet fabric of her robes around her. There was no other chair to sit on. So Gavin remained standing.

He turned his head back to the far wall and then blinked. He was looking at himself.

The Elder One had bought along a mirror.

A fucking mirror.

With the Elder One looking on, an amused expression on her face, Gavin stepped across the tent, staring at his reflection. Through his shock at her transformation, Gavin realised that she must have known that if the curse were breaking apart, her appearance would change. He could see the Elder One drop her eyes to her hands, examining them. Incredible. Her arrogance was breathtaking. He'd seen a whole company of Elves dragging heavy bundles through the forest; never thinking it was this monstrosity. He assumed the strange bundles were weapons. No wonder ponies had eventually been taken from a small, nameless village on the way to assist.

Frowning at his reflection, Gavin stopped himself from chewing the inside of his cheek. At his sides, his hands clenched instead.

Just how much *did* the Elder One know about this accursed magic barrier? And why was she so at ease when they still had a battle ahead?

As if reading his thoughts, the Elder One frowned at her hands and raised her eyes to Gavin in the mirror. The hairs on the back of his neck prickled under her even green gaze. His palms were sweating, so he crossed his arms over his chest. She raised an eyebrow.

"I have to warn you," he blurted out, turning to face her.

Her eyes narrowed further, and she dropped her hands to her lap.

"About what?" her voice was cool.

"My brother... Fox."

Her wintry smile returned, and she raised an eyebrow.

Gavin stood up straighter, clearing his throat. "He isn't who you think he is."

Tilting her head, the Elder One reached up to grab her green pendant. She danced the charm back and forth along the chain, and watched him thoughtfully. She spoke again, her once dry rasp a deep velvety purr.

"Don't you mean," she said, leaning forward, "Fox isn't *what* I think he is?"

Ice slid along Gavin's spine at the calculating look in her eyes. She laughed again, her white teeth scraping over her thick bottom lip. This wasn't how he thought this would go.

The Elder One stood up slowly, rising as if lifted by many hands. Her movement was careful, calculated and infinitely threatening.

He hated himself for it, but Gavin took a step backwards.

The Elder One appeared to glide forward, her velvet robes whispering as the hundred candle flames flickered around them. Her green eyes were like bright emeralds, cutting into him as she hissed.

"I know exactly *who* and *what* he is."

"But-"

"So leave it to me. Stay away from him. Him and his power both are mine to deal with as I please."

"No, you don't under-"

"If that's all '*Commander*'?"

Gavin uncrossed his arms, palms sticky with his fear.

"Please, Elder One! You don't-"

"Get out."

"But Aurelia-"

"I said *get out*."

His vision blurred, and not knowing how it was happening, the Elder One seemed to grow tall, filling the space of the tent. Her form as it grew and spread blocked out the candles around them, the bed behind her and the ground and the draped ceiling above. Green eyes filled his vision, and he tasted ashes and salt in his mouth.

Her words echoed in his mind.

"*Get out, fool.*"

Gavin, desperately clinging to his sanity, trying not to cry out or vomit or worse, realised something. She was *enjoying* herself, enjoying his terror.

Enjoying the return of her powers.

As realisation of her cruelty dawned, a force like searing heat from a giant furnace sent him backwards, back out through the flap. He landed with a curse on the damp needles of the forest floor.

The same guard was there, her gaze carefully trained on the trees above. As Gavin watched, her red spear lowered to carefully cross the doorway again. Once again on the ground, this time he didn't care. Not about the shame of his seeming exile from plans and talk and progress. His mind was spinning and his heart was racing. He was just glad to be away from *her*.

Brushing himself off as he staggered up, eyes on the tent, Gavin heard a soft laugh from within. The guard's eyes flickered to him.

"She's gone mad," he whispered, hand wiping away what felt like mud on his chin. The guard's eyes dropped to his mouth, widening, before they flickered quickly away.

Was he only just seeing it now? How long had she been so... caught up in herself? And then what were they really here for?

He wiped his face with a trembling hand and glanced down at the stickiness there. He'd bitten the inside of his cheek so hard that even the guard had seen the blood on his chin. Gavin hadn't even noticed doing it. He backed away, returning the way he had come.

Whispers followed him as he stumbled back into the trees, lost, looking for his bedroll.

Aurelia.

Aurelia.

Aurelia.

As he finally found his bedroll, the murmurs behind him didn't stop. When sleep finally claimed him, the whispers followed him into fitful dreams of green eyes, dark hair.

Dreams filled with feminine laughter, loud, cutting and cruel.

6

Rhydian

Year 367

Aneirin Castle

The guard's unseeing eyes stared at the dawn sky as his body jolted around in the back of the horse-drawn cart. It seemed impossible that one day he could wake and see the glow of new light creeping across the kingdom once more. Fox had said something about some of the guards surviving whatever he had done to incapacitate them. Judging by the greying tinge to their skin, it seemed unlikely.

Rhydian turned away from the unconscious man, one of many in the back of the cart. He wiped his tired eyes with a sleeve that smelled like minerals and river water. And faintly of flowers.

As the farmer's cart trundled into the gateway of the great courtyard, Rhydian raised his gaze. Above and behind the various towers of the silent castle, low mountains surrounding the long arched valley of Aneirin were turning pink and gold. Colours changed as he watched, creeping down the rocky slopes like split wine. The air was cool and crisp, and it seemed like any other morning he had returned from a ride.

Usually he was on his horse, without a pile of guards, all unconscious or worse.

Unable to help himself, Rhydian turned his gaze to the back of the cart as the farmer urged the horses to cross the cobbled yard. The entire journey back up the terraced city of Aneirin, his heart had tightened with each turn up silent streets. Each time they had stopped to load more guards onto the back of the cart, Rhydian's earlier determination had sharpened into anger.

Why had any of this had to happen? And where was everyone? Where was his father? It seemed impossible that he didn't know what his son had done. Rhydian's chilled fingers grazed his throat in an unconscious gesture.

Finally, the cart rumbled to a stop. The farmer who he'd flagged down on his lonely journey back to the city called out to the team of horses to hold. He had most likely never been this high up in the city to venture through the castle gates. The farmer's eyes were wide as he stared down and across the fields of grains where he no doubt spent most of his days. Beside him on the driver's seat, Rhydian stood up, his damp boots squelching uncomfortably. The golden glow of morning was rolling across the land. Gifting life as it spread, creeping along the forest. Creeping along the river.

As Rhydian dropped onto the cobbles, he realised that, for the first time, the vista of his homeland did not move him. It was no longer a beloved valley of long rides, quiet walks, and thoughtful days of solitude. There were bitter secrets here, and as he rubbed his throat, he thought of his father. His blue eyes shone with a dull light, and he blinked slowly.

Rhydian's voice was barely a whisper as he murmured, "All gone. Buried in the earth like that dagger, under layers of rotten magic and cruel lies."

The driver of the cart hopped down and stood by uncertainly. He took off his baggy brown cap, and his grey-tinged brown hair spilled to his shoulders in soft curls.

"My prince?" the farmer asked quietly, his hand on the side rail beside the guards on the flat bed of the cart. "I don't understand."

Rhydian turned to the farmer. His smile was sad. "It's all gone."

"What is, my prince?"

Rhydian wanted to shout it out into the courtyard; the echoes hopefully disturbing his father if he was anywhere close by.

This kingdom is not what we think it is, a kingdom that was bound by a curse!

But who would believe him? Magic was outlawed, decreed by the king no less.

The journey through the town had confirmed it. Seeing it with clear eyes, no cursed fog in his mind, Rhydian could finally see. The town was deserted; hardly anyone was about. Not because of the early hour, because half the houses were empty. Where the townsfolk had gone, and even when, was beyond him. Some of those left were peering around from shutters and doors, no doubt awakened by the breaking a part of the curse.

Rhydian had made it to the few shacks that were built outside the walls, and hailed a farmer to bring his cart around. There were dead and unconscious men to collect on the way back to his home.

He wanted to laugh. His home! He wanted to cry. Rhydian rubbed at his throat again, feeling the bruise of Fox's hand coming out, and the farmer gasped.

"Your neck, my prince..."

Dropping his hand, Rhydian walked up to the man, placing a hand on the farmer's broad shoulder. Rhydian eyed the fallen guards in the back of the large cart.

"I'll call for these guards to be taken care of, and you can go back to your family. Thank you for your help."

"But your neck..."

"Don't worry about me, good sir," Rhydian murmured, looking from the man towards the barracks. "Worry about the king."

The farmer shook his head, mouth ajar, his hat twisting uncertainly in his soil stained hands.

"I don't understand," the man repeated, eyes full of concern.

Heading to the barracks to get help, Rhydian touched his throat again. He thought of Aurelia, Fox and a tiny purple dragon.

He thought of the curse, and the blood spilt on the castle stones in order to break it, and hope the truth came to light. A truth that showed that his father was a hypocrite, a magic user in a kingdom where magic was punishable by death.

"Neither do I," said Rhydian. He made his way up the stairs to the main doors of the great hall, his footfalls heavy on the bleak stone.

Perhaps the king would finally care to share his secrets.

"War is coming, father."

His father didn't bother to look up at Rhydian's sober words. The king was sitting on the floor in front of the thrones, at the top of the steps. He was dressed plainly, no hint of rich fabrics, no crown. But even as casually dressed as he was, there was something about him that screamed power.

Or arrogance.

"I said war is coming, father," Rhydian repeated, eyes on the man sitting on the steps before the thrones.

He approached the king across the great hall, carefully stepping on his favourite stones on the ornately polished floor. Across the empty room, Rhydian's voice echoed, its timbre filling the silence, yet his father's eyes remained fixed on his hands, tightly clasped between his bent knees.

Behind him, the two thrones sat lonely and neglected, echoing the emptiness that pervaded the rest of the castle.

His father remained silent, staring down at his hands. Rhydian paused halfway across the hall.

"What do you have to say to that, my king?"

At Rhydian's mocking tone, his father raised his head. Despite the silver lacing through his brown hair, with his bright blue eyes and sun-kissed skin, the king looked more like Rhydian's brother than his father. How Rhydian had never noticed before seemed unfathomable to him.

Rhydian bit his lip, something stirring uneasily within him.

Of course.

"The curse," Rhydian murmured, the words dropping bitterly from his lips.

The king's hands clenched. The only change in his expression was a slight curve of his lips. It might have been a smile. It didn't reach his eyes.

Rhydian resumed his measured walk across the great space. The candles around the hall were made of fine beeswax, but all he could smell was river water in his clothes. Rhydian stopped at the foot of the stone stairs, back straight as he met his father's measured stare.

Instead of answering Rhydian's question, the king asked one of his own.

"That Elf. Do you know who sent her?"

Rhydian placed a damp boot on the lowest step. So his father wanted to deflect questions? Fine.

"Where did they go?" Rhydian asked, tilting his head. His father's eyes narrowed.

"Do you know?" the king repeated, a sinister gleam shining in his eyes. "Do you know who sent that Elven girl?"

Taking a couple of steps up, Rhydian tossed his head. "Does it matter? She's working for the truth." His father's eyes narrowed as Rhydian paused. "Against liars," Rhydian went on, his voice quiet, "like you."

His father's eyes widened a fraction. Then he threw back his head and laughed. Taken aback, Rhydian unwillingly took a step down. The chilling sound of his father's laughter rang around the empty hall. Still chuckling, the king rose. With the strange smile on his handsome face, he started down the polished steps of grey stone.

Rhydian's skin prickled. He could feel something in his chest, something unpleasant, as his father approached.

"What did you do to me?" he whispered. His father stopped halfway. "What did you do to our people?"

Blue eyes searched Rhydian's, and the silence of the hall seemed to ring in Rhydian's ears as their gazes locked.

"What did *I* do?" the king hissed.

"Yes!" Rhydian spat back at him. "Do you know what I had to do to be free of your curse? To free our people from you?"

The king snorted, his expression incredulous. "Of course I fucking know."

"You do?" Rhydian whispered, taken aback. "Aurelia spilled my blood. I asked her to, in order to be free of this fog, this... darkness that has covered Aneirin for however long it's been. And you say you know! Like it doesn't matter? What did you do to us here? Why?"

His expression turning thoughtful, the king stared past Rhydian's head.

"Why? To protect you all, of course," said the king. His gaze dropped to his son, the look on his face like that of someone explaining things to a simpleton. "Isn't that obvious, Rhydian? And you broke that protection. It's funny. I think I knew that you would one day. You're so much like her. I love you, my son, but I hate the sight of you just as much."

All at once, Rhydian's rage deflated. There was little doubt about whom the king was talking about. Rhydian swallowed, refusing to acknowledge that the ground had fallen away beneath him as his guts turned to water.

Apart from the cruel words, his father had known what was going to happen? As if to confirm his thoughts, the king shrugged as he spoke again.

"It's nearly over, all this waiting for her to come," his father murmured. "I've been looking for her all this time. That flashy prick Cas was right. She was always coming back to me. With weapons, alas, not open arms."

His father's pale blue eyes sharpened and met Rhydian's once more.

"She'll be back for me." His father smiled. "Back for you. It took longer than I thought. I hoped to find them first."

"You bloody bastard," Rhydian spat, horrified. "You knew what the Elves wanted? What they *needed* to do? To *me*?"

With a chilling laugh, his father shrugged again. "Or to me."

"What?" Rhydian cried. He took a step down. "What are you saying?"

The king took two stairs down in quick succession. Rhydian stared, appalled fascination racing through his body.

"The curse," his father murmured, licking his lips. "It could have easily been my blood to break it. But that's right," his father's eyes narrowed in disgust, "you can't remember the family motto, can you? Blood Binds All. What a wonder that you survived. Did that Elven girl make you kneel at her feet, like your mother had me do for her? By the gods, women are as cruel and deadly as the most insidious, glittering wasps of that fucking forest."

Rhydian shook his head. He'd assured Aurelia that it would be okay, that he'd known the curse wouldn't let him die. But he hadn't known at all. He'd just wanted to help her people, and his own.

"So you let them take my life instead?" Rhydian whispered, not expecting his father to answer. What could his father say to that?

The king inhaled through his teeth. "It's the least my son could do for me, don't you think?" He took another step towards Rhydian. "I'm your king, after all."

Rhydian took another step backwards, feeling as lost as he ever had, when he wandered the meadows at dawn alone. But this wasn't the gentle peace of solitude. This was terror of the unknown. Realisation crept over him like a burial shroud. There was more than lies here at work. His father was staring at him as if his son were a stranger in this hall.

"She didn't die, did she? Are you why my mother left?" he choked out, his words echoing around them.

Moving so fast that Rhydian was unprepared, his father stalked down the last steps between them. A strong, feverish hand grasped his throat. Burning fingers closed over the bruise left by Fox, and the painful line left by Aurelia.

His father's eyes were wide, wild. All trace of cruel mirth was gone.

"Your mother?" the king hissed, spittle lining his lips. "Do not speak to me of your *mother*. She is coming for both of us. And she will *win*."

Rhydian gurgled, a painful, pitiful sound and tore at his father's feverish grip until he was abruptly let go. It took all of his will, but Rhydian held his ground, refusing to back down further. Panting, he didn't trust himself to speak. The words about his mother had dropped from his lips like bait dangling on a hook, and his father had swallowed the barb.

Something Aurelia had said, or almost said, had sat in his guts like spoiled food. Perhaps that's what his father had been trying to say? Aurelia really was on *his mother's* side, meaning his mother was waging a war against her own family.

"Why?" Rhydian finally gasped. "Why is she coming?"

"We had everything taken from us! Dragons, magic, Elves, if I could wipe them from this continent, I would. The curse was for our protection! But she asked too much. And when I finally said no to your mother, the curse broke while it was being forged! She had to run, unable to live this side of the line of magic that was there to protect *us*, to protect *you*," the king sneered. "And thanks to you, my son," the king spat out, "you invited her minion to step across our threshold and *break* it."

With a curl of his lip, his father pushed past Rhydian and stalked across the hall. Rhydian's trembling hand touched his burning throat. Aurelia and Fox hadn't given him all the information he'd needed. Perhaps, like before, Aurelia had needed him to find out for himself, to really *believe*.

But there were still things left unanswered.

Aurelia, he thought. *Was it like this for you? Are you even now discovering there is more going on that we do not understand?*

Raising his gaze to the golden light that was sliding down the high walls of the hall, Rhydian felt a shiver of fear and anger roll through his guts. He needed more light. Cursing himself for the fool, Rhydian turned, trailing after his father from the hall.

The king stalked out to the courtyard and stopped at the farmer's cart.

When Rhydian reached him, the king was watching the scene before him silently, arms crossed against his chest. Merion was helping some of the guards unload the dead, laying them on the cobbles, while others were being taken away on simple stretchers of leather and wooden poles. Chase stood nearby, his arms around the shoulders of his two brothers, all three of their faces wet.

The early morning sun hadn't reached the ground yet, so the dead lay in shadows, two rows of lives cut short. Rhydian gritted his teeth.

Fox, you bastard.

Surely there was another way?

As he stalked down the steps and across to the cart, Rhydian's gaze slid to the king.

This is on you too, father.

From the stables, a loud whinny and a thump indicated that Blackthorn had somehow sensed Rhydian approaching. Merion raised his head, his gaze meeting Rhydian's. Merion, his face white, flicked his gaze to the king before sliding his gaze back to Rhydian. The groom shook his head with the slightest of movements.

Rhydian ignored the warning and went right up to his father. Merion's beard worked around his mouth, like the man was chewing it. The groom hung his head and went back to his grim task.

His father turned to him, face cold and blank. A muscle in his jaw twitched as he eyed Rhydian's bruised neck. Rhydian's gut twisted, needing to hold it together.

"I'm listening," Rhydian said quietly.

His father exhaled, his breath a long and shuddering sigh.

"I've known it was your mother since that Elf of yours appeared," the king paused, aware of the ears of the guards turned their way. "When she forced my hand on the tower."

Rhydian bit his lip, scowling.

When Aurelia sent you *over the edge of anger and reason, showing me who you really are.*

When you sent her over the edge of my tower in return.

It hurt that Aurelia had known his mother was alive, and that Fox had known. Perhaps Aurelia had tried to tell him, but she hadn't quite, had she? Although, considering the layers of deceit, he was slowly unravelling. There was a good chance, though, that Aurelia hadn't known at first either. Had she?

Rhydian coughed, his bruised throat throbbing. "And why does she come? Now, after all this time?"

The king turned to face Rhydian fully, his chilling smile not quite meeting his pale blue eyes. This close, it was clear that his father was under some heavy strain. There was a grey tinge to his normally tanned skin. Something dangerous flashed in his expression.

"Your mother comes now because it has taken her this long to recover, to plan."

"Recover?" Licking his lips, Rhydian tried to keep his voice even, but he could hear the tremble in his words. "From what?"

The king's sharp intake of breath was all the warning Rhydian had as his father grabbed him by the front of his shirt, bringing their faces so close that their breaths mingled. The surrounding guards had paused.

"The curse that backfired when she tried to fucking kill you!" his father hissed into Rhydian's face.

The only sound amongst the shocked silence was another whinny from the stables.

Rhydian shook his head, speechless and numb.

"I thought we were protecting our family. Protecting this entire kingdom." The king's voice was loud, raging. More guards appeared from the barracks, and from their watch along the castle walls.

Two of the guards standing behind his father stepped closer. Their hands were on their swords. But the king whipped up his right hand, and they paused, frozen to the spot. Their eyes darted around wildly. Merion cursed loudly, and no one else moved. The king pushed Rhydian away, his lips twisting, eyes full of a dark light.

"And so I did it," the king hissed. "And so I did it!" he yelled, raising his arms up and out, turning to face the guards all around.

Oh no.

"I made it so she would receive the sting of the magic binding. A magic that was supposed to keep us safe! But in order to do that, a dragon told her she had to sacrifice you! Like a fucking goat for Mabon, like a fucking pagan!"

The shocked silence of the courtyard was almost deafening.

The king laughed, his eyes wild, and he spoke to the horrified faces around them, waving his arms around, inviting them to hear. "And you know what? She *wanted* to do it! To live without fear, or of a repeat of what happened in the City of the fucking Seers."

She wanted to? His own mother?

The woman of his dreams flashed through his mind, even as his eyes filled with tears of sadness, fear, and rage.

Rhydian stepped forward, eyes watering. Despite the tumult within his heart, he had to know. His voice was quiet.

"If you didn't want to, why didn't you just tell her 'no'?"

Merion and the guards were staring at them both with horror. Chase and his brothers were crying now. The sun was rising above, but the courtyard was covered in long grey shadows.

His father turned back to face Rhydian, his smile cold.

"I've never been able to refuse her anything."

"Until now," Rhydian whispered.

His father's smile grew wider. "Until now. She can't have you. Even though like a bloody fool, you invited her to try."

"I didn't know-" Rhydian began, but his father ignored him. The king turned back to the guards. They seemed to have broken free from whatever had immobilised them and quickly retreated. One of them swallowed, her hazel eyes wide.

"Finish cleaning up my son's mess. We have preparations to make."

"But father-"

"An Elven army, foul users of magic, are bringing war upon us," the king interrupted again, raising his voice. A guard gasped, the sound audible over one of the young boy's sobs. Merion was edging closer to them. "We will prepare as best we can."

There was a soft murmur of shocked voices as his father's gaze locked on Rhydian's.

"And see to it that my son remains in the castle."

"What?"

Ignoring Rhydian's shocked question, the king stalked away in disgust.

The guards shifted uneasily before one of them gestured towards Rhydian with his spear.

"My prince, I'm sorry, but you heard the king."

Distracted, Rhydian nodded. The guard looked relieved.

As he followed the silent guard back to the great doors of the castle, Rhydian caught Merion's expression. The man had made it to his nephews, and was crouched down, his enormous arms hugging all three of them at once. The groom looked miserable.

"Why did you come back, my prince?" Merion mumbled, his face flushed.

"Because of that. I *am* your prince," Rhydian murmured as he passed. "I will not leave you alone to deal with *him*."

As Rhydian was ushered up the steps, his mind was reeling.

How can I prevent a battle from within a locked *castle? How can I work to prevent the deaths of my people, and Aurelia's?*

At the top of the steps, Rhydian turned to face the guard as the man shut the doors behind him. The man's expression was grim.

Rhydian rested his face against the back of the ornately carved wood.

I can't.

7

Fox

Year 367

The Forest, South of Aneirin

Sullen yellow eyes watched Fox from across the campfire.

Fox returned the stare without blinking. Eventually, the wary gaze looked away first with a scowl, as they always did.

Jessikah's hands were clutched together over her chest. She was huddled deep into her thin cloak. Apart from the usual simmering resentment, barely contained just under the surface, Jessikah's expression was carefully blank as she turned to stare into the dark spread of towering forest around them.

Fox wondered what she was thinking. About him, or their lush surroundings? In Mionlach, homeland of the dragons, there were no trees at all. If the forest had ever covered that barren place it had been aeons ago, now it was a land of black mountains and volcanic, rocky wastes. The air there was bitter and dry, unlike the fresh and uplifting air of the forest.

Flare was nowhere to be seen, which suited Fox just fine.

"Fox?"

Aurelia's soft voice roused him from the dark thoughts curling through his mind. Standing up, he stretched, narrowing his eyes at the crouched woman across the flames. Fox smiled as Jessikah shrank further into her cloak, before turning to where Aurelia was emerging from the trees. She glanced up at the call of an owl passing overhead, but didn't smile at it like she usually would.

"I'm here," he murmured.

Aurelia had hardly spoken since they had left Rhydian far behind, as they had headed back south, towards where the so-called Elder One and her army were marching north. Aurelia was clearly anxious about the fate of the prince, and his decision to head back to help the people of his kingdom. Fox had to give it to him. The young man had seemed like a pure-hearted idiot at first. But the man's heart was more than just pure. It was full of courage. And strong enough to share what love he could with Aurelia.

Even by the light of the flickering fire, Fox could see her clearly. Aurelia's green eyes were dull, dark circles underneath weighing down their usual brightness. Her clothes were dry after a day of hard riding, but her pants and tunic were rumpled. With her disheveled hair and slouched posture, she appeared tired and defeated.

But her expression worried Fox the most. He held out his arms.

Her green eyes blinked at him, her expression grim, and her hands hanging limply by her sides. Eventually she stepped over the roots of the giant tree they were camped amongst for the night. Fox closed his arms around her, pressing her to his chest. Aurelia sighed.

Fox tightened his arms around her. "That bad, hmm?"

Her voice was muffled as she spoke into his shirt.

"I can't figure out what I could have done differently."

Not daring to answer, Fox remained silent. There had been many choices both of them could have made to end up somewhere else. But in the end, they were here now.

Aurelia's voice was a hum against him. "Do you think that the Elder One knows Rhydian is still alive?"

Jessikah was staring at them, still clutching her chest.

"If you're going to have a heart attack," Fox snapped over Aurelia's head, "just fucking get it over and done with, or go stand behind a tree. *Now*." He bared his teeth, jerking his head at the darkness beyond the light.

Jessikah, her jaw tense, followed his command. As she stepped past the first tree, Fox uncoiled an icy thread of his power, and coiled it around her ankle. Giving it an exploratory jerk, he smiled at the thud of someone tipping over amongst the thick roots of the crowded forest.

Keeping his arms around Aurelia, Fox led her to the tree. He sat, resting his back against the broad expanse of the mossy trunk, and nestled Aurelia between his legs so she was closest to the fire. One of the seemingly endless bubbling creeks was nearby, so the night air was cool.

"I suspect she knows," Fox murmured into Aurelia's hair, answering her earlier question.

"What can Rhydian possibly do now? How could he choose to go back there?" Aurelia said, angry now.

"Don't think of that," Fox said, giving her a squeeze. Aurelia cursed, then sighed against him. He tapped a finger on her arm.

"Can I get you anything?" he asked.

"I'm thirsty."

Fox smiled and squeezed her shoulders. "If you could have anything you wanted right now, what would it be?"

She snorted into his arm. "This old game?"

"Too old?" he teased, trying to ease her tension. He was relieved that she was finally talking. Aurelia shook her head against him, although her sigh was almost a soft laugh.

"How did it go?" she eventually murmured.

"I know you know it," Fox said, and kissed her head. Aurelia cleared her throat.

"Shadow Man, let me see,

Bring me something,

What will it be?"

"That's right." Fox grinned despite himself. "So?"

"Only water, please." Aurelia paused. "From *our* pool."

Fox shifted his hips against her, and Aurelia smacked his chest.

"You idiot," she huffed as she pulled back from him, meeting his teasing gaze. Her eyes were still haunted, but they were brighter. "To *drink*."

Her eyes simultaneously misted over and widened at the lewd expression on his face. Carefully, she leant forward and pressed her lips to his.

"You are my dearest friend," she whispered against his mouth. "And I regret nothing. But I am *thirsty*."

Moved by her words, Fox nodded and swallowed, his teasing smile fading. He didn't trust himself to speak at the shining gratitude in her eyes. She knew exactly what he was trying to do.

Clearing his throat, Fox closed his eyes. Raising his right hand, palm up, he let his magic uncoil. Frost curled around his fingers as the energy moved through his body, with a slightly painful edge to it. He pushed through the ache, and eventually a solid weight formed in his hand. Most metals shied away from coming to the call of his magic. But gold was never an issue.

Aurelia's gentle sigh was one of awe, and he opened his eyes, pleased at her wonder. In his hand was a golden cup. He placed it in Aurelia's hand, and she took a sip.

"Shit. It's cold."

"Would you assume it to be anything else?" Fox asked dryly, flicking the frost from his fingers.

"Hmmm." Aurelia swallowed some more of the mineral rich liquid. "Where's your cup? It's cold, but delicious."

"That was enough for now," he began, and then shrugged. Aurelia was his dearest friend, too. "It hurts," he admitted. "The curse affected me." He held up his hand, and the faint tremble was visible. Aurelia grabbed his hand and pressed it to her lips.

"That's big of you to admit. Here, have some of this."

"No. It's for you."

"Well." She took another sip. "Thank you, I needed that. It's good. Like our time in the pool was good." She grimaced, her eyes searching his face. "Although I know you tried to scare me. All those hearts. You were a beast to scare me."

Fox said nothing, listening to the fire crackle beside them. He could feel each heart as a spark of endless magic within the bitter confines of his own sore organ, his heart surely a blackened, shrivelled thing. Closing his eyes, he rested his chin on Aurelia's hair. It was a while before Aurelia spoke again, her voice quiet.

"Why does someone have to die, so that others may live, Fox?"

His eyes snapped open, and a sudden burst of laughter erupted from him as a loud snort.

"Are you questioning the entire way of this forest, Aurelia?" Fox asked, incredulous. "Of the entire natural order of this world? If you are, believe me, I am absolutely the fucking last creature that should answer that."

While Aurelia absorbed this in silence, Fox wondered at it too. The answer did indeed lie in the natural order of the world. Didn't it? Is that why he was here now, assisting with the breaking of a curse where more would surely die? An uncomfortable feeling, something akin to foreboding, was coiling through his heart. He ignored it. He'd made a promise to help. There was no other course. He tightened his grip on the dark ache within and focused on the young woman in his arms as she worked through what was surely a struggle of thoughts inside.

"Who were they?" she asked at length, the subject change catching him off guard.

"Who?" Fox nuzzled her hair, inhaling her warmth, his eyes closed to the watching giant trees.

"Who were the owners?" She moved her head away from his face. "The owners of all those hearts that you ate."

Fox's eyes opened.

"That's not a bedtime story, Aurelia. You need to rest." He nuzzled his cheek against her hair. "Without nightmares."

"You... never mind. Then tell me this instead. How did the curse affect you?"

Fox sent a tendril of awareness along the energetic cord that bound him to Jessikah amongst the trees. She was dozing.

"The pain of crossing into Aneirin," Fox murmured quietly, "was like coming up against a wall of spiked barbs. We... repelled each other. It was like a war of wills and flesh. That's how the curse was designed, to keep most magic users out. Ironic isn't it?"

"Why didn't you say anything? And why is it ironic?" Aurelia's eyes were wide, and she sounded breathless.

Fox chewed his bottom lip with uncertainty. But she deserved to know. He scanned the trees for any sign of a flash of purple. There was none. He lowered his voice further.

"Aurelia, it was dragon magic."

Aurelia stiffened against him. "But there aren't any... there haven't been any other dragons for..." her voice faded away. She glanced up, probably looking for Flare as well.

Fox waited.

She froze and then turned back to him. "And just how do *you* know that it was dragon magic?"

He smiled blandly, showing his even, white teeth. Aurelia scowled. She looked around quickly again, before leaning close to him once more.

"A long time ago, Flare told me that Rhydian's father had something to do with the dragons disappearing."

"What?" Fox sat up straighter, his smile disappearing in a chilled instant.

"Calm down, Shadow Man. That's all Flare said. That the Elder One had told him that." Aurelia shook her head, and the light in her eyes dimmed. "I think it was when we first spotted Rhydian in the woods. I nearly shot Rhydian with a black arrow."

"That's all Flare said?"

"Yes. Why? What do you know?"

What did he know indeed? And the Elder One had told Flare… this was interesting. Lies and lies and *lies*.

"Forget it." Fox shook his head. "Rest, Little Thing. We'll get you back to your people."

Aurelia's eyes narrowed. "*Our* people, you mean."

Fox's mouth thinned.

Aurelia poked at his chest. "This, all of this, was for our people. Before we knew there was more to it all."

Fox shrugged, his gaze on the fire.

"I don't understand you," she muttered, and collapsed back against him. Fox understood her hurt tone, but he just couldn't be bothered explaining. The memories cost him too much. His head was full enough as it was.

"Fox," Aurelia tapped her hand against his chest; sounding exhausted all of a sudden. "It didn't look like the king was preparing to bring his army to the caves, was he?"

Fox closed his eyes. "It appears that way."

"That means that while there was a curse, more information has been held back from me, from you. Like the Elder One being the queen," Aurelia murmured. "The Elder One said that the king was a monster, and his son too."

Fox tightened his arms again, hating the bitterness in her weary voice. He'd wonder how long it would take her to realise.

"But Rhydian, he was the sweetest man I ever…" her voice faded, thick with unshed tears.

"Thanks," Fox said wryly, opening his eyes.

"Shut up," she snapped. "You and sweet are not two things that go together." She shook her head against his chest, her sob turning into another soft little laugh. "Except that first time you asked me what I wanted. 'Anything at all,' you said."

Fox smiled against her hair. "I remember."

"And so my parents came home from their day in the mines, to find me playing with a mountain pony, right there in our chambers."

Unable to hold it in, Fox laughed, his lips catching in her long hair. "That was the only time I've been yelled at by an Elf, besides you and O-" Fox cut himself off just in time.

"Who?" Aurelia murmured.

Fox exhaled slowly. "No one. Just you. You yell at me *all* the time."

"I do not," Aurelia whispered, a soft snort accompanying her words. "Although I'm glad you're not sweet. I can't remember if I said it, but thank you for saving me." She took a breath. "For saving him."

Fox closed his eyes at the memory of seeing her disappear beneath the churning water of the whirlpool. Fox also saw her fool of a prince, desperate and unthinking, throw himself in afterwards.

"You're welcome," Fox said, his arms tight around her. He opened his eyes, willing his limbs to relax, knowing that she was safe. "However, at the risk of your yelling, let me repeat, don't *ever* do that to me again."

Pulling back from him, Aurelia nodded solemnly, firelight catching the silver trails of moisture down her cheeks.

"I was lost. Even now, I don't know how to hold this heavy weight inside of me. When I think of him." Her eyes filled again. "It hurts."

"I know, Little Thing. I know."

"What side are we on, that this must take place...?"

"Follow your heart, Aurelia." Fox cleared his throat. "That's all you can do."

Urging her to lie back against him, Fox let her cry silently for them both. Chin on her head, he stared at the tall trees reaching up for the majestic sky, hard to see amongst the shifting canopy. A cool breeze stirred the branches. Unable to help himself, Fox wondered idly if Owaen had ever come this far south in his wanderings. What it would have been like to travel with him, if only the world had fewer monsters running loose.

Just like him, cold, heartless and capable of almost anything he cared to do.

"I won't let you go," Fox whispered, thinking of Aurelia and Owaen both, not sure whom his words were for.

Aurelia wept for hours.

Mostly it was silent, and Fox, awake the entire night, could hear the small animals in the undergrowth as they scampered past. But eventually, she quietened, exhausted.

"Aurelia," Fox murmured. "I've got you."

Her voice was hoarse. "I know."

But did he?

Fox was painfully aware that it might be too late to save her from more heartbreak. How the hell could this end in anything but a battle between a king and a queen and their armies?

Fox snorted quietly, as he remembered meeting the Elder One for the first time all those years ago in the forest. The fact that the *Elder One* was with Flare should have tipped him off. Fox had recognised Flare straight away, even in his small form. But Fox's ego, rage and the poison of betrayal had left him reeling for further revenge. Even after feasting on it, it was still not enough. The ash that still fell from his chaos in Mionlach wasn't enough.

Did that mean Aurelia had indeed chosen wrong, under Fox's own guidance? Did that mean Fox should have gotten rid of Flare, like the rest of them, and ignored the Elder One's call for revenge?

Fuck.

He truly didn't know. What he did know was that he should have dropped Jessikah, and then himself into a dark hole. The low fire seemed to wink at him in agreement. Even the earth below seemed to hum.

"You've come so far," Fox whispered. "Any choices that you made, with my guidance, with the Elder One's, with…" he fought the urge to spit, "the help of Flare as well, any wrong choices, that's on us too."

"Flare?" Aurelia sniffed, then yawned. "I guess he helped."

"He got you across the curse line, didn't he?"

"Mmm. He wasn't originally going to come," Aurelia murmured.

Fox paused. That was true. The Elder One had intended for Fox to go, but he had refused. Had that refusal set the chaos in motion they were slowly spiralling towards?

"That's true." Fox tried to keep his voice light, even as his thoughts whirled. "Did Flare… when he didn't think he was going with you, did he give you something before-hand? A token perhaps?"

Aurelia shook her head. "No, no token." She yawned again. "Only my bow."

Ah.

Fox had never held the bow, but if his growing suspicions were correct, there was likely magic bound within it somewhere. Magic to help Aurelia across the curse line, into Aneirin, the very city from which Flare had fled straight after the curse had struck.

"Your bow," Fox murmured. "I see."

No wonder Flare was staying away. Flare must have realised his scaly footprints, all over this mess, would eventually be discovered.

"Either way," Fox went on as Aurelia stretched against him, "the curse *is* breaking if not broken completely. I could feel it straight away. And Rhydian, his mind is clearer now, which is a good thing, as I don't think he's as sweet as you think."

Aurelia stilled mid-stretch. "What does that mean?"

"I'm not sure. But Rhydian..." Fox searched for the right words. "He has a shadow inside of him, deeper than the fog. It was working against him, but perhaps now the curse is finished, the prince might be able to work with it. For protection."

"That's..." she began. "Actually, I don't know what that is, Fox." Aurelia settled back against him, her body sinking into her exhaustion.

"Do I have a shadow?" she asked, her voice heavy with weariness.

"Of course you do." Fox's arms tightened around Aurelia, his words a chilly breeze in her hair. "Me."

8

Aurelia

Year 367

The Forest, South of Aneirin

Aurelia peered into the water, her heart like a fragile weight in her chest.

Standing amongst the circle of stones in the meadow, Rhydian's expression was hard to read. He looked lost in thought, head lowered. The sky was covered in drifting clouds, and the early morning sun shone beneath them, the sky a cool blue above. The grass was a dark green and the fields of grain beyond swayed in a silent breeze. It was a serene morning, but the peace was deceptive.

With his simple cloak draped over one shoulder, and his golden brown hair stirring softly around his face, the prince looked like any young man lost in thought. Rhydian's left hand was on his heart, his other clenched by his hip.

Aurelia frowned. His belt, normally loaded with both a sword and knife, held no weapons.

Also unusual were the six guards, in full armour, waiting just outside the circle of tall stones. The prince paid them no attention; his gaze appeared to be focused solely on the disturbed tuft of wet grass at his boots.

With the toe of his right boot, Rhydian nudged the grass, revealing an indistinct shape of dirty blue. With a wince, he sunk carefully to his knees. The hand on his heart slid up to his throat, where a mottled purple bruise had blossomed. As his fingers probed the swollen skin, his right hand reached out and touched the disturbed earth. A pained expression marred his handsome face.

After brushing his fingertips over the disturbed mound, he lifted grass stained fingers to his lips.

Hanging his head, the prince closed his eyes as a single tear graced his cheek.

"The prince has some new companions," Fox said, quietly. "It appears the king is keeping a close watch on his son since you," he coughed, "visited him with that dagger."

"It's curious that Rhydian is standing amongst those stones," Aurelia murmured, her voice hoarse. "He refused to when I recovered the dagger." She sighed with an uneven exhale, watching Rhydian kneeling on the grass while the guards stood by with uncomfortable expressions. He looked incredibly young. "Can you imagine growing up in that castle? With that king for a father? I think Rhydian has willfully forgotten a lot, or else he is more affected by the curse and his father's magic than he realises."

Kneeling beside her on the bank of a small stream amongst the wet rocks, Fox let his magic ripple across the surface, allowing them to watch over the prince. A faint mist clouded around the image of Rhydian, giving him a strange, ethereal appearance. Nearby, Jessikah tended to the horses, and Aurelia assumed Flare was up in the treetops, catching the sun. Unthinking, Aurelia reached out to the rippling surface, towards the wavering form of the prince.

Fox's pale hand shot out.

"Don't." Fox's voice was as cold as his hand on hers.

Aurelia frowned, and when Fox dropped her hand, she pulled it back reluctantly.

"I'm not going to jump in," Aurelia murmured.

Turning to face her, Fox looked her over, his expression unreadable.

He was clad in his usual black, the long sleeves of his shirt rolled up over pale forearms. His black pants were rolled at the ankles, with his heavy boots discarded behind him. Aurelia sighed, disgusted at her flash of jealousy. Fox's bare feet looked as if sculptured out of the finest white marble. Whilst being both icy and dangerous, Fox was beautiful, his deadly attractiveness at complete odds to Rhydian's golden light and shining warmth.

After travelling through the forest for a few days, slowly, so she could get a hold of herself, Aurelia was already missing the prince's warmth. She was surprised to admit it, but for once, was being perfectly honest. She'd loathed what she'd felt she had to do to him, even with his consent, and her heart was aching for the want of him.

Fox raised his eyebrows under her scrutiny, and Aurelia shrugged. Fox's calculating expression softened, likely well aware of who she was comparing him to.

"Well, you might have," Fox said, eyeing her closely. His lips twitched.

Aurelia gave him a look. Fox merely returned her even stare. Closing her eyes, Aurelia pinched the bridge of her nose.

"Bloody hell, Fox. Please explain what you mean. Explain to me like I have just woken up after barely any sleep, back in this giant, looming forest, on my way to an unknown fate after cocking up a lifelong mission."

Fox's glittering black eyes blinked once, the gold sparkling even in the dim light below the crowded trees. There was the barest hint of a smile over his finely shaped lips.

"Are you sure, Aurelia? That you're not about to jump in?" His smiled widened.

"Fox, don't be a bastard," she snapped.

Throwing back his head in a burst of laughter, Fox's smile was the brightest thing Aurelia had seen for days.

"That's better," Fox said with a smirk, and turned back to the stream. Rhydian was still crouched in the grass, head down.

Carefully, Fox held his hand over the rippling image. The image of the prince and the meadow wavered, faded, and then dissolved. Through the clear water, the rounded stones of the riverbed were visible once again. The surface was covered with reflections of the sparkling canopy far above, painting it a dark shade of green as the sun rose higher beyond the thickly crowded trees.

Resting back on his bare heels, Fox gestured at the stream, his gaze thoughtful.

"Actually, I don't know what would happen if you reached for him."

Aurelia frowned, although she shouldn't be surprised. Fox's magic was vast, wild, and apparently not always under his control.

Raising narrowed eyes to the far bank, Fox bit his bottom lip, and Aurelia followed his gaze while he thought about how to explain.

Across the stream, and around them, giant trees crowded as far as the eye could see. Some of the trunks were so wide that ten Elves couldn't circle them with joined hands. There were all manner of rich colours and textures and shapes, and most were covered with some type of lichen or moss. All of them were tall, and undeniably ancient. There was oak, ash, pine and species she couldn't name. A mysterious, spicy scent lingered around them from the closest brooding trunk.

When Fox broke the gentle silence around them, his voice was soft.

"I've watched him before," he said. Aurelia's eyebrows rose. "For the Elder One," he added quickly. "And the prince turned towards me..."

"Like he knew you were observing him?" Aurelia finished for him.

He nodded, not meeting her gaze.

"Do you think that has to do with his father's magic, or magic within his family?" Aurelia asked, trying to wrap her mind around it.

Fox nodded, his lips pressed together in a thin line. Aurelia's own lips parted as she stared into the forest, unseeing. A thought struck her.

"Fox."

"Aurelia."

"Does that mean that Rhydian is Elven by birth? Because he was born into a bloodline that has magic?"

Fox nodded slowly. "That's how magic works in families. Yes."

Aurelia expelled the breath she had been holding. Damn. What would Rhydian think of that? Had he already thought about it? He was an Elven prince, in a kingdom where magic users were put to death. Aurelia frowned. Was that an ancient law, she wondered, or something the king and contrived to mitigate any threat to his power?

Cupping water to splash his face, Fox closed his eyes. He shook his head out as droplets ran down his face and wiped them through his black hair.

"Magic is unpredictable," Fox continued. "The first Elves were gifted it from dragons, in partnership. That was the only way for humans to have any kind of power. But in time, children were *born* with magic." His lips curled in distaste. "Not *gifted* it by a *dragon*, a creature who needed slaves with better eyes and longer lives to mine their crystals for them."

Aurelia considered his sour expression. Fox knew full well her parents were miners, even now, when dragons had stopped arriving to exchange magic for crystals.

"You say that like it was a bad thing, sharing magic. What's your problem with dragons, Fox? And aren't you the least bit concerned about where they went?"

Ignoring her, Fox cracked his neck, his mouth tightly closed. She watched a muscle twitch in his finely shaped jaw.

Aurelia crossed her arms against her chest in frustration. Fox had so many answers, but shared them so rarely that she was tempted to push him into the stream. Glancing down at herself, Aurelia sighed. *She* needed to jump in and wash. Her clothes were rumpled, and her long hair a tangled mess. While Fox was sitting there, hands in the water, looking pristine, like some Elven prince of shadows.

"It's a bit hypocritical, isn't it? You being so full of their power?" Aurelia mused, frustration and fatigue loosening her tongue. "Who are you, to scoff at the dragons in such a manner?"

With his hands still cupped beneath the surface of the water, Fox froze. The temperature plunged around them, and Aurelia's breath fogged in front of her.

Oh crap.

Aurelia rarely saw this side of him emerge, especially from something Aurelia had said or done.

Fox's voice was tightly clipped, and he turned cold eyes her way, the gold all but gone. "I am whom I am."

Hesitating, Aurelia nearly apologised. Instead, she took a breath and forged on.

"You know what Fox? That answer isn't good enough, not anymore. Not for me."

Staring at his dark eyes, Aurelia sat up straighter.

"Why do you have so much power, when the rest of us are just Elven miners who can see better in the dark? *Who* are you?" She paused. "*What* are you?"

Something cracked, startling her. Looking down, her stomach flipped over. Fox's hands were full of cracked ice, the river water having frozen solid in his cupped hands. His barely held control had cracked the ice into shards.

"There are no words for me," Fox bit out, narrowed eyes hard on her face. "Do not try to find any."

"But-"

"I said *do not try.*"

Unable to move, Aurelia slowly shook her head. She wasn't afraid of him. What she was feeling instead of fear was *grief*. The private internal hell that Fox seemed to dwell in rose to the surface like this occasionally. It seemed to be a hell that she would likely never understand, that he'd never, *ever* share with her.

Standing up, his tall form unfolding like a solid shadow of pale flesh and darkness, Fox threw the ice shards across the water. They shattered against rocks on the far bank. Not looking at her, he headed back to the tree where they'd spent the night.

Staring at his back, Aurelia called hoarsely after him. "Fox, I didn't mean to pry."

Fox slowed his steps, and then came to a stop, pale hands splayed out and trembling by his sides. His chest was heaving with deep breaths. The temperature was still cold, but it was slowly going back to normal.

"Fox, I'm sorry," Aurelia called out, her voice raw.

Looking over his shoulder, his pale, beautiful face in sharp profile to the surrounding gloom, Fox's voice was just as raw as hers.

"I'm not."

9

Flare

After catching sight of the smoldering glare on Fox's face, the dragon was tempted to fly off again. But, on hearing Flare above, Aurelia had glanced up and caught sight of him.

Reluctantly, Flare landed on a great wide oak that the three figures were passing beneath. Fox was in the lead, and as he glanced up, Flare's grip on the branch tightened. A muscle twitched in the man's jaw, but thankfully Fox said nothing. Jessikah was next, and as her gaze slid over Flare, her lips thinned.

Bringing up the rear was Aurelia. The relief on her face was clearly visible as her horse approached the oak. Reaching up, Aurelia adjusted the hood of her cloak.

Landing on Aurelia's shoulder, Flare could sense her weariness and a new tension as well. Murmuring through the long tendrils of her hair, Flare leant his cold snout towards her ear.

"Are you feeling any better?"

Aurelia raised her eyebrows, but kept her gaze straight ahead, watching the two horses in front of her pick their way along a barely running creek.

"I'm just *great*, Flare. How are you this fine morning?"

Flare ignored her sarcasm and tried again. "I know this isn't what you expected-"

Aurelia cut him off, her voice strained. "This isn't what I expected? You're damn right it isn't. Nothing is like I expected, but it could have been if I'd been told more of what the hells was going on." Her voice sounded hurt. "And where the hells have you been? I thought you were catching the bloody sun, but you've been gone for days!"

Flare sighed, a small puff of air that barely disturbed Aurelia's hair. Fox must have procured some more of her favourite soap, because its floral scent was strong around her.

No, *none* of this was going like anybody had expected.

"I've been scouting ahead."

"How far?"

"Towards the army. I, ah, I needed to stretch my wings."

"Why didn't you say that before you left?"

Before you left me, her tone implied.

"You were asleep when I woke," Flare protested, shaking his wings.

"And Fox?"

"Er, Fox was down by the river..." the dragon said tentatively.

"And you thought it was best to fly up and away, and I'd be okay with that, after everything that happened?"

Aurelia sighed disgustedly and shook her head, her lips pressed firmly together. This close, Flare could see a flush over her cheeks. From anger or fear, he couldn't tell. Likely, it was both.

"Aurelia," Flare murmured. "The army isn't far now. I was making sure that we wouldn't miss each other-"

"Flare," Aurelia interrupted, her voice calm. "I don't believe you."

Flare opened his mouth and then closed it. Unable to stop himself, his gaze slid to the back of the man in black, riding at the head of their party.

Fox didn't turn around, but his head tilted back to gaze upwards as Flare watched. His black hair was a shining shadow above his black cloak, at odds with the vibrant greens and rich browns of the thick forest. The air was calm, with only the occasional birdcall above them.

"What did he say to you?" Flare eventually demanded, his voice low.

"What do you think he said?" Aurelia replied, refusing to look at him.

"Tell me," he insisted, hating the pleading note in his voice. He was thinking about tugging on her hair when Aurelia finally turned her head towards him.

"Fox hasn't said much to me for days," Aurelia admitted. "But as we mounted up this morning, he was slightly less of a bastard. '*Trust no one, not even me*' was all he said."

"No one?" Flare bristled, resisting the urge to hiss at the man in front. "Anything else?"

"If you'd have been here, you'd have heard."

Flare spread his wings for balance, as Aurelia urged her horse into a trot along the creek bed, swinging wide past Jessikah. As she passed Fox, the brooding man remained silent. Flare could feel his scowl follow them.

Aurelia obviously needed Flare's guidance, but he *had* left without warning. He rustled his wings and settled down into Aurelia's hood. He really hadn't left to escape Fox's volatile presence. Flare really had flown to meet the Elven army. The Elder One had been pleased to see him, before telling him to turnaround and make sure Fox made it back to them. Not Aurelia, Fox.

Despite his misgivings, Flare, like the good dragon he was, had done what she asked. All the while musing over the changes in her appearance. She wasn't back to her usual breathtaking self, but Flare suspected she would be by the time he met up with her again. The slow unbinding of the curse, which she had born the brunt of, was fading her wrinkles and darkening her hair. Her voice had strengthened, too. The bright gleam in her green eyes told Flare she was aware and well pleased too.

But now that he was back on Aurelia's stiff shoulder, Flare anxiously wished he were somewhere else. Aurelia didn't believe him, that Flare had seen the army? His tail twitched. She knew Fox could hardly stand Flare, and that the feeling was entirely mutual. Flare could *almost* understand if she'd thought that little of him.

As they passed beneath another giant oak, so old and crusty it looked as much like stone as a tree, Flare shook his wings but stayed where he was. He was too proud to fly off, and too worried about where to go if he did. Crystals were required to be on hand, after all.

The bitter taste of resentment that sparked into life in his heart surprised him. It was true that he had done some things that he wasn't entirely proud of. But he was still a dragon, with great power, and worthy of respect.

So why did he feel like there was none left for him now?

A drizzling rain caught them after a tense night of little sleep.

They had ridden onwards after a scant breakfast of some small mammal, which Fox had procured somehow, as he was would do occasionally. Jessikah had been made to skin and gut it before cooking it on a stick over the fire. As Flare had returned from taking a drink at a small stream, Aurelia had been sipping from a goblet. She had offered it to Flare, but Flare had shaken his head quickly when Fox had glared at him from across the fire.

It was now heading towards later afternoon, and the air was chilly, tasting of wet mosses and damp earth. The rain seemed to be annoying the horses, but Flare was snug enough in Aurelia's hood that was up over her hair.

Suddenly, a voice called out, and two other voices answered. On his horse in the lead once again, Fox raised his head, peering through the trees. Flare stuck his head out past the hood, not sure if he felt relieved or even more anxious. Aurelia sighed beside him, possibly feeling the same.

With a dry sniff, Flare knew they'd fit right in with the Elven army, as an undercurrent of tension could be felt amongst the soldiers. The Elder One had marched them hard through the thick forest, and the toll on the soldiers was obvious. They were fit and healthy, but they were not creatures of the forest. Most had lived their whole lives in the caves of Lolihud. The uneven, mossy ground and dappled light hadn't suited them at all. When Flare had made a quick visit to check their location, he had been taken aback.

The soldiers had been resting, slumped, and tired, faces pale from the march. They had been training for years, but most had never walked this far. Efforts to polish weapons against rust and moisture seemed half-hearted, while others simply sat and stared at the alien, green landscape around them.

Someone else shouted nearby, realising it was Aurelia who had returned. As the three riders picked their way across the edge of the camp, another shout went out, and even more voices joined in. And then the shouts turned to cheers.

The Elves got to their feet, gathering close to Aurelia's horse, their weary eyes now bright and excited. Someone even threw a hat into the air. It got stuck high up in a tree and laughter erupted. A call went out for Flare to fetch it down, but he pointedly ignored them.

Fox ignored the gathered Elves too, and slid off his horse, throwing his reins at a startled young Elf with white hair. Fox's glare was gone, but he was frowning, his eyes on Aurelia.

"We're here, Aurelia," Fox raised his voice to be heard above the cheers. More Elves were drifting through the trees to see what the noise was about.

Aurelia sat frozen on her horse, seemingly stunned by the attention. Flare poked her cheek, trying not to scratch her. Her green eyes were blinking rapidly.

"Aurelia?" Flare's query was tentative.

Touching her cheek where he had poked her, Aurelia turned to Flare. "Is... is this for us?"

"No," Fox said, amusement colouring his voice. He raised a hand to her. "It's for you."

"But..." her voice trailed off. She looked around in a daze, the smudges under her eyes at odds with their green depths.

The cheers continued, and Fox helped her dismount. They'd come to a larger than usual clearing in the forest. The canopy far above still obscured the sky, but there were easily a hundred Elves gathered around, standing on fallen branches or on the shoulders of their mates.

As she slid off, Aurelia's cloak got stuck on the saddle. Fox yanked it free, a stiff smile on his lips as Flare had to fly free to avoid getting twisted up in the material. Aurelia hadn't noticed. With a scowl of his own, Flare landed on Aurelia's other shoulder, further away from Fox. As he was righting himself, the cheers softened, and then died altogether.

"So. You have all returned."

The Elder One's voice rang out through the crowd, even richer and stronger than only a few days ago. But the tone was less than warm. Around them, the hush seemed to deepen.

Fox, with his back to the Elder One, frowned at the voice. He stayed facing Aurelia, pitching his voice low, for Aurelia's ears alone.

"Don't forget what I said."

Aurelia nodded, a slow bob of her head. Satisfied, Fox narrowed his eyes at Flare before unhurriedly turning around. Fox's sharp intake of breath was loud enough for all to hear.

The Elder One had stepped forward, Elves parting to allow her through.

Oh yes, Flare realised with a coil of unease in his heart. There was no doubt the curse was receding, and her power returning in its stead. Getting to this point, after so long, should have filled Flare with relief.

So why do I want to fly away and hide?

Stopping before Fox and Aurelia, the Elder One stood there like the queen she had been, resplendent with glowing life. As both Aurelia and Fox continued to stare in shock, bright green eyes flashed, clearly pleased by their reaction.

The Elder One was no longer a wraith of stooped shoulders and colourless hair. Dressed in red and gold furs, her eyes burned a dark emerald, and her hair was darker, fuller and thicker. Her skin was smooth and the sickly pallor was now a warm, glowing cream. Her voice was a rich purr.

"Fox."

"Elder One," Fox murmured, barely tilting his head. His voice was calm, but Flare, peering under Aurelia's chin, could see his lips were a thin line. Light rain had started again above them, but Fox didn't move to brush away the droplets from his cheeks.

Green eyes scanned him up and down before turning to Aurelia. The Elder One's gaze cooled.

"Aurelia."

"Elder... Elder One," Aurelia stammered. "You're... healed?"

She started to drop to one knee, but Fox grabbed her arm without taking his eyes off the Elder One. Fox was frowning again. Eventually he averted his black and gold gaze from the Elder One, staring past the Elves into the trees beyond them.

"Almost." The figure before them smiled with a mocking twist of lips. "You may call me the Lady now."

"The Lady?" Aurelia said, hesitantly. Her cheeks were pink and her mouth was a thin line.

"Yes. The Lady. A lady with no other name. I am no longer an aged shell of myself, but I am not yet fully healed. So nameless I shall stay." The woman's full lips widened into a dark smile. "Until I get back what is coming to me. And then I shall claim my name."

"The curse is broken!" someone cheered, unable to help himself. Others joined in. Aurelia staggered back into the horse behind her, but Fox held her steady. Flare could just make out Jessikah dismounting quietly beside them, eyes down.

The Lady's smile darkened further as she looked around. "But I don't think you deserve all this fuss, considering it was a team effort, hmmm?"

Her chilling green eyes snapped back to Aurelia. Fox casually turned from frowning at the trees back to Aurelia, and he shook his head slightly. Ignoring his caution, Aurelia shook off Fox's hand and straightened. Flare drew in his wings as Aurelia stepped past Fox, away from the horse, to stand in the small clearing the Elves crowded around.

"I agree." Finding her voice, Aurelia's words rang out. "I don't. But my companions do. Without them, the plan would have failed."

The Lady's smile appeared to be stuck on her face. "Indeed."

The silence was so thick that Flare held his breath.

What was happening?

He didn't understand the Elder One's... no, the Lady's, he corrected himself, cold reception. The hush was interrupted only by the gentle drops of rain on leaves above. Flare watched in fascination as the Lady's eyes darkened and flashed. Her teeth seemed too bright a white against her lips. She looked quite different from the original young woman he'd known. Had that dark flash always been there? Flare's wings drooped, thinking of Fox's words of caution to Aurelia. What did that man know?

"So humble," the Lady murmured, and the closest Elves shifted uneasily. There was a cough, quickly stifled. No one spoke.

Moving without a sound, Fox walked forward, coming to stand beside Aurelia.

"Why don't you come closer, Flare? My brave warriors, let Flare lead through to this rather special camp."

Flare coughed, the sound a tiny puff amongst the rain and the hush of the crowd. He was riding on Aurelia's shoulder, and could hardly lead her. But the point was clear that Aurelia was under Flare's direction. Elves were shifting uneasily, and Flare recognised their expressions. They were mirroring his mixed feelings, anxiety and unease. Unsure of the cold welcome by their leader, towards the one who had helped get this far.

"Come now, dragon," the Lady said, stepping aside and raising a shapely arm, her sleeves cut so her smooth skin could be seen. "Let her see what type of king rules this land, what he does to folk and creatures of magic. I saw it with my own eyes before I was banished, my magic stolen."

The Lady turned slightly, at first appearing to gaze out forlornly at the irregular shaped clearing. But her gaze was carefully keeping an eye on Flare, making sure he went along with her words. Fox stiffened beside them, spotting the shapes rising from behind them, and Aurelia made a small choked noise.

"Flare and I saw the king strike this dragon from the sky with magic. Is that the kind of threat we should let go unpunished?"

Behind the Lady, rising from the forest floor, were dragon bones. Flare's breath left him in a panicked gasp.

The dark shapes, twisted and scattered amongst the undergrowth, were the same as before, rising in long arcs, reaching for the treetops above. The same mosses and lichens growing along their jagged forms covered them, adding a strange beauty to the fallen creature's earthly remains.

These were the same bones that Flare had first seen years ago, already dead. Not part of a living dragon falling from the sky as claimed, but when he was fleeing Aneirin with the queen. They had come across Fox here, the man idly seated amongst the jagged shapes, camped with only Jessikah for company.

Flare didn't dare to turn around to stare at Fox.

These were also the same bones where Aurelia, Fox, Flare and Jessikah had been camped on their way back to Aneirin. Where Fox had summoned the prince to meet Aurelia in the forest.

"Oh, my," Flare breathed.

Both he and Fox knew that this dragon hadn't been stuck out of the sky by a magic-fuelled king. The dragon had in fact been laid down with a black Elven spear. Flare's eyes darted back to the bones.

A spear, which was now gone from where it had once lain.

Flare's tail twitched, furious at the Lady for taking advantage of a fallen dragon this way. It was dishonourable and disrespectful, even if Flare didn't know who the noble creature had been.

Had Fox told Aurelia about this place, about how this poor creature had died? If The Lady underestimated Fox's relationship with Aurelia, then she had just exposed herself in a blatant lie. Shifting slightly, Flare looked back at Aurelia. She was standing at the front of the Elven soldiers, all of whom were staring at the bones with solemn eyes.

"The king, you say?" murmured Aurelia, her voice calm.

Flare's wings drooped.

Spotting the red flush rising along Aurelia's neck, Flare realised that, yes, Fox had told Aurelia exactly what this place was, and how the dragon had met its end. Fox's advice, hard as it was to admit, had been correct.

Flare's unease spread, realising he needed to heed the advice as well.

Trust no one.

10

Rhydian

"*Blood binds all*," Rhydian murmured to the breeze at the top of the tower.

Barely lifting his hair from his forehead, the air was strangely calm. To the north, the sky appeared golden, its pure expanse a mockery of the lies he was living amongst. He ached to be away and amongst a place where none knew him, or what type of family he belonged to. Inhaling slowly, Rhydian tried to ignore the ache he felt with each beat of his tired heart. He could hardly detect the thick aromas of the city up here, just the occasional scent of smoking meat and boiling grains from a brewery outside the castle wall.

Shutting his eyes to the vista of Aneirin spread out far below; Rhydian let himself be drawn back to his memory. He replayed hearing his father's yell echoing through the great hall, Rhydian leading Aurelia to the top of the tower.

All the while Aurelia suspecting what would happen if she forced his father's hand, so that Rhydian could see. But was it too late? Was it too late to avoid further conflict? Enough harm had been done. It was impossible that Aurelia was unaffected mentally, as well as physically, from her ordeal.

Rhydian's hands tightened on the balcony wall. His fingers traced the marks of Aurelia's cloak dragging through the accumulated grit, as she had been flung off the tower with magic.

Rhydian's lips curled, and his eyes opened. He stared down at the disturbance in the grit, evidence of the magic wielded by his father, who had openly condemned the use of it.

His father's words played over in his head. So much just didn't add up.

Lifting his head, Rhydian gazed out at the kingdom below him once more. His gaze wandered over the quiet city. Generations of families had made the place a home, but so many had fled, sensing something dark at the heart of it. Where had they gone? His gaze lowered further, examining the great cobbled courtyard and fortified walls, shining brightly in the noonday sun. Great stone blocks had been used to surround the city. How it had been built, he couldn't guess. Only a few guards patrolled the catwalks.

His gaze paused at the spot Lord Cyrus had met his violent end. How many guards remembered seeing that? Rhydian's knuckles whitened. Or did they still not know, was that a separate binding of their memories, unlinked to the dark magic of the curse?

Tearing his gaze away, Rhydian lifted his head to examine the jagged mountains. They surrounded the expansive valley of the farms and fields, and at this moment they were clear of clouds. Turning to look south, over the forest, Rhydian could see a dark line muddying the horizon.

"South," Rhydian muttered, exhaling slowly.

The rain clouds may have been the ones from yesterday, and Rhydian wondered if Aurelia was caught beneath them somewhere as she rode to meet her people.

Rhydian had welcomed the rain on his journey to the stones a few days before. Blackthorn had been kicking up such a fuss in the stables that Merion had bravely petitioned the king for the prince to take the horse out. Not just for exercise, but to prevent him from spooking the other horses. The king had reluctantly agreed, likely knowing they'd need the horses as steady as possible for what was to come.

So Rhydian had been allowed out, for a short time, and only if he was accompanied by half a dozen 'honour guards'. Rhydian snorted.

All of the guards had been uncomfortable with the arrangement. But he had welcomed the short taste of freedom and the rain. It had made the tears on his face harder to spot. The fear in his heart, of approaching war, and for Aurelia had him on edge and it felt he was crying like a lost child.

"My prince?"

Startled, Rhydian turned around. A small head was peering around the half-open door. Rhydian tried to smile.

"Chase."

The boy bobbed his head, staring past Rhydian, to the mountains and open sky beyond. His youthful face looked troubled.

"Chase, are you alright?"

The boy's eyes darted to his, and Rhydian raised his eyebrows.

"Yes. I," the boy stopped and sniffed noisily. Rhydian realised the poor boy was trying to hide his tears in much the same way as Rhydian. "Rhydian, oh, sorry, my prince, I mean. I-I don't like it up here. Not anymore."

Rhydian flicked a glance to the drop behind him, not needing the boy to explain. They both knew what Chase was referring to. All of it.

Stepping away from the balcony, Rhydian wiped his face and stopped at the door. He ruffled the boy's hair, which usually got him a smile, or a laughing protest at least. The boy looked down at his scuffed boots instead.

"The king is looking for you, my prince. He came to the stables."

Rhydian's hand stilled. "I'll come down." He cleared his throat. "Do you know what he needed me for?"

Chase refused to meet his eyes. "I was hiding behind the lost horse, I'm not sure. Uncle was grooming it, and then I was sent to fetch you to the library."

"Huh. What lost horse?"

"It came in a few days ago, still saddled and everything."

Rhydian frowned. "Did your uncle recognise it?"

"Yeah. It was here not long ago. It belonged to a guest of your father."

His father's guest? Perhaps the blonde man that had been rushing from the castle before his father had thrown Aurelia off the tower?

"We might have to send out a party to check they're okay, lad."

"Uncle already requested one of the captains to take care of that."

"Ah. Merion's a good man. Down you go."

Dropping his hand from the boy's hair, Rhydian allowed Chase to precede him down the steps. Rhydian closed the door behind him and followed.

"How did the king seem today, Chase?" Rhydian asked as they descended.

Chase's small shoulders shrugged as he wound his way down. They passed Rhydian's closed chamber door, and he averted his eyes. He hadn't been back inside, not wanting to see his blood over the floor. He'd been sleeping in Aurelia's empty chamber. Chase's voice roused him, answering his question.

"I'm not sure, my prince. But…"

"It's okay lad," Rhydian softened his voice. "You can tell me."

They wound down and around, past the chamber Aurelia had stayed in. Chase's steps slowed slightly. The chamber still smelled faintly of wintery, gentle flowers. Dreading the day when that scent would fade, Rhydian passed it, his heart aching.

They finally reached the last of the stairs. The two guards at the bottom saluted Rhydian before returning to their formal stance, spears upright.

Rhydian nodded politely to them before drawing Chase back into the tower.

"Chase?" he said, crouching down. "Please tell me."

The boy shifted uneasily on his feet. He reminded Rhydian of Blackthorn and that had him smiling, which seemed to calm the boy's unease.

"The king is different," Chase whispered.

Rhydian kept his face neutral. "Yes, that's to be expected. There's an army-"

"*No,*" Chase turned to glance behind him. The guards were still on either side of the doorway, facing away. But both were leaning closer to hear what their prince was saying, and Rhydian didn't blame them in the slightest. They were good men. Chase shook his head and his earnest gaze met Rhydian's. "That's not it."

"What is it then? It's okay. I won't be angry."

Chase licked his lips, dark eyes solemn. "I heard my uncle talking with my mum last night about the king." He lowered his voice. "And about magic."

Rhydian winced.

Merion, shut it around your nephews.

Their ears are too big.

Nodding solemnly, Rhydian urged the boy to continue.

"Well," Chase murmured. "Its just that since Aurelia… we knew something was going on. Then the king… he…Lord Cyrus…"

"I know, lad, I know." Rhydian placed a hand on Chase's shoulder. "Go on."

"Well, we didn't think twice about it all. But then our minds cleared, and now we know things aren't right. And the king, he knows we know. But we all have to act like everything is all right, and…"

A metallic clink interrupted him.

One of the guards had tilted his head closer, so much so that the top of his helm collided with the tip of his spear. The other guard hissed at his companion. Rhydian sighed.

"It's okay, you two," he said, loudly.

Rhydian squeezed the miserable boy's shoulder as the guards shuffled towards the door, sheepish yet eager to hear what their prince had to say. Waiting for him to clarify the strange situation they were all in.

"Look," Rhydian said, speaking from his heart. "I know we've all realised something is… off here."

The guards looked at each other guiltily, but both nodded. Chase bit his lip. "And we know who is responsible." Rhydian ran a hand through his already tousled hair, choosing his words carefully. "A battle *is* coming, and we need to be prepared. But I *am* going to sort it out."

The guards looked relieved, and one of them actually saluted him again. Rhydian nodded at them, but laid his fingers to his lips.

Treason, along with magic, was punishable by death, after all.

The king was alone in the library, sitting at the main table in the centre of the room.

A fire was burning in the grate, and as Rhydian stepped through the double doors, he was greeted by the soft scent of old parchment and fragrant smoke. It was no wonder Rhydian had loved it here as a small boy. It was the kind of space that welcomed you, and invited you in to sit, read and listen to stories by the librarian. Rhydian paused halfway to the reading desk, glancing around with a frown.

Lady Hywel, where in the hells are you?

Meeting his father's dull gaze, Rhydian's frown faded. The king looked unwell, and Rhydian broke the silence first.

"Is there any chance this battle can be won?"

"No." His father shook his head, his head jerking oddly. "There will be no victory, not on either side. I don't believe anyone will walk away from this."

Rhydian took a step closer to the table, his heart beating fast.

"Why can't you stop this?"

"There are only a thousand of them, did you know?" murmured the king. He belched regally and Rhydian glared. "But we are only five hundred soldiers."

"How do you know how many they have?" Rhydian demanded.

"And they have at least two dragons-"

"*Two*! What?"

"-that we know of," his father continued, running a hand through his silvery brown hair. His cheeks were flushed pink, but the rest of his face was grey. "It's far too late."

Rhydian stepped forward again, resisting the urge to wring his father's neck for his cryptic words. Unconsciously, his fingers grazed his own throat.

Flare, no matter what happens, I owe you.

Rhydian straightened, deciding he had to find out whatever he could, no matter the cost.

"Who's the blonde man that visited you?" Rhydian asked, and the king looked startled, his eyes glazing over slightly. "Where is *he*? Is he a magic user as well? Can *he* help Aneirin?"

His father narrowed his eyes, his head shaking slowly, clearly amused. "You don't deserve to know," the king smirked. "You revoked that privilege long ago."

Rhydian wanted to howl in frustration, and he dropped his hand from his neck. "For fuck's sake, father! What does that even mean? Is this because of Aurelia?" He swallowed. "I didn't know where she'd come from!"

But did that matter now? Because even when you knew, you let her carry out her grim task, anyway.

Rhydian swallowed, pleading with himself.

I had to; I had to break this dark magic over us.

Lowering his gaze to the desk, the king said nothing. He waved an unsteady hand at Rhydian to join him. Biting down on his resentment, Rhydian reluctantly obliged. He crossed the rug and the aroma of aged brandy met his nose. A half empty crystal decanter sat discarded on the library floor.

Rhydian blew out a sigh. That seemed to explain why his father looked so ill.

At least his father had the sense to not leave his drink on the table, because in front of the king was a large, beautifully illustrated scroll. Unrolled, it was spread out and held down at the corners with glass weights. The parchment was yellowed with age, but the pigments were still bright. Gold leaf shone in embellishment across the cracked surface.

Rhydian inhaled sharply. It was one of the most magnificent illustrations Rhydian had ever seen, and he wondered why it wasn't hanging somewhere grand. Perhaps in the throne room?

Tilting his head, Rhydian could see the main design depicted a shimmering copper dragon. It was fighting horned figures amongst thickly leaved trees. The lines were strong, the colours vivid, and it was easy to imagine the sounds and smells of the violent clash playing out.

"Do you know who this is?" His father's voice was quiet. He belched again. "Who this was?"

Rhydian nodded, eyes on the beautiful work of art. Everyone knew the myth of the great copper dragon, Dawn of Fire, defender of the weak, slayer of demons.

"She was one of the characters in my childhood stories," Rhydian muttered. "What does that have to do with anything?"

Reaching out to touch the dragon, his father exhaled slowly. "We found her, not too far from here, in the forest."

"You... found her?" Rhydian looked up, his heart turned heavy, weighted down with dread. "But she was just a myth. Wasn't she?"

After tracing the claws and wings, the king's fingers stopped over the heart of the brilliantly rendered dragon.

"She was quite real, son. But when we found her, she was dying." His father tapped the drawing carefully with a blunt finger. "A cursed Elf had used one of their damned black spears."

Rhydian's mouth went dry. The soft pop of sparks in the great hearth behind them was the only sound.

"You said 'we'?"

"Your mother and I."

"Oh. I see." But he didn't.

"Dawn of Fire was dying, unable to move. This was during the chaos right after the sacking of the City of the Seers." His father laughed, a bitter sound in the stillness. "I don't know why an Elf would attack a dragon, especially Dawn of Fire. She was a champion of the weak, or so the stories that were true went."

Rhydian waited, hardly daring to breathe. His father's finger tapped the dragon's scaled chest. His eyes blinked rapidly, as if he were in a daze, and his usually handsome face appeared sickly.

"Dawn and your mother, they talked."

The dread in his heart was spreading, and Rhydian grabbed the edge of the table. The drawings of the dragon in the old armoury below came to mind.

"The pair of them came to a life or death bargain. We were lost in the forest, you see, after the city fell," the king took a shaky breath. "So she shared her magic with us, so we could try and save her. To remove the spear with our newfound strength."

His parents lost in the forest after the fall of a city? Rhydian had no idea what his father was talking about. All he could think of was the dragon, taken down with a black spear. Aurelia's red-fletched arrow flashed in his mind.

Is that what the black one meant? Death?

"You met Dawn of Fire, the great dragon warrior," Rhydian murmured, his mind spinning. "And she shared her magic with both of you? *That's* how you got your power?"

His father's expression darkened, and suddenly his hand shot out, grabbing Rhydian by the wrist.

"And do you know what we did?" his father hissed, his eyes wide and bloodshot on Rhydian's face. "When it was time to pull the spear away?"

His father shook Rhydian's wrist.

"*Away* from her heart?" the king repeated, spittle on his lips.

Gods, please no.

Knowing he was unable to break free, Rhydian closed his eyes, wrist throbbing. The king's voice dropped to a whisper, curling through Rhydian's mind with words like poison.

"Sophia couldn't do it by herself," the king hissed. "Even with the glow of dragon magic inside of us..."

"Stop," Rhydian whispered. "*Please.*"

The king ignored him. "I put my hands around Sophia's, and we..."

His father's hand tensed further around Rhydian's wrist. Ice slid down Rhydian's spine. "Please don't say it," Rhydian repeated, mouth dry, tears clogging his throat.

"Oh, gods," his father groaned.

The grip on Rhydian's wrist disappeared.

Rhydian's eyes sprang open. His father had covered his face with trembling hands, elbows on the table, head hung low. The silence lengthened, the unspoken words were like a wasp buzzing around, ready to sting. Rhydian remained frozen in horror as he stared down at his father, a man who had become a stranger.

"We didn't pull." The king's voiced was muffled, even in the bitter silence of the room.

Rhydian swallowed, feeling a hot flush of shame crawling up his neck. Tears slid down his cheek, and he had to swallow the bile rising in his throat. His father was crying silently, unable to finish. Rhydian pushed away from the table, hands clenched, and spoke the bitter words that his father could, or would, not.

"You pushed."

The king nodded, head still in his hands, his royal tears falling to the noble face of the fierce warrior dragon before him. Her scales were a brilliant coppery red, a fine pattern of alternating shapes. The artist had depicted Dawn of Fire's expression with mastery; she stared back at them, proud, fierce and determined.

Rhydian licked his lips, blinking at the bitter taste of his tears.

"Son..." His father said hoarsely. He dropped his hands from his face and pushed his chair back to stand. Without thinking about it, Rhydian's hand shot out.

Clamping his hand on his father's shoulder, Rhydian slammed him back into his seat. With his free hand, he pointed a shaking finger at the illustration before them.

"Don't you *dare*," Rhydian hissed. The king looked up, his face pale, eyes red.

"Rhydian, I-"

"*Look* at her."

"Rhydian, please-"

"I said fucking look at her!"

Rhydian's outraged yell rang out like a battle cry. His father mouthed words, unable to respond, trembling before the fury in his son's eyes.

A dragon.

His parents had killed a dragon.

Jerking back from the table, releasing his father, Rhydian kicked a chair across the room. The sound of it smashing against the wall was jarring, but didn't quite cover the roaring that was growing louder in Rhydian's ears. He turned slowly, pointing a shaking finger at his father.

"You sit *right there*," Rhydian hissed through his teeth, "and you *look* at her."

His father, frozen in his place, kept his eyes on Rhydian's face. The king flinched at his son's words, but said nothing. Rhydian talked on, shaking his head in a sort of horrified wonder.

"You and my mother! *Blood Binds All*!" he laughed, roaring in his ears and a hysteria coming over him. "Oh my gods, that means I am the son of murderous Elves! Not just a prince at all. I am the son of an Elven king pretending to be a human, in a kingdom that believe magic does not... No. Let me rephrase that... in a kingdom that believes magic *should* not exist?"

His father flinched again.

"Oh my gods," Rhydian breathed, walking backwards to the wall, tripping over the smashed chair. "Are you even... are you even a member of the royal family?"

The flush of shame over the king's cheeks was enough for Rhydian to choke out a shocked laugh.

"It just gets better!" Rhydian flung up his hands. "What happened to them? Did you murder them too!?"

His father shook his head. "I don't know what became of them. But the opportunity-"

"You bastard," Rhydian hissed, approaching the table once more. "*Who* are you? And did you pass on your tainted heart to *me*? Am *I* the same as you? Tell me, father, what am I? What does that make *me*?"

The king sat up straighter, his pale blue eyes still bloodshot, but hard. "You are *my son*."

Crouching down, Rhydian grabbed the crystal decanter off the floor. As he straightened, he took a swig to burn away the bile in his throat.

"To Dawn of Fire." Raising the decanter high with a shaking hand, Rhydian toasted the scroll. He took another swig, the alcohol spilling over his lips. "And to *my family*."

His father sobbed once at that, but Rhydian ignored him.

Lowering the decanter, Rhydian admired its beauty for a moment before he whirled, throwing the decanter across the room. The bottle smashed into the fireplace in a chaotic chime of broken glass against the stone. The flames dimmed at first and then rose as the alcohol ignited.

Stalking towards the library doors, Rhydian had grabbed his chest, trying not to throw up. He was cold, shaking. Numb.

A chair scraped behind him, and the king cried out.

"Rhydian! Stop! Your mother and I, we were desperate, *lost*. Rhydian! *Come back here!*"

Rhydian slammed the doors shut so hard that it sounded like one of them cracked.

Once he was alone in the hallway, Rhydian had to lean against the wall, a hand over his mouth, holding in his scream of rage, of shame. It was hard to think beyond the roaring in his ears and the racing of his heart, and he could feel a numbness spreading through his body like a cold tremor. His mouth had dried up, his throat burnt by the alcohol.

He couldn't shed another tear even if he'd wanted to, which, in a way, was good.

If he started crying again, there was a chance he'd never stop.

No longer afraid of what he'd find, Rhydian jerked open his bedchamber door. He stumbled inside, slamming it behind him.

As his eyes roamed the silent chamber, a laugh escaped his mouth, as he was simply unable to choke it back. The sun was shining through the window like the world was all at peace. The rays were bright, warm, and illuminating everything with a loving golden touch. His rumpled bed. The cold fireplace.

Along with the dried blood under his chair, now a dry, rusty stain, the edges flaking.

Biting back another hysterical laugh, Rhydian addressed the empty chamber.

"I regret smashing that liquor," he admitted. "At this moment, I think I would find it quite welcome."

Rhydian stayed where he was, letting his breathing slow, the roaring in his ears dim in volume. It took a while, but eventually he took a breath, and crossed the room to crouch down. He made himself study the blood. It had run under his chair and covered a substantial area of the flagstone floor. His blood had flowed along the stones, was darker in the cracks, and the coppery red pattern reminded him of something.

Nausea crashed over him like a downpour of rain. Grabbing his chair for support, he hauled himself up, and then around to collapse into it.

"Scales," he whispered, dropping his head into his hands. "My blood has turned the stones into copper scales! Oh Dawn. I'm sorry," he coughed. "My parents... Oh gods. Dawn of Fire, I'm sorry."

No.

This was no time for tears. He had to think.

Think!

Swallowing away the shame of his family, Rhydian slumped back in his chair. He was grateful that his riding pants were dark; as it was likely he was sitting on more bloodstains.

Biting back another hysterical sob, Rhydian's gaze travelled through the golden glow across his chamber, sliding along the rays of light, past the chest in the corner. His gaze came to rest on Aurelia's bow, propped in the corner of his room, where he'd left it after she'd been flung off the tower.

Rhydian sat up straight, the breath pausing in his lungs.

A quiver rested beside the bow, nearly full of arrows with fletching in a variety of colours. Red, purple, white, and yellow.

And just one arrow fletched with feathers of inky black.

Rhydian blinked, and his vision doubled with that of first meeting Aurelia. He saw her arrow, red-fletched, sticking out from the doe. He saw one with white feathers in the driftwood at his feet. And he also saw Aurelia's relief at not having to use the black arrow. Was the colour black cursed? Or was it Elven superstition? Rhydian didn't know. It didn't matter to him.

It just had to matter to *her*.

"Aurelia," Rhydian whispered. "*We* will fix this."

Not daring to breathe, Rhydian pushed himself up, making sure he placed his boots onto the bloodstains below as he made his way towards the door.

He stopped in the centre of the room, with the light spilling in the window, golden rays pouring across the floor and over him.

"I've *cursed* by the gods often enough," Rhydian began, his breath hitching. "Maybe it's time to try something else."

Rhydian closed his eyes.

"Please," he whispered, humble. "Please help me."

Reaching out his hands, he let the faint warmth of the light wash over his skin. He spoke louder, willing the gods to listen.

"I have been trapped. The woman I love has been trapped. Both of us with lies, with deceit, and with the *betrayal* of those who should have been protecting us."

Eyes still closed, he stepped out of the light, towards the corner of the room. Shadows washed over his closed lids, and they reminded him of his dreams.

"My mother," he whispered, "tried to kill me, a sacrifice for some kind of power, for some gods-be-damned hope of protection! When it failed, she somehow found help to seek revenge. And she sent Aurelia here to kill my father. But Aurelia found me. And..."

Rhydian took another resolute step towards the corner with the bow.

"And we came together, and I love her. Now I need to protect her and my people. From my father, who will ruin this kingdom to protect himself from shame. He killed a man in front of us with a bloody whip of magic! And made us forget!"

Rhydian took another step, and his hands touched the cold stones of the two walls. Exploring with his fingertips, he found where the chilled surfaces met in the corner.

Kneeling, eyes closed all the while, Rhydian traced the stones of the wall as he sank down.

"Please," he pleaded. "They killed a dragon, a creature of magic and majesty. They…" he cried. "I'm sorry, oh, I'm sorry."

His fingers left the stone, touching something warmer. It was the smooth wood of the bow. Closing his left fist, Rhydian dragged the bow close to his chest and slung it over his shoulder. He lowered his right hand further.

"Please. *Help* me," Rhydian gasped out and then swallowed, feeling his frustration rising. "I *deserve* this! I sacrificed myself for Aurelia! I sacrificed myself for my people!"

His fingers touched the oiled leather of the quiver, and the quills rustled softly as he made contact with their soft feathers.

"*Guide* me, show me this is the way."

Pushing his hand into the quills, his fingers touched one colder than the rest. Rhydian wrapped his hand around it carefully and pulled it away gently from the rest.

His heart racing with traitorous beats, Rhydian opened his eyes, letting his gaze wander over the arrow clutched tightly in his grip. His smile was grim.

"Thank you," he whispered as the golden sunlight caressed his shoulders.

Standing up, Rhydian opened the door. Slipping the arrow under his shirt, the prince made his way down the steps of the silent tower.

He didn't look back.

11

Flare

Year 367

Aneirin Castle

"Dark magic users are coming."

Silence followed the king's words. Those gathered in the great courtyard to hear them were townsfolk; servants from the castle, the rest of the soldiers and guards. Most were shifting on their feet, fidgeting with hat or helm; many of the people from the town below were holding the hands of the person next to them.

Even from his high perch amongst the highest gargoyles on the prince's tower, Flare could see that their expressions were similar to some of the Elves he had left behind in the forest. Both sides knew something was afoot here, more than what they were being told. Flare's wings drooped, and his tail flicked back and forth like a cat's. The difference here was that there were far fewer soldiers than there were Elves.

"We must be ready." The king's voice echoed off the high walls around them. "They are in the forest, just south of us, and will likely be here by tomorrow, bringing their dark powers to our land. Bringing their foul magic to our soil."

Flare searched the faces again. There wasn't a spark of admiration for their king, nor trust, and no eyes of devotion. The king forged on in spite of their less than trusting gazes.

"They will bring their lies and their dragon-infused magic, trying to pollute us with their dark hearts." The words bounced around the courtyard, and a few mutters started up. The king's voice hardened. "The Elves should have stayed in their caves, mining their crystals of lies, for the beasts that they serve! Instead, they bring about a so-called ending to a curse! I say to you now, the only curse is the one they bring, death and lies to all of us!"

Pausing, the king scanned the crowd. His expression was calm, but his hands were clenched tightly at his sides.

"It wasn't supposed to have been a curse. You knew that, Aran," Flare muttered, his nose wrinkling at the bitter tang of faint magic still seeping from the stones below him. "What we did was supposed to keep you all safe. At peace, not out looking for trouble and chaos in the forest."

Images of ruined cities clouded his mind, and guilt throbbed deep within his heart. The City of the Seers, once a shining marvel. Its parent city, Baile Mara, or The City of the Sea, fallen to chaos even earlier, was lost beneath the waves of the far eastern shores.

Shaking his wings, Flare bristled to himself. "Dragons *never* meant for these things to happen."

His words were carried away by the strong breeze, bringing with it a faint whiff of hot smoke. Flare, tasting the rich minerals, realised it was smoke from the forges behind the armoury. His purple tail twitched again, and he lowered his eyes back to the gathering below, ears straining to catch the king's words.

The king was clad in shining gold armour over pale grey furs, standing atop the steps that led from the courtyard into the great hall. One of his hands was clasped casually over the ornate hilt of the sword hanging at his side. The breeze picked up his silvery brown hair, and swept it over his forehead, and around his simple golden crown. The man was speaking like he believed every word that dropped from his lips, but something about his hard gaze indicated that the man was under strain. The king was a handsome man, who looked more like Rhydian's older brother on occasion. But today, he looked very much like he was feeling the weight of his crown.

Halfway through a sentence about faith in your fellow townspeople, the king frowned, and the crowd shifted again. Flare dared to reach his head out further from behind a grimacing stone monster. It took a moment for the sound to reach him, a low rumble vibrating up the stones from the earth. Flare pulled his head back to the gutter and the gargoyle.

So they still had earth tremors here too, did they?

Interesting.

Idly snapping at a passing fly that was trying to land on his snout, the dragon peered back over the edge. The prince stood by his father's side, his expression carefully neutral.

Rhydian was the same height as his father, but slimmer in the shoulders where his father was broad. His hair was a more light brown, and the sun highlighted the prince's hair with streaked gold. The prince's stance was stiff and formal, with his hands behind his back. Rhydian was attired in dark clothing, not armour, under a rich black fur coat. The blue-black fur was reminiscent of Fox's dark cloak that seemed to eat the light around it. But it wasn't just the prince's dark clothing that reminded Flare of Fox. Rhydian was the same young man, but... Flare squinted. Rhydian was stony faced, his expression unsettlingly similar to the grim stare that Fox usually wore.

Thinking of Fox, Flare shuddered. He was seriously thinking of abandoning whatever came next. He wished no part in any upcoming chaos. And the bones! The *dragon* bones. Flare hadn't had the courage to talk with Fox about the Lady's outright lie.

What was Fox thinking? Was he going to tell everyone the king had nothing to do with them? But the Lady certainly didn't know the king had been responsible.

Flare looked up from the courtyard, his gaze towards the forest.

Or did she?

Flare hadn't encountered her until during her time as Queen with Rhydian's father. What had gone on before?

Below him, the murmurs quietened down as the king had finished his speech, and a new voice spoke up. The prince was speaking to his father; however, Rhydian's crisp voice was pitched loud enough for all those gathered to hear. Rhydian was asking about a parley, his hands now unfolded from his back and tightly furled by his sides.

Flare tilted his head. A parley? That was unexpected.

"Negotiate?" the king asked, his eyebrows rising. Rhydian's back stiffened further.

"Yes," said Rhydian, lightly.

"With the Elves?"

"Yes."

"Why?"

With the sun reflecting off the golden lines of his armour, the king turned from his son to face the crowd, judging their reaction. The great courtyard was silent. Not even the guards, in chain mail and full armour themselves, made a noise. Instead of answering his father, Rhydian faced the crowd as well, addressing them directly.

"We shall give the magic users a chance," the prince called, stepping to the edge of the top step. "A chance to keep their honour. If they refuse, then we will take it from them."

A few people cheered, but the sound was quickly stifled. Flare couldn't quite work out the expression on the king's face, but it was grim. He could see that his townspeople and the guards had responded more warmly to his son.

"Because in Aneirin, we will always have our honour," finished Rhydian. He scanned the crowd, meeting as many shining eyes as he could. The king was unable to back out, and Rhydian knew it.

"Fine." The king's voice rang out, his words clipped. "We will give them a chance to avoid bloodshed. Although I don't see-"

"Thank you, father. I suggest-"

"*No.* That's enough from you. I need two men. No weapons. They can leave now."

After a pause, Rhydian bowed stiffly to his father, and moved two steps lower than the king. Before his father could speak again, Rhydian turned to the guards closest to the stairs.

"Who will go?" the prince called, ignoring his father's narrowed eyes.

The first man to volunteer did so with haste, almost as if he had been waiting for this opportunity. As the man stepped forward, Flare's head poked out further.

Even from his perch high up, he recognised Davyn. Flare hadn't realised Davyn was a soldier or a guard, but the man was now dressed like one. His posture was straight and his brown hair was tied back with a leather thong. Under one arm, he carried a metal helm. In his other hand, he held a bow.

Flare's mouth dropped open.

He knew that bow; after all, it had been his gift to Aurelia, right before their departure from Lolihud. He'd had it made especially for her by a master craftsperson. It was beautifully carved, expertly balanced. It also contained a touch of Flare's magic as well. He'd hated to spare any, but for her he'd shared the tiniest amount to help her make her way under some protection across the line of the curse, like a magical key to fit a dark lock.

"No weapons," snapped the king to Davyn. "If you wish to parley, leave it here. Otherwise, they'll kill you on sight."

"It's ornamental, sire."

"Ornamental?"

"My mam gave it to me, sire. I'll tie a white cloth to the top."

"That's a great idea, soldier. Show them we mean no harm for now," Rhydian said loudly, beaming tightly at the man. The king stared at his son, incredulous, before turning back to Davyn.

"Take no arrows," snapped the king.

Davyn stood up even straighter. He saluted with his hand that held the helm. "I will take no arrows, sire," he agreed.

Flare's scales itched with dread as Rhydian's smile turned sickly.

Another man stepped forward, but Flare didn't recognise him. He was tall, stocky and had sandy coloured hair under his helm.

"I will," the other man said, licking his lips. He coughed when Rhydian turned to him sharply, and the man turned to stare at the king. "I meant, I will go, my king."

Flare watched as the prince's stiff posture relaxed slightly, and the prince turned his face towards the sky. Flare froze, not daring to move. The prince's eyes narrowed as his gaze shifted towards the tower.

The king didn't notice. "You will go?" he asked the tall man.

"Yes, sire," he replied, nodding.

The king paused a moment, surveyed Davyn and the other man.

"Very well," the king said, raising his gaze back to the crowd. "See these men off, with terms of surrender. We will do the honourable thing."

Rhydian finally lowered his gaze, and Flare sighed with relief. The king looked his son up and down before turning to retreat through the great doors of the castle. Behind his back, Rhydian and Davyn both slumped with what looked a lot like relief.

As the crowd slowly dispersed, a loud murmur erupted, and a small boy came running from the stables with white cloth. Flare stuck his head back out past the gargoyle to watch before he flew back to report to the Lady.

The men busied themselves with tying the white cloth to the top of the bow, along with another off-white scrap. It was hard to make out what it was, something that the prince had already prepared for, Flare guessed. The two volunteers handed over their weapons to another guard, mounted up on horses brought forward by the bearded groom and adjusted their armour.

Flare was about to fly away, under the shadow of a passing cloud, but he paused. Rhydian was standing by himself on the steps, his hands clenched by his sides again, and his face pale, haunted.

He was staring after the two riders who had crossed the courtyard, their horse's hooves echoing through the tunnel under the wall, leading to the town.

It was a long time before Rhydian slowly made his way back inside.

"Aurelia?" Flare called. There was no answer.

Where was she?

Flare wanted to see how she was before he reported back to the Lady. He'd flown back to the Elven camp above the giant trees, wishing there was more time to explore. It had been too long since he'd been able to wander and investigate the forest in this part of the continent.

Now would be a good time, Flare, his frightened heart whispered to him. *Before this all blows up in your face.*

Twisting his head behind him to scan the trees, Flare huffed a tiny sigh, his claws scraping on the boulder where he'd landed.

Again.

It would be so easy to just fly away. If not for the fact that he'd helped create this mess, and Aurelia needed someone other than Fox to influence her. Was she still going to fight? Stand across a battlefield from the prince? Wondering what Rhydian had planned, Flare sighed again. The prince's behaviour at the king's speech had worried him. He was a man who'd willingly sacrificed his life for the woman he loved, and was taking more steps to... what?

Stretching his wings on the mossy boulder near Aurelia's bedroll, Flare had no idea. An attempt to see the prince would have been too risky, and besides, Flare's wings were aching from all of his scouting around.

Turning back to examine the bulk of the other Elven campsites, Flare was grateful that Aurelia and Fox had set up bedrolls on the edge of the army. Elven warriors would dice away for chips of semi-precious stones, long into the night, and loudly, despite their weariness. Here, near a little brook and fragrant trees, their tidy cluster of bedrolls was almost peaceful. It was also the furthest away from the Lady's tent.

Checking a claw for blemishes, Flare snorted, idly wondering who'd chosen the location, Fox or Aurelia? She would have chosen it for privacy, while Fox simply would avoid others because, well, that was Fox. And likely no one, except for Aurelia, would want him next to them while asleep, even surrounded by a thousand Elven warriors.

Flare's next snort of laughter ended in a frightened chirp.

Icy fingers appeared from nowhere and slid around his neck, cutting off most of his air. Even before frost bloomed around Flare's scales, he knew whose hand it was.

"Unhand me!" Flare squeaked, his heart just about frozen in his chest.

"Why were you laughing, lizard?"

Watching the forest spin slowly around him, Flare's eyes widened in horror as the icy hand rotated Flare on the boulder. His claws scrabbled at the mossy surface to find traction, but to no avail. Flare was turned to face a glittering pair of black eyes, and lips twisted in a sneer. Fox was leaning on the boulder with one hand under his pale chin, the other around Flare's neck.

"Unhand me!" Flare repeated with as much dignity as he could muster, whilst feeling cold seep into his scales.

"Why were you laughing? Were you laughing at Aurelia's pain?" Fox's eyes narrowed, his even white teeth appearing with his menacing smile. "Or the prince, perhaps? What did you find out?"

"I was not-"

"No more lies, little snake."

The hand around his neck tightened. And while it cut off Flare's refusal, his snout still managed to catch the fresh scent of floral soap approaching.

Thank the gods!

Flare choked out a wordless plea for help. Aurelia spotted them straight away.

"Fox!" Aurelia shouted, jumping over a crowd of green ferns, one hand on her belt. "What the hell are you doing?"

Aurelia's voice was furious, and the chilled hand around Flare's neck twitched, loosening just enough for Flare to take in another gasping breath. "Aurelia!" Flare squeaked again, gulping down air. "Tell this... this b-"

The hand twitched again, and Flare's protests were cut off once more.

"This what?" Fox asked, his smile growing wider, even as his glittering eyes narrowed. "This *what*?"

Her mouth open in shock, Aurelia was almost upon them, finishing doing up her belt. Her hair was damp and loose, her face flushed. She halted, panting, to stop and stare.

Twitching his head, Flare glanced in shock up at Fox. The man's pale face wasn't flushed, but his fine lips looked darker than usual. Even in his precarious position, Flare's mind began jumping to all sorts of conclusions.

Had the two of them been...?

As if reading his mind, Fox's smile disappeared.

"That's none of your business, lizard," Fox purred, lowering his face to Flare's.

"Aurelia!" Flare hissed, eyes wide, clawing at the boulder. "Get him-" he gasped, "-off me!"

Taking in the situation, Aurelia shook her head and grabbed Fox by his hair.

"Let. Him. Go." she hissed, furious, giving his black locks such a fierce yank that his head would have snapped back if he was anyone normal. As it was, Fox didn't move. Instead, he only laughed, his smile returning, the icy hand twitching around Flare's neck even as his hair was pulled.

Aurelia yanked his hair again, harder. "Right now!"

Finally, Flare could see the strain of Fox's muscles as he fought against her fierce hold.

Looking down his nose at Flare, Fox ran his tongue over his top row of teeth. There was a moment of stalemate, and finally, the cold seeped out of Flare's scales. One by one, the chilled fingers lifted away. Then Fox's choking grip disappeared altogether.

Flapping wildly and bristling like a wet cat, Flare scrambled wildly away from Fox, landing on Aurelia's shoulder.

"I wish you hadn't had to see that," Flare sniffed, trembling. "The cheek of-"

"Flare, that was inexcusable of Fox," Aurelia murmured, as she reached up to touch one of his claws with a finger. "But I'm sorry, we'll sort it out later."

As Aurelia's other hand let go of Fox's hair, the man stretched his head from side to side. Adjusting his black cloak behind him, Fox hopped up and sat down on the boulder that Flare had vacated, his smile still playing across his lips.

Flare couldn't help it. He bared his teeth at Fox, despite the trembling still rattling his bones. Fox laughed again, crossing his arms over his chest.

Fuck you, Fox mouthed. Flare's claws sank deeper into Aurelia's shoulder.

"Fox," sounding resigned, Aurelia shook her head with a wince. "I know it's hard for you, and that you're more irritated than usual, but can you stop being a bastard for just one moment?"

Fox's smile faded slightly. He shrugged. "I doubt it. But I'll try for you, Little Thing."

Breathing in the clean, damp scent of Aurelia's hair, Flare used a claw to poke bruised scales along his neck. Thankfully, no one was close enough amongst the trees to have seen. The thought of someone seeing that man's hand around him was too much to bear. With his wings still shaking slightly, Flare knew better than to ask for an apology. So too, it seemed, did Aurelia.

She turned slightly away from Fox and scooped a startled Flare up and cradled him to her chest.

"Flare, please," Aurelia's voice was low. "What's happening in Aneirin? Did you see Rhydian?"

Flare was still trembling from shock, embarrassment, and the chilled hands on his scales. He shivered, wondering why Fox was so cold. Sensing Flare's ongoing panic, Fox's lips tilted back up in a knowing smile.

Get a hold of yourself!

You are a dragon!

"Flare?" Aurelia prompted, holding him up to her face. Her green eyes were bright, although there were dark circles beneath.

Trying hard to ignore the man in black behind him, Flare cleared his throat.

"The king and the prince," Flare mumbled, "are to send a small party here for negotiations."

There was an exasperated noise from behind him, but Flare refused to turn around.

"The king wants to negotiate?" Aurelia asked, also ignoring Fox. "Did he say why?"

"It wasn't the king's idea," said Flare, leaning into Aurelia's warmth.

Aurelia's eyes widened. "Rhydian suggested this?"

Flare nodded, noting the grief on her face and not sure what else to say.

Almost distractedly, Aurelia sat Flare down next to Fox, and it was hard not to claw at her cloak to hang on. She tucked her long hair away from her face. The ends were curling as it dried slowly, as no sunlight reached down here under the trees.

Out of the corner of his eye, Flare could see Fox uncross his arms and casually place a pale hand next to Flare on the boulder. Flare resolutely kept his eyes on Aurelia, as she stared into the trees. Soldiers nearby laughed at a game they were playing around their fire, and the rich aroma of cooking meat wafted past Flare. He really needed to eat, and crystals would be welcome, too.

"We still don't know everything that's going on," Aurelia murmured, wrapping her arms around herself. "Fox, do you know what the prince has planned?"

"Me?" Fox's voice was low. "I've no idea."

Turning to face him, Aurelia raised her eyebrows.

Fox's hand twitched and Flare wanted desperately to fly off, still hating being this close to Fox. He smelled like ice and ash.

"Aurelia," Fox snapped eventually, "Do you really think that there was time to discuss that? After your water adventure?"

Biting her lip, Aurelia stared at Fox for a moment, and then nodded. Flare couldn't look up to see what had passed between her and Fox, but her expression softened. She's tired, Flare realised, and perhaps that was why Fox had taken his time getting her back to the army.

Greetings and a single loud cheer from the trees, towards the middle of the camp, had all three turning to face the sound. They could just make out an emerald-green clad figure moving through the groups of soldiers. Behind her was a small woman with yellow hair, holding what looked like the bottom of the green figure's robes off the moss.

Aurelia moved back closer to Fox and lowered her voice.

"That's interesting, that looks like Jessikah by the Elder... the Lady's side."

Fox made no reply. Flare risked a quick glance. Fox had leant back on the boulder to peer through the trees, and Flare could see tendons straining along the pale skin of his neck.

"Did the Lady specifically ask for Jessikah to attend her?" Aurelia murmured.

A muscle in Fox's jaw twitched. "Yes."

Interesting.

Flare had seen Jessikah occasionally come and go with wine and treats from the Lady's chamber, back at the caves. But watching Fox's tense jaw, Flare had never realised it had bothered the man so much. Flare was amused. As much as he found Jessikah a strange sort of soul, it was nice that the Lady was taking the time to help her. Apparently Jessikah had once been a fierce woman, while now she was like a shadow of her former self.

Without a word, Fox slid off the boulder and stalked over to a tree, peering around it, and Aurelia stepped up beside him. Flare hopped up and landed on her shoulder.

They watched the Lady walk around the trees and around the campfires. Her dark hair was shining, even in the darkness of the forest. Her expression was that of delight and triumph. Unmarked hands were continuously touching her youthful face. With a twitch of his tail, Flare realised that she now looked even younger than the last he'd seen her, before flying off to scout at the castle, which was only a few short hours ago.

Elves rose from their bedrolls and logs to greet her and the other army leaders accompanying her, while somehow managing to ignore the young man trailing behind. It was Gavin, Fox's younger brother, an army officer of some sort.

The young man was attired in black like his brother, but the clothes didn't cling to him in the same way as Fox. They were quite a distance through the trees, but before he stepped between two great trunks, Gavin's eyes swung their way. His face was expressionless. The young man stared at the three of them for a moment, his mouth a thin line, before following along behind the Lady. Although Gavin was far enough away from the Lady, that Flare wondered if he was really a valued officer after all.

Those closest to Fox and Aurelia muttered louder. The Lady's voice was fading as she moved off in a different direction, avoiding Fox and Aurelia. She sounded amused and eager for the battle, unconcerned by the tension in parts of the camp.

Risking a glance at Fox, Flare tilted his scaly head. The black-haired man was gazing with a dark intensity after Gavin. Flare wasn't surprised. Their relationship had been strained for years, even before Fox had embarrassed the man on Aurelia's unexpected and painful return to the caves.

As Fox made his way back to the boulder, his black and gold eyes turned to Flare, who was still staring openly at Fox. Fox bared his teeth while crossing his arms over his chest again. Flare jerked, unable to stop the trembling again. Aurelia followed Fox to the boulder, but didn't sit down next to him, remaining standing before him.

"Fox!" Aurelia hissed. "What's wrong with you?"

A smirk was her only reply.

Once again, Aurelia reached out and Flare hopped onto her wrist, welcoming being pressed back against her warm chest. Flare was enveloped in her floral scent, a welcome aroma against the smoke of the surrounding campfires.

"Flare, I know this has been a strain for you too," Aurelia murmured, caressing his neck, something he did not normally allow. But her hands were soothing, and his eyes drifted close. "I think you're realising that the Lady is up to her own game, not one for the good of the Elves."

Flare's eyes sprung open.

Wait.

What was she talking about?

White teeth flashed as Fox smiled once, and the man raised his pale face to the dappled canopy above, pale lids almost completely closed. But Flare could still see a thin sliver of glittering irises, and Flare wasn't fool enough to think that Fox wasn't paying attention to every word.

"I know who she is," Aurelia said, her voice soft with her head bent low, her lips close to Flare's face. "And you've figured it out as well, haven't you?"

Flare's shivering started all over again.

What else did she know?

"Wh-what are you talking about?" Flare stammered. Aurelia's hand stopped stroking his back. There was a snort from the boulder beside them, but Flare kept his gaze on Aurelia's. Her green eyes were wide.

"I know who she is," Aurelia repeated. "I suspect you do, too. What else do you know?"

"Oh. Oh. Um. Yes, it seems... obvious now... the shared likeness with the prince..." Flare stammered, wanting to twist away and disappear into the trees. A waft of thicker smoke drifted past them and a muted cheer came from across the Elven camp.

"Flare, please."

"That's all I know." Flare shook his head, squirming in her arms. "I have... I have only been keeping my word to help her."

Aurelia's eyes widened at his admission. Or perhaps it was the fact that his claws were digging into her hands. In this size, it was more of a sting than the slicing open of her flesh when he'd caught her in midair, but he was clearly agitated. Aurelia's eyes narrowed at him.

"And Rhydian?"

Another snort sounded beside them, and Flare cringed. This was not ideal at all. What did Fox know, and how much had he told Aurelia? Did she know Flare was lying through his teeth? Aurelia's green eyes continued to search Flare's purple ones, looking for something he couldn't give her.

"When the king threw you off the balcony," Flare mumbled, his voice cracking. "Ah, things became clear." He cleared his throat with a sheepish cough. "Clearer."

"Your lies sustain you like crystals," Fox's frosty voice cut through Flare's desperate words. Cracking his neck, Fox uncrossed his arms, his slitted eyes sparkling with some dark emotion. "Typical, typical, behaviour for a dragon."

The scorn in Fox's voice cut through Flare's fear in a wild moment of anger.

"Have you known so many then, to have formed such an opinion?" Flare snapped in automatic defence of such slander about his race, but he regretted the words as soon as they left his mouth.

Fox opened his eyes slowly, and gold flecks appeared to dance across the black. Moving with a relaxed air, Fox pushed himself off the boulder as a hand drifted down to the hilt of the sword against his leg. Closing the distance with one lazy step, he caught Aurelia's waist in his hands, holding her still when she tried to pull back.

Looming over Flare, eyes like the midnight sky, Fox's voice was surprisingly calm.

"Oh, Flare Shining One, I have known them all."

Flare froze at the sound of his full name. Aurelia stopped struggling too; her tired face, centimetres above Flare's, was staring at Fox.

"What are you talking about?" she whispered. "What did you call him?"

With his dangerous gaze still on Flare, Fox spoke to Aurelia.

"He's a part of this, and he's a liar."

"Flare? A part of this?"

Flare's wings twitched and, unable to help it, Flare closed his eyes. Aurelia's voice sounded close to his burrowed head.

"Flare? Flare?"

Hating himself, Flare wriggled deeper into Aurelia's arms, hiding his face from Fox's gaze, from the name on the man's cold lips.

A bitter laugh barked above. "He can't speak right now, Aurelia. He's facing the truth inside of him."

"Fox, for hell's sake! What are you talking about? Where's your proof? And where's your respect?" Aurelia demanded, sounding exasperated. "Flare saved me from the king!"

"He did, no doubt in someway saving himself."

Aurelia's arms jerked around Flare, the only warning he got when a cool finger stroked Flare's back in one long, frighteningly tender caress. Flare squeaked, and hated himself for it straight away.

Above, Fox's voice was soft. "Open your eyes Aurelia. It's not just the Lady who was holding information back."

The cool finger disappeared, and Flare's whirling mind tried to work out what in particular Fox was referring to. There was too much Flare wanted to forget.

Was that demon spawned man talking about the distant past? Fox knew his name! Or was Fox talking about the curse, and now?

Flare burrowed deeper into Aurelia's arms in vain, thinking, could he still leave? Aurelia might survive without him, with Fox's protection, in the coming battle.

But the thought of losing her was just enough to keep him where he was, ashamed for the moment at his fear. Aurelia's normal joy, and her inner light, reminded him of a most precious dragon, lifetimes ago, it seemed. And Flare had run away from protecting her, leaving when he should have stayed.

So Flare had to stay now, as if in some way saving Aurelia would make up for the past.

Aurelia's distressed voice was urgent as she tried to coax out more information from him.

"What is he talking about? Flare?"

Unable to speak, Flare burrowed deeper into her cloak.

Fox's frosty voice called out from a short distance away, sounding like he was heading through the trees, away from camp.

"Flare knows the time for lies is over, Aurelia. Especially his."

12

Aurelia

Year 367

Elven Camp, South of Aneirin

Flare refused to speak to Aurelia for the rest of the morning.

Unable to get any more sense out of either him or Fox, Aurelia had drifted into a much needed sleep, as the Elves rested around her. Fox was off in the trees, away from the rest of them. She had the distinct feeling he was avoiding the Lady as much as Aurelia.

Not opening her eyes after waking from a fitful rest, Aurelia exhaled slowly through her nose. Who was Fox to say such things about Flare? That Flare was a part of this? The only thing he had to do with it, as far as Aurelia knew, was that he'd found the Lady, and been there for her after she'd lost her magic.

"But that's what Fox meant. As far as I know," Aurelia muttered to herself. So much of the truth had been kept from her.

The most recent untruth had been the Lady's explanation for the dragon bones. Since realising that the Lady was actually the queen, Fox had mentioned to Aurelia about his first meeting with the Lady and Flare when they had been fleeing Aneirin. The dragon bones had been where Fox, Flare and the queen had crossed paths, at the bones of a poor creature who had died by an Elven spear, not struck out of the sky by magic. The spear, which was now missing from the dragon's ultimate resting place.

Had the Lady arranged for that little detail beforehand?

Something else struck Aurelia. Flare's dragon magic had helped get them across the line of the curse. But how had he done that, exactly? Flare went on and on about not having a lot of magic to spare. So how had he been able to cross the curse? When Fox, a veritable well of magic and power, had struggled against the power of the king like a butterfly heading into a storm. Is that what Fox meant, about the curse being so much stronger than the king?

"What else are *you* holding back from me, *both* of you?" she whispered, refusing to let her hot tears of frustration fall. She was done with weeping.

Rolling over amongst her blankets, Aurelia opened her eyes, staring at the softly curling smoke of the small fire. Elves nearby were smoking a slightly toxic fungus that they had smuggled with them from the caves. The spicy aroma had her scrunching up her nose. The mild high would settle nerves, so she assumed more than just a few of the soldiers were feeling the same roiling in their guts as her. So many preparations had been made to get the army here. Most of them were young; meaning that over half the army had lived most of their lives knowing their society was preparing for a war. Most of them had been trained by Fox, who was now shirking his duties by avoiding them. So what reasons did he have? Just that the Lady had withheld information from him?

Aurelia wanted to scream in frustration.

If she was being honest, she was angry with herself. She had missed what was right in front of her, the *Elder* and shadowed plans, blinded by the idea of some distant claim for peace. When really wasn't this some kind of long-winded strike for lost power?

Folding her hands under her cheek, Aurelia stared across the camp at nothing. The sensation of Rhydian's throat giving way to the dagger, and the absolute confusion, panic and fear afterwards, was fuelling her confused rage. Her self-loathing was growing, knowing that even if her intentions had been true, the method was absolutely barbaric. To sacrifice an innocent man! Because as if the king was ever a possibility? He was far too powerful.

The cost of her blind spot had nearly been Rhydian's life. She had no idea that Flare would fly in to save the prince. Did Flare even know that he'd try? Having seen that Aurelia had panicked?

Either way, Rhydian's certainty that his father's magic wouldn't let him die seemed entirely misplaced from her point of view.

Lips twisted in a bitter smile, Aurelia's anger sharpened into something darker. Only by chance was Rhydian still here. Because if she'd been slightly more in control after slitting

Rhydian's throat, she might have gone *up* the steps outside Rhydian's room, instead of down. Flare wouldn't have been able to save her from that. And her lover would be dead. They both would be.

Her, and the sweet young man who had trusted her with his life. A man who wanted the same for his people as she did for hers. Peace, and to live without a threat of misused magic over their lives.

Examining her thoughts, Aurelia went cold. She had called Rhydian her *lover*.

Did that mean she was in... love? Frowning, Aurelia pushed herself up onto her elbows.

"I don't know," she whispered, staring at the fire, the camp, and the trees. Her gaze hardened. "But that's not good enough, is it?"

She was done with this indecision. But hadn't she already chosen? She had completed her mission. And now she was back with the Elves, ready to descend on the kingdom. To what? Wipe them out?

Cheerful faces, Rhydian's men and young Chase, flashed across her mind. They weren't monsters; they were simply the subjects of one. Turning her wide eyes towards the centre of the camp, far off between the crowded, giant trees, Aurelia licked her lips. Just like the Elves were likely the subjects of another threat, right here, right now.

"Aurelia," she whispered to herself. "You chose... *wrong*."

Embers pulsed bright orange. Intoxicating smoke from the Elven soldiers continued to mix with the wood smoke from the fire.

"So now?" her voice lowered to a breath that mixed with the curls of smoke passing by. "Now, I'm changing my mind."

She didn't know how, or in what form her change of mind would, or even could, take. Aurelia closed her eyes.

The Elves had little in the way of religion, only stories of virtues related to various phases of the moon. The people of Aneirin seemed to pray to multiple gods, or swore by them at the very least.

"Help me," she murmured, tasting ash. "Help me stop those that need to be stopped. Please, give me a sign."

Something in the fire crackled, and Aurelia jerked, her eyes opening.

Exhaling, muttering to herself, she stared back across the camp over the fire.

Through the grey curls of smoke, her gaze met a pair of tawny eyes.

"Bindy!"

The woman across the fire smiled. She was sitting on Fox's blankets with her arms crossed around her knees. Aurelia sat up fully, stretching and cracking bones that ached. Fox had healed her cuts, but there were still bruises beneath her skin.

"I've got to be quick, my friend." The woman's voice was quiet, her voice a naturally velvet purr. "But I wanted to see you."

Aurelia moved to push herself up, but with natural grace, Bindy hopped up, jumped over the fire and sat down on Aurelia's blankets. Scooting close, Bindy gave her a one-armed hug, resting her ashen head on Aurelia's shoulder.

"You stay right there." The arm around Aurelia tightened. "You've been through a lot."

"I want to tell you all of it," Aurelia began, but Bindy cut her off.

"It's not the time now, but you will. I just wanted to see you before-"

"Before we fight?"

Bindy's head nodded against Aurelia's shoulder.

Before they attacked the city. Or met the Aneirin army outside.

Either way, a battle was wrong.

Oh gods, Aurelia said under her breath, *please help me stop this.*

"I've missed you," Aurelia murmured. "So much has happened, I... I don't even know where to start."

"Hey, shhh," Bindy twisted, hugging Aurelia with both arms. It was a good hug. Bindy was an archer like Aurelia, and also a great cave climber. She was strong, lean and used what little magic she had passed down to her from her parents to enhance her muscles.

"We'll get time, you just rest." Bindy paused. "I'm supposed to be falling into final drills with the archers. My fellow soldiers aren't quite sure of the Lady's feelings for you. They're restless. Not ideal before... well, you know."

Aurelia nodded.

"Restless," Aurelia murmured. "They should be. Just keep yourself safe, okay?"

Bindy, not afraid of a fight with anybody, stiffened slightly. "Aurelia?"

"I'll explain later." Whenever that would be.

Bindy snorted. But let it go. She was too excited to be here after all this time. There was no way Aurelia could explain all that was happening without causing panic, besides there was no proof. Most Elves adored the unity the Elder One had bought to their lives. Aurelia needed to be smarter. Beside her, Bindy cracked her neck and looked around.

"Where's the beast?"

Aurelia laughed under her breath. "Which one?"

Bindy joined in, her throaty laugh much louder. "Take your pick."

Unlike most of the Elves of Lolihud, Bindy wasn't quite as intimidated by Fox. Bindy didn't spend much time around him if she could help it, but she trusted Aurelia's faith in him, even if she didn't quite understand it.

"Flare is ignoring me, and Fox is hiding in the bushes."

"Hey creep," Bindy called out, her deep voice a silky purr.

A quiet snort sounded from the trees to the left. They both laughed.

We're both nervous, Aurelia realised, wiping her face.

After so many years of preparation, we're here. Ready to fight our way through a dark army. Defeat a dark king.

Wyll, Davyn, and Chase's smiling faces came to mind once more.

Except it wasn't like that at all, was it?

Aurelia blew out a deep breath.

"In all seriousness, Flare is worried. Fox is angry. I know that there's more going on here than what we've been told." What else could she say?

"More going on?" Bindy murmured, lowering her voice.

Aurelia turned to face her friend, trying to sum up in her mind what was likely to sound mad about all that had happened. She paused, catching sight of a glaring face approaching. She cursed.

Gavin.

Sensing Aurelia's mood change, Bindy looked around. She caught sight of the man heading their way. After squeezing Aurelia again, Bindy stood up in a hurry.

"Good luck with that." She winked, but her smile was brittle. "I'm off."

"Bindy," Aurelia hissed, "don't you dare leave!"

"Love you, bye," Bindy called as she stepped under a low branch, and then around a wide tree. She was gone.

Aurelia didn't blame her, not entirely. Gavin had pursued both of them as they had grown up. Both of them had never welcomed his sleazy advances, and he had never let it go. How was he so different from his older brother?

Aurelia cursed under her breath, standing up. She would not let this man stand over her. Gavin, dressed in black but wearing it nowhere near as well as Fox, had stepped right up to her bedroll. His glare turned into a smug grin.

Oh gods, Aurelia realised. *He thinks I'm here alone. More fool you.*

Aurelia said nothing. She tried to summon a cool expression, when really she was trying not to laugh.

"Not happy to see me again, are you?" he smirked.

"Gavin." Aurelia replied in greeting, her smile winning out. She flicked a glance at his groin. "I'm happy to see that you're in one piece."

Gavin's smirk disappeared. Apparently, this was not the reaction he had been looking for. His eyes narrowed.

"Where's Fox?" he snapped.

Aurelia smiled at him.

"Behind you," she snickered.

Aurelia let her laugh bubble free as Gavin's eyes widened before he spun around with a curse to see that there was no one there. His hands had gone to his groin while he frantically searched the trees. In the meantime, Fox made his way quickly and quietly to appear by Aurelia's side.

Gavin whirled back to Aurelia, his fists clenched.

"Fuck!" he swore, catching sight of Fox. Gavin paled and stepped back in a hurry.

Fox stepped forward to follow him, putting himself in front of Aurelia, shielding her from having to look at Gavin. Fox was full of contradictions, but he knew as much as she valued her independence, she would welcome any protection from Fox's ludicrous younger brother.

"Speak quickly, boy. No one wants you here," Fox drawled, and Aurelia wanted to hug him. Despite their familial relationship, Fox no longer had time for his cruel younger brother.

Fox's pale hands were clasped loosely behind his back. As Aurelia's gaze lowered to admire his form, Fox waved a hand playfully at her. Despite the seriousness of everything, she poked one of his palms in response. His cool hand caught her finger, squeezed it once in reassurance before releasing her.

Gavin cleared his throat, eyes full of repressed fury.

"The Elder One..." Gavin shook his head in what looked like disgust. "The *Lady* has asked for *you*," his eyes slid past Fox's shoulder to Aurelia, "to accompany *me*. We need to meet with envoys coming from the Aneirin army."

Aurelia didn't even think.

"No," she snapped.

Fox turned back to stare at her, one of his finely arched eyebrows raised.

She shook her head at him.

"I said no."

She hardly knew why she was refusing, but it just seemed so... wrong, after the role she'd played in this already. Could she face Rhydian if he was there with his men, if they knew what she had done to their prince? Even if it was with his consent to break their king's dark curse?

"It's not optional," Gavin snarled, avoiding Fox's eyes, looking over his shoulder at Aurelia.

After a quiet snort, Fox turned his back to Gavin. Behind Fox, Gavin's eyes widened, but wisely, his mouth stayed shut.

"You should go," Fox murmured, glittering eyes searching Aurelia's face.

"I said no."

Eyes still on her face, Fox casually raised a pale hand and rubbed his throat. As understanding dawned, Aurelia's lips thinned. The message was clear. Rhydian was most likely behind the envoys, and likely for good reason.

Aurelia straightened her spine.

"Fine. Let's go."

Out from under the shaded green of the thick forest, Aurelia blinked at the sky. The majestic expanse was startling, encompassing the entire valley of Aneirin with blue, gold, and white.

She had followed Gavin through the camp, her face expressionless. An unknown soldier in Aneirin livery was waiting for them, staring with wide eyes at the Elves. They stared openly back. As Aurelia made her way over to one of two other saddled horses, the Aneirin soldier's eyes had watched her silently.

"What's the plan?" Aurelia's voice was expressionless as she took the reins from the groom.

Gavin mounted up beside her. "Get on your horse and find out."

The soldier raised his eyebrows, his expression full of distaste. Aurelia ignored them both and mounted up.

Clicking to his horse, the soldier let his horse pick its way back through the tangle of undergrowth. He had to walk it carefully along a narrow track created by the Elves as they set up camp. They watched him ride past without comment.

Behind the soldier, Aurelia was impressed. The man sat upright and looked unperturbed. Better than the sick feeling she was suppressing in her guts.

But Fox was right. Aurelia was in the midst of this, not with all the information, but more than most other soldiers. If the Elves needed a clear mind and seeing eyes to listen to negotiations, then she would do it.

I am here to make sure Gavin's arrogance doesn't cock this up.

I am not *going because there might be a chance to see Rhydian.*

As the Elven army had slowly marched to the edge of the forest over the past couple of days, the ride to the river was short. They exited the line of trees at the river, and Aurelia could hear the whirlpool humming downstream. She kept her gaze on the sky above until they approached the wooden bridge. Reluctantly, her gaze lowered, wishing Fox was here.

Aurelia shifted uneasily in her saddle. Gavin was bound to find out Rhydian was alive. Therefore, so would his mother. But it couldn't be helped. She just had to keep calm.

The soldier had urged his horse over the bridge, to be met by another man halfway. It was Davyn. Why he hadn't come with the first soldier, she wasn't sure. The unnamed soldier turned his horse, so both he and Davyn faced Aurelia and her glowering companion.

Bracing herself, Aurelia urged her horse onto the bridge. The bright light was a shock to her eyes after being back in the perpetual twilight of the forest. The trees were just so damn close together that here at the river; the light was like a shimmering wall around them.

She stared straight ahead and ignored the railing to her right.

No.

Do not *think of that now.*

"Davyn," Aurelia murmured, nodding at the tall man.

His eyes studied her a moment, flicking once to Gavin. He nodded, his eyes hard. Aurelia expected nothing less. She wondered how much Rhydian had told his men.

Davyn was dressed in his usual clothes, a dark brown tunic over black riding pants, with thick black riding boots. He wore no cape or armour like the soldier beside him. A long bundle was tied to his saddle, wrapped in what looked like a blanket. Something white peeked out at one end, flapping in the faint breeze.

As the silence stretched while they sized each other up, Aurelia snuck a glance at Gavin. He was sneering, like the egotistical little shit that he was. Urging her horse closer to the men from Aneirin, Aurelia decided to begin on her own terms.

"Tell me," Aurelia called. "Does your king ever say where he goes?"

The soldier next to Davyn looked confused. Under his helm, his dark eyes slid a look sideways at Davyn. The taller man shook his head.

"No," Davyn replied cautiously. "But I don't see what that has to do with anything."

Aurelia urged her horse forward a few steps.

"Can you think clearly now, Davyn?" she asked, hoping he could read the pleading on her face. "What direction did I come from when you met me in the forest?"

Davyn frowned, but made no reply. The river gurgled under them, the only other sound besides the soft flapping of the white fabric poking out from under the blanket.

"Aurelia, what the fuck?" Gavin hissed angrily, walking his horse up to hers.

"Shut up, Gavin." Aurelia turned back to Davyn, her throat dry. "I tried to warn him. Did he tell you that?"

"Right," Davyn murmured. "How did that work out for you? Or any of us?"

"Davyn, I-"

Davyn cut her off, holding up a hand. His cheeks were pale, and he shook his head. When he dropped his hand, he reached down to unlace the long bundle.

Gavin started to speak again. "Aurelia-"

"Shut the fuck up, Gavin!" Aurelia snapped, cutting him off.

Shocked, Gavin actually did what she asked. Aurelia knew she'd likely pay for it later if she didn't find Fox fast. She could best him in a fight, of that she was sure. But not if he tried something on the ride back. But too much was at stake.

Ignoring both of them, Davyn finally got the wrappings free. He threw them to the other soldier, who watched the exchange with wide eyes. The soldier caught the blanket with one hand and bundled it in his lap.

Davyn held up the item, his expression grim. Aurelia's breath caught in her throat.

Was that..?

It had a white cloth tied to the top, but the beautiful carvings were unmistakable. It was her bow, her gift from Flare for the mission. The precious item had been left behind in Aneirin at the castle, after the king had attacked her. She had never expected to see it again.

"Oh Rhydian," Aurelia breathed. "Why now?"

Unable to stand the tension any longer, Gavin sighed impatiently.

"What do you want from us?" snapped Gavin. "We're here to negotiate. Open your gates, send out the body of your king, lay down your arms. You get the idea."

The Aneirin soldier sat up, his mouth dropping open, his hands freezing on the blanket in his lap.

"Tell your leader the negotiations failed," Davyn snapped in return. "My prince merely wanted to return this to Aurelia."

Davyn urged his horse forward, the soldier following suit.

"The *prince* wanted to return that thing? We're not here to negotiate?" Gavin's voice was incredulous. Aurelia bit her lip.

"Correct," snarled Davyn.

Gavin sat back in his saddle, shock across his face. Then he laughed, guffawing over his saddle.

"The prince is alive?" He slapped his thigh, his cheeks red.

Aurelia stared straight ahead, watching the mixed emotions play across Davyn's face. Something like understanding crossed Davyn's eyes as he met Aurelia's flushed face. Aurelia refused to break his stare.

"I don't believe it," Gavin gasped. "I don't fucking believe it. You fucked it up again, golden girl? Wait until the Lady finds out about *this*."

Ignoring him cost every ounce of her will, but Aurelia walked her horse up to Davyn's. Carefully, Davyn held the bow towards her by the bottom. Aurelia grasped the top. Meeting her eyes, Davyn murmured quietly, just for her ears alone.

"*Our* prince said you would know what to do."

Davyn released his grip, and the familiar weight of her bow was a comfort to her trembling hand. Aurelia nodded, even though she didn't know, turning Davyn's words over in her mind.

Our prince?

Did Davyn know what had passed between her and Rhydian?

She lifted the bow and rested the base of it in her stirrup against her leg. The white cloth at the top continued to flap lazily in the cool breeze. She stared at it until a soft cough interrupted her whirling mind.

The other soldier held out the blanket.

"For your ride back, miss." He licked his lips, and risked a gaze to Gavin, before meeting her wide-eyed stare once more. "In case you wanted to wrap it... again... or some such."

Aurelia shrugged, reaching out a hand. The soldier's hand was trembling too. She took the bundle from him, not unwrapping it. He nodded, swallowed, and finally let go. Behind the soldier, Davyn was gazing into the trees behind her, a faraway look on his face.

"Thank you," Aurelia whispered, not entirely sure what she was thanking them for. Her horse danced sideways, sensing her tension.

When the soldier turned his horse and made his way back to Davyn, the two men locked gazes. Davyn nodded as the soldier who had given her the blanket continued his horse to the far side of the bridge. His back was straight, but Aurelia could see he was sitting so stiffly it was a wonder he didn't fall off. Her hand tightened on the blanket, still bundled in her hand. Frowning, she dropped her gaze, pressing her fingers into the material. It felt like...

Aurelia peeled back a corner.

Oh.

Her face paled.

Oh Rhydian.

Raising her gaze, Aurelia could see the soldier still letting his horse pick its way up the road on the far side of the bridge, grasses long on either side. Davyn hadn't moved. Aurelia was thinking desperately for something to say. There was nothing, but she didn't have to.

Gavin had had enough.

"What the fuck is that for?" he finally snapped.

"The prince... he knew it had been made for me," Aurelia murmured.

"For fuck's sake," Gavin rolled his eyes. "What kind of sop is he?"

"The prince? A sop?" snorted Davyn. "You filthy, lying Elf-"

"Yes, a sop, a fool even, to fall for *her* tricks." Gavin's chin jutted at Aurelia.

It took all her will not to jab him with the bow. The only thing stopping her was the risk of damage to the precious carvings.

Davyn's face paled and then flushed a dangerous pink. "You little-"

"This negotiation is over," interrupted Gavin, curtly. "We are here to *fight*. We're not waiting until you reach the caves to steal what doesn't belong to you." He laughed coldly, not reading the confusion spreading across Davyn's face. "We *know* what your king had planned, what your king and army have been planning for *years*."

"What are you talking about?" Davyn hissed. "We don't have an army-"

Aurelia cut in, feeling sick again. "Gavin, wait, can't you see-"

"Shut it." Gavin wheeled his horse around. "Tell your king and his fool of a son to prepare for battle on the morrow."

Davyn's gaze lingered on Aurelia's a moment longer.

I'm sorry, she mouthed.

Without another word, Davyn turned his horse, his expression grim. He walked his horse back to the far end of the bridge, following the other horse along the road. The valley of grasses and grains spread out beside him in a green and yellow sea, all the way to a barren stretch of land around the outermost wall of the city. Above the wall, the city stretched along elegant terraces all the way to the base of the immense castle, a symbol of strength and might.

Aurelia's hands tightened, one on her bow, the other on the bundle in her lap.

"I'm sorry," Aurelia repeated, letting the breeze carry her words away.

Today Aneirin was peaceful, calm and serene.

Tomorrow, it would be filled with the sounds of war.

13

Fox

Year 367

Elven Camp, South of Aneirin

"The prince is... what?" the Lady hissed, her green eyes blinking rapidly.

"Alive," Gavin confirmed. "Aurelia even admitted she tried to warn him."

"Alive," the Lady repeated, licking her lips as if she could taste the word.

"Yes. And-"

"Be quiet," she snapped, eyes flashing as she held up a hand.

Gavin, who was standing before the Lady, in front of her tent, flinched at the snap in her voice. From where Fox was leaning against a tree, arms crossed over his chest, he could see Gavin's jaw was twitching like the man was grinding his teeth together. The breeze was low and only occasionally lifted the pennant on a lichen covered black flagpole before the tent. The cloth was plain black, the Elven colour for death, ready to lead the army to victory.

Aurelia, standing next to Gavin, was holding an intricately carved bow with both hands. An old blanket was wrapped around its middle section. Fox frowned, his gaze intense in its examination of her. She was dressed as she had been when she'd ridden to meet the human envoys, and had only just returned. The bow in her hands appeared to be the one that Flare had given her. Fox hadn't seen it since Aurelia had left Lolihud. He wondered if Flare could see it from his perch up amongst the canopy above. The beast was still hiding, but Fox could sense him there, listening to every word.

Stepping forward, Aurelia opened her mouth to speak.

"I said BE QUIET."

Fox straightened from the tree behind him. Sensing the tension in the air like a ripple of heat against his skin, he uncrossed his arms, hands flexing. He had Aurelia's belt slung over his shoulder, as weapons had not been permitted at the meeting. As soon as Gavin and Aurelia had returned, Gavin had been waving his arms and yapping on about what had occurred on the bridge. Aurelia had stood by, silent, her hands white knuckled around the bow.

The Lady, dressed in dark red robes, was standing before her elaborate tent. One hand was pressed to her forehead, and she was breathing deeply, eyes closed.

"You killed the prince, Aurelia." The Lady's eyes snapped open, the green a stark contrast to her ruby coloured attire. "And we know the curse is coming apart. So how is he still alive?"

Mutely, Aurelia shrugged, her hands clenching on the bow.

Around them, Elves were scattered amongst the trees, just like Fox. All were silent, eyes round and ears towards this confrontation. The breeze rustled the canopy far above, muting the soft sound of a tiny dragon rustling their wings in unease. But Fox knew that sound.

"What did you really do?" the Lady asked, stepping forward. Fox's hands flexed again, but the Lady had stopped a few paces away from Aurelia. "And did you really warn him about us?"

Aurelia, still mute, shook her head. Gavin noticed and threw up his hands.

"You admitted it in front of me just now!" Gavin shouted. "What is wrong with you?"

The Lady's eyes flickered over Gavin briefly before scanning Aurelia once more.

"And to think, Aurelia, I had so much faith in you," she murmured, her voice low. "Explain, Aurelia."

Fox raised his eyes at the sound of the distressed moan in the leaves above. No one else had heard it. Disgusted, Fox shook his head and stepped forward, pushing soldiers aside without care as he made his way across the moss to the clearing in front of the Lady's tent. An Elf cursed, but after Fox's glare, the Elf ducked his head, stepping behind another soldier.

"For fuck's sake. Aurelia slit the prince's throat. He bled," Fox snapped, adjusting his sword angrily as he steadied himself on a slippery rock. "The curse cracked. We didn't know exactly what would happen, did we? What else did you want? To fling him from the tower, perhaps along with the king?"

The Lady's cool green gaze slid Fox's way. He realised immediately from the gleam in her eyes that yes, she would have preferred *exactly* that. Unable to control the rage rising in his chest, Fox closed his eyes, willing the ice to recede from his flesh. But the temperature under the trees dropped significantly, and quickly. The crowd of Elves around them began muttering, and Fox could hear the Lady's breath quicken.

A warm hand slid into his. Fox opened his eyes.

Aurelia was next to him, her back to the Lady, her gaze calm.

I'm fine, she mouthed.

Trust me.

Behind Aurelia, the Lady had paled, but she hadn't moved away. A flash of sulphur yellow hair through the tent flap had Fox frowning, but the warm hand tightened around his. Aurelia smiled, just a gentle twitch of her lips, but it was enough. The day slowly warmed once more. Aurelia let him go and faced the Lady again.

The Lady was still pale, but her eyes held something dark that Fox couldn't quite interpret.

"Are we clear that what we wanted has come to pass?" Fox asked, his voice even.

The Lady cleared her throat. "Yes."

"Are you clear that I have held up my promise to you?"

The Lady's eyes narrowed, and she glanced at the Elves around before her gaze rested back on Fox's. Now her expression was easy to read. She was furious he had mentioned such a thing before them at such a time.

"Yes," she hissed.

"Good."

An awkward silence filled the trees and the Elven soldiers shifted uneasily. The scent of cooking meat drifted across the clearing, and it turned Fox's stomach. He was still fuming. Yes, Aurelia had withheld information from the Lady. But the same had been done in reverse. And Fox was all about fair being fair, wasn't he?

A shimmer of purple scales glided above them, and with a soft murmur of wings, Flare landed on the pole with the black flag, his claws searching for purchase. Obviously, Aurelia was still out of favour, or her shoulder was too close to Fox. When Flare had steadied himself, the first person he locked gazes with was Fox, as if he was unable to avoid it. After a quick sniff, the dragon looked away, however, his tiny eyes wide.

"Anything to add, Flare?" the Lady asked, turning away from Fox.

Flare arched his neck, and his tail twitched where it hung down around the top of the flag. "I know that the curse has started to unravel."

"Go on," she urged. Flare nodded, eyeing Aurelia before sliding his eyes away. *He looks guilty*, Fox realised. *What's changed? Or is this too real for him now?*

"The curse line is broken," Flare went on. "The army *can* cross into Aneirin without falling to the effects of the curse. Their bodies, their memories, and their minds will not be harmed. The magic that was bound here is now... free. Ripe for reclaiming."

"How do you know?"

All eyes turned to Fox at his quiet words. Flare tried to meet Fox's gaze, but he ended up staring at Fox's boots instead.

Not caring, Fox walked over to the pole and grabbed the wood. Flare tensed, but stayed where he was. The Lady's sharp intake of breath was all Fox needed to continue. Fox lowered his voice, just for the few of them before the Lady's tent to hear.

"How do you know this, Flare?" Fox repeated, his voice a quiet hum.

If only Flare would admit to being behind it all, that would make Fox's life so much easier. Maybe it would break apart Aurelia's strange attachment to the creature. If Fox told her himself, it would be too much like fighting over her, wouldn't it? Telling Aurelia about the Elder One being Rhydian's mother had been hard enough. Not that he'd been able to decide what to do with that revelation just yet.

Would Fox just come out and admit he knew that Flare was responsible for the curse? Would he demand to know why a dragon would do that for a petty queen and vicious king?

There was still time, wasn't there?

Satisfied with Flare's tense silence, Fox let go of the pole. Before he stepped back towards Aurelia, he spoke for Flare alone.

"I think Aurelia deserves to know, don't you?"

Flare's eyes flashed to Aurelia. Fox couldn't take his eyes off the way Flare was simultaneously holding onto the pole for dear life, as well as bunching his wings, ready to take off. Fleeing once again when things were real. Fox shook his head.

"Don't you know, Fox?" the Lady murmured, not quite understanding what had passed. "Flare has more magic and insight than you give him credit for."

"I doubt it," Fox muttered. The Lady ignored both him and Gavin's frustrated snort behind.

"My magic didn't just leak away," the Lady continued with a cruel laugh. "It was taken from me. *Stolen.*"

Fox sighed, nodding. "Yes. But overcoming the threat from the human king is more important than getting your power back, isn't it?"

The Lady laughed again, colour returning to her cheeks. "Of course," she murmured as she stared straight into Fox's eyes. "*Of course.* But it's a close second."

"Of course," Fox repeated, the words bitter on his tongue. He sighed, sick of all the deceit. "Are you really going to do this?"

"Do what? Win?" Her green eyes were wide, innocent. Challenging him.

It was subtle, but Fox realised something had changed between them. The Lady had always been in awe of him. But while her caution was still there, her respect was gone.

"I am owed this," she continued. "I am owed this win and my power *both.*"

Flare shifted on the pole, his eyes tightly shut. Fox stayed silent, letting his glare say what he thought of her statement. She smiled, her teeth a bright white against her pink lips.

"Fox, come now." She waved a smooth hand around her, inviting him to look around. "Surely you'd understand if I said I want all my power back? After being... *helpless* for so long, in my poor, broken, female body," she spoke the words slowly, eyes on his face, "almost a *prisoner.*"

The aroma of spicy incense was filling the clearing from the tent, and the door flap behind the Lady twitched. Fox wasn't sure if he'd imagined it, because his ears were ringing, and he could feel how white his face had gone. He bit his tongue, tasting copper and ashes in his mouth. The surrounding temperature stayed the same. It wasn't rage he was feeling. It was fear.

What did she know? Fox wanted to scream, but the words wouldn't come. Not here, not in front of all these witnesses. Is that why she was so sure of herself? Because of his damn pride? Or was she twisting more of her lies into black arrows, ready to fire aimlessly in the hope of piercing a dark heart? He held his silence, shovelling as much of his normal indifference over his bruised heart as he could.

"Come now, my brave warrior," the Lady purred. "We must finish what we start. No betrayal must be left unreturned after all."

Flare shifted his wings above them, looking like he was about to leave. The Lady's eyes snapped to stare at the dragon.

"You shall not leave!" she hissed. "You will stay, and tomorrow when we fight, you will burn that city to the ground!"

Fox was barely listening, the ringing in his ears only just subsiding. He could feel his palms were sticky from where his nails had etched themselves into his flesh.

What was he doing here? Why was he still here?

Flare cleared his throat. "I can not burn the city, my Lady."

"What?" she snapped, hands clenching in her skirts.

"I have no power for that," Flare mumbled. "Ev-even if I chose to. The army can still meet them on the open ground," his voice gained some strength. "But I can not burn the city before, during, or after."

Eyes wide, the Lady was breathing rapidly and her gaze snapped back to Fox's.

"Well. We have other powers with us," she muttered, obviously disappointed. "And I will have mine, once the king... hm." She licked her lips, standing straighter. "We will meet them as planned, and perhaps the city will fall once I am at my *best*."

Fox shrugged, hands still clenched. Aurelia gasped by his side, but thankfully, she said nothing.

"If that will be all?" Fox bit out, his mouth was working again. He didn't wait for a reply. "Good."

Not paying attention to Gavin's glare, Fox turned to go, his hand held out to Aurelia. The Lady's soft voice stopped him as another wave of sweet incense wafted out of the tent flap behind her.

"Aurelia."

"Yes... my Lady?" Aurelia's voice was soft, as if she'd been hoping to get away without any more notice. Aurelia's eyes were on Fox's outstretched hand.

"Where is your pendant?"

"My... oh."

Fox cut in to save Aurelia a lie of her own. "It came apart when she slit the prince's throat, my Lady."

The Lady's lips thinned, her eyes assessing him coldly. "Did it now?" It wasn't a question. Her gaze flicked to Aurelia, and the cruel smile returned. "He's kinder to you than most, so make the best of it while you can. Tomorrow is a big day. Anything could happen."

Fox could feel his teeth threatening to crack from how tightly his jaw was clenched. He watched Aurelia's hand tighten around the bow, as her gaze drifted from the Lady to Flare, and back to Fox. Exhaling slowly, she took his outstretched hand.

"I always have," Aurelia murmured. "I always will."

Feeling some of the tension leave him at Aurelia's words, Fox turned his back to them all. He tugged on her hand.

"Come."

Flare, still barely holding his shit together on the pole, refused to look at them as they left the clearing. The surrounding Elves were solemn faced, whispers following as they parted to let Fox and Aurelia through.

Neither of them spoke as he led her through the trees, the sky getting dark far above the canopy. As they walked, Fox offered Aurelia back her weapons belt, and she slung it over her shoulder the same as he had. Watching her from the corner of his eye, Fox wondered what she was thinking. Or was she as mixed up as he was, full of thoughts and images and memories that danced with the present?

Fox inhaled slowly, tasting the moist, rich air. It was soothing in one way, but also full of too many bright memories for this time of dark plots, at odds with the fact they would finally be in battle tomorrow. Fox shivered, his hand on Aurelia's back, as much for his need to touch her as she needed him.

When they made it back to their bedrolls, Fox relit their fire with an idle spark of power, and conjured forth a goblet of cool water without Aurelia asking.

"Thank you," she murmured, sipping it with a sigh.

"Don't you want a tent like the Lady's? Wouldn't it be more comfortable, more private?"

"No. I want the trees above me."

Fox shrugged casually. He knew Gavin was waiting in the trees nearby. For Aurelia or himself to be alone, Fox couldn't tell. He moistened his lips with his tongue, feeling his anger still aching deep inside, from seeing the Lady lie to his face, from seeing Flare's cowardice in action.

His thoughts turned back to Gavin. He was a useless, cruel, and spiteful man. Perhaps Fox needed to deal with that man once and for all? Tonight seemed as good a night as any, considering the well of rage inside that the Lady's words to Aurelia and himself had stirred.

Fox eyed Aurelia, who was almost swaying on her feet. He could wait until she had fallen asleep.

Aurelia sat down on her blanket, dropping the weapons belt, the plain knife and sword both of a simple and unadorned design. Should he find her a better one? The idea was attractive, to gift her something better than the bow that Flare had given her. Realising what he was feeling was a spark of jealousy, Fox snorted at himself.

The sword Aurelia had was just fine, wasn't it? She had knocked *him* out with this one, after all. And really, there was no reason to compete with a ridiculous creature like Flare, no matter how reverently Aurelia treated the bow. Laying it carefully across her legs, wrappings still bundled around its midsection, her fingers played over its carved wooden design, while she stared at the fire, unblinking.

"Are you okay?" he murmured, settling next to her, sliding an arm around her shoulders. He probably should be overseeing something or other, but he no longer cared. The Elves were as ready as they ever would be. There were officers to see that the finer details were taken care of. He was just where he wanted to be.

"Strangely, I think I am," Aurelia sighed, settling into his side, and brushing a lock of stray hair away from her face.

Fox hummed, not sure what else to say. Was there anything left? Soldiers nearby were quietly returning to their bedrolls as well. None looked their way. Fox ignored them, leaving them to their last few games of dicing for offcuts of precious crystals before the battle tomorrow. His eyes wandered to the flames, and then down to Aurelia's lap.

"Why?" Fox murmured against Aurelia's hair, tapping the bow with a finger.

Aurelia breathed in deeply, holding it in a moment before sighing. "Can't you guess?"

Rising his eyebrows, Fox nodded once against her. It seemed the prince had come to terms with how this needed to play out. Aurelia twisted her head against him and reached up to touch his jaw. He kissed her fingertips.

"Your eyes are so black the gold is almost gone," she whispered, her eyes a dark emerald in the fading light.

"Good."

With a snort of her own, Aurelia shifted against him and reached into her pocket. She pulled something out, turning it over in her fingers. Fox held out his free hand. Without a word, Aurelia dropped the object into his palm. When he held it up before the fire, Fox whistled a low note of appreciation.

"A garnet," he said, surprised.

Aurelia turned her face away from it, pressing back into Fox's chest.

"Rhydian found it, and then he gave it to me," she mumbled into his shirt.

Fox twisted the stone to catch the warm glow of their campfire. The smooth facets winked in a mixture of deep reds and purples. He could feel a tiny spark of energy inside, waiting to be harnessed.

Thinking of something that he could give Aurelia, Fox closed his fingers around the gemstone, frost forming as it always did. He ignored the chill and squeezed tighter, sending his awareness along his arm, letting his power flow. Aurelia pulled away from him, sensing that he was up to something. She reached for his hand, but Fox pulled it away, feeling his power gathering what he needed from the riverbeds amongst the aged trees nearby. As the air shimmered before them, Aurelia's sigh of awe had her reaching for his hand again.

"Wait," Fox hissed, his fingers burning in icy pain. He exhaled slowly, his breath misting before them both, feeling the simple shape of the garnet change to a heavier, bulkier object. Pleased with himself, Fox smiled. At last, the particles he had called forth had reformed to his desire to give Aurelia a gift from both himself and the prince.

"Alright," Fox murmured, and Aurelia held out her palm.

He let the garnet slide out first, so it dangled. The thick yellow gold chain that was now attached to it slowly uncoiled from his hands, unreeling like a metal rope as he dropped it slowly. Aurelia hissed as the cold jewel hit her palm, but he could feel her warmth travel up the chain that was still half in his fist. Eventually, he let the whole necklace drop, and Aurelia's sharp intake of breath at the simple beauty of it almost warmed his heart.

"A chain for you, Little Thing, to hold a stone as red as the blood of your prince," Fox said, quietly. He kissed her hair as Aurelia clutched the chain to her chest. "Don't waste it."

"Thank you," she was murmuring. "Thank you."

Shifting slightly against him, Aurelia slipped the golden chain over her head, her hands trembling.

"Thank you, Shadow Man," Aurelia sighed, dropping her head back to his chest.

"Don't thank me yet," Fox sighed, ignoring her use of the name he hated. "Let's both get through tomorrow first."

With a quiet sigh, Aurelia's hands drifted back to the bow, fingers playing over the wrapping. She nodded, biting her bottom lip.

"Lie down, Aurelia," Fox soothed. "Dream of nothing and get some rest."

With one ear on the trees nearby, Fox helped Aurelia stretch out on her side before him, hugging the bow tight to her body. As he wrapped another blanket around her for comfort, Fox realised Jessikah had yet to wander back to their camp. Fox sent out a coil of power, sensing she was still attending to the Lady. Fine. She could sleep there or in a tree for all he cared tonight. He'd deal with her later.

Let's get through tomorrow first, Fox repeated silently, reaching for some kind of reassurance. Because there was just no way of knowing just what it would bring.

They'd both chosen to be here, hadn't they? The Lady's words came back to him, unbidden.

Helpless.

Prisoner.

Fox's arm tightened around Aurelia's shoulder as he listened to Gavin tiptoeing around in the trees. The man's stink of fear, mixed with his rage, was offensive. Aurelia wasn't quite asleep, so Fox continued to wait.

Fox had given his word to help the Lady when they had first met, when Fox was reeling from his own bittersweet revenge. But she wasn't as helpless as she had seemed. That was now more obvious than ever. The Lady had spoken in half-truths, along with that ridiculous dragon as well. Both she and Flare were liars. So wouldn't it be fair if Fox took back his promise to help? Could *he* become a liar as well? Considering this whole bitter affair was just so damn close to its tragic outcome.

Before him, Aurelia's breath had evened out completely as she drifted into a deep sleep, exhausted. Just beyond the closest trees, Gavin had circled around to the far side of their lonely encampment at the edge of the entire army. Fox's gaze rose to the shadows, a plan forming in his mind, the burning rage inside of him agreeing wholeheartedly.

Fox poked one of his incisor teeth with his tongue, feeling the need to prove how helpless he *wasn't*. Not anymore.

"Don't worry," he murmured to the trees, getting up without making a sound. "I'm coming, *brother*."

14

Rhydian

Year 367

Aneirin Castle

An echo of familiarity filled the surrounding darkness.

Standing in the great hall of the castle, Rhydian bit his lip and gazed around. The vast space seemed to suck out all warmth, leaving a chilling coldness in the air. Above him, the broad sweep of giant stone blocks rose in wide arches that faded into deep shadows.

How was he here? He was supposed to be resting, as hard as that might be. He'd need his strength on the morrow. They *all* would.

As he peered into the inky gloom, the back of his neck was tingling, like a spider's egg had hatched from the base of his hair.

A soft sound, a feminine laugh, sounded from the far end of the hall. Rhydian's gaze dropped to the shadowed end of the great space, and squinted, willing his eyes to see. All at once, the shadows faded, and his eyes adjusted at his command. That shocked him slightly, but the figure caught his attention.

On one of the thrones, a woman was perched like a queen. She was dressed in red, and her red lips were sickeningly bright. Her back was as straight as a sword.

At first Rhydian thought it was Aurelia. The likeness was uncanny. But then the woman smiled.

Rhydian let out a slow, deep breath.

Aurelia would *never* smile at him like that. She was on a mission to bring light and truth into a place of dark lies. Aurelia would never smile at him, so cold and so cruel.

He began cautiously walking along the marbled floor, feeling like he was walking through black honey that had been left in an unstoppered jar. He paused halfway to catch his breath, pushing through the shadows that resisted him, had worn him out. Looking up, he had stopped directly under the Aneirin family crest on the wall, halfway down the length of the hall. Bright green eyes stared at him, and the soft laugh sounded once more.

Who was she? How had she got inside?

You know who she is, a dark voice murmured, curling around inside his mind like a bitter vapour.

Rhydian's hand reached through the viscous energy that seemed to bind his movements, reaching for his sword. But with a start, he glanced down. He was bare-chested, barefoot, dressed only in his riding pants. Meaning his weapons belt was nowhere to be seen.

His hand dropped from his side, and her smile widened. White teeth gleamed between the seams of blood-red lips.

Yes. I know you. I know who you are; he whispered out loud. But the words made no sound. Rhydian hardened his heart, willing his mouth to fill with sound.

"I am not afraid of you."

As his voice rang out, the hall lightened, torches flaring. The dark soup of resistance against him lessened before fading away completely. The woman on the throne frowned, her lips thinning.

As if in response, from a window high above, the sun came out, and a ray of golden light surrounded him. Dust motes hung suspended in the air, illuminated like tiny flakes of gold.

Rhydian blinked at them, transfixed. Through the frozen sparkling flecks, he could see the woman's smile turn triumphant.

The thick, viscous soup had frozen him once more. Not with shadows this time, but with light. He couldn't move, and images of being a small child came to him unbidden, unable to move from terror. Of being a small boy, watching in horror as a crystal blade flashed down towards him.

"Oh my god," Rhydian breathed as realisation dawned. Something from his dreams became sparkling clear.

It was *her*.

The woman before him was the woman from his dreams. The tingling sensation across Rhydian's neck intensified, as if the tiny spiders were spreading webs across his shoulders.

Here before him was the woman from his dreams.

His mother.

Even as the shock washed over him, he felt a stab of shame. The woman in the dreams wasn't Aurelia. It had never been. How could he *ever* have thought that?

Aurelia was a woman who had fought to set her people free. And before him now was a woman who was emanating something toxic, something bitter like ashes on his tongue... Rhydian closed his eyes, watching a green dagger flash against a rainy sky, clutched in the hand of the woman before him now. But in his nightmares, he'd never seen the killing strike.

A helpless child on his back, up high on the roof of a tower while rain and lightning flashed around.

And a bared arm, a dagger falling towards him, slicing the air as it fell.

Eyes watching the expressions play across his face, the woman laughed.

"Oh Rhydian, *my* Rhydian," she whispered, her voice low. "My poor lost, helpless Rhydian. How did you survive? *Twice*? Are you craftier than I realised?"

Swallowing, Rhydian couldn't look away and she laughed once more, a gentle purr. If he'd been able to block out the sound, he would have.

"I'll see it done myself," she continued. "For you and your father."

He closed his eyes, trying to block out her words, concentrating on another pair of bright green eyes. Eyes that gazed upon him, if not with love, at least with fierce compassion. His lips formed words silently once more.

Aurelia.

I'm trying. I will break free of this, this horror, this dark bloodline.

"The curse is almost broken," the woman murmured, sitting forward, red robes catching the light, green eyes flashing. "And I will take back what is mine."

As Rhydian's whirling mind continued to piece things together, the image of the child blended with Aurelia, and the place that she had come from. This woman before him was part of the Elven invasion, wasn't she? But how had she taken control of Aurelia, one so full of justice and light? When this woman, his mother, was emanating cruelty and spite like she was filled with dark passions?

He struggled against the light that bound him.

No!

I will not be caught here.

Something dark inside of him resisted the light that enveloped him like amber.

"Aurelia," he whispered in prayer. This time, his words had weight and sound.

The golden light of his prison throbbed. It contracted and then throbbed again.

Sensing his opportunity, Rhydian stepped forward, out of the light. And the woman's smile vanished.

She sat up straighter, the red robes flowing around her like spilled ink.

Rhydian took another step, and then one more.

"How are you doing this?" she hissed. After glancing towards the golden light where it flowed in from the window, her green eyes flashed back to him again. "How are you doing *this*?"

Unable to think of an answer, because he truly didn't know, Rhydian focused his eyes onto something just behind her. The hall was light, but the area behind the thrones was draped in a thick gloom. More sensing than seeing, Rhydian paused, willing himself to see. It looked like a piece of midnight sky had taken on a vaguely human shape. He blinked, his eyes narrowing. Staring back at him were two tiny points of glittering light, minute gold stars, observing him with a lofty coolness that seemed achingly familiar.

Glancing back to the woman on the throne, Rhydian's mouth parted slightly. Her eyes were wide, still scrutinising him and expecting him to answer. He shifted his gaze back to the presence behind her.

The two stars turned side to side carefully, just once.

Ah.

The woman in red did not know there was someone else here in the hall.

Rhydian blinked in understanding and made his way out of the cloud of suspended dust motes to the edge of the steps. At the top, the woman's frozen emerald glare seized him up. And he noticed something different.

There was no black marble here, like in the Aneirin great hall that he had grown up with. Here, in this dream state, it was now transparent, like glass or ice. Sighing, Rhydian smiled to himself. Here was somewhere he was used to, where he came every night, and then to wake in guilt and fear.

"Are you such a coward, *mother*?" His voice was the only sound. "To try and trap me here?"

The two pinpoints of light behind the woman brightened momentarily while the woman licked her ruby lips. Rhydian stared up at her without expression. She seemed to be struggling to speak; eventually she swallowed, narrowing her eyes.

"You've grown since we last met, my son," she finally spat out.

"Have I?" Rhydian shook his head. "I don't think so. I see you every time I dream."

She sat up straight at that. "You do not."

He stared at her, incredulous.

"I'm no longer a child. I've seen you in my dreams for years now."

As she paled, something hot and dark stirred inside of him, not the usual guilt that followed him from dreams into wakefulness. Placing a barefoot on the bottom step, he spoke again.

"What kind of mother does that? Haunts the dreams of the son she tried to sacrifice for some kind of rotten, useless power?"

A low hiss sounded from her throat, and her pale hands gripped the transparent arms of the throne. Droplets like tiny diamonds dripped away from her hands. Rhydian laughed, and the spiders crawling over his neck and back melted away like the ice of her throne. This meeting was obviously not going to plan.

Rhydian took another step higher and closer to his mother. She shrank back into the throne at his advance. She opened her red painted mouth to speak again, but he got there first.

"Why not come yourself, instead of appearing in my dreams? Why send a young woman in your place?" he snapped, the rage in his voice surprising even him. His words filled the space of the empty hall and echoed around them. Her head snapped back in shock. Behind her, the dark figure, and the two glittering stars, seemed to solidify for a moment before becoming shadows once again.

Seizing on her uncertainty, Rhydian took two quick steps higher, and now he was halfway up the stairs, his gaze was at last level with his mother's. This time, he let her speak.

"Why?" she hissed as she leaned forward. "I'm a queen, that's why. Everything here is mine-"

"No," Rhydian interrupted with a low laugh, his body and his mind coming to life, the last remnants of numbness falling away. "It is *mine*."

His mother's face went completely white.

Stepping over the last rise, Rhydian now stood before the throne, towering over the woman who sat there seething like a wet cat. Water was running in tiny rivulets down the clear arms of the throne, melting under her even as he watched. He could feel the cool liquid reaching and caressing his bare toes.

"Everything here is mine," Rhydian repeated. "Come to me tomorrow, *mother*. I will show you the same mercy that you have shown your *son*."

"How dare you-"

She shrank back as Rhydian stepped as close as he dared, catching the faint scent of perfume or incense.

"I dare because I am your son, after all. Blood binds all, doesn't it?"

The only warning Rhydian had was her lips parting in a silent scream, before he was pushed back by a wave of furious force, sliding him on his bare feet to the top of the stairs. He teetered there, heels threatening to slide back, before he was caught by a cold burst of air, surrounding him and holding him still. Rhydian's feet planted firmly, catching his balance and finding their grip on the top step.

"What did you do?" his mother hissed, her eyes so wide that their white showed all around. Before he could answer, like a snake, she lashed out, too fast for Rhydian to follow. She caught his face with a hand so hot it almost burnt his flesh. Her nails bit into his skin.

"I will take it back," she screamed into Rhydian's face, her gaze heating. "I will take it *all* back!"

He winced from both the heat of her words and her flesh, but he refused to turn away, refused to struggle. He licked his lips and stared her straight in the eyes.

"Our family is a poisoned well," he gasped. "And the guilt stains my soul."

Her green eyes searched his face, glowing brighter, hotter. Thinking of how many people had had him by the throat, all Rhydian could do was laugh, which made her eyes blaze like green suns. A thought came to him, and he spoke the words in his mind.

I am done here.

Ripples of shadow and light wavered across his vision, and his mother's eyes dimmed while staring around with wild confusion. Her hand squeezed his face so hard that her nails pierced his flesh.

"I will take it back!" she hissed again, her voice frantic. "With your spilt blood, the curse is undoing itself, and I have taken my magic back from your father!"

"I am done here," he said out loud.

Unconsciousness danced around the edges of his vision. The dark figure behind her faded, stars winking out one by one. The throne behind her melted, a silent collapse of ice and sparkling clear water, the coolness splashing violently over his feet.

His mother's voice lingered even as she disappeared.

"And now I will take it back from *you* as well..."

Rhydian sprung up and out of bed, landing with a curse on his knees, his bare feet twisted in sheets still draped over his bed.

His heart was racing, and his breathing was shallow.

Scrambling up off the floor, he raced over to his fireplace. He ignited a dry piece of kindling and lit a candle on the mantelpiece above. There was a small bronze mirror he used for shaving nearby.

His pale eyes were wide with wild fright. Peering closer, heart still pounding, he could see the marks of nails across his cheeks. His sharp intake of breath was almost a sob. Raising a hand, he wiped at his face, and his fingers came away sticky.

Shit.

How had she affected him within a dream? It was a magical dream, the most powerful he had ever had. But to affect *real life*? And was that shadow behind her really who he thought it was, a coolly amused man who had saved him from falling backwards? And would he have died in real life, if he had broken his neck in her dream?

As her words came back to him, chilling his racing heart, there was a noise behind him.

Holding a brass candle lantern, a sleepy guard had stuck his head around the partially open door of his chamber.

"My prince?"

Swallowing, Rhydian waved him away. The guard looked around the room curiously, but the young man eventually nodded and stepped out.

Rhydian met his gaze in the mirror once more. What had she said?

Touching his bleeding face again, thinking of the magic that had wounded him through a dream, Rhydian licked his dry lips.

His mother had said she would take her power back.

From *him*.

15

Gavin

The man that looked like his brother moved like a dark fog through the trees, his cloak an opaque shadow.

From the edge of the camp, Gavin watched Fox take his time, like the tall man was out for a nighttime stroll. For once, Jessikah was nowhere to be seen. The low light of multiple campfires glinted on the golden-hilted sword at Fox's hip, and also the small smile playing on the man's lips. As he made his way around groups of sleeping soldiers, Fox cracked his neck once, stepping sure-footedly into the darkness between two impossibly wide trees, his gloomy form blending with the night.

Shit.

Gavin, nearly tripping over a sharp rock in the moss, hurried through the trees at the edge of the camp, aiming for the place where Fox had disappeared. Behind him, the camp was mostly quiet; a sea of faint lights across the edge of the forest and farms. Gavin knew there were sentries posted beyond in the darkness, and he idly wondered if he should tell them he was... what? Chasing his brother into the forest?

Clenching his fists, Gavin decided against it. What would the sentries think about that, really? If he told them by following Fox, Gavin would be taking a risk. *He's your brother,* they'd say, laughing at him to his face.

He's fucking not, Gavin hissed under his breath, his fingers tracing the rough bark of a lichen-covered tree, hearing water gurgling nearby. Apart from that, the forest was silent. He paused; using what little magic he possessed to hone his eyesight to the surrounding gloom. The stars and the sky were too far away to provide any light, but a faint movement caught his gaze. There, to his right, further in amongst the silent trees. Even the leaves had stopped rustling, and all was still. Gavin, chewing the inside of his cheek, edged his way closer.

It took some time to pass between another dozen or so trees until he caught it, a faint, vertical line of golden light, growing as he watched. Frowning, Gavin rested against a damp tree, thinner than the rest, which smelled of something like the pines near Lolihud. Gods, he wished he were there now, amongst the familiarity of the caves, the ice and the snow. Not here amongst the watching trees, stuck in the moss and the muck, chasing a phantom that wore his brother's face.

As his eyes adjusted, the line of light became clearer, stronger. As he realised what he was looking at, Gavin choked back a curse.

A tent, black as the night around it, smaller than the Lady's but just as out of place, was pitched amongst the thickly crowded trees. Even with his Elven eyesight, it was hard to focus on, as if the fabric it was made of wasn't quite of the same substance as the rest of the world around it. It was basic, with a front flap for a door. It was from the middle of this front flap that the golden line of light had appeared, as if from nowhere. The glow dimmed and then pulsed just once as he continued to stare.

Beckoning.

Fox knew he was here.

Taking a breath, Gavin stumbled over the ferns and the moss to the entrance and paused. His heart was beating a wild rhythm, and it was an effort of will, for the love of his missing brother, to stand there and not run screaming into the forest.

It's now or never, Gavin, you need to know.

He yanked the flaps aside and stepped through.

"Where's my brother?" Gavin demanded, scowling. "What did you..." his words faded into a dry croak, his eyes adjusting to the dim interior, a sweet scent infused the humid air, arresting his senses.

A single lantern was lit in the centre of the tent. Perched on a small table of finely carved wood, the lamp was a delicate object of coloured glass and finely wrought gold. A single flame glowed steadily from within the faceted panels, giving out a gentle glow. The warm light that spilled forth from the single flame was gentle, but the objects it caressed were not. Flowering bushes, taller than Gavin and full of finger-long thorns, formed a dense garden in a ring around the flame. He didn't know what they were. Their like had never been seen in the icy caves that he knew of. The flowers themselves were sweet, exuding a deep, sweet perfume, at odds with their petals of the deepest velvety black. Fox was nowhere to be seen.

What the fuck?

Gavin spun around, reaching for the flap, but the split had disappeared. He scrabbled at the slick material of the wall, trying to find a grip. But the tent was made of some dark material, almost like stretchy leather. It made him gag to touch it with his bare hands. Even as he clawed at it, the material slowly reformed back into a smooth wall, like some living thing retreated to its original form. He wanted to vomit, blood coating the inside of his mouth from where he'd bitten both of his cheeks wide open in his terror.

Behind him, behind the thorny bushes and the single lantern, someone sniggered.

Fox.

Gavin whirled, wiping his bloody mouth, gagging at the musky scent on his fingers from the tent's weird material.

He could just make out a tall pale, figure standing on the far side of the densely packed shrubs. Over the tops of the velvety flowers, Gavin could see the man was facing away. The tops of his bare shoulders were just visible, a colourful tattoo painted across his flesh. The hair on the back of Gavin's neck rose. He shut his eyes tightly, not wanting to relive the horror that he himself had witnessed all those years ago. The image of pain and death, undulating and moving across pale skin and lean muscles, as it was needled into Fox's bare back in the deepest, darkest caves of home.

Opening his eyes, Gavin's hands drifted to his sword belt and his dagger, even as he knew both would be of no use to him now.

"Where is my brother?" he pleaded hoarsely, the sweetly perfumed air thick and cloying.

Bones cracked as the man rolled his head side to side, black hair flopping from left to right with the movement, and a soft sigh could be heard. Gavin's eyes widened as he watched the top of the tattoo ripple, not just from the man's stretch. He stepped back, pressing himself into the sickening, fleshy wall behind him.

"Where is he?" Gavin pleaded, desperate words escaping him in a bitter rasp.

"He is where he belongs."

The deep voice was quiet, full of dark threats and the promise of violence.

Gavin's heart was beating so fast that dark spots were dancing before his eyes, but he kept them open. The figure rolled his shoulders once more and Gavin sobbed out loud as the colourful images of the tattoo writhed in agony between the black flowers.

"Wh-what did you do-"

"Be quiet," Fox hissed and spun around.

The humid interior, full of spiked thorns, seemed to shimmer with oily currents, confusing Gavin's vision. As his shining eyes glittered from the shadows across the tent, Fox laughed once more, taking in the expression on Gavin's face.

Sweating now, his back drenched, Gavin shuddered in a deep breath. He wanted to leave. He wanted to run. But more than that... he had to know. Even as a roar was growing in his ears from his fear, that was threatening to black out his vision completely. Did their Lady know that this was a creature of darkness, walking amongst them every night? Ignoring the man's warning to quiet, Gavin inhaled sharply.

"What did you do to Jessikah? And my brother?" Gavin bit out. "And what..." he licked dry lips, the blood in his mouth not helping at all, "the fuck are you?"

Fox's dangerous eyes narrowed, and he shook his head. His pale cheeks were flushed, and straightening his spine, Fox stepped forward. He stepped straight into the thick bushes full of sweet black flowers and sharp back thorns. Gavin hissed, unable to help it, but the man's eyes merely fluttered slightly as the thorns dragged across his flesh. Fox's lips parted slightly, and he bit his bottom lip; as if he was savouring the way the spikes tore into his flesh.

"Your brother," Fox murmured, pushing through the shrubs and coming to the lantern, "was a beast."

Gavin was finding it hard to breathe, and his whole body was covered in sweat now, chilling him and stinking of fear.

"He was my b-bro-"

"He was a *beast,*" Fox roared, pausing his slow advance, his chest heaving with fury. "And beasts do not deserve free rein to prey upon the innocent!"

By the dim light and with fewer shrubs between them now, Gavin could see the man was completely naked, his pale body slim but finely muscled. With his eyes on Gavin, Fox lifted a pale hand and brought it down to rest over the open top of the lantern. After a moment, smoke coiled upwards from the man's hand, and Gavin gagged at the scent of burning. Fox threw back his head, eyes tightly closed, muscles in his white neck straining.

"Fuck! Stop! Stop!" Gavin cried. The bittersweet smell, not of burning flesh, but something more like the sharp aroma of a lightning storm, mixed with the floral aroma of the black flowers and he choked back the bile rising in his throat.

What the hells was happening? What was the man doing to himself?

Gavin bit his raw cheeks again, knowing he should have told someone where he was going.

Carefully, Fox withdrew his hand from the flame, glancing down, rubbing his thumb over his fingers. He murmured something, lifting his gaze to Gavin once more, eyebrows raised above eyes that looked completely black, full of shadows.

"Wh-what did you say?" Gavin choked out, dreading the answer. Fox's voice was a gentle whisper now, uttered right against Gavin's ear.

"I said, little brother, do you want to know where he is?"

Gavin flinched. Fox hadn't moved. He was still in the centre of the tent by the lantern, thorny bushes still between them. Fox smiled, his expression one of playful violence, his white teeth catching the light. The flame pulsed once again.

"N-no..." Gavin whispered, his eyes tightly shut. "No...I won't tell... your secret is safe with me, I won't tell, I-I don't care..."

Realising he was rambling, Gavin's eyes opened. Fox was gone.

"Oh, fuck," he gasped, as the black spots over his eyes threatened to fully black out his vision.

"Let me show you," Fox murmured, his chilly lips pressed directly against Gavin's ear.

Gavin cried out, just before an icy grip grabbed his throat.

"Let me show you," Fox crooned, and squeezed his hand together.

Bones cracked, and flesh tore. Through blinding pain, Gavin lost all control of his body. But he was still aware of the surrounding tent; of the lantern being blocked as Fox placed himself in front of the single flame that burned steadily behind the sweet, dangerous flowers.

As the air left his body in a violent, agonising shudder, Fox jerked what was left of Gavin's neck towards him. Fathomless black eyes glittered right before his own, their depths filled with only a few golden flecks suspended across an impossible midnight sky.

Even as Gavin's bladder and bowels emptied in a stinking rush, he knew they would be the last eyes he'd ever see, a violent mockery of his brother's knowing gaze.

Icy lips pressed against Gavin's.

"Let me show you," Fox repeated, inhaling the last gush of Gavin's air.

There was darkness.

At first, there was nothing.

Then there was pain.

16

Merion

Year 367

Battle of Aneirin

"People of Aneirin. Our queen is alive."

The silence of those gathered in the courtyard was tense, and after a moment, a shocked hum spread through the guards, townsfolk, and servants. Merion tightened his grip on the king's horse as it danced sideways over the cobbles. He felt the same. The king's words were a heavy weight upon his heart.

The king was mounted, already in his armour, facing the crowd with his helm under one arm. Rhydian was mounted beside him, looking like he hadn't slept a wink. His face was flushed, and it looked like he'd cut himself shaving in multiple spots. Merion blinked away the salt water in his eyes; thinking the dawn ride that the prince would take today was one of battle, not of peaceful reflection.

"Since the parley, you may have heard the rumours," the king continued from the steps where he addressed his people. From Merion's vantage point below the king, he could see the man's face flush with displeasure. As he faced the crowd, Merion was glad of his thick beard hiding his pink cheeks. He knew *exactly* where the rumours had started.

"I am here to tell you that they are true."

As the indistinct murmurs gained strength with this statement, the king held up a gauntleted hand. But the voices continued, growing louder and travelling back to those spilling out into the tunnel that led to the town. The king cleared his throat, his pale blue eyes looking grey in the dawn light.

"People of Aneirin, do *not* fear."

There were newly conscripted soldiers at the front of the crowd, cobbled together from the families that hadn't yet fled. They were young and old men, in dusty armour and cracked leather jerkins. Slightly better trained pike men were behind them, and cavalry lined up at the rear. Family members were crowded against the castle walls. Merion said a quick prayer under his breath for his prince.

Gods, please bring him home safe to us.

The confused and angry voices of those assembled rose as the king's words were passed around. Merion watched on, hopeless and grim, as the people of Aneirin reacted to the words of their king.

"I said, my people-"

Beside the king, Rhydian urged his horse forward, placing a hand on his father's arm. The king jerked, yanking his arm away. Rhydian's exasperated sigh was loud enough for those around them to hear. The prince shook his head, his tousled golden brown hair shifting around his face.

"One moment," the prince interrupted.

Without waiting for the king to go along, Rhydian urged Blackthorn further forward. He raised his voice, sounding every bit like a leader, even as his eyes betrayed his weariness.

"People of Aneirin! Your king is speaking," Rhydian called. The murmuring died. "Pay him your respect, as is his due."

Silence rippled out across the crowd. Merion watched the faces of those closest bite their lips or narrow their eyes in confusion. His own included.

Why was Rhydian paying his father any respect? Merion had made sure that his fellow townsfolk knew, along with the insight that the queen was alive, that the king was responsible for their dark dreams and isolation from the outside world.

A bloody curse!

Merion wanted to weep at the injustice, not understanding Rhydian at all. Must they *all* pay a bloody price for the king's lies? While two dark souls, the king and his missing queen, both magic users, waged a war for power around them?

The negotiation with the Elves had gone pretty much as Merion had expected. Nothing had come out of it. They had demanded the body of the king be handed over, and to lay down arms or some such nonsense. He was happy with the first demand, but not the second. Merion's hand tightened on the reins. If he had the chance, he'd hand the body of the king over himself.

Even as he flushed with shame at the treasonous thought, his ears were listening to the rest of what the king had to say.

"We go today to defend our kingdom from her threat, a queen who left us to fend for ourselves while we wasted away here, under a dark veil, for so long."

Merion's eyes widened, even as he noticed the prince hang his head, biting his lip and taking a long slow breath in.

"We take our honour with us, and refuse these magic users, these wild Elves, and their dragons, we-"

Whatever the king was saying next was completely drowned out by a roar of surprise from just about every single member of the crowd. Merion cursed to himself,

even as he could hear the king swearing out loud above him.

"People," the king shouted, raising his voice.

"Leave it, father," the prince called out, jerking his horse closer to the crowd. "You've said enough." Behind him, the king sat on his horse, mouth a thin line as he stared at his son's armoured back. Rhydian ignored him and pushed his horse through the crowd. Sensing him approaching, a ripple of silence spread away from his progress like a quiet wave.

"I go to break free of lies," Rhydian called. The silence grew as they watched Blackthorn carry him through the crowd. The king was staring at Rhydian with open hostility in his gaze, and Merion could feel his already sick stomach flip over.

Oh beware, my prince, beware!

"I go to protect you, my people, and you may join me if you can," the prince called even louder, making his solo progress to the far side of the courtyard, away from the castle steps.

Some folks raised their lanterns and torches to see him better, and the lights winked over the prince's armour and his shining, golden hair.

"I choose to do everything in my power to protect you, and it will always be," Rhydian stopped his horse, turning to face his father across the crowd, "my honour."

The king cursed again as the prince urged his horse into the tunnel through the thick wall of the courtyard, which would lead him to the town. The crowd parted, letting him through, as caps were doffed and some folks wiped their eyes.

They know, Merion thought.

They know who their true leader should be.

"Merion," the king said above the hum that was starting up once more.

"Sire?" Merion snapped his gaze to the man mounted on the horse above him.

"Reins."

"Oh, yes, of course my king." Swallowing, Merion passed up the reins, his clammy fingers coming into contact with the king's armoured gauntlet. Merion dropped the reins before the king could grab them, and pale eyes flicked down to Merion in annoyance.

"Apologies, sire," Merion muttered, his mouth dry, his heart riding with the prince. He would fight if allowed, but his abilities with injured people and horses both meant that he was ordered to stay behind.

Pursing his lips, the king gathered the reins as the crowd shifted to let the soldiers and cavalry form up.

"You will not have his blood, Sophia," the king muttered to himself. "Or mine."

Merion, wiping his shaking hands on his apron, dared to respond.

"My king?"

The king's gaze dropped to Merion's once more, and the man's handsome face was twisted into a dark grimace.

"She will not have our blood," the king repeated, a dark light igniting in his gaze. Merion took a step back.

"Of course she won't," Merion said, desperation filling his voice. "You'll be there to protect him, sire. The gods, too."

Without comment, the king pressed his knees into his snorting horse, and the beast pushed through the soldiers as they shuffled into order around him.

"Sire?" Merion called, but the king ignored him, narrowed eyes following the path that the prince had taken. Dread coiled with the sick feeling he was already experiencing in every single organ of his body.

As the king rode into the crowd, soldiers formed up behind him. Merion spun on his heel. Unable to help himself, he pushed families aside, racing up the steps beside the barracks that would take him to the top of the wall. The crowd behind him was forgotten when he reached the top.

In the low light of pre-dawn, the city of Aneirin dropped away in slopes and terraces below him, the castle and mountains high and jagged behind. Despite the city not as full of people as it once was, there were still weeping townsfolk lining the roads that led down to the impressively built outer-city wall. Merion's eyes drifted over the sight, and out to the farmlands beyond, past the fields of grains and meadows, looking black and grey as the night faded.

There, at the edge of the dark line of trees and along the river, an army waited.

His breath caught. It was hard to tell, but it looked like there were far more of them than there were soldiers of Aneirin. He wasn't sure how long he stood there. Others were crowding up the steps behind him, spreading out along the wall. No one had run inside at the idea of a dragon come to attack with the Elven army.

What would hiding matter, then? Folk knew of the dragons of old folklore, since members of the town and castle staff had woken from some dark, veiled nightmare. Whispers had spread about what people had seen in the fog when Lord Cyrus had died. They *knew* there was nowhere you could hide from such a beast.

As Merion tried counting in vain, his eyes straining, the sun broke over the horizon from his left. It broke over the valley, catching the waiting army with golden rays and long shadows. Merion bit his lip as the sun winked over endless line after endless line of spears, illuminating the colourful clothes of the Elven soldiers. An eerie war cry went up, and the spears rattled as one as the sound rippled along the line.

A sob catching in his throat, Merion prayed once again, this time out loud.

"Gods, please, *please* bring our prince back home safe," he choked out. "But welcome our king and queen to the deepest icy hells with open arms."

17

Rhydian

Year 367

Battle of Aneirin

As Rhydian exited the city, a low war cry rolled over the valley before him, and beneath the layers of his armour and leather undershirt, his heart just about shriveled up and died.

Blackthorn tossed his head, and Rhydian patted the dancing horse's neck with one hand, the reins held tightly in his other. Concentrating on taking even breaths, Rhydian stared out across the farms of his homeland, across the river, to the faraway lines of spears held aloft to greet the dawn. Gone was the peace and solitude of the early morning meadows. In his dry mouth, he could taste the distinct flavour of the breeze. It tasted wild, cold and bitter, like salt and ashes on his tongue.

"Gods have mercy on us all," he breathed; watching the sun catch the lines of spears, row after row of glittering weapons.

Not realising from Aurelia and Fox's dark clothing, the Elven army was a brightly coloured shock. Even from the vast distance across the valley, Rhydian was fascinated with the riot of colours, all shades, all the way along the lines.

Why did Aurelia wear dark clothes?

And Fox, why was he dressed like a shadow?

Rhydian shook his head, wondering if perhaps because of the nature of her mission that Aurelia had dressed in such conservative colours. Trying to shake off the chill of the early morning, he chewed his bottom lip, lost in the spectacle before him. The sound of marching and multiple hoof beats on cobbles getting louder behind had him finally break his stare, to twist in his saddle.

The army of Aneirin, as he had hoped, had followed him out of the castle and down to do battle.

They had followed their prince.

Not his father, their king.

Cold with the fierce delight of the knowledge evoked within him, Rhydian tossed his head and schooled his face into a semblance of calm. He didn't want to be here. He didn't want this for his people. But even less, Rhydian didn't want his father to get away with any more lies, manipulation or deceit. It was a betrayal of trust to the people he was there to rule over, rightful king or not, and it was a betrayal to his family.

Both my parents have betrayed me, he realised.

They have betrayed all of my values, all that is important to me.

The single shining ray of light out of their betrayal was the fact that it seemed like his mother had taken power away from the king. Ignoring what she had said about Rhydian himself, he examined her words in his mind. She had taken power back from his father? So she would be more powerful, but his father less so.

Would that tip the battle in Aurelia's favour? So she could do what he needed from her?

As his thoughts turned to her, Rhydian walked Blackthorn along the dusty farm road a bit, giving the army more space as they filed on foot and horse out into the clearing beneath the walls. As he stared with dry eyes, it was obvious. There weren't nearly enough of them compared to the colourful soldiers across the river.

The mustering was a solemn affair of low curses, hissed words and bated breath. Their prince watched from the road, his thoughts on two women with dark hair and green eyes, one filled with misplaced hope, the other with violence waiting to be unleased. He turned his eyes upwards, seeing the sunlight painting the castle, his home, with a golden glow. It looked serene, a noble place full of justice and wisdom. His thoughts turned to the heartbreakingly beautiful, noble illustration of Dawn of Fire.

Lies, all lies.

Rhydian's eyes filled at last, his grief winning out over dry-eyed fear, as his eyes dropped to the main structure of the magnificently impressive castle, the great hall and the thick, high stone walls around it.

He wiped his face on his gauntlet; the metal plates catching on the crescent moon shaped scratched on his cheek.

"Get a hold of yourself," a furious voice hissed.

Blinking slowly, Rhydian lowered his gaze from the golden stones above, meeting the pale blue eyes of his father. The king had ridden out at last, and was sitting on his impatient horse before Blackthorn. The black horse beneath Rhydian snorted in warning, and the king's horse tossed its head in response.

"Do you expect these soldiers to follow a bleeding heart into battle?"

Staring at the king for a moment, Rhydian eventually tossed back his head and laughed, the sound rolling out over the shocked silence of the Aneirin army.

"Yes," Rhydian finally choked out. "Yes, I do." He turned Blackthorn away and called loudly over his shoulder. "I have *already* bled for them, by my mother's far-reaching hand and your nearby one as well."

And as his horse started down the road, the soldiers arranged themselves behind him to follow, avoiding the fuming gaze of their king as they passed. Rhydian's shoulders itched the entire time he rode at the front, and even when the king galloped his horse forward to ride next to Blackthorn, Rhydian still didn't quite feel safe.

Not long, he prayed, not long.

Aurelia, I need you. Please!

Please.

As their march gained pace, Rhydian was wondering, how will this battle even work? The Elves are still on the far side of the river. But all too soon enough, he had his answer. He called a halt not far from the water, as the woman in red from his dreams urged her white horse onto the bridge.

The king, beside Rhydian once more, straightened in his saddle and hissed something under his breath.

Rhydian was too far away to read his mother's expression, but the triumphant aura that surrounded her was as sickening as it was sobering. She raised pale arms above her head and seemed to speak. Rhydian didn't hear the words, as his army was forming up a wide line on either side of him, only a few rows deep. Not nearly enough.

At first, nothing happened, and the men on either side of him shuffled and snickered, their bravado masking their desperate fear. Rhydian wanted to show his bravery once more, but with his father's fuming presence by his side, he realised he was shaking. With anticipation, anxiety, and horror.

Wait, Rhydian wanted to scream. *This cost is too high, I take it back! Stop!*

Two things happened at once.

The first thing was that his mother dropped her arms with a dramatic slice through the air. A loud cracking filled the valley, centred on his mother, firing out to the left and the right with a shattering echo. Around the Elves, a fog was rising, and as one, the Elven army walked forward onto the river itself. She had frozen the waters.

The gasp that spread along the lines of the Aneirin soldiers was quickly swallowed by a frantic group of cries behind them from the city. Rhydian twisted in his saddle, his heart stopping in his chest.

Oh my gods...

Rhydian had a flashback to something large and impossible, swooping in thick silence through white fog, the day his father had thrown Aurelia off the tower. He'd not quite seen what had happened, but in his heart, he knew.

Now was his chance to appreciate the frightening beauty of Flare, at full size, as the dragon swept over the jagged peaks and swooped low over the castle below. Screams of the citizens scattered in all directions. From this distance, tiny ants running for their anthills.

Flare was enormous, perhaps the length of twenty horses from nose to tail. He was a brilliant, metallic purple, glittering with gold overtones as the dawn sun reached higher in the sky. His wings were even more iridescent, and the tips of the vast leathery structures were so dark that the rich purple was almost blue.

Heart in his mouth, forgetting the Elves as they advanced, Rhydian waited for Flare to dive and wreak havoc, as the beast circled once, twice, and then a third time overhead. His father beside him shook his head, drawing his sword, muttering words under his breath. The air shimmered around them, but Rhydian's focus was above.

Flare, please don't do this!

Rhydian, speechless, watched the dragon arch high overhead. To his right, Flare's great shadow painted the eastern facing peaks with a mimic of himself as he flew by, blocking out the sun. Finally finding his voice, Rhydian roared for all he was worth, over the noise of the Elven army, calling out war cries as they advanced closer still, merely a minute away at the pace they were now racing to.

"Flare! Don't do this!" Rhydian screamed across the fields, in vain over the chaotic noise. "Not to Aurelia, not to me! Not to my people!"

18

Aurelia

Year 367

Battle of Aneirin

As much as the combined sight and sound of the two armies colliding was horrifying and heart stopping, Aurelia couldn't tear her gaze away from Fox.

Aurelia was on the bridge with a small group of Elves. There were about two-dozen brightly clad soldiers and Elves there, deemed unnecessary to the fighting before them. All were smiling, certain that their years-long campaign to mitigate the human threat was reaching its culmination. Jessikah was there too, silent, standing by herself on the far side of the bridge and holding the reins of three riderless horses.

The Lady was in the centre, clothed in bright red on a white horse, her gaze eagerly tuned to the battle. Once she had frozen the river, in the first large-scale feat of magic that Aurelia had ever seen the Lady enact, the Elven armies had crossed and met the human army at a run. Aurelia had been desperately searching the skies for Flare, but when the sound of clashing armour and weapons, along with war cries, had reached her ears, Aurelia's gaze had fallen to Fox.

He wasn't looking at the battle; he wasn't flinching at the sounds of men and women fighting and dying. He wasn't even looking at Aurelia. Fox, standing by the rail of the bridge, was staring at the Lady. His normally pale face was flushed, and he looked... troubled.

Aurelia, distracted as she was by the battle, was still shocked as she caught sight of his face. Fox was normally indifferent at worst or smirking at best. But now, a whole spectrum of emotions played across his face. It was all there and easy to read; anger, confusion, and desperation.

Along with fear.

Fox was still staring at the Lady, not paying a single second of attention to the chaos before them all. He was also absentmindedly rubbing sooty fingers together. A moment ago he had trailed them in the dirt on the bridge railing, a self-satisfied smile on his face. But then he had looked up, his lips slightly parted as the Elves charged. The colourful warriors had crossed a frozen river in full glory; to claim what they thought was a victory over lies and threats to their way of life. They had charged with battle calls on their lips, calling out in the name of Lolihud, calling out in the name of their Lady.

No, not the Lady, Aurelia whispered to herself, rubbing the rough pad of her thumb against her index finger. *The queen, Rhydian's mother.*

Her guts were full of lead and her vision was wavering from unshed tears or lack of oxygen, she wasn't sure. It was difficult to breathe, while the battle raged on and she was standing here waiting for a dragon that had seemingly disappeared. Aurelia's hands tightened on the bow, her knuckles white.

"Flare," she whispered, shutting her eyes to the things she didn't understand on Fox's face. "Come back."

Removing one hand from the bow, she pressed a hand to her chest, searching for the garnet. It was easy to feel, vibrating as it was from the rapid beats of her tortured heart.

"Hold on Rhydian," Aurelia murmured, wondering if she needed to beg for a horse. "Hold on."

At her near silent words, Fox's gaze finally broke free from the Lady's triumphant grin. His eyes searched Aurelia's. As he examined her face, his calm expression changed. She stared back, entranced. Fox's expression became first a look of longing, before morphing into confusion and despair.

She shook her head. Glancing at the battle, Fox wiped his hands on his black shirt. When she noticed Fox's fingers trembling, she hissed under her breath. His eyes, black and barely shimmering with gold stars, were wide as they returned to hers.

Do something, she mouthed, eyes wide, clutching her chest. *It's a slaughter on both sides.*

Fox's gaze dropped to her hand, clasped desperately over the garnet inside her shirt. As if in a dream, one of his hands drifted to his own heart, and his breathing was ragged as he closed his eyes. He shook his head.

"I promised," he whispered, opening his eyes, unable to meet her gaze.

Aurelia jogged over to him, keeping out of sight of the Lady, risking a kick from the white horse.

"Words!" Aurelia hissed, smacking his hand away from his chest. He stared at her, his sparkling eyes fading to something dull, numb. "*Words*. They can be blown away like the ash on your hands. *Do* something."

"But your whole life was for this…" he breathed, his gaze flicking to the battle as the cries of dying Elves and humans alike reached them.

Aurelia jabbed the top of her bow under his chin, exposing his straining neck, and Fox shut his eyes to her fury once more. She bit off the words that fell off her tongue like daggers of her own, making sure he felt every single one as she jerked the bow into his flesh.

"I've. Changed. My. Mind."

Fox slowly opened his eyes, looking down his nose to meet her own. She was relieved to see some of the gold flecks shimmering as the sun caught them both, spreading its rays across the valley as it rose. A crack sounded under them and off to the sides. Aurelia, breathing fast, looked down through the wooden slats of the bridge. It looked like the river was finally tearing the ice apart. But it didn't matter, did it? The army was across. Four Elves for each human, tearing them apart by the sounds of it.

As Fox blinked at her, a new sound joined the cracks of the shattering ice. Somewhere, deep below the river, the earth was trembling. Fox licked his dry lips and just before she heard it, Fox broke their stare, turning to face the castle at the far end of the valley. As if he had sensed the dragon approaching, Flare appeared over the red tumble of peaks that surrounded Aneirin.

"Late," Fox mumbled with a sour twist of his lips. "As fucking always."

Aurelia, wanting to cry with relief at the sight of the purple shadow growing closer, and laugh at the return of Fox's characteristically sardonic expression, withdrew her bow from Fox's chin. Wiping her hair away from her face, she exhaled a long, ragged breath. Fox pushed Aurelia away from the white horse and shuffled her to the side of the bridge, his back to the Lady. His gaze flicked to her bow and back.

"Do you have what you need?"

"Now that Flare is here, yes," she replied, standing straighter. She opened her cloak, showing him the arrow fastened to her side with leather ties. The shock across his face as he examined its colour was so uncanny that she almost forgot where they were. But soon enough, his face cleared. Fox nodded once, his solemn eyes on hers.

"Go help your prince," Fox murmured.

Above and behind them, the Lady's voice interrupted.

"Aurelia! Why are you here!?" she snapped, sounding breathless with excitement.

Beside her, Fox opened his mouth to speak. Aurelia got there first.

"I was waiting," Aurelia said loudly. "Flare will take me to where I need to go."

Her green eyes shimmering with dark glee, the Lady looked shocked at first, then pleased. She threw back her head, laughing loudly, a shrill noise even over the cries of the wounded from the fields before them.

"Will he now?" the Lady trilled, shaking out her shining black hair over her shoulders. "Good! He's here now, so go and get me back my throne!"

The closest Elves on the bridge turned from the battle, eyeing the Lady with confusion. A tall man in dark blue tilted his head at Aurelia, an eyebrow raised. She smiled at him.

Good, Aurelia smirked to herself, *good. They heard it from her, not from me. Fox, are you watching?*

"Surely you meant get out there and stop their advance?" Aurelia said, archly. "Weren't they coming to attack us?"

The Lady opened her mouth and then closed it, eyeing the surrounding Elves. The white horse danced under her a few paces before she jerked the reins hard and it calmed down, eyes shifting nervously. Eventually, the Lady swallowed and her expression soured and her red lips pulled back to expose her white teeth.

"Aurelia," she hissed, leaning over the saddle, her voice dripping with disdain. "Just get out there and kill the Prince!" She sat back in the saddle, turning back to the battle raging across the farms, her smile back once more. "For *good* this time."

Staring at the Lady's youthful profile, all Aurelia could do was shake her head.

Did she really hate her son so much?

The large shimmering form of Flare swooped low overhead before he circled once to land across the bridge. Not far from the whirlpool, whose low hum had been silenced at first by the ice, and then the battle.

Nodding to the Lady who wasn't paying attention to her, or the Elves murmuring amongst themselves, Aurelia took a breath, about to head over to Flare. A cool hand grabbed her arm, holding her in place.

Fox's free hand rose to her face, and she could see it was covered in ash once more, like he'd swept more off the wooden railing. Eager to get to Flare, Aurelia blinked at his hand in confusion until he touched his fingers to one of her cheeks. He swept the soot along under her eye and smiled.

"War paint," Fox murmured, his eyes shimmering full of memories. "For the heroine, triumphant on her dragon, riding to war."

Aurelia choked out a laugh, feeling cold suddenly. "Is this war paint as special as your tattoo ink?"

Fox's eyebrows rose, and unexpectedly, he laughed. The sound wasn't a bright burst of joy, though. It was more an outburst of disbelief. Aurelia's heart throbbed with the sound and the strange light in his eyes. He looked sad.

"Even *more* so," Fox said directly against her lips, not caring who was watching. His voice lowered as he pressed his forehead to hers. "More than you can ever know."

It was her turn to face him solemnly, and she pulled back to give the Lady a quick glance before returning to Fox's embrace.

"Good. Then follow my lead, Shadow Man."

He pulled away, glancing down at their feet as more ice cracked and broke away from the river below. With one last look at her, he smiled, still sad. Her heart gave an uneasy twist. But he shook his head at her questioning glance. Breaking their stare and running a sooty hand through his black hair, Fox spun on his heel, his smile gone. She watched him stalk back to the Lady's horse. Jessikah's acid yellow eyes stared at Aurelia for a moment before she tossed her head, turning back to the battle with a small smile playing across her lips.

Aurelia wanted to see what Fox might be planning, but she had lingered long enough. Taking a breath, her mouth drying at the thought of the task ahead, she jogged across the bridge. As her boots hit the dirt road, Flare's shining eyes swung her way, away from the carnage that was taking place across the once pristine farmlands.

"Flare," Aurelia shouted, running towards him, "I thought you weren't coming!"

The rustle that he gave to his wings was an impressive sight, as the outside of his wings caught the morning sun. He was breathtaking. His guilty expression ruined it.

"Aurelia," he rumbled. "I don't know what to do."

"I do. The king," she puffed. "Help me end this, please."

The entire scaled length of his tail twitched as Flare nodded, clear lids sliding over eyes, making them look like wet amethysts.

"Yes," he sighed, the sound a low hum that she could feel emanating from his chest as she reached him. He was gazing at the ring of tall stones, opposite to the way Aurelia had run. They were only just being caressed by the morning light.

"Yes," he repeated, lowering his head, his closest eye now on the bow she held. "I cannot do this without you."

With that, he lowered himself for her, his chest pressing into the trampled meadow. He offered her a scaled leg. Glad she would be on his back and not within his sword-sharp claws, Aurelia scrambled up with one hand, her other one holding desperately to the bow.

A great leap took them into the air after she had wedged herself between some spikes; feeling like she left her stomach on the grass below. He flew towards the peaks in the west along the river, gaining height. The forest spread out like a spiked carpet to her left, endless and touching every horizon, even behind the burnt orange peaks that ranged around Aneirin. The view was vast, and for the first time, Aurelia realised that the valley of Aneirin was a wide, shallow crescent, with mountains and peaks heading further off into the north. She couldn't see where the curve headed back towards the east, as the sky was too hazy even for her keen Elven gaze.

The amazing view quickly soured as Flare circled back to his right, facing the sun and the battlefield below.

A sob caught in her throat.

The once lush farmlands were a chaotic scene of colourfully robed Elves and darkly attired humans fighting for their lives. There was no glory down there, just pain, blood, guts and death. The dreadful noise reached her as Flare swooped lower, and Aurelia cried out as a human man looked up in shock as they passed, only to catch a spear in his chest.

"There!" Flare called, not realising she was trying not to be sick on his scales.

"What!?" Aurelia croaked back to him, her stomach heaving from the sight of the man's death as well as the sharp turn Flare was making.

"The prince!"

Clutching the bow, Aurelia held on to Flare's spikes as he circled once more, and she realised with dread that he was going to land behind the now scattered lines of the human army.

"Get ready!" Flare roared, causing Aurelia to panic.

They weren't here for the prince; they were here for the king! What had he seen?

Aurelia couldn't make sense of the wild chaos below, people and horses alike crying out. The dust was rising too, kicked up from beneath the once undulating fields of thick grains and crops. Her dry mouth was no help in trying to spit it out, and it clogged her nostrils too.

"Get ready?" Aurelia panted to herself, trying to find a grip on the shining purple spikes before her as her palms became slick with sweat. "How?"

"There!" Flare rumbled as his clawed feet touched the ground about fifty paces from the central fighting. Many humans and Elves alike scrambled away from the dust his steadying wing beats were raising.

"What-" and then she saw it.

A shimmering, only faint, but it was suspended above the ground amongst the dust.

Now that Flare was down, Aurelia was able to stand up, perched on the toes of her boots. In the centre of the fighting, a concentrated heap of dead soldiers in colourful armour and clothing were sprawled. Dead horses made up the tangle of bodies. No animal had been left standing, and no fresh animal was able to be sent in for the human soldiers.

In the centre of the heap, Rhydian fought, his helm gone and his golden brown hair plastered to his forehead with blood and gore.

Beside him, only a couple of metres away, stood the king.

"Oh my gods," Aurelia breathed, watching the prince fight for his life even as his father seemed to manipulate the air around just himself, meaning the Elves that came for the human king were weakened by some unseen, sickening force.

The man was such a bastard, protecting himself, but not his son. The last of Aurelia's fears and doubts dried up and blew away into the dust rolling around them.

Remembering Rhydian's words when they had parted last, he would do anything she asked of him. And he had. He had touched her dagger to his neck, helping her crack open a dark veil that covered all of them, Elves and humans alike, keeping them from the truth that both races were being manipulated. Especially Rhydian, and her as well.

He had chosen to give his life for his people. For her people.

For her.

She had done the worst thing that she had ever expected to do, and they had both lived through it. Now what was been asked of her was much simpler in return.

Watching him fight, like he was born to protect his realm, was an honour. But one that had to end. She was here now, and as her hand reached inside her shirt, untying the arrow, she realised she was honoured to be here. For her people. For his people.

For him.

Knowing she could do what he could not.

As she knocked the arrow to the string, her hands as steady as they had ever been, the king's eyes rose and met hers, the decapitated body of an Elf falling at his feet.

Rage crowded his expression. She was close enough to see him sneer at Flare first, his gaze rising to her perched upon the dragon's back, staring straight at him as Flare twisted his neck to the side.

Aurelia raised her bow, and the king's rage turned into something darker, more cunning. A twisted, violent bitterness.

Rhydian stumbled away from the closest Elf, kicking the young male with a heavy boot to his leg. The Elf collapsed with a shrill cry. Aurelia didn't hear the Elf's bone snap, but the man's agonised wail was proof enough. Wincing, the prince looked up, and his regretful expression turned to shock.

Had he really *not* seen Flare land? There was no time to wonder, as Rhydian's shock changed to relief. He lowered his sword.

"No! Not yet! Rhydian! Not yet!" Aurelia cried.

Movement behind the prince caught her eye; the shimmering in the air was fading away.

And the king was turning towards his son's back, his expression hard.

Flare gasped and froze beneath her, for which she was grateful as she raised the bow. They could both see what was about to happen.

"No!" Aurelia screamed. "Rhydian!"

Behind him, the king was raising his sword, angling it just so, for another precise decapitation. The prince blinked at her and Flare, not knowing how close his father was, mouthed something and dropped his sword into the dust, his face full of hope.

Inhaling until her lungs felt like they would burst, she roared the only thing she could think of, hoping Rhydian spoke true when he'd said he'd do *anything* she ever asked of him. Aurelia put every ounce of frustration, confusion, and rage that she could into the command.

"RHYDIAN, KNEEL."

Unable to hold another second, Aurelia let the arrow fly.

19

Rhydian

Year 367

Battle of Aneirin

There was a vast wave of pressure and pain; there was a burst of light, and then darkness.

Confused with pain radiating from his heart to his limbs, Rhydian's eyelids fluttered open. He was staring at the ground, kneeling, his hands clutching his chest. It was hard to breathe. As his vision returned, he could see the once vibrant field was now churned and bloodied beneath him. There had been fighting, hadn't there? A battle? The ringing in his ears, along with the pain, had turned his thoughts to thick stew.

Around him, soldiers, Elven and human alike, had been blown backwards, fanned around him like some macabre pattern. With a sob, the image of the old armoury wall flashed into his mind, the pattern of daggers on the wall.

He shut his eyes tightly, not understanding why the soldiers had fallen in such a manner, or why it was so hard to breathe. Maybe it was the bitter dirt that coated his face and his mouth? Or was that the blood of his so-called enemies, iron and copper like the war paint of old stories, splashed across his face?

Suddenly, he was frightened. Those stories scared him, and he needed his wits about him to discover what was going on. The ringing in his ears muffled all else, cutting off what could be happening, so Rhydian opened his eyes once more.

A beautiful woman with long, dark hair was emerging from the clouds of dust blowing past, thick clouds of brown and grey. Her mouth was moving. Rhydian shook his head, touching an ear with a bloodied and trembling hand.

Behind the woman, an impossibly colossal head appeared from the dust as well. The head was topped by sparkling peaks that caught the sun. As the front half of the creature emerged, Rhydian inhaled another ragged breath.

It was a dragon.

Rhydian blinked, his mind reeling.

Flare!

Normally so tiny, here and now the dragon was *big*. Flare had flown over the battle just now, hadn't he?

Rhydian's mind was struggling with the pain and the ringing in his ears. He swallowed, trying not to be sick, tasting copper and dirt in his mouth. He broke his gaze away from the cautiously approaching woman and the dragon, trying to piece together what else had happened.

Other soldiers, further out from those knocked down by whatever had happened to him, were pausing, sensing that the battle was over. Expressions were dazed, some less so than others. All were covered in blood, and there were a lot more of the soldiers in colourful armour than not.

As the ringing in his ears faded, Rhydian glanced down at himself. He was dressed in dark clothes under plain armour. The woman, still making her way towards him, was dressed the same, minus the armour. But she wasn't on his side... or was she?

It just hurt to think. Everything hurt, everything felt like he had been scalded. But he needed to find out what was going on. Clutching his chest, Rhydian tried to push himself up, crying out at the pain. He pushed through it, standing up with a stagger, dark spots clouding his vision.

"Rhydian," the woman called, the dragon close behind her, "wait."

Her gaze shifted past him, to the ground behind where he had been kneeling. A wave of nausea and cold washed over him. Rhydian didn't want to, but he turned.

A man in bloodied golden armour was lying on the ground, his legs and knees twisted up, as if his fall had been sudden and violent. His arms were thrown wide; one gauntleted hand was still clasping a richly adorned sword. The man's golden helm had rolled back into the dirt, exposing his face and the black arrow protruding from his throat. Bright red blood was bubbling from the wound, from the cruel gash the arrow had made on impact.

Rhydian's legs buckled beneath him as the day came crashing back to him.

Aurelia?

The arrow.

Rhydian sobbed aloud, a cry of grief and relief both, as he turned to the sky in gratitude. It was done. His father was-

A wet gagging below had Rhydian's gaze fall to the man, his stomach lurching.

His father was still alive.

Rhydian stared down numbly, meeting his father's wild and bloodshot eyes.

"Father."

Unable to help it, Rhydian lowered himself back to the ground, grabbing his father's hand. The man gasped in pain as the arrow in his throat bobbed.

Oh gods!

Why did it have to be like this?

"Don't move, father... I-"

"Rhydian," the king gasped, spraying Rhydian with blood. "Your mother-"

"Don't talk," Rhydian mumbled, feeling the hot droplets of his father's blood sliding down his cheeks.

Should he call for help? Except, this was what he wanted, wasn't it?

Breathing through the pain, both physical and otherwise, Rhydian risked a glance behind him. Flare and Aurelia were closer, and Aurelia's dusty face was solemn. Her bow was hanging limply in one hand. Dragging his eyes off it, Rhydian looked back down.

"Why did you do this to us?" Rhydian whispered, not bothering to specify, because he meant all of it.

But even as his life leaked away, the king seemed to understand. His father shifted slightly with a gasp, the ground below them soaking up his blood, mixing with that of the other fallen soldiers.

"The curse... *her* curse..." The king swallowed, his eyes blinking in pain. "It was to keep..." he coughed as more blood bubbled over his lips. "It was to keep *all* of them away from *us!*"

"Who?"

"The elves! The dragons! All of them..." his father's eyes closed, overcome with agony.

"But..." Rhydian wasn't sure what he was going to say. His father's eyes snapped open, searching wildly for his son's.

"They consume, they destroy... everything... people, cities, each other... We had to keep ourselves *safe*!"

More blood sprayed across Rhydian's face and his father's clammy hand jerked in Rhydian's grip. Rhydian pulled back slightly.

"By sacrificing your *son*?"

As soon as the words spilled out, Rhydian wished he could take them back. The shame of it was coiling in his guts, like the black Elven arrow that even now was leeching his father's life away.

"I didn't... I realised too late, we were in too deep, she wanted to be... untouchable..."

His father was gasping for air now, and his other hand relaxed around his sword.

Rhydian stared at the king, the man before him looking more like a stranger than ever. His ears were still ringing, but his hearing was almost back to normal, and the pain in his chest was slowly fading to a dull throb. He sniffed, blinking to clear his eyes.

Did a dying man such as this deserve his tears?

Considering I engineered his demise?

Seeing something in his son's eyes change, the king was still frantically trying to speak.

As the hush over the field filled his hearing now, he realised how close Aurelia was, by the dragon's heavy steps. It seemed like they could have made it to him by now, unless they were taking their time, waiting for his father to die. Rhydian wasn't sure if that was something he wanted to be alone for, or not. Perhaps this was something he needed to witness by himself. His father's wet voice tried again.

"Son! Look at me," his father ground out, straining, blood leaking from his nose.

"No matter what I could try to explain, you could *never* understand. You're just like her..."

"Stop talking, father... just stop..." Rhydian pleaded and squeezed his father's hand, feeling the warmth leaving the clammy flesh. His father shook his head. The arrow bobbed cruelly with the jerked motion.

"Let me talk!" His father wheezed. "She knew! That you're just like her! She knows..." he was gasping for air now.

"Stop! You're not making sense-"

"Damn you Rhydian! Damn you both!" his father roared, lips turning blue.

With his face covered in his father's blood, Rhydian stared, shocked.

"You're just like her!" his father cried out. "And she knew! Full of so much... full of..." the king coughed again, his eyes staring at the sky. "And *you* knew!"

Rhydian shook his head, not understanding, chills creeping along his spine.

"Yes... I know that, that you used magic..."

"You fool boy! You bloody knew what she did, what we did-" more gasping and red foam passed his father's darkening lips. "You knew! And I took that knowing from you..."

A shudder ran through the king's body, his gaze full of rage as it found Rhydian's wide-eyed gaze once more.

Rhydian was numb. His father's icy hand slipped from his grasp. Rhydian made no effort to grab it again.

"Wh-what did I know?" Rhydian asked, his voice hoarse. "Why did you take it from me?"

His father shuddered again, his body twisting in pain on the grass. His father was trying to speak, and the arrow bobbed as his mouth worked. Dreading what he might hear, Rhydian leant closer.

"You knew we laid the curse," his father wheezed. "You found out..."

No.

"... and you made me take that knowledge from you."

NO.

The chill creeping up Rhydian's spine crawled inside his skull.

"That's a lie!" Rhydian hissed out, even as every morning since he could remember had him waking up crushed with guilt.

With a sudden wild grab, his father caught Rhydian's shirt, pulling himself up. Rhydian tried to free himself, but the king's icy grip was strong, despite how close he was to death. Pressing his face to Rhydian's cheek, his father hissed back.

"Yes! You found out, you bloody *knew.*"

Rhydian's thoughts faltered at the dark revelation. Before he could think of anything to say, one of his father's chilled hands grabbed Rhydian's, forcing Rhydian's fingers to make a fist around the slippery arrow in his father's neck.

"*You coward,*" the king spat the words, and they left his blue lips in red mist.

With a grunt, his father released Rhydian's hand, falling backwards to the ground. Rhydian watched numbly as the wound, now torn open, pumped his father's life away into the grass, into the soil of his people.

With one final gasping exhalation, his father's eyes rolled towards the sky.

The king was dead.

Rhydian's gaze lifted from his father's body, landing on the only thing that he could.

The black arrow clutched in his own bloodied hand.

20

Cas

Year 367

Battle of Aneirin

Cas frowned, the hairs on his neck prickling as terrified cries sounded across the town.

Amused, Cas followed the gazes of the city folk to glance up. After a moment in which his jaw dropped open of its own accord, he got a hold of himself. He gaped for a bit, laughing in shock as people screamed and ran for cover.

To his unexpected delight, an enormous dragon of shining purple with darker purple wings had appeared from the mountains behind the castle.

"Holy, fucking *shit*," he breathed, glee filling him up like warm honey as his gaze followed the creature's path in the sky.

Considering the renewed war cries that his sensitive hearing had picked up from the field of battle, things were about to go down. If Cas' suspicions were correct on whom that purple dragon was, it would get even more interesting from here on. There was more powerful work here to be undone, not just the breaking apart of a royal house.

Enjoying the flush of magic within his veins, Cas shivered in anticipation. Leaning against the outside wall, out of the way, he was watching the frantic chaos at the main gates of the city. Although it was hard to see the whole layout of the day as it unfolded. Being mounted would give him a better view, and he could make a quicker getaway if he needed. His eyes roamed over the row of riderless animals shifting uneasily beside the city's gates.

"Hmm," Cas murmured thoughtfully, pushing off the wall.

Straightening his blue velvet cloak, Cas stalked up to the tallest horse of all, a large grey beast with intelligent eyes. As he reached for the reins, intending to slip them off the rail, a woman's harried voice called out.

"Hey! What are you doing there?"

"This is my horse," Cas replied, flashing his most charming smile at the young woman hurrying over from helping a big bearded man in an apron. The groom, Cas thought, I think I've met him. The woman, almost at his side, pointed at him.

"I doubt it! They're for the soldiers! Now get lost."

Clearly, his smile was the wrong approach. The slim woman, in a guard's uniform with her brown hair braided on each side of her dirty face, was frowning at him in disbelief. She brushed a fly away from her face. The bugs were gathering already, like the black crows circling above, here for the guts and the blood.

"I said, this is my horse," he repeated, careful to keep his power from lashing out. Not because he needed to. But because he *wanted* to.

"What the fuck are you talking about?" the guard spat out, her hand wiping over her face, spreading the dirt raised from the battle. She eyed him up and down. "That's a horse from the royal stables. Who the fuck do you think you are?"

Frowning, Cas looked down at himself. Clearly, he looked more royal than any of the peasants running around waving their swords. But also clearly, he was not part of the battle. He tried a different approach.

Ignoring the dirt across her mouth, over lips that would have been quite pretty if she were clean, he closed the distance between them with a single step. Uncoiling a thread of power from his centre, not really because he had to, but just because he could, Cas pressed his lips to hers. He threaded his magic at the confused thoughts running around in her head. Her eyes fluttered in shock.

Pulling away from her gritty lips, Cas smiled once more, ignoring the stink of horses and battle around them. The guard blinked up at him in wonder. She wiped her lips again, fingers lingering on her lips.

"That's better, beautiful," Cas murmured. Her eyes widened a fraction and his smile almost faded into a smirk. He willed himself to keep eye contact as he caressed her face, backing her up to the grey horse that turned its head to eye them with a startled expression.

"I'm going to ride you all day, sugar," Cas whispered, trying to contain his laugh as the woman's eyelids fluttered once more.

She pulled away from him, catching the saddle on the grey horse for support.

"Wh-what?" she mumbled, her free hand playing with one of her plaits of hair.

Cas licked his lips, leaning closer, teasing her nose with his own. He reached an arm past her head and patted the horse's dusty neck.

"I am talking to the *horse.*"

She was still reeling from the fog he'd planted within her mind, but her eyes narrowed at his jest. But he was still able to brush her aside like a weed. But, somehow, a small part of her was fighting him. Her hand dropped from her hair to her sword as she stumbled away.

Straightening to his full height, pulling the horse away from the rail, Cas wiped her dirt off the tip of his nose with the sleeve of his shirt. Dropping his arm, his eyes locked to hers, Cas tilted his head.

"Do you really want to draw that?" he asked, his tone mild.

Her hand tightened on her sword, so he bared his teeth at her. It was a simple thing to drop the glamour from one of his eyes as well, and he was pleased when the guard flinched. Her hand jerked away from the sword in a hurry.

"Good girl," Cas murmured, turning the horse away. The guard watched mutely, hands limp by her sides.

Checking under his horse for a moment, Cas straightened up, and he patted the grey beast. "Good girl," he said to the horse with a smirk. "Lets go."

He mounted up, feeling better for the extra height already. It had been too long on the ground for him, and despite the horse not being quite what he wanted in terms of a better view, he'd deal with it for now. He was *so* close to getting what he needed, which was why he was still hanging around like a creep.

Walking the horse past a group of frantic surgeons by the side of the road, Cas pulled the horse to a rough stop, cursing in shock. A petite woman with bright red hair was leaning over an older man with a spear sticking out of his thigh. Cas' heart flipped over in his chest. He knew he was staring, but he couldn't help it.

Was that...?

The woman, sensing his fierce stare, raised her face to his. She was covered in spots of blood. Cas' nostrils flared as he stared down at her, examining her face and her slim body. Slowly, the anxiety threatening to rise within him eased. It wasn't *her.*

Thank the icy hells; he didn't need any distractions just now. Not now, not at this time, when so much was coming together. Even as he had the thought, a cry went up on the battlefield, even as the earth beneath his horse's hooves heaved unsteadily.

Clutching his throat, Cas cried out wordlessly at the agonising pain across his neck. Feeling more pain lance deep within his chest, Cas slumped forward in the saddle until his face was pressed into the horse's sweaty neck. Something was happening, and by the way his magic was heaving, roiling and rejoicing within his body, Cas came to the realisation that Aneirin had lost its king.

His heart churned again, his guts burning, his hands feeling hot and cold all at once. The daylight around him was too bright all of a sudden, and the calls and shouts from the battlefield were too loud, even as far away as they were.

"Oh my gods, oh my gods," Cas gasped, the pain even more severe than his recent experimentation with quartz crystals. There was no way to tell, with stolen or shared magic, if this was good or bad. The magic within him throbbed again, and black spots covered his vision.

"Ow, fuck," he croaked, pulling the horse away from the battlefield. As he did, the pain receded noticeably.

"Come on, good girl, go," Cas was finally able to gasp, as the pain faded quicker the further his horse travelled away from the carnage behind. He leant over the saddle to spit out horsehair and dust.

"We'll come back after things settle the fuck down."

21

Fox

Year 367
Battle of Aneirin

Follow my lead, Shadow Man.

Fox stared blankly at the raging battle, his expressionless face at odds with the rush of his emotions within. He felt uncertain. And he hated it.

"I can't make you go out there, can I?"

The Lady's voice was full of barely contained excitement. Lowering his face, Fox shook his head, arms crossed tightly over his chest. His voice was calm.

"You're here. I've fulfilled my promise to you."

"Perhaps. I am almost where I should be." Her green eyes darkened with amusement as they flicked to his belt. "But don't you want to wet your lovely sword?" The Lady jutted her chin at the pageant of colourful Elves overrunning the human army before them.

His mouth a thin line, Fox uncrossed his arms and one hand drifted down to the ornate sword hilt at his hip. He'd never used it. And he'd never intended to, had he? There had never been a need to, full of other's magic as he was.

Fox turned away from the amused gaze appraising him, his other hand brushing over the ash of the bridge's wooden railing. Rubbing the pad of his thumb across his fingertips, the silky ash sliding over the ridges of his skin was such a gentle sensation, opposite to the jarring sights and sounds close by.

Follow my lead, Shadow Man.

Making himself look up, Fox opened himself to the sound and sights of the slaughter on the battlefield, a complicated and chaotic vista. Soldiers and horses fought and screamed and died. Nearby on the bridge, the Lady on her white horse was watching intently, her bottom lip caught between white teeth. She seemed to be about to shout out, her eyes flashing with eagerness so acute that it was akin to a sickening kind of lust. But as the play of blood and guts reached a peak, a hush fell, spreading like a dark sun over the field.

Averting his attention from the Lady, Fox followed the line of her gaze to the fields. A muscle in his jaw ticked.

A great metallic purple dragon had landed not far behind the lines of the human army.

Holding his breath, Fox's keen eyesight watched as a figure stood up from the great spikes of the dragon's back, simultaneously raising a bow.

The king raised his sword to his son's exposed back. The prince was facing the dragon, unaware.

Something was shouted from the figure on the dragon, desperate, raw. At the words, without hesitation, the prince dropped to his knees.

There was the arching flight of a single arrow, a spinning and elongated barb.

The king stumbled backwards, collapsing, clutching his throat.

As the man collapsed to the ground, there was an immediate blinding light.

Bright and radiant, bursting forth over the field, the golden rays spilled from the king, spreading out in a circular wave, erupting in heat, accompanied by a low but deafening roar. The wave crested over those on the bridge, radiating from the king as he fell, releasing, opening, freeing and loosening his magic.

Fox closed his eyes and braced himself against the rail, knowing what was coming.

The final remnants of the curse had broken, and the remnants of the unwinding power were approaching fast.

When Fox came to, slumped but still standing, the first thing he saw was the Lady. Her face was wild with mad delight, laughing while her terrified horse danced beneath, spooked from the light and the roll of the roar as it faded. The other horses tied to the rail on the far side were shifting in fear, eyes wild and round.

Straightening his spine, it was clear to Fox that the Lady was absolutely full of unleashed power, full of life. Ignoring the crowd of unconscious Elves around them, Fox watched her, fascinated, as she held up a hand, something gripped tightly within. He snorted on seeing what it was. It was a gold tiara, fitted with red jewels, as ruby red as her dress. It was obvious that the Lady felt that she was queen once more, not even waiting for the battle to be called.

As she placed the tiara over her dark hair, she looked as fierce as when Fox had followed her thread of power into the great hall of Aneirin the night before. He'd been awake, satisfied with finally taking care of Gavin. He had felt the air shift with a hum when he had made it back to Aurelia, to their campfire. And so, watching half from sleep, half from a trance, Fox had observed the Lady on the throne as she taunted her son.

But the prince had broken her hold on him. Summoning a strength or something darker within, he had torn himself away from her grasp.

Fox examined the woman before him now, full of power at the moment of her triumph.

Can I do that?

Break away from the promises I made?

Watching her face, Fox realised he had likely once looked as she did now, after taking revenge on all those that had broken him, those who had stolen the lives of countless others. Could Fox sacrifice his pride? Could he admit that what he had been doing here was likely worlds apart from when he took his revenge on the dragons that betrayed him?

Fox touched his face, feeling the ash leave his fingertips to stain his cheek.

I looked like her when I wiped this body's soul from the earth.

I looked like her last night, when I sent Gavin to meet his brother in the darkest hells, where they both belong.

Was the cycle of unchecked revenge worth it?

Aurelia's words came back to him once more.

Follow my lead, Shadow Man.

After all this time, Fox felt that yes, revenge would *always* be worth it. But this... this was something else, wasn't it? Fox hadn't yet untangled all of the threads that made up the curse. But the Lady's mission wasn't just about revenge... Fox's gaze slid back to the battlefield, where hundreds of men and women were dead, or sorely wounded.

This wasn't a cause for justice. This was a *betrayal*.

The innocent had been used as stepping-stones to cross a vast abyss, while the Lady grasped for the return of what she had lost. All of her arrogance had swept aside those in her way, in the name of her greed.

As the hush descended around them once more, Fox realised he was certain of one thing, at least.

Once an Elder, once a queen, and once a simple serving girl, whatever she had been or was or would be, this woman had brought this on *herself*. Fox's breathing hitched as he examined all the pieces, and how they had come together for the one he cared about. Feeling that the only choice left to her after failing in her task, the wild reach of this vicious woman had resulted in Aurelia throwing herself into a river.

Somehow Aurelia had risen above the apparent failure, learned something about herself, and had examined the situation with new eyes. And then she had changed her mind.

Follow my lead, Shadow Man, she had urged him.

So he would.

Pushing himself away from the wooden rail, his feet only partially unsteady from the backwash of the broken curse, Fox walked calmly to the Lady's horse. With a slow, deliberate movement, he reached out and grabbed the stirrup. One of his fingers brushed the leather of her boot. His voice was quiet, but she heard him.

"Sophia."

Her laughter died off with a startled choke. Turning from the stillness of the battlefield to look down at him, her bright green eyes were wide and incredulous, her lips slightly parted.

"I have not heard that name in a *long* time, Fox." Her lips curled, and her eyes flashed with warning. "Careful."

"Sophia," Fox repeated, enunciating the name clearly, pulling the name from the past. "It's over."

The Lady, Sophia, raised one single perfectly groomed eyebrow.

Straightening her posture, she twisted in the saddle to gaze behind her. Fox broke his attention from Sophia just long enough to look. Jessikah stared back at Fox, her normally sullen expression now radiant, brilliant for all its wicked delight. Her yellow eyes were wide with anticipation. Fox ripped his gaze back to Sophia, confused.

"Really," said Sophia, calmly.

Fox tilted his head back. His fingers twitched on her horse's stirrup.

"Yes." Fox said, eyes on the Lady's, all the while unsure of the change that had come over Jessikah, the back of his neck itching. "It's over."

"I see." Sophia pursed her lips, green eyes glinting with malice. "Now Fox?" She held up an arm, the red sleeve of her dress falling away to expose her smooth skin, to indicate the battlefield with a broad sweep. "After all this time?"

Fox shrugged, a single shoulder lifting and falling, not breaking away from her gaze. There was a tightness in his chest, and his hands felt numb. The Lady's eyes blazed. He watched as her incredulity eventually soured into bone chilling rage.

"After all that we've both been through?" Sophia hissed, her eyes cruel. "Both of us, victims of the darkness that seeps from the *males* of *both* our species?"

Fox broke away from her fiery emerald stare, turning to Jessikah, quite unable to process the wicked smile on Jessikah's beaming face.

What?

As he stared at Jessikah, the flesh across Fox's back rippled, his tattoo shifting, its ever present ache a constant reminder of the trauma he'd been through. His breathing coming in hard won gasps, Fox tore his gaze from Jessikah to face the triumphant woman above. The Lady's dark hair, lifting in the dusty breeze, framed her sickly sweet face.

"Yes," Sophia purred. "I *know* what happened to you."

Even as his hand tightened on the stirrup, Fox stumbled back a step. Sophia leaned down from the saddle. The red gems in her tiara winked in the rising sunlight.

"Not everyone needs a voice to share their secrets with me," she whispered. "I know what happened to you. And I know what you did *afterwards*."

That wasn't possible. How-

Sophia's voice lowered, barely a breath between them. "I know what you did in Mionlach," she said, her voice thickening with cold glee.

Fox's mouth opened, but no sound escaped his lips. It was hard to think, hard to see.

What was happening to him?

Sophia was leaning so far over in the saddle Fox could have yanked her off her horse. But he couldn't move from shock. She knew it too, letting words drip from her venomous tongue like poison.

"I know what you did to the *dragons*... to your *family*."

What.

The.

Fuck.

Sophia straightened in the saddle. The look of satisfaction on her face, at the effect her words were having, had Fox feeling like the curse was breaking over him once more. He was completely eviscerated, inside and out. A very small part of him was left thinking rationally enough, wondering if he had ever been quite so utterly and completely lost for words.

The fingernails of his free hand dug into his palm as he stared at Sophia, unable to turn to look at Jessikah.

I'm finally going to kill that monster.

I'm really going to do it. I don't need a reminder anymore.

Fox inhaled slowly, his nostrils flaring slightly.

I don't need a reminder of who not *to be.*

Whilst watching Fox trying to control himself, Sophia reached into her bodice. Fox stared numbly, his mind spinning, as she withdrew a long glittering object that caught the sun. She held it up and all final rational thoughts left his head.

Sophia let the charms swing free, hanging from the chain around her neck.

The breath left Fox in a choked rush.

Owaen's chain.

There was no mistaking it. The faceted golden topaz, and the tiny wand of solid gold, swung freely in the light, mocking him. Sophia's expression was vicious, her eyes cold and cruel. The flush in her cheeks told him that she was enjoying this, and she knew Fox was well aware of it. He was amazed at how calm his voice sounded when words finally came.

"How do you have that?"

Sophia's smile turned darker, wild, and she bared her teeth at him. The horse danced beneath her again, and unconsciously, Fox gripped the stirrup tighter in response. If he had looked down, he might have seen his knuckles were so white they matched the snowy coat of the horse.

"That's mine, Sophia." Fox's voice was quiet. "That was my... that was Owaen's."

His expression chilled from numb to flinty, and Fox had to grit his teeth lest more words fall out of his mouth unbidden. As his beloved's name dropped from his lips, however, Fox had felt the stirrup jerk as her boot twitched.

Owaen.

Sophia's feral grin faltered. Eyes of crushed emeralds narrowed at him.

"Owaen? *Owaen Carter?*"

Fox licked his lips, trying to remember how to breathe.

"Yes."

"I don't believe you," she snapped. "That's not possible."

"It was a gift from a dying woman," Fox bit out. "Owaen eventually entrusted it to me." Not quite the truth, but close enough. There was something wrong with Fox's heart. His free hand found its way to clutch his chest.

At his words, Sophia bit her lip so hard that a drop of blood appeared at the corner of her mouth, ruby bright. She flicked a glance to Jessikah, then back to Fox, and jerked her boot once more, this time on purpose. Fox held the stirrup firm.

"You filthy liar," Sophia hissed eventually, her voice rising. "That charm was my *mother's*. And I *know* it was Owaen that killed her."

Of all the lies, this was too much.

At her statement, Fox, his eyes just about bugging out of his head, finally turned to stare incredulously at Jessikah. The small woman stepped back, flinching, and he was pleased to note that her smirk disappeared. Seeing the expression on Fox's face, Jessikah tried to retreat another step. Fox gathered himself together and sent out a cold thread of power to trap her and hold her in place.

"No," Fox murmured, finding his voice and meeting the Lady's gaze once more. "Owaen didn't kill your mother."

Unable to hold in the hysteria rising from his guts, he laughed. Fighting the fit of laughter that he was unable to bite back, Fox jerked his thumb over his shoulder at the frozen form of Jessikah. Uncertainty flickered across Sophia's face before it was covered with a sneer.

"Liar," she hissed.

Shaking his head, Fox looked down. His hand was still clenched on the stirrup, pulsing, trembling, as he tried to catch his breath.

I'm trembling, he realised in wonder.

My face is numb.

I can't breathe.

What's happening to me?

He thought of Aurelia and Rhydian. He thought of Owaen. Some lives are worth sacrificing for. Rhydian had taught him that. Aurelia had taught him that.

Follow my lead, Shadow Man.

Fox's hand tightened further on her stirrup. With a calm shift in his posture, Fox's other hand reached up to wrap around the ankle of her boot. She hissed at the icy burn of his grip, the icy fire reaching her skin even through the leather.

"Sophia," Fox said, a trembling overtaking his legs, knowing where this would lead. He had never felt this cold. "I'm giving you a chance to end this now. You can't, neither of us can. We can't go on like this."

Silently, she stared at him, and he could feel the air thicken as her power gathered around them. The wind picked up with a rush that gained momentum in the space of a few moments, and horses tossed their heads. Sophia's horse stamped uneasily and her hair whipped around her face.

Sophia smiled.

Without further warning, Sophia called to herself a furious surge of power, enabling her to jerk her boot free of Fox's iron grip. Fox cursed, his hands stinging, the air crackling between them, and sparks like stars gathered in her hair.

"You're not a fox," Sophia said, green eyes flashing. "You're a scaly bitch."

Then she kicked him in the face.

Fox was flung backwards, without time to block or even curse, the heated burst of her magic lending such force to the blow that he landed on his back. Blood flowed immediately from a deep gash above his eyes, his sword and dagger digging in painfully under his thighs.

As he blinked through the blood, he watched, dazed, as Sophia brutally jerked her horse around, causing it to rear and squeal in pain from the bit cutting into its soft mouth. One of the other horses nearby whinnied in fear at the sound. Sounding like rocks tumbling down a mountain, her horse raced to the end of the bridge, and once the hooves had touched the dirt road, she jerked its head to the left.

With his ears ringing, Fox stared after her, watching with morbid fascination as the woman wielded her newly regained magic. She charged her horse through Elven soldiers, and whether they were standing or fallen, it didn't matter. Jets of green bursts blasted dazed soldiers out of her path. Their broken bodies scattered as she passed.

She knew what she was doing. She was taunting him.

Follow me, if you think you can silence what I know about you.

The way was as clear as the path of the rising sun above.

I dare you.

There was no longer the need to make a choice.

Fox pushed himself up, eyes straining. He groaned, realising that Sophia was making for the forest, the shelter of the vast sea of endless trees that lapped against the southern end of the jagged mountains. In her wake, the waves of her passing had rippled across the battlefield, leaving a trail of broken bodies and blasted earth.

Fox stared through the blood on his face at the decimated farmlands before him.

But at least one battle was over.

The king was dead. The prince was alive.

And Sophia, betrayer of her family, betrayer of Aurelia's kinsfolk, the reason they were all here, bloodied and raw, was getting away. Sophia knew that there was no one else left to end her campaign for power, for victory.

Only him.

Getting up with a stagger, Fox ignored the blood on his face, but sent a cold burst of magic to the gash in his forehead to staunch it. The numbness had left him, but he was still shaking, the rage in his mouth tasting like ash.

Ears still ringing, Fox spat out blood from his mouth. Taking his eyes off the white horse racing for the vast network of forest, he turned around.

Jessikah was staring at him; her expression a mixture of fear, hatred, and vicious triumph.

Yanking a horse's reins from the rail, Fox paused. He needed to take care of *this* problem too, once and for all. After Sophia, if he was able. Perhaps he would enjoy it.

Fox walked over to Jessikah, her expression faltering. He stepped in so close that she was crowded against the far side of the bridge, her back pressed against the railing. The bridge felt like it was vibrating beneath his boots, perhaps due to another deep tremor from the earth below.

"Hopefully, I'll see you shortly," Fox said, and smiled. Then, with brutal calm, his fist connected with Jessikah's stomach.

The punch had the full force of all his fury, his fear, and his rage.

Without a sound, Jessikah folded like a dropped square of dirty linen, sprawling face-down on the boards. Her back would be bruised from the railing as well as his punch. But while the sight filled him with cold satisfaction, he had no time to waste in incapacitating her further. Fox mounted the horse, and kicked the poor beast's sides, making for the end of the bridge, and then swinging left. He was thinking of dragons, of humans, of greed.

What an idiot he'd been. He should have just killed them all when he had the chance. It was doubtful that he'd get another.

As Fox's horse galloped past the rear line of scattered soldiers, wide eyes from both armies followed his passage. A mountain of ice inside his guts taunted him, even as he wondered what he rode towards. He had nothing left to offer anyone anymore. Not even Aurelia. Only his death, the cold revelation of his true, inner nature that just *might* stop the woman who had caused the death and pain of so many around her. Who would continue to do the same until she was stopped. Perhaps it would be easy to let go, to take her with him, to drift away from the cold that consumed him.

To find *any* kind of peace.

Fox choked back a sound that might have been a sob, lost to the pounding of his icy heart inside, the hot hooves pounding the dusty earth below. The giant trees loomed closer, their heights crowding over him as his horse darted between the outermost trunks to the green hush within.

What if there was no peace?

As the shadows of the forest flashed around him, Fox followed the white shape darting before him through the greenery.

What if there was only a kind of dark rebirth?

The thought of transforming into another kind of darkness gave him pause, even as he raced towards the possibility. His desire to lash out at anyone, for the injustice of everything he had seen and experienced, might win over the desire to just let go and die. He might rise, a vengeful, scaled phoenix, intent on paying back every single dark heart in kind.

Anything was possible.

He had risen from the welcome arms of oblivion once before, after all.

22

Aurelia

Year 367

Battle of Aneirin

I have killed a prince.

And now I have killed a king.

This time, there was no doubt in her heart that this had been the right choice. Placing a steady hand on Rhydian's shoulder, Aurelia tried to pull him away from the body of the dead king. Resisting, Rhydian didn't move, the black arrow still clutched in his bloody fist.

They were both kneeling; Flare a silent, looming shadow above. She had dropped the bow to the mud beside them, not caring that the wood would stain. The now silent fields around them were churned into mud, and full of wandering horses, Elves and humans, dazed, bloody, wounded. And dead.

Looking up from the dead king, Aurelia brushed dusty hair away from her face, blinking to clear grit from her eyes. A flash of hair so blonde that it was almost white caught her eye. Far off, a tall man on a grey horse was watching them from the road. Aurelia narrowed her gaze, focusing on the strange figure. His spotless velvet cloak was at odds with the mud, blood and ruin around them. Ignoring her, the man stared at the king. He did not look upset.

Flare edged closer. "Rhydian?" Giant leather wings fluttered. "Can you hear us?"

"Rhydian," Aurelia murmured, dropping her gaze from the blonde man. "It's over. You've won. *We've* won."

At that, Rhydian's fingers twitched, and he dropped the arrow. It landed in the red earth and Aurelia reached for it.

"Don't!" Rhydian exclaimed. She froze.

Withdrawing her hand, Aurelia placed it back on Rhydian's arm instead. "Fine, that's fine." She brushed his blood-splattered hair off his forehead and pressed her lips there. "That's fine."

Above them, Flare cleared his throat, a deep rumble from amongst the smoke that drifted past from something burning nearby. "Rhydian, did you see him?"

"Who?" Lifting his dull eyes to the dragon, Rhydian shook his head in confusion.

"Your father," Flare said. "He was going to kill you."

Closing his eyes for a brief moment, Rhydian shook his head slowly. When his eyes opened, they were haunted, dull and empty.

"No," he whispered, and then swallowed. "He... no."

Rhydian reached up to cover Aurelia's hand where it clutched his arm. His hand, trembling slightly, squeezed hers. She nearly sobbed with relief at his reassurance while Rhydian's gaze dropped back to the body of the king.

The awkwardly sprawled corpse, with its golden armour covered with the blood of its owner, along with the blood of others, was a garish sight. Aurelia cleared her throat and tugged at Rhydian's shoulder again.

"We need to get up," she said, grimacing. She spat some dust. "We need to get you away from here."

Flare interrupted.

"Why would he do that, Rhydian? Why would he try to kill you?"

Aurelia glared at Flare before tugging Rhydian again. This time, the dazed young man rose with her, slightly unsteady on his feet.

"I don't know," he mumbled. Something flashed across his face before she could name it. "Maybe he... he knew I was going to kill him."

"I killed him, not you." Aurelia pulled him close, wrapping her arms around him. Rhydian hesitated at first, but his arms eventually rose and wrapped around her in return. He pressed his face into her hair, inhaling deeply.

"No," he sighed, staring down at his bloody hand. "I was too weak to do it in person, but I killed him all the same."

Aurelia pulled back to cup his face, her hands smearing the drying blood on his cheeks. A bruise was blossoming in purple and yellow across one cheek.

"Then *we* killed him," she whispered. "Like he deserved-"

A startled roar from Flare had her twist around. The sudden noise, amplified by his proper size, made her bones rattle.

"Oh..." Flare cried, his voice shocked. "Oh, my... Aurelia!"

"Flare, what is it?" Rhydian demanded, his dazed expression changing immediately into one of concern.

"Your mother," Flare cried, staring across the field towards the river and the bridge. "Oh..."

"What! What, Flare?" Aurelia demanded, going cold at the shock in Flare's voice.

Spinning with her, Rhydian followed the dragon's gaze.

The Lady could be seen, making some kind of mad dash behind the lines of the Elven army.

Where was Fox?

Why hadn't he stopped the rogue queen already?

Even as she thought the words, Aurelia's breath hitched in her throat. The Lady, a bright spot of red on her white horse, was making a run for it, parallel to the river, heading towards the line of trees where they met the south end of the mountains. And as her horse crossed the rear of the Elven army, she wasn't hiding her passage. She was making it known to all that she had her power back once more.

Green bursts of light and raw magic left her raised hand, scattering and clearing a path. Not bothering to dodge the Elven obstacles in her way, the Lady ploughed through them, as Elves watched, horrified, some too shocked to jump clear.

She must be mad, Aurelia thought, watching with shock and dismay.

How could she?

After all we had done for her?

Revolted, furious and unable to look away, Aurelia bit back a frustrated sob.

Where was Fox?

Wait-

There.

Straining her Elven eyesight, Aurelia watched as a figure in black raced a brown and white horse after the fleeing figure along the river. Aurelia tasted fresh blood in her mouth.

She was startled to realise that she had bitten her lip, hard. Something about this wasn't right.

"Fox?" Aurelia breathed, and Rhydian's arms came up around her.

"He'll be fine. If anyone can take care of her, it'll be him."

Above them, Flare made a strange sort of noise.

"What do we do?" Aurelia asked, not sure which of them she was addressing, as the white horse reached the trees. Elves were picking themselves up from her passing. Some of them, anyway. The others were left charred or in pieces, lifeless.

No one answered her. All of them watched silently as Fox's horse made it to the trees and darted in between the giant trunks.

Instead of helping the wounded, neither of them moved, still watching Fox's horse reach the trees. Nothing happened at first. There was obviously a wild dash amongst the thick trunks and undergrowth of the forest. But something changed. Aurelia wasn't sure what, but a slight pressure or wordless hum seemed to vibrate in the earth below.

Aurelia turned from the trees to stare up at Flare, frowning. His nostrils were twitching, and his eyes were blinking rapidly.

"Flare?" she asked, knowing he could sense something that she couldn't.

As she watched, his enormous purple eyes widened, his wings opening slightly. Rhydian swore and pulled Aurelia out of the way as one of the great leather appendages nearly knocked her over.

"Flare! What is it?" she demanded, watching Flare's jaw open, thinking he was about to say something. He didn't. Flare just stood there, shock rendering the dragon silent, frozen, struck dumb.

"Flare! For fuck's sake!" Rhydian yelled. Reaching out before Aurelia could stop him, Rhydian punched the dragon in his scaled jaw.

Flare's mouth snapped shut, missing Rhydian's fist by centimetres and his eyes, still wide and wild, swung his way.

"Answer her!" Rhydian demanded, unheeding of the danger. Aurelia was impressed with his courage, even as she wanted to push him out of the way. She glanced back at Flare.

"F-Fox... is..." Flare stuttered, his dazed eyes back to the trees. "He's..."

"He's what!?" Rhydian cursed, waving his hand at Flare to go on.

A low throb reached them, and had them all turning towards the trees, away from Flare's staring eyes, back to witness something that was simply too impossible for Aurelia to make out at first.

There, amongst the towering canopy of the forest, a great golden dragon with shimmers of emerald green burst forth towards the sky. Aurelia cried out, her hands over her mouth.

Another dragon, after all this time?

Larger than Flare, shining like a faceted emerald in the morning sun, the dragon arched over the trees, outspread wings a brilliant golden green, shaking off chunks of wood and forest with its flight. Soaring in a tight circle, it pulled in its wings and dived back into the forest below.

"*Who* is that?" Aurelia breathed. There was an odd sensation in her guts.

Flare shook his head, unable to speak, while Rhydian choked out a mad laugh.

"That fucking better not be my mother!" he yelled, pulling Aurelia towards Flare. The purple dragon shook his head, his great mouth of shining teeth hanging open.

"It isn't," Flare croaked.

"What?" snapped Aurelia, her mind racing towards all sorts of impossible conclusions. "What are you saying?"

"I knew it!" Rhydian crowed, punching Flare's flank. "Leg!"

Startled, Flare swung his great head around to Rhydian. Aurelia was prepared to jerk him back from snapping jaws once again. But to her surprise, after a pause, Flare closed his mouth. And blowing out a hot breath, Flare extended a clawed foreleg, allowing them to scamper up.

Without hesitating, Rhydian hoisted Aurelia up first, and then crawled up behind her. Once they had settled, slotted between two of Flare's spikes, Rhydian kicked his heels in. A hysterical laugh threatened to burst forth from Aurelia at the thought of Rhydian trying to treat a dragon like a horse. However, the thought left her as quickly as it came, as the seriousness of the situation returned, and Flare took a running leap to catch the wind.

With a lurch and a loud drumming of wings through the dusty air, Flare rose into the sky, the sun behind him as he headed west towards the forest.

They could see more green lights bursting the tops of the trees apart, but of the dragon, there was no sign. Aurelia, clutching tightly to Flare's spike as Rhydian clutched tightly to her, couldn't even tell if it was dragon magic, or the queen's, that was breaking apart the canopy.

As Flare approached the forest, what looked like the top half of a tree was bursting apart as an ear-splitting roar rang out from below.

"Shit, shit, shit," Aurelia was gasping, unsure of how or what they were doing getting close. Rhydian was unperturbed.

"There!" he called, slapping Flare's flank as they wheeled high over a giant crater of desolation below. "The sideways tree!"

In answer, Flare dipped and headed to where Rhydian had indicated. As they dived, Aurelia was only half aware that her stomach was left in the sky behind her. She had caught sight of the two opponents below.

An awesome and terrible dome of greenish light was glowing over a figure inside. Trees and branches were ripped up by a significant force from behind the dome, flung like giant spears at the dragon that tore against it. The dragon was somehow suspended over the shield of magic, its claws ripping away at the wall of light, fighting for entrance.

Aurelia could smell smoke and flames even as the wind picked up, stirring strange dark flames that licked the edge of the broken mass of trees. Branches and trunks twisted and shattered like broken bones across the forest floor. The wasted arena of chaos was about a hundred metres across, and Aurelia felt sick at how much power each fighter below must hold in order to cause so much destruction in so little time.

Flare landed with a jolt, his wings spread behind the brilliant gold and green dragon on a giant pine that had been broken and toppled away from the dome. The golden, emerald dragon's scales were covered with soot and ash, and Aurelia choked on the smoke that whipped past, even as another tree was ripped up, the forest groaning. The tree was torn apart in midair with a lazy twist of the golden green dragon's foreleg. It roared in fury, and the hemisphere of power on which the creature crouched pulsed brighter, heat reaching them all the way to the crater's edge.

His colossal head shaking back and forth before her, Aurelia realised Flare was moaning, something about the sky, while he stared at the violence before him. She couldn't make out the words. Even as she tried, thinking the safest place was exactly where they were; Rhydian unhooked his right leg and slid off Flare onto the broken trunk below. Aurelia tore her eyes away from the magnificence of the dragon, to stare horrified at Rhydian, as he held out his hand, beckoning to her. She shook her head, eyes wide, and he frowned.

"What are you possibly going to do?" Aurelia yelled.

"Whatever I can!" he called back, urging her down beside him.

But it was too late.

Flare reeled back as a great trembling shook the ground, and a woman's ear curdling scream sounded amongst an ear-splitting roar.

The gold and green dragon had broken through the dome of light.

Still, it was held back by some force, and the massive dragon tore and gnashed its sword like teeth at the air in front of it. The giant tail, full of golden spikes shimmering darkly, whipped back and forth. Flare had to duck swiftly to avoid a blow to his face.

Screaming wordlessly, the queen began to glow. Not green like the failed dome of protection, but fiery, wicked red. Her skin and hair were now red like sunset over a burning field. As the red glow turned hotter and brighter, she grew in size. As her figure expanded, her face was clear to see, the cruel smile of triumph on her face horrifying in size, a signal that she clearly thought she would win. The wind picked up around them, and more chunks of shattered trees spun by.

"Fox... Fox," Aurelia chanted, hands wrapped around Flare's spikes, wanting to but unable to shut her eyes.

Roaring in frustration and rage, as the grotesque woman threw her head back and laughed, the great dragon lunged forward, golden scaled mouth open wide, ivory teeth sharp, giant wings spread, gilded claws outstretched. The violence of their collision knocked Flare sideways towards Rhydian. Aurelia cried out in terror and held on to Flare, her arms locked around his spike, as the hurricane of detritus, wind and magic split the world apart.

"Rhydian!" Aurelia screamed, shoving a branch away from her.

Somehow, she was still on Flare's back. Flare was limp under her, and Aurelia forced her limbs to work. She half slid, half jumped from his back to the wreckage below.

"Rhydian," Aurelia sobbed, pulling aside branches and rocks that had landed around them.

A cough sounded, and a sooty face appeared in the silence.

"I'm okay," Rhydian coughed, "I'm... oh my god..." his eyes widened as he stared at the scene behind her. Whirling, Aurelia prepared to dodge another branch. She froze instead.

The air had stilled. All was silent, and somehow... all the chaotic particles flung up by the short-lived hurricane had stopped in place. Leaves, rocks, branches and parts of splintered trees were suspended in midair around them.

At the centre of it all, the gilded green dragon was wrapped around the giant form of the limp queen, and the two figures had spun around so that the dragon's back was no longer towards them. Aurelia's gaze travelled up over the sight of great claws piercing clean through the queen's torso. Aurelia's gaze kept rising; up along the great, shining mass of wild, tangled long black hair to the dragon's head, pressed against the queen's. The dragon was staring at Aurelia, and her eyes widened even as her heart stopped. Its beautiful scaled head was topped with golden spikes, like a crown.

A great pair of golden eyes, the exact same gold normally found glittering amongst the darkest of blacks, blinked at her, just once.

Then the dragon pounced, jaws snapping over the queen's head, claws ripping the queen's body apart.

"Fox!" Aurelia screamed, as the world exploded around them once more.

This time she forced her eyes to stay open, risking blindness as all that had been suspended in the air flashed outwards. Amongst it all, the burst of white light consumed the dragon and its prey, white light eating over them hotter and hotter, and Aurelia was unable to watch anymore.

Rhydian launched at her from behind, knocking the air from her lungs, his body protecting her from the aftershocks of power uncoiling around the wrecked clearing like furious streaks of green lightning.

With the stink of ozone and a final rumble from the ground below, all was still and silent once more.

Aurelia raised her head, drawing in air, panicking.

The queen was gone.

The glittering gold and green dragon was gone.

She pushed up and away from Rhydian, stumbling over logs and splintered trees, cutting her hands and arms, as she slid and ducked and clawed her way through the wreckage of the forest.

"Fox!" she screamed. "Fox!"

Crashing and cursing behind her, Rhydian followed her mad fight to the epicentre of the smoking crater. There were no flames, just the stink of burning ash falling.

Rhydian slid to a stop, as Aurelia dropped to her knees, hands to her mouth, holding in words and tears and shock at the ground below. This couldn't be right. Her heart wailed, even as her eyes stared.

"Oh Fox," Rhydian gasped with a low sob, collapsing to kneel beside her.

He reached out; gathering up what was left, holding it up between them.

The gold chain with its sparkling yellow gem, its miniature glittering wand, caught the golden light of the sun, even as Rhydian's shaking fingers wiped soot and ash away from the dangling charms. There was nothing else left to find.

"No," Aurelia sobbed. "Fox, no..."

She pressed her hands to her face, digging her heels in hard to clear her eyes.

When she was brave enough to open them again, nothing had changed.

Her Shadow Man was gone.

23

Fox

Year 367

Battle of Aneirin

Aurelia's beautiful face was distorted into a mask of anguish. Eyes on hers, the dragon blinked, just once.

The fact that she had come with the prince, on Flare no less, meant something to him. They were of no help at all. Even so, it mattered. It was far, far too late for him.

The queen had far too much magic for him to simply kill her. She had to be completely destroyed, otherwise she might come back.

Just like he had once before.

Sophia had taunted him, sounding in her mind all the terrible things she would do to all the humans of Aneirin who had let her wither away. It was garbled; it made no sense. The humans who had been around when the curse had fallen would have had no idea of the means of her demise.

So Fox had launched one last desperate attack against the woman who fought like a dragon, or like she had almost the entire magic from one. And now, locked in a last embrace around the red clad figure of the queen, his claws in her sides even as her great hand had pierced his chest, her hot fingers around his heart, Fox's great pink tongue tasted the ash that covered her ear. He relished in the taste, even as he whispered against her hot, heaving neck.

"It's over for both of us." He licked her sweaty neck, tasting the bitter salt of her fury. It was as familiar to him as his own rage. "As it should be."

As her fingers closed around his heart, the weight of her fiery emerald gaze, a fount of raw power, scalded him. Ignoring the agony in his chest, Fox sank his gilded claws in deeper, reared back and closed his jaws around her head. He closed his eyes.

As the magic from their bodies ripped them both apart, Fox's last thoughts were of a different pair of emerald eyes, a dark forest green, sparkling with joy, while familiar arms wrapped tightly around him, keeping him safe.

Keeping the cold away.

24

Cas

Year 367

Forest of Aneirin

"Don't you dare," Cas hissed at the bee.

He allowed it to fly closer, but before it could land on his hair, he fried it with a flick of fiery energy. It dropped to the mud, a crispy ball of soot. His lips thinned with disgust.

"I warned you."

Staring at the tiny black speck, now just another corpse in the blood and muck of the battleground. The other bodies were much larger, and not turned into black and twisted shapes like the bee had been. Cas frowned, squinting at the trail of Elven bodies blasted into smoking pieces, left behind in the queen's wake as she rode towards the trees. A man with black hair rode after her, his horse risking broken legs as they raced over the uneven ground.

Taking his eyes off them, Cas returned to appraising the figures crowded around the dead king. He was surprised to see Flare in his normal larger size. It had been *so* long since the last time.

"Hello, old friend," Cas murmured, his heart beating faster.

Amongst the carnage of the battlefield with Flare was a young woman, along with a young man whose wild hair was plastered with blood. Cas assumed it was the prince, from the man's expensive armour and his numb expression.

The three of them were talking, but broke off at the same time Cas' eyes widened, lifting to stare at the forest where the queen had fled.

He knew his mouth was hanging open unattractively. He knew his eyes were bugging out of his head like some virginal teen seeing a pair of breasts for the first time. But the muscles in his face were simply not responding to his brain. There was no other expression he could school his face into, except one of deep, crippling shock.

As the golden green dragon broke from the trees, a pulse of deep power rolled out across the battlefield from the forest. Cas was ashamed at the hysterical giggle that burst forth from his open lips.

"A day," Cas breathed, "for seeing old friends *indeed*."

Flare and the two figures with him had exchanged heated words before jumping into action, taking flight and heading towards the chaos erupting from the forest. Cas watched in fascination, wondering that Flare would let the two people ride him so easily. He also wondered what Flare thought he could do to help if he was brave enough to try.

Eyes on the trees, Cas urged his horse forward. Fallen soldiers moaning in pain called out to him as he rode by. He didn't glance down at any of them.

His mind was reeling with all the possibilities that this latest revelation could lead to. Cas had discounted the gilded green dragon from his plans long ago. Cas had thought the creature had been lost to the chaos in Mionlach, as so many others had been. And very nearly himself as well.

Clearly, the emerald gold dragon hadn't been lost at all.

Merely hiding.

As he reined his horse by the body of the king, Cas raised his eyes to the looming city on the mountainside, and the walled castle above. Who and what else was hiding from him? How could he get back inside the castle now, without causing a scene, when Flare would likely claw his way through the stones to get away from Cas? If there was any possibility of getting Flare's attention, Cas needed to catch the purple dragon *away* from the castle.

Dismounting, Cas grimaced as his boots squelched into blood and wet muck. Before him, the king's corpse was on its back, lying where it had fallen. A pair of human soldiers were heading toward the king, frowning as Cas stepped close enough to nudge the king's limp arm with his boot.

With the air tasting like ash and blood, he wondered if it would be too unmanly to pull out his scented handkerchief. Probably, but the idea of vomiting in front of witnesses was even less ideal. Cas was reaching into his cloak when one of the two human guards called out.

"Hey!" a grizzled older man yelled at Cas, waving his spear. "Get away!"

"Don't touch him!" the woman with him called, carrying an old-fashioned sword. Under her helm, her long hair was braided in two.

Withdrawing his empty hand from his cloak, Cas waved a hand at them airily

"Leave me be. I won't be long."

They reached him, puffing. When Cas didn't move, the woman laid her free hand on his velvet cloak, attempting to tug him away.

He didn't even stop to think.

Cas' airy wave turned into a sharp slice down. Both guards dropped to the ground, silently, their arteries drying up inside their bodies.

Not sorry at all, but hoping no one had seen, Cas sighed impatiently.

"I warned you too," he began, thinking of the bee, and then he paused, mildly surprised. "Oh."

Gagging at the surrounding mud, Cas leant over to tilt the woman's face towards him by using one of her braids. He nudged off her helm. It was the same guard who had tried to prevent him from taking the grey horse.

"It's you again." He released the woman's hair and tugged her helm back on.

Straightening up and stepping aside to avoid a dismembered hand near his boot, Cas stood awkwardly. He pursed his lips, eyes narrowed on her unseeing gaze.

"Um. Thank you for my horse." Tilting his head to the side, Cas chewed on his bottom lip for a moment. Then he smiled. "And I'm sorry that you're dead."

Putting all further thoughts of her out of his mind, Cas flicked another glance towards the forest, feeling the low hum of power there. He would prudently wait on who triumphed before going to investigate further. His gaze dropped back to the king's corpse, experiencing a sudden rush of anger. The emotion welled up from so deep that it startled him, and his breath hitched. He gave the king's head a vicious kick.

"Why can't you humans just get by with what the gods gave you?" he hissed.

Obviously the corpse made no reply, the pale blue eyes glazed over, dull and bloodshot. Having come to see that yes, the king was indeed dead, Cas turned to go, when a thin, dark object in the mud caught his eye.

He dropped his horse's reins, looking the animal straight in the face.

"Stay," Cas commanded.

The horse's ears went back, but did as it was told.

Dreading what was about to get stuck on his hands and the hem of his cloak, Cas took a breath, and then reached carefully into the muck. Despite the blood and dirt caking his fingertips, he whistled, impressed at what he extricated from the mud.

"I'll keep you, pretty thing," Cas murmured, turning the arrow around in his hands. Pointing it upward at the rising sun, he smiled.

"The higher we are, the further we can fall," he said, tracing the sun with the point. His gaze dropped back to the lifeless body before him. "It's a bitch. I know, because it happened to me too."

Not far away, more people were going past, catching his attention. It was a pair of stretcher-bearers puffing loudly. As the man in the lead looked up, Cas let the tip of the arrow drop towards the ground. The man locked eyes with Cas, and he stopped up short, recognising Cas immediately. The man in the rear, along with the wounded soldier they were carrying, swore and cursed at the sudden halt.

It was the shopkeeper who had sold Cas the crystal phalluses.

Cas smiled, and the man's eyes widened. Unable to help himself, Cas raised his free hand, and very deliberately blew the man a kiss from his middle finger. He barely avoided the filth that caked his fingertip. It didn't matter. The man's look of horror, along with the fact that he nearly dropped the wounded soldier into the mud, was reward enough. With a frightened yelp, the shopkeeper jerked the stretcher upwards and took off at a fast jog, the man in the rear cursing once more. Feeling playful, Cas poked the king's cold cheek with the arrow.

"You played me for a fool. Too bad for you, *I'm* the one still playing."

Watching the arrow press into the dead man's face, Cas smiled once again.

"Hmm," he hummed, leaning forward, dropping his cloak to hold the king's head still. It was hard not to laugh and break his concentration, but he persevered, the tip of his tongue poking out of his mouth while he got the shapes *just so*.

Sitting back, his hands tingling with mud and blood, Cas smirked.

Finally satisfied, he tucked the arrow into his cloak, regretful that he'd have to throw the fine garment away. Before he could rise, something else in the mud caught his eye. It was the king's sword. Willing himself to forget about all the mud and blood and shit that now covered him, Cas leaned down and reached out once more. He undid the weapons belt, complete with scabbard, from the king's waist. After pulling the sword out of the filth, he rose.

At the same moment as he lifted the weapon up to examine it, another enormous burst of magic accompanied by a thunderous roar, rolled out from the forest. It was shocking, violent, and the world seemed to heave beneath Cas' boots.

Cas stumbled back into the horse, grabbing the reins as the animal reared and whinnied in terror. Thankfully, he was full of the king's magic, and it kept him conscious, on his feet and able to hold on to the terrified animal. Others around them weren't so fortunate. Newly gathered horses had scattered, and most of those who had been on their feet were now flat out on the ground.

Blinking and cursing, Cas watched a green burst of light fading from the treetops, the king's sword clutched tightly in his hand. As the light faded from the forest, Cas looked down at the weapon.

"That was a fucking omen and a half, wasn't it?" he muttered, his eyelids fluttering to clear the after glow from his eyes. He coughed, spitting out the dry taste of ozone and sulphur from his mouth. Behind the bitterness, another flavour coated his tongue.

Yes, Cas thought coolly, his tongue running over his lips, idly patting the still crazed horse to calm it down. He'd never forget that blend of icy power.

The gold and green dragon was indeed someone he'd like to see again.

Cas tucked the scabbard and belt under one arm, wiping the blade clean with the inside of his blue velvet cloak. He slid the sword with practiced skill into the richly adorned scabbard. There was no need for a sword where he was going, but it brought back memories brimming with satisfaction. There had been a time when he had been marked out for greatness with his skilled swordsmanship. As he buckled the belt around his waist, he was smirking at what was left of the king.

"By the way," Cas said to the corpse. His sniff was one of disdain. "You were a lousy fuck."

Throwing one last look over his shoulder as he mounted up, Cas admired his handiwork, his wide grin at odds with the desolation around him. He winked at the king's neatly carved forehead.

"*Sire.*"

The prince was covered in ash, his face a blank mask. He seemed to be barely containing his shock as he half-carried, half-dragged the equally numb young woman through the trees. Of Flare, there was no sign.

After dismounting, Cas risked sticking his head out further as the couple passed him. They were only a few metres away. Now that he was closer, the young woman looked familiar. To Cas' eyes, the faint sheen to her complexion, and the brightness of her green eyes, meant she was likely Elvish, from Lolihud.

Watching them retreat to the once pristine farmlands of Aneirin, Cas pursed his lips. It would be interesting to see what they planned to do next, if he could use them to get back inside the castle without a hassle. But equally important was investigating the left over magical residue, hanging about the forest like sticky threads of light, perceptible only to creatures like himself.

Once he was alone, Cas placed a dirty hand on the soft pink muzzle of the grey horse. "Remember our last talk, yes? Good girl."

The horse watched him, ears forward this time, as Cas edged his way to where the shattered forest ended abruptly. The horse stayed where it was.

Peering into the giant crater, at least a hundred metres across, it was hard to keep himself together. The residue here was strong, and his hands were tingling. Not from the mud, but from the ache to scoop up the power from its source. The source of which was unfortunately now missing. Cas ran a trembling hand through the grey streak in his hair. Gods, could he imagine what it would have felt like to find them again? The glittering gold and emerald dragon and the king's magic *both* becoming a part of his wildly unpredictable powers?

Nearly tripping over a fractured branch, Cas stepped forward, before pulling back into the shadows with a silent exclamation.

Flare was still here after all.

The dragon was back to his pocket size form. He had landed in the epicentre of the desolation. Wondering why Flare had waited until the prince and his lady friend had departed, Cas narrowed his eyes.

Needing to see better, Cas grabbed a low branch and hopped up into the tree he was hiding behind. Pine needles broke off with a pungent aroma as he climbed. From his new height, Cas could see that the dragon's normally glittering purple scales were dull, coated with soot and ash.

Cas smiled maliciously.

Flare would *hate* his scales to be sullied so, almost as Cas hated the crap that pretty much covered him from head to boot now as well.

As he watched Flare poking at the still smoking ground, Cas wondered if Flare could feel the echo of something still vibrating around them. Magic... and something else. An awareness? Perhaps it was the trees, the giant heights and trunks indicated that they were so old it was likely they'd developed some kind of conscious mind. Something like a passive observational quality hung about the place.

It didn't feel like the queen's magic. Hers was second hand and unpredictable, which definitely still lingered here. But her magic was more like the silence after an echo, not the echo itself. He wondered where that magic had gone, now that the king had died. Cas had absorbed the leftover magic in the backwash of the breaking curse, and the king's death, but as for the whereabouts of the queen's power, he had no idea. The prince was a likely candidate, but the man had shown no magical aura as he passed Cas without knowing only moments ago.

Whatever had happened to it, Cas had to act quickly. Of all his plans and travels to come, whatever he did next needed to happen fast. Now the curse was broken, it was likely that all those who were once shut out, magical creatures, would return. Sniffing around.

As Flare came to a stop right at the centre of the crater, hanging his tiny head, Cas bit back a bitter snort.

Cas never thought he'd thank his parents for anything, especially the fact that he had been born *without* magic. But in this case, in the case of the curse, it had come in handy indeed. According to the threads of magic that had held the curse together, Cas had been able to come and go as he pleased, unlike Elves and most dragons. He wasn't a magical creature really, and the magic from his last dragon-sharing had long ago faded. Enabling him to pop through the Aneirin bubble, like a drop of water coming up against a waterfall. Unnoticed, but still essentially made up of the same stuff.

Because even if he'd been born with magic, he'd be on the same path. Only he would have been unable to claw his way into Aneirin. He sighed. Not that he'd been able to make much progress.

Growing tired of watching Flare mourning a creature that he had failed to protect once again, Cas idly withdrew the arrow from his coat. He could remember what it had been like to arch through the air in the same way, although in a much more pleasing colour. His eyes flicked to the crater below, thinking of emerald scales, along with a pair of breathtakingly beautiful, golden eyes.

"Where did you go, you little tease?" Cas murmured. "Was I wrong to give up on searching for you? On all the power that you hold?"

Frowning, Cas chewed on his bottom lip. Was it possible to adjust his plans? If he could find whatever was left of the emerald and shimmering gold dragon, and combine their endless well of power with the treasure he had hidden away? Well, that would be something he had never dreamed of. He had never thought to use both, just one or the other. Staring unseeing at the trees around him, Cas let go of his lip, exhaling as slow as he could. Why not use two sources of magic for his requirements? Both were of the same essence, weren't they? All Cas had to do was retrieve them, and get them back to where magic had been born.

But.

His lips parted slightly, emitting a gentle laugh, while his heart quickened with the growing thrill.

Even if he *could* remember where magic had been born, and even if he still had access to dragon wings, it would not be an effortless task.

Was the risk to his person worth it?

Because if he *were* successful, there was none on this continent who could hold him back or pull him down from greatness ever again.

The possibilities left him breathless, and more than a little aroused. Surprised, his gaze lowered to his groin. He was amused that the thought of being the most powerful magic user on the continent had affected him in such a way. He could be someone, something again.

"There you are, my shy pipe of pleasure," Cas murmured, one eyebrow raised in a delicate arch. "After our desperate measures with the king, I was worried that I'd lost you for good, my sweet charmer."

In the crater, Flare let out a small mewl of distress. After getting himself together, the tiny purple dragon shook his wings and took off, heading in the direction of the castle. Up in the tree, Cas tucked the arrow back in his cloak to his arousal. He wanted to wash his hands. But he couldn't wait. He closed his eyes as his hands picked apart the laces of his trousers with delicate and precise movements. Red hair flashed behind his closed lids and Cas smiled wistfully as his hands caressed his silken, engorging flesh. If only more creatures from his past could return to him once again.

"Hmm," Cas murmured thoughtfully, his breath catching as his pleasure grew. "Flare Shining One, it really *is* the time for the return of old friends."

25

Rhydian

Year 367

Aneirin Castle

This time, waking was different.

When Rhydian awoke in his bed, the dawn was still far off, and the bitter tears on his face weren't from a dream. He wrapped his arms around the sleeping Aurelia, weeping silently into her hair, *remembering*.

When he was not quite ten summers old, the king had discovered his son where he was not supposed to be. Rhydian was a prince who was used to getting away with a lot. That day he had been playing in an off limits part of the castle. He had found an old armoury, and taken an unusual dagger off the wall, the centrepiece of an ornate display of weapons.

Holding the dagger aloft to catch the light from his tiny candle flame, he could feel the gold of its roughly worked hilt warm to his touch. It scared him, even as it called to him. The dagger brought back images of things best forgotten. But he could not.

Using the chalks that the young prince carried in his pocket, kept to graffiti hidden places that made Lord Cyrus throw up his hands in frustration, he had drawn a pageant of events on the wall.

When he had finished, his bottom lip between his teeth, he tried to make sense of the images the king had found him creating.

His father's face was flushed with something dark. Perhaps he had been worried that his young son had hidden himself away far too well this time. The king had startled the prince so badly with a yell of furious exasperation that the child had dropped the dagger in fright.

As he raged, the king's lantern flame reflected across the green blade. And suddenly the prince was reminded of a detail that he had locked away. Of lightning flashing across its jagged green blade as it arced down towards him.

The prince started to cry, demanding answers from his father.

Who had tried to use the dagger on him?

The prince pointed to the wall.

Who was the dragon?

Was someone coming back to kill him even now?

As the prince's terror grew, he became insensible, uncontrollable.

Grabbing him roughly, his father had tried to explain the events of the past, to a child who didn't understand, who was lost to the terror of being attacked by a woman in the rain, holding the crystal dagger above him.

As the prince wailed louder, shaking with shame at his fear and unable to do anything but cry and shake, the king yelled at the child about his mother's sins, about how they had tried to protect their family... not end it.

But the magic had failed; it had rebounded at the moment when the woman tried to sacrifice her son.

The prince had cried and cried.

No, father, it can't be true, he wailed, louder. *You're a liar!*

A hard slap connected with the prince's face.

His father's own face was crimson with anger as he screamed at his son that yes, Rhydian *would* believe it, because it was true.

The child, lost to rational thoughts, was screaming endlessly.

No no no! I'll tell everyone no it's not true! You're a liar! Where is my mother? I hate you! I hate what did you do to her! Don't hurt me! I will tell them all! They don't like you, they will believe me, they are afraid of you!

The king had clapped a hand over the prince's mouth, his own breaths shallow and fast as he narrowed his eyes at his son.

Stop it, the king had hissed, dropping his hand. *Don't be such a coward!*

The child calmed down, more from shock than obedience. But he was crying again, sobbing under his breath, trembling in the shadows of the old armoury, buried away and forgotten under his family home. Words had tumbled in a shocked flow from the boy's lips once more, as his child's mind tried to make sense of it all.

It can't be true... my mother loves me, and she will come back... won't she? I saw her in the rain... with the dagger... and you were there and she wouldn't do that, would she? But I saw it... oh no, mother where are you? What did you do to me?

Collapsing, heartbroken, the prince could deny it no longer. He had drawn it on the wall. Under the dragon, it was clearly a woman with the tiny swipe of green chalk in her hands.

Silently, the king watched his son's mind unravel into deep shock, blue on blue eyes staring blankly as the shame of his mother's betrayal cleared in his mind, a hot knife to his childlike, innocent sense of honour.

The prince had quietened.

What is wrong with me? He had finally whispered. Am I broken? I don't want this. I don't want to be your son! He had ended up shouting, his trembling beginning once again. I don't want this!

The king's face hardened at his son's bitter words. *If you must forget. I will help you.*

A choked sob. *What, father?*

The prince had stared up at the king, meeting his father's pale blue eyes that were shining almost silver in the dim light.

Rhydian. Look at me, come here. Come here. If you can't handle this... if you can't be a man... Look at me.

The boy, not quite understanding, but responding to the soft tone of the king's voice, nodded.

Yes.

His father's eyes, bright in the shadows, shone with disappointment.

A firm hand grabbing the boy's quivering chin.

Look at me, boy.

Forget.

Getting up from his bed as carefully as he could manage, Rhydian was glad for the fact that his tower faced the north. It was very early morning. As he wrapped Aurelia's cloak around him, he hopped up onto the windowsill with the glass partially open.

Facing north meant that he didn't have to stare at the great bonfires burning in the south, in the fields that once gave life with the harvests each season. He could smell the smoke though, but thankfully not the burning flesh as the dead souls were sent to the wind and the sky, blending with a soft aurora that was painting the sky with greens and blues. There were too many dead to bury. So their bones would be turned to ash, to fertilise the ground on which they had died.

It was a morbid thought, but Rhydian was secretly glad that the earthly remains of those who had died here would become part of the land.

There was so much to think about. Not just his father's dying words.

His tower was the last silent place left amongst the chaos. Wounded soldiers were being carried into the town, into the castle, Elves and humans alike. When they caught their breaths, when the dust had settled and the blood stopped flowing, he would address them.

All had seen the king die, the magic erupt from his dying corpse.

All had seen the queen leave, the brutal violence to her own people as she fled.

There was a necessity for him to address them, just... not yet.

Unable to make peace with his mother's ultimate goal, Rhydian gritted his teeth with a dark satisfaction. Whatever she had expected, to die amongst the forest surely wasn't it. But her violent passage had done what she had likely not expected. The Elves had thrown down their weapons as their leader had carved through them. The dazed soldiers from both armies were wary of the other, but enough heads had been left intact that a common ground had been forged.

Rhydian leant against the glass.

He had opened the castle to the wounded from both sides. Tensions were high, but the word was spreading. All had been affected by magic, by lies.

The Elves from a queen bent on a mad dash for power. The humans, under a curse, trapped in some isolated bubble meant to keep them safe. But it hadn't, had it? All of them had been affected. All of them had lost someone.

Rhydian glanced back to Aurelia, curled up in his bed, hopefully still asleep.

His hand rose to his chest, to touch the heavy golden chain hanging around his neck, caressing the pendants warmed from his flushed skin.

After his mother and... Fox... had gone, Rhydian had gathered Aurelia in his arms. Their progress back towards the valley and the bloody field was slow, silent and he could not recall a single step that he had taken. Only that one of his arms had been around Aurelia's shoulders as they stumbled beneath the watching trees, and his other arm had been curled against his chest, Fox's chain held tightly within his bloody hand.

A soft flash of light and sound had Flare turning back to the size Rhydian was used to, and the purple dragon had flown off without a word.

Rhydian almost hated him for it. But really, who could blame him after what they had all witnessed?

They had followed the trail that Fox had taken into the trees back to the battlefield. Along the way, Rhydian had discovered Fox's discarded sword with its ruby topped pommel lying amongst the ferns. His eyes had watered, and he'd collected it without a word.

With Aurelia silent and unresponsive beside him, they had made it back to the battleground, full of soldiers from both sides staring numbly at those they had moments before been trying to hack or spear into pieces. Rhydian had taken command of the chaos. Rumours had spread. Dark magic. But it helped keep the peace. Finally rousing from her daze, Aurelia had commandeered Davyn and Wyll to take the strange mute woman to the dungeon. Despite favouring her midsection like she had been part of the fighting, Jessikah had been smiling as they led her away.

An uneasy truce between Elves and humans had been called, and Rhydian had opened the city, and his castle doors to all.

His castle.

But was it?

The conversation with his father in the library came back to him. Were they even really part of the line of royals who had earned their place here, in Aneirin?

Unsure how to answer, to even find out, Rhydian turned back to the window, inhaling the bitter smoke of the fallen, welcoming the ash of Elves and humans into his lungs. It was the least he could do.

When night had fallen, at first Rhydian had slept like Aurelia, dreamless and bone weary from shock and fighting. At first his dreams had been murky, before turning into something he realised that he *remembered*. Finding the dagger. His father's icy reaction to his son's terror.

The final words of his father as he died seemed a likely catalyst, as the magic that had bound his memories away had broken apart.

Perhaps I can deal with this guilt now. To not wake from dreams that bring forth my tears of guilt, but perhaps I can rebuild something that my father broke. Perhaps I can find us both absolution?

If he deserved any.

Rhydian dropped the chain to run the fingers of both hands through his hair. He had washed before bed, and he was sure that by sleeping on his hair while wet had left it looking like a bird's nest. But he didn't care. His thoughts had turned to the person, or creature, out of all of them who deserved absolution.

Fox couldn't be dead, could he?

The man was a dragon!

He could be anything, he could be... alive.

It was hard to catch his breath. Rhydian wished he could ride out with Blackthorn, into the fresh air and peace. But there was none to be had. No untouched fields of grass or farmlands that hadn't been churned up by the feet of soldiers fighting each other because of lies and lies and lies.

"Fox, where are you?" Rhydian whispered to the night, watching the sky above change colours. He had never seen the night sky filled in with shades of pastels. Merion had predicted it, when Rhydian had watched the solemn groom cover the face of an Elven woman that had just died only a few hours ago.

"The sky will glow tonight, with all this magic about," Merion had said.

"The sky?" Rhydian had asked.

"Yes, my king."

Rhydian had stood up in a hurry, stepping back into a startled Chase, who was walking by. Rhydian had nearly knocked the clay jugs from the boy's hands.

Sire.

Without another word, Rhydian had fled the hall, running all the way to his tower. He had been there since. Aurelia had finally found him, along with a young woman, each of them carrying a bucket of hot water. Rhydian had stared at them wordlessly from the floor in the middle of the room. He was sure that even though he had stopped crying, his eyes were likely still red. Aurelia hadn't said a word, her expression the silent mirror of his. The other Elf had left just as silently, her beautiful eyes kind.

They had washed before curling up against each other, each as empty of words and tears as the other. They had slept.

Now Rhydian was awake, breathing in the ashes of the dead, thinking of another.

"Fox," he breathed, feeling unsure of himself, but needing some kind of speech to match the measure of the man who was no longer here. "You saved us. The stars and the sky are shining above, bathing the cold ground where your ashes lie in light as pure as your sacrifice."

Rhydian swallowed, knowing it was mad, but there was something inside of him, a faint... spark... that still connected him to the strange man who wasn't just a man. Fox had been a man whose heart had been wrapped in shadows, but who had sacrificed himself for them all.

Touching his chest once more, Rhydian sat up straighter, trying to concentrate on the spark. It wasn't something he could see, touch, or explain. But it was a knowing, a pulsing beneath the beat of his heart.

"Fox, I think as all my parents' magic finally broke apart... the magic woke in *me*. I don't know if that makes me an Elf like Aurelia... or you..."

His voice dried up at the memory of the brilliant emerald gold dragon, lighting up the forest with its beauty, with its rage. Tears welled in his eyes and his throat was hot.

"Fox. I saw you let go, I saw you choose. But I need to know about my mother. I... I don't understand..."

Blinking, he let the tears paint his cheeks with salt.

"Please. Your aura of coiled rage, I felt it, I felt it change. You let go... you were finally free, you were glad to die."

Strength left him. Rhydian slumped against the window, hands braced on the rusting iron.

"I saw that look on your face. That relief, thinking it was your time to go," he sobbed. "But there is a light here that burns even now for you."

Shutting his eyes to the shifting colours in the sky, Rhydian pressed his hands together to stop them from shaking.

"The afterglow of your disappearance lingers, and I can almost hear words amongst the smoke on the breeze. The spark, the knowing inside of me... it tells me..."

Rhydian's tears ran down his face and the words he needed to say were locked behind his teeth, but he needed to let them go.

"It tells me you are *alive*."

Rhydian's shallow breathing was almost a pant, and he opened his eyes.

"I'm not finished with you. So you *need* to come back. You need to tell me once and for all... am I like them? Like my father? Am I like my mother? And can I change? You said I wasn't, but..." Rhydian gasped, his inner fears spilling forth. "You were dark... yet you changed, you did... we saw you!"

Wiping his face, Rhydian slid off the windowsill, to stand instead, hands braced against the cold stones.

"I can't do this...I'm not ready. But if I have to play at king for now, I will. And do you know what? I declare the first act of Rhydian the First is to curl up into a ball and cover my ears," he whispered. "I'd rather be amongst your ashes, paying my respects."

The knowing beneath the beat of his heart flared slightly before fading to something nearly imperceptible once more.

Rhydian's breath caught, his mind tumbling in all sorts of directions. Settling on one radical and momentous thought, he pushed himself away from the window, his hands dropping to his sides.

"But we both know that your ashes are only a skin that you've shed."

He rolled his shoulders, his strained muscles burning, and the bruise on his face a dull ache.

"Fox," Rhydian said, his words barely a hum in the silence.

He smiled into the dark, a bruised hand clutching the golden chain again. "I *know* you're alive. Last time you summoned me, but this time you don't need to."

I am coming.

26

Rebirth, again

Year 367
The Forest

A soul drifted.

Drifting through nothing, it was an inferno of thoughts and fears and chaos. And at the centre was a core of stillness, of peace.

The peace of letting go.

The magic that bound the soul to the wind pulsed in time with the grace of the peace that flowed within. A gentle emptiness, along with a yearning.

The soul slowed in its directionless drift, its soft dance now a hovering disturbance amongst the trees. It remembered crystals, gemstones.

A golden topaz.

Emeralds.

It remembered emerald scales, like the fresh green gems of the raw earth, and emerald eyes that welcomed a lonely heart with a warm embrace. There was also a pair of flashing green eyes that challenged it and made it laugh.

There were also sapphires. The strange blue eyes, ringed with lighter blue, watching in horror as a dragon ripped apart chaotic powers, spilling from a mad figure. Crushing the life that glowed red with chaos, and absorbing that power within itself, and discarding the life it held.

Saving them all from further chaos.

Sapphires, no... blue eyes.

The prince.

Rhydian.

Aurelia.

The soul throbbed with memories.

Shadow.

Friends left behind to face an unknown threat, one they didn't realise was right there amongst them.

The soul spun around, frantic, pulsing, its core of peace disturbed. It felt once more that it was called, that it *must* take action on behalf of the innocent who even now were caught up in matters of great consequence that they were helpless to overcome.

The soul rebelled momentarily.

Hadn't it done enough?

No.

It had more to do.

What it should have done, years and years and lifetimes ago.

It yearned to do better, to show that it was deserving of the honour of a friendship not yet quite forged.

The soul, drifting once again, floated lower out of whatever higher plane it traversed. It sunk down into a familiar ache, into a familiar cold.

There, it called forth the life and breath of the forest. Molecules clung to the soul, following an imprinting along a pattern impressed upon an icy heart. The particles were sucked into a tornado of sparkling dust, life and flickering lights. Gradually the frequencies of the soul tuned the particles into a familiar form, tuning them like a bard tuned his harp. Into a form that had scared some but soothed others.

The soul didn't care.

The mass of energetically vibrating particles and matter became a body, and the body became a man.

A man with black hair and black eyes that glittered with yellow gold.

It hurt.

A lot.

Rebirth, again.

Opening his eyes, the man coughed, laughing at the twist of fate, listening to a river bubbling nearby. He had no idea where he was. Something tugged at his heart, but he wasn't afraid.

As he stared at the strip of coloured night sky that followed the canopy edges along the river, the man smiled. It was a genuine smile this time, not mocking.

He was looking forward to finding out what spending time with bright hearts did to a black one.

27

Aurelia

Year 367

Aneirin Castle

T he bucket brimmed with bloody water.

As the morning dragged on, Aurelia had changed bandage after bandage, and the bucket of clear water had slowly turned a dark, murky red.

Wiping a loose tendril of hair from her face with the heel of a bloody hand, Aurelia wondered if life was the same. Did you start off innocent, sparkling, and clear? Only to become muddied with pain, heartbreak, and loss? Ignoring the void in her chest, Aurelia went back to her work. Around her, row after row of moaning soldiers, Elves and humans alike, were laid out like batches of loaves ready to be baked in some giant oven.

Chase wheeled an old three-wheeled cart along the row of wounded, exchanging the blood for water yet again. Murmuring her thanks, she set to the next soldier, secretly glad that she was relatively safe, unharmed. On the outside, anyway. She was desperate to find some glow wort or similar drug, to disappear into a dull haze of numbness for a while. Lowering her gaze in pity, she grimaced.

She'd hate to be laying here, dependent on someone else for help. So Aurelia chose to stay busy, not thinking about anything else except the next wound, the next pointless cut or slash, which had to be cleaned and covered. That morning she'd pulled on some older dark clothes of Rhydian's, to hide some of the blood she knew that she'd be dealing with that day. It was only a day after the battle, and blood was still flowing. Now she was desperate for a bath.

The next time Aurelia looked up from the next soldier, a clay cup of warmed wine appeared in her vision.

"Thank you, Chase," she murmured, rinsing her hands in the bucket of red liquid once again.

Staring blankly at the soiled floor of the castle's great hall, Aurelia reached out to take the offered drink. A quiet sigh over her shoulder had her look up. Aurelia blinked. It was Rhydian, a sad smile on his bruised face.

"Oh, thank you." She took a sip. Thankfully, it was strong.

She could do with ten more.

Crouching down on his knees beside her, Rhydian watched her drain the rest in one go. When she gasped the last of it down, he held up a jug. Her eyes watered, the fact that he had understood what she might need right now, and she nodded.

Wordlessly, Rhydian held her hand steady while she held the cup. She quickly drained that, too. It burned, it felt good. He held the jug up without judgment, only a question in his eyes.

"No..." Aurelia cleared her throat, indicating the wounded around her with her chin.

"You've done enough," he said, refilling her cup despite her refusal. "I've been in talks all afternoon with some of the Elves and my officers. I know you've been here all day, and Chase said you've not eaten, and hardly drunk anything."

"Afternoon?" Aurelia blinked. "All day?"

Rhydian lifted his chin to the windows high up on the western side of the great hall. Chase was leading a group of other boys in lighting the lamps along the wall, and above them, the sky was a burnt orange through the glass. They were carrying charcoal braziers filled with some kind of perfumed resin as well, to clear the air of the sickening aromas from the wounded.

"Shit," Aurelia sighed.

Where had the hours gone? She stared at the bucket of red liquid, knowing that was where the day had run.

After making sure that the young man she'd been attending was comfortable, Aurelia finally rose. Rhydian put down the jug to help her stand. Her knees were sore; her back was on fire, and her heart- she shut that thought off straight away.

Nearby, someone groaned loudly, and a woman's soft voice could be heard urging a wounded soldier to breathe. She met Rhydian's gaze, intending to ask him how the peace negotiations were going, when he turned away, giving her a better look at his face.

"What is that?" she gasped, touching the bruise coming out on his cheek, but also an arc of scabbed scratches that looked red, angry.

His fingers came up over hers as he turned to kiss her palm, not caring about the state of her hands.

"From the battle," he murmured, not meeting her eyes.

"They look like someone scratched you." Aurelia's eyes narrowed. Had she seen them last night? "What else happened?"

He shrugged, the light blue that ringed his darker blue irises looking grey in the low light. "Far too much."

Unable to help the welling in her eyes, Aurelia nodded, not able to speak. Wrapping his arms around her, he pulled her close. She inhaled his warm scent, pressing her face to his chest. He was dressed almost the same as her, dark, simple clothes. Nothing of note to mark him out as different or above anyone else here in this hall. Apart from the natural golden highlights in his brown hair that drew the eye, he acted like just another young man, doing his best to mop up after the battle. Her arms tightened around him.

"Have you seen Flare?" he eventually murmured against her. Aurelia shook her head against him, inhaling him deeply once more, clearing the sickly, coppery blood smell from her nose.

"No. He was deeply affected by what happened."

"I know that," Rhydian said, pulling her towards the base of his tower. "We all were. But I need to ask him for a favour." He paused. "An important one."

"I think we've both got a lot to talk with him about," Aurelia replied, intending to say more, but a curse from behind them interrupted.

Rhydian sighed, running a hand through his hair. It was wild and tousled, liked they'd done more in bed last night, other than just hold each other and weep. Biting that thought away, Aurelia turned with Rhydian to see Davyn hurrying over. The man's face was grey, his expression ashen.

"Sire, I know you're needing rest... but..."

Sire.

Aurelia could feel Rhydian tense beside her at the word. She placed a steadying hand on his back. He reached behind him to squeeze it in return.

"It's fine, Davyn." The weariness was clear in the set of Rhydian's shoulders, but his voice was firm. "What do you need?"

The man stood there awkwardly, his normally neat plait of dark hair frazzled and unkempt. While one of Davyn's hands fidgeted with his belt, a small sob had Aurelia looking past him. Chase was behind Davyn, his eyes red, and holding the older man's other hand. Unsure what to do, Aurelia stayed where she was. At the expression of both the man and the boy, her grief and weariness darkened into warning.

Beside her, Rhydian frowned down at the boy, before raising his gaze to Davyn.

"Davyn?" Rhydian pressed, stepping forward.

Biting his lip, Davyn glanced at Aurelia, then back to Rhydian. He tried to speak, failed, and shook his head.

"It's... it's your father's b-body, sire," Chase stammered, quietly.

Davyn, his gaze locked on Rhydian's, nodded slowly.

"His body?" Rhydian repeated, confused.

"Yes." Davyn finally began, swallowing "Ah. We went to collect him from the battle-field." Davyn cleared his throat. "To take him to the crypts."

"Go on."

"With no ceremony, like you asked."

"Yes. Go on." There was a hint of warning in Rhydian's tone. Impatience? Aurelia wasn't sure. Davyn closed his eyes, hearing it as well, dreading the exchange ahead.

Aurelia tried to think back. Had she been there for that conversation? That Rhydian wanted his father interred, with no ceremony? It was understandable, considering. But she honestly couldn't remember.

A low wail came from the hall. Aurelia licked her dry lips and ignored the sound of grief. Someone else's loved one wouldn't be rising with the dawn.

"Did you find the arrow?" Rhydian asked. Davyn shook his head, opening his eyes.

"No, sire," Davyn managed, shifting awkwardly. "It was gone."

"Gone?" Rhydian repeated, his tone not giving away his feelings. "Interesting. I would have liked to have it framed and mounted on an abandoned wall somewhere."

Aurelia examined his profile; he looked calm enough under his bruises, but a muscle in his jaw twitched. Rhydian scanned Davyn and Chase with a long glance.

"What else?"

"His sword... was gone too, sire," Davyn added reluctantly.

"His sword?" Aurelia asked, surprised.

Chase nodded, his eyes solemn, and he sniffled. She could see Davyn's hand squeeze the boy's as both of them continued to stand there, faces pale and ashen, eyes wide.

"Davyn." Stepping away from Aurelia, Rhydian grabbed the man by his shoulders. "What else aren't you telling me?"

Chase buried his face in Davyn's side, and the man wrapped his arm around the trembling boy. Aurelia could see the larger man trembling as well.

"The king's f-face..." Davyn whispered, sweat breaking out on the man's forehead.

"What about his face?" Rhydian snapped. Aurelia placed a hand on his shoulder. Rhydian ignored it, his own hands squeezing Davyn's shoulders tighter. "Tell me."

"Someone... carved..."

Another sob from Chase.

"...on his forehead, like a crown..." the man's face paled further, his voice fading.

"For fuck's sake, man, tell me!" Rhydian exclaimed, shaking the man. "Someone carved... something... on my father's forehead? Well, *what* was it?"

Davyn stared at Rhydian, lost for words, eyes wide.

A small voice, muffled against Davyn's shirt, uttered a single word.

"What?" Rhydian asked, blinking rapidly at Chase. "*What* did you say?"

"You heard him correctly, sire," Davyn mumbled, miserable.

Rhydian, breathing heavily, dropped his hands back to his sides.

"I see. That will be all."

"Sire-"

"That will be all, Davyn."

Davyn flicked a shaken glance at Aurelia. She hadn't heard what Chase had said, but mouthed '*go*' at the man just the same. With obvious relief Davyn hurried back to the hall, Chase close by his side. Rhydian remained frozen in place, hands clenched by his sides.

"Rhydian?" Aurelia asked, her voice tentative.

Shaking himself, Rhydian inhaled carefully, his chest rising with his deep breath.

"Truly," he muttered, eyes distant. "It's naught less than he deserves."

"Are you alright?"

"No. But I will be. Hm." Rhydian's voice hardened. "Change of plans." His curt voice caught her off guard. "What?"

Rhydian indicated a flash of purple heading their way, Flare, tiny again, gliding in from wherever he'd spent the day.

"No rest just yet. I need to speak to him. And you."

Spotting them, Flare circled lower. He was aiming for her, like always. He landed with a soft rustle onto Aurelia's outstretched arm, and she met his shining gaze, both of them unsure what to say to the other. Flare tilted his head, his slender neck twisting back and forth between them.

"The library," Rhydian said. "Now."

"Uh. Are you sure?" The dragon's voice was tentative as he climbed to Aurelia's shoulder. "Perhaps-"

Rhydian gave the dragon a long look, then spun on his boot heel.

Without waiting, he strode off across the hall, grabbing a lantern off a startled guard. A few people bobbed their heads to him. He ignored them all.

Taking a breath, Aurelia set out after him, her mind reeling with questions for him and the brooding dragon both.

"Where in the hells is my bloody librarian?"

Aurelia paused in between the double doors of the library, staring.

Rhydian was on the opposite side of the table in the centre of the room, his jaw clenched. On seeing them, he closed his eyes and shook his head, waving them in.

"I'm sorry," he murmured, pulling out a chair for her. "I am not myself."

"Rhydian-" Aurelia began, but he interrupted.

"Nothing that has happened is an excuse to behave," his gaze dropped to an illustration of a copper coloured dragon on the table, "like *him*."

Not needing to ask whom he meant, Aurelia nodded, her hand covering his trembling one as he sat down beside her.

It was dark here, the fire unlit, the small bronze lantern he had bought up the only source of illumination. Aurelia could see perfectly well, however. She wondered what the room looked like to Rhydian. It was silent, calm despite the hall of wounded nearby, and she guessed he had asked them here for that very reason. Flare, still looking dazed, had left her arm for the mantelpiece, staring at an old engraving.

The silence dragged on, and as Rhydian's trembling hand brushed back his hair from his forehead, she realised he was having more trouble controlling himself than she had thought. Thinking she could distract him, she asked the first thing that came to mind.

"What did you mean when you said *you knew it*?"

It was the wrong thing to say.

Rhydian withdrew his hand from under hers, sitting back in his chair. Tilting his head up to stare at the ceiling, looming and dark above, he shrugged. He didn't ask what she meant; he knew. Not being able to stand the silence, and frustrated with absolutely everything, Aurelia tried Flare, twisting around to face him.

"Flare. Did you know, or suspect, that Fox was," she had to force herself to say it, "that he was a... dragon?"

Flare turned away from the items on the mantelpiece to stare at her, his eyes wide. The flash of Flare's shimmering purple scales was faint in the lantern light, but they were beautiful nonetheless. She wondered if the emerald of Fox's scales would look just as pretty in the same light. Aurelia held back a sob, her throat full of heat.

"Aurelia, I..." Flare began. He stopped at the sight of her tears falling, even as she fought them back.

"Oh," Aurelia gasped, pressing the heels of her hands into her eyes. "I'm sorry, I..."

There was the gentle scrape of a chair beside her. Warm arms gathered her close to a broad chest.

"Hush, lover," Rhydian soothed, holding her tight as he knelt on the floor next to her chair. "It's going to be okay."

Hiccupping, Aurelia pushed him away. "No." She swallowed, sniffing. "I don't think it is. He was a fucking dragon! He was my friend. And now he's *gone*."

"You've been so brave," Rhydian murmured, as small wings above her head disturbed the air. Rhydian continued, "I need you to be brave for a little while longer."

"I c-can't..."

"Yes." Rhydian kissed her damp cheek. "You can."

She shook her head, gazing at Flare's solemn eyes from the table. He'd landed right in front of her, careful not to set his claws over the copper dragon, his expression unreadable.

"You've done so much for me, for all of us," Rhydian sighed, rubbing her arms. "So I am going to do something for you, for all of us, in return."

Aurelia stared at him, not understanding.

"I'm going to find him."

Aurelia continued to stare, Rhydian's words not making sense.

"Wh-who?"

"Fox, of course."

Blinking, Aurelia looked back at Flare, who had gone very still, then back at Rhydian. He had calmed down and was staring at her intently. She touched his face, lightly running her fingertips over his bruises.

"How hard were you knocked on the head?"

Gently, Rhydian brushed her hand away, kissing her fingers as he pressed her hand to his chest.

"Aurelia," he said, calmly. "Fox is *alive.*"

"I-I don't understand."

He nodded. "Me neither, to be honest." He pressed her hand to his chest, and she could feel the steady beat of his heart. "But I can... feel it."

"Rhydian." Flare said, his voice uncertain. "What are you talking about?"

Pulling out the golden chain from his shirt, the topaz and golden wand shining in the lantern light, Rhydian met Aurelia's gaze and held it steady.

"I can *feel* he is alive."

He let that sink in for a moment, watching her digest the information.

"And I am going to find him."

Aurelia stared at his hands as he tucked the necklace and charms away. Flare's mouth was hanging open.

"Oh," said the dragon, as his mouth of sharp little teeth slowly closed.

"H-he's not gone?" Aurelia whispered, squinting at Rhydian.

"Correct."

"He's not gone," she repeated. The fierce light in Rhydian's gaze was all she needed to trust, even if she didn't understand. She tried to stand.

"I'll go-" she began, but Rhydian pulled her down. He kissed her lips to keep her quiet.

"No." He pulled back, tucking some of her hair behind her ear. "I've already decided."

"But-"

"I am going. You're needed here. You're better with my people than I am with yours."

"But you're the king-"

Rhydian sat back on his heels, sighing. He cleared his throat.

"Don't," he murmured, his eyes dark. "Not yet. I can't be that, not yet. I need you here for me."

All she could do was stare at him.

"Please trust me. You did before. Please, trust me again."

"Okay," she whispered after a moment, nodding, even as her mind was still trying to catch up with his words. "I'll wait here for you. For both of you."

"Thank you," Rhydian said, holding her tight, his boots creaking as he stayed next to her, kneeling on the floor.

Her mind, her heart, was reeling.

Fox could be *alive*.

"I know you need him," Rhydian was saying quietly. "So I'm going to find him for you. For I have a few questions of my own."

"You'll need *some* help, at least," Aurelia said, just as softly.

"Yes."

As one, both of them turned to Flare.

The dragon was still on the table, clearly stunned at Rhydian's revelation. He was staring at the copper dragon in the illustration beside his claws. Feeling their gaze on him, Flare looked up; purple eyes hooded with something Aurelia couldn't name.

"Flare?" she urged.

Flare stared at them a moment longer before slowly nodding.

"Thank you," Rhydian said with a sigh, pushing up from his knees. "We'll get a few hours rest, then leave with the dawn."

Looking back down at the dragon below him, Flare's tail twitched. Aurelia frowned, sniffing away tears. Rhydian held his hand out to her, and she took it, rising to be once again pulled into his arms. His lips moved on her hair.

"We'll talk when this is over, when Fox is safely returned to us."

"Yes," she murmured against his chest, relishing his warmth even as her heart ached for the cool body of her oldest friend.

Was it really true? Rhydian was convinced. She had trusted the wrong person before, they all had, with the Lady playing with them all. But now, she held someone full of light and truth, who had just as much to thank Fox for as she did.

"While I'm gone," Rhydian said against her hair, "keep an eye on that woman."

"Jessikah?" Aurelia clarified, narrowing her eyes on Flare, who had frozen again.

"Yes, that's her."

"There was a reason Fox kept her close," Rhydian sighed. "And even if I don't understand that, I will respect it, for now."

"I agree," she murmured, eyes still on the dragon. Flare looked up, looking like he was going to be sick. "She's still in the dungeon. I took her food and water this morning. I'll leave her there."

"Good idea. I took her some food before I sought you out. She'll be fine until tomorrow."

"Okay. Maybe I'll get Chase to help me with her."

"Get one of the men too, please."

"Mmm," she murmured as Rhydian helped her up from the chair. She caught sight of Flare's pained expression as Rhydian pulled her to the doors. "What?"

Shaking his head, Flare swallowed, finding his voice.

"I'll see you with the dawn," the dragon croaked, turning away. His tail was flicking back and forth like it did when he was lost in thought.

Rhydian pulled her out of the room into the hallway, and she lost sight of the dragon.

"Aurelia," Rhydian said, his voice low as he pulled her along.

"Rhydian?"

"When we get to bed, I'd love to say that we are going to have a really, really *nice* goodbye..."

Aurelia squeezed his hand as he tugged her through the crowded hall, not stopping or answering anyone's questions.

"But in actual fact, I am going to pass out, staying awake only long enough to dump water over myself."

Despite it all, despite her grief, her fears, and her hope, Aurelia laughed softly. Rhydian looked back at her, his eyes serious.

"I understand," she said, as each of them grabbed the buckets of warm water left by someone thoughtful at the base of his stairs.

"I understand," Aurelia repeated, as the pair of them puffed up the stairs, both of them ready to collapse. "Bless your sweet heart for letting me know."

In front of her, Rhydian didn't look back, but his words affected her like he was saying them against her bare skin.

"I'm glad you think my heart is sweet," he murmured. "It's still yours, and it always will be."

I know, Aurelia said silently, climbing after him as the stairs continued around and upwards.

And when I find the courage, after everything that I've done to him, I'll tell him that I feel the same for him.

"I can't believe I'm about to do this," Rhydian muttered.

Flare was crouched low on the cobblestones, the sun not yet over the horizon. It was cold out. So cold that the local guards that met them at the castle's great entrance had commented how unseasonal it was.

Aurelia was wrapped up in her cloak, along with one of Rhydian's, as well. He was wrapped in his thickest one, a thing of furs he had never worn, carrying another, wrapped around a pack of food. A few guards, Elven and human, watched them from the wall. Aurelia could see the human's eyes were wide, staring at Flare in awe.

"You flew not two days ago," Aurelia said, by way of encouragement, proud of what he had set out to do.

Rhydian really was a man of inner strength, to do this in the face of his fear. She only wished she could be there, to see Fox's face when Rhydian finally found him. Would an inky haired man laugh at a prince come to rescue him? Or would an emerald gold dragon bow their head regally in gratitude? After a dreamless night of restless sleep, she had no idea about how to feel, or what to think, this early. The idea was too new, and her heart too bruised.

Rhydian threw Aurelia a dark look, the faint sheen of nervous sweat across his forehead. Large and shining beside them, Flare said nothing, still avoiding Aurelia's gaze.

"That was in the heat of the moment."

Aurelia reached up to grab Rhydian's face. "You've got this."

"I've got this," he repeated, the words leaving his lips even as he shook his head as if no, he really didn't. "Remind me, why am I doing this?"

"Because you're brave and sweet," Aurelia smiled, wearily, "but if you're too sweet for this, we can swap places if you need."

Rhydian swallowed, his eyes closed. "No. You know that appealing to my fear of being too sweet won't work on me. I'll be the first to admit it, how weak I am."

"No," Aurelia said, pulling him close, "not weak. *Gentle*. Full of light."

"Hmm." Rhydian grumbled, his eyes still closed when she pulled away.

"You can be both brave and gentle, strong and light, Rhydian."

"Light? Pffft. But what about you?" he asked, finally opening his blue eyes to gaze down at hers, his expression heated. His feelings for her were unashamedly clear, momentarily trumping his fear of being back in the sky. "What will *you* be, if I am light?"

"That's easy," Aurelia murmured, Fox's words coming back. "I'll be here for you, behind you all the way. I'll be your shadow."

Flare's outstretched leg jerked at her words before holding steady as Rhydian scampered up. She frowned at Flare, stepping away. What was wrong with him?

"Bring him back safe," Aurelia said instead. "Yourselves as well."

After pulling himself up Flare's scales, Rhydian flashed her a nervous grin, which was half a grimace. Aurelia stepped back as Flare shook his wings, careful of his tail as he walked away, giving himself more room to lift off.

"Please Flare, don't drop me," Rhydian pleaded, wedging himself between two dark violet-hued spikes.

Flare twisted back, giving Rhydian an insulted look. The dragon muttered under his breath as he straightened.

"Don't worry, I'll take better care of you than I did your mother-"

Even as he spoke the words, his gaze finally met Aurelia's.

There was a startled heartbeat of silence between them, while Rhydian, oblivious, settled himself securely.

Something missing clicked into place amongst the unanswered questions still bubbling away in her heart. Something so bloody obvious that Aurelia's eyes widened, matching Flare's horrified expression. Flare's mouth snapped shut and his colossal head swung away.

"Flare!" she cried. "Stop!"

The dragon reared up with a jerk, the beat of his wings knocking her sideways. She landed on her side on the cobbles with a painful grunt. Above her, Flare lifted off, gaining height so fast that she expected to see Rhydian rolling off.

Shit!

Scrambling back to her feet, Aurelia waved her arms wildly, knowing it was no use.

"Flare! What did you do!?" she yelled, her heart about to burst from her breast. "Come back here!"

Fox had said more magic was needed to enact the curse; the king and queen weren't strong enough. The only creature anywhere close by was Flare. There was no one else. All along, he'd been there, right here where she was now, in Aneirin.

Before the curse.

And after the curse failed, when the queen had come across Fox in the forest. Rhydian had even drawn a dragon on the armoury wall, with his mother holding the dagger up in some kind of sick offering.

Shit!

Aurelia hadn't seen it because... why? Because Flare was helping them undo the curse? But he hadn't been helping only the queen, had he? He had been attempting to undo a momentous mistake, his mistake. If a mistake was what it had been?

"Flare!" Aurelia cried, devastated, as the dragon gained height. "You *liar*! Come back!"

The dragon circled wider and further away into the dawn sky, the son of the queen on his back. The son of the queen, whom Flare created a curse for, where Rhydian had been the sacrifice.

"*Flare!*" Aurelia screamed, the purple flash of scales fading into the grey sky. "*How could you?*"

28

Flare

Year 367

Aneirin Castle

He was glad for the fact that Rhydian was on his back, unable to see his face. Aurelia's eyes, horrified pools of misery, would stay with him forever.

"*How could you?*" she had screamed, not knowing that he could still hear her, hear the anguish in her voice, the betrayal of all the things he had never admitted.

Because I thought it was right, Flare pleaded.

Because I thought it was best, after what magic did to two other shining cities, once so full of life, now dark and cold and empty, all thanks to magic.

And because I didn't realise the king and queen would get the weaving of the magic so wrong.

Flare shook his head, and Rhydian cursed, his balance thrown.

"F-Flare?" Rhydian called over the beat of shining, leathery wings. "Are you... are w-we okay?"

Swallowing, Flare croaked out a "yes", flying west as previously agreed.

"What did Aurelia s-say?"

Gazing out at the forest below, as the sun broke the horizon behind them, the world turned into a tapestry of bright, mottled, dark and shining green that took the breath away.

Flare closed his eyes for a moment, feeling the wind dry his tears. When he opened them just a crack, Aurelia's horror at his lies was all that he could see.

Clearing his throat, Flare called back to the frightened man clinging to his spines.

"Aurelia, ah. She wanted to make sure that I took good care of you."

29

Rhydian

Year 367

Forest of Aneirin

"**A**re you watching, Rhydian?" Flare shouted into the freezing wind.

Rhydian shook his head, holding on even tighter.

Flare had said little to him as they flew steadily west. The sun was higher now, and Rhydian estimated that the journey of a few hours would have been a few days by horse or foot in the thick forest below. One of the few times that he'd opened his eyes, he'd peeked quickly behind, seeing the tall reddish mountain range of Aneirin slowly fading.

"No. I'm," Rhydian replied, trying to raise his voice through gritted teeth, "trying to concentrate on where we need to go. We aren't far."

He sensed the charms on the chain against his chest and the deeper, dull ache within. Further, not by much. He tapped the scales near his left thigh. Flare's scales shuddered beneath him as he adjusted their path.

The last time he had been this high, adrenaline from the battle had sharpened his nerve, the desperate flight over in seconds, it had seemed. This was vastly different. He risked a glance through slitted eyes, his stomach heaving immediately.

Nope.

Flare was the only one using his eyes. Rhydian couldn't bring himself to look. He'd tried, felt his vision darken and his stomach fall away. Besides, Rhydian *did* need to concentrate. Through the wind, and the cold frost that peppered the air with a tangy aroma, he had to feel their way forward.

Tucked against his chest was a pack of food and supplies, along with another cloak. He was glad for the one he wore over his normal riding attire. It was *cold*. But, if he was honest, and despite the terror he was experiencing, to be out here was a freedom that was sorely welcome. Eyes closed or not. There was a lot of sorting out at the castle. *His* fortress. The bowing and murmurs of 'yes, sire' that should have been for his father were now directed at Rhydian instead. He knew he had to step up to the responsibility. It was what he had planned, wasn't it? Should he be grateful that things had gone as they had, and not the other way?

There was just so much to process. Rage and grief were clouding what should have been his relief that the battle was over. And there was nowhere left to ride out with the dawn to clear his head. So he was now riding out in a way. Just on a dragon, instead.

With a greater purpose than just running away from the mantle of power.

Unwelcome thoughts came to him, of his mother. So close, and then gone.

His mother.

Rhydian gripped the scales below him tighter, wishing he'd worn gloves. Knowing she had been the one to instigate all of this, this horror, he wasn't sure how he could even unpack that. Would time really help? Could Aurelia?

Could he help himself? He was feeling so much shame and guilt. His parents had betrayed each other, along with himself, and the good people of Aneirin.

The shame was tricky. The guilt over being directly responsible for his father's death, and partway for his mother's, was perhaps a moot point.

Both of them had tried to end his life after all, he thought dryly, the freezing wind and empty air below forgotten for a moment. So perhaps they were even. Aurelia seemed to think so.

His heart eased a fraction, thinking of waking up with her again this morning. With her green eyes and long, dark hair, she had kissed him sleepily when he had sat down on the bed to pull on his boots. He realised now that Aurelia looked a lot like his mother had, comparing Aurelia to the woman of the throne room the night before the battle. He suspected that Aurelia had been chosen for that similarity alone.

Shame ate at him again. Aurelia had been doing something, believing it was the right thing, even misguided by lies and deceit as she had been. She'd not sat back like Rhydian had done, ignoring the bigger, and muddier, picture around him.

"Oh, my."

Flare's moan broke into Rhydian's musings. His stomach dropped further, and he risked opening his eyes.

Nope.

He slammed them shut again, against the sparkle of the river and the blur of the trees.

"What is it?" Rhydian asked, his voice hoarse.

"I see he-" Flare coughed, his deep voice rumbling. "I see him."

The dragon altered his flight, and they dropped suddenly. Rhydian, already feeling cold and clammy, swore under his breath.

"By the river," Flare called back. "Ah, I'm not going to be able to land. The river isn't wide enough, and the trees are too close together."

The dragon didn't sound the least bit disappointed about this.

"What does that mean?" Rhydian shouted back.

"You're, ah, going to have to jump."

WHAT THE FUCK.

Rhydian was pretty sure his whimper wasn't audible.

"Not far. Okay? Rhydian?"

Rhydian shook his head, cold air whipping around him. He thought he'd cursed out loud, but apparently his voice had gone completely.

"Rhydian?" Flare called again. "Rhydian?"

"Mm." His voice was tight. "F-fine."

His balance was thrown again when he could feel Flare circling, swooping lower in a great arc.

"Nearly," Flare cautioned. "Nearly, hm, when I tell you to let go, you let go, alright?"

"S-sure, why not," Rhydian gasped out, his voice an embarrassingly high pitch.

"I'll circle for a bit. Raise an arm if he is… uh… alive, and I'll go back to let your men know as discussed. It may take a few days, I can't see any paths-"

"They'll find their way," Rhydian croaked. "F-fine."

"Good, good, nearly there."

Rhydian hoped he wasn't going to cry, as Flare dropped lower again.

"Loosen your hold now. Get ready to slide down my leg in three, two, oops. Uh, okay, there you go…"

Rhydian cracked his eyes open and somehow he scrambled backwards down Flare's great purple foreleg. Thankfully, the river was only a few metres below, so that when he fell, the drop was short. With a splash, he ended up on his arse in the shallows. It was less than waist deep, so he wasn't injured, but he was now a soaking mess.

Shallow water was fine, but heights were not.

Shaking his head to clear his ears from the splash, Rhydian dug his boots in amongst the slippery rocks to stand. Flare rose away, the air swirling above Rhydian in choppy gusts, as great wing beats lifted the dragon to circle higher above. Rhydian blinked, examining the river and the surrounding shore. Flare had done an amazing job getting him down, but surely the wide swerve of this river was greater than the courtyard? Surely Flare would have been able to land?

Rhydian splashed to the shore, his heart still racing from the drop. He spat out the mineral rich water from his mouth, about to call out something about Flare making a go of landing, when he turned to his left. Rhydian froze.

About ten metres away, beyond a scattered group of rounded boulders, a naked man was face down on the shore.

His face was just out of the water, thank the gods, his left arm bent under his chest, his right arm outstretched beside his tousled, damp black hair. It looked like he was severely sunburnt.

Trying to go faster without breaking an ankle on the slippery rocks, Rhydian hurried over, eyes on the shore below his boots. His mouth was dry and his palms were sweaty. Would he have to poke Fox with a boot this time?

Cursing, Rhydian nearly rolled an ankle and forced himself to stop, his hands on his thighs. Swallowing, he looked up; Fox was only a few metres away now.

"Holy shit," Rhydian breathed. Fox wasn't sunburned.

He was tattooed.

Vaguely aware of Flare circling overhead, Rhydian squinted as he approached, more cautious now. Fox's entire back, from his shoulders to his buttocks, was a riot of colours, shapes and *movement*. It was hard to focus on. Surely it wasn't movement, but the thing shimmered, and seemed to undulate with layers of- what, exactly?

Rhydian stepped closer, his head tilted. Flare passed overhead once more, a great shadow crossing his path.

"Fox?" Rhydian called. He cleared his throat. "Fox, it's me. It's Rhydian."

There was no reply. There was only the sound of his breath; the wing beats above and the gentle gurgle of the river.

"Fox," he called again, feeling like he was approaching an unbroken horse. "It's me, I'm here."

Flare's giant shadow swooped overhead again even lower, and Rhydian ducked as his heart flipped.

As the shadow passed, the pale outstretched hand had twitched.

Thank the gods.

Rhydian wasn't crazy after all.

There had been a tiny part of him- Rhydian touched his chest, the pendants under his shirt. The relief of this mad mission was dawning. He realised he was afraid the whole time that he'd be wrong about coming. Delirious. But Fox's hand had moved.

Fox was alive.

Rhydian slid to his knees, bruising them on the rocks. His pack dropped away with a wet thud, his gaze focused on the hand that had moved. Carefully, Rhydian gathered up Fox's hand between his own.

And as Flare passed overhead once more, the cool hand between his twitched again.

And through the weird shimmering tattoo, Rhydian could see the man's ribs had expanded with a slow inhalation.

Reluctant to break contact, Rhydian raised one hand to signal to Flare. Fox was indeed alive. Rhydian blinked to clear his eyes. *Fox was alive.* The knowledge left him reeling. Flare was wheeling above, his great wings beating the air, the river at Rhydian's back giving up a fine, cool spray. The droplets covered them both, landing on the tattoo before him like diamonds that dazzled in the late morning sun.

Rhydian glanced up, frowning at the dragon.

Circling above him, Flare's mouth was agape, and his deep purple eyes were wide. Rhydian couldn't decipher his expression. The dragon seemed fascinated by Fox's tattoo as well.

What was he waiting for?

Rhydian waved his arm again. Flare met Rhydian's gaze, his mouth snapping shut. After one last glance back at the man on the ground, Flare rose higher. With great sweeps of his wings, he passed up and over the top of the forest.

The river bubbling and the soft sigh of the canopy far overhead were the only sounds to break the silence. And Rhydian's ragged breaths.

Flare would go get the men, and Rhydian would stay here and do whatever he could. He glanced back down at Fox, his gaze coming to rest upon the chaos of colour and shapes. A sick feeling, oily and dark, lurched inside his guts.

In a rush, the image came together, to make an appalling, disturbing sense.

Rhydian's breath caught.

Holy, holy fuck.

30

Aurelia

Year 367

Aneirin Castle

The crypts were cold, stale, and gloomy.

Aurelia paused at the ornate stone archway, its once pristine marble now pock-marked and greyed with dust. It would have been best if she'd asked someone to come with her. But she needed to be alone.

"Flare, what did you do?" she muttered, stepping through.

Holding up her small lantern, Aurelia took a breath, tasting mould and the gods only knew what else. The crypts, not far from the forgotten armoury, where Rhydian had had his revelation about the dagger, were almost as vast as the great hall above. There were sarcophagi in all manner of coloured stones, red marble, white granite and something black that may or may not have been black obsidian. She shuddered. If it was, and she had a strong enough lantern, she'd be able to see the body inside, through the black volcanic glass.

The layout seemed to be simple enough, the older burials close to the archway, and getting more recent as she walked down the wide corridor. She was surprised there were no bats. That was curious. Looking up, the ceiling was too far for her lantern to penetrate, and her Elven eyesight could only just make out a combination of natural cavern roof and stone vaulting.

As she passed the older sarcophagi, some with figures carved into them, Aurelia said a prayer for each one. Who knew what horrors these silent royals had witnessed, while a king and queen had ruled with lies above them?

It was a solemn space. One of quiet reflection.

But as she reached the last occupied resting place, her boots disturbing the bare earth floor, Aurelia couldn't help her wild, mad burst of laughter. All thoughts of Flare and his years of withheld information fled. Holding her lantern above her, Aurelia stared down at the king's face.

Containing the next laugh threatening to burst forth, Aurelia shoved her free hand over her mouth.

Rhydian's father had been stripped of his clothes and armour. His body had been laid to rest on a plain stone block, no arrangements yet in place for a more formal sarcophagus. The blood and dirt of the battlefield had been washed away, most likely with a careless bucket of water. The body had then been wrapped loosely in a black shroud from shoulder to toe. Leaving his face and his head bare, for all to see what had been carved there, under his silver streaked brown hair. Leaning closer, breathing shallowly around her hand, Aurelia stared. The detail was extraordinary.

A steady hand had precisely, almost lovingly, carved a line of cock and balls across the greying flesh of the king's forehead.

"King of Aneirin," Aurelia whispered, her hand falling to her side. "A dickhead in life, a dickhead in death." She lowered the lantern, straightening up. "I hope you and your mad wife rot for all time for what you did to him."

Without a further glance, Aurelia spun around, her boots crunching over the loose ground as she headed back to the entrance. Stopping to catch her breath at the archway, Aurelia wondered. She wasn't sure if she'd like to meet the owner of the hand that had carved the mocking crown for all to see.

Nearly turning right to head up the marble steps, Aurelia looked across the corridor. Taking a breath, she passed the steps and made her way through another arch, this one leading to the dungeons. Strangely enough, the air was fresher here, and the floor paved with slate.

There were no guards down here, as there were no cells full of prisoners.

Only one.

Some of the Elves had discovered Jessikah on the bridge after the battle. She had been conscious, but wheezing and unable to stand. They had carried her on a stretcher to Aurelia, as Fox was missing by that stage. Aurelia, in shock, had simply muttered 'dungeon', and they had obeyed.

She had already asked Wyll to help with food and water for their solitary resident; he'd likely be along soon. So Aurelia had slipped away in the meantime for what answers she could find. About Fox, Flare and even Jessikah herself. Despite the fact that Jessikah no longer spoke.

Her boots on the slate floor sounded loud in the silence, in time with her heart. As she made her way down the hall, with empty cells on each side, Aurelia wondered at that. Rhydian had put Jessikah in the last cell. For all his distaste at locking up someone, Fox clearly kept a very close eye on her. So Rhydian had made sure Jessikah was furthest from the door. There were no windows, but the lanterns along the walls had lots of oil, so the woman wouldn't be left in darkness at least.

Coming to the last door on the right, Aurelia cleared her throat.

Jessikah was in the middle of the clean cell, seated on a small three-legged stool, polishing her brown leather boots with a cloth. She ignored Aurelia, her long yellow-blonde hair looking clean for once, and hanging around her head in voluminous waves. The cell was tidy, its brick walls clean and unmarked. There was a grill for fresh air, high up on each side, and a bare hook for hanging a lantern on the back wall, if the detainee had been granted one. Jessikah hadn't, so only the light from the main corridor illuminated her cell.

Aurelia cleared her throat again.

At that, the woman looked up, one eyebrow raised.

"Did you know?" Aurelia asked, her voice low.

Jessikah looked Aurelia up and down, curled her lip, before going back to wiping down her boots.

"Did you know Fox was a dragon?" The words felt unreal.

In front of her, the cloth stilled. The woman didn't look up, however, and after a moment, she continued polishing.

"Did you know where he came from?"

Silence, and more polishing.

"Do you know why he was with us in the caves?"

More silence.

"Was he in hiding from someone?" Aurelia hedged.

The cloth paused, and didn't move again. Jessikah looked up, a soft smile on her pink lips. Aurelia swallowed. She'd always felt sorry for this woman. But an uneasy feeling was causing the hairs on her arms to itch.

"If he was hiding, do you know from whom?"

Jessikah stood up with slow, deliberate movements, her strange yellow eyes full of shadows. Aurelia took another breath, unable to help herself, knowing that the woman couldn't answer. Perhaps Aurelia could read something on her face.

"Did you... did you know about Flare? And what he did here in Aneirin, years ago?"

The woman stared at her, silent; her gaze heavy with scorn.

"I'm sorry that you're here," Aurelia ventured, lamely. "But it's for your own good, until we work out what to do, and where to put you."

Jessikah snorted, her eyes ranging over Aurelia once more. With a twist of her top lip, she sat down, primly shook out her cloth. And went back to cleaning her boots.

Feeling like she had been dismissed, Aurelia stepped back from the bars and made her way towards the archway at the end. Of all the things she'd ask Fox when he returned, who the hell that strange woman was would be right up there.

As she was going back up the stairs to the main floor of the castle, she met Chase coming down. He called down a tentative hello, a tray carefully balanced in his hands, a small lantern in one fist. The food was something warm and spiced, and steam curled from under the white cloth that covered it.

"Hey Chase," Aurelia murmured. "Where's Wyll?"

"He's busy, but he told me what to do."

"Ah." Aurelia bit her lip. "I can come down with you, though."

Chase shrugged, his cheeks pale. "I won't be long."

He clearly felt this was something he could handle amongst all the mess above them. Aurelia sighed. She had little experience with young boys. Not wanting to make him more uncomfortable, Aurelia changed the subject.

"Lunch time for our silent guest?"

He bobbed his head, his bottom lip between his teeth. He was avoiding looking her in the eye, and the tray of covered dishes rattled and clanked as he came to a stop. Aurelia wanted to reach out and tousle his head. The sick expression on his face from earlier still lingered, but as much as the boy had sought comfort from Davyn earlier, a relative stranger patting him on the head was unlikely to be received well.

"It's okay, Chase," she offered instead. "I saw the king."

His startled eyes snapped to her face.

"It was pretty grim."

Chase nodded. "Yeah."

"If it helps... It would be normal to think that he deserved it."

The flush over the boy's cheeks told her that she had said exactly the right thing.

What had been done to the king's body was horrific, yet considering what the man had done... who could blame a young boy for thinking in his secret heart, that he had been glad to see some final revenge, no matter how small, or how petty.

"One day we'll look back on all of this," Aurelia continued, "and realise these challenges made us stronger."

"I think so, too," he finally offered, the tray rattling and clinking as he took a deep breath.

"You need help?" Aurelia jutted her chin at the tray.

"Nah, it's ok, I've got this."

Aurelia glanced behind her, debating internally.

"Would it be okay if I wait here?" Aurelia offered the boy a tentative smile. "She is your king's prisoner, after all, and potentially a scary monster."

Chase finally laughed, almost himself again, and continued down the steps.

"Only if it makes you feel better, sure," he called behind him.

Aurelia checked the stairs for spiders with the lantern, and then sat down on the cold stone, thinking hard.

So much had happened. To all of them. She wondered if her words to Chase were true. That their *challenges*, as she had worded the battle, would forge in them all something stronger. Better adept at dealing with whatever else might lie ahead. Would that be true for Rhydian?

For Flare?

For Fox?

Wondering what the woman had done to cause a dragon to keep her so close, Aurelia frowned. Would that be the same for Jessikah?

As a petite woman of silence, it was hard to tell. Aurelia had been little when Jessikah had left the caves with the other Elves, sent out to rescue Elven refugees from some far off devastating event in the north. Only two had returned. After a *very* long time.

Aurelia scuffed the marble with the toe of her boot, staring down the stairs.

Only two had returned.

Jessikah and Fox.

Aurelia stilled, her wandering thoughts grinding to a halt.

Fox had returned all right, as someone, as *something*, completely different from who had left.

Aurelia dragged herself up off the step, her hand going to her belt. *Shit.* She hadn't strapped it on, thinking she'd not need it here in the castle. Her knife and plain sword were back in Rhydian's room. They were discarded on the floor, along with Fox's ruby adorned sword.

Taking a step down, her heart beating with sickening speed, Aurelia was cursing herself for a fool. If Fox was no longer Fox-

"Chase?" Aurelia called, her voice cracking in fear.

There was no answer.

As she rushed the rest of the way down the stairs, she realised something else was bugging her. The noise of the tray as Chase had come down, the rattle of clay crockery, wasn't the only noise it had made. There had been a clinking, a jingling. Like metal.

Like *keys*.

"Chase?" Aurelia yelled. "Chase! Did you have the keys with you?" She rounded the bottom of the stairs. "You don't need to open the door to feed her..."

Aurelia skidded to a stop.

There was no sight of the boy. All the lanterns lining each side of the corridor were out, the smoke from the extinguished wicks scenting the air with a bitter aroma.

Her keen eyesight noted that the barred door at the end was now open.

"No," Aurelia moaned, lurching forward, her lantern forgotten on the stairs, "no no *no*."

She sprinted down the gloomy hall, hyperventilating, her nose smelling something metallic over the savoury spices of the food. At the end of the hall, now that she was closer, she could see the tray. Its cover was gone, but the tray was placed neatly on the floor by the door. So he could indeed unlock the cell, not knowing there was a gap in bars on the floor for such a purpose.

Aurelia reached the cell, her heart wild in her throat, her breath hard to come by as her brain tried to piece together what her eyes were seeing. She dropped to her knees, the last of her breath leaving her in a rush.

Faintly aware of someone wailing in horror, Aurelia crawled into the cell, knees immediately soaked with blood, still warm. She grabbed at her face, at her chest, knowing there was no hope that her garnet had powers, but called on Rhydian just the same.

"Rhydian," Aurelia croaked, "Rhydian, come back-"

A soft footstep sounded from beside her, where they had been waiting while Aurelia had collapsed in shock. Pain burst across the back of her head.

The cell, its dark walls and shadows tilted, as Aurelia toppled sideways, one hand flung out as she choked, having bitten her tongue as she fell. Low light flared, as if someone had lifted a cloth away from a small lantern. Her out-flung arm was yanked back as she sobbed, and her arms tied roughly behind her.

A pair of brown leather boots entered her field of vision, their laces gone, and their owner jerked something like a sack down over Aurelia's face.

It didn't matter, though.

She could still see Chase, hung up on the lantern spike in the back wall like an animal carcass after a hunt, the only warmth left of him cooling in red puddles on the cold stone floor.

PART TWO

The Snag

"A snag is a tree in the final stages of its life. It can be a dying tree, or a dead tree still standing. While possibly at the end of its own lifecycle, a tree's usefulness to other life cannot be underestimated. A dead tree can still contain other forms of life."

Taken from 'Plant Lore for the Continent of Beinacoilia' by Hypatia Carter, commissioned for the Library of Seers.

Added underneath in an expressive scrawl:

'My dear wife, your capacity for the lore of the natural world cannot be surpassed. But as our children grow old, will they surpass our long years? Did we do the right thing?

x Illarion'

31

Rhydian

Year 367
Forest of Aneirin

Fox stared at the enchanting golden sky, visible through the break in the canopy above the river. Gold glittered amongst the black of his fathomless eyes. His expression was hard to read, but it appeared to be a mixture of weariness, confusion and fatigue.

Whatever Fox had been through, Rhydian hadn't yet had the courage to ask.

Swaying slightly on unsteady feet, Fox was standing next to where Rhydian was seated by the fire. After a deep cough racked his body, Fox cracked his neck in a slow roll, and stretched his pale arms wide. The heavy velvet cloak around his shoulders fell open, exposing bare flesh beneath.

The warm glow highlighted the hollows and shapes of Fox's sculptured form, mere centimetres away from Rhydian's face.

"I'm not *all* scales," said Fox dryly, noticing Rhydian's flushed cheeks.

"Apparently not," Rhydian replied, averting his gaze from Fox's smirk as well as his display of skin.

Fox's soft laugh dissolved into another racking cough, and Rhydian turned back in alarm. Fox had bent over, head hanging with his hands on his thighs as he gasped for air, his breath a white fog before him. Eventually he straightened, spitting into the fire, his face screwed up in disgust.

It was Rhydian's turn to smirk. The man was clearly trying to make him uneasy, but instead had ended up gasping for a breath. It was petty, the situation serious, but Rhydian was still amused. Shaking out his wet hair, Fox readjusted the black cloak around his shoulders, clearing his throat. The sun had now touched the canopy above the river, and the man's face was a play of firelight, dusk and shadows.

No, not a man.

A dragon.

Earlier, on the shore, as Flare had disappeared, Rhydian had carefully rolled Fox's limp body over. Rhydian had slid an arm behind Fox's shoulder, gathering him to his chest. At the sound of his name, repeated urgently, black eyes had finally opened to stare coolly at Rhydian's face above him. A cool, trembling hand had reached up and caressed Rhydian's cheek.

"Kiss me," Fox had said, cracked lips twitching.

"No," Rhydian had replied, smiling, his heart turning over with relief and a wild kind of giddiness.

"Help me up, then."

Rhydian had bitten back his questions and complied.

"Water," Fox had murmured.

Rhydian had helped him stagger over the wet rocks, to let Fox slide below the surface of the rippling water. Rhydian had eyed the tattoo as it passed him by, resisting the urge to touch it. The design was as awful as it was magnificent.

After soaking under the surface for a few alarming minutes, Fox's head, his eyes barely visible through soaking hair, had broken the rippling surface a couple of metres away.

"Build a fire," he had said.

Rhydian had stared at him until Fox had cleared his throat.

"Please," he said eventually. Rhydian had bobbed his head, staring as the inky head of hair disappeared back under the cool water.

So Rhydian had trudged up the bank, gathered driftwood, and built a ring of stones. He'd dragged over a larger log for them to sit on and lit a fire. And then he had sat down watching the flames changing colours as the driftwood burned with different minerals from the river. Red, orange, and gold were infused with bright flashes of blues and greens.

Rhydian simply sat there for a long time, throwing branches and logs into the fire to keep it burning for hours. Fox had been so long in the river that Rhydian wondered if he was expected to join him. But he had sat at the fire instead, the sun arching overhead, until it was now dropping behind the dark green forest around them.

Fox, finally satisfied with his soak, had splashed unsteadily over the shore to the fire. Rhydian had handed him the spare cloak, shirt, and pants. He hadn't thought to bring boots. Fox didn't seem to mind. He discarded the shirt and pants, and had draped the cloak about himself, sniffing to clear his nose, dropping water all over Rhydian.

It had been strange to sit there, watching him. After all that had happened, they could be two friends out on a hunting trip. Rhydian touched his hand to his lips, thinking of how his mother had died. It had been right, but the situation was still awkward, considering the manner in which Fox had gone through with it.

Fox coughed again, the cloak draping open as he wiped his hands through damp hair. Fox turned to face him fully, his next cough more of a snort.

"Blushing, are we, princeling?"

Rhydian raised his gaze from the fire, both eyebrows raised.

"That's *kingling*, actually."

Black and gold eyes narrowed. "Ah."

Rhydian shrugged, glancing back to the fire, watching the flames lick over the fragrant wood. He drew his dagger from his belt and began to clean his nails, avoiding having to look anywhere else.

"Well." Fox muttered awkwardly, pausing. "I'm sorry."

"Don't be," Rhydian murmured, holding up a hand to feel the heat from the fire, thinking of Lord Cyrus. "He was your enemy, the enemy of his people. He was a monster."

Sighing, Fox moved gingerly to sit beside him on the log, pressing against his side. Rhydian glanced down; Fox's thigh looked luminous, his skin so pale it looked like the marble that was used in the staterooms of the castle.

He was burning to ask questions, but he kept his mouth shut for now; aware Fox was still struggling to hold his next cough in. Glancing up instead, Rhydian examined the sky as the temperature was dropping. Fox sniffed, dropping his head to Rhydian's shoulder. With a sigh, Rhydian slid his dagger back into its sheath.

"Not all enemies are monsters," Fox murmured, wiping his face with a corner of Rhydian's cloak. Not the spare one that Fox wore, but the one Rhydian was wearing. Aware that Fox was teasing him, Rhydian shook his head. He said nothing.

Fox sighed with disappointment.

"The king," Fox said eventually, "wasn't my enemy. No matter what he was guilty of."

Rhydian didn't know what to say to that. "I don't understand."

"Put your arm around me," Fox said instead. "I'm cold."

"You could put more clothes on."

"I could."

Knowing he would lose the battle, Rhydian sighed. Reaching his arm carefully over the cloak, he slid his hand along Fox's shoulders. He was aware of Fox's intense tattoo, only a layer of fabric beneath him. As he was trying not to twitch his hand, something pale fell past from the sky. Then another.

"What the hell?" Rhydian cursed, looking around.

Fox sniffed. "What?"

"What the hell is this?"

Fox followed Rhydian's gaze and laughed until he coughed again. Rhydian drew back, narrowing his gaze.

"Rhydian, you twit," Fox said, smirking. "It's *snow.*"

With a flash of insight, Rhydian thought back to first meeting Aurelia on the banks of another river. The trees on the far side, her side, had been dusted with white. Her dark hair had been covered in the same.

"This is *snow*?" Rhydian repeated, his eyes brightening. "I've only read about it. It doesn't snow in Aneirin."

"I think that blasted magic bubble took care of more than isolating you from other people." Fox's voice was amused. "The weather seems to have been affected too."

A few more flakes drifted past them, and Rhydian frowned.

"But are we outside of the curse line here? Or is the weather changed all over?"

"I'm not sure."

Rhydian held out his hand, catching a flake that melted before he could quite see it. "It's beautiful." He caught another flake. "Shit, it's cold."

"Some things can be both."

Rhydian snorted, shaking his head, refusing to be baited. He dropped his arm back around Fox's shoulders, squeezing.

"Not all monsters are enemies," Fox murmured with a yawn and a shiver.

"Are you still talking about yourself?"

"Yes."

"I see."

"Do you?"

"I saw you in my dream," Rhydian said, ignoring the question. He touched the fingernail scratches overlaying the bruise on his cheek. "You were behind my mother. You heard her say that I had magic *too*. Because she wanted to take it back."

"She did."

"I came to find you, because... I need help with that. And also because you *saved* us, all of us, from her mad grab for power. I don't know what she might have done. So, thank you."

"You're welcome." Fox yawned again, adjusting his damp head against Rhydian. "I'm not here to be thanked, however, I don't want that. I'm here to finish things. Things that I should have finished a long time ago."

Rhydian had no idea what Fox was talking about. He took a deep breath, tasting the smoke of the fire. The smell reminded him of the funeral pyres, burning in the kingdom he had left behind to find this strange creature. There was a lot of confusion back home, but most of all, relief. Two armies that had been led by tyrants were hopefully listening to reason, to each other, and to Aurelia.

"How did you find me, kingling?" Fox murmured after a moment of silence.

"I felt a pull," said Rhydian, not mincing his words.

Fox stiffened slightly. "Interesting. Go on."

"That's it, really, I felt a pull. Flare helped me, and we found you."

Fox tensed against him at Flare's name, and then laughed.

"Is Flare coming back to rescue us?"

"That was the plan. I jumped. He flew off. He couldn't land."

"He couldn't land after you'd jumped? Not even in his ridiculously small size?"

Rhydian blinked. "Um, we didn't discuss that. But he'll be back with help."

"Did Flare see my tattoo?"

"We both did, um, it's-"

Fox laughed once more, a choking bark. "Flare isn't coming back."

"What?"

Fox blew out a sigh, shrugging. Rhydian shook his head.

"Flare will be back. He would've seen it for what it was."

"And what is that, do you think?"

"A commiseration of sorts?"

"Rhydian, you're too sweet for this world."

"Why?"

"My tattoo is not a commiseration."

"What is it then?"

"Quite the opposite." Fox cracked his neck. "It's a *celebration*. Of what I did. And also of what I stopped myself from doing. I could have taken my revenge so much further." He sighed. "But I held myself back, just enough. The pleasure needed to be prolonged. Perhaps too long, though."

Rhydian had no reply to that. He glanced down.

"I have your chain," Rhydian said, quietly, patting his chest where the charms lay under his shirt. "I'd seen it on you when we first met."

"What?" Fox drew back from him, his face unreadable.

"Your golden chain," he repeated.

Fox stared at him, blinking rapidly, staring at the glint of gold around Rhydian's neck. Clearing his throat, Fox blinked a few more times before he could speak.

"I'm glad. Your mother stole it recently, I think Jessikah..." Fox's voice faded into a hiss of frustration, and he shivered again. "I was unhappy to find that it had gone."

"Well, I found it. I've kept it safe for you."

Rhydian moved to take it off, but Fox moved to grab Rhydian's thigh, stilling him.

"No," Fox said, his voice low. "Keep it safe for now. Please."

"Oh. Okay." Rhydian dropped the chain. He took a breath, not knowing where to start. "I need your help," he settled on eventually.

"Was all of this not," Fox said, lifting his hand off Rhydian's thigh to indicate himself, "enough?"

With the fire hissing in front of them, and the river gurgling nearby, Rhydian wasn't sure how to say, no, he wasn't sure that it was enough. It sounded unspeakably selfish, but there were still too many questions that needed answering.

"I need more help. With my... magic."

"That might be a problem."

"Why?"

"Because I don't seem to have any at this moment."

"Oh."

Fox laughed, but the dry sound turned into a choke, then a wet cough.

"Okay. We'll find a way to deal with that," Rhydian continued, mildly alarmed. "But it's not just that. Aurelia needs you."

Fox nodded slowly. "I need her too."

"You also need to deal with Jessikah."

"My dear Jessikah," this was said in a hiss. "Yes, I really do."

The snow appeared to have stopped falling, but the air was still bitterly cold, but not as cold as Fox's voice. Rhydian was surprised at his reaction, having to hide his shiver.

Fox hadn't seemed to notice, as he was shivering again instead. Rhydian flexed his hand, not daring to drop it lower to Fox's back. Fox wiped his face with Rhydian's cloak once more, blowing his nose into the corner. Rhydian rolled his eyes.

"Is she secure?" Fox said with a cough. Rhydian really wished he would put on clothes, not just for modesty's sake.

"She's locked up in the dungeon."

"Good. When we get back, I need to finish him off for good."

"H-him? What?"

"It's a shitty story. With more than one monster."

"Tell me," Rhydian murmured.

"Will you cry for me?"

"Why are you such a bast-"

"Fine, fine. Let me tell you. Hmm," Fox paused, thoughtful. "Not even Owaen knows everything that happened."

"What? Who?"

Fox paused for so long that Rhydian was afraid he wasn't going to answer. When he finally spoke again, Fox's voice was subdued.

"Owaen."

"Who is he?"

"He was someone who tried to hold me back."

"An enemy?"

"No. Never that."

"A monster?"

"No."

"Then who?"

Fox stretched his feet towards the fire, and Rhydian found it hard not to stare. The man... dragon... who gave off more masculine energy than anyone Rhydian had ever met, had extraordinarily beautiful feet. They were as pale as the rest of him and finely formed.

His bare skin looked luminous as the sun disappeared, and his flesh took on the warm glow of the burning wood. Rhydian closed his eyes. Against him, Fox coughed again.

"Owaen was someone who tried to hold me back," Fox continued, exhaling slowly, "Holding me back from what had to be done." He swallowed. "He also tried to hold me back from what I needed to become in order to do it."

The hairs on the back of Rhydian's neck rose at the dark undertone of Fox's words. Opening his eyes, Rhydian bent his head, his lips brushing the top of Fox's damp hair.

"What did you become, Fox?" he whispered.

Fox shifted so he could stare at Rhydian. The gold glittered in his black irises like the sparks above the fire. Fox stroked a chilly finger down Rhydian's bruised cheek, causing him to wince.

"One of the monsters in my story," Fox said, smiling gently at Rhydian's pained expression, "was me."

32

Fox

Year 367

Forest of Aneirin

Fox paused, examining Rhydian's face, eyeing the line of faint crescent-shaped scratches over the colourful bruise on his cheek.

"Like I said, kingling, this is a shitty story. Are you sure you want to hear it?"

"A part of me," Rhydian admitted quietly after a pause, "is almost relieved to hear that you have a shitty story."

"As well as you, sweet king?"

"Yes." Rhydian nodded, his blue eyes solemn. "But not because of whatever happened to you. Only that it might help explain why you're so..."

"Charming? Desirable? Mysterious?"

"Ha ha, no. The phrases that came to mind were more along the lines of 'cruelly aloof', or 'happily murderous'."

"Brutal," Fox muttered, settling back under Rhydian's warm arm. "But points to you for honesty."

Staring at the warm flames, Fox knew he owed Rhydian an explanation. He was struggling however, not with the sharing of it, but the feelings that sharing his story would evoke. Being open, transparent and vulnerable were foreign concepts to him after so many years of living behind closed walls, even from Aurelia.

The smoke had died down, and embers glowed hotly amongst the ring of stones. Wishing the fire was even hotter, Fox wiped his face with a shivering hand. Clothes would have been smarter, but the feel of the cloak on his new and sensitive skin was irritating enough.

"I'm sure your royal lessons covered history, Rhydian. So you know that long ago, the great City of Seers was built. This new city was founded far north and west so as to be away from the coast, where the ocean had heaved, rising to wash the original great city away."

Rhydian tightened his arm around Fox, a warm blessing of reassurance. It felt like ice was creeping through his extremities, the cold air around them not helping.

"I'm not," Fox paused, as his back shivered in an unwelcome spasm. "I'm not sure of the timeline, to be honest."

"How old are you?" Rhydian interrupted, adjusting the cloak over Fox's shoulders.

"How old do you think I look?" Fox replied, archly.

"Fox," Rhydian said, not bothering to raise his cheek from Fox's damp hair against Rhydian's shoulder. "I think we might have established that what you look like, and what you actually are, may not necessarily be related."

"Fair enough. Where was I?"

"Timelines."

"Yes, I don't know how far back this was," Fox said with a deep, crackling inhale, clearing his throat.

"At that time, dragons, hating the cold, lived in their homeland, Mionlach, a place of scorching sun and dry heat, north of the City of the Seers. They burrowed into their mountains, creating vast caverns to live in, but more importantly, mining crystals. These crystals were what they needed to keep their magic burning within their hearts."

Licking his chapped lips, Fox shifted slightly to get closer to the warmth against him.

"From what I can piece together, the dragons mined the most sought after of crystals into extinction. Other rich deposits were available, but too far south, in the ice and the cold, for them to mine. But this gave them an idea. If they *shared* their magic, just enough, they could create helpers to mine the crystals that they desired."

With another dry cough, Fox paused and wiped his hand across his mouth.

Rhydian straightened his leg to hook his boot into the strap of his pack and dragged it closer. Reaching in, he bought out a metal flask of clean water, and wordlessly passed it to Fox. Murmuring his thanks, Fox drained the bottle in one go, but didn't let it go.

"So," Fox continued, rolling the flask in his hands. "From what I could gather, the dragons hatched a plan. Certain select humans from the beautiful city on the coast were chosen. If it worked, the dragons would have a whole civilian army of helpers to mine their magical sustenance-"

"Hang on," Rhydian interrupted, drawing back slightly to look at Fox in the eye once more. "Did you know Flare? Does he know you?"

"I've known him all this time."

"But Flare didn't know who you were? I mean, who you are now?"

"Not until now. He'd be more of an imbecile than I thought, if he didn't know by now."

They both knew what Fox had left unsaid.

After I ended your mother's life.

"I see. Please, go on."

"Thank you." Fox cleared his throat. "So the dragons created a race of *better* humans."

Rhydian swore softly. "Holy shit."

"Do you see?"

"Yes... The *Elves*... Does Aurelia know?"

"Yes, correct. And no, she doesn't."

Fox let that sink in. Rhydian absorbed it in silence.

"Nice of them, wasn't it?" Fox wiped his face again. "Out of the not so goodness of their cold, magical dragon hearts. You see, magic is just a manipulation of matter, through the contained energy within each tiny piece. The dragons manipulated humans. And the Elves were born."

Rhydian made a strangled sort of noise. Fox went on.

"But this caused dissent. And there was fighting amongst the humans. I think this is when the city on the coast was destroyed. I don't know how. The dragons didn't really speak of it. Eventually, along came a treaty. A council was formed, with representatives from each race. Magic, the sharing of it and the mining of crystals, would be better managed. To replace the destroyed city, which fell to the sea, The City of Seers was built further inland, with the help of the dragons. It was supposed to be a place of refuge for all," Fox murmured.

"What happened?" Rhydian's voice was soft.

"I did."

"What?"

With careful aim, Fox threw the flask back onto Rhydian's pack. It landed with a soft thud.

"Ever since I was young, I was different." Sensing Rhydian was holding in another question, by his sharp intake of breath, Fox sighed. "What?" he snapped.

Rhydian shook his head.

"Out with it."

"Were you born a dragon?"

"Yes. But I don't have family that I know of." Fox took a breath, not sure how much it was right to share. "I think my origins differed from the other dragons."

"You don't need crystals, do you?" Rhydian guessed.

"Clever little kingling. No, I don't."

"Why?"

"Stop."

"But-"

"Rhydian, be quiet," Fox snapped.

Rhydian muttered something that sounded like *that's be quiet, sire*. Pursing his lips, Fox continued.

"When I was old enough, some of the dragons noticed, and decided it would be a good idea if I was elected to be their *special one*."

Fox stopped to clear his throat again and pulled the cloak tighter around him. The sun was well and truly down, and the snow had appeared to have stopped for now.

"I hated it. I was esteemed but ignored. Their pride, their egos and their way of life, in turn, repulsed me. Dragons are cruel, first and foremost. Don't ever forget that," Fox said, his voice firm.

Rhydian nodded against him, his cheek warm against Fox's slightly damp hair.

"One day I'd had enough, knowing there was more to life. I'd gone to sleep, my yearning so deep and wide that when I awoke, I had been connected to... some kind of golden thread within. I..." Fox's voice wavered, and Rhydian squeezed his shoulder.

"I made my way south, to the City of the Seers, to follow that thread. And I met..." Fox wiped his face, unsure why his eyes were leaking. "I met Owaen."

"Owaen," Rhydian murmured, repeating the name as reverently as Fox had.

"I arrived in disguise. When we got there, as I slid off of Shadow-"

"Wait! What? You, a dragon, rode another dragon?"

"Like I said," Fox snapped. "I was in disguise. So I went as..." Fox closed his eyes.

Rhydian stayed silent, sensing the wave of memories threatening to overwhelm Fox.

"I went as someone else, eager to meet that blasted Elf, joined to me inside my heart by a shining thread of golden light."

"That's..." Rhydian's voice was full of awe. "That's *amazing*."

"Is it?" Fox's voice was flat. "Don't forget what type of story this is, kingling."

Rhydian sighed. "A shitty one."

"So we met," Fox continued, "in innocence. But soon enough, finding that we had similar opinions about equality, we thought we could make a difference, about the innate racism, and sense of entitlement within all the races. But..." a new round of deep coughing interrupted him this time, not Rhydian's questions. He wiped his mouth when he was finished, struggling to catch his breath. "But as Owaen and I grew close, we upset a dragon named Shadow Light."

Fox closed his eyes.

"This dragon was obsessed with me, my *purity*. It was his will that I should never share my magic with any of the lesser races."

"Did you?"

"No. But Shadow Light thought I did and caused great harm. The city was torn apart. I tried to help them. But."

"But you couldn't?"

"Owaen convinced me to flee. He was trying to keep me safe." Fox's hands curled into fists, his nails carving half moons into his palms. He opened his eyes, welcoming the sting.

"What happened?" Rhydian barely breathed the words.

"I was captured."

Rhydian's sharp intake of breath was exactly what Fox didn't want to hear.

"By Shadow Light?"

"Yes," Fox whispered. "He captured me. And a lot of Elves were captured as well, and died because of him, because of what he did to me."

Even after all these years, it burned his heart to speak of it. He cleared his throat and concentrated on breathing carefully, lest his fury rise in a wave of crimson over his vision.

"Shadow Light, in his cunning, convinced me that he had taken Owaen. It was untrue, but the only way to make me go with him. Partly in rage, partly as a distraction perhaps, he destroyed the city. He took me captive, and from the fleeing Elves, mostly the younger ones, children. He took all their magic away from them."

Rhydian stiffened in understanding. Fox nodded.

"Yes," Fox confirmed. "And then he gave it all to me."

"On top of what you already possessed?" Rhydian whispered in horror.

"Yes." Fox pressed the heels of his trembling hands into his eyes. "I told Aurelia something of it, that I ate their hearts one by one. Really, their hot little magical hearts were forced unwillingly down my cold throat."

"Oh, my gods..."

Ignoring Rhydian's horrified whisper, Fox went on.

"I think Shadow had something like this planned for a while. Risking my magical purity spurned him on. It took Owaen a long time, but when he finally found me, I didn't want to go with him. I felt like just a shell, something different." Fox took another long breath, dropping his hands from his face.

"You'd been through a lot," Rhydian mumbled. "Of course you weren't the same."

"You have no idea. I was..." Fox hating the pain that choked him as he forced out the words. "I was more of a dragon than ever. All those lives lost, because of me."

Without warning, Rhydian pressed his warm lips to Fox's forehead. Fox's throat tightened at the gesture.

"So Owaen freed me," Fox murmured. "But the dragons were still free as well. The same dragons who had helped, or stood by and watched as Shadow Light destroyed whatever he needed to, and do whatever he wanted to me."

Fox inhaled slowly through his nose.

"I knew only I could make it right. So I did."

"Did Owaen help you?"

"No." Fox swallowed, an ache rising from his chilled heart. "No, he couldn't have. I needed to do it alone. He was... too good for such a task. I acted alone."

"He was okay with that?"

"I didn't give him a choice."

"Oh. I'm guessing he was pissed off at that?"

"I assume so." Fox bit his lip.

"You don't know for sure?" Rhydian pressed.

"I haven't seen him since. It was a long time ago."

Rhydian twisted to face Fox, the different blues in his eyes dark and hooded in the light of dusk.

"Fox, what do you mean?" he asked, his brow furrowed.

"Like you said," Fox shrugged, avoiding the other man's strange blue gaze. "He'd be pretty pissed off."

"If he was an Elf, he could still be alive though? You've lived a long life. He could too, right?"

Fox rubbed absently at his chest. The golden thread was dormant, but still there, as always. A dry cough shook him as another round of shivering overtook his limbs once more. "He was Elven by birth, not because dragons shared magic with him. And he is alive, yes."

Fox could sense Rhydian raising his eyebrows.

"But he's," Fox blew out a deep, slow breath. "He's sleeping. Dreaming of things besides me, hopefully."

"I highly doubt it," Rhydian muttered darkly.

Fox snorted in spite of the guilt welling inside his heart, his voice a dry whisper.

"Like I said. Dragons are cruel."

Rhydian shook his head, unable to respond.

"Anyway," Fox continued, the memories burning his throat as he raised his voice. "I took it upon myself to make it right. Nothing could bring any lives or the city back. But I could get their justice for them and take revenge on their behalf."

Rhydian's voice was hesitant. "What did you do?"

"What I had to."

The words were so simple to say. The doing of it was very different. Rhydian was silent, obviously thinking about all the things left unsaid, not quite brave enough to ask. Fox glanced down at his hands clasped together to stop them from shaking.

The surrounding forest was full of birds singing their night songs as they went to roost. The thick canopy above them allowed only a few stars to peek through, casting a faint, twinkling glow. It would have been a beautiful evening, with the river bubbling, the embers glowing warmly, if their conversation hadn't been full of darkness.

Conflict was clouded over Rhydian's face, and his wide blue eyes searched deep into Fox's.

"The dragons," Rhydian whispered, "you killed them all, didn't you? That's why there's no more of them?"

"No."

Raising his gaze from his hands, Fox met Rhydian's searching gaze, not looking for absolution. Fox smiled at the memories.

"But I'm sure they wish I had."

33

Rebirth, before

Year 336

The Cave, North of Aneirin

Was he crying? Or laughing?

The man gasped down gulps of magic-charged air, pressing his face against the still rumbling stone. His eyes were watering, and his chilled breath misted away into the gloom of the cave entrance. There was muffled pounding from the other side of the thick rocky wall that he leant against.

The man kissed the stone with deep reverence. What was locked away was safe, never to experience the horror that he had. With his pulse rushing through his new body, modelled on someone who had already met their end, the man pressed his face harder into the rock. The surface grit scraped his forehead and his nose.

His hand tightened around the gold chain in his fist, yanked off the one who held his heart before the living tomb had been sealed for good. Around him, tiny motes of multi-coloured light flared in the shadows, in time with his breathing, before winking out. The energy in this place was still hissing softly in the atmosphere.

Scanning his awareness slowly along his new body, the man's mouth twisted with amusement. This new body was aroused. The collision of forces, wielded by himself against the dark creature who had caused all of them to be here, had left him unspeakably pleased with himself. But it was obvious that there was so much to learn, and so much to do. He would have to get used to this new body quickly, overcoming the dark desires of the original it had been modelled upon.

A rasping groan simmered from the shadowed cave floor below.

"I," a gasp, "what did... no, no..."

The man ignored the plea. Shifting his head against the gritty stone, behind which the pounding continued, the man could feel a graze open up along the flesh of his forehead. It hurt. It felt good; a reminder that hurting was only temporary.

The naked man pushed away from the rocks, stretching his arms wide. Muscles twisted, sinews and joints popped. After a deep exhalation, he crouched in front of the gasping woman below.

His nostrils flared, and he licked his lips, tasting salt, sweat and blood. Striking out, the man grabbed the tiny woman by the throat. More dancing sparks of bright, rainbow-coloured light burst into life, fluctuating with the rapid movement of his pale hand. With one hand, he dragged her face to his. Despite the gloom, his new eyes could see fine. The yellow of her hair, so like the original colour the new man had modelled this new woman on, was like a wild mess of sulphurous smoke around her face.

"Do you remember," the man murmured, "who I am?"

Their icy breaths mingled, and the sparks around them bounced between two pairs of wide eyes. Her strange yellow eyes reflected them. His wild and gold-flecked black eyes absorbed them. The man bared his teeth in a wicked grin. The woman clenched her eyes shut, but nodded, trembling all the while.

"Do you remember," the man asked next, examining her face, "who you are?"

A tear appeared at the outer corner of one tightly closed eye, the salty liquid reflecting tiny rainbows from the particles of lights flashing around them. The woman nodded once again.

"And do you know," the man whispered, his face pressed intimately to hers, forehead to forehead, "what is going to happen now?"

Like salty opals, more tears made their way down her flushed skin. Almost violently, she shook her head. The woman continued to tremble, unable to speak. He had left her with a tongue, but she was unable to use it because he did not wish to hear her excuses.

"Well, my sweet *Jessikah*," the man laughed, calling the woman by the name her body was modelled upon. "It's going to be *epic*."

The rustling canopy of leaves outside the cave was the only witness as the man, who now called himself Fox, dragged his trembling companion to the tunnel mouth. Before their descent to the dark forest floor, far below, he paused. He carelessly dropped Jessikah onto the rocky floor at his feet. She landed with a gasp of pain.

The figure, once a dragon but now a young man with inky black hair, gazed out at the dark heart of the forest. The giant trees, reaching for the dark sky, met his new eyes. He stared out at them, running a pale hand through the blood drying in his hair, feeling his magic within conforming to his new body. Exposed skin registered the cool air, and he turned his gaze to the cold stars above.

"He was called Fox, wasn't he?" the man mused, his new voice dry as he ran his hands over the pale skin of his new body. "Jessikah's companion? That name will do well enough now for me. Hm. Maybe we'll find his fox hole one day."

He nudged the woman at his feet with a toe. Unable to reply, all she could do was tremble. With a snort, the man raised his gaze to the stars once more, peering through the break in the trees. Even without being able to see it from here, he knew the northern sky was stained with a bloody glow, lit by the volcanic land beneath.

"Stained crimson, like your claws, *Jessikah*," Fox whispered, his voice a thick purr, thrilled by the thought. "And soon enough, these icy hands shall follow."

34

Rhydian

Year 367

Forest of Aneirin

Fox watched Rhydian intently, the whites of his eyes faintly bloodshot around the captivating gold and black of his irises.

For some reason, the memory of the small doe trapped amongst the rocks on the riverbank crossed Rhydian's mind. Lowering his gaze from Fox's, Rhydian stared into the dying fire, and could think of absolutely nothing to say. The crack of burning wood as it was transformed into red embers was the only sound. The sun was gone. It was dark and cold. He waited for Fox to speak again. He didn't have to wait long. After a thoughtful sigh, Fox continued.

"I went north to Mionlach and did what I needed to do. Afterwards, I wandered the forest for a *long* time. Eventually, I found your mother in the woods with Flare. She had been changed, too, but I didn't know who exactly she had been before. Flare was much less powerful. I could have taken care of him then and there. But I was dazed."

A snort broke the silence of his weighted pause.

"I decided to go with them, to follow. I eventually made a promise to her. It seemed right. After what I did in Mionlach to the dragons, your mother gave me the opportunity to help her with a situation that, at the time, seemed very similar to mine." Fox's voice was flat. "The rest, you know."

Unable to look away from the hot embers, Rhydian took a breath.

"But what did you do to them?"

"I didn't kill them." Fox swallowed. "But they can't hurt anyone ever again."

"Do you know who that poor dragon was in the forest? The bones, I mean?"

"No."

Rhydian chewed his bottom lip. "I think I might."

Fox stiffened a fraction, and Rhydian thought he was going to ask, but Fox just settled back into Rhydian's embrace with a snort. "No, don't tell me."

Rhydian tried to think of something else to say.

"Now do you have questions, kingling?"

"Yes, actually." Rhydian cleared his throat. "What's your real name?"

Fox's eyebrows shot up, eyes wide as he pulled away, flinging Rhydian's arm away from his shoulders.

"That's what you want to know? What's my *fucking name*?"

Fox laughed, the horrible rasping quickly descending into a mad gasp for air. It took him a while to catch his breath, pulling the black cloak tight, shaking his head. His pale hands were trembling. Fox muttered something under his breath. It sounded a lot like 'you idiot'. Rhydian smiled.

Slowly, Rhydian stood up, not just to clear his head, but needing to stretch. Travelling by dragon was unnatural; he'd prefer a horse any day. He walked around a few steps, glancing at Fox occasionally. Fox's eyes followed every move he made.

Sighing, Rhydian came back to Fox, standing next to him, looking down. Neither of them said a word out loud. They merely examined each other, blinking occasionally. Inside, Rhydian was learning something about himself. He was still cautious of Fox. Only a fool *wouldn't* be. But his fear had morphed into a breathless kind of awe.

Carefully avoiding the long bare legs stretched towards the warmth, Rhydian added more logs to the still hot embers, and then wordlessly sat down at Fox's side. Aware of glittering eyes upon him, Rhydian slid his right hand under the folds of the cloak, along the bare skin beneath. Fox shivered at the touch, the smooth muscles rippling, the flesh freezing. Rhydian sighed. Why hadn't Fox put on more clothes? The man was beautiful, naked, and Rhydian was- what? Confused? He could imagine Aurelia's laugh. She wouldn't be concerned. He was sure it was more likely that she would find this situation hilarious.

Rhydian's fingers tingled as his hands brushed the top of Fox's tattoo. Fox made no comment. It had obviously been inked with some kind of strange magic. The sight of it was burned into Rhydian's memory, never to be forgotten, shifting like a play of light across the man's skin.

Aside from the magic that powered it, the design was a hideous, chaotic, and beautiful thing. Closing his eyes, Rhydian hung his head, remembering each detail. Across Fox's shoulders spanned a row of impossibly detailed figures, weak humans and bright eyed Elves, all with arms raised, faces afraid. Below them, in a dark cave that glowed a sickly blue, an emerald and shimmering golden dragon sprawled across the cave floor, bloody and defeated. Further below the broken creature, other broken winged creatures lay in twisted contortions. Dead dragons, stacked like the strata of ancient rocks, were piled in layers and layers of jeweled colours with claws, spikes and scales gleaming, eyes dull, each and every one of them.

It was terrifying, and Fox had created it specifically to never forget what had been done to him, and what he had done in return. So full of rage, the man had done something to an entire race of magical beings, all by himself. It sounded like Fox had locked away the one person who may have been able to help him crawl out of the darkness of his imprisonment.

The man had eventually found a friend in Aurelia, but he was still, essentially, alone.

Opening his eyes, Rhydian gently reached across with his free hand to catch Fox's cheek. The crackling firelight showed up the dark circles of fatigue under his black eyes. Sliding his fingers into Fox's thick, black hair behind his ear, Rhydian gently pulled Fox's head towards him.

Rhydian kissed the inky strands on Fox's cold forehead, and Fox sighed.

"I'm sorry about what happened to you, Fox."

Ignoring Rhydian's quiet words, Fox extended an arm from the cloak, and slid it around Rhydian's waist, curling into his warmth. Rhydian rested his chin back against Fox's head.

Rhydian wondered at himself. He wondered at the... creature... that he held close, needing comfort after so much violence and chaos. Rhydian pressed another soft kiss to the black hair against his lips; there was no other comfort that he had to give.

I am holding a storm.

A dangerous storm.

Unable to help himself, Rhydian smiled. He'd finally thought of something else to say. He laughed, shyly.

"What?" Fox's voice was muffled.

"It scares me, but," Rhydian said, shyly, "I like your tattoo."

Fox laughed, pressing his face against Rhydian's heart, his shivering somewhat calmed down for now.

"Hush," Fox said. But he sounded pleased.

Unable to help himself, Rhydian felt just as happy. He had found Fox, and would return him safe and sound, back to Aurelia, who was waiting for them both.

Watching the flames consume the fresh logs, despite everything, Rhydian was content, eager to get back now, looking forward to the more peaceful times ahead.

35

Flare

Year 367

Forest of Aneirin

"I mpossible," the dragon breathed.

Flare had sat shivering on the side of the mountain the whole night, with the image of Fox's tattoo etched into his mind. Now the sun was rising in the east, and Flare stared into the fiery ball, trying to burn the image away.

He was crouched on a rocky outcrop amongst the lower slopes of the mountains behind Aneirin. At the south end of the range, Flare could see the devastated fields of the farmlands below. He was also high enough to see where part of the canopy had been destroyed by Sophia and...

Fox.

It was the day after he had left Rhydian in the forest, after he had seen Fox's back, the weird rippling image of the demise of Flare's race. He didn't quite understand it, but it was clear Fox had seen something, or knew more than Flare did, about what had happened to them all. Something Flare had never been brave enough to fly north and find out about. So Flare had stayed south of the mountains of Mionlach, living as a tiny thing, dependent on others to survive.

And Fox had known.

This whole time!

Flare still wasn't sure what he was going to do about it. Now he was here, sitting and shivering in the cool air, breathing in smoke from the fires and damp air rising from the forest. A lone wasp buzzed past him, something dangling from its long legs. He looked away.

"Impossible," Flare repeated, his eyes watering, dark purple eyelids lowering of their own volition. The dawn light was too bright to stare at, but not bright enough to burn away the horrific image that he was unable to forget. And that it was inked on the back of... The noise that escaped Flare's throat was partway between a gasp and a snort.

How was it possible that all this time, Fox was...?

"Impossible," Flare repeated once again, this time the word coming out as a dry sob.

Small rocks rattling on the slope below his rock interrupted his musings. Flare ignored the quiet tumble of stones, likely a small landslip, but opened his eyes to stare blankly at the pastel colours washing the sky. The blue was mixed with dazzling streaks of gold and pink.

There were many situations in his past that filled Flare with shame. And this meant, because of who Fox really was, he *knew*. Fox knew that Flare could have stayed behind in the City of the Seers to stand against Shadow Light. But Flare had fled instead.

Weeping now, Flare's wings drooped further, the tips of his underwings brushing the red dirt that sprinkled his rocky perch. He turned from the breathtaking view of the valley, staring at the peaks above. After fleeing the City of the Seers, he'd come to Aneirin, a place he'd always wanted to see kept safe. But, again, he had been part of the reason so many had suffered instead. He had fled with Sophia into the forest, only to be found by the very one whom Flare had left behind so long ago.

The contempt in those glittering black eyes was suddenly all too real, all too clear. And all too *deserved*.

A quiet rattle of small stones shifting in the dirt of the ridge below came again.

"I'm sorry," Flare whimpered, his nostrils flaring as great dragon-sized tears rolled down the scales of his face. "I... I... What?"

Stopping mid-sob, Flare raised his head.

He had caught the scent of something else, something at odds with the mountain air and the forest nearby. Strangely, it reminded him of Aurelia. Dipping his head to wipe his eyes with the back of a scaly claw, Flare peered around him. What was it? He raised his snout, inhaling deeply.

Soap?

That's why it reminded him of Aurelia. It wasn't floral, but it was still soap.

Flare was still blinking in confusion at the red peak above him when a man's breathless laugh came from behind.

"Found you!"

After spinning around, wings spread wide, the dragon froze in shock.

A blonde head had appeared at the edge of the rocky outcrop on which Flare was crouched. Moonlight blonde hair was partially covering the young man's face. It had been a *long* time, but there was no mistaking who it was, however. The disturbing, mismatched eyes, full of wild delight, gave him away immediately.

"You!" Flare screeched in horror. "C-Caspian!"

Scurrying away from the edge, Flare's sharp claws gouged at the rock in his haste to put as much distance between himself and the man before him.

Caspian threw back his head, laughing with mad delight.

"I *knew* that you'd be pleased to see me," Caspian said, grinning as he pulled himself up the rest of the way onto Flare's rock.

When he stood up, Caspian carefully dusted himself off, before spinning around, arms wide, as if showing off his cloak. The material was rich velvet, its dark purple colour suspiciously similar to the colour of Flare's scales.

"It's new. Do you like it?" Caspian asked. He grinned, his teeth white and perfect in his exceptionally handsome face. "When I knew you were back around these parts, I realised I needed to look my very best for our *most happy* reunion."

Flare just about tripped over his tail, scrambling back as far as he could go. He came up against the uneven wall of the ridge behind him, avoiding Caspian like someone might scurry back from a giant and deadly spider.

Caspian lowered his voice, his eyes narrowing at Flare's retreat. "Do we look too similar? Hm. Perhaps we should have conferred with each other before we made love to the world with our presence this morning." He raised his blonde eyebrows suggestively.

All Flare could do was croak nonsense.

"But you... you're..."

Striding forwards, Caspian stopped right in front of Flare, his expression thrilled.

"I'm sorry to disappoint you, Flare Shining One. But I am not dead. In fact," the man tilted his head and poked Flare's trembling snout with his finger. "I am *quite* well."

Flare jerked his head away from the man's touch, the side of his face pressing into his wing. But even staring at Caspian with one eye was too much; the man's unpredictable aura was like an intense shimmer in the air between them.

Tall and slim, Caspian was the kind of man that both women and men ogled when he entered a room. His slim frame was still finely muscled, from all of his years as a highly skilled swordsman. Caspian was handsome, almost pretty, with sensuous lips, white blonde hair and creamy skin. But when the man dropped the glamour over his eyes, like he had now, people usually placed a hand on the closest weapon.

Caspian's eyes, ever since he had been born, had been... different.

Each one was a different shade of blue. The left eye was pale and icy, the right a dark sapphire. That was unusual enough, and would leave anyone facing him unsure as to which one to look at. That wasn't all, though. Each one was iridescent, and when the light caught them just right, or *wrong*, they shone with a quicksilver, metallic sheen. Not always at the same time.

Flare couldn't stand to look at them. It had always been hard to meet Caspian's gaze, as his expression was usually either inappropriately amused, or a mask of unspeakable cruelty.

At the moment, they were sparkling with dark mirth, shining with quicksilver in the light of the dawn sun. Flare could just see himself, a tiny purple speck, reflected in each. He gasped out the only thing he could think to ask amongst a crowd of questions, which were making it hard to focus.

"If you're h-here now, where are... *they*?"

The mirth disappeared, and Caspian's dangerous gaze narrowed. The purple flash of Flare's reflection disappeared, leaving just slivers of two different blues.

"I assume you mean Illarion and Hypatia?" Caspian clarified, lips thinning. "They're still *quite* dead. Don't be alarmed. They can't hurt you now."

"But you? H-how? Where have you b-been?"

"The same as you, precious," Caspian purred, his smile back once more. He waved a hand airily about his head. "Avoiding Shadow Light's mess. Making plans."

Flare, unable to handle his terror any longer, rallied himself and rose up, spreading his wings wide, looming over the man.

"Get away," Flare cried weakly, "you don't belong here, not here, not in Aneirin!"

"Shut up," said Caspian, calmly.

And just like that, Flare's brief show of bravery deflated, and his wings dropped, his heart thudding in time with his shallow breaths. He had no idea how to escape, this man, this *fiend*... if Caspian had found him here, he could find Flare anywhere. And worse, the man had the ability to take away everything that Flare held dear.

Magic.

Caspian likely had abilities he didn't even know that he was capable of, and Flare was perfectly content to make sure it stayed that way.

"H-how did you find me?" Flare whispered, wishing the man would move away.

Ignoring his question, Caspian asked one of his own.

"The gold dragon, with the green shimmer... Tell me, am I mad, or was that our shining sun, rising in the *sky* after all this time?" Caspian laughed, amused by his own joke.

"No," Flare mumbled, lying through his teeth, "No. I don't know."

The expression on the handsome face before him told Flare that his lie hadn't gone unnoticed. A pale eyebrow rose delicately.

"Interesting. But not good enough, sweetness. I need to find out."

"Wh-what? And how do you know if it *was* them, after all this time?"

Caspian continued, his expression thoughtful, his flinty eyes glazed.

"Flare, oh great Shining One, I know more than you think. Well, except for how to get back inside the castle without the wrong kind of attention. I'm not quite sure I can manage that, no matter how much magic I've scooped up from the king."

"The king is dead," Flare said, with no idea of what Caspian was talking about.

"Yes," Caspian said, speaking to Flare like he was a small child. "And the bitch queen too, sweetheart. But the castle is now full again, and I do not want to attract any attention. Who knows what traps the king has left inside, hmm?"

Silently, Flare stared, still without a clue what the man was talking about. Caspian returned his stare, unblinking, his shining purple cloak flapping in the cool breeze. One hand rested on the hilt of an elaborate sword at his hip, the other in his cloak. Caspian continued.

"But as for *our* esteemed royal one, after rushing in to save the day, they are hiding once again."

"B-but, Fox... died," Flare stuttered, caught by the cunning look over Caspian's face.

Caspian had withdrawn a thin object from his cloak and tapped it against his lips.

"Fox, hmm? Clever. But no. I think *Fox* is in hiding, once again. But I will find where." Caspian pointed the object at Flare, his face solemn. "With your help."

Seeing what was being pointed at him, Flare cried out.

"Where did you get that?" he gasped, eyeing the black arrow in Caspian's hand.

"The battlefield, of course," Caspian said, a small smile playing across his lips.

"The one that...?"

Caspian's smiled widened. "The very same."

"That means that, on the king's face..."

Looking immensely pleased with himself, Caspian winked.

"What are you going to do?" Flare managed to get out, swallowing back the bile in his throat.

"Tsk tsk, Shining One," Caspian scoffed. "Nothing as bad as you." He pointed the arrow over his shoulder at the battlefield below. "That's on you, after all."

Flare grasped for anything to say.

"N-no!" he managed to bite out, "I didn't mean for this-"

"Don't try that with me. I know it was you who helped those fucking idiots create that stupid spell. You just didn't realise how dumb they'd be to get it so wrong, did you?"

"N-no, that's not what-"

"Come now, my scaley poppet, that's always been your weakness, the adoration of others. Trying to buy loyalties with a magical blessing of protection is all you, baby. Pah! But it turned into a rather spectacular curse. Well done, dragon. It was *really* well done."

Caspian laughed at that, clapping his hands together with the arrow between them. Like Flare's shame was the most hilarious thing in the world. Flare, despite his colossal size, wished he were small enough to disappear into a crack in the rocks and wither away to die. Just as suddenly as it had started, Caspian's laugh broke off. The man took another step forwards and stroked Flare's cheek lovingly with the tip of the black arrow.

"Fret not, dear one. I might have a way you can finally make amends for *all* of this," Caspian murmured, pointing at the battlefield once more. He gave Flare a secretive smile. "Or are you going to run away like you did to *both* of your families?"

"What are you talking about?" Flare whispered, fear chilling his bones.

"Oh, Flare," Caspian murmured, his voice tender. "As the child of your maker, what kind of question is that?" Caspian poked Flare with the arrow once more. "Now, lend me your foot. I'm coming up."

"NO!" Flare cried, eyes wide, rearing up once more.

"That's cute," said Caspian, and slashed the arrow through the air, eyes locked on Flare's. Despite the arrow being metres below, and not having touched him physically, Flare called out in pain.

A searing stinging cut opened up beneath Flare's right eye. On feeling his cold, reptilian blood flow freely down his face, Flare whimpered with fright. Crooking a finger, Caspian urged Flare to lean down. He had no choice but to obey. A warm touch at the gash had Flare whimpering once more. Caspian had pressed his fingers into the cut, only a hand's breadth away from Flare's sword like teeth, knowing Flare wouldn't dare to try anything stupid. Drawing his hand away, Caspian smiled sweetly, lifting his fingers to his lips.

"Mmm," he purred, eyes closed, licking the fresh dragon blood off his skin. "Straight from the source."

In the next breath, Caspian's eyes snapped open. He focused his quicksilver blue gaze on Flare's. With a sickeningly loving caress, Caspian patted Flare's face. The cut stung with the gesture, but the blood stopped flowing, and the small overlapping scales of his face rippled together as if it had never happened. The dark sheen on Caspian's lips told another story.

"Flare," Caspian said, quietly. "Don't ever speak like that to me again." He paused. "I might take out your eye next time."

Hanging his head, Flare swallowed, eyeing his claws clenching at the rock below. What else was there to say? Caspian went on, his tone thoughtful.

"Hm. Although, if I did, I could *eat* it. And then what sights might I see?"

Flare snapped his head up, only to see Caspian smiling yet again.

"A joke, precious. Now." Caspian pointed the arrow at Flare's leg. "Don't be shy."

"Why?" Flare whispered, gingerly extended his foreleg. Caspian adjusted his matching purple coat, out of the way of his legs. "Why do you need me?"

"I need your wings, sweetness," Caspian said, his voice a dark purr once more. "Mine are buried *far* too deep."

Gulping, cringing, and with eyes closed, Flare shivered as Caspian climbed up, pulling himself onto Flare's back to wedge himself amongst the spikes, some of which were quite sensitive.

"Off we go," Caspian called, as happy as a child on their first pony ride.

Obeying, Flare spread his wings and took off, rising with a gentle thermal.

A very soft, very delicate touch on one of Flare's spikes felt like Caspian had kissed him, just once, with deep reverence. Flare shut his eyes for a moment, entirely repulsed.

I am heading out of one disaster, Flare thought.

Only to head directly into another, and I suspect this one might be worse.

The quiet laugh from his back, almost a sigh of the wind, indicated that Caspian knew exactly what he was doing.

I'm doomed.

36

Rhydian

Year 367

Forest of Aneirin

"Thank the bloody gods!" Rhydian cried out through the trees, relieved to hear the jingle of tack and horses approaching. "Over here!"

It had been a long, frustrating day. Rhydian had woken up with Fox curled around him yesterday morning. After a chilly night of alternative shivering or coughing, Fox had finally agreed to put on the spare clothes that Rhydian had brought. And so, wrapped in the cloak as well, Fox had stumbled along barefooted with Rhydian, too impatient to see if Flare had returned to Aneirin or not. He didn't quite believe Fox when he said that the dragon wouldn't, but he was eager to see Aurelia. So they were making their way along the wide, shallow river, back to Aneirin.

Their slow journey through the day had halted early, as Fox had worryingly not stopped coughing for the entire afternoon. Rhydian had built another fire, while Fox had stripped without a care to wade out into the river once again.

"Why?" Rhydian had grumbled, certain the water was doing Fox more harm than good.

"My skin hurts," Fox had said, disappearing beneath the rippling surface as the dusk light turned the forest into a dim, shadowed and silent wonderland.

They had spent another icy night beneath a sliver of starry sky, this time without talking. Rhydian had held Fox while the man coughed so hard he had a burst blood vessel in one eye. Rhydian had laughed in shock at first at the sight of it; until Fox had glared at him so darkly, with the red glow from the fire across his pale face, that Rhydian had hid his sniggers in his arm. There hadn't been a lot to smile or laugh at recently, and this was hardly a joke. But it had struck Rhydian as so unexpected, because of how vulnerable Fox looked, that he'd been unable to help his reaction.

It wasn't funny anymore, however. Whatever Fox had done in order to come back... to life... in the same form as before, hadn't quite gone to plan.

"Where's your magic? Why can't you fix it?" Rhydian had said when he got up that morning, pointing at Fox's trembling body.

"Fuck you," Fox had choked out, coughing until he could hardly breathe.

After nearly two full days of half dragging, half carrying a dragon, who was at this point an ill man, Rhydian was ready to pull his hair out in frustration. He wanted proper food, a hot bath, his bed, and Aurelia. Not necessarily in that order.

"Over here!" Rhydian called again, peering up the banks into the crowded and moss covered ferns and trees.

"Calm down, sire," a familiar voice called. "You're caterwauling will disturb all the ghouls out amongst these parts."

"For fuck's sake, Dav. Don't say that!" Wyll's voice admonished. "You'll catch us a jinx just by joking about it."

Finally, the two men appeared from amongst a patch of tall ferns, thankfully on the same side of the river as Rhydian and Fox. Each man was mounted on a sturdy horse, and leading another behind. The disapproving glare of Blackthorn, being led by Davyn, was enough to lighten Rhydian's heart by leaps and bounds immediately. He hadn't actually seen his horse since being knocked off of him in the battle. Merion had sent Chase to him that night, however, advising Rhydian that the wise horse had made his way back to the city with barely a scratch, but Rhydian had regretfully not been down to greet his old friend.

Both Davyn and Wyll looked tired and worn, which was fitting since they had been through the same battle, and had now ridden through previously unexplored forest. Each wore odd bits of their normal riding clothes, cloaks, and tough boots. All four horses had packs tied to their saddles.

Ignoring Fox's protests, Rhydian dragged the limp man up the bank.

"Flare found you, then! Thank the gods," Rhydian panted, setting Fox down on a boulder. Fox sat down with a groan, his black hair hanging limp, and his face more grey than its usual luminous white.

"Flare? The dragon?" Wyll said, sliding off his horse. "He never came back."

"Told you," Fox croaked, his head resting on his arms that were folded over his knees.

Rhydian ignored Fox, slipping over the rocks to greet his horse. "But Flare left us here two days ago." He wrapped his arms around Blackthorn, who tossed his head, but settled immediately as Rhydian tugged the animal's forelock. "Hello, I missed you too."

Davyn cut in as he dismounted. "Merion couldn't wait. Flare didn't come back, so he took matters into his own hands. There's some," he hesitated awkwardly, eyeing the rather woeful form of Fox sitting on the boulder, "magic in his family. He did some kind of a spell. With your horse, a rutilated quartz crystal, and a big compass drawn in chalk in the courtyard."

"It was bizarre to watch," Wyll interjected. "Um, but you're not going to hang him for it, are you, sire?"

Rhydian lifted his face from Blackthorn's mane, examining Wyll. The man's dark eyes were serious, his normally shining hair a tousled mess.

"Why the fuck would I hang Merion?" Rhydian demanded, at a loss.

"Because magic is outlawed, sire, isn't it? His family is full of it," Davyn said, kneeling in front of Fox. Fox raised his head, but only a fraction. "Here, looks like you could use more than water, eh?"

Davyn held up a large leather flask, and Fox stared at it at confused After a moment, Fox raised his weary gaze to Davyn, and carefully, like he was expecting Davyn to jerk it away, Fox wrapped his pale fingers around the flask.

"Thank you," Fox murmured, lifted the flask to his lips. He sipped cautiously. He coughed at first, and then brought the flask back to his lips, gulping much quicker.

"Ha!" Davyn said, rising to his feet and nearly tumbling over on the slippery rocks. He regained his balance, beaming, tugging on his thick plait of hair. "I knew I'd like this one!"

Rhydian kissed Blackthorn's muzzle once more and slid off the mossy bank onto the rocks. "No more magic users are ever going to hang," he murmured, turning around. He frowned at Fox, who was still drinking from the flask, eyes closed.

"Davyn, what's in that flask?"

"Fire wine, to warm you up, of course."

"What?" Rhydian stalked over to Fox and snatched the flask from his hands. "That's enough of that," he hissed at Fox, who scowled back, looking worse than before.

Rhydian turned back to Davyn. "He can hardly stand. How's he supposed to sit on a horse if he's drunk?"

"Give that back," Fox said, hiccupping. He reached out, but overbalanced and started to sway to the side. Rhydian grabbed the collar of Fox's cloak to hold him upright. "It's *magiiiiiic*, like M-Merion..."

"For fuck's sake, this is all we need," Rhydian snapped. He closed his eyes briefly.

Wyll was staring at Fox. "Why do you need him at all?"

Rhydian twisted around, still holding Fox upright by his collar. Fox squeaked as he was spun about. "Are you kidding me?"

Wyll jutted his chin out. "Why is *this* Elf so important?"

Fox snorted. "Don't be *jealous*, little man," he said, hiccupping again, causing Davyn to slap his hands on his thighs, going into fits of laughter. Obviously, Davyn was eager to lighten the mood since the battle and its stench of death as well.

"You don't... didn't you see?" Rhydian asked, hesitant, pointing at Fox.

Both Davyn and Wyll stared at Rhydian. Davyn looked interested, and Wyll looked suspicious and wary.

Fox cleared his throat. "Shhhh, I'm in disguise," he said in a mock whisper before dropping his head back to his arms with an ominous groan. "Oh, I don't like f-fire wine."

Pinching the bridge of his nose with his free hand, Rhydian sighed, his eyes closed. This was not going to get them on their way back to Aneirin as fast as he would like. As he listened to the murmur of the canopy above and the water beside them, he let it slide for now, not wanting to explain just how much Fox was more than met the eye. Rhydian wondered, had he or Aurelia, or even Flare, wherever he was, explained to anyone who the gold and green dragon had been, or was? No Elves had asked after Fox either. Perhaps he'd just keep it to himself for now.

"We owe our lives to this-" Rhydian paused.

To this what?

"This *lovely* creature," Fox hummed below him.

Fox raised his head, smiling now, looking dreamily up at Rhydian, before resting his forehead against Rhydian's chest. He was murmuring something Rhydian couldn't make out. As Fox's trembling arms slid around Rhydian's waist, Davyn laughed harder, taking a swig of the flask himself. Wyll looked on with something like disbelief mixed with disgust.

"We owe our lives to this *Elf*," Rhydian said, his voice firm. "And we shall treat him with all due respect, like all the Elves, along with his companion, Jessikah." He took a breath, eyeing the top of Fox's blank hair. "Although she must be kept under guard for now."

"Jessikah, oooh, she's *so* bad," Fox mumbled against Rhydian. "Really, *really* terrible."

Rhydian reached down and tried to get Fox to stand up, but the man was a dead weight, humming to himself.

"Fox, please, get up now, we have to go," Rhydian urged, and Davyn tossed the flask to Wyll so he could give Rhydian a hand. Davyn grabbed one of Fox's arms.

"Oh shit," Davyn said, noticing Fox's eyelids fluttered closed. "He's going to faint, sire!"

"I told you that was too much," Rhydian snapped.

"I'm not going to faint," Fox gasped, and then promptly passed out.

Rhydian glared at Davyn over the limp form sprawled between them.

"Oops," said Davyn, and grinned.

"Water," Fox hissed, his eyes shut tight against the dim light of dawn.

Rhydian, his water flask ready, held it up.

Fox jerked it from his grip, and drunk the lot.

"More," Fox gasped.

"Lets see if you keep it down this time, okay?"

"This time?" Fox mumbled. "What's that smell?"

Across the campfire, Davyn smirked.

"You've been in and out of waking three times now," Rhydian explained, his voice pained. "That smell is your vomit. I do not wish to hold your hair away from your face again while you spew. So, trust me," Rhydian took the empty water flask back and set it down amongst the moss. "That's enough for now."

Rhydian was lying on his bedroll, with Fox wrapped up against him before the fire. Wyll had been bug eyed when Rhydian had set Fox's bedroll directly next to his own, but had thankfully said nothing. Which was just as well, as during the day Rhydian had to sit behind the barely conscious Fox on Blackthorn to stop him from tumbling headfirst from the saddle. Rhydian had just about had enough of Wyll's dark eyed glares at them both. Davyn, as usual, was amused.

They'd made fast progress with the horses picking their way along the banks above the mossy rocks of the river, but the previous day's ride had still been slow. Rhydian, frustrated at the pace, had tried to be content with the fact that he was heading back towards Aurelia. He'd ridden with his arms around Fox on the same horse. But the shaking, intoxicated form of Fox, who thankfully hadn't got any vomit on Blackthorn, had been an unwelcome hindrance. Their return to Aneirin just might not be as spectacular as Rhydian had first imagined.

Across the fire, Davyn smirked at Fox, and raised his own water flask, taking a long satisfying drink.

"I h-hate you," Fox mumbled, pressing the heels of his hands to his eyes. One of them was still bloodshot, but was fading back to normal.

Wyll, blinking sleepily, said nothing. He was occasionally throwing pebbles into the red embers, waiting for their dried bread to heat on the stones warmed by the flames.

Sighing, Rhydian rubbed Fox's back, glad that his mates couldn't see his hand. They sat in silence for a while, and when Fox didn't turn to the side to heave, Rhydian took it as a good omen. He coughed occasionally, and his body still trembled.

"Hm," Fox murmured, dropping his hands away from his face.

"How do you feel?" Rhydian murmured quietly.

"I feel," Fox said eventually, "*wrong*."

"That's to be expected," Rhydian sighed. "I assume without your... magic or whatnot, that you've never been drunk before?"

"You assume c-correctly," Fox said, as icily as he could manage. "But that's n-not it." He coughed again, and spat out something dark. Rhydian frowned, not liking the look of it. Fox was still cold and trembling, but at least he was conscious.

"I feel something else," Fox said, pushing away from Rhydian to sit up.

Hearing a note of concern in his voice, Rhydian sat up as well, keeping Fox against his side. Wyll rolled his eyes and looked away, but Davyn sat up as well. Fox was starting to shake, worse than before.

"What is it, mate?" Davyn asked, full of concern. He was fiddling with the end of his thick braid, his prior amusement gone.

"Aurelia, w-where is she?" Fox mumbled.

"Aneirin," Rhydian soothed, "waiting for us both."

"N-no," Fox coughed, his sputtering a deep, wet sound. When he wiped his mouth with the back of his hand, Rhydian stared at the blood that came away. Fox saw it too, but said nothing as he dropped his hand to his lap.

"That's not good, mate," Davyn said, his eyes meeting Rhydian's.

"No, it most certainly isn't," Rhydian muttered. "Fox? What's wrong?"

Hunching over, his arms now wrapped around his stomach, Fox groaned.

"Fox?" Alarmed now, Rhydian got up onto his knees. Blackthorn snorted from where he was tethered nearby, noting the concern in Rhydian's voice.

"J-Jessikah?" hissed Fox, his eyes shut tight, as if in pain. "Where is sh-she?"

"Jessikah is being looked after by Aurelia, in the dungeon."

"Oh," Fox opened his eyes, their glittering blackness staring past Rhydian, unseeing. "That's g-good."

Unwrapping his own cloak from his shoulders, Rhydian wrapped it around Fox. Rhydian wasn't sure if the man was still drunk, cold or experiencing some other side effect from all that he had been through.

"No, she isn't," Wyll interrupted, hesitant. He shrunk back from the three pairs of eyes that locked onto his face. "I mean, Jessikah *is* in the dungeon, but Aurelia was helping the wounded. She asked me to help with the prisoner. But I had other... chores to do. So I got more help. Aurelia knew that, she was fine with it."

"Who?" asked Rhydian. "Who else is helping?"

"Chase," Wyll answered, shifting uncomfortably. "Why?"

"Ch-chase?" Fox asked, swaying, his lips bloodless. "Who's Chase?"

"He's a fine *human* boy, unlike those..." At the look on Rhydian's face, Wyll changed tack. "He's Merion's young nephew," he finished lamely.

"Merion?" Fox asked sharply, inhaling quickly.

"He's the one who used magic to find you both," Davyn interjected.

"And Chase is his relative?" Fox asked, squinting, his brain trying to piece things together. "So Chase might have some m-magic in his blood too?"

"Yes," Rhydian said, his heart thudding uncomfortably. "Why?"

"He's a ch-child! And you left him with-"

"What's going on?" Davyn asked, his brown eyes darting between Fox and Rhydian.

"Oh fuck, no," Fox hissed, his head slumping.

"What? Fox? Shit." Rhydian cursed as Fox lurched up, trying to stand.

He couldn't. Legs collapsing beneath him, Fox had fainted again. Davyn wasn't grinning this time when he met Rhydian's gaze, who had lunged forward to catch Fox's head before he came into contact with the ground.

"I'm sorry s-sire," Davyn was muttering. "I didn't know, the wine…"

"No, it's not you, it's more than that," Rhydian hated the snap in his voice, but he couldn't help it. "Hold him," he said to Davyn and rose, gathering things from their rough camp into a pile. "We need to leave immediately."

"What about him?" Wyll asked, sitting up straight, eyeing Fox with worry. "Even you can't ride with a dead weight like that and make any kind of speed. Not through these trees."

Stopping mid-movement, Rhydian looked at Fox. His gaze rose to Blackthorn, at the tether that connected the horse's bridle to a low branch. Davyn followed the direction of Rhydian's gaze, before his eyes returned to those of his king. Davyn's eyebrows rose.

"We will be faster if we are not doubled up," Rhydian mused, his nose scrunched up. "Fox needs to ride on his own."

"Is this really the kind of man," Davyn said, giving the unconscious man in his arms a shake, "that will appreciate you tying him to his horse, sire?"

Rhydian pursed his lips.

"No," he said, calmly. He was thinking of the dread in Fox's voice on realising that Jessikah was being looked after by only Aurelia and a boy.

"But we shall do it, anyway. Let's go."

37

Fox

Year 367

The Forest

Despite being bound by rope instead of the magic-saturated chains of his past, violent and disorienting flashbacks consumed Fox's mind.

Unfortunately, his nauseous stomach thought watching the ground speed by was worse than the horrifying memories of his past, so his eyes remained closed. He had no wish to vomit on horseback. Therefore, the grim imagery played over and over within his mind, thin wrists chafed from irons, sensitive ears raw from the screams of others.

The silky neck of the horse below his cheek rippled in irritation as he exhaled slowly, his breath cold against the sweating animal. Fox's bloodless lips curled in wry amusement. Thinking about how much Rhydian's horse wanted to throw him off its back was as good a distraction as any.

Blackthorn, Fox mouthed silently, his cool lips tickling the neck against which he was slumped. The silken coat rippled again, muscles bunching. Fox wanted to laugh and scream all at once.

Don't bite me when I finally dismount.

Trust me, my bite is worse.

Fox snorted, nearly choking on the bitter reality of how untrue that was at this point in time. He could hardly breathe, never mind bite the head of a horse.

Rhydian was on another animal, leading Fox's stubborn but sturdier mount beside him. Fox was slumped forward in the saddle, his hands tied around the horse's neck to keep him sort of upright, and from falling off. He just felt so... useless. Gritting his teeth against the jarring of the fast trot they were making through the trees, Fox wondered if he had ever been sick in this form? No, he hadn't. So the present ache of his head, the dry ache in his guts, was new.

He'd been delirious once before, in Shadow Light's cave, when Owaen had carried Fox out, a rescue that had come far, far too late.

No, don't think of that.

Leave Owaen out of this current mix of fuck ups.

Deliriously, his mind wandered to Aurelia. She hadn't been sick often. But she'd been intoxicated a lot growing up. Fox had carried her back to her chambers once, when she and Bindy had drunk or smoked something far too strong for her teenage body to handle. He couldn't remember what it was. Or when it was, either. Everything just hurt too much to focus on the details.

The only thing crystal clear was that he should have taken care of all of his loose ends long before now.

Loose ends.

What a thing to call the chaos left behind by a black dragon. Shadow Light, before Fox had gifted him the current form of a tiny woman, had tortured, killed and experimented on so many innocents. And Fox hadn't simply ended it; he'd made his revenge last years, decades, even.

Fox smiled, tasting blood from biting his tongue at the pain. He welcomed the pain and the aches. He deserved all of it. More even, especially if Aurelia had been harmed.

"The end of the ridge, sire," Davyn called from the front. "I see it."

Rhydian cursed with relief. By ridge, Fox assumed Davyn meant the mountain range that spanned the valley of Aneirin, and beyond. He didn't bother opening his eyes. Fox kept them tightly shut, content to concentrate on his endless pain, his burning shame.

An unanswered questioned remained though.

Just one.

If he went through all of it once more, his captivity, his torture... would he retaliate in the same way again? He knew what *he should* have done.

But *would* he?

Despite where the consequences had led him, racing back to try to prevent more innocent lives from being taken, would he choose the same path again?

His icy hands twitched, the rope far heavier against his flesh, heavier than any regret.

The next time that Fox drifted partway to consciousness, it was because the cadence of the hooves below him had changed. Their pace had also quickened, and the sound was now more pronounced. They had left the crowded, shadowed, winding paths of the forest and were now on a dirt road.

"We've reached the farmlands, Fox," Rhydian called from beside him. "We aren't far, not much longer."

Fox didn't reply. Still slumped forward, he kept his face pressed to the sweating horse-flesh beneath his chilly skin. His back was burning with pain, but the animal's warmth was welcome because he was just so fucking cold. The flashbacks had stopped, which was welcome, he supposed. But only because his mind was working so sluggishly, it was becoming harder to think.

He was still in his right mind enough to note that his ego was having a hard time. There was more than one lesson here, besides examining past choices because of how they affected others in the present. His dry lips cracked against the sweating horse as he grimaced.

I will never take magic for granted again.

Even if it is the cause of all this shit.

The cobbled streets of Aneirin echoed with a clatter as their horses wearily made their way up the steep streets. With each switchback turn, Rhydian cursed, and Fox wouldn't have been surprised to hear him ride off with impatience.

But he didn't. Rhydian kept his horse beside Fox, and as ill as he was, Fox was grateful.

He was reasonably sure that he hadn't vomited on the horse, not once. But the pain in his chest and back from his awkward position was now excruciating. The coldness in his limbs hadn't numbed the pain; it had only made each jolt worse. His bare feet also ached, feeling like they were entombed in blocks of ice.

They passed under and through various city walls; the hooves echoing with a different timbre at each level of the terraced city they climbed. Fox remained unaware of the identities of the city folk as they passed until they eventually reached a standstill. Voices rang out, and torches flickered behind his eyelids, which meant it was late. He didn't know how late. Amongst the bitter smoke of the torches was the sour tang of stale blood. His eyes dry and irritated, stung as he swallowed back a sneeze.

"We're here," Rhydian murmured, his boots landing on the cobbles near where Fox was still tied around the neck of Blackthorn. Boot heels clicked closer and warm hands fumbled at the rope on Fox's wrists. Fox hissed and was unable to help his jerk at the sudden pain.

"I'm sorry Fox, I'm sorry," Rhydian was mumbling, trying to get the ropes unbound. Humiliated, Fox made no reply, and kept his eyes tightly closed until the last of the ropes came free. His hands started to tingle immediately, and he bit back another hiss of discomfort, hating to be seen like this.

Rhydian's sharp intake of breath told Fox that he had noticed what it cost Fox to stay silent, but thankfully Rhydian said nothing. He simply reached out, and with Davyn's help, Fox slid off the trembling and sweating horse.

"Here, what's happened, sire?" a new voice rang out, deep and shocked. Fox couldn't see the man; his eyes were still shut, avoiding the black spots in his vision.

"Oh shit," Rhydian gasped as he took Fox's weight with an arm wrapped around Fox's shoulders. "Merion, have you seen Aurelia?"

"No, sire, not today." The man's deep voice grew worried. "Why, what's happened-"

"Um, I'll fill you in later," Rhydian hesitated. "Don't follow us, please just see to the horses for now."

Fox bit his tongue as the living agony that was his shivering body was jostled up the castle steps, and into the cool shadows of the great hall. Voices were murmuring nearby, but the silence that struck quickly was like a soft wave of peace spreading out from the doorway in which they paused. Fox cracked a gummy eye open. Elves and humans alike were bedded alongside each other, all bandaged in some form or another. It was orderly and efficient. Aurelia had likely had a hand in it. He could smell the blood here, stale, neatly bound under clean linens.

"I'm back!" Rhydian called to those closest to the entryway. "Where's Aurelia?"

A flurry of voices called out to each other. Someone cleared his throat.

"Not seen for days, sire. We wondered if she'd gone after you."

"What? Fuck," Rhydian hissed. "And Chase?"

No one had seen Chase.

"Oh shit," Wyll cursed nearby. Fox's lips curled at the bitter odour coming from the man. Fear, along with something else.

"The dragon?" Davyn called, sounding hopeful.

Definitely no one had seen the dragon.

"Keep going," Rhydian ordered, puffing as he pulled Fox with him. "The dungeons."

With Fox dragging his bare feet between Davyn and Rhydian, they rushed from the hall. Startled voices picked up behind them, and a guard or two cheered when finally realising their young king had returned. Rhydian ignored them all. Fox was dragged to the left, along a corridor. The noises dropped away behind. With another turn, an eerie calmness descended upon them, leaving everything silent.

Fox cracked open a dry eye. Flickering torches lit the plain stone walls, but the black archway at the end of the wide hallway was dark.

"I told them to leave Jessikah with light," Rhydian muttered, his pace slowing.

Fox hissed, a low wisp of sound.

"What is it?" Wyll called, trailing behind them.

"Blood," Fox ground out. "A lot of it. Old."

Davyn groaned beside him, the man's sweat turning from musky to sour.

Reluctantly, Fox finally opened both eyes. They had stopped at the black void of the archway, a series of steps disappeared down into shadows.

Rhydian cursed, pulling away from Fox, clearly intending to step down first. Fox coughed, grabbing uselessly at Rhydian's hand.

"Wait," Fox rasped. Rhydian cursed, but Fox held his hand tight. "W-wait, please."

He planted his bare feet on the white marble floor and took a few breaths to steady himself. The trickle of magic Fox gathered from somewhere deep felt like he was cracking open his ribs, but he didn't care. After a moment of nothing, eventually the torches lining the bottom of the stairs flared to life.

As the light spread out, Fox could see a doorway to the left of them, close to the top of the stairs, smelling like stale air and old deaths. Not like the fresh one down the stairs somewhere.

"Rhydian, let m-me go," Fox gasped, "D-don't, it's bad…"

Wyll, unable to control himself after Fox's warning, forcefully pushed past the others. He took the steps two at a time, risking a broken neck. He reached the bottom, sprinting around the corner to his right before Rhydian and Davyn had dragged Fox a third of the way down.

Wyll's wail of anguish reached them while they were only halfway down.

"Fuck, fuck, fuck," Davyn chanted, his breathing fast.

Rhydian was silent, but Fox could feel the thrum of his tension. They reached the base of the stairs and dragged Fox around the corner. As one, the three of them stopped, staring at the far end of the corridor.

Wyll was on his knees outside the last cell on the right. His head was down, hands over his face. The man was sobbing, mumbling. Fox frowned, making out some of the words, not understanding their meaning.

Davyn let go of Fox, making his unsteady way down the corridor alone, hands over his face. Rhydian, breathing rapidly, dragged Fox the rest of the way by himself, knowing there was no point in hurrying. They were far too late. As they made it to the end of the corridor, Fox saw just how late they were.

Rhydian's hold on him went slack, and Fox hit the ground hard. He didn't care. With the side of his face pressed to the stone floor, Fox's gaze was on the back wall of the cell. Davyn stepped straight into the small dark chamber, past Wyll, and stood there silently. The man was breathing heavily, his hands clenching and unclenching by his sides.

Beside him, Rhydian collapsed to his knees, turning away, retching, one hand on the icy wall to support himself.

Fox blinked, his eyes no longer dry.

"I'm sorry," he whispered.

But his words weren't enough. They never would be.

The small cell was sideways from his position on the floor. But Fox could see the macabre spectacle within well enough. The body of a young boy, maybe ten or eleven winters old, was hung up on the wall by something. The boy had clearly been there for days. There was nothing peaceful about his grisly end.

No one had known where the boy was, because Jessikah had been a secret.

Fox's shameful, and *dangerous*, secret.

"This is my fault," Fox whispered, his body numb, his heart shattered.

Wyll, on his knees beside him, turned around, one hand on the hilt of his short sword on his belt.

"Your fault? You filthy Elf," Wyll spat the words, his eyes wide and full of shock. "You black-hearted, magic using-"

"Wyll," Rhydian cut in, staggering into Fox's line of sight. "Stop and go, now. *Quickly.*"

Wyll's sullen gaze snapped to Rhydian. "But he-"

"Merion!" Rhydian snapped, wiping his chin with his sleeve, his eyes bloodshot. He turned his back to the cell, listening to the sound of boots, most likely guards summoned by Wyll's wail of grief, coming down the stairs. "I am ordering you to *go*. Make sure Merion doesn't come down here. Go, *now*."

Fox watched from the floor, limp, as Wyll pushed himself up off the ground. He spared the days old corpse a quick glance, his face grey. He turned back to Fox and spat noisily on the floor. Rhydian didn't notice, his gaze was on the grisly sight. Wyll stormed off.

Fox noted with confusion that Wyll's pants were different colours. The back was different from the front. The blood, he realised. It was dry, but it had still stained Wyll's clothes where he had knelt in it. There was a lot of it, after all; it was likely there was none left in the body. The boy's slit wrists and open wound in his belly had seen to that. Fox hoped the lad had been dead this time. It hadn't always happened like that in the cave of his nightmares.

Davyn still hadn't moved. Rhydian had stepped forward, and carefully took something off the body, from around its neck. Fox blinked, too weary to move. It took him a moment to place what the object was. As Rhydian sobbed once, Fox realised it was Aurelia's gold chain, by the garnet swinging brightly in the flickering light.

"This is my f-fault," Fox whispered again. He made himself stare at what was left of the boy. "Aurelia, I'm sorry. Chase, I'm s-sorry."

Reaching out a trembling hand, Fox touched his fingertip to the edge of the dried puddle of the boy's blood. The cold, flaking blood froze immediately. Fox stared, fascinated, as the frost crept along the dark brown stain.

This *was* his fault. Chase, an innocent boy, was dead.

His greatest weakness, his enemy, bound in what Fox thought was an impenetrable lock, was gone.

Aurelia was gone. The garnet chain left behind was clearly a message for Fox.

Come get me, if you wish to trade.

Give me back what you took from me, in exchange for what I stole from you.

"The d-dagger," Fox croaked suddenly, the cold from the floor seeping up into his already tortured bones. "Where?"

"Fuck the fucking dagger," Rhydian hissed, whirling to face Fox, the garnet clasped in his hand. "Fuck this fucking woman! And fuck you too!" Rhydian was shouting now, his eyes wild, no longer innocent shades of blue.

"Rhydian, p-please, the dagger-"

Rhydian didn't hear him. He walked right up to Fox and crouched down. Fox shut his eyes, but could still hear the frozen blood shatter under Rhydian's boots.

"The fucking dagger is in my room!" Rhydian shouted so loudly that Fox's eyes cracked open of their own accord. "But Aurelia isn't up there, is she? She's bloody fucking gone too," Rhydian shook the chain, dangling the garnet in front of Fox's face. "And for what? For the sake of *what*?" He was screaming now, spittle flying.

Davyn had backed out of the cell, his hands clasped on his forehead.

"Sire, p-please-"

"No!" Rhydian shouted, standing up, hands on either side of his face. "No! Don't call me that! I can't do this!" He had backed up to the far wall of the corridor, flinging the chain to the ground. A small noise escaped Fox's mouth as the garnet bounced instead of smashing. It was all Fox could do to stretch out and grasp it as guards came running down the hall.

By the time the group reached Rhydian, he was screaming and clawing at his chest. A guard, an older man who was clearly distressed, tried to pull Rhydian's hands away. Like a cornered animal lost to pain, Rhydian swung wildly, punching the man in his jaw. The man dropped like a sack of grain. Rhydian lurched forward like he intended to plough through the rest of them, but three others jumped on him while he thrashed and kicked and cursed. The melee rolled onto Fox, and he curled himself into a ball, the garnet chain against his aching chest.

Davyn was shouting, "I'm sorry lad, I'm sorry, we'll find her, we'll catch them, hold him down, easy, lads, easy-"

Fox wasn't sure how long they fought to calm Rhydian down. Someone's elbow or fist connected with his face, and the last thing he heard was someone calling for chains for the king.

The morning light through the window was as beautiful as any morning. The sky behind it was blue, clear, and mockingly sweet. Fox hated it.

From the bed, Fox stared at the glass, and the crude star shape scrawled upon it. A simple enough shape was outlined on the glass pane in a dirty crimson. He stared numbly for a long time, listening to the air wheeze in his lungs. Something was definitely broken deep within his chest and not healing. He ignored it.

Fox hadn't been inside the castle of Aneirin before, but he knew the chamber he was in was high up. The tops of the mountains that surrounded the valley were visible in the window, a rusty red like the taunting star on the glass.

Shifting painfully, Fox couldn't help his groan of discomfort. Someone had washed him while he was unconscious. He didn't know whom. He would never ask. There was no point, he didn't want to know if he'd lashed out and caused another innocent bystander any harm. But he still felt caked with filth. Whoever had washed him had also dressed him in a soft, white shirt. That had surprised him, so used to black as he was.

He had held up a shaking hand, tracing the star from across the room. It was the exact shape of the wall that surrounded the City of the Seers. Instead of giant blocks of stone like the real thing, this was made of blood.

Sighing, his breath rattling, Fox wondered if it was Chase's or Aurelia's.

Fox grimaced as he adjusted his neck. There seemed to be about ten layers of fur piled over him. But he was still very, very cold. He ignored that, too. His mind was less fogged today; maybe his body had finally rid itself of the fucking wine that Davyn had given him. Unfortunately, his magic was practically non-existent. The deep, icy well that it bubbled from was simply a black hole somewhere behind his numb heart.

Fox licked his dry lips and dropped his gaze from the window.

Across the chamber, Rhydian was sitting dejectedly on the floor beside the fireplace, his legs sprawled out before him. The young man was dressed in the same clothes as the night before, head resting back against the wall, his eyes closed. Rhydian's wrists were locked in iron cuffs, resting in his lap. The cuffs, in turn, were chained to the iron grate of the fireplace.

"Rhydian," Fox croaked, his mouth gritty. "I know you're awake."

Rhydian swallowed a few times. When he spoke, his voice sounded as hoarse as Fox's.

"I'd prefer not to be."

Rhydian finally opened his eyes, the different blues of his eyes reddened, swollen. It took a long time for his gaze to reach Fox. When he did, the young king winced at what he saw.

"That b-bad, huh?" Fox hummed, moving gingerly to unfold his arm from his cocoon. He touched his own swollen eye with an unsteady hand.

"Fox, I-"

"Don't be s-sorry. It was an accident. You were understandably n-not yourself, Rhydian."

"It wasn't, though."

Rhydian's gaze was cool. His right hand twitched, and Fox was strangely pleased to see bruises across the young man's swollen knuckles.

"Ah," Fox said. "I see." He smiled faintly, his first in days. "I'm g-glad it was you."

"Me too," said Rhydian, and burst into tears.

Fox waited for a long time. He didn't look away.

"The d-dagger?" Fox murmured eventually, swallowing past the tightness in his throat.

"Gone," Rhydian breathed, his face red and blotchy.

"Aurelia?"

"Gone," this said quietly, barely a sigh.

"The key?" Fox asked next, and Rhydian looked up, confused.

Sitting up, masking his groan of pain, Fox slid sideways across off the bed, feeling as old as his years for the first time in forever. Dragging some of the furs with him, he stumbled upright, gasping with each new shift his body had to make. When he was upright, Fox looked pointedly at Rhydian's hands.

In turn, Rhydian jerked his chin at a table just beyond his reach.

"Behave?" Fox said archly, attempting to lighten the infinitely shitty situation. It didn't work. Rhydian, avoiding his gaze, shrugged. The young man's eyes were ready to spill once more.

It took a long time, but Fox shuffled his way to the table, still covered in layers of fur. If he fell, they were fucked until someone came to check on them. Fox almost smiled again. That would be a sight.

After grabbing the key, Fox shuffled carefully to Rhydian, and dropped the key in his lap. Fox's bones cracked as he tried to fold himself down on to his knees. His lips were so dry that his scowl of pain cracked them open in at least three places. Ignoring the way his body was screaming at the need for water, he sank down to the floor. Rhydian hadn't moved, hadn't reached for the key.

Neither of them could be bothered to make a joke as Fox's trembling hand retrieved the key from Rhydian's lap.

When Fox's weak hands finally got the key in and the cuffs open, Rhydian still didn't move. His blue eyes were dull. He was ignoring Fox, his cheek on the wall so he could stare at the window. The window was large enough that Rhydian could surely see the star from his position on the floor.

"I'll get her back," Fox said, licking the blood off his lips.

A muscle in Rhydian's jaw twitched. He kept his gaze on the on the window.

"What is that?" Rhydian asked eventually, his voice hoarse.

"The City of the Seers," Fox answered, his voice just about gone. "That's where he's taken her."

"He?"

"Jessikah, I mean," Fox said tightly. The words cost him, the strain of holding in his fear and his rage. The strain made him cough, and at the effort he could feel something tear free inside his lungs. He ignored that, too.

"I don't understand any of this," Rhydian said, blinking. Two shining trails leaked down his cheeks.

Fox turned his face to the side, trying to spit out the fresh blood without Rhydian seeing. His faint smile was more of a wry twist of his cracked lip. At least his mouth wasn't as dry.

"I know you don't understand, but I do," Fox said. Slowly, Fox reached out to wipe Rhydian's cheeks with a one of his blankets. "He's not going to hurt Aurelia, not if he wants to bargain."

Rhydian's eyes closed at the touch. "Bargain for what?" he whispered.

"Something that only I can give b-back. Something that he wants desperately."

Fox sat back, unsure of how much more of his past he needed to explain. Feeling the need for space, he tried to stand. He failed.

Fox's hoarse shout of surprise as he tripped over his own feet had Rhydian's eyes snapping back open. Lucky for Fox, Rhydian caught him, half rising from the floor. Rhydian's expression was one of disbelief.

"You are a fucking idiot if you think you are in any position to help her!" Rhydian yelled suddenly. "This is the person who held you prisoner, wasn't it? What are you going to do? Cough up a lung on them?"

"I d-did not cough up a-"

"I saw you spit that crap out on my floor just now-"

"This is your ch-chamber?"

Fox's hoarsely amused voice cut through Rhydian's diatribe, as Rhydian dragged the bundle of furs, complete with the limp Fox rolled inside, back to the bed.

"Yes," Rhydian hissed, tumbling Fox onto the mattress. "Why?"

"Aurelia will l-laugh so hard at this," Fox mumbled, trying to find an opening in the ball of furs to get some air into his tortured lungs. "She'll l-love this."

"Will she? Really? You're saying we'll find her, and she'll laugh at this?"

Fox nodded, finally finding enough of a gap between the layers of fur and blankets to breathe.

"Yes. Believe it, or n-not, Aurelia is in no immediate danger."

Sounding exasperated, Rhydian settled down on the bed beside him. "You're really sick, aren't you? Fuck. You're not thinking straight."

"I'm fine," Fox said, coughing again, ice running through his veins. "Mostly f-fine. I'm sorry about... Chase... I'm so s-sorry. But I'll fix this."

Rhydian pulled Fox against his chest.

"You fucked up, Fox, with this, with Jessikah, with Shadow Light."

"I k-know." Fox was glad of the warm arms around him that his sigh of relief was almost embarrassing.

"You were wrong, not to just... end it."

"I know," Fox hissed, eyes shut against the truth of his failures to protect those that should be protected. "Shut up and let m-me think." He was shaking hard. Rhydian hugged him tighter.

"Aurelia might not feel safe," Fox said, haltingly. "But she is, for n-now. It's the only thing left her abductor has that I will bargain for."

Rhydian sniffed, his head shifting above Fox's.

"So Jessikah is a magic user?"

"Yes, sort of." Fox didn't want to elaborate, but explained what he could. "Jessikah might have been able to... take some s-spark out of... Chase, to help in the escape with Aurelia. I took it, Shadow's magic. I know he wants it back."

"For Aurelia's life?"

"Yes."

"And you can do that?"

Not right now and not easily. Fox inhaled, ice eating away at his insides.

"Yes."

"So you took Jessikah's magic?"

"Yes."

"And Jessikah is the... person who held you captive, right?"

"Yes. Sh-shadow Light." Just saying it was like peeling back a wound near healed, to expose all the sinewy and pussy workings of a sick body within.

"Shadow Light, Jessikah, stole it from the Elves? Like my parents? With the dragon they killed?"

Fox tried to ask him to elaborate, but his croak of surprise left him choking. The force of his coughing had him spraying fresh blood over his chest, and Rhydian's too. Fox tried to make a joke out of it, horrified as he was, but couldn't.

He couldn't get the air in to breathe.

Sensing Fox gasping for air, Rhydian rolled Fox onto his side, pulling furs away and thumping his back.

"You're dying," Rhydian cried out.

The reality of his words was so dark, so serious and so inappropriately hilarious to Fox, that he managed to gasp in a desperate mouthful of air.

After a long while, he could finally talk.

"I know," Fox said, calmly.

Rhydian held him tighter, as if trying to hug the ice away.

"But not just yet, kingling." Fox smiled faintly as Rhydian's warmth seeped into his broken body. He raised his gaze, eyeing the bloody star on the window.

"Not just yet."

38

Flare

Year 367

City of the Seers

"Stop it, *please*," the dragon begged.

"Stop what, my spiky amethyst jewel?"

Trying to keep his wings spread evenly, Flare dipped around a group of dark green pine trees so impossibly tall that they towered over the rest of the forest below. Caspian had only been wedged between Flare's spikes for less than an hour, but was already amusing himself at Flare's expense.

Flare's hind legs brushed the tops of another line of trees. They weren't as tall as the soaring pines behind them, but the irritating tingle in one of his neck spikes had him lose his concentration enough that his wings twitched. Flare dipped through a cooler thermal, and the thrilled laugh from his back was almost as annoying as whatever Caspian was doing to his spike.

"I can't concentrate," Flare mumbled.

Another laugh and the scent of something acrid, like hot minerals, tingled in Flare's nostrils. Considering they were moving, the scent of whatever Caspian was doing was dropping behind them in the cool air. Another tingle had his spikes twitching, almost like Caspian was-

"Caspian!" Flare exclaimed, too scared to look behind. "Are you trying to set m-me on *fire*?"

The pleased chuckle caused Flare to jerk involuntarily as revulsion rippled along his scales.

"Took you long enough," Caspian sang out. "Not as sensitive as you used to be, are you, hmmm?"

Too shocked to answer, Flare flew higher into the sky, his wings beating as hard as his heart. Thankfully, the tingling ceased. He should never, *ever*, have made acquaintances with this man.

Not even for the sake of getting to know Hypatia and Illarion, where your magical journey began?

The thought was so shocking and sudden that Caspian called out, sensing Flare's tension in the set of muscles under his purple scales.

"What's wrong, baby?" Caspian crooned over the sound of Flare's wings.

"Nothing, I... nothing."

"I don't believe you," Caspian sung out. "Tell me where it hurts. Come on."

Hoping Caspian would let it drop, Flare glanced to his right, towards the north. This high up, he could see the mountain range that was the foothills for the dragon's old homeland, Mionlach. The morning sun was at just the right angle to both paint the normally black, jagged mountain tops with gold, whilst also lighting the underside of a thin line of clouds. Flare squinted. It wasn't a normal layer of clouds, though, was it? It was a layer of ash. Flare flicked out his tongue, his nostrils working as he realised with dread where it was from.

So much had gone wrong, so much chaos. But the riddle of what had come to the other dragons after the fall of the City of Seers still eluded him.

Because you are too afraid to go see for yourself.

Yes, Flare admitted to the tiny voice that spoke from his frightened self, *yes I am.*

Caspian shifted his legs around Flare's back, and Flare had to fight the urge to buck the man off of him. Flare had no idea if Caspian would survive, but the risk was too great. Caspian was too unpredictable, far too wild. Caspian had said that his wings were buried too deep. But Flare suspected that if he threw Caspian off his back, the man would no doubt cast some kind of net, a violent web of sticky magic, which would pull Flare down from the skies after him. Not out of anything more than spite.

What had Caspian said, lifetimes ago?

If I burn, you burn too, serpent.

Flare blinked with a longing that cut through him like a sharp blade, still looking to his right at the north while he headed northwest, thinking of all the things he had left behind to get where he was, to be what he was. Was it worth it? It really didn't seem worth it now, magic. Power, the adoration of others. He'd had that once, the simple love and respect of his family. But he had given it up, willingly, for this: for the sky, for wings, for magic. But to think that none had been affected adversely by his rise into magic would be a lie.

He adjusted his height once more, his gaze fixated on the winding path of a wide river cutting through the vast expanse of the forest. This waterway had a road alongside it, and Flare moaned with quiet dread, realising where the road would lead them.

To the City of the Seers.

Caspian hadn't said where they were going, or why, only to head in this direction. Perhaps a part of Flare had known where they were going... suspected and dreaded. The road below was a thin brown line, an arrow of confirmation, pointing their way back to a city ruined by dragonkind.

A thoughtful hum sounded behind him, loudly. Flare shut his eyes for a moment, knowing that anything could drop from those finely shaped lips.

"A lucky escape," Caspian sang out.

"What?" Flare opened his eyes, blinking at the horizon. Whatever Caspian could have said, Flare wasn't expecting that.

"Mionlach," Caspian clarified. "You know it was our sparkling queen who did it, don't you?"

"I-" Flare inhaled sharply, the image of Fox's tattoo clear in his mind.

That would make sense of it, all the layers of dragons, overthrown, defeated, and dying. He didn't know if that made it easier to understand Fox, or worse. Certainly the... man... had been through something directly related to Shadow Light's insanity at the City of the Seers. But Flare had fled to safety afterwards, not heeding the call to help their most precious jewel.

Another sin, another creature in his care, left behind.

For this.

For magic.

Was it worth it?

He didn't know.

A warm hand patted the scales at the base of his neck.

"There, there," Caspian soothed, his voice gentle. "I know it's a shock. I would have done the same if I were her." A mad laugh danced over the sound of the wind. "Except for the fact that Shadow was only doing what I told him to. Pity he fucked it up."

What?

There was too much to unpack from a statement like that, so Flare asked the most important question he had for now.

"Did Skye really... kill them all?" Flare hated the catch in his voice.

"Kill?" Caspian scoffed. "Whatever do you mean, precious one? The dragons aren't *dead*."

Shocked, Flare's wings faltered for a moment. He didn't know what to say.

But the tattoo-

"Whatever gave you that idea?" Caspian called, sounding smug. "They're certainly no longer part of this fine world. They've been... left behind, like so many of us," this last was said on a bitter exhalation of breath. Caspian muttered something else, but it was too quiet for Flare to hear over the wind. He could barely make out the words, sounding like bloodlines and family loyalties.

Thinking about Caspian's family added another layer of fear to Flare's already mounting anxiety. Before he could judge the wisdom of asking such a thing, he blurted his question out in a rush.

"What happened to Owaen?"

The mumbling stopped abruptly. A very, very long silence followed.

Oh dear.

Flare opened his mouth to apologise, but Caspian finally deigned to reply by asking a question of his own.

"Why does everyone care for him?" Caspian muttered, his voice dangerously low.

"I'm sorry, I-"

"Fuck off, Flare, don't lie to me."

Another pause. The strong legs adjusted themselves on Flare's back and he bit his tongue, expecting one or more of his spikes to start tingling again. The sensation didn't come. Which was almost worse.

"He's out of my reach," Caspian sighed eventually, tapping the heels of his boots against Flare's sides. "Locked *tightly* away."

"What do you mean?"

"I tried to get to him. Mmm, not very hard though," Caspian admitted, sounding sheepish. "I had a *lot* of things to say to that brute-"

Caspian's words cut off mid sentence, and the tapping of his boots ceased.

"Caspian?"

No answer.

"Caspian?"

No answer, just the sound of the man-

Flare narrowed his eyes, as if somehow that would help his ear holes try to determine what the madman on his back was doing. Flare dipped lower, trying to avoid the loudest gusts of the wind.

It sounded like the man was sniffing?

"Oh, my gods," Caspian finally purred, "no *way*."

Flare's own nostrils twitched, only just now scenting what Caspian had detected. Which meant Flare was right in his caution. Caspian might have claimed his wings were buried far too deep. But the man was certainly full of more power than Flare, if Caspian's senses had detected that aroma before Flare had.

Excitedly, Caspian called out. "Can you smell that? Can you taste that?"

Flare nodded, sensing more than one aroma on the breeze. There were two. Both were oddly familiar. Both wrapped in magic, strange that it was out in the middle of nowhere.

"Yes," Flare mumbled, "I-"

"Go back!"

Dreading the glee in Caspian's tone, Flare twisted his neck painfully to look behind him. Caspian, his blonde hair a wild mane in the breeze, his brilliant purple cloak flapping, was looking over Flare's side down at the road behind them. As Flare's nose sorted through the complex scents, he caught sight of figures on the road. The faint scent of something floral filled his nose.

No.

No!

"I said go back right this instant, Flare!"

Caspian's voice was so full of violence that Flare whimpered.

"Please, Caspian," Flare whispered. "No-"

A sharp, hot pain burst into life on Flare's tallest neck spike, followed quickly by a cold sensation at the tip. Looking down, Flare whimpered again, catching sight of a glittering object. It looked like a dark purple crystal falling away from them.

It was the tip of one of his shining purple spikes, dropping into the trees below.

Flare sobbed in shock. And then slowly circled back around.

There was barely enough room to land and when his claws touched the ground; it was half on the road, half in the river. Flare hung his head, aware that the sensation of being half in the rushing water and half dry was exactly how his heart felt. Torn between what was right, getting the hells away from this madman, or staying out of fear. He closed his eyes, unable to face the two riders; one gagged and bound, her deep green eyes full of hope, the other with yellow eyes just about bugging out of her head.

Sliding off Flare's back, Caspian called out.

"Holy fuck Shadow. Is that you?"

Flare raised his head, avoiding Aurelia's gaze, instead watching Caspian standing in the road, his hands on his hips.

Jessikah, fury overriding her shock, slid off her horse. With short, efficient strides, she stormed towards Caspian. He bowed, the purple cloak swirling. Jessikah was not amused.

When he rose, Jessikah slapped him across the face.

That simple action confirmed one of his suspicions. Fox had been keeping Jessikah close by him all these years. But they were really other creatures, weren't they?

Fox was their missing emerald gold dragon, betrayed by most of dragonkind. One in particular, Shadow Light, who had somehow been transformed into the body of a petite woman. Flare had no idea of the details, but Fox was obviously responsible. The venom in Fox's treatment to Jessikah meant that something dark had happened long after the City of the Seers had fallen.

Flare cringed, waiting for Caspian to retaliate against the slap. A red mark was blooming across his cheek.

Instead of a violent eruption, Caspian threw back his head, laughing like he'd been told the most hilarious joke in the world. He was trying to speak, but he couldn't. He bent over at the waist, guffawing, one hand on his thigh, the other held up as if to say, *wait, I'm nearly done.*

Aurelia was still on her horse. She was bound and gagged so tightly that her cheeks would likely bruise, and was watching Flare with wide eyes. Flare turned away, unable to stand the confusion in her gaze. She wouldn't understand that two of the darkest creatures either of them would ever know stood face to face. Caspian was wiping his eyes, getting his hysteria out of his system. Jessikah stood by with narrowed eyes, full of rage, her slim arms crossed over her chest. Her lips thinned. Whatever she had been able to conjure for her escape, restoring her voice hadn't been a part of it.

Good grief.

To think that arrogant beast had been so close to Flare, all these years?

His scales rippled with shock, apprehension, and more than a little fear.

Flare examined Jessikah with a morbid fascination, now that he knew who she really was. She was tiny, thin and her yellow hair was wild and mussed like she'd spent days on horseback, fleeing Aneirin. She was dressed in a simple tunic with pants underneath, her boots scuffed. Her expression was flinty. She shook her head at Flare when she noticed him examine her. He quickly looked away.

His gaze met Aurelia's once more, and she held up her hands, moaning something through the gag. Flare caught the name *Chase*.

His eyes widened, and he could smell blood on her plain dark clothes that were too big for her, likely Rhydian's. Flare smelled the same on Jessikah, but had dismissed it, too worried about how Caspian would be received.

Aurelia struggled some more, so much so that she slid off her horse without using her hands. She landed with a painful sounding thud. Caspian stood up straight at that, his metallic gaze finally landing on Aurelia. He said nothing. The blonde man just watched, eyes flashing with curiosity.

Making a mad dash, Aurelia ran at Flare, eyes wide, screaming through the fabric wadded and bound to her mouth. She was trying to dislodge it with her bound hands, which were bound in turn to her belt.

"Jessikah... Chase... killed..."

Whirling, Jessikah slashed out a hand, and Aurelia tripped over, falling painfully to the road once more. It was a pitiful sight, her dirty face full of anger and grief, and her long dark hair a mess and full of what looked like dried blood on one side.

Flare glanced at Jessikah, who returned his stare coolly.

So Jessikah, Shadow, had broken free of some of the magical threads that bound her, *him*, to Fox?

Swallowing the acidic bile threatening to rise in his throat, Flare realised the boy, Chase... that sweet, innocent boy, had likely had some spark in his blood. Just enough to be the key, which opened a very tricky lock. Jessikah had likely been waiting for such an opportunity. But why had she taken Aurelia?

Flare's guilty gaze dropped to stare at Aurelia, who was on her knees, trembling likely not with fear, but fury. Her desperate green eyes were fixed on his face, waiting for his help.

He ruffled his wings.

And did nothing.

Aurelia's eyes widened. Flare made himself watch, seeing the shock and confusion fade to something darker.

Understanding.

Anger.

Betrayal.

Blinking rapidly, Flare finally looked away, his claws digging into the cold water on one side of him, rough, unkempt dirt road on the other. The trees around them provided a lot of shade, but the dappled light was enough that before he looked away, the flint in Aurelia's expression was a shard of crystal to his heart.

Jessikah, staring at Caspian now, pointed to her own lips impatiently, as if to say, *well*?

Watching with a bemused expression, Caspian ignored the obvious demand.

He brushed off a speck of dirt from the shoulder of his cloak and adjusted his leather satchel against his hip. He was grinning like the wicked, handsome prince of magic that he was, his teeth white and his malevolent eyes sparkling. One finely shaped hand came to rest on the elaborate sword hilt at his side.

He sighed, obviously pleased with this new development.

"Shadow Light," Caspian crooned, "I just *love* what you've done with your hair."

39

Rhydian

Year 367

Aneirin Castle

You coward.

Rhydian's eyes opened, his father's words ringing in his ears.

You knew.

Sitting up in bed, he glanced around; it was still dark. The last few embers in the fireplace glowed a dull orange, and the soft glow with only a few weak flames was the only illumination in the silent chamber.

Throwing off some of Fox's blankets that had fallen across his leg, Rhydian dragged his hands through his hair, trying to ignore the irregular beat of his heart. One of his hands touched his chest, fingers tracing the two pendants he now wore under his shirt. One was the garnet that had been left like a challenge around Chase's icy neck. The other was the strange green shard that he had taken off Aurelia himself, seemingly ages ago, when they had come together in shared intimacy. There was no comfort in touching them now, however. His father's voice echoed through his mind.

You knew what we did.

Licking his dry lips, Rhydian hung his head. His grief was mixed with anger, feeling like a dull ache in his guts. But his father's words were likely true. Why waste your dying words on a lie? And along with the words that had been full of disappointment, Rhydian had been left with a bloody arrow in his hands.

Rhydian stared at them, barely visible in the low light. They were clean, but they would forever feel like they were coated with his father's blood. If *he* died right now, what would *his* last words be? Biting his bottom lip between his teeth, Rhydian didn't have to think about it long.

Aurelia, I love you.

Hold on.

Before the battle, he had returned the black arrow to her in a wordless plea for help. Asking her to end the dark legacy of a king who'd held his people under an oppressive cloak of magic for years. Rhydian had been well aware that he couldn't do it by himself.

So was he a coward then?

Undoubtedly so.

But if you died with no last words, what were those that were left behind to think? That you died easy, with no regrets? Or would it mean that you'd die in pain and full of fear? Rhydian's hands clenched, tucking away the shame of his father's admission deep within his heart. He had to keep going. He would deal with them, with what it meant about himself, but just not yet. Now was about finding Aurelia, and taking care of that strange creature that had stolen her away from him.

Rhydian felt rather than saw a tear land on his tightly furled hands.

Chase, I'm so sorry.

Merion's wail of grief was still a haunting echo from hours ago. Rhydian had heard the groom's cry from his bed, as he had held the shivering Fox in his arms. The pain of Merion's wordless cry was close to the terror that Rhydian had been biting back. How was he going to get all of them through this? Because he had to, didn't he? After all, he was the king.

Wasn't he?

In the dark chamber, his sharp intake of breath was loud. Behind his closed eyes, his father bled into the land of their people. Was this why his father had been a cold and distant man? Was the weight of a crown too heavy for a gentle heart and mind? Aware of his own limitations, Rhydian lips curled in a wry smile, tasting salt water on his lips.

"If so," Rhydian whispered, "we're fucked."

Dragging his gaze down to the bundle of furs by his side, Rhydian sighed. He clutched the garnet against his heart. Flare was missing, Aurelia was taken, the dagger was gone, Chase-

Chase was *dead*. And the one person who *should* have been able to help was a mess. Fox had come back to take care of things, but something hadn't gone to plan, when he had come back from wherever he had been.

"You need to fucking fix this, Fox," Rhydian mumbled, dropping the garnet to poke the blankets. He frowned, pressing harder. There was no shivering body within.

"Fox!" Rhydian cried out, rolling to his knees and clawing at the pile. "Oh fuck no, fuck... Fox!"

Rhydian sat back on his heels, breathing rapidly. He had to-

An indrawn breath rattled from across the chamber.

"Miss m-me, kingling?" a hoarse voice rasped. "I'm t-touched."

Rhydian's head jerked up. There was a figure perched on the windowsill.

"You stupid fuck!" Rhydian yelled. "Fuck! I thought that you were gone. Shit. *Shit*!"

With a hand over his racing heart, eyes closed, Rhydian was willing himself to calm down. A laugh that morphed into a wet cough accompanied his heaving breaths.

"You're so s-sweet."

Cursing, Rhydian opened his eyes. He slid off the bed, dragging a blanket across the floor, stomping over to the window.

"No," Rhydian snapped, throwing the blanket around Fox's shoulders with a grumpy tug. "I didn't miss you at *all*."

Fox had somehow managed to drag himself from the bed to the window still. It was dark outside, but his face was lit faintly by the last of the starlight before the dawn. He was still dressed in Rhydian's white shirt and thin wool pants. His feet were bare. Rhydian bit back his pang of guilt at having forgotten to find socks. *Socks for Fox!* He wanted to laugh at the stupid rhyme, laugh until he cried.

"You've got it wrong," Rhydian said, ignoring Fox's smug expression. "I need you to get Aurelia back safely, before you die of fucking dragon flu."

With a low snort, Fox raised his head from where his cheek was pressed against the glass, centimetres from the bloody star scrawled on the glass. Fox's cool breath was turning the red stain into rust coloured frost.

"That's cold of you," Fox rasped, blinking at Rhydian, his eyes glittering like gold flakes in black oil. "I'm *h-hurt*."

"You're useless, that's what you are," Rhydian hissed, hating the fear in his voice. His heart was still beating like a drum, and under Fox's appraising gaze, Rhydian could feel his cheeks turn pink. But if he also lost Fox now, what would happen? What could he do? Confused and sickened with fear, Rhydian turned and crossed to the fireplace, his socked feet quiet on the cold floor.

Coward.

Rhydian swallowed, throwing more kindling and small logs of wood over the embers. As he watched the fresh wood catch, he realised that he had no idea what he'd have done if Fox was gone for good this time. Even with Fox as sick as he was, it was better that Fox was here. But if Fox was gone?

Padding back to the window, with a sigh, Rhydian braced his hands against the sill next to Fox's leg. Keeping his head down, away from Fox's stare, Rhydian examined the grit of the stone windowsill beneath his hands. The grains and the stone gradually became clearer as the warm glow from the fireplace increased. It was hard to think straight. Trying not to let his nausea rise, he dropped his head, pressed his face into his trembling hands.

"I'm useless too," Rhydian said quietly. "Both of us are."

"I'm not-" Fox's wet cough ripped through his words.

"We need help," Rhydian mumbled, his eyes shut against the racking cough beside him.

After Aurelia was safe, all he wanted was to crawl under his bedcovers and hide from the expectations everyone had of him. He inhaled unsteadily, praying to the same gods that blessed him with a black arrow, praying that Aurelia, wherever she was, was as safe for now as Fox had claimed.

Something cool touched his shoulder, causing Rhydian to flinch. It started to move in slow circles. Fox was trying to soothe *him*, as if *he* was the sick one. Behind his closed lids the warm glow from the fireplace brightened. But one of the logs he had thrown on the fire must have been a bit damp, as he could taste smoke on his tongue. It was as bitter as the nausea and fear that he was struggling to bury.

"I don't know what to do, Fox," he whispered. "I can't help her. I can't help you."

"She's going to be-fine," Fox mumbled, "I just need to-"

"Do what, Fox? I appreciate all that you've done... truly," with a near hysterical laugh, Rhydian opened his eyes. "But Aurelia is *gone*. We don't have time to wait for you to get better. You've got little magic left, however the fuck *that* works, and you're getting *worse*. We need *help*."

Fox's voice was thick with emotion. "She's going to be okay. I-"

"So you say," Rhydian interrupted. "But I've only just found her. How can she be gone already?"

"It happens more often than you think," Fox muttered. Louder, he said, "She's not gone. She's just gone from here. I-"

His next words were cut off by another violent round of gasping for breath after a great cough racked his shaking body. Rhydian didn't bother to look, despite the violence of it. There was nothing more obvious than Fox's present condition to validate Rhydian's point. He doubted Fox was someone who was humble enough to take help when it was needed. But this was not the time for dragon-sized egos.

"Is there anyone else?" Rhydian's voice was soft. Fox had caught his breath and the hand on his back settled. "Another magic user who can help us?"

The hand on his back stopped mid-movement.

"Fox? Is there someone else?"

The cool hand disappeared.

Without raising his head from his hands, Rhydian turned to glance up. Fox's expressionless face was half hidden in shadow, and a trembling finger was tracing the red star on the windowpane. When he finally answered, Fox's voice was calm.

"No."

"I don't believe you," Rhydian said, watching a muscle twitch along Fox's jaw.

"Fuck off, kingling," Fox muttered, not meeting his gaze.

"Fuck you. Why are you so mean?" Rhydian hissed, pushing himself upright to slouch against the wall.

"Am not."

"You are! Fuck you."

"I don't care," Fox snapped. "And you swear too much."

"I blame you. And I still don't believe you," Rhydian snapped straight back. "Who else can help us?"

Fox closed his eyes, dropping his head back against the stonework beside the glass.

"Shit," he breathed, raising a shaking hand to rake through his inky hair. "I *can't*."

"Can't what?"

Fox shook his head, the gold in his eyes indistinguishable from the black as his eyes opened a fraction. Rhydian forced himself to not look away, letting Fox read the desperation on his face.

"Please, Fox, who?"

"I can't," Fox whispered, his voice raw.

Rhydian slid closer and captured Fox's trembling hands in his. The difference in temperature between them was startling. Holding Fox's gaze, Rhydian jerked his chin at the window, the red star barely visible in the dim light.

"How do we get there? Who can help us?"

Shaking his head, Fox swallowed, clenching his eyes shut once more.

"Tell me, what do you need?" Rhydian urged.

Gently folding Fox's hands against his chest, Rhydian pulled Fox towards him. He pressed Fox's forehead into the warmth of his neck, his arms wrapped around the cool shoulders. Rhydian wasn't sure at the small noise Fox made, choke or sob.

"Fox, what can I do?"

Rhydian could feel the soft hum of Fox clearing his throat against him.

"I need..." the unsteady voice against him was soft.

"What?" Rhydian whispered into the silky black hair against his lips.

"I need warm arms around me," Fox murmured, his voice barely audible.

"I'm here," Rhydian murmured around the lump in his throat. He squeezed tighter. "I'm right here-"

"Not... not yours," Fox gasped, trembling.

"Whose arms, then?" Rhydian struggled to keep his voice even. "Who do you need?"

Fox made a noise against him, a low, reluctant moan.

"Owaen..."

The name fell quietly from icy lips, a soft sigh against Rhydian's neck. Fox shifted against him.

"I need Owaen."

40

Merion

Year 367

Aneirin Castle

The king's mouth was set in a thin line. There were dark circles beneath his eyes, and his cheeks were hollowed in the light of the lanterns. Rhydian was clad plainly, not quite his usual riding attire, but there was nothing to suggest his ascension to kingship. His head was bare, his golden brown hair a tousled mess.

Merion blinked slowly, wondering why Rhydian's expressionless face reminded him of Blackthorn. As Rhydian continued to stare at the small body wrapped in clean linens on the stone bench before them, he realised slowly that the resemblance might have something to do with the fact that a spark had gone.

Blackthorn had been behaving himself over the past day, his stall quiet. The horse had lost some of his temper. From the battle, or sensing his human's distress, the groom couldn't say. Merion, unable to look down at the body, continued to examine the king. The young man's blue eyes were dull, strained. Like all of them, Merion supposed.

There were a few gathered in the crypts for a simple service. Only a few lanterns were lit. The scented oil was a welcome cover to the faint aroma of rot from where the king's body hadn't been taken care of yet. Unlike Chase.

Merion inhaled sharply, unable to lower his eyes and witness the remains of a young life cut short.

Nearby in the gloom, Wyll was standing with his arms crossed over his chest. He didn't look dull or lifeless. He looked angry, his eyes visibly reddened even in the shadows. His usually shining hair looked unkempt. Realising Merion was looking at him, Wyll's gaze flicked up from the body before them, before flicking quickly away. Davyn was beside Wyll, shoulders slumped. Like Merion, Davyn hadn't said much since-

Merion sighed.

A few others were gathered in the royal crypts. It was where their new king had insisted the boy should be laid to rest, amongst what was left of the nobles and royals whose names had long been forgotten.

Was it right that Chase's two younger brothers had been kept away? Chase's mother was sedated in her bed. A small noise escaped Merion's throat at the thought. Across from him, Wyll swallowed and Rhydian closed his eyes. How did one cope with a loss like this?

Lord Cyrus had also been cut down in the place he had called home for longer than the rest of them had been alive. There had been a battle and bloodshed outside the castle gates. And there was a new king because Rhydian's father had fallen in the battle. Merion frowned, examining Rhydian's shadowed face.

"Merion?" Davyn's voice was quiet. "Do you wish to speak?"

Merion shook his head, glad for his beard to hide the quiver of his lips.

"Wyll?" Davyn asked next, shifting in his boots.

Wyll's shoulders tensed, and he looked away from Davyn's raised eyebrows. Wyll muttered something unintelligible.

There was a moment's silence. But, thankfully, Davyn began to speak.

He spoke about Chase's love for his brothers, and his love of all things new and strange. Listening to the solemn words of his friend, Merion inhaled slowly, his throat tight, his mouth dry.

He was only vaguely listening to Davyn speak, his deep voice the only sound in the cavernous natural hall that was the crypts. Merion was remembering a bug squashed on the stable door. He thought of Chase scraping it carefully off the wood to wrap it up in the same rag it had met its end with, to be taken off to show his brothers. Behind his beard, Merion chewed his bottom lip, wondering where the half squashed wasp was now.

Aurelia had been there, laughing, her green eyes full of mirth. Merion's gaze wandered from Davyn back to their king. Aurelia had spoken of flying rats that day, bats, or some other name. Back in the place she had come from. Lolihud. A name so strange that it had stuck with him. But perhaps somewhere they should never have forgotten, if not for their queen, and their recently dead king.

One of Merion's hands twitched involuntarily. He wanted to fiddle with his apron, or a tool from one of its deep pockets. But he was without it today. The first day without it since, well, a long time. Horses were his life, the stables were his home. And his apron was part of that. The familiar smell of the old leather calmed him.

Davyn's voice faltered for a moment, but he cleared his throat and continued on. There were no priestesses left in Aneirin, so Merion was grateful that someone was able to speak. The lanterns flickered slightly as cool air from outside came through in a soft breeze, stirring the flames. Rhydian's gaze flickered to the doorway, then back down. Merion kept his gaze straight ahead. He refused to lower it.

Beside him, Davyn continued on, and Merion's mind wandered back to Aurelia.

Were there any holy women or men in her caves, her home? Besides stories of flying rats and a breed of horse that Merion had been overjoyed to see, she had also brought a dragon.

His chest rising and falling with another deep sigh, Merion stared at the shadows beyond his king. A dragon that was now missing. The previous king had known there was a dragon with the Elves. What else had he known before sending his people to battle where they could not hope to win? The speech that he had made before Rhydian had led them out of the city seemed to indicate the man had known more that may have helped. May have prevented the need for prisoners or anyone to be locked up. Where the after battle chaos had meant that a boy was helping feed someone who had best been left behind bars.

Merion shook his head. He didn't understand that at all. He also didn't understand what he had seen when the body of Rhydian's father had come back from the battlefield. The desecration on the dead man's face had been clear, as was the wound in his neck. It was a cruel tear, not the clean slice from a sword. Even though the Elves had been using bows and arrows during the battle, Merion glanced at Rhydian, his mind shying away from the negotiation that the prince had organised. His mind also shied away from the bow, and the white flag that Chase had fetched to tie upon its tip. On the men's return to the courtyard, Merion had met them, and the bow had been missing. Davyn hadn't been able to look the groom in the eye.

As if sensing Merion's gaze on him once more, Rhydian looked up. His blue eyes were dark, his face still expressionless. One of the king's hands twitched, and Merion looked away. And with a start, realised they were alone apart from Wyll. The rest of those who had gathered here were gone. Even Davyn.

The king straightened under Merion's silent gaze.

"Merion," Rhydian said, his voice quiet. "I'm sorry."

Blinking against the wetness in his eyes, Merion stared at him. Wyll cursed softly beside them. Glancing his way, Rhydian's chin tilted up, appraising Wyll before his solemn gaze focused back on Merion.

"I can't fix this," Rhydian murmured. His hand came up to rest on the hilt of his sword at his hip. "But I'm going to get justice for him."

With a slight shrug, Merion blinked. He wanted to wipe away the moisture that had run into the top of his beard, but he kept his hands limp at his sides. Rhydian watched him struggle, saying nothing.

"So you're still leaving?" Wyll's voice was a low hiss. "For Chase? Or for that Elven woman?"

Rhydian turned to face Wyll, his face finally showing something besides fatigue. Something dark flashed in his gaze. Tension filled the stale air.

"I'm going to find her, yes-"

Wyll cut in, gesturing angrily with his chin at the small body in front of them.

"Leaving us here, yes, with the bloody Elf that is responsible for this?"

Rhydian's eyes narrowed. He seemed to be about to speak, thought better of it.

"Well? My *king*?" Wyll snapped, his cheeks flushed.

The hand on Rhydian's sword tightened. Merion glanced at the king's face, seeing a dark expression there that he hadn't seen before. He wasn't sure what it meant.

"If Chase was missing, would you bring him back safe if you could? Aurelia has been taken and I must go. I love her."

Wyll's snort cut through the shock of silence that followed that admission.

"Love?" He laughed, a frosty bark. "I don't believe this. *We* need you, your *people* need you, and you leave to go find an Elf that has most likely bewitched you?"

As Rhydian let go of his sword, Merion released his breath slowly and quietly. Rhydian wiped his face with the hand that had been clasped around the hilt.

"I can't stay here while-" he started, but Wyll cut him off once more.

"You *must*! How can you leave now? Like your father did all the damn time!"

At that, even in the shadows, Merion could see Rhydian's face pale. Rhydian's hand dropped back to his sword, knuckles white. Wyll stepped forward, dropping his crossed arms to his side. They were eyeing each other off with enough tension between them that Merion cleared his throat. He finally looked down.

"Enough," he croaked.

The two of them broke their stare, apparently startled.

"Enough," Merion said again, swallowing. His eyes were frozen on the small body below him on the cold stone bench. He hoped there would be some kind of carved covering, like the older burials, but for now, it was enough that the boy had been cleaned and carefully wrapped in fresh linen. Before his family had seen what was left.

Chase had been small for his age; most people thought he was younger than he really was. Merion choked back a sob and lifted a trembling hand to rest it on the cold stone by the boy's side.

"Enough, lads, please." Merion swallowed uncomfortably. "Not here."

Rhydian dropped his hand from his sword. "I'm sorry," he whispered.

"I know, sire," Merion rasped, tearing his eyes from Chase to stare at the troubled face of his young king. "Believe me, I know."

With a huff, Wyll stepped close and grabbed Merion's arm. He tugged Merion towards the faintly lit opening that led back to light, and to life.

"Come on, Merion," Wyll muttered. "Leave our *king* with his thoughts of *love*," he said darkly.

Before he allowed himself to be led away, Merion watched their new king's cheeks flush white, then pink. Not bothering to reply, Rhydian lowered his gaze to stare at the small body before him and closed his eyes.

"What are we doing *here*?"

Merion's croak was so low that he was surprised Wyll had heard. On the steps of the old temple beside him, Wyll paused, turning to face the groom.

"Trust me," Wyll replied, his dark eyes unreadable. His grip tightened on Merion's arm, and with his free hand, Wyll hooked one thumb at the imposing stone building looming above them.

Shaking his arm free, Merion glared at Wyll, stubbornly refusing to move. Even in his numb daze, he knew that the old place of worship was not somewhere they should be.

"What," repeated the groom darkly, "are we doing here, Wyll?"

The younger man raked a hand through his hair. He glanced around, his gaze furtive. In the low light of the overcast morning, Merion could see that the other man looked like he hadn't slept in days. Like all of them.

"There's a meeting," Wyll finally admitted. "And I think you need to come too."

Merion continued to stare at Wyll, his lips a thin line behind his beard, frown lines marring his forehead.

After leaving the crypts behind, Wyll had dragged Merion through the castle, his hand firm on Merion's arm. When leading Merion past the stables through the courtyard, Wyll had looked so secretive in his haste to leave that he may well have had yelled 'I am up to no good'. Numb and unsure of his spinning thoughts, Merion had let himself be pulled out of the castle gates and down the city streets.

Despite the recent battle, and the fact that Rhydian had opened the castle to their so-called enemy, the streets were reasonably quiet. Human soldiers and Elven soldiers hung out in their own groups, feeling safer with their own kind. Some of them had bandages on various limbs. Wyll had dragged Merion past all of them, not saying a word. And now they were here, at the foot of the old temple where no priestess had served for years.

Eventually, tipping his head back, Merion blinked up at the looming stone structure. Even in his grief, he could appreciate that the building was a solemn place. And if he was honest, a tiny part of him, deep within, burned brightly to see the wonder of the crystals within once more.

The tall building looked as old as the castle and made of the same large, pale stone. The slight green tinge of moss could be seen marring the lower half of the outer wall, darker in the rough joinery between the large pieces of rock. A wide set of steps at street level led up to a broad open space. Tall and wide, undressed columns of stone ran along the width. In the centre of the front of the building, a single doorway, as tall as the temple itself, perhaps the height of five men standing on each other, led into the darkness inside. There had never been a door. Even if one could be made to fit, there likely never would have been. The temple had once been open all day and night for those who needed guidance.

It was empty now.

Or it should have been, however from the lowest step, Merion could hear the soft, hushed voices of many people within. His frown deepened. Their previous king had decreed magic outlawed. So the priestesses and their strange rituals had left. Like so many others. Most with no clue to where they would end up. Merion chewed on his bottom lip, his thick beard moving with the gesture.

Perhaps my family and I should have left too.

"Please," Wyll urged, "trust me. Come on. You can leave at any time."

Not liking this at all, Merion shook his head. But he let his arm be caught up by Wyll's firm grip, as the man pulled him up the steps and through the giant door.

It was cooler inside, and dark. A few paces beyond the entrance, visitors were faced with a plain stone wall. Supplicants could turn either left or right, as either led to the same place. What direction you took used to depend on what you needed, if Merion remembered rightly. It had been a long, long time since he had been here. He had been a very small boy when the last priestess had left. He didn't know what either side meant. Without hesitating, Wyll chose left. At Merion's grunt, he finally let go of Merion's arm, but kept checking that the groom was following. They turned left inside the first doorway, then right, then right again and finally a last left out into a central space.

The smell of old incense was strong, and it was brighter here. The single square opening to the sky in the roof above was long and wide, and the overcast sky above tinged the room with a sickly light. More wide columns supported the plain stone ceiling, ringed around the four walls of the space. The temple had been built hundreds of years ago as a simple building. It hadn't needed any adornments. The breathtaking crystals had been enough. Each of the gods and goddesses had had their own rectangular altar of plain stone. Upon each one of them had been a human-sized point of quartz, with the different colours representing the attributes of each deity. As they paused at the edge of the inner chamber, crowded with about forty people, Merion paused in shock.

The crystals were gone.

Wyll stepped forward to clasp hands with those huddling close to where they had exited the short tunnel. Merion stayed where he was, eyes darting amongst the columns to the altars. Each one was bare.

Searching around the space, Merion swore. They were too large to be missed, and hadn't been moved. The crystals were simply gone. Taking a step forward, he froze as something crunched under his thick boots.

A few paces into the room in front of him, Wyll turned away from the other city folk he was talking with, glancing back at Merion. He opened his mouth to say something, but paused at the expression on Merion's face.

"Merion?" Wyll asked.

Breathing carefully through his nose, Merion looked down as a soft moan escaped his lips.

"By the gods…" he breathed.

Merion lifted his boot, wincing as tiny shards of crystal fell away from the sole.

His horrified gaze lifted to Wyll's.

"Did they do this?" Merion hissed, his chin jutting to the folks who had turned to watch.

"No!" The exclamation came from a young woman in a dark green robe behind Wyll.

"Merion," Wyll gasped, coming back, his eyes searching Merion's gaze. "How could you think that?"

Shaking with anger, Merion shook his head, unable to speak. He glanced back down, his gaze sweeping the wide expanse of the stone slab floor. He could see the glitter now, a fine covering of tiny crystal splinters. Not just under the feet of the crowd, but amongst the columns, too.

"It was like that when we first met here," the woman in green muttered.

Hands clenched by his sides, Merion said nothing, glaring at the desecration.

No one knew how much old magic had been here in the temples, or exactly what the priestesses had practiced after dark. But there had been healings and guidance, the power channelled from the giant crystals that had once been held in reverence here. The priestesses and their power had gone, but old families still remembered and said their prayers in secret, hidden from their previous king. Magic may have been outlawed, a hypocritical act that filled Merion with bitterness, now the veil of the curse had been broken and revealed. But the gods and goddesses had not been forgotten.

"It's true."

His glare still marring his brows, Merion turned to his left, from where the quiet voice had come. The soft, feminine voice was familiar as it continued.

"Although what is left isn't the entirety of what was here. Most of it was… taken."

A small woman, slight of stature and height, blinked at him from between two columns to his left. Her green eyes appraised him expressionlessly. She was dressed in well-made but plain clothing, pants and a short tunic, plain homespun linen in brown and grey. A black headscarf was wound around her forehead, but a few wisps of hair had escaped in front of her ears. The bright shade of red was startling amongst the grey light. There was a scatter of freckles over her nose, cheeks and the backs of her hands. She was holding a tall staff of pale, twisted wood. Its jagged top had something wrapped around it, a discoloured piece of fabric.

Merion blinked.

"Lady Hywel?"

The librarian of Aneirin acknowledged him with a curt nod.

"Our young king has been looking for you," Merion began, but she interrupted him, her voice just as soft.

"I know. But he's not ready," she said calmly.

"For what?" Merion asked, his glare fading back to a frown. "And what are you doing here-"

"He's not ready," Lady Hywel repeated. She glanced away from him and nodded at one of the crowd, a tall man closest to the altars. She raised her voice. "Hurry up. I don't have much time."

The man narrowed his eyes at her command, but said nothing as she stepped back into the outer edge of the large room, ducking between the giant columns.

Wise of him to keep quiet, Merion mused, remembering Lady Hywel's temper. It had been a long time since he had seen the librarian. But he had never forgotten her tirade at a young Rhydian, when the curious prince had once snuck his favourite history of swordcraft out of the library into the hayloft.

His gaze wandered back to the librarian, and he tilted his head. She would have to be older than Merion, but she looked the same. *Exactly* the same. His frown deepened. He crossed his arms over his chest, unease warring with the numbness within. All he wanted to do was get back to his room, the familiar smell of horse, and his bottle of spirits. This, this temple, the shards of crystal on the floor, and now realising the missing librarian was still around but looking... the same, was too much.

Had she always looked that young?

What else have I missed while we were under a blasted cloud of magic?

Beside him, Wyll poked his arm. The tall man, a guard named Joseph, was talking.

"I heard the soldiers," the guard was saying to the crowd. "They were miners once. Did you know that?"

"From the far, far south," someone said from the back.

"Banished there for a reason," said the woman in green.

Lady Hywel appeared closer to the altar, but hadn't joined the crowd. She was still amongst the columns, hands on her staff. Her face was a mask of disinterest as she assessed those assembled.

"Exactly," said Joseph, "some weird place, full of strange things-"

Lolihud, Merion thought to himself. He kept his mouth shut. The unease in his guts grew at the same pace as the faces in the crowd grew angry. He uncrossed his arms, and shifted on his feet, not daring to step further onto the desecration on the floor, or into the tension filling the once holy space. He tuned back into the angry words of Joseph.

"I heard the Elves talking," he was saying, his eyes flashing with bitterness. "They've been training there for years to wipe us out their whole lives. And I was there, with Davyn, when we went to negotiate. But they wanted bloodshed, no doubt about it."

A murmur of dissent rippled through the gathering.

"The Elf we spoke with, *he* wanted war. Not just the... queen." The man faltered on the word. Most of the townsfolk were still reeling over the news that their missing queen had returned with an army. For some, it seemed unbelievable. Merion's frown deepened.

"It was him, them, *all* of them. Not just the queen! They weren't under a curse like us!"

The murmuring was louder now. Merion eyed Lady Hywel. She returned his stare evenly. He averted his gaze back to the man at the altars who was talking louder. The man's face was turning red.

"And you know what!?" he was saying, his eyes flashing. "They knew what they were doing! When they saw us, and how few soldiers we had, they bloody attacked anyway! Where's the honour in that?"

Voices were cursing now, and an older man with grey in his hair, on the closest edge of the crowd, wiped his eyes with his folded cap.

"Honour!" Joseph spat. "Our new king wanted to give them a chance to show their honour, and they tore us to pieces!"

"True!" someone shouted.

"And what did our king do?"

The curses were louder, crueler now. Merion took a step back, cringing at the sight before him as well as the crunch under his boots.

"He let them inside these walls! Into our homes!"

"The son of the man who cursed us now rules us, and let them in!" a man shouted from the middle of the crowd.

"Exactly!" Wyll called. The crowd turned their way. Merion kept his face carefully blank as Wyll ranted on. "And that woman? That Elven woman, swanning around with our *king*? She's the worst! She let in the very same Elf who killed poor Chase after the battle was done!"

Cries of anger followed his words.

"She's corrupted him!" the woman in green robes shouted.

"And he plans to leave us to follow her," Wyll spat out, "while we wait here in our homes with the army that came to destroy us!"

The shouts were wordless now, and the stale tang of dissent hung on the once per-fumed air.

"We need to do something," a young man called.

"Yes!"

"We will!"

"We must!"

Wyll nodded. "It's true. We must. We need help though, considering who they are, what they are..."

"Who would help us, though? And how?" At the altars, Joseph spoke over the calling voices of anger. "Where would we even start?"

As the faces of the crowd turned back to Joseph, Merion took his chance.

Aware of the librarian's steady gaze upon him, Merion took another step back between the columns. He'd seen enough. He'd *heard* enough, especially from Wyll. Merion might not understand all that had happened, and his heart was a stone for poor Chase. But he would have no part of this or of anything against Rhydian. No matter whose son he was. Merion knew what type of men they both were.

With one last curious glance at Lady Hywel, Merion turned and followed the dark passage back to the temple entrance. His heart ached at the last of the crystals crunching under his boots. However, before he could step outside, a rough hand grabbed his shoul-der from behind.

"Wait!" Wyll's voice was a hushed plea.

"No. I have to go. The king is leaving this morning-"

"*Damn* the king!"

Merion jerked his arm out of Wyll's grasp, whirling to face him.

"What's wrong with you?" Merion hissed.

Wyll took a step back, eyeing Merion up and down.

"What's wrong with *me*? Why don't you ask what's wrong with our bloody *king*?"

"That's *treason*!" Merion said, still hissing. Wyll glanced behind him, then back to Merion, his gaze turning from shock to defiance.

"No, it's not," he spat back. "It's what we need to do to save our city. I'm shocked at you Merion. Where's your loyalty?"

"Loyalty?" Merion wanted to laugh and weep at the same time. "To my *family*! To *our king*!"

Wyll took a step forward and poked Merion's chest.

"Our king? Really." He scoffed. "And what family? Where is everyone? There's hardly anyone left, which is why we need to protect them. We don't even know where our families went. So we *must* fight for those who are *left*."

"You're mad," Merion muttered. "I trust the king-"

"Do you?" Wyll hissed, jabbing at Merion. "Why? I know you know that he sent Joseph out with the arrow that slayed Rhydian's father! You know it was Aurelia that talked him into it!"

Merion spluttered. "That's ridiculous-"

"Is it?" Wyll asked, his face red and screwed up. His hand slid from Merion's chest as he took a step back. "You know it's true."

Merion shook his head, all too aware of what he'd been thinking about, staring at his young king over the body of Chase not long before. No. There was another explanation. There had to be. Rhydian would never do anything against his people. Surely he'd felt it necessary to take steps?

Wyll's sour expression turned triumphant as he watched Merion, the sound of hooves passing on the street outside breaking the silence.

"That's right, Merion. And we need to do something about it. I know someone who can help us, rid us of these Elves, who even now are likely plotting to get rid of the rest of us that are left."

Taking an uneven breath, Merion chewed his beard, dreading the fierce light in Wyll's eyes.

"Who do you know?" Merion asked eventually, his voice low.

"A man," Wyll replied, the red of his flushed cheeks fading.

"What man?"

Wyll smiled, and something dark crossed his face. Merion's unease deepened.

"I heard him at Cora the tailor's while I was getting more fabric for bandages. The man was there, paying in gold coins." Wyll's eyes brightened. "Gold coins, Merion, for information on the Elves."

Eyebrows raised, Merion waited for Wyll to explain further. Merion had no need for gold coins.

"He saw me listening, so he asked me about the Elves and the castle. He said he would pay for information."

"What kind of information?"

"Where they were in the castle, what rooms they had been allowed in, the hall or the library, like he has a plan to flush them out."

"Flush them out?" Merion repeated dully.

"Yes!" Wyll exclaimed. "Like we want."

"How?"

"He has..." Wyll licked his lips and glanced over Merion's shoulder, likely checking there was no one else nearby. No one should be, as this place was off limits. Or it had been until now, Merion thought darkly. "He has *power*."

"Treason," Merion mumbled. "You're mad. Is he an Elf, turning against his own kind?"

"No," Wyll murmured, his voice low. "That's the best part. He said he's not. He's, uh, different. But he's got magic too."

Tipping his head back to sigh at the stone far above them, Merion bit his lip.

"Wyll," Merion said, and lowered his gaze. "Elves are humans with magic. That's what they are."

"No," Wyll insisted stubbornly. His eyes flashed. "He's not an Elf. He wants them gone, and he said if we can get him into the castle, he could help us. He showed me his power. It was... he used his magic to tear up the linens for bandages. It was crazy." Wyll looked unsure for a moment, but hurried on. "Yes, he was odd, but he can help us., I know he will. We need someone like him against the magic users that have corrupted our new king."

"Where is he now?" Merion asked, biting back his defence of Rhydian for now.

"He's not here in the city, but he'll be back. He's keeping an eye on things for us, gathering more like him to help us."

Merion's doubt must have showed on his face, because Wyll bit his lip.

"He'll be back, and we are going to take back our city, and *our* honour."

Going along with Wyll for now seemed the best bet. With a sigh, Merion nodded at the passage behind Wyll.

"Fine, I'll find you later." He chewed his lip. "The king is leaving this morning, whether you like it or not, so I'm off now. But when I see you and your *friends* again, all I'll do is listen. That's all."

"Yes Merion, that's all I ask."

The relief on Wyll's face was at odds with the strange expression in his eyes, one that Merion couldn't read. The groom swallowed back the bitterness rising in his throat. All of them were experiencing things they had never expected. Wyll, he supposed, was right in the middle of grief and shock as well. But something struck him as odd, even amongst all that had happened and come to light.

"Wyll," he said, lowering his voice. He'd noticed a shadow approaching them from deeper within the twisting tunnel, light footsteps barely audible. "What was this man of yours doing in the tailors after the battle? With *gold* coins?"

Wyll scrunched his nose up in distaste while running a hand through his already mussed up hair. Angry voices echoed toward them from deeper inside. Merion peered around Wyll, noting that the shadow that was approaching had stopped nearby, the figure just out of sight.

"Well," Wyll said, shaking his head. "Would you believe it? In the aftermath of a war, he was buying a fucking purple cloak."

41

Fox

Year 367

Aneirin Castle

O waen, I died.

And maybe you'd laugh at me, but I was pleased to learn something. Death was better than when you rescued me.

All those years ago, when you found me a husk in Shadow Light's cave, I knew I'd have preferred to die. When you came back for me, and found me like that, as delirious as I was, I wanted to press you down into the earth. I wanted to escape your pity. I wanted you to disappear like claw prints in the dirt washed away by winter rain. I was ashamed of my weakness, ashamed of all dragonkind. You came for me. But I only made it out halfway from that cave. A part of me was left behind, beyond even your own great spiritual understanding.

Did you know that I regretted it, that I was still alive? I didn't deserve to be. By then I had given up. It burned me that you saw that, the shame of my new existence, my dark rebirth full of power and wrath.

So when I shut you away in return, I convinced myself that you would understand why I had to. I couldn't allow any other witnesses to what you dragged out of that hell. Besides, I needed to keep you safe.

I survived. I did what I had to.

But then, I eventually fucked it up.

And I died.

At first there was peace, and I was right. It was safe.

But it was only fleeting. Because there was also remembering.

There was a mess I left behind. I owed those I loved to fix it with whatever was left of me. Maybe there will be something left of me for you as well, Owaen, locked away in a betrayal of our love. Or will you hate me?

Do I care? Of course I do.

Except I hate that. I hate that I wonder if there is anything left of you for me.

Perhaps you will choose to continue to dream and not wake up for anything but the final days of this magic-cursed continent. Either way, Owaen, I am coming for you.

For your help.

When I died, I had to come back to fix my mess, my loose ends. Would you laugh? My ego got in the way of the final knots of my revenge. Because Owaen, I fucked up with Shadow Light. Even deep down, I know that he deserved every second of his new role that I bestowed upon him. I was happy to return the favour of his dark deeds with my own. But it went wrong. The innocent have once again been caught up in the dark. Truly, I'm trying to fix it.

But I think I'm dying again.

So as much as the thought of breathing the same air as you once more makes me choke on my shame, I need your help with him.

With me.

I'm cold, Owaen, I'm still so fucking cold.

When I'm so cold that I can't think, all I can do is feel, and what I feel is you stirring in your dreams. Your goodness threads its way into my lungs like tiny, permeable filaments of justice trying to choke the furnace of my revenge.

Do you remember before I shut you away? Full of wrath, I had been reborn, filled with the deaths of too many innocent creatures to count. Wanting to die, I realised I had to live for them. So I took them with me, inside my black heart, north to Mionlach. In much the same way as I took care of Shadow Light, I took care of the rest of them as well.

I can still see your deep green eyes pleading with me. When I had my hands around the one who had broken me, you knew I wasn't going to kill him. You could see me plotting, even then. You said to me... Don't...

I did it anyway.

And I got it wrong.

The potent smell of horse against Fox's cheek was welcome. It was warm, alive, and full of strength. A welcome distraction from the winter chill in his lungs.

After a few hours of fitful sleep, Fox had been conscious enough to notice Rhydian disappearing in the early hours of the morning. Later, when Rhydian had returned with Davyn, the pair were solemn eyed but determined. They had helped Fox dress warmly, thick socks and boots covering his icy feet. Then, with no consideration of his dignity, they had carried Fox down the tower stairs. He'd had no strength left by then, his skin icy and his lungs tortured by deep, racking coughs. He had bitten his tongue at some point. The copper taste was still fresh even now. At some point, Fox had blacked out. The motion of being carried around and down, around and down, had been too much.

When Fox had finally risen back to a semi-conscious state, he was being carried through the great hall, his mind echoing with words and jumbled thoughts and memories of the one they were setting out to find.

Owaen.

Fox pressed his lips against the silken neck of the horse, his eyes shut tight, inhaling deeply. It was a tenuous way to sort out if he was still dreaming, or delirious. Because no matter how hard he tried to ignore it, the face of the one who had seen into the depths of Fox's soul was right there in his mind. Knowing that it would soon be real was as bad as being carried down the stairs. The anticipation and the dread of seeing that face in person felt like he was slowly going mad.

"Mad," Fox whispered, fur sliding across his bloodied lips.

The horse stamped on the cobbles beneath Fox as his lips irrigated its neck. Cracking an eye open, Fox groaned as his stomach shifted with the movement.

He was slumped over in the saddle, his forehead on the animal's neck; his shaking hands limp on his trembling thighs. They were still within the castle walls, not yet on the road under the cloudy sky. From his awkward position, he could just make out that the courtyard was crowded with humans, Elves, horses, carts and supplies.

Normally, it was hard to tell humans and Elves apart. Most Elves had brighter eyes and unblemished skin. But Fox's blurred vision showed him that some folks were walking around like they were enveloped within a faint mist, tinged with pastel violets and pinks and blues. Fox closed his eye, willing the faint auras of what little power the Elves carried to fade.

Mad.

The noise of hooves and shouts that normally echoed across the space were muted by the yard being filled with so many. He'd gotten enough of a glimpse to know that his horse was still by the stables. Louder voices nearby jarred against the meandering of his spinning thoughts.

"I don't know, Wyll," a low voice rumbled, thick with fatigue. "Perhaps a horse was taken. How could I tell at such a time as this?"

Rhydian's tired voice cut in, soothing the agitated man.

"Don't worry Merion, however, the prisoner made it out with her. They're gone. But we know where they're going."

"Yes, sire," the low voice rumbled, then paused. "Please, be safe, my king."

"I'm sorry." Rhydian cleared his throat. "There's more going on that I can explain. But once we are back, I'll sort this out. I don't know how long I'll be gone-"

An angry voice interrupted. Fox frowned. He knew the voice, but his aching head couldn't place the man it belonged to.

"That's what happens when you have magic users on the loose," the man hissed, his voice bitter. "You're needed here, sire, and the magic users can take care of themselves. For fuck's sake Rhydian, she's just a fucking *Elf*!"

The sound of Rhydian inhaling slowly had forced Fox to open his eyes wider, the light and the sensations acutely painful. Straining to push himself upright, Fox bit back a groan. His eyelids fluttered as he tilted his head to look around, willing the swaying of the sky to cease.

The day was overcast, the air cool. He was thankful for the multiple cloaks he was wrapped in, and the thick socks and heavy boots on his feet. The cold was still seeping in, but the weight was soothing. As the swaying eased a fraction, Fox eventually found the face he was looking for.

Rhydian was pinching the bridge of his nose. A man stood nearby, glaring, his chin jutting out. Eventually Rhydian dropped his hand away from his face, his normally sweet blue eyes flinty.

"Wyll."

"What?"

"I dare you to say that again."

Wyll stepped back, his cheeks flushing white, then pink. After a moment, he shut his mouth and shook his head. He turned to leave, but paused on meeting Fox's bleary-eyed stare.

It took a moment, but Fox realised who he was. Wyll was the man who had spat on the cell floor when they had found the body of the boy. Aware that his mouth was stained with fresh blood from his bitten tongue, Fox widened his lips, baring his teeth. Wyll flinched. He shot one last glare at Rhydian before disappearing into the crowded yard. He didn't look back.

"Mad," Fox whispered, blinking at the retreating man, the world around him spinning again. As firm hands came around him, Fox realised he had slumped sideways. The surrounding sounds went quiet for a moment, and his vision dimmed. When he came to once more, another voice was talking.

"...are you sure about this, sire?"

"No, Dav, but I need to fix this mess. This is the only way I know how."

"Go, sire," the first voice murmured, close to Fox's head.

Fox opened his eyes, the dim light still strong enough to make him squint.

A man with a bushy beard was holding the head of the horse he was slumped over. His tired eyes were peering at Fox, but he was speaking to Rhydian. "The guards and the Elves you've spoken to know what to do, sire."

The horse beneath Fox danced and tossed his head. Fox winced at the sudden movement.

"I hope so, Merion." Rhydian paused. "And if Flare comes back, tell that blasted dragon where we are. If he doesn't help us, he's not welcome here. Ever."

A grunt from Merion was the only reply.

Boot steps on the cobbles sounded, and Rhydian appeared in Fox's vision. The young king was carrying something slack in one hand. His other hand appeared to pat the horse's neck. "Hush Blackthorn, behave."

Fox groaned. So he was on Rhydian's great black warhorse, was he? Eyes on Rhydian, Fox planted a kiss on the animal's neck with a wry twist of lips. Rhydian's mouth twitched at the gesture before his eyes turned serious.

"I'll ride on my second best animal and lead Blackthorn. So. Are you ready?"

"I'm ready," Fox croaked.

Rhydian held up the bundle in his hand. It was more rope.

"No," Fox rasped, closing his eyes. "I'm not ready."

The man with the bushy beard, Merion, sounded like he stepped closer as he spoke, his voice quiet.

"It is necessary, sire? He looks like he's about to have a fit."

Fox opened his eyes. Merion's weary gaze turned to pity at the glare Fox was trying to summon.

"Yes, it is."

Rhydian hesitated, though, his warm hand resting on Fox's thigh, his expression conflicted.

Fox pressed his face into Blackthorn, knowing that rope was indeed necessary. They needed to move, and he needed whatever strength he had to assist them with this task once they were away from the castle. He couldn't think here, he couldn't concentrate. He also needed to not fall off the horse he was slumped over. But the idea of being bound once again left him gasping for air, faces clouded his vision.

A young boy, dead in his cell.

A young woman, asking him to choose.

A blonde Elven man, fathomless green eyes pleading.

I am heading into madness.

"Do it," Fox mumbled, rolling around fresh blood with his tongue against the inside of his cheek.

Rhydian was weeping silently.

From his awkward position against his horse's neck, Fox squinted across the distance between Blackthorn and Rhydian's horse. A single tear was sliding down the young king's cheek. However, Rhydian paid no attention to it. His gaze was fixed straight ahead, mouth set, as he rode the brown horse whilst leading Blackthorn down the steep cobbled streets of the city.

Rhydian was wearing his usual riding clothes, white shirt and dark pants with tough boots. Fox was dressed much the same, in cloaks as well. He had demanded to wear his ruby topped sword when Rhydian presented it to him, no matter how uncomfortable it felt. With the awkward position of his seat in the saddle, the uncut stone in the pommel poked his ribs painfully with each shift of the horse.

As for Rhydian, he was also barely holding it together; in much the same way as Fox. Fox could feel the strain of holding on to sanity, to reason. This was a long shot, a mad endeavour. But it was his only shot. The tiny spark left inside of him was a single tiny kernel of power, barely keeping him functioning, and the end of the thread that tied him to Owaen.

But he would hold on, because he had to.

For Aurelia.

For Rhydian.

And for Chase, although it was far too late for him.

"Too late," Fox murmured, tasting old blood on his tongue. Needing a distraction, he tried to concentrate on the bustle of the folk around them, the city still functioning despite the battle. It was quieter than the castle courtyard, although not by much. The aroma of the streets was more pungent and rich than the castle. Cooking food, incense, and smoke stung his sensitive nostrils.

Rhydian's gaze remained firmly in front of them, even as they passed an impressive stone building to their right. Looking past Rhydian's tense jaw, Fox frowned. He didn't remember seeing it before. Although by the look of its aged stone columns it had been here a while, and the last time he was here and in full possession of himself, they had been chasing Aurelia back down the streets in the dark.

"Aurelia, gone again," Fox muttered, before all thoughts left his head.

In the shadows amongst the giant columns, a diminutive woman watched them ride past.

Jessikah?

Fox tried to shout, his head half raised off Blackthorn's neck. Rhydian jerked their horses to a halt and Fox cursed at the sudden motion, blinking wildly. When he looked again, the woman was still there, but she had retreated further into the shadows. She was gripping a tall staff tightly, her mouth a thin line as she met his stare easily.

"What is it?" Rhydian asked hoarsely.

In his delirium, the hazy aura around her was different to the others Fox had seen. It was the colour of heavy sunsets, a dark shimmer of copper, as bright as the red hair that poked from the black headscarf she wore.

Not Jessikah.

Not Shadow Light.

"N-nothing," Fox mumbled, dropping his head back down. He lost sight of the woman as a group of people crowded out around her from the building. Rhydian was looking at Fox intently; unaware of the furtive looks the city folk were throwing them as they hurried away. Fox's gaze met Rhydian's. The man's blue eyes were alarmed. Funnily enough, there was a haze around Rhydian too, but it was colourless, like a shimmer of heat.

"Are you sure?"

"Let's go, kingling."

"Don't call me that today," Rhydian muttered as he urged the horses back down the steep street. He guided them around a cart with a broken wheel. "I don't feel like it."

"Okay, *kingling*," Fox taunted with his best attempt at a smirk, his eyes drooping with fatigue.

An irritated sigh sounded beside him over the hooves that echoed around them.

"I should have addressed them all, the Elves too, before we left. But I... my father..." his voice faded into a wet sniff.

Fox said nothing until Blackthorn jerked under him as a flock of honking geese was ushered up the hill beside them.

"Fuck," he spat, biting his tongue again as he was jostled in the saddle.

"Hush Blackthorn," Rhydian soothed.

Fox would've laughed if he were able. His black heart was amused that both he and his horse were being led on the end of a rope, held by a king who didn't want to be king, to a place where neither of them wanted to go.

"Aurelia," Fox whispered, his lips pressing against the irritated animal beneath him. "Only for you."

Earlier, warm arms had been wrapped around him.

But they weren't enough.

"Don't let me go," Fox mumbled into the blankets, his lungs aching. A deep voice soothed him, right against his ear.

Never.

The sensations and the aches in his body were enough that, as they made their way down the city streets, Fox slipped back out of consciousness. As careful as Rhydian was being in trying to get them out of the chaotic streets into the open fields of the north, it was taking them longer than they had imagined. But Fox hadn't slipped into delirium. He was fully aware that he was reliving the darker, earlier hours of that same morning.

"Don't let me go-" a cough interrupted his muttering, the first fit he'd had in hours.

"Fox?" A different voice broke through his ringing ears, and his coughing settled down. "Fox?"

Warm arms supported him, holding him up so he could spit out the vile filth he'd coughed up into his mouth. After spitting it out to the floor beside Rhydian's bed, Fox allowed himself to be laid back down. The arms settled back around him, holding him tight as he shivered.

"I'm h-here," Fox rasped. "I'm awake."

A relieved sigh broke the silence from right near Fox's head. Not Owaen at all, but Rhydian, the king's voice nowhere near the deep timbre of his dreams. Inhaling deeply, Rhydian spoke once more, his voice a whisper that rustled Fox's hair.

"Can I ask you something?"

"No," Fox croaked, his eyes shut tight as he trembled. Rhydian ignored him.

"What magic does he have?"

There was no reason to ask whom Rhydian was referring to. Fox licked dry lips.

"Does it m-matter?"

One of the arms wrapped around Fox tensed.

"I think it damned well does at this point," Rhydian muttered, bitter amusement laced over the fatigue in his voice. "Since without it, we're fucked."

Fox opened his eyes; dismayed he couldn't make out the ceiling. His eyes weren't working. He blinked, trying to clear them. It didn't work. He took a ragged breath.

"I think Owaen was one of the first Elves," Fox began. Rhydian's sharp intake of breath beside him pleased Fox, and his lips cracked as he smiled. "He has a lot more magic than most, more potent. He was born with it, not shared it by a dragon. Not unusual in itself. But to possess the quantity that he had, that was unusual."

"Go on," Rhydian whispered as Fox paused. "Please."

Fox cleared his throat as best he could without inciting another fit.

"And when he and I were together, his magic seemed to ignite mine. Like we had something similar burning inside. I don't know what, or why. Magic is just the manipulation of the energy within crystals. And he could wield a lot of it."

"Was he a great and powerful figure, then?"

Fox's snort nearly had his controlled breathing give way to more gasps for breath.

"Absolutely n-not. The other Elves avoided him."

"Why?"

"Because he looked down on them, as much as they looked down on him."

"Why?"

"Because they used their magic for themselves. And he used his for others."

Rhydian was quiet for a moment. Fox blinked again at the ceiling, feeling as blind as he had ever felt, unable to see his way clearly.

"Where is he," Rhydian murmured eventually, his voice weary, "exactly?"

"From here, north." Fox closed his eyes, swallowing against the hard lump in his throat. "North."

"And he'll help us?" Rhydian's voice was small.

"He will help *you*, I'm sure of it."

"But he wouldn't help you?"

"I doubt it, not after what I did to him." Fox shuddered. "I won't blame him, though. It was my fault, not his, for what happened."

The warm arms around him shifted.

"Do you really believe that, Fox, after all this time?"

"Yes."

Another sigh ruffled Fox's hair. "You're the most infuriating person, or creature, that I've ever met."

Fox's snort startled them both as it quickly turned into a dry choke.

"Wait until you meet Owaen," Fox gasped out eventually, his lungs burning. "He was a bastard when he needed to be."

"You're cruel too, when you want to be," Rhydian hissed, his fingers tight in Fox's hair, keeping it out of his face as he spat out another chunk of filth.

"I don't care," Fox huffed, collapsing back to the bed. He wiped his bloody mouth on the blankets. "Sometimes cruelty is necessary."

"I disagree."

Fox had nothing to say to that, and the quiet surrounded them like an extra blanket. Fox shut his eyes to the shadows, and focused on his next trembling breath, and the steady breaths of the warm man against him. He swallowed, the last spark of his magic dangerously close to snuffing out. But for Aurelia, he'd risk it.

"Rhydian."

"Fox."

"There's a chance that I might be able to s-speed the journey to Owaen."

Rhydian exhaled through his nostrils. "I can sense a 'but' to this, Fox. What?"

"Well. I might be w-worse than this when we arrive."

A bitter laugh cut through the silence following his statement.

"Worse than this?" Rhydian sputtered, eventually. "If you were any worse, you'd be," he broke off with a sigh. "Just tell me she's going to be okay."

"She's going to b-be okay," Fox murmured, opening his eyes just a crack.

She had to be.

Instead of responding, there was fumbling beside Fox. After a curse, Rhydian twisted to lean over Fox, and Fox caught the glint of gold before warm metal slid past his face.

"What are...?" Fox groused, feeling Rhydian settle the gold chain and pendants around his throat. Unable to speak, Fox reached up through the blankets, swaddling him and grabbed the familiar weight of the topaz, the pad of his finger sliding along the tiny golden wand.

"I'm guessing Owaen gave this to you."

"It was his, actually. I t-took it from him without his consent, when I..."

"Well, you should definitely have it back now," Rhydian mumbled. "In case Owaen gets the wrong idea."

"Are you scared to meet him, k-kingling? Ha. Perhaps you should be."

"So damn cruel," Rhydian mumbled. His arms slipped back around Fox and squeezed. "Cruel as well as useless."

"That's b-better," Fox murmured, pressing his trembling body into Rhydian's warmth and the surrounding blankets that smelled like sunshine and a peace that was only a lie in the end.

Fox smiled.

"You're learning to be a king already."

Now, the warm scent was gone.

In place of the soothing musk of Rhydian's skin was the sooty aroma of a burnt-out farm. What was left of it stood beside the road as more a pile of rubble than a cluster of buildings. It was to the north of the city, almost the furthest farm that spread along the valley below the steep mountain range to their left. The road kept meandering north, but Fox had croaked out that here was as good a place as any to stop and do what he needed. They were a couple of pain-filled hours from the castle, and the clouds were still great and low down. The light was washed out, and the colours were a mix of dull greens, greys and dry yellows of old fields of grass.

The landscape was eerily quiet and sad, at odds with the chaos and noise of the city and castle.

Fox wrinkled his nose, listening to Rhydian dismount nearby. Fox's eyes were making the world waver around him, but his nose was doing just fine. The smell of ash and smoke was old, but not by much. The scents were bitter and wormed their way into his brain, making him want to turn away. With his face still pressed to the horse, he couldn't.

Underneath the aroma of ash and soot, another scent danced on the breeze that drifted under the low clouds. Fox relaxed his face, trying to discern what the strange smell was over the taste of old blood on his bitten tongue. It wasn't familiar, but it wasn't unfamiliar either. It carried the mineral aroma of old magic.

"How far does this road go?" Rhydian asked as he appeared in Fox's vision. He waved a dusty hand to the north. "I always rode south. I never thought to venture this way." He pursed his lips. He was close enough to Fox that the dark blue ring around his paler blue irises looked grey and silver in the dull light.

Fox's vague twist of his shoulder was supposed to be a shrug. Rhydian didn't see it. His gaze was far off, following the road as it scraped along the base of the reddish mountains on their left. The gold in his hair was a dull bronze and the slight breeze was blowing strands around his face. He turned to Fox, knowing he was being watched.

"The curse," Fox murmured, adjusting his chest on the horse's neck, feeling the small press of the golden chain and gem under his shirt, against his heart.

After a moment Rhydian nodded. His gaze was steady as he studied Fox's expression. "Perhaps."

"It goes north a fair way, I think. There was a town mentioned once, south of the City of Seers. Not Aneirin." Fox closed his eyes against the grey day and searched what little memories he had of his time with Owaen. "Baile Fuar."

"Baile what? Where?"

Fox searched his jumbled memory. "A quarry town. I think Owaen said something about the s-stone for the City of Seers came from there-" Fox paused to cough as a spasm rocked his lungs. "There's a fork in the road up ahead. North and east."

"East?" Rhydian turned to face the valley's edge to their right, his face a mask of confusion. "What the fuck else is there east?"

Forest, thick and green but not as tall as the woods to their south, spanned to a blue green haze on the horizon. Low hills and shallow valleys were interspersed with short mountain ranges that didn't quite form a broad arch like the steep reddish range behind them.

Blackthorn shifted and whinnied under Fox as he tried to push himself up, failing with a pain filled slump. Rhydian sensed the horse's unease, soothing the beast's nose with a pat, before he realised Fox was trying to move. A sheepish grin broke the thin line of Rhydian's weary face as he realised he was more concerned for his horse. He met Fox's glare and huffed out a soft laugh.

"Sorry, I love this beast."

"Clearly," Fox muttered, his voice dry. "As for the east, I think there was a city out there somewhere. On the sea."

"The sea?" Rhydian looked at him blankly.

Fox stared. "Please t-tell me you know what an ocean is?"

"Of course I do," Rhydian snapped, his blue eyes flashing. Blackthorn tossed his head. Rhydian prevented the horse from doing it again, kissing the animals's soft nose. Fox cursed as he was shifted around. Rhydian let out a cool breath. "But there's none... I mean..."

"Your parents," Fox muttered, "were bad, *bad* people."

Rhydian bit his bottom lip again and his cheeks flushed. "Right. The curse."

"Either way, from here, Aurelia is north." Fox sighed. "And so is Owaen."

"Are you sure?"

Fox let his awareness wander inwards, tugging at the last kernel of power inside of him. His hands trembling again as the rope around his wrists chafed, stinging.

"I feel it. Or h-hear maybe. Like a dull chime has been rung far off. The notes ring true when I think of them in the north."

"Where does this chime ring?" Rhydian asked, his voice low. His hand dropped from the horse to his side.

"Inside," Fox murmured, "in my heart, like you f-felt when my magic called you to yours in the forest. Before all of this."

Swallowing, Rhydian nodded, his expression solemn. The wind blew his hair back over his face and absently he brushed it away. The scent of ash drifted past. Fox sighed, running his dry tongue around his copper tasting mouth. There was no reason in stalling. He was already in pain, limbs twisted and aching, his lungs and chest on fire.

"Untie me."

Rhydian didn't move. A single golden brown eyebrow rose. Fox choked on his pleased laugh. Even in the midst of all of this, the young king had found something to hold on to. Stubbornness or a sense of righteousness, Fox wasn't sure. Cracked lips bled afresh as his mouth widened with a dark smile.

"Please."

42

Morgan

Year 367
Aneirin City

A purple coat?

"Caspian," Morgan sighed. "You fucking idiot."

A throat cleared around the last corner of the passage that led from the temple to the street. Her hand tightened on her staff as she made the last turn to meet the two men near the temple entrance.

The older man's eyes widened, his mouth opening behind his beard.

"Lady Hywel," Merion murmured. His eyes were red and weary, but still burned with questions.

"Groom," Morgan replied, calmly. "And Wyll." She raised her eyebrows at the startled man next to Merion.

"Where have you been?" Wyll asked, his mouth hanging open.

Morgan tipped back her head to stare at the stone ceiling far above. She didn't have time for this. Being out in the open, even here under all this stone, was risk enough.

Not looking at either man, her gaze followed the soot stains of old incense on the shadowed ceiling.

"I've been avoiding the man that apparently wants to help your cause."

"Wait, what?"

"Is the king definitely leaving?"

Morgan dropped her eyes to Merion's curious gaze, uncaring about the flush of pink over Wyll's cheeks as she ignored his question and asked one of her own.

"Yes, my lady."

Nodding, Morgan peered past Merion to the street outside. Voices and hooves echoed up the broad steps into the columned space before the temple entrance. Possibilities ran through her mind while her fingers smoothed the edge of the faded fabric wrapped around the top of her staff.

"Thank you. I'll head back to the library. If I don't see you later on, let me say this now." Her green eyes met Merion's once more. "I'm sorry about Chase, Merion. I truly am."

Merion nodded, unable to respond.

She turned to head back into the temple, but Wyll called after her.

"Lady Hywel, wait, please."

Cursing under her breath, Morgan paused before turning back. Wyll was fidgeting with his belt. Merion was wiping his eyes with a scrap of fabric. The pang of sympathy that flared in her chest for the groom quickly faded as she met Wyll's narrow-eyed stare. He was clearly suspicious of her presence here.

"How do you know him?"

Morgan eyed the man up and down, trying not to show how much Wyll repulsed her. Not for any particular thing he'd said or done. It was only that the magic coiled within her heart was very, *very* good at letting her know when people needed to be avoided.

"I could never explain it to you," she replied, darkly amused by the anger that bloomed across his face. Wyll opened his mouth and closed it a few times before he finally settled on something to say.

"How *long* have you known him?"

Her reply was as noncommittal. "A while."

Merion cleared his throat and interrupted. "Do you trust him?"

Unable to help herself, Morgan laughed, startling both of the men. Thinking upon the last time she had seen Caspian and what he had done, Morgan shook her head, slowly. A dog barking from outside on the street broke the silence while she considered her words.

"The man is a liar," she mused. "But when he *does* tell the truth about his intentions, he does exactly what he said he would do."

Lines around Merion's eyes appeared as he frowned. He seemed like he was about to comment, but shook his head instead. He cleared his throat.

"Lady Hywel, it was good to see you, but I've got to go. I hope to see you again soon."

Morgan nodded at him, and Merion returned it before eyeing Wyll. Saying nothing, Wyll gestured to the street with his hand. Merion's frown deepened. But he left without another word.

Watching the groom leave, Wyll ran a hand through his hair. His gaze slid back to Morgan, eyeing her up and down in much the same way as she had done to him a moment ago.

"How can you tell if this man is speaking the truth?"

"Poor Wyll," Morgan said, her tone mimicking that of an adult speaking to a small child. "You can't."

Morgan darted back into the temple passage before Wyll could pester her further. Raised voices echoing around the turns from the crowd within continued. About what, she couldn't tell and she didn't care. Whatever came out of the aftermath of this ridiculous battle would happen no matter what she did. So she would ride it out as she always did. In much the same way as Caspian was doing.

As she ducked behind the columns closest to the altar, Morgan wondered about that. Would he still be looking for her? Passing into the temple, she stepped from column to column, checking behind her to make sure none of the townsfolk followed her into the dark corner behind the altar. Her words to Merion and Wyll came back to her. It was true. When Caspian said he'd do something, there was no point in stopping him. The gods only knew that she'd tried.

A choked laugh escaped her as she felt blindly for the narrow gap in the corner. Where one wall *supposedly* met the other. If you didn't know the tunnel entrance was here, you'd likely never see it, not with the way a light buzz of magic blurred the opening. The crystals of the temple were gone, but some of the magic remained. If she hadn't known who had desecrated this temple, the next likely candidate would have been Caspian. He was always looking to fill the void inside, where he felt magic should have welled within, deep and endless. Just like he was likely looking for her.

"Yes," she murmured, her boot finding the top step leading down into blackness. She tapped the next step below with the base of her staff.

Caspian would still be looking, even after all this time.

Perhaps not actively, but still keeping his quicksilver eyes open.

But it wasn't just about his longing for her, was it?

She might have needed him to be saved from herself once more.

Morgan followed each step carefully, descending into the forgotten chamber below the altar. It had once been full of priestesses deep in prayer and meditation. As she let her boots and the staff guide her progress in the gloom, Morgan was aware that the descent into the shadows was a fine metaphor for the choices she had made willingly long ago. Decisions that Caspian had yanked her right back out of. It was the single most hard and easy admission to make. He was likely the only reason she was still alive, taking care of her in a way that no one else had bothered.

It hadn't been her fault. She had been charged with the care of a fucking library full of knowledge in which she had no interest in. Raised an orphan, a priestess had recognised her keen eye for details from a young age. *Too* young. She should have been playing on the beach with the others, looking for shells and crap that the sea bought to shore. Instead, she had been taught to count, write and memorize.

And when the priestesses had aged or left for the City of the Seers, with less and less young ones joining in the worship of the various gods, the library had been left to Morgan's care.

A library on the cliffs, once overlooking a sparkling turquoise sea.

A library full of nonsense that had been written by old men, men who had died centuries before she had been born.

A library that she had been forced to love, but instead, had *hated*.

Caspian had taken care of that, too. But like the fool she was, she'd fled his attentions, thinking she could hide. To the City of the Seers, still being built, back to the priestesses and the new library under construction. To a den full of poppy smoke.

As the steps evened out to smooth flagstones beneath her boots, Morgan was still unable to separate horror from amusement at Caspian's actions taken on her behalf. Not just with the old library, now a pile of ash on broken cliffs in the east, but with her addiction as well.

Crossing the chamber below the temple, Morgan paused at the far wall, listening. The voices above were faint. The only other sound was her breath, along with the occasional drip of moisture from the low stone ceiling. It was colder down here, smelling of moss. There was no light reaching down from above. Not even her magic could help her see. Her staff could have helped with a soft glow if she chose. But she'd come to know this tunnel well over the past few weeks. So she chose the shadows instead. The light would be reached soon enough, but for now, the darkness was familiar. Potentially infinite.

It was the closest she could get to Caspian for now.

His darkness was endless.

Endless, lethal and *pure*, a force to be reckoned with, especially when he used it for her.

The dark days of her past even now were a blur. Her keen mind hadn't failed her, but the poppies that she'd been smoking had. Angry and resentful, instead of making adult decisions, she'd made poor ones. In choosing to avoid her *sacred duties*, of caretaking thousands of aged books and scrolls, Morgan had chosen oblivion, and to leave her body. She had chosen to let her mind drift with sickly sweet smoke and pleasures of the flesh. At the time, it seemed to be the only option to avoid her responsibilities. It worked for a while.

Until a blonde sixteen-year-old boy had disagreed.

Caspian's darkness had shone like a ray of light in the poppy den. He had thrown back the curtains to the room she had let herself go in. His expression wasn't disgusted when he had found her. It had been calm, knowing, even then. Swaggering in like some pirate from her mad dreams, stealing her away.

How old had she been? Twice his age, at least. It was hard to tell with the way his parents had experimented on them all, honing their discoveries with magic on their once human bodies. She should have known better. But she'd been as high as a newly morphed dragon, her mind lost in the clouds that last day in the den.

Exotic eyes, both blue but one dark and the other light, had filled her vision. There had been an amused laugh before the room had tilted around her. Rook, her dealer, might have put up a fight. There had been swearing, at least. Caspian had said something sharp that she remembered, and then there had been a strange silence. Rook's face, normally scowling, was etched into her memory for the comical look on his face as he blinked at whatever Caspian had murmured to him. With another soft laugh, Caspian had swanned out with her in his arms.

Morgan didn't know what Caspian said to Rook to let his best customer, her, go free. He'd never offered, and she'd never asked, but she had a fair idea.

Soon enough perfumed incense breezed past her as they exited the curtained doorway, coloured silks feeling blissful as they caressed her face. Despite the fact that she had been thrown over his shoulder, like a ridiculously beached seal. Her laugh echoed up the tunnel as it rose under her boots, heading directly to the castle. She couldn't be certain, but it was likely that the smack on her arse was real, and not some figment of her imagination while she was high.

Had Caspian even known how dangerous Rook was? And the danger he'd put himself in by strutting in like he had? If he did, he hadn't shown it or cared. Caspian had swanned into that hateful place full of poppy smoke and hashish, scooped her up and then carried her back to his half built chambers in the new City of the Seers.

The city had been in progress before the old city on the sea fell to the waves, but people forgot that. The new city wasn't built especially to replace the old, but its progress had been sped up to take the refugees from the chaos on the sea. Her memory knew, but there was hardly anyone left to care about the details, was there? So his family's chambers were crude and unfinished. It didn't matter. Thank the gods the place had been devoid of builders. There was still only rudimentary plumbing, and Caspian had laughed as he held back her hair while she'd vomited over the drain.

He'd thrived even then, amidst any chaos that came his way.

She hadn't thrown up because she had been nauseous. He'd been suspicious of what she'd been high on. She'd thrown her guts up simply because he'd made her.

"Did you smoke it?"

Morgan had half laughed, and half sobbed at him from the chamber floor. His gaze had darkened.

"Did you eat it?"

Another giddy wail of grief and joy had fallen from her numb lips. It shamed her now to remember. Caspian would no doubt still laugh fondly at the memory.

"Be a good girl and, you know..." Standing above her, Cas had waved obnoxiously to the corner of the room, bright-eyed and expectant. She followed the direction of his wave. He was pointing to the still unfinished drain that was yet to be covered over by stone masons.

"Fuck off, you spoilt little sh-shit."

"Oh my gods," Cas had wheezed, clutching his chest dramatically. "When you say those things, my heart splutters just so."

"I hate you," Morgan had hissed as her eyes closed. The room had been spinning, the smoke fogging her mind, leaving sticky cobwebs and strange echoes behind. But closing her eyes was worse. She flickered sticky eyelids back open.

"Beautiful woman," Cas had crooned. "My heart flutters like leathery bat wings, dangling in the caves where cold stones are torn out by dragons to build this fucking city."

"Shut up, you f-freak."

His beautiful eyes had widened at that. The thoughtful look on his face had caught her by surprise. As had his question.

"Why aren't you a dragon, Morgan?" he had whispered, eyes curious. "Is it because you're already a snake?"

"Get lost."

His concern had sharpened into something darker.

"So you can choke on your vomit and die? Not today, serpent."

Morgan tapped the staff carefully on the slightly uneven flagstones underneath. The tunnel hadn't quite collapsed, but the ground was uneven, the floor undulating up and down a few metres like the foothills of the Aneirin valley. This was likely from the tremors that had been striking more and more frequently.

Taking a shallow breath, Morgan made her way over the stretch of miniature hills and valleys in the gloom, remembering the thoughtful look on Caspian's teenage face. The tip of his pink tongue lightly touched his teeth as he spoke.

"Trauma bonds are in no way healthy," he'd said seriously. "But I fall for you a little more each time I see how broken you are." A warm hand smoothed her hair. "Broken at birth, just like me."

Morgan had been lost for words by that point, unable to look away from his mesmerising, iridescent eyes.

"I promise I'm going to kick this fucking habit with you, my tiny ruby jewel," Caspian had said, eyeing her calmly. Taking off his weapons belt, his beautiful sword had clanked in its sheath as he placed it on the tiles. He'd knelt by her side with a graceful fold of long legs, and then urged her gently towards the drain. The room had reeled, and Morgan had to shut her eyes as the room span in colourful circles.

When she'd finally opened them, she'd been propped up over the open drain that ran with fresh water, directed from some underground source from the gods knew where. Cas was still on his knees beside her. A hand tightened in her hair. The fingers of his other hand had gently stroked her brow. Callouses from sword practice wandered in a tantalising path across her sweating flesh.

"I promise that I'm going to make you see what a waste of our lives this nonsense is, Morgan."

The soothing caress of his calloused fingers travelled tenderly from her brow to her cheek, then further down to clasp her chin. Sounding like he was biting back a laugh, she'd never forget the solemn hum of his quiet voice.

"And I promise that I'm going to enjoy this much more than you."

She'd had no warning as he'd shoved his fingers down her throat.

He'd been right.

Caspian had done exactly what he said he would, his wild smile ever present. Morgan had been free of the need to lose herself in sickly sweet smoke in only a matter of weeks. Unheard of to most of those that were caught amongst the web of drugs and the oblivion they promised.

Thinking of that time didn't cost her any shame in remembering how lost she'd been, and how earnest Caspian had been in return. How careful with her, how patient no matter how sick, angry or violent she'd been with him. His laugh had always been both sting and balm. In the midst of one city crumbling on the coast, and one city being built far inland, there had been no sign of uncertainty in his bright eyes. Even as a teenager, Caspian had known exactly what he wanted. Simple things, really.

Power.

The world.

And her.

With Caspian's laugh echoing in her chest, Morgan's staff bumped into the end of the steep, uphill tunnel. She had come to the door under the castle. The flagstones were especially uneven here. She almost tripped headfirst into the wall, before she managed to fling a hand out to catch herself. Realising what she was touching, she swore. Yanking her hand free of sticky cobwebs, she edged her way over the uneven ground. The scent of old dust seeped in from the crack below the wood as she pressed her shoulder against it, grunting with effort.

The heavy wooden door had no working lock. The rusted metal of the old mechanism was still there, but it had been unlocked when she had first discovered it. At the temple end of the tunnel, there was no door, the priestesses had likely seen no need. All they needed was solemn, unhurried access from their place of worship and veneration to the crypts of the castle's lower levels. But unlocked didn't mean easy to open.

Scowling, Morgan pushed as hard as her slight frame would allow, her slim shoulder straining against thick oak. With a low humming scrape, the door eventually shifted and gave way with a quick burst. The suddenness had her stumbling into the solemn silence of the crypt.

"Fuck," she hissed, uncaring of the dead royal family members around her in the dark. As she found her feet, the low light from a single lantern flickered.

She froze.

Cool air washed over her, noticeably drier than the faintly humid air of the tunnel. She reached out, fingers touching the chilly stone of an old burial, and she crouched down behind it in the dark. While her heart beat a wild rhythm, she held her breath, waiting. But there was no one else here besides her. The lantern had been left at the far end of the crypts, towards the entrance up into the castle. It must have been left in vigil for the most recent internment.

Grateful that she was alone, Morgan wiped what she hoped was hair off her face but halted the movement, a soft prickle of awareness touching her subconscious. No voice called out, no steps were headed her way to investigate. It was something more ephemeral, not quite anything at all, really. Even so, Morgan waited. And eventually she sensed something. It wasn't someone moving in the shadows. It was instinctual, more of a feeling.

Straightening from a crouch behind one of the oldest stone sarcophagi, Morgan blinked into the cavernous space, a line marring her lightly freckled brows.

The feeling, almost a sound, was stronger now. She glanced up, unable to see the ceiling from the dim light at the far end. Something landed softly on her face. Biting back a scream of fright, Morgan stumbled back, catching the wooden doorway of the tunnel to steady herself. Wiping a trembling hand across her cheek, she scrunched up her nose. Her fingers came away gritty, dry earth crumbling between them. Dirt was quietly raining down from the roof above, the underside of the great hall.

And then she heard it again. This time from behind.

Eyes widening, Morgan slowly turned around.

Something was travelling along the tunnel towards her.

Dismissing the risk of Caspian sensing her magic if he was close by, Morgan ripped the tattered scarf off the top of her staff. With a sharp flick of her mind, a blinding, red light spread out in her dark corner of the crypt. She hefted the staff up, spreading the light as far as she could from the red orb at the top. The light played over the old carved stone walls, patterns marked directly into the rock of Aneirin itself. The light spilled into the tunnel as she passed the staff through the opening. Her mouth dropped open at the sight before her.

It wasn't something coming down the passage; it wasn't something moving within it.

It was the tunnel itself.

"Earthquake," she breathed. "Fu-"

Even as the thought registered, her mouth forming words, the wave of force rippling along the tunnel towards her collided. The sides of the tunnel heaved, the flagstones cracking and splintering as the energy blasted past and over her. Morgan was thrown onto her back, away from the opening, her bones protesting. Her staff, thankfully still shining, rolled away from her fingers as she landed.

The sound reached her, a violent rumbling and groaning. With her eyes stinging as more dust rained down from above, Morgan pushed herself up, watching parts of the tunnel ceiling collapse. Chunks fell and slid downwards, along the slope of the cracking and heaving floor.

She watched for the gods knew how long as grit clogged her mouth and nose, bones jarring and flesh shivering with the deep roar of the earth shifting and protesting around her. As the wave finally passed over, various cracks and pops rang out in the cavernous crypt behind. It was likely more of the oldest stonework on the wall and sarcophagi were cracked beyond repair. But she was unable to look, unable to tear her gaze away from the devastation within the tunnel before her.

By the red glow of the fallen staff, it was easy to see that the way was no longer safe. It was only by mere chance that she'd exited when she had.

"Hells," Morgan whispered, staring at the almost solid mass of jumbled rock, wall, and floor. There was no way she could shut the door now. She glanced up. The blood red light reached the underside of the roof above. Thankfully, no cracks were visible. There were only a few great natural columns of stone fluted from ground to ceiling to support the great space, but they seemed unharmed, solid enough to not crumble. But now she was trapped inside the castle, without an invisible way to get in or out. She hoped that Caspian was as far away as she thought.

As she pushed to her feet and dusted off what she could, Morgan paused as she bent to collect her staff. Her heart was still beating wildly. Tremors had always been part of the way of life here. But a full on quake? She hadn't experienced one of those since before the City of the Seers. It was unusual, and likely related to the curse, or something close to it. It required meditation and further study, but for now, she was here for something else.

It took a careful amount of manoeuvring, but once the red glow from her staff had been snuffed out, Morgan made her way up to the chaotic lower levels of the castle. She passed the single lantern, left near the body of Merion's nephew, pausing long enough to use a faint mist of power to blow the fallen dust and soot off his wrapped body. The king's corpse, she ignored.

There was a shocked quality to the air as she reached the top of the stairs that levelled out to the main floor. Elves and humans alike were picking themselves up and dusting off. Using their distraction as cover, she walked as fast as she dared in the shadows.

Back to the library.

Her library, as the young prince had once called it. Scowling, Morgan pushed open the doors. The large space was empty. Tearing off the scarf that bound up her long red hair, Morgan rested back against the inside of the doors after she locked them from the inside. A soft sigh escaped her as she examined the room.

The spiral staircases, the mezzanine above, the armchairs and central table were as familiar as her hands. Her eyes trailed over the room, landing on the unlit fireplace. It was cold and dark, and the mantle above it was full of the trinkets she had collected over the years. The many, many years she had been here, quietly existing until a young king and queen had turned up when so many of the royals were thought lost.

Pushing off from the door, Morgan crossed the room to the cold hearth, taking her time on purpose. The soles of her boots crunched on something. Smashed fragments of glass were scattered outwards from the fireplace.

"That's annoying," she muttered, knowing it would be hers to clean up.

Other items were scattered on the floor in front of the fire. Some of her trinkets had been knocked off the shelf by the quake and had come to rest amongst the sparkling remains of glass. Frowning, Morgan lifted her gaze to the beam across the top of the hearth. The engraved plaque had fallen on its face. Reaching up, she set the map upright to lean back against the chimney. Even in the grey light from the overcast day seeping in from the windows across the wall on either side of the hearth, she could see the finely made features of the engraving. The lines were similar to fingerprints, sinuous records of all the pain and disrupted memories that the old city on the sea held for her.

"Give it up, Caspian," Morgan said to the empty room, eyes following the contours of the brass map. "As much as I'm curious, you'll never do it."

It was fascinating to think back on her long life, about how the highs and the lows had been shaped by only two things. Her so-called life purpose, bestowed upon her at birth as an orphan. And him.

Reaching up with the ruby at the top of her staff, Morgan poked the side of the engraving. She closed her eyes, imagining the salt and the crisp air of the sea from where this plaque, and her, had originated. Even those memories were intercepted with memories of blue eyes, one light and one dark, shining silver and bright, intent on her face. The pride and the pain within them had always taken her breath away once she'd seen past her own limitation and ego to recognise it. Something that looked back at her when she bothered to find a mirror and look. No one else had understood. Their rage. Their hunger for more.

Their absolute disregard for letting others in, not needing to prove their worth to anyone but themselves.

Her earlier words to Wyll at the temple seemed appropriate.

Morgan spoke them aloud once more.

"I could never explain it."

She tapped her staff to the plaque; the quiet tap of crystal onto bronze was the only sound besides her slow exhale.

"Even now, I feel no need to try."

No matter what he'd done, she had always been there for him. Equally appalled and amused by his actions. But she had always been there.

Except for now.

Because the last time she had seen him, *that* had been unexpected. Even for him.

"Oh Caspian," she had sighed, eyes on his bare feet and his bloody hands. "Tell me you didn't...?"

His calm expression had been the only answer she'd needed to know what he'd done. His parents, blind to their work, likely hadn't seen it coming.

"Hypatia, my old friend," Morgan breathed into the empty library as the clouds passed by outside the windows. One of the glass panes had a new crack from the top of the square to halfway down. "Your son is a beast, just like you were."

A faint tremor, hopefully just an aftershock, rumbled through the room. The crack in the window forked like lightning to reach the bottom of the pane. Morgan stood still, unmoved by the shouts of alarm from outside in the various courtyards below. She eyed the sharp angles of the fissure in the glass.

"But he's *my* beast. Just like I am *his*."

43

Rhydian

Year 367
The Forest

What was a story, and what was real?

As Rhydian dragged an unconscious Fox off Blackthorn, a small voice inside asked a thousand questions. But this one was the loudest of them all. The strange events unfolding around him seemed like part of some endless loop of mania inside his broken mind. Living under a curse, his parents' war for power, Aurelia taken from his home. And now he had travelled with some kind of ripple of power, generated by a dragon that looked like a dying man. But to where they had travelled, he couldn't say. It was a blur that his mind couldn't process, his stomach still churning. He knew they had headed north, but to where he simply had no idea.

I can't be here, this can't be happening, kings don't get lost in the woods.

"Fox," Rhydian panted as he placed Fox on the moss, "stay with me, *please.*"

He was now on his knees in the moss and the mud, with two spooked horses, and had no clear idea what the fuck had just happened. Tilting his head back, Rhydian's gaze travelled up the black cliff face above.

The jagged, natural wall was slick with rain that was no longer falling. It was not quite vertical. He had never seen rock like it before. It was glistening with droplets that looked like a thousand stars in the low light of the overcast day. It hadn't been raining when they had left the farmlands earlier, on the exhausted sparks of Fox's magic. But now they were somewhere it had rained quite recently.

Before Fox had passed into unconsciousness, he had somehow transported them to this place. Near silent, the air felt eerie, as if tiny mites were leaving little bursts of ice while crawling over exposed flesh. The after effects of however they had travelled? As he brushed a sweating hand over his cheek at the phantom sensations that had yet to fade, Rhydian remembered a roar in his ears, a bright glow behind his tightly shut eyes, and the shuddering of his horse beneath him. Aftershocks and tremors, great ripples under their feet, still hummed and boiled below. The horses were rightly scared, and so was he. He closed his eyes to the wall of rock.

This is just a story, a nightmare told by my librarian when I'd sat still long enough to listen, strange tales of knights, kings and queens.

They had arrived in a blur and nauseous inducing motion of colour, sound, and cold. And blood. The coppery tang was as strong as the life affirming aromas of soil and foliage. Rhydian opened his eyes, blinking tears of frustration out of his clouded vision.

The forest crowded thick and tall around them, cool, rich and silent apart from the fading, rumbling violence within the earth below. Opening his eyes, he could see that the trees were just as tall as those south of Aneirin. But the trunks were darker; the most common species of broad-leafed pines was one he'd never seen before. The air was humid despite the low temperature. Above the clearing they had arrived in, the canopy was a rippled of shifting shadows and dappled grey light.

Is this real? I'm searching for Aurelia, but I am in the mud of a strange forest with the unconscious creature that brought us here.

Rhydian cursed as his eyes roamed over the man in his arms for signs of life. Fox was bleeding from his mouth, nose, ears, and even his eyes. A shallow breath rattled in his throat, and Rhydian's heart turned over in alarmed relief that Fox was still with him. His white face was completely colourless, except for the dark circles around his eyes.

"Fox," Rhydian pleaded, shaking the man in his arms. "Where?"

Fox's reply might have only been an indrawn breath, a mere gasp of pain. It was faint, but Rhydian sobbed with relief at the sound.

"Up..."

Rhydian tilted his head back once more, taking in the wall of rock before them.

This can't be a story; the stories in the library had better endings than this, because it looks like I'm fucked right now.

"Up?" Rhydian repeated into Fox's inky black hair tickling his jaw. There was no reply. Not only was Fox as cold as the ice that cracked under Blackthorn's hooves in his field during a winter ride, Fox was no longer racked by shaking tremors. He was limp, completely still.

Up.

Rhydian eyed Blackthorn. The animal's ears were still pointed back as far as they could go, and glossy black muscles twitched and trembled. The other horse was just as wide eyed. Laying Fox on the moss for a moment, Rhydian pushed himself up with a groan and secured their reigns loosely to a low-hanging branch on the closest pine tree. He hoped it was the right thing to do, and that he was coming back. If he didn't, he was sure Blackthorn at least would free himself.

Stepping back to Fox, Rhydian slid his hands under Fox's arms and dragged him to the base of the cliff. He set Fox against an irregular shaped boulder and assessed the steep rise. The jumble of ferns and moss that made up the forest floor butted right up against the black sheet of rock to his left and right. But to go up? A trail of loose rock and pebbles that twisted steeply up to a series of low, natural shelves of black rock to his left was the only option. Rhydian bit his lip.

It was possible, but only barely. Except that if he dropped Fox at any point, there would be broken bones at best. A snapped neck at worst. Carefully, he leant forward and placed his hand on the smooth, black outcrop nearest his head. He immediately snatched his hand away.

The rock was *alive*.

No. Not quite alive. But it was humming with a low vibration that he could feel not quite with his fingers, but in his bones. Any doubts about this seemingly lost cause evaporated. Above their heads, a slight breeze stirred the dark leaves around them and a faint creak of wood broke the silence.

This must be the place.

With that thought, Rhydian took a breath, lifted one of Fox's arms and ducked his head underneath. Placing one hand on Fox's elbow near his face, his other hand around the man's hips, Rhydian staggered upright. With Fox on his shoulder like a sack of grain, he rested against the cliff, puffing. When he took his first step, his boots slipped and with a grunt, he collapsed, narrowly avoiding Fox's head on the boulder he'd been leaning against.

"Fuck!"

Rolling Fox gently to his back, Rhydian puffed out a few breaths whilst on his knees, running his hands over his sweating face. His own hands were trembling now. From the exertion, or from the anxiety of how precarious this attempt for help was becoming, he wasn't sure. Either way, he had to move. He thought of a tiny purple dragon telling him to poke Fox with his boot. If only Flare were here now. Although, considering what he was about to do, it was good there was no one to witness the indignity.

Stumbling a little, Rhydian stood back up and gripped Fox by his chilly wrists and raised them past the damp, black hair. He cursed again as he caught Fox's weight, but at least there was no chance of breaking Fox open like a cracked egg. It took him a moment, but they were moving. Walking backward onto the steep and uneven trail that was barely there, cursing and grunting, he was able to progress up the steep slope, albeit slowly. It was one boot step at a time, dragging Fox's dead weight. But they were rising. Aware of his frustration at having to drag Fox up a steep cliff, a small part of him was finding satisfaction in how his sword occasionally poked Fox in the ribs.

It might have taken hours, Rhydian wasn't sure, but the higher he managed to get, passing jagged outcrop after jagged outcrop, the hum of the surrounding cliff could now be heard without touching it. Roughly ten metres up, his arms and back were practically screaming with the weight of Fox's unconscious form, but his bones were vibrating inside of his body. Like ants crawling through his sinew and muscles, the magic of this strange place was trying to burrow inside of him. It didn't hurt as such, but it made him want to scrub himself all over, inside and out, with Blackthorn's favourite stiff bristled brush.

Rhydian's arms and back were burning by the time they reached the largest shelf of black rock. Its surface was coated with patchy splotches of grey lichen, growing thick in deep grooves that could have been giant claw marks. He dragged Fox off the loose rocks, laying him down gently onto the hard surface. This outcrop, whilst still uneven, was mostly level. One edge brushed up against the steep slope they had been ascending, the other two sides of its roughly triangular shape retreated into the cliff face, into shadows. It was a cave. The opening was large, about five metres high and the same width, almost a perfect arch. The blackness was not quite absolute, because deep inside the tunnel, a light was glowing a soft and steady sky blue.

They had arrived.

Sobbing with relief, his back protesting, Rhydian couldn't help himself.

"Knock, fucking knock, Owaen," he rasped, wiping his face with the hem of his soaked shirt.

Below him, Fox was still as limp as ever, his shirt and layers wrecked and torn from the drag up the trail. The once shining green of his sword's scabbard was scratched and scraped by the rocks. Fox looked like he'd been punched in the face days ago and the bruises had come out dark purple instead of green and yellow. There was fresh and dried blood smeared with black grit over his face and neck.

Swallowing, Rhydian adjusted his grip around one of Fox's icy wrists. His fingers pressed into the soft inner skin below Fox's palm. Holding his breath, Rhydian waited, eyes closed. It was faint, but it was there. A weak pulse, like butterfly wings, fluttering with irregularity beneath the cold flesh.

Rhydian's sigh of relief mixed with the sound of the canopy rustling before the cliff face. A fresh breeze was competing with the humidity, leaving cooler air in its wake. He glanced back towards the mouth of the cave, staring out at the forest beyond, while addressing the unconscious man below.

"Fox," Rhydian whispered. "I'm going to poke you with my boot once more... or at least slap you very... *very*... hard. And you are going to wake the fuck up."

Catching Fox's weight again, Rhydian dragged the unconscious man into the cavernous passage, the rocks glowing and humming around them.

"*No.*"

Fox's anxious croak might have been lost outside amongst the breeze passing through the trees below. But here, surrounded by black rock, there was no mistake.

On his knees with his hand stinging, Rhydian hung his head.

He had carefully laid Fox to rest as close as possible to the wall of glowing rock at the end of the dark tunnel. The forest was barely visible outside. The low light of the overcast day left little light illuminating the trees, barely any made it down to the far end. Rhydian estimated the tunnel was roughly twenty metres deep, and it had widened out, not narrowed like he had expected once inside. The tunnel itself looked the same as the cliff, black and smooth in patches. The end of the passage, a featureless wall, was different, however. It was emitting a blue light, cold and clear, that made Rhydian's eyes hurt to look at. The hum of the rock was all around them too, and Rhydian wanted to drag Fox the fuck back out and away. He grit his teeth instead, and shook Fox more roughly.

"Fox," he hissed, raising a shaking hand to slap Fox's icy cheek once more. "Do your thing. We're *here*."

Black eyes opened, slits barely wide enough to reflect the blue glow around them.

"No," he rasped. "I've changed m-my mind..."

"WHAT?" Rhydian's roar echoed around them like a disturbed flock of bats screaming through the shadows. "Do it, damn you, do it *now*!"

The black slits disappeared as Fox tried to turn his face away. Rhydian grabbed Fox's hair by the roots in one hand and his jaw with his other.

"Fox!" Rhydian hissed directly into Fox's face. "Open this cave up right the fuck *now*!"

Black eyes opened, this time wide enough for gold flecks to reflect the blue light. The scatter of strange sky blue flecks made Fox look sicker, wilder. Something was mumbled from cracked lips.

"What? What was that?"

"You swear too... much..."

"What the f-" Biting back his curse, Rhydian adjusted his grip to grab the front of Fox's shirt. He jerked Fox towards him, their foreheads touching. Rhydian ignored the sharp gasp of pain.

"Open it!"

"No..."

"Why?" Rhydian cried, shaking the man roughly. "Why the fuck not?"

"I don't w-want to. I'm..." Fox mumbled, his dry lips cracking, red seeping between the seams. Black and gold glowing eyes darted back and forth between Rhydian's. "I'm afraid."

Rhydian froze. Crimson washed across his vision.

"Afraid?" he hissed, teeth flashing in the blue light. "Oh, you're *afraid*, are you?"

Unable to turn away, Fox's eyes stayed locked on Rhydian's face.

"Guess who else is likely afraid right now, Fox?"

The tip of Fox's tongue darted out to lick the fresh drops of blood away from his lips. Rhydian watched the movement, then snapped his eyes back to Fox's own.

"No idea?" Rhydian hissed. "You can't guess?"

"P-please... no..."

"*Aurelia!*" Rhydian roared, tasting the metallic blood on Fox's lips. "So get over your-self," he grabbed one of Fox's icy hands, holding him up just by the grip on Fox's shirt, "and open this fucking cave, before I toss you off this fucking cliff!"

Not waiting for an answer, Rhydian slammed Fox's palm against the end of the passage wall.

The result was instant, and both of them cried out.

A blistering cold, so icy that it burned, seared into Rhydian's hand where it was joined with Fox's. A deep pulse sounded around them, ringing in their ears, feeling like a sharp ache in their bones. The loose grit and rock on the tunnel floor seemed to rise momentarily, just a fraction, before falling back down. The low, ever present hum of earlier faded away. For a moment, all was silent.

Their panting and shallow breaths filled the tunnel, and just beneath that, a soft hiss of shifting sand could be heard.

"What-"

Before Rhydian could finish, the earth below them heaved with a deep roar and the wall they were collapsed against disintegrated.

"Owaen," Fox croaked, trembling. He was half buried in black sand, eyes closed. "Owaen, I'm sor-"

Rhydian smacked his burning hand over Fox's mouth, wobbling on his knees as the tremors subsided around them. His other hand was supporting Fox so that he didn't sink beneath the shifting rubble around them. Fox's eyes widened in alarm.

"Hush," Rhydian hissed, spitting out grit.

Fox opened his lips to protest, but at the look on Rhydian's face, closed his mouth un-der Rhydian's hand. Satisfied Fox wasn't going to say anything else just yet, he carefully let go of Fox's mouth before brushing the grit and dust off Fox's face. They were surrounded by a mound of black sand. Fox's bloodshot eyes were now wide with confusion. Mutely, Rhydian shook his head. The blue glow was brighter inside the cave.

The cavern was enormous. It was easily bigger than Aneirin castle's great hall, maybe three times as long, twice as tall. It was cool, smelling faintly of minerals with a freshness that was unexpected. The giant chamber was full of the sky blue glow, and completely covered in giant clear quartz crystals, many meters in length. Even the black floor was interspersed with giant columns piercing up from the ground, to almost reach the ceiling in soaring points. It was hard to tell if they were the source of the blue light, or if they only enhanced it. Either way, they reflected the light back and forth; the glow was a bright, icy blue, aqua at the base of each giant quartz cluster, but a paler hue at the tips.

"My gods," Rhydian muttered under his breath. His heart felt like it was trying to force its way out of his chest.

All of the crystals and their cold, breathtaking beauty would have been stunning enough on their own. But what Rhydian had seen to cause him to cut off Fox's desperate plea immediately after spitting out a mouthful of sand, was two things.

In the centre of the chamber was a giant crystal that was more of a rectangular prism than a regular quartz point. It reminded Rhydian of the sarcophagi in the royal crypt, but not hollowed out. It was barely bigger than a table that would seat ten people. On the flat surface, another unnatural clear crystal block, shaped like a cushion, was positioned at one end.

It was clearly intended as the final resting place for someone of high esteem, likely the person they were here for. But it was currently unoccupied. Rhydian swallowed, his mouth dry from the gritty air, anxiety spiking up along his spine.

The second thing that he'd noticed was the incredibly lifelike statue, only about two metres away from where they were crouched at the chamber entrance. It was made of the same quartz as the rest of the chamber, with a wash of colours highlighting the details, especially the woman's long and curling emerald green hair.

As his gaze wandered over the life-sized figure, Rhydian couldn't think of a single thing to say. He swallowed, blinking.

"Who is *that*?" Rhydian eventually breathed.

Fox mumbled something, pushing himself with weak movements towards the crystal figure. While Rhydian's gaze was riveted on the golden eyes of the breathtaking woman, Fox reach out a bloodless hand.

Too late, Rhydian's shout broke the silence of the glowing cave.

"Wait-!"

As soon as the tip of a single finger touched the crystal hem of the woman's dress, the statue cracked. A dull chime rang far off.

And then the quartz woman shattered.

"No!" Rhydian cried out, grabbing Fox around the waist. He jerked Fox backwards as quartz exploded into razor sharp shards, bursting outwards. They rained down with the sound of a thousand windows shattering. Rhydian covered Fox as best he could, his arms and back bursting with bright spots of fire as the natural glass rained down around them. Even as the stings made his eyes water, his heart burst with an ache for the loss of the artefact that had stolen his breath.

The statue had been the most incredible piece of art he'd ever seen. It was likely made by magic. The statue had been a woman, wide-eyed and impossibly beautiful. Along with the shining, transparent emerald green of her hair, jewel like tones in rainbow hues had coloured the cascade of gems down the front of her simple gown. Even the bare arms had been decorated. Faint green tattoos had wound down and around crystal clear limbs. But it had been her expression that Rhydian had been unable to tear his eyes from. Her wide golden eyes had been sparkling, her soft lips and been smiling, and her cheeks were rosy tinted with the glow of pure, unconditional love.

It had been the statue of a woman in love, as she had stared adoringly at the viewer.

Now it was broken shards glinting wickedly sharp around them.

A quiet sob echoed around the chamber.

"I'm s-sorry," Fox gasped.

He was barely upright, on his hands and knees, with his head pressed into the clear shards and black grit below them. The end of his scratched scabbard scraped amongst the sparkling pile. White fingers shook as he grasped at the chunks of crystal around him. Breathing fast, Rhydian stared, shocked at the surrounding devastation. Fox raised his head, his eyes completely black. He opened his bleeding mouth to say something else, but the black eyes widened, fixed on something behind Rhydian.

"Ow-"

Without any further warning, Rhydian was tackled from behind. He was torn away from Fox and thrown bodily across the cave. With a groan, he blinked with confusion from where he landed.

"Oh fuck," Fox whispered, barely able to move.

He coughed up blood that looked purple in the blue glow and collapsed into the shards of grit and crystal below.

Rhydian blinked up with confusion at the man who had knocked him away from Fox, knocking the wind right out of him.

He was holding Rhydian down with powerful hands, pressing Rhydian's shoulders to the chamber floor, the man's body on Rhydian's thighs. Blonde hair fell over eyes of the deepest green that Rhydian had ever seen, darker and wilder than Aurelia's. They were also clearly full of rage. Bared teeth were clenched as he glared expectantly down at Rhydian. With his head ringing from the impact of being thrown across the chamber, Rhydian realised the man had said something that he'd completely missed.

"Wh-what?"

Green eyes widened slightly before narrowing into thin slits.

"I said," was the venomous reply, "what did you do to her?"

Unable to break his eyes away, Rhydian shook his head.

"The statue? I'm sorry," he wheezed. "That was an accident, we-"

"I don't care about the statue, you fucking prick!" the man spat out. "What. Did. You. Do. To. Her?"

All Rhydian could do was blink.

Her?

A weak gasp interrupted them.

"O...Owaen..."

The man's nostrils flared. He squeezed Rhydian's shoulders, hard enough that Rhydian thought his bones would snap, before releasing him. The man had stalked back across the chamber before Rhydian could draw in an uneven breath. It was a struggle. The muscles in his arms, chest and shoulders were still on fire from dragging Fox up the cliff. Now he was bruised from being thrown across the softly lit cave. Finally, pushing up onto his elbows with a curse, Rhydian stared across the giant space.

Despite how sorry he felt for himself, hope flared within his chest.

The blonde man had gathered Fox into his arms, and Fox looked... better. Not great, but already soothed. Fox's face was still a ghastly sight, but the anxiety was gone. Eyes closed, Fox let himself be held, the arms around him gathering him close with tender care.

Even crouched beside Fox, it was easy to see that the man was tall. Toned arms and shoulders were clearly defined under his long-sleeved shirt. He was dressed in soft colours; a mixture of whites, beiges and browns. Dark brown boots were laced with leather bindings. For some reason, Rhydian was surprised that no sword hung off the thick leather belt at his waist. As bruises continued to bloom across his back, Rhydian realised wryly that perhaps the blonde man didn't need one.

The blue glow of the chamber and the crystals cast the two figures in an ethereal light, but they couldn't have looked more different. Fox's black hair looked midnight blue, his skin as pale as ever. The man who held Fox against his chest had skin that looked tanned in comparison. His long blonde hair reflected the blue glow, even the shaved section above the man's ear. He was holding onto Fox like he'd never let go, lips pressed into Fox's hair. Feeling the keen observation, the man turned his head to the side, eyes glaring at Rhydian with naked fury.

Inhaling deeply, his lungs protesting at the mineral rich air as he held his breath, Rhydian nodded to himself.

So that was Owaen.

With his jaw set tight, Owaen narrowed his flinty eyes at Rhydian before dropping his gaze. The change in his expression was remarkable. The fury was gone in an instant, to be replaced immediately with a concern so obvious that Rhydian wanted to look away. But he couldn't. He was fascinated with what he was seeing, the giant of a man with his arms around Fox. It was also Fox's expression. Rhydian bit his lip. Fox, even in his weakest moment, even unconscious, had been guarded. But the lines of pain, of fear, were gone, his mouth soft.

Owaen's lips brushed softly over Fox's. Fox sighed, limp in Owaen's arms, his breathing easy.

"Can you speak?" Owaen murmured.

Fox nodded slowly, not opening his eyes.

"Good." Owaen's expression hardened slightly. "Then tell me. Why do you still look like that? Why are you covered in blood? Where's your magic gone?"

As a faint smile twisted Fox's lips as he pressed his cheek into Owaen's chest.

Owaen raised his head, flinty green eyes burning darkly at Rhydian.

"And," Owaen continued darkly, "who the fuck is that?"

Rhydian's lips thinned, refusing to look away. Something unexpected passed over Owaen's face, but cleared just as quickly as it came. A pale hand reached up, soft blue in the cool light, long fingers taking hold of Owaen's jaw.

"Calm down," Fox croaked, weakly pulling on Owaen's jaw to face him.

Owaen's eyes tightened, but he allowed Fox to tug his face down. As the flinty gaze left his face, Rhydian carefully pushed himself up, keeping his hands well away from his sword.

His mouth a thin line, Owaen stared down at Fox with one eyebrow raised.

"That's…" Fox's voice was faint, but less of a rasp than only moments ago. "That's the k-king of Aneirin."

Rhydian edged closer, the toes of his boots had just started to crunch on the pile of dirt and rubble near the two figures. He froze as Owaen threw back his head and laughed. The sound of his mirth was a mocking echo around the crystals that crowded the cave. Fox winced, and Owaen tilted his head sideways to eye Rhydian up and down.

"That's not the king."

At the expression on Rhydian's face, Owaen's laughter died abruptly. He opened his mouth, then shut it. Licking his lips, he stared blankly at Fox. Rhydian had the distinct impression that Fox's cheeks may have been flushed with a faint wash of colour.

"I see." A muscle in Owaen's jaw twitched. "How long?"

With his eyes on Fox's face, Rhydian edged closer. The crunch of his boots on the shards below slid against the leather of his soles, but neither Fox nor Owaen glanced his way.

"How. *Long*?" Owaen repeated.

Fox licked his dry lips and cleared his throat.

"A little while," he replied.

Owaen absorbed that noncommittal remark in stony silence. Eventually, his nostrils flared.

"Shadow Light?"

"About that," Fox said, and hesitated. He bit his near bloodless bottom lip, the gold in his wide-eyed stare a pale mockery of its normal burning glory.

Burning emerald eyes narrowed as Owaen took in Fox's expression. Alarmed by the wash of fury that passed over Owaen's face, Rhydian's hand darted to his sword. But as his hand touched the cold metal of the hilt, he paused. Owaen closed his eyes, one of his hands coming up to his face, and strong fingers pinched the bridge of his nose. It sounded like the blonde man was counting whilst taking long, deep breaths. Finally, his eyes opened. His expression was grim as he stared down at the black-haired man in his arms.

"What's wrong with me?" Owaen sighed, eventually. His hand dropped away from his face to caress the side of Fox's slightly flushed cheek.

Fox momentarily shifted his gaze away, his glittering eyes searching until he met Rhydian's. Rhydian was still a few metres away, and he was unable to comprehend the depth of emotions in Fox's gaze. Still covered in blood as he was, his hair a wild mess and his clothes torn and wrecked, Fox grimaced. His eyes flicked past Rhydian, darting quickly around the cave before turning back to Owaen.

"Where are all the others?" Fox swallowed. "The others that Shadow Light had here? Where are their remains?"

Looking confused for a moment, Owaen looked around the chamber. As his gaze fell on Rhydian, Rhydian tensed. But Owaen's gaze left him just as quickly, almost dismissive. Rhydian narrowed his eyes, withdrawing his hand from his sword. He wanted to walk over there and shake them both to move, to hurry. He crossed his arms over his chest instead, sore arms protesting with the movement.

Owaen's touch was tender as he wiped Fox's hair back from his face, smoothing his hand across the bloody forehead.

"You left me with *some* magic that I used wisely when I woke occasionally," Owaen murmured. "They are at rest now."

Something dark flashed in Fox's wide-eyed gaze before he closed his eyes.

"I didn't mean to leave them here with you, but I was not quite myself," Fox's voice faded, and he murmured under his breath, too soft for Rhydian to catch. Owaen heard it, and he leant closer to press his forehead to Fox's.

Forcing himself to turn away, Rhydian moved towards the closest crystal wall. Reaching out carefully, he brushed his fingers over a point of clear quartz, taller and broader than him as it jutted from the cave floor. He examined the smooth edges before peering into the clear, blue-lit depths. He frowned. There was something, multiple things, inside the crystal. Not just close to him, but further back, embedded within.

Pressing his face against the cool surface, his mouth dropped open.

Stacked neatly inside the quartz were bones.

Hundreds, possibly thousands, of bones.

"Oh, fuck," Rhydian groaned.

With his nose pressed into the crystal, Rhydian's eyes darted around, trying to take in what he was seeing. There was no mess or jumble, just row after row of all sorts of bones, not arranged by body, but by type, impossibly preserved and set within the quartz like a dried out butterfly sealed under glass forever. Each one was clean and blue tinted. These just weren't displayed as if under a layer of glass, they were *embedded* within. And at the very top of the stack that stretched out from side to side were skulls. Their lower jaws were still attached, and skull after skull, neatly, and facing forward, stared back at him. They weren't the same sizes, though. Occasionally, some were large and adult sized.

Most of them were not.

His breath misted the clear surface and his hand flew to his mouth.

"Oh my gods, *no...*"

The reality of what this place was, of what horrors Fox had been through right *here*, hit Rhydian with full force. With a choked sob, he staggered away from the quartz wall, away from the staring skulls of the gods-only-knew how many dead children.

Panting, he stumbled away, turning his back to the glowing crystals and the silent victims within. Bent over, his hands grasped his knees while he struggled to comprehend what he had seen. The horror explained, at least in part, the cold fury just simmering beneath the surface in the way Fox spoke, acted and behaved.

Owaen was watching Rhydian, his face cold. Rhydian shook his head, unable to speak.

"This cave," Rhydian gasped. "It was here, wasn't it? When Sh-shadow..." his voice gave out and he cleared his throat. He straightened up, using the hem of his ruined shirt to wipe his eyes. "I'm sorry Fox, I didn't realise..." his voice faded.

A faint tremor vibrated under Rhydian's boots as he met Fox's unguarded stare. Fox nodded, his mouth a thin line. Rhydian pressed the heels of his hands into his eyes.

What exactly had happened here? When Rhydian had found Fox in the forest, Fox had admitted some things that had happened. Just not exactly *how*. But the bones were evidence of how bad it had been. And Owaen had made it here, and somehow pulled Fox out from whatever violence had occurred? Finally, beginning to understand what connected Fox to Owaen, Rhydian raked his hands through his gritty hair as he stared at the ceiling.

Could he do that? Is that what was about to happen when they tracked down Aurelia? They were facing the very same creature who had trapped Fox here, after all. Shadow Light, even in the form of a tiny woman, was the same creature who had done the gods only knew what in the quest for some fucked up grab for power.

Just like his mother. Rhydian swallowed the hot lump in his throat.

"Aurelia," he whispered to the giant crystals overhead. "I'm trying, I'm coming."

Still sniffling, Rhydian stared at the men before him. A pair of black and gold eyes, full of things Rhydian could never expect to understand, focused on dark green eyes full of light.

A light which Rhydian could only hope filled his own gaze as he got to see Aurelia once again.

With his heart bruised and his mind swaying from the overwhelming events around him, Rhydian cleared his throat. Daring to interrupt, he edged closer once more. Stopping as close as he dared to the protective aura that emanated from Owaen, Rhydian sank to his knees. A soft shift of the earth under his legs hummed against him.

"Please, Owaen," he said quietly. Green eyes broke from Fox's and travelled almost lazily to Rhydian beside him. "Please, we need your help."

A blonde eyebrow rose. Rhydian bit his lip.

"As king of Aneirin," Rhydian said, his mouth dry, "I'm here before you on my knees, begging. I need your help. My friend Aurelia. She needs your help."

Owaen said nothing. His gaze continued to bore into Rhydian's. He might have stayed like that for a while, but Fox jerked in Owaen's arms as he coughed. Blinking rapidly, Owaen shifted his focus. He helped Fox lean sideways, his face showing no sign of disgust as Fox leant over to cough out a fresh gob of blood. The purple-red liquid splattered over the black sand and glittering shards of quartz.

"Fox," Rhydian murmured, "he needs your help, too."

The man seemed amused at that. His intense stare was fixed on Fox's pale face.

"Obviously," was Owaen's cool reply.

Fox reached a weak hand inside his ruined shirt, fumbling for a moment. Eventually, he pulled out the golden chain. Owaen's eyes widened slightly. The charms they sparkled blue gold in the dim light. He reached out to wrap a minutely trembling hand around Fox's pale fingers. The pair of them held the charms together, and the cave became very quiet. Rhydian held his breath.

"I know I d-don't deserve it," Fox mumbled. "But *he* does." Fox's gaze rose to meet Rhydian's for a moment before he met Owaen's gaze again. "He's like you."

"Lost for wanting you?" Owaen murmured, his expression a little sad.

"No," Fox breathed, "he's good."

Watching a play of dark emotions wash across Owaen's face, Rhydian doubted the wisdom of such an admission. Expecting jealousy or rage, it seemed like the time to shout something like *don't say that, not to this wild giant, it's not like that between us at all!*

He was mistaken.

Remaining quiet, something softened in Owaen's expression. He pressed his lips back against Fox's hair. Rhydian wanted to look away from the intimacy, but he simply could not, not with his heart burning in love and fear for Aurelia.

Aurelia, please hold on.

It had seemed like the most unlikely plan, and the glare that he had received from Owaen had left him doubting. But seeing and sensing the connection between the two before him had the tiny flare of hope inside his chest ignite into something brighter. After a long, low exhale, Owaen's voice was quiet.

"Of course I'll help."

Fox nodded with a wince, and both hands let go of the chain. He sank back into the muscular arms wrapped around him, eyes locked on the emerald-eyed stare that had barely left his face.

"Owaen," Fox whispered. "Get me out of here. I can't... I can't stand it."

Wordlessly, Owaen nodded. One arm reached under Fox's knees, the other reaching around his shoulders. Owaen rose in one smooth, impossibly strong movement, scooping Fox up as he stood while the blue hued beauty of the cave throbbed around them. Fine particles of dust moved through the cool glow, soft scatters reflecting the light as they settled on the cave floor. Dust, all that was left of the tunnel door and the achingly lifelike statue.

Still kneeling on the cave floor, the cool air a balm to his burning lungs, Rhydian wiped his face again. It was likely he was just smearing the dirt and grit around rather than clearing it away. His eyes stung with salt and water.

Across from him, despite the sweat, the dirt and the blood, the expression on Fox's face was as clear as day. One of Fox's pale hands was on Owaen's cheek as he stared up at the man who held him tightly. His white face held the same expression as the crystal statue that was gone forever. In return, the masculine beauty of Owaen was unmatched as green eyes stared into glittering black. Owaen leant forward, his lips close to Fox's ear.

But Rhydian heard every word.

"I've got you, keeper of my heart," Owaen breathed, his voice low and sweetly sad. "So this time, for fuck's sake, don't let go."

44

Owaen

Year 367

The Forest

Everything was the same. Everything was different.

The creature in his arms was the most obvious example. It was the same soul, the same heart, albeit in another form. Owaen would have recognised Skye anywhere, of that he was sure. But he had seen a glimpse of this disguise, glittering gold and black eyes locked on Owaen's face as he had been sealed away.

Safe, Owaen muttered bitterly to himself, *to keep me safe.*

When it should have been the other way around.

Owaen pressed his lips together tightly. Perhaps his chance to make some kind of amends to all that Skye had been through had come at last. But at what cost? Owaen had been shut away from a fight that was rightly his, shut away from the world longer than needed. That was clear. One look at the road before them said as much.

The winding forest road disappeared around a tree that was growing from the middle of the way. No matter how many Elves had despised his role as a type of warden of the forest, they all appreciated a clear road. The tree, a tall straight pine at least thirty metres tall, rose high enough that its top was not too far behind the crowd of its companions thick around it. So it had obviously been growing for a long, long time. He said nothing as the horse he was riding, a tall black creature that clearly didn't like the way he sat, veered around the out-of-place tree.

Owaen rested his chin on the black hair against his chest, attempting to choose his words carefully. He gave up, a million questions and thoughts vying for expression.

"Skye," Owaen began, but realised his mistake as the figure in his arms stiffened. Dropping his eyes from the shadows and the surrounding trunks, Owaen met the wide black eyes, throwing sparks his way.

"Don't call me by that name. *Ever.*"

He could feel his jaw tensing, but Owaen nodded sharply. *Fox* would do. For now. Skye, no, *Fox's* eyes narrowed, before he settled back into Owaen's arms. He tilted his face away, staring out at the darkening gloom beneath the thickly wooded forest. It felt like evening, but Owaen wasn't sure. He was happy to be awake and surrounded by life once more. Not death.

The young man riding beside them remained silent. He had clearly heard the exchange, slowing his horse and shooting Owaen with a dark look. Owaen shot him a stare with the same amount of warmth, which was none, and Rhydian's hands tightened on his reigns. As Owaen continued to watch him, the cool evening breeze tousled Rhydian's golden brown hair, lines of worry marring the skin around his eyes. The young man had strange eyes, his irises a gentle blue ringed with a darker shade. Fox had said this was the king of Aneirin. Rhydian actually looked somewhat familiar, but the feeling sat like coal in Owaen's guts. Because the woman that Rhydian reminded him of was long gone.

Cool fingers caught his chin to lower his gaze from Rhydian back to Fox's appraising stare. Owaen was unable to help the wry twist of his lips at the hum that warmed his heart at the touch.

"So," Fox murmured, staring at Owaen's mouth, his expression clouded.

When Fox hesitated, Owaen rolled his lips inward over his teeth, eyebrows raised. Fox cleared his throat, his breath still wheezing with each inhale.

"So," Fox repeated, raising his eyes back to Owaen's. "I need your help. Shadow Light has, ah, he has taken someone dear to me. To us. Rhydian and I."

Owaen absorbed this a moment. "In the cave, a name was mentioned."

"Aurelia," Rhydian said, his voice cracking on the name.

Owaen spared a glance at the young man. Rhydian was staring straight ahead.

"Fox said this creature had taken Aurelia to a city in the north," Rhydian continued. "There was a battle in Aneirin. My parents, uh. Things happened, and Fox disappeared, we locked up-"

Fox interrupted, the catch in his voice sharp despite the rasp. "You can say it Rhydian. I fucked up when I left Shadow Light behind like that."

His gaze darted between them, but Owaen made no comment. His opinion of the king wasn't as high as it perhaps should have been.

"Um. Well. I went to find Fox. I found him like this, his magic gone. But when we came back, Aurelia was taken by this creature."

"Because," Fox interjected again, "I fucked it up-"

"We get it!" Rhydian snapped, his blue eyes flashing. "I agree, but let's focus on where we are at right now."

When Fox had the grace to look slightly chastised, Owaen's estimation of the young king rose. Slightly.

"Anyway," Rhydian huffed. "I've tried to help Fox get well again to get Aurelia back, but he said he needed *you*. He needed *your* arms around him. So here we are."

Ignoring the edgy tone in Rhydian's voice, Owaen kept his eyes on the black pair so close to his own. But he allowed himself a snort.

"'Him'?" Owaen scoffed, ignoring Fox as he shook his head, eyes widening with alarm. "This is not a *him*." The black eyes closed, a frustrated sigh leaving cracked lips.

Rhydian reined his horse to a halt. Smirking, Owaen followed suit. He waited for the king to say something, but Rhydian was simply staring at the man in Owaen's lap. He seemed to be about to speak, but closed his mouth. Owaen shrugged, inhaling the rich air so full of life, different from the mineral coolness of the cave he'd spent gods only knew how long inside. With a toss of its head, the black horse snorted, glanced back towards the king. Owaen's gentle nudge had it walking forward once more. He counted to ten before he could hear Rhydian urge his horse to follow.

"Be serious, please," Fox murmured against him. "Shadow Light got free of his bindings, and took Aurelia."

Inhaling against Fox's black hair where it was pressed against his cheek, Owaen wondered at that. His arms tightened around Fox, also wondering at the coolness of the weight against his lap, familiar while yet still so different.

"So Shadow light is still alive," Owaen mused. "I didn't expect that of you."

"I am more than happy," Fox hissed against his chest as Owaen shifted slightly on the saddle, "to continue to surprise you."

"No more surprises," Owaen said calmly. "I think you've given me enough."

Fox muttered something under his breath.

"You sound like you're feeling marginally better already," Owaen murmured. He shifted his hips again.

"Stop that," Fox demanded with a crack in his voice, his eyes widening.

Owaen's reply was a smile full of promise. Fox looked away, eyeing Rhydian, who had caught up. The king seemed lost in thought. While Rhydian was distracted, Owaen's smile widened.

"You need a bath," he said, his voice low. "I'd be happy to help."

Shocked black eyes snapped back to his. The dim light was fading quickly, but the smudges of blood across Fox's face were still visible. But that's not what Owaen was offering. Both of them knew it.

"I... my magic..." Fox's voice trailed away.

Owaen laughed quietly at the look on the white face so close to his. Fox avoided his gaze, blinking at the dark canopy rustling above.

"Hm," Owaen murmured. "I thought you needed my help. Isn't that why you're here? Why I'm here? Helping you recover?"

"But," Fox spluttered, "I'm-"

"You're covered in dirt." Owaen snorted. "Obviously, being around me is doing wonders already, but you need to get your shit together." He smoothed his fingers over Fox's forehead. His temperature was chilled, but not freezing. Pleased, Owaen continued. "I think a bath might be a good idea. And then perhaps you'd feel well enough to show us your scales and fly us to the city afterwards?"

"No!" Rhydian shouted beside them, startling them both. Rhydian had the grace to look sheepish at his outburst, showing he'd clearly been listening. "No flying..." he paused and looked down at his horse. "I mean, not that I don't want to get there quickly," Rhydian's laugh was weak, sounding like more like a choke. "I can't... I don't want to fly. I mean, you need to reserve your energy for when we get to the City, so you can take care of Shadow Light. And I can't leave these horses here, not Blackthorn, if you changed back... into a dragon. How could we take my horses?"

It wasn't the reaction Owaen had been going for, but he ran with it, nonetheless. He smirked at the fear playing across the king's face before Fox poked him hard in the chest.

"Stop it," Fox muttered. He shook his head at Rhydian. "Owaen is being a beast. I'm nowhere near that level of magic yet. And don't worry, kingling; it is very, *very* rare for a dragon to carry people, to be ridden like a horse, let alone try and carry some. You should count yourself lucky that Flare allowed it."

Rhydian ran a hand through his hair, refusing to look at them.

Owaen snorted.

"Even you did, *Fox*. When we first met, you were riding Shadow Light."

"Don't remind me," he said, wincing.

Feeling reckless, Owaen leaned in, but kept his voice loud enough for the eavesdropping little king beside them to hear.

"Don't forget," Owaen purred. "I've ridden you too."

Fox was speechless; his shocked gasp more of a spluttering rasp. Owaen sat back in the saddle, pleased with himself. Until Fox coughed, struggling to regain his breath. Cursing, Owaen helped him lean sideways to spit another fresh mouthful of blood over their legs to the mossy road. He sat back against Owaen, muttering. Suitably chastised, Owaen wrapped his arms back around Fox.

Unable to keep his mouth closed, though, he pressed his lips against Fox's black hair.

"I'm not done with you," Owaen said patiently.

Fox shook his head, either not bothering or not able to reply.

The silence was welcome enough, however. The fading light above cast a haunting ambience, causing the surrounding forest to darken and fill with an eerie stillness. The air temperature was dropping and neither of his companions seemed to have packed anything beyond extra cloaks. He hoped the saddlebags at least contained some food. Owaen bit his top lip. How long had it been since he'd eaten? His Elven magic was strong. Surely that was one of the reasons he'd stayed alive, locked in a cave. Or perhaps his jailor had left too much magic behind, keeping him safe.

Safe.

His lips curled. But he said nothing, listening to the wheezing breath against him finally relax into a healthier sound.

They'd need to stop soon to camp, near water. The city was still a couple of days away. He wondered how this Aurelia was faring, and how quickly he could help Fox recover from however the fuck he'd lost his magic. He examined Rhydian's back in front of them. There was more that needed to be shared. A lot had happened, that was obvious. He didn't care where they were headed, or into what. Only that this time, they were facing the chaos together. This was enough.

For now.

A cool hand reached up to take one of his. As his breath misted in the evening air, Owaen dropped his gaze to Fox's. Carefully watching Owaen's face, Fox placed Owaen's hand on the hilt of the sword at Fox's hip, fingertips brushing the single, uncut ruby in the pommel. He didn't say anything, but the message was clear.

"I don't want it back," Owaen murmured.

"You should have it. I took it without asking."

"I said I don't want it."

Fox's eyes narrowed. "This sword is *not* the cause of this. Or you. It was Shadow Light, and all of dragonkind's fault. Mine, even."

The cool fingers were still weak, but they pressed Owaen's into the cold metal. The old ache in Owaen's chest flared, as it always did when he thought of his brother.

"What happened wasn't your fault." Owaen paused, watching Rhydian stare out at the silent forest, listening to the quiet snuffs of the black horse as it pulled towards the king. He sighed and nudged the horse to keep its head straight. "The Elven elders were responsible too."

"But not you?" Fox dropped his hand from Owaen's and the hilt of the sword.

"Fuck no," Owaen snapped. "I've been trying to keep the heads of both races out of their own arses-" he paused. Fox looked better than before, and was clearly holding in a laugh. Owaen blew out another sigh. "Don't do that."

"Do what?"

"Provoke me." His eyes roamed over Fox's face. "I told you I'm not done with you."

In the low light, it was hard to tell, but Fox's eyes appeared to change colour. The black heated, morphing to all gold for such a fleeting moment that Owaen wondered if he'd imagined it. Fox licked his chapped lips.

"I tried to f-fix it, Owaen. I really did."

At the dark tone of Fox's words, a chill crept up Owaen's spine. He tried to keep his voice neutral.

"Skye-," Owaen cursed under his breath, his jaw clenched. "Fox, what did you do?"

Ignoring the question, Fox squirmed against him. "Stop squeezing me."

Owaen let it go. This was another thing he'd need to address, but not now.

Apart from the occasional cough and fresh mouthful of blood that was spat over the side of their horse with a disgusted hiss, Fox was improving. They'd left the cave behind only hours ago, but his pallor was not as frightening. It was a far cry from the green-haired woman who had descended from the heavens one day, full of life and laughter. But it was better. Owaen had no expectations of Skye for anything right now, other than that the improvement continued. He was going to help in any way he saw fit to help get that spark back. Not only the magic that was lost, but also the shining light inside the once sparkling heart and bright soul as well. The soul he'd never fail to recognise, no matter what vessel it was dwelling within.

Seeing Skye for the first time was still something he would never forget. Even in the cave, locked away by the very one who had captured his heart, his dreams had been of her. Alighted from a back of a black dragon, she had stepped into the sun, the cascade of coloured gems over her tunic like an exploding constellation of rainbows across the main courtyard of the city. How long ago was it? He still refused to press further and find out. Besides. His family was already gone, long before Skye had appeared. The only person that mattered was wrapped in his arms, albeit in a different form.

She had also shown him her scales after their first tryst at his parents' cabin. Would it still be standing? With his brother's grave among the roses? And what of the city as well? Had the forest overtaken the once majestic city of stone arches and lofty towers in the same way the forest was encroaching on the old forest road?

"I thought I was dying again," Fox spoke suddenly, interrupting his thoughts, the quiet words stopping his heart.

"What do you mean *again*?" Owaen hissed, blinking rapidly. "What the fuck?"

Ahead of them, Rhydian looked over his shoulder. After assessing the expression on Owaen's face, he averted his gaze just as fast. The young man looked tired, worn out, and pale. Owaen didn't give a shit.

"Skye! What. The. Fuck?" he repeated.

"I said," Fox groused, "don't call me *that*. And I also s-said stop squeezing me so tight."

Owaen bit back a laugh even as his heart raced inside his chest.

"Stop squeezing you so tight, huh? You're lucky I'm not squeezing your-" he cut himself off. Taking a long, slow breath, Owaen hesitated, then began again. "Stop squirming. How about you just explain how you fucking *died*?"

"No."

"*No?*" Owaen spluttered. "Are you fucking kidding me-"

"I don't feel like it," Fox huffed. "I've changed my mind. You're too p-pissed. I'm tired. Stop talking to me."

Gritting his teeth, Owaen shook his head, aware that ahead of them Rhydian had slowed his horse down once more, not bothering to hide that he was listening. Cursing under his breath, Owaen changed tactics. He pressed his face into the back of the black hair before him. Fox, sitting stiffly against Owaen, didn't acknowledge him.

"How can you be sure that this Aurelia is safe for now?"

When they came alongside Rhydian's horse, Owaen struggled to keep the black horse he and Fox were on from idling closer to Rhydian.

"She is," Fox muttered, his voice actually sounding like it was fading after all. He nodded and cleared his throat. "All Shadow has left is to bargain with her. He knows only I can f-free him to his preferred form." Fox attempted to continue, but his breath wheezed and the wet cough began again, deep in his chest. He slumped against Owaen with a muttered curse. That reluctant gesture of surrender was enough for Owaen to swallow back the rest of what he had to say. Which was a lot.

Watching beside them, Rhydian started to say something, but Owaen cut him off. As much as he wanted answers, a lot of them, and immediately, he had enough sense to recognise that now was not the time.

"That's enough," Owaen said, eyeing the king with irritation. "This fox needs to rest."

Regaining control of his breathing, Fox said nothing. He twisted slightly to stare at Owaen, his black and gold gaze filled with the same soul that once wore another face. Owaen met his stare evenly, until Fox turned his gaze to the distant hoot of an owl in the silent, watching forest surrounding them.

"But we-" Rhydian began.

Owaen shot the man another glare, not caring whether the man was a king or not. Rhydian bit his lower lip and nodded, eyeing the possessive way Owaen had gathered Fox close.

"That's fine," the king sighed, clearly unhappy. "For now."

Fox was gone.

Owaen sat up, his head clearing immediately. One thing about sleeping for however the fuck long it had been, seemed to mean that he was wide awake instantly, as soon as he had realised Fox was gone from beside him.

Across the soft glow of the campfire, Rhydian blinked sleepily, his eyes clearly bloodshot even in the soft glow of the low fire.

"He's not far," the king murmured.

"How could you let him go? And why didn't he wake me?" Owaen groused, blowing his hair out of his face.

"Let me see." Oddly coloured blue eyes narrowed. "Perhaps he thought you needed to get more *sleep*."

Owaen tilted his head.

He didn't know whether to snort at Rhydian's snide remark, or punch it off his handsome face. Rhydian shot him an exasperated glance before he rolled over, leaving Owaen muttering under his breath.

Inhaling slowly, he looked around. It was fully dark, perhaps a few hours yet until dawn. Barely visible above the thick canopy, points of cold light sparkled amongst the leaves. There was a layer of thin frost over the moss around them and the air tasted crisp and full of greenery. He pulled the cloak tighter around himself, lost in the memories of how many nights he had roamed in the forest alone. The forest during the day was full of living beauty. The forest at night was a wonder.

The horses were tethered nearby, and they shifted quietly as Owaen pushed off the ground to his feet.

"Where?" Owaen eventually demanded grudgingly.

Rhydian didn't reply, but he raised a lazy hand to gesture towards the creek. Owaen made no comment about the middle finger that Rhydian pointed with, although a muscle in his jaw ticked.

They had all cleaned up there earlier; black grit stuck in places Owaen had been amazed at. But the water was barely a stream, shallow and icy. Leaving their clothes on, they'd refreshed as best they could before Fox had staggered and Owaen had to catch him before he toppled over.

As he set off to track Fox, Owaen froze. Fox's boots and socks were discarded carelessly in a pile. Not only was he out in the forest without a cloak, Fox was barefoot as well.

"You didn't dress him?" Owaen snapped, glaring at the back of the young king's head. This earned Owen a snort.

Rolling back towards him, Rhydian stared at him, eyebrows raised.

"We are talking about the same person," Rhydian murmured, "yes?"

Owaen bit his lip. "Skye, fuck, *Fox*, is still stubborn, I assume. Fair enough."

Clutching his cloak, he ignored the sudden sympathy in Rhydian's eyes and set out through the thick, rough trunks of the trees. There was an ache in his bones, like he hadn't ridden for years. Owaen halted. Well, he hadn't, had he? He resumed walking. He wasn't ready to ask Fox for how long, not just yet.

Feeling almost as if he was dreaming again, Owaen slipped through the forest. If he'd been dreaming, Skye would have been wrapped around Owaen in her guise of an Elven woman like when they had first met, her long green hair stuck to his sweating flesh. Instead, he was following the vague directions of a sad eyed king to find his lover who now looked like some dark knight of bad dreams.

Scowling, he walked on. If he really thought about it, he'd be able to find Skye without asking. The connection, the pull they had, was that strong. Even after all this time. Coming to the little creek, Owaen halted.

Fox was standing in the ankle deep water, not moving.

Owaen nearly called out, but paused. Fox was half turned away from him, staring across the narrow waters. Glancing away from Fox, Owaen cast his gaze over the water. He smiled. A red fox, complete with bushy tail, was standing on the far bank. It had stopped on top of a lichen-covered boulder. The animal had a dead rabbit in its pointy little jaws, as yellow eyes assessed the black-haired figure before it.

The legs of the lifeless rabbit dangled as the fox turned to face Owaen.

"Its alright, little brother," Owaen murmured.

The animal blinked at him, blood staining the fur under its chin. It looked back at Fox, who hadn't moved. The black nose twitched.

Moving slowly to remove his boots, Owaen kept his eyes on the fox as he stepped into the water. The water was *cold*. One of the fox's ears flicked sideways at his curse. It continued to stare. It watched without moving as Owaen slipped off his cloak to wrap it around Fox's trembling shoulders.

"What's wrong with me?" Fox murmured, his gaze on the calm yellow eyes of the fox across the water. "I'm cold. Powerless. I *hate* it."

"I'm here," Owaen whispered, settling the fabric around Fox's icy skin.

"It's my fault," Fox went on, unblinking, his voice low. "She was taken, and a boy was killed. I told you, this is my fault. My pride, my fucking dragon-sized ego."

It was hard to disagree with that last part, considering what Fox had done to him. Owaen kept his voice low, watching the fox assess them, black nose twitching.

"We need to talk about the dragons-"

"No."

"Please. Tell me," Owaen breathed, "tell me what you did to them-"

"No."

He sighed, brushing his nose against the damp patch in Fox's hair.

"I think I can guess," Owaen murmured.

"I doubt it."

"You did what we talked about, didn't you, concerning magic, and the greediest magic users of them all? Dragons."

The stony silence from Fox was blended with the quiet gurgle of the clear water, rippling over dark stones and shadows. Owaen shifted his foot from a sharp stone and tried again.

"What did you do? Why didn't you let me help you?"

Fox shook his head. "I get that you're angry-"

"Oh, I bet you do," Owaen murmured, hating the coldness in his voice but unable to rein it in. "Do you know why?"

"No." Fox's reply was a whisper. "I don't actually, I was keeping you safe-"

"Safe?" Owaen hissed, his hands tightening on the shoulders he held onto. Across the water, one of the fox's ears twitched. "You took away *my* choice, like Shadow did to *you*."

Fox jerked at that, trying to turn around. Owaen held him still.

"But it's n-not the same-"

"No? Maybe it's not the same, but it's fucking close."

Fox shook his head, the trembling back in his body.

"Don't say that," Fox whispered, the pain in his voice as transparent as the cold water around their feet. "Don't say that."

Closing his eyes, Owaen dropped his head onto Fox's shoulder.

Owaen bit his bottom lip. "We're not done with this."

Sliding his arms around Fox's shaking figure, Owaen pressed his chest against the chilled back before him. Bright yellow fox eyes continued to appraise them.

Inhaling slowly, Owaen tasted the familiar aromas of the forest that had once been his home. But home wasn't really a place now, was it? Not anymore. Home was the soul bound tightly to his, despite all that had come between them. He wanted to wrap all of himself over and inside the creature against him.

Not quite regretting his harsh words, but daring to make a peace offering nonetheless, Owaen pressed his lips to the back of Fox's icy neck. The cool skin reacted immediately, softening and warming beneath him. Despite it all, what Skye had done, taken away; there was no chance that Owaen could be anywhere else but here. Trying to force himself away would have been like cutting out his lungs and tossing them to the wild animal across the creek.

Carefully, Owaen manoeuvred his lips to Fox's chilled ear, his heart sinking into the energy that crackled between them. Fox shivered as warm air bathed the cool shell of his ear.

"I'm here," Owaen whispered, his eyes closed. "I'm not going anywhere."

Fox inhaled like he intended to reply, but instead of speaking, he let out a slow breath instead. Owaen opened his eyes.

At their feet the water ran endlessly with a cool gurgle, the forest above cool, quiet. Across the creek, the boulder was empty.

The fox was gone.

45

Aurelia

Year 367
The Forest

What type of people were those who died with too many words on their lips?

Fools, Aurelia thought bitterly.

Who were those who died while keeping their mouth shut?

Also fools.

Kneeling in the dirt of the old forest road, Aurelia breathed through the pain in her ribs and her knees. Head hanging, long dark hair a mess around her, tears of anger threatened to fall from closed eyes. One of the horses snuffed at her hair.

It was obvious which type of fool she was. If she died without telling Rhydian that she loved him, impossible as it seemed after so short a time together, then she would likely be the biggest fool of all. Her feelings for him had been subtle, watching actions, not listening to words.

Aurelia had set out from home with a single goal in mind, not a final destination. But so many variables had occurred along the way, truths and untruths, and careful, simple plans had turned to ash. The young man, son of the man she had been sent to manipulate for the sake of her people, had showed her who he truly was. Not what he was. He had shown her the best of an innocent heart. Even taking a leap of faith to find her missing friend, for answers, yes. But also for her.

Hands still bound together, she pressed them against her chest, rubbing her calloused fingers over her shirt. Where her garnet should be hanging was empty space, echoing her bruised heart behind. The loss of the jewel seemed minor in comparison to everything else. But it was something that Rhydian had given her, hung on a chain conjured by Fox's magic. His ease with conjuring elements and metals had always been a delight to her. Maybe that's why a pang of guilt twinged deep within. Had she caused all of this, in demanding he choose right over wrong? Fox, *her* Fox, was a man who had been a dragon all along. And he had used that part of himself to fight, and thankfully defeat, Rhydian's mother. Who had an agenda all of her own, not a bid for freedom for the Elves of Lolihud. But a dark bid for power and twisted revenge. It still just seemed too surreal to process. So much had happened and there was just so much she was unaware of.

What was most concerning was if Rhydian had found Fox by now. Or not. Flare refused to talk with her even now. There was no way of knowing if the dragon had kept his word, taking the grieving king to find whatever was left of Fox. Was Rhydian even aware of-

Aurelia gasped at the image of a boy hanging on a dark cell wall etched into her mind. Along with the horror, fear rippled through her body in a fierce wave. What if Rhydian was back to find her gone, and thought she had left on her own? The only way to answer any of these questions was to get back and find out for herself.

But first... shame ate away at her from the inside. The last couple of days were a blur, and she wasn't sure when the last time food had passed her lips. Hunger was starting to rear its furious head and her mouth tasted funny. Short drinks at rivers and creeks that tasted like the forest along the way were simply not enough. And relieving herself whilst keeping hygienic with bound hands had been mortifying.

Opening her eyes to stare at the grit and moss on the overgrown road, she wondered if there was a way to turn back the days, to do things differently. She'd asked Fox something like that once, back in Lolihud. He had looked at her with humour in his beautiful eyes when she'd asked, then told her to go back to training. And she had her whole life. To end up kneeling in the dirt, lost in the forest, staring at the dragon who had betrayed her.

Her green eyes rose from their blind appraisal of the road to meet with wide purple eyes that stared at her with alarm. After a nervous ruffle of his wings, Flare looked away.

Which was *fine*.

Aurelia's mouth tightened into a thin line. While there was potent magic in her family, it wasn't enough to soothe the bruises that were blooming along her ribs and legs. That was fine as well. She welcomed the fury burning through her aching body, fuelling her determination to get past this. Concentrating on not tipping sideways, Aurelia gathered her strength. But as she was pushing to her feet, the blonde man standing beside Flare said something that caught her ear.

"Shadow Light," the man had almost purred, "I just love what you've done with your hair."

Aurelia froze. *Shadow Light*? The man was clearly talking to Jessikah.

Trying to draw as little attention to herself as possible, Aurelia stood up at last, trying to make sense of the scene before her.

The blonde man was tall and slim, but not thin. He was richly dressed, complete with a vibrant purple cloak that was almost an exact match to Flare's scales. White teeth flashed as the man smiled, smooth blonde hair windswept across his head. There was a darker blonde streak, almost silvery grey, slightly off centre, at the front. His long fingers were covered with sparkling rings, noticeable as he rested one hand on the hilt of his sword. A sword that she was *positive* that she'd seen before. And the man himself, too. Something about his pale hair and slim stature tugged at her memory.

Against her will, she had to admit that he was exceptionally handsome, almost to the point of being pretty, although something about his eyes seemed off. Even with her Elven eyesight, Aurelia wasn't quite able to see what. It had something to do with his expression as well. It was just past the point of beyond wild.

Jessikah glared up at him without fear. Her yellow hair was as tangled as Aurelia's. Petite hands were crossed over her chest as she shook her head. It was obvious that they knew each other, despite the chilled expression on Jessikah's face.

What had Fox said once, about black dragons and shadows? Is this what he meant? Is this *who* he meant?

Fox had hardly let Jessikah out of his sight, ever since Aurelia had been a child. She could remember how protective he'd been. But he had never been kind about it. Considering Fox had been more than what he seemed, it seemed likely that Jessikah wasn't only a refugee from the chaos of old. Jessikah was something else. Just like Fox. Her actions in the cell had had Aurelia thinking. This just confirmed it.

Aurelia shifted her gaze back to Flare. His immense purple eyes were still wide, his mouth hanging ajar. The man's smile had faded, and he was muttering something under his breath. As he waved his arms, Jessikah scowled. The man narrowed his eyes in return. His hand dropped to his sword once more.

Unable to understand just what the fuck was happening, Aurelia inhaled slowly. The air was turning cool, thickly scented with the earthy musk of deep moss that covered the forest floor. The sharp scent of foreign pine trees added a deep spice. It was cool enough to raise goose bumps on her exposed skin. Frost was likely, and soon. The light was already dim from the overcast day, and above the high canopy, she could feel the sun heading towards the west.

Flare shifted uneasily, his gaze bouncing between the two figures glaring at each other on the road. The blonde man finally shrugged and muttered something. He waved a lazy hand towards Jessikah. To Aurelia's astonishment, Jessikah, or whoever that was, shuddered once, all over. Flare's mouth fell open further, his sharp teeth visible.

And Jessikah spoke for the first time since Aurelia could remember.

"You are *not*," the woman rasped, using vocal chords that had not worked in years, "going to interfere with *this*."

What.

The.

Fuck.

Aurelia stood there in the road by the horses, in much the same pose as Flare. Eyes wide, mouth hanging open. Her hands started working frantically at her bonds. There was more going on here than she could fathom, and she needed to get as far away from whatever it was as fast as possible. If there was any dignity left in Flare at all, he wouldn't allow himself to be used to track her. It was doubtful, but she had to try.

Aurelia took what she hoped was a casual step towards the edge of the trees along the closest side of the road. No one looked her way, and she took another step with her boot barely above the uneven surface of the road, less she dislodge any loose pebbles. One of the horses shifted. She took another step, eyes glued to what was happening.

Jessikah cleared her throat and continued.

"So kindly," she coughed dryly, "get the fuck out of my way."

"Caspian," Flare hissed, his eyes darting to the blonde man.

The man, Caspian, held up a hand. Flare's mouth swung shut, and his wide eyes shot back to Jessikah. Aurelia used the opportunity to take another step back towards the forest.

"Excuse me," said the man calmly. His eyes were cold now. "I think what you meant to say was '*thank you* Cas, you're so wonderful, quite amazing really, to grant me back the power of speech-'"

"You ignorant fool," Jessikah hissed, gesturing towards Aurelia. "This is the only way I'm getting back to myself, and you," she coughed again, "*you* of all people are not going to mess this up-"

"*Me* mess this up?" Caspian shouted suddenly, cold to hot in an instant. "After your little experiment in that fucking cave with Skye, you have the balls to accuse that of *me*? What exactly did you intend? What did you even do?" He pressed his hands into his cheeks, sliding them lower until his fingers cupped his jaw. "You are more of a sick, misguided creature than I thought."

Jessikah's eyes widened. "Misguided? It was you-"

Caspian cut her off with a loud scoff, his hands dropping to his hips.

"Sometimes adjustments must be made, common sense and all that crap." He paused, eyeing the small woman glaring at him, a smile playing across his lips. "Tell me, how long have you lived as a woman? Hasn't *any* of your time owning a vagina left you with *any* sense at all?"

At this, Jessikah gasped, and Flare choked loudly. Aurelia's bound hands flew to her mouth, holding back a bubble of horrified laughter. Ignoring them, Caspian's expression turned serious, almost concerned.

"Wait," he murmured, tilting his head, pale brows furrowed. His strange eyes travelled down along Jessikah's body while she bristled. He waved a hand towards her. "You do have one, don't you?"

Even as Aurelia edged further away, she could see Jessikah's eyes practically spitting fire. The tiny yellow haired woman had uncrossed her arms and stepped forward.

"You are a *disgusting* and *disrespectful* little *shit*. It is one of life's great mysteries that you are still alive, let alone able to-"

"Yes, yes. And you're acting like a cock. But it doesn't really matter at the moment, does it?" Caspian's laugh had the hairs on Aurelia's neck rising. "Not when your precious little bargaining tool is trying to make a run for it, hmm?"

Shit.

Just as Aurelia made a dash for the closest towering trees, hoping to duck behind the widest trunk to get lost in the shadows, Caspian turned a chilling smile her way. Iridescent eyes bored into hers, as shocking as if she had woken up to find a glittering scorpion beside her face on her pillow.

Caspian's laugh was loud behind her as she sprinted uselessly for the trees. It was her only warning. This time, Jessikah didn't use magic to knock Aurelia over. Jessikah sprinted after her, cursing, grabbing Aurelia around the hips so they both landed in the rocks and moss beyond the edge of the road. Aurelia's bound hands were useless at preventing the shock of the impact. Aurelia cried out as they landed heavily, her head bouncing on moss only centimetres away from a scatter of black rocks.

Aurelia's scream of fury echoed around the trees. The horses shifted and whinnied at the sound, and Flare shouted something. She wasn't sure what because, while she had pushed herself up and away, something heavy hit the back of her skull. Pain shot out from the impact. Red, black, and white shapes danced in her vision. Aurelia was knocked sideways, this time colliding with the sharp rocks right over her bruised ribs. She ducked away from the rock in Jessikah's hand as the woman went for another blow, using her foot to kick it away. She failed.

It was unclear if the tiny woman was going to kill her or at least try to knock her out. Either way, Jessikah's face was a blank mask of rage. Aurelia cried out as Jessikah scrambled over Aurelia's chest, legs spraddled around Aurelia's hips with the rock raised once more. Aurelia tried to remember her training, but the pain throbbing from the back of her head was too much. She closed her eyes to the cold fury in the yellow eyes above. Jessikah's expression took Aurelia's breath away, much like the impact had. It was raw, unexpected, and violent.

"Tsk, tsk," Caspian said from above them.

Aurelia's eyes flew open. Baring her teeth, Jessikah halted. The rock was gripped tight and held above her.

"I was correct," Caspian murmured. "A vagina hasn't helped you out with more sense after all, my dear Shadow. So, let me be clear." He paused. When he spoke again, his voice was dangerously low. "Hit her like that again and I'll rip off whatever balls may or may not be left under your skirts."

Cursing, Jessikah narrowed her eyes at Aurelia. Then she threw the rock into the trees. It landed with a dull thump somewhere over to Aurelia's right. The pain in Aurelia's head was making her want to vomit, but she held still. Jessikah squeezed her thighs around Aurelia's aching, panting ribs once and hard before finally pushing herself up with a curse. Chest heaving, she turned to Caspian and eyed him up and down.

"I'm not wearing skirts, you orphaned little fuck."

Something flickered within the iridescent eyes that were now glued to Aurelia's face. But to her surprise, Caspian merely shrugged.

"I'm sure you've thought about it. Now. Get your spicy little lady bits over to Flare. I'll deal with this. You are too soft when you needed to be hard, Shadow, and far too hard when you need to be soft."

Jessikah cast one last sneer at Aurelia before heading back to the purple dragon. Flare was shivering on the road, his wings held slightly off from his body as if he might take off at any moment. Aurelia was confused as to why he hadn't. It was clear from the fear and shock on his face he didn't want to be caught up in whatever this was. But how much of it was his fault, Aurelia wasn't yet aware. Either way, she would never trust him again.

Glaring at the branches above, she caught sight of a gigantic owl. Round orange eyes blinked multiple lids at her before dismissing the scene below. Unlike the snowy owl that Fox had rescued, this one was brown, with large yellow talons and a stubby tail, striped in yellow and brown. She wondered where the white owl was now. After being healed by Fox and let go, there was a chance it had only been caught in the sharp talons of a more powerful creature such as this one. Just like her.

A quiet rustle came from beside her. Nudging his sword away from his legs, Caspian had crouched down. Eyes, two shades of blue that shined in a way she'd never seen before, peered into hers. His voice was soft.

"Are you alright?"

Aurelia blinked at him, unable to look away, unsure how to reply.

Was she? Fuck no. She was bruised, covered in dirt, and the back of her head was throbbing with spikes of pain. Biting back the bile in her throat, all she could do was cough out a brief burst of laughter, an incredulous snort.

Pursing his finely drawn lips, Caspian nodded sagely. "Fair enough."

His lids lowered to halfway closed over his scorpion gaze, his eyes wandering over her. As much as Aurelia wanted to throw moss into his face and get him to look away, his attention seemed merely appraising. He appeared neither interested nor disinterested. His eyes roamed back to her face.

"Can you stand?"

She flexed her legs and winced, but nodded. Caspian's expression didn't change. He pushed himself up and reached out a hand, rings sparkling mutely in the soft filtered light beneath the trees. When Aurelia stared up at him, he flexed his fingers.

"Don't be shy now, little finch. We're about to get a lot closer."

"What do you mean?" she asked suspiciously, eyeing his beckoning hand.

"You're obviously valuable to that yellow-haired cock over there." He grinned at her snarl. "I'm Cas. Who are you?"

"No one," she snapped.

"Unlikely," Caspian replied, clearly amused. "I saw you with the new king at that fun little battle. You're more than just his lover, aren't you?"

Swallowing, Aurelia closed her eyes against the wave of nausea rising again.

"I don't know what you mean," she protested weakly. With one blonde eyebrow raised, Caspian opened his mouth, but Aurelia cut him off. "I saw you as well."

The surrounding light was getting greyer and darker, but the flash of interest in his mismatched eyes was unmistakable.

"Go on."

Licking her lips, Aurelia winced as she brushed some hair out of her face.

"Before the... fun little war," she mumbled, her head throbbing. "Just before the old king threw me off a tower."

Caspian perked up at that.

"He *what*? And you didn't break?" Looking impressed, he waved a hand lazily behind him as Jessikah called out something Aurelia didn't catch. "Well done. How?"

Looking past him, Aurelia glared at Flare. Unsurprisingly, Flare was facing away. She filled her voice with as much venom as her aching skull would allow.

"Flare caught me. I knew he would."

"I'm sorry I missed it. Come on." Caspian flexed his long fingers at her impatiently. "I remember something else, too. You're the Elven queen's little bitch, aren't you? You've grown up."

Aurelia stared at his graceful hand, the meaning of his words settling around her heart like ice.

"Wait, what-"

"Hush," Caspian interrupted, smiling strangely, as if at some joke. He leant over to grab her arm, ignoring her futile attempt to knock his hand away. His patience was clearly gone. "If you behave, we'll make sure you don't plunge to a near certain death again, hm?"

She was hauled unceremoniously to her feet as whatever momentary concern he'd had with her had disappeared. She bared her teeth, sucking in the cold air of the falling evening through them.

"I don't care what you do to me," Aurelia hissed.

Caspian used his firm grip on her arm to direct her towards the others. His tone was playful.

"That's fine." He made a popping sound with his lips. "But Flare might."

Glancing at the dragon, Aurelia sucked in a gasp of irritation as Flare's nostrils twitched, his purple eyes darting between them. Clearly, this man was going to use her behaviour to keep Flare in line. Which was interesting. It meant that a part of Flare really didn't want to be here. Aurelia sniffed. Might she be able to use that, even if she couldn't trust the dragon with anything?

Her resolve was pushed aside as a sneeze shook her unexpectedly. Above the trees, the sun was fading and the air below grew chilled. She sneezed again. Beside her, Caspian paused.

Without a word, he unclasped his ridiculous coat. After a sad glance at the plush material, he drew it around Aurelia's shoulders with a one armed flourish. Narrowing her eyes at him while he stepped close to do up the clasp, she said nothing. Neither did he. He merely winked at her when he smoothed it over her arms. Aurelia caught the scent of a strong soap, spicy and clean. He smelt wild, like an effervescent mineral pool.

"It's going to snow up here for the first time in a long time," Jessikah muttered.

Eyes on Aurelia, Caspian nodded. "Yes. Interesting timing."

"The curse?" Jessikah asked, her tone grudging. Aurelia shifted her gaze from examining Caspian's eyes up close to Jessikah. Her arms were still crossed over her chest where she stood by the quiet dragon. Aurelia looked back to Caspian, her gaze darting between his eyes, one light and one dark blue. The quicksilver shimmer within each iris was hard to focus on. Calmly, he let her look, widening his eyes slightly for her appraisal. His hand tightened on Aurelia's arm.

"Why?" Aurelia murmured eventually, unable to keep the question in.

"The snow?"

"Yes."

Keeping his eyes on her face, the debate playing across his face on whether to answer her question was obvious. The fact that he might filled her with a fear that she might later be disposable. But she wanted to know.

"Because the curse is broken," Caspian eventually admitted. He fluttered long, blonde eyelashes at her. She refused to look away. He looked pleased as he continued. "Aneirin won't be in a toasty little bubble, not anymore. The real climate will return, along with magic."

Nearby, Flare choked out what sounded like a moan and a sob.

Laughing, Cas winked at Aurelia before shifting his gaze to the dragon.

"Don't worry, precious, I'll keep you warm-" He paused. Looking down at his feet with a frown, his hand twitched on Aurelia's arm. "What the fu-"

The ground heaved with sudden violence, and they were thrown up like leaves scattered on the wind.

Flare bellowed out a warning and Jessikah swore in alarm, both sounds swallowed by the loud groan and heave of the earth below. At first, the ground felt like it dropped away, before rising back up to meet them with a violent shudder. The horse's whinnies were almost a screech, but Aurelia had no time to catch either one of them. The road rose to meet them in a wave. Both Aurelia and Caspian were knocked off their feet. Aurelia's eyes were wide with shock as she caught a glimpse as the wave of force rippled through the surrounding forest, the great trunks creaking, the far off canopy shivering above. A loud cracking and ripping of wood was followed by a bone-jarring thud not far from their position.

Rocks and pebbles were kicked up, larger boulders in the moss nearby, shifting with loud cracks. Leaves and small branches rained down. Aurelia cried out as a cold pressure pressed against her ears, momentarily blocking out the cacophony of wild sounds.

It lasted for a long time before the churning eased to a slow heave and then finally ceased. From the bubbled up dirt road, Aurelia watched the horses galloping away, tossing their heads in terror. She groaned in pain, unable to stand.

Beside her, Caspian blinked groggily. He didn't look alarmed, more curious than anything. He rolled to his side before pushing up to his knees, checking over his sword. Along the road behind him, one of the horses whinnied again as it raced away. At the sound, a bored expression crossed his face. One of his hands shot out with a severe cutting motion. Aurelia cried out in alarm for the poor beasts. But while they stumbled, they didn't drop like she had expected them to. Whatever this strange man had sent their way wasn't a bloodthirsty death. What happened was that both horses kicked out in terror as both their saddles slid sideways, before coming apart to fall away from their bodies. She only saw one bridle fall before the horses disappeared, but it seemed likely that the other one was now free as well.

Panting, Aurelia stared at Caspian, thoroughly confused. He met her stare coolly in return as he picked himself up, carefully dusting off his pants. He grimaced as he picked out dirt from his fingernails. Eventually he looked up and around, tilting his head back to eye the sky.

"Well. That was fucking something, wasn't it?" he mused. He dropped his gaze back to Aurelia.

Mutely, Aurelia shook her head. She'd never experienced anything like that before. It had come from the south, and it seemed likely it had something to do with every other gods-damned thing that had gone on. She stayed where she was, on her arse for the second or third time that day, and wondered. Was that Fox? Rhydian? And why had this strange, cruel man let the horses run free like that? A loud rustling had her turn away from Caspian's profile while he stared around the forest, his eyes narrowed in thought.

"Flare?" she mumbled.

The dragon was adjusting his wings, using his snout to clear away debris from his spikes. He refused to look at her. Aurelia was glad he seemed okay, even after everything he'd done. Or not done. But there was so much that she needed to know, her heart was barely contained within her ribcage from how fast it was beating.

Near Flare, Jessikah hissed something about the sky.

Caspian lowered his head, nodding at what Jessikah had muttered, his gaze intent on the looming forest around them. "Yes. I think you're right."

"Which means I need to move. I need to get to the city before them." The smile she flashed Caspian was cruel, her voice oddly deep for such a petite figure.

Caspian turned from the forest with a smirk, a weird twist of his lips that had him looking like he was simultaneously smiling and frowning.

"A fitting coincidence, actually."

"Why?" Jessikah asked suspiciously, her yellow eyes narrowing.

"Because that's where we were going, too. Now your horses have *sadly* bolted, you have to join us."

"What-"

Caspian pointed to Flare, his smile brightening.

"Get up."

Jessikah took another step back, shock washing over her face. "*Fuck* no."

"*Now.*"

"No... n-no, Caspian, *please*, don't-" Flare pleaded, his voice cutting the tension. But his cry faded almost immediately.

All Caspian had done was turn to face the dragon, his expression calm. Iridescent blue eyes narrowed. But Flare shut his mouth. As Aurelia watched, the spikes on the dragon's back rippled with unease.

Jessikah looked horrified and repulsed. Caspian said nothing else. The woman opened her mouth and closed it twice, her yellow gaze dancing between him and the dragon. Her caution won over her complaints. As she stalked to Flare, he averted his eyes, his head and wings drooped down towards the road. Aurelia laughed nervously at the tension rippling between them. Turning her way at last, Caspian smiled. He'd heard her laugh, correctly interpreting it for what it was.

"If you don't actually know who that tiny firecracker is," he smirked, "it's even funnier than you think."

He took her arm again, his touch surprisingly gentle this time. Guiding her to Flare's leg, he stopped and undid the binding on her wrists by hand, not magic. Holding still while his firm hands undid the knots, she was under no impression about how bad it would go her way if she tried to run off again. Caspian glanced up, a wry expression on his fine features.

"No ropes until we both consent," he teased.

"What? Ugh. You're unbelievable."

His weird smile came back. But as she watched, it changed. It turned ominous. His right eye twitched, and his hands stilled while still holding hers.

"Um. Caspian?"

He blinked at the forest behind her, the weird smile fading very, very slowly. Aurelia wanted to turn around and look, but his eyes widened and seemed so unfocused she kept her eyes on his face. He seemed to be looking at something far away, his eyes glassy. Bewildered, he mumbled a word. Aurelia watched his lips move, but no sound came out. It looked like a two syllables, starting with the letter M.

After a sharp inhale, his smile returned just as slowly as it had faded. The reappearance of his even white teeth chilled her heart as Caspian's eyes locked back on hers, his expression bland. It was worse than the darkness she'd seen.

"Get up," he said, eerily calm.

Rubbing her wrists, Aurelia turned to face the dragon, inhaling deeply.

"Flare," she hissed as she started to climb. "What of Rhydian?"

She knew Caspian was following her up, but she didn't care. She turned to spare him a glance, the top of his blond head below her boot. She might have imagined it, but Flare's shining purple scales rippled at his touch. Caspian glanced up, made a dismissive shooing motion, so she set back to getting up to the strongest row of spikes where Flare's spine met his neck. One of them looked oddly formed compared to what she remembered. She ran her fingers along it. A quiet groan sounded from the dragon.

"Aurelia," Flare finally mumbled. "Please, just do what he says. Don't worry about Rhydian, not now."

"What does that mean?" Aurelia hissed as she arranged herself between two spikes. She had purposely avoided getting anywhere near Jessikah. The small woman was looking sick and shocked. As she settled down facing forward, Caspian wedged himself between the two women. His arms slid over the cloak around her ribs.

"There is a joke here," Caspian murmured. "But after that, I am too distracted to come up with anything good."

Aurelia leaned forward, daring to raise her voice. "Flare! *Answer me.*"

Caspian's voice tickled her ear, his lips irritating her soft skin like a wasp buzzing in her hair.

"Shut up now," Caspian said, quietly. "Please."

"Flare!"

She was pulled back against Caspian's chest, one of his hands brushing back her mess of hair from the side of her face. Cool lips pressed against her cheek in a chaste kiss.

"I said hush now. Or I will gag you." He sounded distracted, no longer playful. She wondered what he'd sensed after the earthquake.

"You bastard, you can try," Aurelia murmured, not daring to ask what had worried him. She could feel his shrug as he wrapped the cloak around her more firmly. He didn't respond. She wondered at that, the dark and light of him. His cruel words were at odds with his consideration for her comfort.

Flare glanced once over his shoulder as he manoeuvred into the middle of the road, the forest dark and tall overhead. Aurelia knew he could do it, but his take off would be rough. She closed her eyes; her head still ached, her bruises burned. The pain loosened her tongue.

"Just so you know, being this close to you is distasteful," Aurelia hissed, gritting her teeth as Flare's muscles rippled beneath them. "Whoever you are, you're a beast."

The arms around her squeezed her briefly.

"I know." He sounded unconcerned. "Thank you."

There was a string of muttered curses behind them. Jessikah clearly didn't want to be here, on Flare's back as much as Flare didn't want her there. A nagging thought was growing in the darkest part of Aurelia's mind, and she bit her lip. She hoped she was wrong.

After Flare shuffled and flapped his wings a few times, stirring up all sorts of detritus, he was airborne after a great leap into the air. Her stomach dropped as the ground fell away. She didn't open her eyes until the air cleared, dropping in temperature. Staring at the dark forest below, Aurelia blinked away tears of rage. There was nothing for as far as she could see, just trees that undulated with the hills and valleys to the horizon. It was alarming to realise how lost she was, with no visible town or village around. Her rage mixed with the fear of knowing if she had escaped, it was likely she would die out here.

And the words she needed to share with Rhydian would go unspoken.

Unaware of her distress, Caspian shifted against her with a sigh.

"Hurry up, Flare," he eventually called next to Aurelia's ear. "We don't want to miss out on the family reunion."

"Fuck off," was Jessikah's vehement reply.

"Charming," Caspian muttered.

Hating herself but wanting answers, Aurelia frowned.

"What are you talking about?" she asked.

She needn't have bothered. He ignored her. When she twisted around, she found Caspian twisting in turn to face Jessikah.

"So tell me, how does it work?" he mused, the wind whipping his hair around like a crown of moonbeams. "Having a vagina, despite being a massive cock?"

Jessikah's snarled reply was lost to the cold currents of air that raced by.

46

Fox

"King, huh?" Owaen shifted on the horse behind Fox. "You seem a bit young."

Fox leaned back into the warmth behind him, his cheek brushing against Owaen's chin. Tilting his head, he spared a look at Rhydian. The young man was pale, red eyed and sat on his horse with slumped shoulders. When Rhydian spoke, his tone was clipped.

"Both of my parents are newly dead."

Fox felt more than heard the thoughtful hum in Owaen's chest.

"Fox killed one of them," Rhydian continued calmly. "I killed the other."

"You can say it, kingling," Fox offered softly. "That they both deserved it."

"I see." Owaen blew out a thoughtful breath. "Some believe that violence can be used as a sinister means to a seemingly necessary end."

Fox snorted, ignoring the arms that tightened around him.

Instead of commenting straight away, Rhydian reached out to pat the black horse that Owaen and Fox were riding. When the young king's hand touched Blackthorn's neck, the horse tossed his head in appreciation, quickly stepping sideways into Rhydian's horse. Rhydian muttered a quiet admonishment under his breath and pushed the black horse away with an amused twist to his lips.

"Perhaps they deserved it," Rhydian eventually admitted while staring at the road ahead of them where it curved to the left amongst the trees. "After the things they both did. My father said things, dark things, to me. I'm not sure what I can do to make up for any of what they've done."

"Rhydian." Rhydian turned to face Fox, blue eyes wary at Fox's rare use of his name. "Whatever that bastard said to you, don't think of it."

Raking his fingers through his wild, golden brown hair, Rhydian shrugged.

"Even if his words were true?"

Not waiting for a reply, Rhydian urged his mount to increase its pace. As the distance between their horses grew, Owaen had to prevent Blackthorn from trying to follow. Fox ran his tongue over his bottom lip, pleased it wasn't as cracked. The king's horse was clearly infatuated with his human. Most people were, including himself. Aurelia had been as well, despite the way they'd met in the woods and for what reason.

Fox settled back closer into the warmth at his back, inhaling a familiar, woody scent, and closed his eyes. With Owaen's breath against his cool skin, Fox's mind drifted.

The shimmering colours of energy he'd been seeing around people had gone, thankfully. He'd spied a dark mist of grey around Rhydian, which had worried Fox at first, but it was gone now. Owaen's had been bright and golden. As he listened to the creak of saddles and the dull thud of horse hooves on the forest road, Fox wondered. He wasn't sure what the colours had been. Madness? Or some innate flicker of their power within?

He didn't feel mad. He felt anxious, confused. Owaen was still the same cocky Elf Fox had known. He radiated a peace that Fox had found nowhere else. A peace that was offered freely to Fox, something that he wasn't sure he deserved. It was obvious there were unsaid things that needed to come to light between them. Owaen's eyes burned with questions. And while Fox was grateful that the sparks of his deep magic were igniting, blooming brighter with each moment he spent wrapped up in Owaen's arms, there was much that Fox simply had no interest in speaking of just now.

Or ever.

The bone chilling cold still flowed through him for now. However, an unspoken fear in Fox's heart couldn't be squashed down. If he shared too much, too soon, he was afraid that bright, radiating warmth would be taken away. And with it the power that used to consume him, threatening to spill forth each time he lost control of his inner war. So much depended on Owaen being here. The scowling Elf could easily cut through Fox's ego with a simple rise of a blonde eyebrow, like nothing and no one else ever could, and that scared him more than he cared to admit. With his eyes still shut, Fox snorted. He was aware of his own stubborn nature more now than ever, and his aching vulnerability as well. A soft kiss was pressed into Fox's hair.

"Stop thinking so loud." A warm hand smoothed back the hair that had fallen across his eyes. Fox pretended to ignore the touch. The soft laugh behind indicated that Owaen didn't trust his indifference. Fox's breath had stuttered, a fact obvious to both of them.

It was the second day riding to the City of the Seers, to Aurelia. The last few days had been a blur, especially the ride from Aneirin, as he'd just about used up what spark he had left inside to get them to the cave. He remembered the earth trembling inexplicably in their wake. And he remembered the blue glow of the cave, so different from the flickering red shadows from his time there against his will. Now the fog had started to clear, his heart and mind blooming into consciousness as he'd been carried away from that hateful place for the second time in the same warm arms.

The thought compelled Fox to open his eyes, revealing the lush greenery of the surrounding forest. The vibrant greens and deep, earthy browns blended together in a rich tapestry of colours. So this was a second chance. To do what he should have done years ago. He was still confident Aurelia was relatively safe. Shadow Light was arrogant and cruel, but he'd know the odds for his survival were for naught if anything happened to Aurelia.

Lightly resting a cool hand on one of the cosy arms around his chest, Fox inhaled deeply. Owaen smelled faintly of horse, his own masculine musk, and the cool woods around them. The forest, spread out endlessly on either side of the unkempt road, was quiet. No birds sang here, although the occasional gurgle and rush of water could be heard through the wide trunks. The air below the trees had no warmth of its own, and he was grateful that the tattered cloak he wore still provided some protection. It was hard to tell through the canopy, but along with the faint aroma of ash, there was possible rain on the way. Any sunlight that managed to find its way to the ground was washed out and thin. The wan rays of light were a fine representation of how he felt. His magic was responding to Owaen being so close once again, but he was still unbearably cold. The impatience with himself was frustrating him to no end.

"I'm coming, Aurelia," Fox murmured, his fingers curling into fists. The next kiss against his hair was firmer.

Ignoring the skip of his heart, Fox rolled his lips inwards between his teeth. That was something he didn't know how to approach. What was left between Owaen and himself?

Surely that part of their lives together was past. Fox shut the thoughts down; aware his stubbornness was winning for now.

"Stubborn horse," Owaen muttered, startling Fox with the congruency of his thoughts to the soft words. Fox couldn't help but smirk.

Blackthorn had added just enough speed to his walk that he had almost caught up to Rhydian. Sighing, Owaen urged their horse the last few paces to come alongside the king. A raised eyebrow from Rhydian was his only acknowledgment of Blackthorn at his side. The horse didn't seem to mind. After a little while of riding in silence with the occasional pale ray of light painting his face, Fox realised Rhydian kept glancing at them. Specifically, at Owaen.

Owaen's sigh this time was a hot puff of air against Fox's cheek.

"What."

Rhydian shifted in his saddle and cleared his throat.

"Did you dream?"

Overriding Blackthorn's stubborn resistance, Owaen halted the black horse. Rhydian halted his smaller horse as well. His gaze was defiantly calm. Fox's hand tightened on Owaen's arm in warning.

"Please. It's important," Rhydian said carefully, not breaking off his stare.

Turning in the saddle, Fox's eyes were in line with Owaen's jaw. Muscles twitched under the tanned skin, the faint scruff of his cheek. Owaen's nostrils flared and he let out a long sigh.

"Yes." Green eyes flicked down to Fox for a moment before meeting Rhydian's stare once more. "I did."

After a moment, Rhydian nodded. His expression was thoughtful as he urged his horse to walk on. Owaen let Blackthorn follow on at his own pace. Fox let out the breath that he was well aware that he was holding. It was a slow exhalation of tension, relief that Owaen hadn't leapt off his horse to slam the young king down into the moss for asking such a thing at such a time.

Still a little ahead of them, the grey, dappled light played over the gold in Rhydian's hair.

"My apologies if it was too personal a question." He rode on for a while before murmuring again. "I have dreams. I know they mean things. And that cave... I wonder because of what happened there, if..." his voice faded, barely loud enough to be heard over the quiet rustle of the leaves above.

"Go on," Owaen encouraged, his tone mild.

"I wondered if you dreamt about the things that had happened there."

"Be more specific."

Fox shifted against Owaen, a coil of dread working its way up his spine. He had a dark suspicion of where Rhydian was going with this.

"My dreams are about things that happened at home, when I was young, things I don't know if I experienced there, or not. I wondered if it was the same in the caves for you. Fox never said what happened there. Not exactly."

There it was.

Fox narrowed his eyes at Rhydian's back.

"Do I need to?" he asked icily.

Rhydian didn't hesitate. "Yes, I think you do. I know you spoke of some of it." He slowed his horse until Blackthorn came alongside. "I don't like shitty stories, but I'm living one now. Aurelia is gone. I've left my people alone. I'm not sure what's left back there for me. How do I handle all of... this? You went through something dark, Fox. I want to know how to cope."

Unable to help it, Fox laughed. So hard that he choked. Owaen's firm thump cleared his lungs, and with a wheeze Fox got air back in and out once more. Fox smirked as he wiped his mouth on his sleeve.

"You're asking me?" he asked dryly, as he gestured to himself with a pale hand. "You think this is coping? I-"

Owaen lifted a hand and placed it over Fox's mouth. Startled, Fox's eyelids fluttered while Owaen's musky scent filled his nose.

"Go on, Rhydian," Owaen said graciously as Fox, recovering his senses, smacked Owaen's hand away, his lips tingling. The heavy hand landed on Fox's thigh. Fox crossed his arms over his chest.

"Um okay. Well, there was a battle between my father and my mother with the Elves."

"Who won?" Owaen's tone was curious. His fingers pressed lightly into Fox's thigh.

"No one." Rhydian's tone was bitter. "Aurelia was taken by Shadow afterwards, who had been brought to Aneirin by Fox."

The hand on Fox's thigh twitched.

"I'm trying hard not to think this, Fox. But the closer we get to this damned city, the more I can't help but think you should have killed him."

Uncrossing his arms, Fox smacked Owaen's hand off his leg.

"I thought I needed to keep him close, as a reminder of what I needed to become, in order to stop the other dragons from their greed. I refuse to explain it further."

"You mentioned what happened," Rhydian pressed. "Not how."

His mouth a thin line, Fox shook his head.

"Tell him," Owaen breathed against his ear.

"I can't," Fox snapped, jerking his head away from the warmth that tickled his skin. Something cold and clogged shifted in his lungs and he had to clear his throat as Rhydian pushed on.

"You said innocents died by Shadow's hand to fill you with power."

Turning his face to the side, Fox spat out a fresh piece of whatever sludge was still breaking away in his chest.

"I told you in the forest." Fox kept his tone even. "Shadow Light took me against my will to that cave and experiments were done. Blah, blah, blah. He sacrificed Elven victims that were captured fleeing his destruction of the city, and he made me take all their magic. The end."

"But how?" Rhydian's voice was firm. "I want to know what we're up against. If you were so powerful, how did he take you?"

Fox closed his eyes, not seeing a way out of this, hoping Owaen didn't lose his shit. Unaware of what Fox had to say, Owaen reached back around Fox with one arm, squeezing his side in encouragement.

"He tricked me."

Owaen stiffened behind him, not having heard this before. When Owaen had rescued what was left of Fox from the cave, Fox had been in no condition to share.

"How?" Rhydian insisted. Fox opened his eyes, staring straight ahead.

"What he did is hard to do. Well, for others, not me. But he glamoured someone," Fox sighed. "Someone was in disguise to look like Owaen... Enough that I thought Owaen had been taken. I fell for it long enough to be overcome."

Owaen's hand on his side went still. Fox shook his head, his hands trembling slightly. Oblivious, Rhydian kept going.

"Why?"

Aware that Rhydian really was only trying to prepare for whatever was ahead of them, Fox grit his teeth.

"I think the endgame was to force all the magic into me. He wanted to check I could take it back. And then he was going to take it all from me."

"Huh." Rhydian swallowed. "And how..."

Fox could feel the rage rolling off the chest behind him, and the hand on his ribs dropped to his thigh once more. He had to force the words from his icy lips.

"It was fun. Shadow Light ripped out their hearts and forced them down my throat."

Rhydian halted his horse, choking back a startled sob.

"The bones...?"

Fox grabbed the reins from Owaen's other hand and jerked Blackthorn to a halt. Blackthorn tossed his head until Fox tugged on a lock of the black mane with a sharp jerk. Owaen's hand on his thigh was now a fist, knuckles white as frost.

"It's a shitty story, remember, kingling."

"That's what you're calling it?" Owaen interrupted, his voice a dangerous murmur. "A shitty fucking story?"

"It's true-"

Owaen cut him off, his voice rising in volume. "You were fucking tortured, Elven children were murdered, and you're calling it a *shitty* fucking *story*?"

"Owaen, calm-"

"Don't you *dare* say it-" Owaen barked.

"-down."

"You... ugh." Owaen's teeth were almost audibly grinding together. He jerked the reins from Fox with one hand and urged the horse on once more. "When you recovered, you should have taken Shadow back to the city. You should have-"

As his dark eyes threw off chilled sparks, Fox tilted forward, away from Owaen's coiled rage. But the fist on his thigh rose to become a vice against Fox's chest, keeping him close.

"Stop-" Fox spluttered while Owaen talked over him.

"-taken him to the other dragons!"

Seething, Fox grabbed the hand over his chest and squeezed. Owaen cursed, but refused to let go. Blackthorn whinnied and came back alongside Rhydian and his horse, both of which were eyeing Fox and Owaen with alarm.

"Owaen, let me go. I couldn't-"

"What about the council?" Owaen hissed against his ear. "Why didn't you take Shadow Light to the council?"

Rage both red hot and white cold spread out from Fox's spine, rippling over his tattoo and leaving his hands shaking. His voice was a loud cry of anguish as he twisted to shout directly into Owaen's shocked face.

"Because there was no fucking council left!"

Both horses danced sideways as their hooves touched the road that shook with a mild tremble. Owaen's eyes widened as he looked over the side of the horse, then back to Fox. He blinked, his dark emerald eyes wide.

"What?" he breathed.

"There was no city left." Fox went on, his eyes glittering, the ground below humming like wasps ready to break out of the moss and the soil. "So how could the fucking useless council meet in ruins? They all fled. Like the fucking dragons, who I tracked all the way back to Mionlach!"

Owaen stared at Fox, mouth working, no sound leaving his lips. Rhydian was fighting to get his horse under control as the tremors rolled past and along the road, out through the dappled forest with a hum that had leaves falling in its wake. He reined in Blackthorn again, one handed. Irritated beyond his own understanding, Fox finally smacked Owaen's hand off his chest.

"Stop asking this fucking horse to stop and start walking!" Fox yelled. "It's driving me mad, it's driving him mad. Can we just get to the fucking city already?"

Wisely, Rhydian kept his mouth shut, but he looked faintly sick. His face was pale, his hair a tousled mess. His blue eyes were wide, and sad, looking with pity at the man behind Fox.

Fox twisted around, wincing as his lungs protested. Owaen was staring blankly, his gaze lost on the road as it disappeared into the dark trunks of tall pines and oaks.

"The City of the Seers is gone?" he eventually mumbled, not looking at Fox.

"There's no one there. Shadow Light finished it off while you were looking for me."

There was a moment's pause. One of Fox's hands twitched.

"It's in ruins, Owaen."

Fox was keenly aware of the blank shock on Owaen's face, as the Elf's dark green eyes shifted to meet his. Owaen's throat moved as he swallowed, his eyes closing.

"It's in ruins," Owaen repeated softly.

Fox shrugged, not wanting to let any more bitterness pass between his lips. He was tired, empty as the ruined city and sorry he hadn't realised that Owaen had no way of knowing how bad it had been, because Fox had locked him away. When Owaen finally opened his eyes, his head was tilted back so he could stare up at the canopy of shifting light and shadows above.

As the silence thickened, the canopy above moved like seaweed in the deep rivers that crossed the forest floor. Occasionally, there were weak rays of light that washed over them where it filtered to the road. It was getting dark and cold down below, even though the sun was not long past the midday horizon. The aroma of wet moss and water was strong here; another creek could be heard bubbling away through the thick woods. The trunks were too crowded to see where, possibly to their left. Fox lowered his gaze from the trees, finding Owaen's dark green eyes locked on his face. The green flashed with highlights when the dappled light touched his face, blonde hair falling to one side and touching his shoulder.

"I was too late," Owaen murmured, his voice hoarse. "Far too late."

"Owaen, don't, please."

Shaking his head, Owaen pressed his forehead to Fox's cheek.

"I failed. Maybe that's why I'm not as angry with you as I should be. I deserved to be locked away."

Ignoring Rhydian's sharp intake of breath, Fox touched the shaved hair on the side of Owaen's head. He dragged his fingernails along the skin, feeling the tremble beneath his fingertips.

"That's not why I left you there. You know that. I left you behind, *safe*. Not because you failed me. You had no chance to stand against him."

Unhooking one leg from the stirrup, Owaen pulled away from Fox to slide off Blackthorn in one smooth movement. His boots barely made a sound as he touched the mossy, unkempt surface of the road. Fox watched with confusion as Owaen stalked to the side of the road. He paused and turned to face them, his face blank.

"Excuse me for a moment, please," Owaen said calmly. He turned and quickly faded into the silent trees, like the forest wandering Elf that Fox knew he was at heart.

The silence didn't last long. Fox watched Rhydian flinch.

"FUCK."

The roar of fury echoed in a strangely intimate way towards them from the direction Owaen had disappeared. A moment later, the sound of branches cracking and being torn apart followed.

"Fuck! Fuck! *Fuck!*"

It went on for some time.

Numbly, Fox watched Rhydian wipe damp eyes with the back of his hand. As the cursing and thumping continued, Rhydian slid from his saddle and came to stand by Fox, the reins of his horse loose in one hand. Blackthorn nuzzled his arm. One hand cupped the nuzzling velvet nose, his other hand grabbed Fox's cool fingers. Rhydian squeezed gently, blinking as he met Fox's gaze.

"Do you want to talk about it?" Rhydian asked, his voice hesitant.

Shaking his head, Fox returned the squeeze. They listened to the sounds beyond the trees for a while. A while later, Rhydian cleared his throat.

"I like Owaen for you. Strangely, he's not as scary as I thought he'd be."

Rhydian shrugged at whatever he saw passing over Fox's expression.

"Upright with no rope, you're doing better," Rhydian murmured, sounding brighter than he looked. Pleased with the hope that was blooming over Rhydian's face, Fox smoothed his thumb over Rhydian's palm.

"Owaen is my rope."

Rhydian nodded, seeming to understand he meant that it worked both ways.

"Are you feeling stronger?"

"Fuckity fuck fuck fuck," echoed from the trees as more branches smashed and cracked. A flock of tiny birds flew past them both in a bright scatter of gold and red. Ignoring the destruction from the trees, Fox raised an eyebrow at Rhydian.

"Did you mean to ask, kingling, am I able to kill Shadow Light now? And can I save Aurelia?"

Rhydian shifted on his feet. "Yes, I guess. We'll be there soon. Are you going to be okay?"

Larger birds rose with loud calls of alarm as the chaos of their forest continued. Wings passed through the filtered sunrays like ghosts, and a grey rabbit sped across the road, away from the cursing and cracking of branches. Fox stared into the trees with the sound of destruction warming him as much as Owaen's embrace. With reluctance, he let go of the warmth of Rhydian's hand.

"Yes, to all of that." Fox rolled his head from side to side, cracking his neck. "I'm just about ready."

"Fucking fuck *fuck*…"

Fox licked his lips, considering the sounds of violence close by.

Owaen was as caught up in his fury in much the same way Fox had been, with a rage that needed expressing. Which Fox had, with his own violent revenge, focused directly upon the dragons in their so-called homeland. The bitter ash still fell across the continent from his actions. Perhaps one day he would take Owaen back to Mionlach to show him. If he calmed down enough to let Fox explain what he'd done. Either way, he wasn't sure if his lack of alarm at Owaen's outburst should have bothered him. Because it didn't.

"Yes, I am going to save Aurelia, and yes, I am going to finally end that beast."

"No more keeping your shadow by your side?"

Rhydian's grip tightened again, and this time Fox returned it straight away. Leaves drifted past on the cool breeze, through the dappled light, kicked up from the violence of guilt and rage set free amongst the trees. Dropping his gaze to where his hand joined with Rhydian's, Fox smiled. He'd once had sharp claws, and he'd once had delicate women's hands, soft and gentle. Now they were long and pale, strong and capable. But if he was honest, he didn't know what he preferred. But how they looked wasn't important.

"You're going to get rid of him once and for all?"

Whatever form his hands or claws took now, he wanted to sink them past Shadow Light's ribs. Fox wanted to break the foul creature's body open, tearing out his black heart as it beat with cruel power. He wanted to swallow it down whole, the circle of horror closed once and for all.

"Yes," Fox murmured, eyes glinting with black ice, "it will be my absolute pleasure."

47

Owaen

Year 367
The Forest

*C*rack.

Owaen's palm connected with Rhydian's face.

The blow was sharp, hard enough to split the king's bottom lip. Wiping his mouth, Rhydian staggered back. Blue eyes widened as he stared at his bloodied hand. His right eye twitched. That was the only warning Owaen had before Rhydian charged in a desperate bid to knock Owaen down.

Dodging the wild swing from Rhydian's right fist, Owaen jerked back and sideways out of the way, easily. His laugh was mocking.

"You'll end up in the campfire, little king," Owaen teased. "With a sloppy move like th-"

Rhydian circled back quicker than Owaen had expected. The king swung again, this time close enough that Owaen had to duck, not dodge.

"Better!" Owaen barked. "Fists up! Watch my eyes!"

This time, when Owaen popped up and swung, Rhydian danced sideways out of the way. Owaen held up both hands, palms out.

"Much, much better," he said, impressed, tossing his blonde hair out of his eyes. "Not every fight is won by a charge. You also have to keep out of the way."

"That seems obvious," Rhydian panted. He bent over, grabbing his thighs with his hands. "Too obvious that I never really thought about it. My reach with a sword is good, but without it... well."

"Without it, you're a paddling without an oar if you can't get out of the way, if you don't keep *moving*."

Nodding wordlessly, Rhydian straightened to stretch his back, bones popping while he winced.

Not as winded as the young king, Owaen glanced at Fox. He was sitting on the moss with his bare feet at the fire's edge and his toes wiggling towards the flames for warmth. The tattered cloak was wrapped around his shoulders. An unamused scowl adorned his pale face. Black and gold met Owaen's, the derision in Fox's expression enough to cause Owaen to laugh out loud again.

It felt good to laugh this morning. He wasn't feeling great, and if he was being honest with himself, he actually felt like a bag of hot horseshit. But after burning off some of his rage the evening before on some innocent trees and sparring with the king this morning, he was feeling slightly more in control.

Noticing the direction of Owaen's gaze, Rhydian's eyes crinkled at the corners and his lips twitched. But it wasn't quite a smile. The king was almost as pale as Fox, the strain they'd been under clearly catching up to him. Owaen knew *exactly* how he felt. Which is why Owaen was distracting them both for a short while before they set off through the crowded trees once more.

"Come spar with us, Fox," Rhydian called from across the clearing.

Owaen smirked as Fox's scowl deepened.

Where they had slept last night wasn't quite a clearing. It was where he'd let his rage free out, tearing through the undergrowth the evening before, helplessness pulsing in his veins. Once he'd calmed down, panting heavily, it had made a good enough campsite off the road and cleared enough for the horses to not be crowded alongside them. Rhydian had appeared between two prickly pines when Owaen had finally stopped ripping off tree limbs. Serious, sad blue eyes had assessed him with quiet and determined courage. Owaen had stared down at his bloody hands, blinking at his already healing Elven skin, his estimation of the young man rising. But only just.

"Are you done?" Rhydian had asked. "Fox needs to rest."

The king had known exactly what to say. The red sparks dancing across Owaen's vision had faded.

"Yes," Owaen had rasped, breathing in the bittersweet scents of freshly exposed wood and churned up earth. "For now."

The young king had nodded solemnly. "Good." Rhydian had paused, assessing the devastation.

"This looks like how I feel," he said dejectedly, his careful blue gaze eyeing the splintered, fragrant remains of an oak branch at his boots.

A young pine tree was lying awkwardly in the middle of the narrow but deep creek beyond the wreckage. Owaen had ripped it out by the roots, but seeing it there now shamed him. He hated to see it sitting there, out of place. Like him.

Nothing more had been said. Rhydian had headed back to get Fox as the weight of unspoken words hung heavy over them all.

And now, in the dim light of another overcast day, Owaen was doing his best to share some skills but also to distract them both. They had little time, and likely it would never count. But the king needed something to do. Something to take his mind off where they were headed, what they were about to do. Something that Owaen knew only too well.

"Come on, Fox," Rhydian called again. "Come, move around a bit."

Shaking his head, Fox's glittering eyes narrowed.

"This is not what I meant when I asked for your help, Owaen."

Wondering if the king would take the bait, Owaen turned to face Fox head on, his back to Rhydian.

"I'm helping your *friendly* little king learn to trust himself, not just a sword."

Settling against the log behind him, Fox's gaze contracted into slits. He crossed his arms over his chest, not taking the barb in that comment. Perhaps Owaen had read their relationship wrong-

Something brushed over the soft moss behind him.

Owaen winked at Fox.

He shifted to his right just as Rhydian came barrelling past. Owaen kicked the king in the arse as he overstepped. With a curse, Rhydian corrected his overstepping and whirled around.

"Almost got me, little king-"

Not giving up, Rhydian darted forward, swinging with his right fist. Owaen raised a forearm to block the hit, only realising too late what was really happening. Rhydian's knee connected with his groin, missing his target by only a few centimetres. But the impact would still bruise.

"Oh fuck," Owaen gasped. "That's not like a king at all. Nice work."

"Thank you," Rhydian panted. He charged again, the flush of his near victory bright across his pale cheeks. There was a smudge of dirt under one eye, a bruise blooming across his face, and blood over his mouth. Despite that, in the soft dawn light that barely reached the forest floor, he still looked less haunted than the day before.

Owaen blocked his charge, but only barely. He ducked and caught the king around the waist, and both of them went tumbling heels over arse, into the moss and scattered rocks by the stream. Winded but refreshed by the cold splash from the shallows, Owaen rolled and grabbed the king's hair, straddling the young man over his waist, his heavy thighs on each side of Rhydian's hips. It looked like the king was trying not to laugh.

"I almost," he panted, eyes closed while his bloody teeth flashed.

Owaen nodded. "You got me on the ground. Good boy."

The king's eyes snapped open, and he tried to buck Owaen away.

Ignoring the king struggling beneath him, Owaen spared Fox a glance. His expression was still unamused, but he seemed interested in the pair of them sprawled by the river. He was sitting up straighter. Dappled light from far above was playing shadows across the handsome features, different from what Owaen was used to. But the wintry fire inside was the same. He welcomed the warmth uncoiling inside of him as he allowed his gaze to wander freely over the bare feet, long legs and slim figure by the fire.

"You okay over there, sunshine?" Owaen called, green eyes wide and innocent. He tugged on the golden brown hair in his fists. Rhydian's struggling stopped with a painful curse.

"No," Fox snapped. His eyes flashed with a dark light. "I was feeling better, but the two of you are making me ill again." He slumped back down, closing his eyes, pulling the cloak tighter around his shoulders. "You look like a pair of drunk goat herders on the slopes of Lolihud."

"Goat herders, huh?" Owaen laughed.

Gazing down, he examined the bruise blooming across Rhydian's face. It suited him. "I'm actually impressed with you, little king."

Rhydian tried to speak, but shook his head instead, his half smile fading to a grimace. Blue eyes stared up at Owaen, the weight of his worry shuttering over his expression slowly. A single tear escaped the corner of Rhydian's eye as he watched. With a sigh, Owaen released Rhydian's hair.

"It's going to be fine," Owaen murmured, his gaze darting between Rhydian's eyes. The morning light was weak, but this close he wondered where he'd seen their like before. The king's eyes were two shades of blue, the paler irises circled by a darker blue.

"It wasn't fine though," he murmured, blinking up at Owaen. "It wasn't fine for you, or Fox, was it?"

He tapped Owaen's thigh lightly and Owaen pushed himself up and away, unable to think of a reply. Refusing to meet Owaen's searching gaze, Rhydian pushed himself up and headed to the edge of the clearing. In a few steps he was gone, lost amongst the thick undergrowth and crowded trunks along the edge of the bubbling creek.

"I expect he'll be a while," Fox murmured, eyes still closed. "Especially if your episode last night is anything to judge by."

Glaring, Owaen lowered himself down beside Fox, saying nothing.

"Don't even try to pretend you're not scowling at me," Fox snapped. "I can feel the heat of it without looking."

"You'd know all about that," Owaen muttered before he could stop himself.

He stretched his legs towards the glowing embers and pinched the bridge of his nose. Feeling Fox shift beside him to turn and examine his profile, Owaen busied himself with picking bits of moss and dirt out from beneath his fingernails. When he was satisfied, he sat back and crossed his arms over his chest. He wasn't winded from their sparring. But now that Rhydian had wandered off, taking a moment to sit quietly seemed like an excellent idea.

Shifting sideways so that his elbow poked Fox's arm, Owaen sighed. Beyond the fire, he examined the dark trunks and shadows dance as the heat from the embers hazed the air. The smoke of the green branches that were burning had died down, and a resinous scent drifted around their rough campsite.

Today was their third day of travelling together. Only three days and he was struggling to contain himself. Frustration and guilt pulsed through him, at odds with his attraction to the strange creature beside him. There was nothing he wouldn't do for her, for Skye.

Fox, he corrected himself.

Uncomfortable feelings were eating away at his insides, frustration and regret. They'd had so little time together before Shadow Light had ruined their lives. And so little time now to catch up.

Properly.

As innocently as he could, Owaen carefully stretched his arms over his head, yawning. Lowering them in hopefully what seemed as natural a way as possible, one of his arms ended up around Fox's shoulders.

"Stop that," Fox scoffed. But he didn't pull away. With a faint smile, Owaen left his arm where it was.

Fox wasn't shivering, but his cool body temperature was noticeable even through the faded black cloak. When he'd woken up that morning, Owaen had been unapologetically wrapped around Fox like an Elven blanket. Black and gold eyes that had been examining him while Owaen slept had blinked at him before looking away, as Fox stubbornly refused to acknowledge the evidence of interest pressed against his thigh. Unfazed, Owaen had yawned, feeling warm despite the cold morning. *Any* time that they had together was important. Even waking up in the forest on the bare earth a day before they met the bane of both their existence, hopefully for the last time.

No wonder the young king was a mess. From what Rhydian had and hadn't said, it was obvious that he'd had so little time with Aurelia as well. Listening to the cool bubbling of the stream, Owaen wondered about that. That after all this time, Fox would finally get rid of his tormentor. So who was Aurelia to Fox? And Rhydian too?

Aware that even for an Elf, his ego was impressive. But the jealousy that he was experiencing like a dark ache in his guts was more about the time that Owaen and Fox *hadn't* had together. Time that Fox had shared with Aurelia, and the king who was like a lost soul in her wake. Owaen was feeling less sorry for himself, but some of that concern had passed to Rhydian. There was common ground there. Both had lost their parents, along with the one they loved above all others. No wonder Rhydian had ended up trying to hide tears the first time Owaen had seen Rhydian laugh. The grief was too fresh for anything too bright to shine through without pain.

Owaen's dark green gaze wandered around the rough clearing, his arm shifting along Fox's shoulders. Tearing up the trees had certainly helped him release some of what he was struggling with, and he had figured something similar would do for the king. So Owaen had invited him to train that morning as soon as Rhydian was up, without giving him time to think.

In much the same way, when he'd woken up to the black eyed, grumpy huff against him, he'd acted instinctively. Not giving Fox time to think.

"Cold?" Owaen had murmured as Fox shivered once against him.

"No," Fox said, his lips faintly blue, still avoiding Owaen's gaze.

It had been a frosty morning, the coldest yet. The hot breath from the two horses nearby was a white fog before their velvet noses. Trying not to smile, Owaen had reached out to pick up a sizeable log and chucked it to the dying red embers of their fire. Fox had snorted as it landed. The last of the glow died out as the wood landed with a dull thump, a few sparks of orange rising to wink out as quickly as they had appeared.

"Go on," Owaen had urged, his lips tickling the cool shell of Fox's ear.

Fox had twisted around, black eyes glittering. Owaen narrowed his own in challenge. His smile had been harder to hide by then.

"Light it."

"I'm not ready-"

Fox had tried to bury himself under the cloak, but Owaen ripped it off his face.

"LIGHT IT."

Across the camp, the king had sat upright with a start at Owaen's shout, looking wildly around. His gaze had landed on the fresh log in the ring of stones just as it had burst into flames. Rhydian's blue eyes snapped up, staring in hopeful surprise at Fox.

"Good girl," Owaen had purred, pressing his lips into the back of Fox's head. Rhydian had choked back a snort at Fox's expression. Owaen didn't care. He'd just pushed himself up and pointed at the king.

"I'm going to take a piss," Owaen had said, yawning. "Then you're going to try to knock me down."

Owaen had left the pair of them blinking stupidly at each other while he'd taken care of his needs. Then he'd fed and watered the horses too, from the meagre supply of oats left in the saddlebags, hoping that there were still meadows of grass around the city.

Dragging his thoughts back to the present and the coolly unamused figure beside him, Owaen examined the knuckles of his free hand. The cuts and the grazes of his flesh were almost gone. Unfortunately, it wasn't the same for the wounds that ran deeper. It would be the same for Fox. But Owaen wouldn't stop trying to work out ways to heal both of their scars. No matter what.

Moving slowly, Owaen adjusted his arm around Fox's shoulders, his hand cupping the cool skin of Fox's neck. When Fox didn't acknowledge him, Owaen tugged at the ends of the thick, black hair that tickled his wrist. Owaen's lips curled in a dark smile as gooseflesh rose below his calloused palm on Fox's neck. Fox turned to stare, incredulous. Owaen's smile widened, his gaze dropping to Fox's lips. He tilted his head, letting his keen hearing sense just how far Rhydian had gone off amongst the endless trees. It was a good distance, and the young man was still heading away from them.

"You're still the same to me," he murmured.

Fox cursed and looked away.

"Let me in, Fox. You didn't trust me to help you before you locked me away. But you do now. Please. You're still the same to me," Owaen repeated, studying the finely made profile of the man next to him. "I'm still the same. What do you think is different between us now?"

Silently, Fox shook his head. Owaen tugged at his hair again.

"Sk...ah shit. *Fox.* I will *always* help you. But I need to know why you want that from me *now*." He took a breath. "And not before."

Blowing out a sigh, Fox bent his legs, withdrawing his feet from the fire. He wrapped his arms around his knees.

"I know you're angry. You have every right to be. This is about Aurelia, and Rhydian. Not you and I."

"Angry?" Owaen said, sharply. One of the horses turned to stare at him. He ignored it. "Yes. But that's not what I'm talking about."

"What are you talking about, then? I'm tired and still sore in places. Spit it out."

Owaen pursed his lips at the dismissive tone but let it go.

"You walked the forest. *My* forest. With Shadow Light by your side."

"Yes." Fox sounded unapologetic.

Shaking his head, Owaen's fingers traced a lazy circle over Fox's neck. Black and gold eyes drifted shut.

"You chose to live with a dragon, the worst one of them all. You chose to lock me away. I'm not just angry," Owaen searched for the simplest way to explain the complex emotions crowded inside his heart. "I'm *sad*. That should have been our time. Not his."

Fox was silent for so long that Owaen was afraid he'd said too much, too soon. Eventually, Fox took a ragged breath, eyes barely open, narrowed into slits.

"I told you before. I became a real dragon in that fucking cave."

"You did, didn't you," Owaen mused. "'Cruel', I think, was the word you used."

"Yes," Fox's voice was barely a whisper, dropping his forehead to his knees.

Owaen slid his hand lower, his palm soothing trembling shoulders. Fox was clearly still suffering. Owaen didn't condone violence normally, but the only way he could go on living was if Shadow Light was ash and bones under his boots. Owaen's hand paused, feeling Fox's heart on the other side of his spine, beating peculiarly under his fingertips.

"Cruel," Owaen murmured, sitting up straighter. "Except I know what it cost you to ask for my help after all this time." He leant forward until his forehead rested on Fox's shoulder. "That's not cruel. That's *selfless*. That's *brave*."

A faint noise that could easily have been a sob, or a scoff, sounded from beneath Fox's curtain of black hair. Fox's voice was faint.

"I changed my mind at the last moment. I was afraid. I didn't want to s-see you."

Inhaling slowly, Owaen nodded, watching the fire flicker and twist before them.

"Fear is natural. Brave is facing those fears, Fox. You've done that. I'm here. And I'm going to stay right here and be whatever you need me to be."

Fox glanced to the side to peer through his black hair. He said nothing, but the heat in his gaze had Owaen's voice drop to a mumble.

"Why are you looking at me like that?"

Fox's gaze dropped to Owaen's lips.

"Because despite everything, I *am* happy to see you."

"Are you? Because you're confusing me."

"What? I was at death's door, *again* mind you, when we came for you," Fox muttered dryly, "so of course it's taken me a while to feel..." he waved a pale hand before them like that explained everything.

It didn't.

Owaen grabbed Fox's hand, almost crushing it with his own, needing to get the words out. "Even though I failed you before?"

Fuck, what was he trying to say?

Not that.

Why had he said that?

Fox's heated expression faded to something softer.

Pity, as if he of all of them deserved pity!

"Oh," Fox sighed. "Owaen, no, you didn't fail me."

Suddenly unable to handle the conversation that he'd instigated, Owaen stood up abruptly. He ran shaking hands through his hair, trying to ignore the ache in his chest.

"I'm sorry, I don't... huh. I need..."

Turning away, Owaen pressed the heels of his hands into his eyes. No matter how hard he wanted it gone, the image of a woman in his arms, green hair bloodied while she laughed and cried as he carried her from the cave, was simply unable to be wiped away. Fox's gasp of discomfort was soft as he stood up behind Owaen. Owaen's heart died a little more at the faint sound.

"I can still see you, Skye," Owaen whispered, not turning around, "in the cave. It's my fault, and I'm sorry. I'm sorry for all of it. I failed you-"

"Owaen." Fox's voice was abrupt. "Look at me. Right now."

Unable to do anything else except follow the snap of command in Fox's voice, Owaen turned around. He was immediately slapped across the face with a cold palm. The crisp snap of the slap echoed around the clearing and Blackthorn raised his head, ears back. Owaen, head ringing, staggered back, stumbling over moss and rocks.

"What the fuck, Skye?" Owaen hissed, one hand on his face.

Fox was breathing heavily, a faint wheeze perceptible in his chest.

"You wanted to fight Rhydian? Get your rage out?" Black and gold eyes were ablaze. "Hit *me* then!"

"Are you crazy?" Owaen shouted. "*Never.*"

Fox was shouting now, too. "Even after what I did to you? Are you sure that's not what this is? These tears and words of regret of yours aren't just some misguided fury at me locking you away?"

Unable to think of a single thing to say, Owaen shook his head.

"I will never hurt you," he said.

Fox stepped forward, his eyes still burning, but the dangerous gleam was gone.

"What's different this time you asked? I am. *Me.* I am not the same, despite what you think. I was fine to go out on my own before, and do what needed to be done. But I'm weaker now. Except *you're* still the same. And I know you. That's why you'll help me, because you won't give up on me. That's all you need to do now. Shit happened before, and I made a choice. It got me here. I lost my magic when I needed it most, and I'm here with you because I'm cruel enough to ask for your help when I clearly don't deserve it."

"What? No, you-"

"Shut up. I'm not done. You didn't fail me. I failed us both. And now, even with my magic returning, I still don't know who I am. I've changed. But I just need you to be Owaen. That's all. Can you do that? Can you just do that?"

Running his hands through his hair again, Owaen sighed.

"Skye-"

"My name is not Skye!" Fox shouted, a faint flush of pink in the centre of his cheeks. "Not anymore. Don't call me that."

Blackthorn pulled at his tether at the raised voice. Owaen slid his tongue around his teeth, tasting blood there from the force of Fox's blow.

"I'm sorry," Owaen said. "You're the same to me. You always will be, however you feel, however you appear."

"No," Fox said, his fury fading, fatigue washing over his features. Owaen wanted to gather him up like before, when Fox was still slightly delirious. The thought shamed him slightly. But at least his arms had been where they should have been.

"I'm truly no longer what I was," Fox went on. "What you need... what you want, I won't go back to being..." he took a deep breath, indicating himself with a shaking hand, "*her.*"

So the keeper of his heart was worried about... that?
That was something he could fix easily enough.

Owaen took a step forward.

"I want you, however you feel safest with me," Owaen murmured. "I don't need you to change. I don't need you to be anything else, other than what feels right for *you*," he said carefully. "But first, I want your forgiveness for not saving you from that monster."

"My forgiveness? Is that all?" Fox laughed even as his eyes filled with unshed tears, his expression incredulous. "After what I did to you, I'd say we are just about even."

Owaen's eyes narrowed at that. It wasn't quite what he wanted to hear. He took another step. Fox shrugged, his pale hands rising to grab the cloak tighter around his chest.

"I can't go back," Fox whispered. "I can't feel helpless again. I'm not that creature you knew. I'm not that dragon and I'm not that woman, either."

Closing the distance between them, Owaen clasped Fox's hands. His skin was still cool, but not as freezing as before.

"I said you don't need to change for me," Owaen murmured, moistening his lips. The gold in Fox's black eyes pulsed.

"Wh-what are you saying?"

Owaen let the heat in his gaze speak for itself, not words.

"I-I didn't think you were," Fox stammered, eyes widening, "that way inclined..."

Deep in the woods, Rhydian was still moving away, his boot steps faint now. Owaen dropped his searing gaze to the trembling figure before him. His heated fingers tightened on Fox's cool hands.

"Take off your clothes."

"What?" Fox gasped. He stepped back, the damp forest floor beneath them rumbling with a soft hum. Owaen dropped a hand to Fox's belt buckle.

"I said," Owaen murmured, pulling Fox towards him, "take off your fucking clothes."

"I... I think..." came the delicate plea above him.

Owaen pulled away, slightly breathless.

"Don't," he suggested. "Don't think."

On his knees in the soft moss, Owaen leant forward once more. Coolness on the back of his neck might have been the breeze, but the touch grew more insistent, confirming that it was hesitant fingers sliding up into his hair.

Fox had balked at first, as Owaen's hands slid over Fox's clothes. So Owaen had smacked his hands out of the way and undone Fox's belt buckle with his own trembling hands, their eyes locked on one another. As glittering black eyes locked to him, Owaen had been wishing he could read the thoughts behind them, wishing he had the right words for such a moment as this. He didn't. His actions would have to do instead. He had dropped to his knees, bowing before the one he loved.

"Breathe for me, lover," Owaen had murmured, tucking his hair behind his ear while gazing up.

And now, as soft, shallow breaths came from above him, the forest burned around them. Not with fire. It burned with wonder, the colours brighter and full of depth. Sounds were sharper; scents beyond the salt and musk against him were deeper, richer. Yet the two of them were separate from it all. The pair of them existed within a pocket of calm, cocooned from the storm of sensations around them by the intimacy they were sharing. The inside looking out, the outside looking in.

It felt necessary to soothe, feeling the hesitancy still in the deceptively gentle fingers, one hand in Owaen's hair, one cupping his cheek. Salt water tickled his cheeks.

"You're perfect," Owaen breathed as he pulled away for a moment. The fingers caressing Fox's skin trembled. "*Perfect.* You're so perfect when you come apart for me."

Below his knees, the earth seemed to agree, a deep hum vibrating up through his knees from the rocks and soil. He paid it no mind, and fingers slid deeper into Owaen's hair like frost made flesh, tugging him back to his task. His lips parted in a willing smile, Fox's startled gasp a salve to his ears.

After a little while Owaen slowed, pausing, listening to the sighed word above him, a mere breath.

"Agony…"

Frowning, Owaen glanced up. He was quickly reassured by the glow of euphoria and unmistakable desire within the black and gold eyes that stared down, the pale lips parted slightly.

"Agony?" Owaen teased.

"Agonisingly slow," Fox mumbled. "Hurry up, arrogant Elf, ah…"

Laughing smugly, Owaen obliged.

The wonder of it all was as he remembered, the parts different, the pleasure of their shared sweetness the same. Fastened to his lover, Owaen let himself drift, shivering with the pain of ignoring his own need. Nothing else mattered. He gripped tighter, pressed firmer, his lips swollen. A ragged gasp. And then, not quite suffocating, Owaen felt like he swallowed light, perhaps the light of a cold but shining star.

Panting, pleased with himself, he pulled away at last.

"You are exactly who you need to be," Owaen whispered, capturing Fox in his arms as the inky haired man collapsed to his knees, limp, breathless and spent. Owaen kissed the cool lips that sought his eagerly, uncaring where they had been.

Owaen laughed and breathed against Fox's kiss. "I am here with you, always."

As the colours and the sounds returned to normal, attentive fingers traced Owaen's hairline with reverence. Fox was sitting with his back against a log in the ferns and undergrowth, holding one of Owaen's hands against his chest. Owaen was lying in the moss, his head on Fox's lap.

Rhydian still wasn't back, but Owaen could hear that he wasn't far off. They had been blessed with the time alone despite what yet lay ahead. The forest sounds drifted around them, deceptively peaceful, considering what they were yet to come up against. But that was later. This was now.

Cool fingers traced Owaen's closed eyelids. He smiled at the touch that was as full of wonder as he remembered. Even the cool lips that occasionally brushed his hand were the same.

"Owaen."

"Mm."

"If you're still angry with me, after Aurelia is safe, if you plan to lock me away in return..." Fox paused, a satisfied sigh escaping him, and Owaen's smile turned into a frown. "Just do this for me again, first."

Inhaling Fox's familiar, effervescent scent, Owaen blew out a sharp breath.

"Don't joke about that."

"I wasn't. Really, you can do that again anytime."

"Mm."

They were quiet for a while, listening to the liquid rippling of the creek over smooth rocks. Faint wisps of campfire smoke drifted past, mixing with the pine aroma from the trees. A startled cough interrupted Owaen's dozing.

"Look!"

Head raised, Owaen turned to follow the direction Fox was pointing.

"My little fox is back," Fox said, his voice soft with the pleasure of what had passed between them. "Hm. Do you think it's the same one as before?"

Pushing himself up carefully, Owaen planted a kiss on Fox's cheek.

"As we both know," Owaen murmured, "every fox is uniquely different."

Fox scowled and waved him out of the way. He leant forward, trying to spot the red flash of fur darting through dappled light and shadows, so far that his cloak fell away. Owaen laughed under his breath, only half aware of the animal's swift movements through the trees. He settled on the moss beside Fox, his hand reaching to pull the cloak back up to Fox's shoulders.

"But it's unlikely that this one is the same one as before..." Owaen's voice drifted off, his line of thought forgotten.

Another strange flash of colour had caught his eye, this one much closer. His hands paused their work. While pulling up the cloak, Owaen's gaze had dropped to the soft, torn fabric of Fox's shirt, and the exposed skin beneath. The cloak was forgotten at the unexpected sight of coloured ink and swirling lines.

"What..." Owaen breathed, his heart hitching behind his ribs, his throat choking up with heat.

The colours *moved*.

Oblivious, Fox twisted to follow the path of the animal disappearing into the shadows. Owaen lifted the hem of Fox's shirt slowly, the cloak discarded beside him against the log. As more of the design was revealed, the hotter his throat felt, his eyes burning with salt water.

Oh fuck.

"It might have been the same one," Fox wondered aloud. He cracked his neck, sighing wistfully. "You never know, it might have been tracking us for scraps and the like."

Swallowing, Owaen simply stared. Writhing and shifting with dark magic, the coloured ink seemed to mock all that had been ready to burst forth from Owaen's heart for new beginnings, to replace missed opportunities. As toned muscles rippled and shifted, the movement of each horrific layer, dragons and other figures, twisted further in agony. Fox glanced back, his lazy yawn fading. Not understanding the blank expression on Owaen's face, Fox frowned.

"Owaen?"

Owaen shook his head, unable to speak, unable to think.

"Owaen," Fox snapped, the pleasure that had softened his features morphing into confusion. "What the fuck is wrong?"

"*Skye*," Owaen managed to croak.

Confused, Fox gazed wildly about; barely noticing his shirt had been pushed up. But as he grabbed the hem to pull it down, Fox paused. His gaze rose slowly. Owaen saw the moment that realisation fell like a dark veil over the glittering black and gold eyes.

"Ah," Fox said calmly.

"Skye," Owaen rasped, "what did you do?"

Fox jerked his shirt down all the way, his white teeth biting his bottom lip. The gesture should have been a heated distraction. Owaen wanted to throw up.

"It's not what you think," Fox said, obstinately tossing his head whilst doing up his belt.

"No?" Owaen gasped, his hands trembling. Wide green eyes, full of horror, stared blankly as if he could still see the entirety of the tattoo beneath the shirt. As if it would help snap Owaen out of it, Fox yanked the cloak over his worn shirt. Except Owaen had seen enough. Fox narrowed his gaze at the green eyes searing into his.

"I didn't kill them."

Swallowing against the bitterness in his throat, Owaen stood up and took a step back in one fluid movement.

"What did you do to them?" he whispered.

"I fixed them." Fox sat back, arms crossed over his chest. Hot and cold sparks flickered in his eyes, the barest hint of uncertainty. "Like you did for me."

Unsure how to even begin to interpret that, Owaen took another step away.

Fox stared at him, unrepentant.

"With what Shadow Light gave me, I used it against them," Fox said, as if that explained anything at all.

Trembling now, Owaen tried to rationalise the clipped words with the terrifying vision of devastation imprinted into his brain. Trembling hands swept through his blonde hair, tugging on the ends as if it would help make sense of what should have been a bright afterglow, but had turned to ashes in his mouth instead.

"Owaen?" Hurt flashed in Fox's eyes as he read the disgust on Owaen's face.

But Owaen was unable to explain; his throat had closed, from shame, from fury, from grief. Fox sat up, arms uncrossed, hands dropping into fists on his thighs.

"Owaen! Come back here!"

Words had simply failed him, disgust and guilt rising from his guts to consume him, overriding any rational thought. He stumbled away, following the creek upstream.

Yes, he was disgusted, but not with what they had done. Owaen was afraid, chilled by the realisation of how much both of them had gone through. It was going to be the same no matter how they came together, or went apart. It was simple. He'd been right. Fox had been wrong. Owaen had failed, dismally and epically, to protect him from whatever the fuck that was on his flesh.

Whatever Fox had been through, resulting in the experience of what had been recorded with blood, ink, pain and magic, was something Owaen could never soothe away. Whatever he had been through, Owaen could *never* make it right. Even being here to help now, to ignite whatever had nearly snuffed out Fox's magic, wasn't going to make up for what had happened before. Fox was definitely getting better. But the damage was done.

And no matter what Owaen could do, it would never be enough to undo what had happened. He had failed, and he was disgusted with *himself.*

"Owaen!"

Ignoring the furious shout, Owaen walked and stumbled until he was far enough away that his choked sobs would be scattered and unheard through the solemn trees.

He would never be enough. The evidence was there, in colours that writhed on skin like creatures in hell. Shadow Light had triumphed once before in breaking Fox, in breaking Skye.

And there was no guarantee that Owaen could stop it from happening again.

48

Cas

Year 367

The City of the Seers

"It's better if you hate me," Cas whispered.

Pressing his face into flaming red hair, inhaling the lingering aroma of poppy smoke and ash, he smiled happily.

"I think you should," he continued with a satisfied laugh. "It makes your eyes shine even brighter, my tiny glowing ember. I want to see them full of emerald fire. Therefore, I plan on making you feel so good that you hate me with everything that you possess."

Morgan, barely conscious, stirred against him, still managed to bare her teeth at him. Cas caught a lock of her red hair between his lips, tugging it playfully. His arms held her tight as her body shivered against him. His eyes closed, anticipation filling him like thick, dark honey.

"This is my eternal gift to you, Morgan," Cas breathed. "My Morgan."

With his face pressed into Aurelia's dark hair, his eyes shut tight; Cas could almost pretend he was in another time, another place. When he'd snatched another woman from the pit of despair that she'd fallen prey to. The fury and the fight were the same in both of them. But the scent was not. Aurelia, for all her sweat and bitterness, carried a faintly floral aroma. Morgan had always smelt and tasted of beeswax, mint, and fresh parchment.

Unable to keep the fantasy going, Cas opened his eyes to the landscape changing below. They were still unhappy, crowded on Flare's rippling purple back, soaring through pockets of warm air amongst the cool. They were now approaching the City of the Seers, approaching what he was hoping to be a fruitful showdown. But for all his excitement, his thoughts were far from here, far in the past. His thoughts were with another woman who had once been wrapped in his embrace, a woman who had fought him initially, just like Aurelia. But who had eventually warmed to him. As he knew she would.

Cas pursed his lips.

Well, their path was not without *some* challenges.

And after so long apart, by her choice and not his, Morgan had resurfaced once again.

After the tremor that had rolled under them with all the violence of an underground eruption, her magic had flared from the south. A burning, red spark felt in the darkest recesses of his heart. As he knew it would one day. As for why now, he had no idea. The timing was interesting, however. Perhaps it was another moving piece that he could use. Either way, he would make sure their paths crossed. And hopefully stayed that way.

Flare dipped lower, avoiding an ash grey cloud and small arms tightened around his waist. Laughing under his breath at the sullen cursing behind him, Cas dropped his face back to Aurelia's hair.

There had been no urgency to the spark that he'd felt. He'd know if Morgan was in trouble. Along with taking her against her will from a drug den, Cas had also made another decision for her. He'd barely mastered the art of siphoning off magic from those who had what he did not. But once he had, he'd linked himself to her, a tiny thread between them, heart to heart. It had been necessary to keep her alive. When he'd finally bargained for her debt out of Rook's drug den, Morgan had only been half the woman he knew she could be.

She'd fought it at first when she'd realised what Cas had done. With a shrug, he'd explained that *even* if he wanted to, which he did *not*, Cas knew of no way to reverse it. It was pleasantly simple.

If she died, so did he.

It was the same in reverse.

Neither of them wanted death, as much as they both toyed with it, risked it even. But she'd kicked up a stink so bad he'd added a *minor* detail to the magic that bound them. The one caveat had been that she could always find him if she needed, but not him finding her.

Morgan hadn't yet tugged on that fine thread between them until now with that wild burst of magic from the south.

Or had she?

Thinking back to Rook, Morgan's drug dealer from long ago, and the man's stunned expression when Cas whisked her away from her poppy smoke, Cas had to laugh. Comparing it to the tiny woman behind him now was just too much, even for him.

"You only think that you want this, that you want me!" Morgan had hissed, when she had realised what Cas had done. Unconcerned by her rage, he'd cupped her face, capturing her fiery green eyes with his metallic blue gaze.

"Look at me closely, lover. If you change the way you look at things," he'd whispered, his lips against hers, "the things you look at change. So watch me closely."

Aurelia stiffened against him. Her hair shifted under Cas' lips as she leant forward. His arms tightened around her waist.

"What?" she asked, her voice hoarse. "What did you say?"

Cas blinked. His head was aching; he needed to pay more attention to his surroundings.

"I said, how about this weather we're having?"

Aurelia made an exasperated sound, her long, dark hair whipping around them both. Cas grinned, listening to her curses lost to the wind as Flare continued to descend. Cas was looking forward to getting lower. It was fucking cold up here without his cloak. Although, as much as he hated to admit it, the purple set off the green eyes of the furious Elf in his arms quite nicely. Stretching his neck, Cas stared past Aurelia's shoulder to the city growing larger on the horizon.

They'd flown over the tops of the giant, reaching pines and other spicily scented trees for hours. The landscape barely changed, apart from the occasional valley. A long line of mountains on the northern horizon grew darker, and to their right, a scatter of mountains with sheer cliffs could just be seen above the canopy. Below them the forest eventually gave way to flattened valleys, the pines brighter shades of green. Eventually, the endless forest below had given way to overgrown farmlands, crumbling stone bridges and wild fields of flowers and grass. Once a manicured paradise of Elves and humans, the lands around the city were wastes, wild and abandoned.

As Flare glided low over the fields of blossoms, Cas sniffed Aurelia's hair, comparing her aroma to the riot of blooms and herbs below. Most flowers only bloomed seasonally. But here the magic imbued soil was still as potent as ever. If he remembered correctly, it had something to do with a buried horn, or amethyst. No matter what the time of year, or position of the sun, they bloomed. Even in the cool, grey afternoon, their myriad of scents was so strong that it was possible to taste them up here, even with the cool breeze flapping their clothes and their hair. As he inhaled, Cas idly wondered if the amethyst could be found, dug up, and be of any use to him-

"Whatever you're doing back there, stop it!" Aurelia hissed.

Cas merely snorted, while behind him Jessikah muttered under her breath. Cas laughed outright at that. His mood lifted as the aroma of wild mint met his nostrils. But as Flare coasted over the high wall of the city, more ornamental than anything, his smile faded. It had been a while since he'd been here.

The City of the Seers.

Most of those that had lived here had assumed it was built to replace another city, Baile Mara, Cas' home city by the sea. But Morgan had shared how this one was already planned, already under construction, when his home city had crumbled to the sea. Both of his parents had more than just a little something to do with that cosmic fuck up.

"Fuck you both for that," Cas muttered.

Flare glided lower, circling over the largest open space available. The great courtyard, its paved surface now a cracked map of the continent, rose to greet them. As dragon claws sought purchase on the rough and uneven ground, Cas sighed. The brokenness of this place was beautiful, if a little sad. He'd been here before, during and after its destruction. So much had happened here. So much had *almost* happened here.

The city was made of pale, pinkish stone. Carved from the earth with magic and dragon strength, the blocks were of outstanding sizes. While in ruins now, the evidence of how great a city this had been was still visible. From its sprawling, delicate towers, its vast halls and atriums to its water gardens and fountains. All majestically sized for dragons, all once immaculately maintained and cared for. Now it was ruined by time and cracked by the occasional quake, the likes of which seemed to be rumbling below them now, but not enough to worry him.

But most of the obvious damage was caused by one pissed off black dragon in the throes of a jealous, raging tantrum.

"Happy with yourself, *Jessikah*?" Cas snapped, relishing the scowl that crossed the delicate features which masked the monster within. He could have addressed the creature as Shadow Light, but her continuing glare was worth it.

The little woman was scrambling to get down off Flare as fast as she dared. He slid down after her, his boots kicking up a thick layer of ash, before turning to help Aurelia down, but she swatted his hand away with a glare of her own.

Cas snorted before turning his attention back to the demure, yellow-haired figure. "You were good at destroying things even before you flew, weren't you?"

Jessikah's smirk spoke volumes. As did the quiet sob from Flare. When Aurelia's boots hit the cracked, sooty flagstones, Aurelia looked at the dragon sharply, but said nothing.

Her wide green eyes were a different shade from Morgan's. As she glanced around, he could see the questions and emotions at war within, but she held them behind her lips. He raised an eyebrow at her, expecting her to ask at least one. She shook her head and turned her back on him whilst tilting her head to examine the closest, and tallest, tower. It was clearly leaning at a new and precarious angle. A giant crack forked up the whole length of it, base to top. Cas' eyes narrowed as he casually reached across to wrap his hand around Aurelia's arm.

"Fuck me," he whispered. That wasn't ideal at *all*. But he'd make it work, simply because he had to. He cleared his throat. "Now it's time to make some plans."

Shining purple flashed in his vision. Flare was weeping quietly beside them.

"Now what?" Cas snapped, whirling to face the dragon.

"Don't make me do that again," Flare mumbled. His head was hanging so low the creature could have licked a layer of ash from the cracked flagstones.

"Do what?"

"C-carry him..." Flare whined. "Please don't."

"Oh," Cas said. He flicked a glance to Jessikah. She was still smirking at the ruins, looking far too pleased with herself. An idea that had been itching away inside bubbled to the surface.

Hm, it could *work.*

"Well," Cas said brightly. "Lets hope this goes to plan then, and we get some magic back for *all* of us then, hm, my pretty thing? Don't cry. Cas will make it better."

"*All* of us?" Jessikah frowned at him.

"Fair's fair, sugar," Cas explained. As if it did. "Besides, now that our true identities are finally revealed, my sweet Shadow Light, we need to stick together."

Was that too obvious?

Surely Shadow had been thinking about it.

It was hard not to laugh at the furious, jealous gleam in Jessikah's beady little eyes. Aurelia was staring at Cas, confused. He ignored her. Using his free hand, he drew his sword. Its shining blade flashed even in the low light of the overcast day. He threw it up, inverting the blade with a twist, and caught it deftly by the hilt as it fell point first towards the ground. Cas spun around and held it out to Jessikah, hilt first. She stared at him, bewildered. He shook the sword at her.

"In case there are any creatures here, your little inner spark can't deal with."

Cas smiled pleasantly, eyes wide and blinking innocently.

"What the fuck, Caspian?" Jessikah snapped, confused.

"You know, protect each other, you and Flare," he encouraged. "We're all that we have left, and I know we need to stick together to reap the coming rewards." Cas cleared his throat. "Equally."

Two pairs of dragon eyes stared back at Cas. Flare's were large, purple, and filled with confusion. Shadow Light's were small, yellow in a human face, full of suspicion.

Fuck, how thick did he need to lay it on?

"What?" Flare eventually sniffed. "What are you talking-"

"Aurelia and I need to go freshen up," Cas said loudly, wondering if what he'd said was enough. Was Shadow Light that fickle? He hoped so. "And last time I was here, there were some dragon hating Elven bandits wandering around. I don't want to see either of you hurt. We need to get through this in order to share out our magical spoils."

"Oh," Flare muttered, whirling around. "Oh, no. Maybe you should stay, Cas-"

"You think I can't use this?" the tiny woman groused at Flare, waving the sword as Cas practically shoved the hilt into Jessikah's tiny hand, turning away before she could see his expression. "I'd be more use than you. You've never known how to use your fangs or claws properly!"

"Come on," Cas said amicably, pulling Aurelia away. "This way, please."

He risked a glance over his shoulder as he led Aurelia down to the old dragon guest quarters. Sure enough, the tiny yellow haired woman was examining the blade, as Flare crouched behind her. For all of Flare's impressive size, he was a coward, but leaving them alone seemed almost too obvious. He could only hope.

Unwilling to risk running off like earlier, Aurelia followed willingly enough.

Her gaze examined the ruins they passed, the courtyard, the map that had made up the expansive pattern in the flagstones, now broken beyond recognition. Trees and vegetation from the many gardens had spread, some with flowers, growing in the widening gaps between flagstones.

The ash that blew in from the north provided a rich base for a riot of plants. Even along the walls, ferns had spread their spores and the long, covered walkway that led to the dragon's den was a crowded tunnel of moist greenery. It was cooler and quiet here, apart from the soft scuff of their boots on the sooty, broken flagstones. On their left, the tall open wall led out into a once beautiful garden, large enough for a full sized dragon to wander its paths to the giant circular water feature within. Subtly inhaling the clean, damp coolness of the gardens, Cas continued along the verdant walkway towards the large archway at the far end.

As they reached it, Aurelia's soft gasp of awe had him looking up. The great domed roof was partially open to the overcast day and the cool air had given the large circular space a chilly ambience. Cas pulled her through, manoeuvring her around the fallen blocks of the pale stone roof that had crashed onto the floor. He had been tempted to find one of the open aired water features, but nostalgia had called him here. He was also sick of frigid river water.

"Where are we going?" Aurelia asked as Cas dragged her under a second inner arch. "What is this place?" Her green eyes flashed at him, suspicion and alarm swirling in their depths.

"This is where I stayed sometimes," he murmured, avoiding a slippery patch of dirt and moss. "Hopefully, the baths are still adequate."

"It's size shows this was built for dragons, though," Aurelia protested.

Cas paused, turning to face her. "Clearly," he smirked, his tone mocking. Then pulled her through the arch. A pleased sigh escaped his lips.

This inner sanctum, next to the sand pit area for scale polishing, was the bath chamber. Water had bubbled up into the vast circular pool, large and indeed built for dragons. It was mostly empty now, but wisps of steam near the closest edge gave him hope.

"Ahhh," Cas crooned. "Here we go."

Unwrapping his fingers from Aurelia's arm, he raised an eyebrow at her. Her eyes narrowed, but it was clear she got the message.

"Help yourself," he murmured, kneeling at the edge of the pool.

The stone walls had once held water a couple of metres deep. But the walls were cracked and full of wide breaks, the water only a few centimetres deep. But that was enough. It was still hot, near scalding. Hot springs underneath were still producing clear, mineral scented water. He was sure Aurelia was almost going to refuse, stubbornly, but her thirst won her over. She knelt beside him on the broken paving, shifting until her knees were comfortable, pulling his purple cloak out of the way. Her deep sigh of pleasure as she plunged her hands into the steaming water to drink was satisfying. Cas smiled to himself. The water was hot, yes, but it was as rich and pleasant as anything he'd put in his mouth.

Smirking, Cas unhooked his satchel from his shoulder and dropped it to the ground before reaching behind his neck and pulled off his shirt. Beside him, Aurelia unclasped his purple cloak, letting it pool onto the filthy, cracked tiles. He winced.

"Don't forget to put that back on after you clean yourself up," Cas murmured.

Aurelia snorted. "Why would you care?"

"Runny noses disgust me."

"What in the hells are you talking about?"

Cas vaguely waved a hand at his face. "You know, if you got sick or some shit."

"You're... *ugh*. Don't talk to me."

"You know," he said conversationally, "if you were just a tad more feisty, you'd be spectacular."

"What? I said don't talk to me," Aurelia spat, then paused. She turned to face him, baring white teeth in the fakest smile he'd ever seen. "Unless you can tell me what your aim here is?"

"Ha. Better. You'd get on well with Morgan. Do you have any soap, sweetness?"

Her smile froze. Aurelia didn't bother to respond as she went back to scrubbing.

He knew how she felt. Cas sighed wistfully. A full bath would have to wait, but getting at least some of the dust off was a pleasure he couldn't miss. Plunging his shirt into the hot water, he then squeezed it out to sponge himself clean. His own sigh of pleasure had Aurelia staring at him, puzzled.

"What?" Without looking at her, Cas gestured at where steaming water was bubbling out of a fissure. "Don't drink it from too far out. Get it from just there. It's freshest bubbling out of that crack."

Aurelia continued to examine his face, her arms dripping, along with the ends of her long, dark hair.

"I don't get you," she murmured, a frown worrying her brows. "I-"

Wiping his face, Cas turned to see why she'd stopped talking. Aurelia was still staring at him, her gaze now on his arms and chest.

"Oh." He snickered. "They're almost as lovely as my eyes, hm?"

He dropped his shirt back into the steaming water, squeezing out the dirt he'd wiped off his face. Aurelia was still eyeing the hundreds of tiny round scars that marred his skin. Cas spun around slowly, arms held away from his body. Her sharp intake of breath made him smile.

"Shit. I mean, shit. What happened to you?"

Grabbing his shirt and ringing out the wet fabric, Cas debated making something up. But the truth was fun enough. He shrugged, tilting his head to listen for what was going on out in the courtyard.

"Don't ever let yourself get thrown onto an angry beehive while naked." He shook out his damp hair, meeting Aurelia's alarmed gaze. "I do *not* recommend it."

Smirking at her dazed expression, Cas shrugged. He rarely thought about his scars. He could have healed them, but chose not to. They were a good reminder about what happened when you let your guard down. The king hadn't minded them, although Cas hadn't really given that sick pervert much time to think or speak, had he? He'd made sure the king's mouth had been busy so Cas didn't have to hear *any* commentary. Not about his body or about what it was that he was doing, in trying to claw his way back to some semblance of power. Taking liberties with the king's cold, dead flesh after the battle hadn't made up for it, but it had been worth it.

"Go fuck yourself," Cas murmured. "King of nothing."

"What?" Aurelia snapped, scowling beside him. "Rhydian?"

"His lovely father," Cas said airily. "Now hush, I'm trying to listen."

"But-"

"*Hush.*"

Aurelia eyed him for a moment, shook her head, and dipped her head back down for another drink, not caring that the water was hot enough to be uncomfortable as it went down. It was that good.

A loud screech echoed down the walkway into the broken dome behind them.

"Ah," Cas said, rocking back on his boot heels.

"What the hells?" Cursing, Aurelia stood up abruptly; scattering droplets of warm water, but Cas grabbed her damp hand. Flare's cry of alarm was a balm to his ears as he paused beside her.

"We must wait, little flower, until it gets good-"

"What?" she spat, attempting to yank her hand away. Flare cried out, his voice sounding small. "What did you do?"

"I admit nothing," Cas smirked.

His smirk curled into a wicked smile as Aurelia stopped struggling for a moment. He let out a soft chuckle as Jessikah's shouts grew louder. His pleased laugh was quickly choked back as Aurelia twisted, her knee connecting sharply with his groin.

"*A dick kick*?" Cas squawked, releasing Aurelia in shock and collapsing to his knees.

Stars crossed his vision. Coughing, he pressed his hands to his bruising balls. He winced as the movement made the pain worse.

"B-bad form... fuck me..." he wheezed, watching through slitted eyes as the Elven woman run back the way they had come.

"Is that feisty enough?!" Aurelia shouted behind her, sprinting towards the raised voices from the courtyard along the walkway of ferns and shadows.

Collapsed on the broken tiles, Cas half sobbed, half laughed with the pain. He was impressed, but not worried how far Aurelia would get; she was clearly running to the dragon's aid, despite her fury with him. His vague idea was likely not going to work, anyway. Wiping tears from his eyes and grabbing the cloak and his leather satchel, he breathed deep, staggering upright to hobble after the young Elf who had achieved what very few had.

"A dick kick," Cas muttered incredulously, tempted to heal the pain away.

He chose not to.

The discomfort reminded him of Morgan when she'd done far worse. Especially when he'd asked for it. His frown was almost a dark smile as he navigated the destroyed walkway back to the great courtyard. He eyed the sky through the green, spidery ferns that lined the gaps in the masonry above. The light was fading and as he ignored the throb in his groin, Cas wondered idly how far away Aurelia's rescuers were.

By the time he'd limped to the end of the walkway that opened to the courtyard, things were still heated. As he pulled on his damp shirt, he watched Flare, who for some incomprehensible reason, had shrunk to his tiny form. He was buzzing around Jessikah's head, screeching indignantly, while she was wildly swinging the sword with both hands. Clearly, both were too worked up to achieve any desired outcome. Cas rested against a cracked stone for a while; wishing one of them would just get it done. It would save him having to do it later.

But as soon as Jessikah, the great Shadow Light locked into a petite form, scraped the tip of the sword in a whistling downstroke against the cracked paving, Cas straightened up. *That* was too far.

Jessikah was yelling as Cas stalked over.

"How can you say you didn't know it was me? I was right there! In front of you the entire time, you pathetic waste of dragon scale-"

"Flare! What are you doing? Just go!" Aurelia was pleading and trying to dodge Jessikah while attempting to catch Flare from midair.

"I didn't know!" Flare cried, a tiny roar. "I didn't-"

Why had he gone small? Perhaps his brain never grew big enough to fill his skull, Cas mused, dancing sideways and away from another cringe inducing swing of the sword. Jessikah was still yelling and carrying on.

"-disgrace to all dragons! Illarion and bloody Hypatia should have let you rot with your useless little chil-"

Aurelia was ducking and weaving, fighting to keep her damp hair off her face, trying fruitlessly to pluck the flapping, frantic dragon from the air. The dragon seemed to be trying to protect her, but was in such a state he was like a shiny scrap of useless leather blown about on a wild breeze. Jessikah was stabbing uselessly and had no sense of Cas as he made his way behind her. It was easy to wrap his arms around her and lift the petite woman off her feet. Her scream of outrage was worth it, despite the lack of his desired outcome.

His laugh was just as wild as her flailing, and he spun her around.

"Calm down," he soothed, knowing it would have the opposite effect. Cas winced as she dropped the sword, screeching even louder.

"What the fuck? Put me down, you creepy little shit!"

Aurelia stepped back, eyes wide, panting. Flare landed a few metres away, puffing and rustling his wings amongst the drifting puffs of black ash. Amused and only slightly disappointed, Cas slowed down his spinning.

"Now, now, my happy little Shadow, you'll get me all excited, rubbing up on me like that."

"You vile, filthy-"

Cas slapped a hand over her puffing mouth, his thumb and fingers pinching her nose. Aurelia's eyes widened, her mouth agape. Jessikah struggled the whole time Cas counted to ten, fascinated with the fear on Aurelia's face.

"Stop now," he eventually whispered in Jessikah's ear.

Weakened just enough, Jessikah's struggle died down.

"Good girl." He released the tiny woman and also dropped his satchel to the flagstones, carefully pooling his cloak on top. Cas picked up the sword.

Rapid breaths misted the cool air as Jessikah glared at Flare, disgust evident in her yellow eyes.

"He's a *disgrace*. A fool!" She gasped, whirling to face Cas as he straightened. Her hands were balled into fists. "You want more magic? Magic that doesn't deserve to be disgraced? Here it is!" She gestured wildly at Flare.

Clearing his throat, Cas' tone was mild as he wiped the sword blade on a dry patch on his *absolutely* ruined pants. Only the twinkle of the ornately worked gold hilt stopped his scowl from forming.

"For shame. I can't leave you two alone for one minute, and you're at each other's throats?"

Jessikah's nostrils flared. Flare looked ashamed of himself, his head hanging. Aurelia looked unamused and confused all at once, her hands clenched into fists at her hips. Above and behind them all, the tall leaning tower loomed with promise towards him.

"Shadow Light started it," Flare mumbled, eyeing Cas with shining indigo eyes. "And I can't do anything! I don't have much left!"

Cas ignored the dragon's chatter and slid the sword back into its scabbard. Weighing up his options, it was best to continue using Flare to get around for now. Shadow Light, even trapped as a tiny woman, was too unpredictable. And Shadow Light was not as afraid of Cas as he should have been. So when Cas finally had to choose, Flare had nothing to fear.

"You're a liar," Jessikah hissed at the dragon. "You've got *plenty*."

Flare spun to face her.

"No, I don't! You know Fox, I mean Skye, is the one who holds most of it! All the minerals and metals bow to her," he rambled on, eyes wide with protest.

Cas paused, looking up.

What?

"What a waste," Jessikah was saying, her face screwed up while she yanked her hair out of her face. "All this could have been avoided when this bitch," she waved a hand at Aurelia, "was getting it from the prince. Why didn't you just break that fucking spell, then? You had the dagger in your possession for ages. I saw you, the fucking queen did too."

Looking like she wanted to murder them both, Aurelia was glancing between them, her mouth pinched, green eyes wide. "What? How did you know that?"

Jessikah whirled to face her with a sneer.

"Like Flare said, Fox could do what he liked when it came to magic. We watched you, in that black obsidian slab, and in those bloody, miserable fucking mineral pools!"

Stepping amongst them, Cas held up a hand.

"Excuse me, let's go back a moment, children. You watched *how*?"

"Oh," Flare mumbled, wings drooping. "Oh, it was nothing, um..."

A loud snort from Jessikah had Cas narrow his gaze at her. She paled at first, then tossed her ragged hair over her shoulder.

"We watched the pair of them." She waved a tiny hand, this time at Flare, as well as Aurelia. "We watched them with Fox's magic, making their *lazy* way to Aneirin, and then failing to do what they were supposed to do."

"We didn't fail," Flare protested, hopping from claw to claw. Small puffs of ash lifted with each scrape on the ground. "We..." His voice faded at Aurelia's shocked expression.

"You watched?" she hissed, her cheeks flushing red. "*All* of it?"

Jessikah raised her eyebrows and eyed Aurelia up and down. "I saw what I could, Fox, well, he watched more, I'm sure."

Cas started to blank them out at this point. He walked up to Aurelia and grabbed her arm. Ignoring her muttering about Fox being a bastard, Cas dragged Aurelia back towards the crumbling compound and hot water. His mind was elsewhere, a churning fog of possibilities.

What?

Watching people in obsidian mirrors?

Watching them in mineral pools?

"Why can't I do that?" he wondered aloud.

He halted before they entered the long span of the moist, fern covered walkway to the baths. Spinning around abruptly, Aurelia cursed him now as well. Oblivious, Cas eyed Jessikah up and down.

"Can you do that?" he asked, fighting with himself to keep his voice even. "Spy on people from afar?"

Jessikah flinched under his searing stare and shook her head.

Furious with his fundamental failings, Cas licked his lips. Further thought was required, but not just now. Another hum from the ground was getting louder, and a crack sounded above. Cursing, Cas pushed Aurelia to the closest wall and shielded her from any falling rocks, while staring blankly up at the tower across the courtyard.

As the faint quake rolled under them, he could see the tall, leaning tower was swaying slightly. Another crack popped, and a fine puff of dust drifted away from the side of the enormous stone blocks near the top. Eyes wide, he stared in breathless, horrified anticipation.

But as the earth settled, the hum passing them by without further damage, the swaying slowed, and then stopped. Cas let out his breath very, *very* slowly. The tower was clearly a death trap. Or a death wish. He should have been used to it by now. There were just so many plans within plans that had yet to come to fruition. Sighing with disappointment, he wondered how he'd take care of Shadow Light like he'd vainly expected Flare to do. But there was still hope for their reluctant queen to get here and do it. As his eyes scanned the courtyard and the tower, it seemed obvious a piece on the board had to go. And soon. The way forward was too crowded, too messy to control.

Just what had he been thinking, bringing Shadow along? Likely, it was his ego getting in the way again. He should have left him in the forest. Tossing his blonde hair out of his eyes, he scowled.

Shit.

Shit.

Shit.

Thinking hard, Cas' free hand caressed the hilt of the sword. Flare's wide purple eyes met his, his gaze dropping to the weapon. Realisation appeared to be dawning in the tiny brain, *at fucking last*, about what Cas had tried, and failed, to engineer.

"*I still love you*," Cas mouthed with a wink behind Jessikah's back.

With that, he yanked Aurelia back towards the baths. Good impressions needed to be made.

"Hurry up, Skye, let me see you close up," Cas muttered. Aurelia shot him a strange look, her gaze darting frantically between his fucked up, iridescent eyes.

Annoyed with her rebellious expression, Cas pushed Aurelia in front of him, his mind full of promise at the magic that would come to him. Soon, Skye would be by his side, close enough to touch, and to taste.

Close enough that he would take what belonged to him and maybe, *just maybe, if he could find her*, that which belonged to Morgan as well.

49

Fox

Flying had been a natural part of Skye's life as a dragon. Soaring high, emerging damp and sparkling from low clouds had been an everyday joy. But after everything he had endured at the claws of dragons, that joy had become something Fox had willingly forgone. He rejected the aching wonder of being airborne and filled with light; the ground falling away. Flying seemed too close to the cruel egos and lofty ideals of dragonkind. Being a man on two legs without wings was as far away from being a dragon as he could get, whilst still having some semblance of strength.

But.

Aurelia had shown him differently, hadn't she?

As a confident Elven woman, Aurelia had turned Fox's expectations on their head as she'd grown. Until meeting the tougher folk of the caves, the only other humans and Elven women he'd met were soft, city born creatures. His body may have changed with a deep ripple of power, but his ego had taken a lot longer to shape into something more mature. He was not unaware that there was still a fair way to go.

After unleashing his wrath in Mionlach on the dragons, Fox had chosen to continue his existence as a man on purpose. Except now there seemed to be a lesson there somewhere, about strength not meaning that you had to have certain parts. Fox was also aware that his heart and mind were usually numb, unable to think or feel beyond each day. Because of this, he'd chosen to wander across the continent on two legs, sometimes on horseback. Not thinking, barely feeling. He'd found a cause or two that had spiked his dark heart's interest. He'd found a friend in Aurelia, a little brat who had grown into the capable young woman of today. His dark heart had spluttered to life in those moments. It almost felt like *flying*.

What he'd shared with Owaen when they had first met, though, had surpassed that. Owaen as a cocky Elven man, and Fox as a naïve dragon in the guise of an Elven woman.

Fox bit his lip and blocked out the frustrated muttering beside him. Owaen was stomping his way along the lonely, claustrophobic forest road, Fox riding beside him. Fox could not hold back his sigh of defeat.

Despite their differences now, flying *still* didn't come close to what he'd shared with Owaen only a few hours ago.

The heady combination of assertive yet careful caresses, warm breath on Fox's chilled, sensitive skin had been just as consuming, just as scorching, and just as *right* as years before. Fox's body was still floating with wonder, even now in the afterglow of his release. Except that while his cool, masculine body was light, his heart felt like a dead crystal.

As a young dragon, he'd hatched knowing how to fly. Just as easily as he'd known how to breathe, how to eat. Talking as well from what he could remember, which he'd never given much thought to. There was still so much that didn't make sense when he looked back. He'd had to learn many things.

Mostly on his own.

He'd quickly realised that dragons preferred isolation, that they hoarded magic, and that they were extremely, irrevocably jealous. The jealousy extended to the other races, and to each other. There was no unity, no relationships between any of them that he could re-member, male, female or any other combination. Since he'd been young, Fox had perched in the tall mountains of black rocks and glittering dark sands in Mionlach. He'd wondered at it, what the purpose of life had been, to exist so *alone*. And while he'd wondered, it was always with others watching from nearby. Scaly bodies soared overhead, slitted eyes staring from the dry plains below. Shadow Light was always watching, sometimes with that fool, Flare Shining One, as well.

The idea that he had been studied never bothered him; it had always been that way. What bothered him was when he needed them, when he had questions that his young mind couldn't reason out on his own. The dragons rarely answered them. They told him what they thought he needed to know, and that was all. Nothing was shared that soothed the ache in his heart, the yearning for touch and affection. He ached for something that came close to what he felt when lifting away from the earth, letting the thermals support him.

Alone on Blackthorn, Fox's eyes narrowed in disgust at the overgrown forest road ahead of them. He must have made a noise because Owaen spared a dark glance his way. After checking Fox was *just fine*, the blonde Elf went back to glaring straight ahead. This time, Fox made sure his snort was loud enough for the whole damn forest to hear. So he was pleased to note that Owaen's cheek flushed, and a muscle twitched in his jaw. But Owaen said nothing.

Neither did Fox.

Sometimes the way their minds worked was too different. Had they been doomed from the very start? When Fox had decided that he needed more answers than his scaly family could, or would, share? Their egos had been unable to comprehend it. Their shock had been quite alarming.

No wonder they had kicked up such a fucking stink when Fox had deliberately chosen to head south from the dragon homeland. He'd invited himself to a council meeting in the City of the Seers, much to the protests of his fellow dragons. But he wanted to see it all. The council meeting seemed a likely place to start as any. Elves and humans would share their grievances with the dragons, and resolutions would be attempted. Fox had known the outside world was full of answers to questions he didn't even know how to ask. About dragons, yes, but Elves and humans too. Where they'd all come from, what they thought and felt. What they lived for, what they died for.

Fox's hands tightened into fists around the pommel of Blackthorn's saddle. It wasn't just the dragon's blatant arrogance and racism that bothered him. Even with no role models of compassion, he knew the way they talked of others was wrong. What bothered him most was that he'd found out some had known what had happened to him. They'd *known* that their precious, green jewel of a dragon, their ridiculously named Endless Skye, had been taken against her will. Taken by none other than Shadow Light, one of their eminent own.

And the dragons that had known had done *nothing*.

The same dragons who'd watched him day in and day out as he'd hatched and grown, eagerly waiting for the fuck knew what.

Shadow Light had done the deed, had taken Fox against his will. But others had been just as guilty. Perhaps they too wanted to know what Skye was capable of, how much magic she could take back from those who'd had magic shared with them, and their families. Was that what they were waiting for? It was hard to know. There weren't many left that he could ask. Not that they would have answered such a question, anyway.

Unable to hold it in, Fox tilted his head back to the canopy far above, and let his pain out as a dark laugh. He ignored Owaen's scowl and inhaled the spicy scent of the myriad plants and trees around them. The underside of the treetops was so far above, yet nowhere near as high as he'd once reached on gold-tipped emerald wings. But he didn't regret hiding them away. The dragons could rot in the hells of their own creation.

As a young hatchling, he'd learnt enough at least to survive. Living amongst dragons had taught him that they were jealous, arrogant, and cruel. Tough lessons, but valuable nonetheless.

Which was why, as a dragon in the guise of a young woman, when he had met Owaen, Fox had been instantly curious. Here was someone who was the opposite of a dragon in everyway. Fox had felt in his heart that someone important would be there to meet him, but not who, how or why. In the black mountains he'd felt the pull, the strange golden thread that connected them. His mind had wanted to know and to understand, so he had decided to go. He had gone and met Owaen, knowing there were things about *warmth* and *connection* to be experienced with the tall, blonde Elf. Things that no dragon could teach.

How to love. How to *be* loved.

Both paradoxically easy for Owaen, it seemed, and unspeakably hard for the dragon who had grown up without ever being touched. Without shame, Owaen had shown that he loved what he loved, the natural world and those important to him, for no specific reason, no ulterior motive, only because it was right. Because he wanted to.

Fox's mind normally shied away from thinking of his time under Shadow Light's power, but he forced it back there now. No dragon had come, no dragon had saved him.

Only Owaen.

A lone Elf, frantic with fear, grief and desperation. And Fox, with his mind half gone, had saved Owaen in return. He'd saved Owaen from Fox's own wrath, his ruined heart, and his burning desire to retaliate. As the dragon in their strange relationship, wasn't it Fox's role to make things right?

Fox risked a glance at Owaen beside him, blinking rapidly.

Was that just his own dragon sized ego talking, making decisions for them both?

But how was he to know? When had he ever seen what passed between two hearts as something normal? Dragons weren't paired off in bliss. Dragons were exactly what Fox said they were.

Cruel, proud.

Hungry for power.

Fox stared down at his chilled hands, once claws, now fluttering with barely suppressed rage as his mind wandered down dark valleys. The dappled light filtering through from the shifting leaves high above them covered his pale skin in patterns similar to scales. The illusion turned his stomach.

Cursing, Fox flung the reins at Owaen, and slipped his hands into his cloak so he didn't have to look. Owaen's mouth tightened into a thin line, but he caught the reins that were tossed at his head, and urged the impatient horse to continue walking without comment. Mildly put off by the lack of response, Fox glowered to himself.

The stubborn, brooding Elf was clearly still disturbed by what he had seen. Riding close by, Rhydian was just as silent as Owaen, red-eyed and more tightly lipped the closer they got to the city.

Fox exhaled slowly through his nostrils, wondering at the nature of egos. Dragons were only made up of pride and the endless hunger for magic, for power. They'd had to be to choose the life they led. Fox had discovered that each one of them had chosen to be that way. It was some messed up, misguided dream of two alchemists, in turn becoming a nightmare for the innocent that deserved to live in peace. Fox had been alone in his origins, as a young green hatchling without that choice. He had been alone amongst giant creatures who brooded over his growth and held the keys to his access to the world. Until one morning, he had sat on a black mountain, fully grown at last, and said *enough*. He'd followed a thread made up of self awareness and wonder, south to the City of the Seers.

And at the end of that threat was an Elf at the top of a tower, his dark emerald eyes wide on meeting the creature who Fox had been. A bright creature who no longer had any place in this dark world.

Back then, it had been no surprise to either of them when Owaen and Skye came together. It was just that easy, that natural. The golden thread between them had tied them up into almost one being of curiosity, love, and trust. But the dragons had rebelled. Shadow Light being the worst, mad with jealousy and full of grand, twisted ideas for his dark vision of who that gilded green dragon should have been. A queen, a vessel, a holder of their magic? Fox had thought he'd be able to handle what had come about, foolishly. He'd been too innocent, and far, far too naïve. The city had paid for it. The Elves had paid for it. The humans had paid for it as well.

And Fox had paid for it, over and over, until Owaen had come for him.

Fox inhaled a ragged breath at the memory. He'd barely had enough sense to transform back into the green-haired woman Owaen had come to love in order to be carried from that hateful place.

He snuck another glance off to his side. The scowling Elf's blonde hair was pulled up today in a wild twist, exposing the shorter sides. Fox itched to reach over and run his hands over the spiky hair. Instead, he slumped lower in the saddle, keeping his rebellious hands safely under his cloak.

He blew out another bitter sigh.

Safe.

Fox tried to convince himself that it was possible if the roles had been reversed, Owaen might have done the same, locked Fox away to protect him from further harm.

"Fuck," Fox muttered sourly, sneaking another glance to his side. This time Owaen turned to meet his stare, his gaze intense, making sure Fox was okay.

Owaen frowned, suspicious as Fox scoffed at the concerned glance sent his way.

But who was Fox trying to convince?

No, Owaen wouldn't have done the same.

Ignoring the Elf's confusion, Fox's gaze wandered over Owaen's slightly swollen lips before he glanced over to Rhydian. Fox had seen so much of the young man's tender care towards Aurelia, without judgement or expectations. It was hard to imagine that Rhydian would have locked up Aurelia to save her from his mother, or his father. It was unlikely. They were equals. They had both made decisions that affected them equally, but both had usually been on the same page.

Fox chewed on the inside of his cheek, wondering if perhaps that was what a healthy partnership was supposed to look like. One party stepped forward and did what the other could not, and in reverse, as required. So perhaps there *had* been another way, another way of keeping Owaen safe.

Fox turned to the road ahead, to the way the overgrown surface meandered through the trees. He just didn't *know*. If he wanted to be really mature about the decisions he had made, consideration to how broken his mind had been after Shadow Light's ministrations should come into it. But that seemed like an excuse. Maybe there should be no excuse for what he'd done to Owaen, but at the time... with his mind split open by trauma, his heart scarred for however long he lived, maybe there hadn't been any other way for him. Except for exactly the dark path that he had chosen, and walked alone.

But he wasn't alone anymore, was he?

Owaen still hadn't made any attempt to mount up behind Fox. Not that he cared. Despite that, it would have been *nice*. It was almost too easy to slip back into the chill that kept him constant company instead, despite the arms of the one he loved being *right there*.

Earlier, Rhydian had wandered back to their camp, his eyes dark and haunted as Fox had eyed him coolly. Owaen had stalked back to camp not long after, obviously not gone too far to leave Fox unattended. Which angered Fox for many reasons.

He just hadn't been able to think of any good ones.

Fox assessed Owaen's dangerously blank expression.

Wanting some kind of reaction, he picked up Owaen's discarded sword. Summoning his strength, he launched it at the blonde Elf's boots. Strangely enough, Fox instantly regretted it.

As Owaen watched the weapon land in the moss at his boots, the hurt in his dark green gaze was as sharp as the blade within the scabbard. Owaen had picked up the sword, handling it with reverence. He'd wiped the dirt and the moss off the dark red ruby in the pommel with careful fingers. A small broken twig was flicked off the scabbard. Without a word, Owaen secured the belt around his waist and dropped his hands to his sides, his narrow eyes staring at Fox. By then, Owaen's handsome, stupid face had been carefully impassive.

Tossing his head, Fox had turned his back and shakily mounted the tall black horse by himself, for the first time since, well, since he'd come back to *life*. Since he'd returned to fix what was now a shit storm. Which he was failing miserably at, apparently.

He'd angrily ignored the small voice that admitted that this was a storm of his own creation. In failing to act and take down Shadow Light when he should have, a hundred times over during the past however many years, all of this could have been prevented. The thought had made him even angrier. Rhydian had sensed it, his eyes roaming over how Fox was sitting in the saddle.

"Don't use your boot heels on my horse like that," Rhydian had said, as he turned his own horse back to the road. Whatever else he'd been about to say was cut off by Owaen's curt agreement.

"He's right. Let's go."

After Rhydian had watched the Elf stalk to the road, his blue eyes had met Fox's haughty stare, full of questions. Fox took no notice. Urging Blackthorn with more care than before, Fox had guided the horse after Owaen.

"For fuck's sake, you arrogant Elf. Get up here."

"No."

"Owaen. Look at me." Fox had led Blackthorn into step beside him. Owaen had kept staring straight ahead, his hand on the flashy, ruby-topped sword hilt now at his hip.

"No."

"Why?"

"I'm busy."

"Doing what the fuck?"

"Ignoring you." The Elf's jaw clenched and unclenched. "I can't look at you right now."

Rhydian had urged his horse to catch up to Owaen's fast-paced walk. He opened his mouth to speak, but Fox had jabbed a finger at him.

"Not one word, kingling."

The young man flushed, flicked his eyes between Fox and Owaen before shaking his head. He dropped his horse to walk behind them.

"I was only going to ask how long before we get there," he muttered.

"Tonight, if we push," Owaen called behind him, his tone clipped. "But daylight tomorrow would be better if we want to approach with caution."

"We don't need caution," Fox interrupted snippily. "I'm *fine*." He wasn't.

Owaen's sharp bark of a laugh was loud amongst the silent trees.

"Fine? You're the furthest from *fine* that you've ever been, Skye."

Fox pointedly ignored him for hours.

As he thought of their angry silent travels now, the next snort from the back of Fox's nose turned into air, getting stuck in his throat. After a wild, unexpected cough, Fox tilted over the side of the black horse and spat out the filth that had broken free from his lungs.

Owaen's eyes shifted to Fox immediately, concern shining brightly within the emerald depths of his eyes.

His annoyingly beautiful eyes.

"I'm fine," Fox snapped, using the edge of Rhydian's old cloak to wipe his mouth.

Owaen's lips thinned. Fox glared right back.

Shaking his head, Owaen shifted his gaze to the trees ahead, his expressive eyes thick with barely held in check emotions. Emotions which tugged at Fox's bitter heart, emotions that he was trying to ignore.

Fox had chosen to return Owaen to the world, yes. But the reality of them being together after so long, and after what Fox had done to Owaen, had left the life Fox had chosen completely inside out.

Still glaring at Owaen, Fox had to wonder. Despite possessing a softness that Fox didn't quite understand, Owaen had just as much of an ego as Fox. What had the Elf expected of him? The path to revenge had been a straight road, an arrow pointing north to the dragon homeland, Mionlach. So Fox had taken his time with them, their roars of fury and the subsequent ash fall had been a balm to his aching heart. The result had been a bitter, twisted salve pressed to his wounded soul. His revenge had been necessary, not to heal those wounds, but to at least allow scars to seal them.

He spared a quick glance at the forest, the earthy scent of moss and damp soil filling his nostrils. He hadn't spotted any ash falling just here, but it was still a wild place. The pungent aroma of fungus and spicy ferns permeated the cool air. The wild road ahead was dappled with rays of dull evening light filtering down from the canopy far above.

Another coughing fit left him with an equally revolting gob of phlegm in his mouth. He spat it out as far as he could. Owaen was lucky that Fox didn't aim over the other side of the horse. The bitter copper aftertaste on his tongue was as unpleasant as the direction of his thoughts.

"Fine, huh?" Owaen groused. "You sure about that?"

An exasperated curse from Rhydian had Fox hiss with frustration.

"Are *you*?"

Owaen's eyes flicked to Fox's ribs and back as if he could see the shifting colours through the ruined cloak and shirt. Fox wanted to rip off the layers to expose the design running like honey over his skin, in patterns that felt like old and familiar friends.

"Neither of us is fine," Owaen muttered, brows low over his eyes. Fox spared a moment to note that the disgust from earlier was gone. "I'd like to be wrong. But I'm not."

Fox shifted in the saddle, aching to feel as warm as he had that morning. It had been like nothing he'd felt in a long, *long* time. But there was likely to be less of *that* if he kept talking. But his mouth refused to stay closed.

"You *are* wrong. You're wrong most of the time when it comes to me. You think I'm something I'm not." Fox pointed to himself. "Dragon." He pointed to Owaen. "Elf."

Owaen rolled his eyes and Fox just about broke his teeth by gritting them so hard.

"As if that matters." Owaen turned to glance at Rhydian. The king was riding close enough to hear and was clearly listening. He shook his head at them. Owaen bit his lip and turned back to the road ahead, his pace increasing. "That's not the issue here. Don't pretend you aren't aware."

Fox's bitter laugh had Blackthorn pulling at the bit in irritation. Owaen laid his hand on the animal's neck.

"The issue here is your Elven ego, Owaen," Fox said, his tone sharp. "In thinking you could *ever* have prevented a fucking dragon from doing anything. You got me out of that cave eventually, so thank you. But then it was *my* role to retaliate. So I took their magic away. They got what they fucking deserved. Get over it."

"Fox!" Rhydian shouted suddenly from behind, startling them both. "Owaen is here to help, so calm your shit down. *Now.*"

"What?" Fox hissed, eyes wide. He turned in the saddle, voice rising. "Why don't you just-"

"Don't talk to him like that," Owaen cut in. "That's a bit ungrateful after what he's done for you, don't you think?"

Speechless, Fox stared blankly at Owaen as Rhydian coughed to cover his snigger. The words were almost the same thing Rhydian had said to Fox not long ago. Fox bared his teeth in frustration. Owaen merely laughed and continued on.

"As you can imagine, after I laid the bones to rest, I was worn out. It cost me a lot, magically and emotionally, frantic as I was with worry for *you*. When I finally slept, I dreamt of you in Mionlach. And I saw it, what you did." He went on before Fox could interrupt, gesturing between them with a wave of his hand. "I can't explain what we have between us, what connects us. I don't need to. But I saw you. And how could the dragons have survived that? I saw it. I *know-*"

"No, you really don't." Aware of how petty he was being and not giving a shit, Fox tugged his boot out of the stirrup and poked Owaen's muscular arm with each word he bit out. "I. Did. Not. Kill. Them."

"Stop that," Owaen hissed, grabbing Fox's calf. Using more force than was required, he forced Fox's boot back to the stirrup. Blackthorn tossed his head in annoyance once more. Fox tugged on the animal's mane even though Fox understood the horse's frustration.

"I should have been there. I could have saved you from regret. Fox, I can guarantee it's going to catch up with you."

Fox laughed coldly under his breath, his anger rising with the cold irritation spreading through his face and his hands.

"You don't get it, do you, Owaen? No! Shut your mouth. *Listen.* You say you know what happened after I left you in that fucking cave? Well, let me tell you. You know we talked about wiping the world clean of egotistical magic users-"

"Yes, but not like that! Gods, that fucking tattoo... We didn't plan to wipe out an entire race. The regret is going to catch up with you. How can you look at it, or explain it away as revenge? And you say that you're *fine*?"

Fox yanked the reins out of Owaen's grip and urged the horse to a halt. A scream of frustration was building up in his throat. He laughed instead.

"We are having a major breakdown in communication here, you blonde twit. How can I explain it if you won't let me speak? Are you done?"

Owaen's mouth narrowed into a line so thin his chin jutted out. He nodded curtly, one hand on his sword, the other a fist at his side.

"Do you really think I'm going to collapse with regret? Will that make you feel better? So you can save me again?" Fox forged on, not caring at the way Owaen's face paled. "Mm. I bet it would. Let me help you out there, *lover*. Let me list what I *regret*. Let me share my darkest secrets with you."

Nodding cautiously, Owaen's lips parted in expectation. Fox crooked a finger at him and the fool actually stepped forward. Eyes flashing with fire and sparks, Fox reached out and grabbed Owaen's shirt collar in his fist, making sure they were eye to eye. His voice lowered to a dangerous whisper.

"I regret that Shadow Light murdered your Elven brethren."

Owaen's jaw twitched.

"I regret that an innocent human boy died alone in a cold dungeon."

Next, it was Owaen's eyes that widened a fraction.

"I regret that my Aurelia has been taken."

"And as for Shadow Light, and my other scaled kin," Fox hissed, injecting his words with a quiet venomous purr. "I admit that I fucked it up the way I went about it, but..."

Owaen's eyes widened in alarm as Fox yanked him closer, frost forming on his hands. So his next words were spat directly into Owaen's face.

"I DIDN'T KILL THE FUCKING DRAGONS!" Fox shouted, fingers bruising Owaen's chest. Owaen grabbed Fox's hand on his chest with both hands, but could not pull them away. "THAT'S WHAT I REGRET! I REGRET THAT I DIDN'T KILL THEM!"

Across the old forest road, a flock of black birds took off from the branches above, scattering with screeching calls. Owaen was breathing rapidly, but he'd given up struggling to free Fox's icy grip, which was growing colder. The alarm in the green eyes, so close to his, was tinged with fear now as well. Rhydian called out something. Fox wasn't sure what. He didn't care. His lungs were freezing over. But he wasn't done. He coughed, trying to clear whatever was clogging his throat. It wasn't more bitter words choking him; it was *ice*. He spat out the frosty obstruction and forged on.

"And if I had killed them, do you think I'll ever weep for those creatures? That I'll weep for myself? Oh Owaen," Fox hissed with condescension. His breath misted between them. "I'll shed a lonely tear for the innocents of this fucked up chaos. But regret my revenge? Surely, you jest. I have *never* regretted it."

Fox pushed away Owaen so forcefully that the Elf stumbled back a few paces. Fox sat up in the saddle and raised his face to the canopy above. The giant, majestic treetops appeared to be swaying, although it was hard to tell from so far down below. The wind had picked up intensity amongst them, and Fox's black hair whipped around his face. Laughing and welcoming the leaves that stung his exposed skin, Fox flung his hands up and out, as if to embrace the whirlwind around him.

"Can you hear that, Shadow Light? I regret choosing to keep you by my side! I regret reminding myself of what not to become!"

Blackthorn skipped sideways, away from falling twigs and small branches, skipping over the deep rumbling that was bubbling up from the road. Owaen dashed around to the front of the horse, trying to get the beast under control. Rhydian was swearing nearby, cursing, as he too was stung with needle sharp debris. The breeze shifted from cool to cold, the soft pine and winter berry aromas sharpening into ice and frost.

"Fox," Rhydian cried, his horse in Fox's vision, fighting with his horse to bring him closer. "Fox! Please-"

"Skye!" Owaen shouted, frost forming in his hair. "Stop it! Just stop-"

"I regret every ounce of mercy I showed every single fucking dragon!" Fox screamed into the wind, his eyes watering, the tears forming icicles on his cheeks. "I regret not wiping out every fucking last one of us! I regret the fires that I lit in our homeland didn't burn them all to hell!" He lowered his gaze to Owaen, eyes completely black. "And as for everything *else*?"

Fox was struggling to breathe now, struggling to stay in the saddle, as Owaen finally caught the reins, bringing Blackthorn's head down and holding it low. The Elf was covered in frost, white ice forming over his clothes. He didn't care.

"I DO NOT REGRET ANYTHING ELSE!" he shouted to the trees and the biting wind around them. He laughed, feeling ice crack over his face. "I NEVER HAVE! I NEVER WILL!" He started to choke for real this time on the icicles in his lungs. Coughing and laughter mingled while his body shook with the violence of his outburst. Fox grimaced, wheezing, and took one last, gasping breath in.

"I DO NOT REGRET IT-"

The ice won.

His airways closed.

Realisation that he had gone too far came too late, his magic rising with his rage. Fox grabbed his throat. Panic set in as the next breath didn't come. His eyes widened in shock as the road around them and the trees above started to freeze. The rumbling earth below sent up waves of vibrations that cracked the frozen trees just as fast. Branches that were now frozen solid started to fall and shatter around them, shards of sharp ice added to the debris cloud that whirled around.

"Owaen," Fox mouthed soundlessly, his words forming flakes of snow in the air that were yanked away by the sharp wind that pulled at his hair. "Can't-"

"Oh f-fuck," Owaen hissed, his lips blue. He seemed to be frozen in place, ice covering him, a thin layer of clear blue that was creeping up from the road, over his boots and up his legs. Rhydian was white faced, wide eyed, his own horse going berserk, both of them misting thick clouds of breath before them.

"O-Owaen," Fox wheezed, unable to move, unable to breathe. His eyes shut, freezing over.

He was amazed to find that the only thing holding him to the horse now was ice. His hearing faded. He hoped that the loud cracks that he could still make out was Owaen breaking free of the ice that bound him like vines as the Elf cursed frantically.

If Fox could have sobbed with fear, he just might have. After a final crack from what must have been Elven magic and brute strength, powerful hands grabbed Fox around the waist. More snaps and pops broke over the roaring winds as Fox was pried from the saddle, unable to cry out as the ice cut his exposed flesh. The shock of hitting the frozen road with a painful thud cracked some of the shards in his lungs. While drawing in breaths of fresh, if painfully cold air, Fox struggled against the arms that held him down. He kicked out reflexively, unable to help it, the muffled grunt next to his ear letting him know that his boot connected somewhere sensitive.

"Stop... judging... me..." Fox croaked, wild and mad as he gasped for air and words that would likely never explain how he felt.

Owaen's weight disappeared for a moment, only for the iron grip to reappear more firmly. Strong hands clamped down on Fox's wrist and drag him off the road. Panic started to set in as more ice filled his mouth. The blow on the back of his head from a falling branch cracked it open for a moment. Leaves and wind and snow ripped at their clothes and faces. Fox fought Owaen's hold with such fury that the Elf dropped him for a moment, only to pick him up quickly and efficiently. Fox was thrown over Owaen's shoulder. The indignity of it only spurned Fox on, as he fought with the last of his air to spit out what words he could.

"If you're as guilty of... failing me... as you say you are," he managed to gasp out, his voice a hoarse mist of air, "then you have... no fucking right... to judge me-"

There was a moment of confusion as Fox felt the forest floor disappear, followed quickly by a powerful splash. If he had still been able to speak, or breathe, Fox's next words would have been cut it. A rush of unexpected water closed over his head and pulled him under.

Owaen had thrown him into a river.

Fox roared beneath the surface, and he kicked out angrily, his boots filling immediately. Water filled his mouth, icy at first but quickly warming and despite a mouthful of water; he could feel his lungs expand again. The mineral rich liquid was losing its shockingly cold temperature somehow and was melting the frost of his outburst away. As he processed this, Fox was dragged back up to the surface with a rough jerk by his hair. With one arm around his chest and the other in Fox's streaming hair, Owaen held Fox's head above the surface.

Fox's vision started to return, and he realised the water was steaming around them. Quite unnaturally.

"Are you done?" Owaen jerked Fox's head back, his furious voice close to Fox's ear. Fox blinked, able to see more clearly now as the haze of frost over his eyes melted away like salt in the rain.

His thrashing slowed, the rage leaving him at once. Spitting water from his mouth, Fox glanced down. Owaen's hands were glowing, shining softly like the moon behind silver clouds. The sight calmed him for some gods only knew reason, and just like that, the fight, his wrath, left him. Owaen, taking deep ragged breaths, held on, not trusting Fox at all. The water temperature was still rising, stinging Fox's skin that hadn't quite lost its chill. Owaen held Fox against his chest, breathing fast and deep.

"Are you done?" Owaen repeated, almost snarling. The water was positively *hot* now. Owaen's voice was not.

Aching for the loss of what they had shared between them, Fox finally went limp. He spat into the steaming river before him.

"For now," Fox replied testily, unsure of himself. He cleared his raw throat. "I can't promise-"

"Oh my *gods*," Owaen hissed, his hot breath tickling Fox's ear and his muscular arm tightening around Fox's chest. "Will you just-"

"Are you two bastards still alive?"

Both of them looked up as Rhydian's furious yell reached them, Owaen holding the pair of them together as they floated. The river Owaen had dragged them to was wide and deep but slow moving. Owaen's occasional kick was all that was required to keep them near the mossy bank. The hand in Fox's hair tugged once in warning, and then was gone.

"Owaen? Fox?" Rhydian shouted again, his voice coming from the direction of the old road. "For fuck's sake, answer me. If you kill each other now before we get Aurelia, I'll fucking kill you both again myself-"

"Yes," Fox shouted back, his throat raw. Since when had Rhydian started swearing like an Elf stuck in a mine?

"We're fine, Rhydian," Owaen growled. Fox could feel the glare against his wet cheek, as the iridescent glow faded from Owaen's Elven skin. "Both of us are just fucking *fine.*"

"Good," Rhydian called. There was a pause. "Now get over yourselves, *both* of you, and get the fuck out of there."

Fox wanted to laugh at Owaen's choked protest. "I am *not* your subject-" he began.

"At the moment you are," Rhydian's voice echoed through the solemn trees. "If you're in my service helping me, helping Aurelia, you bloody well *are.* Take a moment to calm your shit and get over it. That's a fucking royal command."

Taking advantage of the loosening grip across his chest, Fox twisted around, pressing his chest to Owaen's front, their foreheads just as close. They breathed together, listening to Rhydian stomp away with the horses through the undergrowth.

"Rude," Owaen murmured eventually, his green eyes on Fox's lips.

The cold wrath of his tantrum not quite forgotten, Fox used the tip of his tongue to sample the various minerals in the droplets that coated his skin. Owaen's eyes darkened, and he dragged his gaze to Fox's black and gold eyes that glittered mere centimetres away. They stared at each other, neither of them moving, the steam rising off the surface around them in ghostly wisps. Certain that Rhydian had taken himself far enough away, Fox slid his hands around Owaen's neck and waited, not blinking. It only took a moment for Owaen's hands to find Fox's hips. His warm palms slid around Fox's back and pulled them together against the bank.

"I'm proud of Rhydian," Fox heard himself say, his own gaze on the droplets of water running down the pale, three-day growth on Owaen's chin. "I... I taught him to swear properly."

Fox watched, enthralled, as the incredulity and alarm faded in Owaen's eyes, the emerald green losing the chill that scared Fox as much as the ice that had choked his throat. Fox inhaled slowly, letting the warmth from the water and the man against him soak into him, hot tendrils brushing the ice in his core, along with his limbs and other extremities.

Letting Owaen support his weight, Fox kicked them away from the bank. Not breaking his stare from Owaen, Fox wrapped his legs around the Elf's waist. Owaen's skin was cooling now, his magic working in some way that was impossible for Fox to comprehend. So much of who they were to each other made little sense. Their differences made what perhaps could have been simple into something difficult. But there were some simple things that were still straight forward enough.

"I'm sorry for how I've made you feel, Owaen," Fox mumbled finally. "For the way I've gone about things."

One wet, blonde eyebrow rose as Fox sniffed.

"But?" Owaen asked warily.

"But I don't regret what I did. I really, *really* don't."

Dark green eyes narrowed. "I think you've made your point."

"You weren't listening to me."

Owaen sighed, his eyes half-lidded. "You're right. I wasn't listening. I'm sorry."

"Pretty caught up in your guilt, hm?"

"I said I'm sorry. I meant it."

They were turning slowly with the current now, the water temperature dropping as they drifted away. Owaen kicked lazily a few times to bring them back to the warmer patch before it faded, Fox still wrapped around him.

"I can't believe you threw me into a river." Hooking his boot heels together, Fox rubbed his face against the warm cheek beside his. "But thank you. I actually didn't know how to stop myself. I don't know what happened. I got cold, Owaen, really fucking cold."

"I know, Skye," Owaen's hands rose in a long slide up Fox's ribs and chest and rested them on either side of Fox's face. "That's exactly what you should have expected when you came back for me."

"Warmth? Or being chucked into a fucking river?"

Owaen's soft chuckle was a gentle rumble between them. "Hm."

Fox dropped his head to Owaen's shoulder, averting his gaze. As his cool lips reached the water level, Fox let the river in, washing away the last of the copper and sourness from his mouth.

"I didn't want to come back to you. I changed my mind at the last," Fox said quietly, letting the warm water run over his lips. "I told you that. I don't... I don't deserve you."

Affectionate fingers cupped his chin. Close to his, emerald eyes burned deeply and brightly. Fox tried to turn away, but the fingers held him still. Another lazy kick had them back into the warm water once more.

"I love you." Owaen lent forward carefully, slowly, until his lips pressed against Fox's. His lips moved again, speaking directly into Fox's mouth, his voice a shared breath. "I love you."

Fox tried to pull away, but Owaen refused to let him go.

"Stop it," Fox whispered, shutting his eyes to the bottomless shining gaze so close to his. "Please-"

"Forgive me for everything," Owaen murmured, his warm lips now against Fox's cheek. His voice was like a free falling leaf hitting the water in gentle prayer. "And know that I love you."

It was getting harder to breathe again. Not from ice in his chest, but from pain, panic. Fox shook his head. This was too much. He didn't understand it, how the intimacy here could be deeper even than the events of that morning. He unwrapped his legs and attempted to kick away. Owaen caught him, his lips pressed to Fox's shivering ear.

"Owaen, p-please stop-"

"I will never stop when it comes to you. I'm here. Tell me what you did. I'm listening now."

"Are you? Then let me go."

"I will, but-"

"I said let me go," Fox snapped. Immediately he was floating free, Owaen pulling his hands away, naked hurt clearly visible in his eyes.

Turning, Fox kicked for the bank, grabbing onto the moss and the rocks, wishing in a way he was back in the mineral pools of Lolihud. Alone with his thoughts. There he knew where he stood, and all the things Fox had done had made sense. He knew what was up and what was down. Owaen's words confused him, his emotions raw and vulnerable. Fox had no idea what to do with them.

He didn't pull himself up the bank. Instead, he turned, panting, forcing himself to face Owaen. As the water rippled between them, Fox's heart ached. The sight was almost too much, Owaen's expression bare, pain, passion and worry at war in his gaze.

"I didn't kill them," Fox said quietly, averting his gaze to the moss and the ferns along the bank. Swimming closer, Owaen grabbed a slippery rock next to Fox. Water streamed from his hair. He flicked his head sideways to clear his face.

"Okay," Owaen replied from beside him, avoiding looking at Fox's semi-exposed back as the wet fabric hung open along the worn out rips. "Okay. I believe you, but explain that. Please, tell me what you did."

Catching his breath, Fox stared at his hands.

Above the gentle gurgle of the river and the rustle of the endless greenery around them, cries for help and pleas for mercy crowded his mind. Along with cries from dragons pleading for *his* mercy. What he'd given them instead was far worse than they would ever have imagined.

Fox bared his teeth, still staring at his hands, remembering them squeezing the power out of each and every dragon. He truly wished he'd squeezed out life instead.

Owaen had expected him to be sorry one day, full of regret. Well, he was. He'd spoken the truth before he'd lost control. Fox *was* sorry now, that every dragon that had ever flown and flashed their scales over the other creatures of this land was still alive. If alive is what you'd call it. Perhaps the mercy he had shown had been Owaen's fault? Fox had known that Owaen would have hated Fox if he'd gone through with it. Which is the only reason why Fox hadn't gone one step further to wipe the creatures from the earth.

If Fox could prevent some heartache for Owaen, he'd keep that last few secrets between them trapped behind his teeth for life. Was that why he had panicked just now? With Owaen pushing him to explain, his impression so wrong about what Fox had done to the dragons. Had Fox lost his mind because he simply didn't want to share what he'd done? Or because that would unveil a whole lot of volatile secrets, that Owaen just might have preferred not to know, about his family that had died so long ago?

"Tell me," Owaen urged, wiping water from his eyes. "Please."

A laugh escaped Fox before he could bite it back. It was all he could do. Or die from weeping, from holding back. Fox turned to Owaen and smiled.

"I'll tell you when I think you're ready to hear it."

There was a moment of silence.

"What?" Owaen blinked rapidly.

"Oh, Owaen," Fox leant over, and pressed a chaste kiss to Owaen's warm lips. He hated to tear himself away, but he did. Owaen didn't need to hear how awful his parents had been. And how else could he explain why and what he'd done? "Just know that my revenge was never about undoing what the dragons did. What kind of a broken idiot do you think I am? My revenge was for *me*."

Kicking back into the water, Fox tilted his head back, his heart shrinking a little at the lost expression on Owaen's face. Fox closed his eyes, sinking back into the cooling river, hardening his heart.

"I did it for me and I," Fox repeated, letting his tears join the river water as he sank, water filling his mouth, "am *quite* satisfied."

Fox allowed himself to sink and water closed over his head. He sunk his boots into the smooth rocks and pebbles on the bottom and hung there, pushing into the lazy current. Welcoming the sting of the rich water, Fox opened his eyes. Owaen's shape was a blur. The Elf was upright in the water, head hanging low, watching him through the ripples. The weeds around them both wavered with the ebb and flow of the river, like green serpents coiling around their legs.

Green eyes searched for his through the sparkling liquid between them, each in a different world, above and below, one light and one dark. Owaen was talking. Fox tried to focus on the muffled noises of the water instead. But through some part of the thread they shared, or Fox's magic, or from the shape on Owaen's lips, Fox caught each and every word.

"I regret not saving you from the dragons, Skye, and I regret not saving you from yourself."

With that, the Elf made his way to the bank.

Wet fabric clung to tanned skin and boots overflowed with water as Owaen pulled himself up the moss covered bank. His boots disappeared in a cloud of bubbles and green plants undulating against the rocks. Still underwater, Fox stayed where he was, relieved to be cut off from the rest of the world, if only for a moment longer. He let himself drift with the river as it cooled, letting his anger build, feeling his magic returning to full, barely restrained fury.

The time to talk of regrets was gone. All that was needed now was rage, the fuel and the power within him to burn away his shadows.

This time for good.

50

Rhydian

Year 367
The Forest

Huddled in his cloak on the moss, Rhydian blinked at the shivering canopy above, lost to his sight in the brisk night air.

During the day, the tops of the giant pines were hard to see through the middle layer of branches and saplings that vied for the dappled light below. After the sun went down, it was impossible to find the crown of the forest. Only the faint creaks and gentle scrapes from high up let him know that there was a canopy above them at all. Being surrounded by the forest for so many days without open sky was something he should have been used to by now. But he missed the open air and blue sky above the valley of Aneirin, with the great sweep of reddish mountain ranges, the city terraced up the sides.

It had been foolish to push on as the sun dipped, so they'd ridden in silence until the shadows were deep and the glow above the trees gone dark. Nearby, the fire popped and threw sparks and Blackthorn tossed his head when something scurried through the undergrowth. The three travellers had hardly spoken a word to each other since they'd resumed their journey after Fox had erupted in a frozen, unhinged outpouring of wild abandon.

Not one of them had spoken a single word. Dark looks had been shared between a relentless pair of black and gold eyes, the other pair dark, forest green, glaring underneath wet blonde hair. Owaen had walked on with his jaw set tight, clothes dripping until he'd steamed in front of the fire. Fox had dried himself off without offering the same courtesy to the Elf. Clearly, Fox was feeling better. Or at least partially.

After a cold meal of tasteless bread and unpleasant dried meat, it was almost a relief to close his eyes. They had lain down by the fire as the night air dipped to frost, the three of them silent. Rhydian was now curled against Fox, who in turn was wedged against Owaen, scowling even as he settled himself to rest. The three of them were huddled together against the cold seeping up from the moss, frigid night air rustling through the giant trunks above.

Blunt nails dug into his palms as Rhydian's hands curled into fists. He was tired, his body aching and his heart a bruised muscle of fear. Fox had scared the hells out of him when he'd lost control, frost creeping away from him like rolling waves of fury. Rhydian sort of understood, especially after visiting the cave of glowing quartz and silent bones. But now, his ire wasn't just from the cold. Or the ever present fear that Fox was wrong, and that Aurelia was in danger. He was frustrated because he was afraid. And because he'd had to... what?

Be a leader.

After Owaen had dragged Fox into the trees, his choked hiss had reached Rhydian, who had told them to get their shit together, commanding them to get their shit together.

Owaen's voice had reached him easily, the scowl in his voice obvious. *"I am not your subject-"*

Rhydian hadn't even thought about his reply.

"At the moment you are..."

But did he want that?

Rhydian was surprised Owaen hadn't appeared to drag him off his horse as well, after the way Rhydian cursed at them. He'd never spoken to anyone in that tone before that he could remember. He hoped to the gods he never needed to again. As he'd stomped away from whatever the hells Owaen was doing to calm Fox down, Rhydian had half expected some kind of frozen lightning bolt to knock him out of his boots.

But it hadn't come.

Whatever Owaen had said, or done, had worked. Even if neither of them spoke to each other over their bland dinner. Owaen had been glaring at Fox the entire time, not breaking his stare as he'd spat a particularly unsavoury piece of dried fat into the fire. Fox had been worse. He'd sat there like he hadn't a care in the world, after demanding Rhydian stack logs so Fox could ignite them, the gold in his dark eyes unusually bright.

As Rhydian had built up the stack of branches, a particularly knotty branch was almost begging to be hurled at the head of inky black hair for the delay in their progress. Until Rhydian had noticed that the black and gold eyes had darted sideways, checking that Owaen had seen Fox ignite their fire.

That tiny movement, that seeking of approval, had told Rhydian what he'd needed. He'd inhaled the bitter smoke from the green wood as it burned, wallowing in frustration with his strange companions.

Fox was clearly processing something neither of them could quite comprehend. Rhydian didn't know how to handle it. After they'd seen to the horses, eaten and wrapped themselves up with their travel worn cloaks and layers, they'd lain down together for warmth, and tried to rest. Fox had turned his back to Owaen, smiling sweetly at Rhydian as he'd settled down beside them. But Rhydian had seen the brittle edge to Fox's expression and had met Owaen's smouldering gaze above Fox's black hair. Dark green eyes that were impossible to read had eventually closed.

Rhydian had lain awake, his face only centimetres above Fox's black hair. Fox was so different from the pale-haired man on his other side. They were completely unique creatures. But somehow, the way they orbited each other, they made sense.

With his mind on Aurelia, his longing a harsh throb deep within his chest, Rhydian finally fell asleep.

You coward.

On the abandoned armoury wall, a dragon and a woman with a tiny swipe of green chalk in her hands for all to see.

I don't want this. I don't want to be your son!

A father watched his son's mind unravel into deep shock, blue eyes staring blankly as the shame of his mother's betrayal shook his core, toppling his innocent sense of honour. His father's pale blue eyes turned bright silver in the soft light, shining with disappointment.

Rhydian. Come here. If you can't handle this... if you can't be a man... Look at me. Look at me, boy.

A firm hand grabbing the boy's quivering chin.

Forget.

But he hadn't.

Rhydian had for a while, growing up as a pampered, but not quite spoiled, prince. He had been prone to wild shenanigans that earned him the occasional belt on his backside, and the threat of no more stories from Lady Hywel. And one day, as he sought mischief while alone, the prince had found the dagger. He had forgotten that it was the second time he had come across the strange weapon. He had forgotten his father's eyes, bitter with shame that his young son was not man enough to handle the darkness it represented. A darkness within his family, a darkness within the blood that ran through his arteries and veins.

Blood Binds All.

Rhydian remembered it now. Aware that he was dreaming, the past was revealed to his mind as his subconscious and consciousness merged, coming together in that special place between deep sleep and wakefulness.

The prince had stumbled into the old armoury, covered in cobwebs. He'd wiped his face, held up his lantern to the wall and cried out, alone and afraid. The shard, the evil looking green crystal dagger, had been on the wall for anyone to see, winking back in the light of his yellow flame.

It was just an object. But it hurt to look at. He hadn't been able to explain it. The icy dread that filled him when his gaze fell upon it could only mean one thing. It was a magical object, full of potential menace to his people. Magic was outlawed though, because all magic was evil. So to be the prince that his kingdom needed, Rhydian could do but one thing.

It had been a silent battle of wills, but Rhydian had turned his back on the evil thing and walked out. His courage was tested further when he had headed back after retrieving his old, child-sized blanket. He'd climbed upon the bench, reached up and tried not to vomit from fear as he'd slid it out of the fine wire fastening on the wall. The young prince, barely old enough to practice with a real sword, had emerged white faced and blinking into a blue sunny morning.

There was no excuse necessary beyond the fine weather to saddle up his old grey pony and ride out. Rhydian made it out of the town, battling to smile and not cry at the folk he rode by, and past sunburnt farmers who raised their hands in greeting to their young prince. He made it to the edge of the farmlands, the giant trees of the forest a little ways beyond the river, stopping only at the silent ring of standing stones where they kept watch over the quiet, green grasslands.

His little pony nuzzled the grass as he'd forced himself to pass between two of the cold stone blocks. He knelt, finding relief in the feel of the grass and the rich soil under his fingernails as he dug, the aroma of earth and life thick in his nostrils calming his rapidly beating heart. And then it was done.

Half awake now, Rhydian stirred, realising how far his father's power had reached.

Some part of his father's power stayed with him and coiled its way deeper within his mind. Each subsequent morning, he rode out to check the dagger lay undisturbed, and each morning he forgot a little more why he went where he did. But the urgency remained; to rise earlier and earlier with the sun, and then before the sun, to make sure his kingdom was safe from whatever strange magic the dagger was part of.

His mind forgot, but his heart did not. Even before the woman with dark hair invaded his dreams, the prince wept every single time he woke.

"Rhydian."

A cool hand snaked around Rhydian's cloak to find his hip, creeping up his back like his own layer of intimate frost. Fingertips slid up his spine and gently tapped at his shoulder blade.

"Rhydian. Wake up."

Clearing his throat, Rhydian shook his head groggily. His mouth was dry, and the rich fresh scent of grass faded from his senses.

"I'm awake," he croaked, as quiet as Fox's murmur.

As his eyes opened, he blinked and saw the nocturnal forest stretching out above him. A cool breath from the lips close to his cheek blew away the last cobwebs of his dream. It had been a dream he'd never had before. Something he'd forgotten, that he'd been made to forget, had been revealed. And what stuck with him the most was a single thought.

He *wasn't* a coward.

As a small prince, he'd taken a serious matter into his own hands, removing a threat from his kingdom on his own. It hadn't quite gone to plan, he thought dryly, but he had done it. And now Rhydian was wrapped around a creature of raging, incomprehensible magic, on his way to a city he'd never heard of, to find the one he loved. His father could rot in hell.

He inhaled sharply. Despite all that had happened because his father was a power hungry monster, he was ashamed of the bitter thoughts which curdled within him like spoilt milk.

"Want to talk about it?" Fox breathed against him, black and gold eyes searching his face.

"No," Rhydian whispered back.

He slid one hand between them, absently fiddling with the tiny green shard through his shirt. The chain was caught up and twisted with the chain of the garnet. Sighing, he gave up trying to separate them. Tilting his head, he faced the surrounding trunks, blinking at the rustling shadows, feeling something caught in his eyelashes.

"Is it snowing again?" he mumbled groggily.

"It isn't snow," Fox murmured, sounding pleased. He blew into Rhydian's face. "It's ash."

"Ash?" Rhydian blinked away the delicate flakes in his eyelashes. "From the campfire?"

Shifting against him, Fox sighed contentedly; the cool hand that had been rubbing small circles on Rhydian's back sliding around to his chest. It stopped, fingers examining the sharp outline of the green shard under Rhydian's shirt. Fox tugged on it as he exhaled slowly.

"There was a big fire in the north, years ago." A cool palm came to rest over Rhydian's heart. Fox's voice was gentle. "The further we head in that direction, the more likely you'll still find ash falling."

"There was? When?"

"A few years before I found your mother in the forest."

"Bloody hell, Fox. What did you *do*?" Rhydian hissed under his breath.

Fox's only reply was a soft laugh. As his chilly fingers withdrew from Rhydian's chest, a disgruntled sigh broke the silence.

"You're unbelievable," Owaen's voice muttered from the shadows beside them. "You know that, right?"

"Thank you," Fox said, smugly.

Rhydian pressed his face into his cloak and the spongy moss below. He could taste it now, the faint aroma of soot. He frowned as Fox shifted. Along with the hint of ash, something else was different.

"You don't feel as deathly cold," Rhydian murmured eventually. "Your coughing has finally stopped as well."

Fox was silent for so long Rhydian wondered if he'd fallen asleep. His voice, when it came, was muffled. He'd tucked his face under his cloak.

"I know," Fox said, sounding almost reluctant to admit it.

"Why can't you warm yourself up, like you soothed me? When you summoned me to you, and we... um..."

"Excuse me, what the fuck?"

"Go back to sleep, Owaen," Fox groused. He lowered his voice while Owaen grumbled under his breath. "My power didn't do that, Rhydian. I simply called yours forth."

"I don't know-" Rhydian began, but Fox interrupted coolly.

"You know what I'm talking about."

Both Rhydian and Owaen said nothing, the silence heavy and weighted.

It reminded Rhydian of the silences that weighed on him when he was alone as a child. When the mad capers of the day were over, he'd find himself in his cold chamber retelling himself stories that the librarian had shared for company. The stories would end, but his imagination would continue. Stories he'd make up, heroes and knights and forbidden magic. He was in one now, but he didn't want to be. He wanted the silence again.

The stories were things he could pick up and put down. They weren't about the complicated Elf and strange creature between them now. Both magical heroes in their own way. Rhydian knew he wasn't the same. He didn't want to be a hero. He wanted peace; quiet and long rides on his horse at sunset, no longer with the dawn. He wanted Aurelia by his side; he wanted to see all the places that existed down roads that were forgotten. Adventures, minus the life or death situations that his parents' legacy had left in their wake.

"Fox?"

"Mm."

Rhydian swallowed, acutely aware Owaen was still awake and listening.

"Why did my mother, um, why did she use Aurelia?"

A long, dark sigh hummed from beneath the cloak beside him. Fox twisted around, Owaen cursing as Fox rearranged himself between them.

"To be honest, I asked myself that early on."

"Early on?"

"I watched Aurelia grow up into the wonder that she is today."

Rhydian's gaze narrowed at the ink black hair in his face.

"I'm a little disturbed by that, just so you know."

"As I was saying," Fox continued, unperturbed, "I think Aurelia was selected because she looked like your mother. Aurelia wasn't special, or some mythical 'chosen one'. I think it was purely out of spite. Your mother picked her because she was growing up to resemble the woman your father originally fell for. It was the king that Aurelia was originally trying to get to. She just happened across you instead."

"Now I'm definitely disturbed by *all* of that."

"Mm." Fox sighed again. "Your mother was a powerful woman, despite being stripped of her power."

"And you never thought it was wrong, what she planned, what she was doing?"

Owaen cursed again as Fox shuffled between them. Black and gold eyes glittered brightly as he stared intently at Rhydian.

"I was sick of thinking, sick of feeling. I'd been through a lot. I was dealing with power that didn't belong to me, coming down from a very, *very* big high on wielding it in the north-"

Fox paused, waiting for something. With only the faintest of red glow from the dying embers, Rhydian watched Owaen open his eyes to stare at the back of Fox's head. Dark green eyes rose to Rhydian for a moment. And then, without a word, Owaen turned his back on them to face the trees. With a small sniff, Fox continued.

"So. I may have been negligent in not having my wits about me. But in my defence, I thought your mother had been through something similar to me."

"Because of what happened to her, the curse?"

"Mm. She had the right to be bitter. Even if what they did was wrong-"

"From what I can make out," Owaen interrupted, his tone icy, "her reaction seemed a *little* overblown."

Fox's eyes narrowed. "Maybe."

Jerking his cloak higher to his shoulders, Owaen snorted as he flopped onto his back. Fox kept his eyes on Rhydian's face, eyes wide.

"'Maybe'?" Owaen repeated darkly, staring at the shadows above.

After a sly wink at Rhydian, Fox rolled over, giving Rhydian his back. His long body wiggled between them a moment before he settled against Owaen's side. Over the head of dark hair between them, Rhydian could see Owaen's nostrils flare as Fox cupped the man's chin and held him still.

"I understand why she did what she did." Ignoring Owaen's searing glare, Fox pressed his face into Owaen's neck. "Can you at least try to understand that?"

Owaen blew out a puff of hot breath and shook his head. Something brushed against Rhydian and he realised that Owaen had snaked an arm around Fox to pull him close. The Elf's voice was low as he spoke quietly into the inky black hair that tickled his chin.

"You fucking died because of her. No. I don't think I'll pretend to understand."

"It was easy to let go, and it was peaceful to die," Fox's muffled voice was firm. "Coming back was harder."

Frustrated eyes the colour of the dark foliage above them flashed as Owaen glared at Rhydian over the top of Fox's head.

"Surely that means something, the harder choice, the sacrifice of your peace. Isn't that a choice that you won't regret?" Owaen asked, his tone accusing.

Rhydian blinked rapidly, urging Owaen to stop talking. There was a tension building that he had no wish to be part of. There was too much at stake.

"I told you. I regret the sacrifice of a young boy in a cold dungeon," Fox said icily, "for the sake of my dragon sized ego, in thinking I could control Shadow Light for any length of time."

One of the horses stamped quietly nearby as an enormous owl passed low over their small campsite. Rhydian watched the slow currents of ash whirl with its passage; the cool air carrying little eddies and puffs of ash around them. After a moment, a long sigh misted the night air. Fox was calm enough, and the tension eased. Owaen dropped his gaze from Rhydian, his expression resigned as he watched Fox burrow deeper into the warmth between them.

"Your parents," Owaen murmured, glancing back up to Rhydian, "were they born with magic?"

The figure between them stilled.

"No." Rhydian shivered. He pressed closer to Fox, who had somehow ended up with most of his cloak. Fox seemed to be hardly breathing. Rhydian shut his eyes, the hateful words he wished he'd never heard from his father rolling around in his mind like bitter ale. "They murdered a dragon for their power."

Owaen's eyes widened, and he mouthed *fuck* silently.

"Rhydian, I'm sorry," he murmured when he could find his voice.

"Fine role models," Rhydian said, aiming for a light tone. It didn't work.

"If it's any consolation, Rhydian," Fox's voice was faint, "if you help me kill Shadow Light, they'll be so proud of you."

"For fuck's sake, Skye," Owaen snapped, squeezing the bridge of his nose. "Really?"

"What do you actually see in him?" Rhydian muttered over Fox, who snorted loudly.

Owaen shook his head, his mouth a thin line.

"I," the Elf began, but hesitated. He sighed. "Strangely enough, I see the other half of me in this remarkable creature."

A different noise, a soft noise this time, quickly stifled, came from the cloak against Rhydian. Owaen's arm brushed Rhydian's chest as he tightened his embrace around the man between them. Fox was still cold, but Owaen was clearly warm enough for the both of them. Rhydian could feel that Fox was slowly settling down.

Yawning, Rhydian tried to think of something else to say. He wasn't ready to settle back down. He wanted to keep talking. He didn't want more dreams; he didn't want to give in to the spike of fear for Aurelia. Fear that coiled around his spine, like a snake ready to strike.

"What about your other family, Owaen?" Rhydian felt it directly this time as Fox tensed against him. He frowned. "Maybe that's too personal. I'm sorry. They must have passed while you were... sleeping."

Owaen was silent for long enough that Rhydian thought he'd offended him after all.

"No," he sighed. "My family was gone long before this shit storm rained down on us."

Fox still wasn't moving. Owaen hadn't seemed to notice, lost in thought.

"Can I ask what happened?" Rhydian asked carefully. "What were they like?"

"Let's go to sleep now," Fox said firmly from where he'd burrowed, yawning obnoxiously. "Big day tomorrow. We'll plan in the morning."

"It's going to be okay." Owaen kissed the top of Fox's head.

Certain that Fox was trying to stall the conversation; Rhydian poked Fox in the ribs. Fox reached around and grabbed Rhydian's finger with an icy grip, squeezing hard before letting him go.

A warning? Rhydian wasn't sure. Either way, Owaen talked on, oblivious.

"My mother was a wonderful, if distracted, geologist and botanist. And my father was a free spirited artist. He was an enthusiastic beekeeper as well. They were good people.

Where I was born, there was a devastating earthquake and subsequent tidal wave that wrecked the city. They were helping refugees head inland to the City of the Seers. But there was a sickness that passed through the displaced folk that even Elven magic couldn't win against. Unfortunately, they both passed while I was helping elsewhere."

"I'm sorry," Rhydian murmured, staring at the trees above them, his cheek pressed to Fox's back.

"Mm. There was so much chaos. My brother died not long after. He was a swordsman, he trained non-stop. Not that he needed to. He was gifted with the blade." Owaen looked uncomfortable for a moment. "It was a natural ability that he had to move and fight. But it wasn't enough to save him. He was fighting bandits in the forest, I think. I'm not sure. It took a long time for refugees to make it to the inland city, and there were some that took advantage of their helpless state." Owaen sighed, his voice full of old regret. "Apparently, my brother tried to help them."

"I'm sorry," Rhydian whispered again. "I never had a brother. I think I would have liked to have one."

Even with his face half covered in shadows, it was easy to see Owaen's smile was bitter.

"He was a big part of my life. But I wasn't there for him when it counted." He sighed. "I should have been. I was supposed to look after him. I still regret that he and my parents-"

"I'm tired," Fox interrupted. "Stop talking. Please."

Drawing Fox closer to him, Owaen nodded.

"Mm," he murmured, green eyes taking a last look at Rhydian before closing.

"But," Rhydian continued, "what about-"

"You too, kingling."

With a frustrated sigh, Rhydian burrowed deeper into what he could of his cloak, moss and ferns pressing into his legs. He shut his eyes to the falling ash and the red glow of the fire.

"I think I prefer being a prince, being a princeling," he muttered, more to himself than the others. Fox snorted gently.

"Don't worry Rhydian," Fox yawned. "I'm sure all new kings, in the history of everything, think that at first."

Not knowing how to respond to that, Rhydian breathed in the spicy mineral scent from Fox's skin, aware that the dramatic imagery of Fox's tattoo was separated from his face by worn fabric. Strangely, it was a comfort. It was symbolic of what Fox's power could do, whatever it was that he had done. Aurelia was going to be saved and protected by the violence that Fox had used before, and Rhydian was grateful. That was what family meant, he supposed. Not what he was used to at all.

"Owaen," Rhydian murmured.

"Mm."

"Thank you for being here."

"Mm."

"Perhaps, being here for us now, maybe this is your chance to make some kind of amends, to appease that regret you spoke of." Rhydian opened his eyes, seeing nothing but the back of Fox's shirt against his face, feeling the inked skin beneath shiver against his lips. He continued, hoping his words could be of some comfort. "Helping all of us now might help you, even if it can't bring your parents, or your brother, back."

They were all quiet for a little while, breathing in the rich aromas of the trees that crowded around them. The fresh, verdant smell was full of life, yet as with all forests came the heady undertone of things buried, slowly returning to the soil.

Owaen's quiet murmur was almost lost to the cool sighing of the night breeze.

"If only."

51

Aurelia

Year 367

The City of the Seers

"You'll be fine," Caspian said soothingly. He appeared calm. Only the brightness in his odd eyes betrayed how excited he was.

The petite woman in front of him gritted her teeth.

Bound and gagged, Aurelia listened while Caspian and the woman she had always thought of as Jessikah argued. But her gaze was elsewhere.

Glaring at Flare, Aurelia was putting all the words she couldn't say into the force of her gaze. It must have been working. The dragon hadn't looked at her once since Caspian had stuffed her mouth with fabric.

"I am sorry about this," he'd said seriously not long before. "That cute little dick kick of yours was really quite impressive."

Aurelia had sworn at the man, her furious *fuck you* muffled.

"In another life," Caspian had said with a smirk as he tightened her gag with infuriating care, "definitely."

Now she slumped on the edge of an ash-covered domed roof, her hands bound and aching, her mouth full of fabric that tasted like dirt and smoke. The purple cloak around her was barely thick enough to ward off the occasional icy chill that lifted her wild hair.

Nearby crouched the tiny purple dragon. A dragon who had once saved her life, but was now unable to meet her gaze.

The domed roof they were on capped some vast building, a once splendid example of masonry and grand vision. Gaping holes in the curved sweep of the once smooth expanse showed a dark space below, with the weak light piercing the gloom in long, pale shafts. They were high enough that Aurelia could see over the silent city, all the way to the crumbling walls, to the forest beyond. The air was charged, loaded with the excitement pouring from Caspian like a hot shimmer from fiery molten rock. The shimmer was almost an aroma that was potently laced with minerals and something bitter, wild.

Swallowing awkwardly around the gag, Aurelia blinked away tears of frustration and rage. Her eyes roamed over Flare's row of spikes along his back to his nervously flicking tail.

"When I am free," Aurelia hissed, her words obscured by the fabric that was drying out her mouth, *"You will pay for this."*

Flare's wings twitched. Her words might have been muffled, but her tone was perfectly clear.

Caspian broke off from whatever the hells he was saying to the small yellow-haired figure. He glanced at Flare, then down at Aurelia. His pale eyebrows rose.

"I like you," he said seriously to Aurelia, blinking slowly. Caspian's unnerving eyes flashed silver, both blue but one pale and the other dark, as he appraised her with lazy confidence. He smiled.

She refused to dignify that with a response.

Caspian's smile widened. "Pity."

52

Owaen

Year 367

The City of the Seers

There *had* been a cautious plan of approach. But that had gone to shit immediately.

"Damn you, Skye," Owaen had muttered as his horse raced after Fox into the City of the Seers. Their carefully thought out approach *hadn't* included Owaen ending up with lurching dread, watching an innocent victim plunge to the cracked flagstones below.

There had been two figures on the edge of the ruined domed roof of the council chamber. Fox was in the courtyard below, impotent with confusion and his rage, making the situation worse. There was a vicious verbal exchange. Rhydian had made a fool's bargain. And then the taller figure, a gagged and clearly exhausted Elven woman, had been stabbed viciously from behind.

And then kicked off the crumbling dome, her cloak a cascade of purple behind her.

Shock vibrated through Owaen's body with such force that he had experienced a moment of complete delirium. It was like being flung into the horror of his past, when Owaen had realised the one he loved had been taken and held against her will.

Some things never changed, while so much had.

As his heart and mind lurched with a sickening wave of incoherence, the woman's scream was muffled.

Fox's roar of terror was not.

And then, adding to the strange wave of incoherence within, Owaen's ears stopped working as reality seemed to *slow*.

All movement, the wan daylight, and the muted sounds of the bleak city ambled to a halt. Owaen felt like he was stuck in a glass jar of his father's prized honey. It confused his senses, and the desire he had to rush in was blocked by the way that the air seemed to thicken. What *wasn't* confusing was the sickening twist in Owaen's chest, on hearing the sound of various bones snap.

Fox had moved indescribably fast, but seemingly on strength alone. Not with his magical ability that moved him from the city gates to here. He had moved through the syrup that surrounded them without any buffer from his power within.

Multiple things happened at once.

Owaen had time to glance at the young king. He had time to wonder if the expression of terror on Rhydian's face mirrored how Owaen had looked, who the fuck knew how long ago. When Owaen had seen Skye, her iridescent green scales bloodied, golden eyes dulled, as she lay sprawled, limp and defeated, on a still smouldering cavern floor.

In the City of the Seers, sounds became muted, time crawled even slower.

Owaen also had time to wince at the sound of Fox's desperate dash across the ruined paving stones of the awe-inspiring expanse of the great courtyard, bones breaking with his speed, arms outstretched. The sound was a painful series of cracks, like ice breaking in the morning sun. Owaen was glad that he was behind and unable to see what was surely a nightmare inducing expression on Fox's face.

Everything went still.

Owaen had stopped breathing as the young Elven woman plummeted from the crumbling roof's edge, long hair streaming like dark flames behind. He had time to watch as Shadow Light, still in the form of a tiny woman, gathered her newly acquired treasure of green crystal to her chest with one hand. The foul creature had a worryingly eager twist to their pale lips as they ducked backwards from the edge. A black fog had begun to form with a dull hum, the scent of ozone splicing through the cold air. Before the little woman disappeared, she had twisted and acted quickly. Both with the dagger and a small, well-aimed boot.

The bitter, black fog thickened around Shadow Light as he ducked away. Time had sped up, sound returned. The chilling, muted day around them was shattered with a horrified roar of terror. It was Rhydian, watching helplessly as Aurelia plunged towards the cracked paving stones below.

Before she hit the ground, Owaen darted around Blackthorn and ran the other way.

This still *wasn't* the plan.

Thinking back to what had happened in the courtyard, Owaen was now ducking around fallen blocks of large stones. As he leapt through the back entrance of the ruined council chambers, he was surprisingly calm. There was even time to think about what the hells had just happened. The charged confrontation between Shadow Light and Skye had been quick, full of things Owaen didn't understand. He wasn't sure he wanted to.

Inside the ruined building, Owaen jumped over a pile of shattered rock, grateful for the weight of his brother's prized sword at his hip. As he dodged another block of once beautifully carved stone, he tasted fresh blood on his tongue. He must have bitten it at some point.

Owaen swallowed the blood, and made his way deeper into the council chambers, following the acrid stink of ozone and dragon. In his mind, he cursed with frustration at the bitter arrogance of a beautiful yet naïve and traumatised dragon.

Before they had reached the courtyard, before the plan had gone to shit, Rhydian, Fox and Owaen had made their way out of the eerily silent leviathan trees. They had been met with a sweet aroma hanging thickly on the chilled air, the forest a looming presence behind them. Frost crunched under the hooves of their horses on the dirt road. Owaen had ignored the ache inside at the familiar scents of flowers, buds heavy with pollen. Open meadows of fragrant blossoms ran right up to the crumbling ruined walls of the great City of the Seers.

Or as it was now, the *once* great City of the Seers was more fitting.

Owaen hadn't been able to take it in at first. The once lively city was now obviously just the cracked and bleached bones of what it had been. He could see through gaps in the shattered outer wall that the place was silent, cold and overgrown.

They had paused at the gateless archway, a soaring expanse of pale stone that was covered in twisted, thorny vines. As they took in the dead city ahead, Owaen had been about to go over their plan to sneak in and circle the edge of the city. But a young woman's desperate shout had echoed towards them. The sound had reached them from deep inside, a strangely muted cry full of frustration and pain.

Rhydian had gasped. "*Aurelia!*"

"Skye-" Owaen had warned.

But Fox had said, "Fuck it."

Not so much with words, but with actions.

Owaen had tightened his arms around Fox, who had been back in the saddle in front of him, stiff, cold and unmoving.

Until Fox had heard Aurelia's cry.

He had thrown Owaen's arms off of him as simply as a horse twitching off an insect. Fox had slid off their horse to the hard ground below, his gasp of pain ghosting after him faintly as he sprinted for the ruined city gates. He had ducked beneath the crumbled archway of the outer wall, moving so fast it was almost impossible to track him even with Elven eyesight.

Tasting the strange ozone scent left behind in the wake of the magic that Fox had drawn on to move so quickly, Owaen cursed. But if he was honest, there had been a moment to be self indulgently pleased. Fox had finally found some inner strength, his inner spark. The moment passed quickly, however, and shoving his ego aside, Owaen had spurred his horse into a mad dash, Rhydian not far behind. It had been easy to follow the soft eddies of disturbed soot on the large frosted flagstones that made up the city streets. Disturbed frost marked Fox's frantic journey. They had followed the stone streets covered with overgrown shrubs and brown moss into the heart of the ruined city. Owaen refused to think about the desecration of what was once a refuge.

But he couldn't think of that now. He had too many things to make up for before allowing any self-indulgent pity.

Like keeping Skye safe this time.

Tumbled walls and broken blocks of stone occasionally obstructed their path. Thankfully, both horses were nimble despite their fatigue. They leapt over the cracked slabs of once shining masonry, shouting reaching them from the great public plaza ahead.

When they had come to the great central courtyard, sized to easily fit bustling crowds and at least a dozen full sized dragons, they arrived at a scene full of crackling tension. In a flurry of dirty white flakes, the two horses came to a halt not far from Fox, and Rhydian slid to the ground. From the saddle, Owaen brushed his blonde hair out of his eyes, his brow furrowed with confusion.

Owaen was not quite sure what he had expected, given the way Fox looked, but what he had come across wasn't it. It was even clearer to him right at that moment that many things had moved beyond his comprehension; the world moving on and changing around him while he slept. Fear lit him up from within.

Skye... *Fox*... was there, hands curled into fists at his sides, perhaps ten metres from the council chamber wall. His cloak was discarded, his once white shirt torn open at one sleeve, the riot of colours on his back clearly visible through the material. His black pants and boots were covered in dirt. He was staring at the crumbling edge of the domed roofline above, yelling at the top of his lungs.

Above them, a small woman with wild, dirty blonde hair laughed callously. She held a green crystal dagger under the ear of a struggling, bound young woman, her dark hair streaming in the wind. The pair of them were on the very edge of the domed roof of the grand council chamber. The edge of the dome was about five metres high, the centre of the dome rising behind by ten times that height at least. The dome curved away in a scarred mess of open masonry. The circular building was so vast it had once seated twelve council members, including three full sized dragons, at a large table of intricately inlaid wood. As with most of the public places in the City of the Seers, the scale was vast, awe-inspiring. Not just to accommodate the dragons, but to *intimidate*. Owaen loved this city. A part of him also hated it just for that.

As his heart beat so fast it was risking escaping through his ribs, Owaen bared his teeth. The gentle rise of the domed roof where they were standing was clearly unstable. The whole place was in a state of decay, lost to rage and time and ruin.

With a quick glance to his right, Owaen's heart stuttered. Even the great tower that had watched over the city, whence Owaen had first seen Skye, was now a teetering column of once breathtakingly carved pale stone. Wild vines of some sinuous plant had snaked its way halfway up its rounded height. As he watched, a small tumble of stones and grit dislodged from the cracked wall around its roof terrace.

Everything was different from what Owaen remembered. He experienced a flash of regret for Skye, once full of joy and shining like the sun with her outrageous outfit of jewels. Now she stood here, broken but not quite beaten with the dangerous eyes of a furious young man, scarred by fear and rage which had caused her to lock Owaen tightly away.

To keep Owaen safe.

But it was *his* turn to keep Skye safe.

Across the plaza, a flock of grey birds rose with a scatter of squeaky wings as Fox raged, his voice echoing around the otherwise empty courtyard. His cool facade was long gone.

"Aurelia better not have a single hair on her head missing, you miserable piece of shit-"

Owaen stared hard at the figures on top of the roof. Realisation dawned with dread that Skye really had contained her tormentor into a vessel that she could drag around the continent alongside her, in some twisted form of revenge. The great oily black dragon Shadow Light was here before him, just not as expected. After a moment of reflection, he realised it didn't matter. Owaen placed a steady hand on the hilt of the sword at his hip as Blackthorn danced uneasily beneath him.

Dragon, man or woman, it didn't matter. Owaen had scoffed at violence as a younger Elf. But after what he had seen, if a creature with a heart as cruel as Shadow Light's was tormenting the innocent, then Owaen *had* to act.

Fox continued to roar, and Owaen winced.

For fuck's sake, Skye, this is not the way we planned to keep things calm.

As Shadow Light laughed disdainfully, inciting Fox further, it seemed obvious that this had the potential to go quite badly. Owaen dismounted carefully, catching Rhydian's eye. The young king was on the other side of Fox, eyes wide, his gaze frantically pinging back and forth between Fox and the two women above. Owaen mimed placing a hand over his mouth and flicked his head at Fox. Rhydian's blue eyes widened. He shook his head.

Fuck.

"Rhydian," Owaen hissed, "shut him up-"

A soft feminine voice rasped from above when Fox finally took a breath.

"Owaen fucking Carter," the voice scoffed. "Of course *you're* here. Back to taint our queen with more ridiculous ideas?"

Owaen tilted his head more urgently at Fox, who had suddenly stopped yelling. Rhydian ignored Owaen, his eyes fixed on Aurelia above. Owaen cursed under his breath. His grip tightened around the reins of his horse while wondering what the fuck to do.

"I can see you, you know," the voice continued, "or are you as deviously stupid as your bro-"

"Don't you dare talk to him!" Fox shouted, finding his voice. "And how in the actual fuck are you *talking*-"

"My queen," the woman above continued with a sneer, "you think your magic enables you to know everything about our race? You're as ignorant now as you were when you unleashed yourself on our innocent brethren-"

"*Innocent*!?" Fox sounded like he was lost for words. He was staring with unwavering intensity at the two women above, the yellow-haired woman who was still struggling to hold Aurelia still.

The young Elven woman looked worse for wear, with her hands bound and a loose gag over her mouth. There was a soiled purple cloak half-off her shoulders that cascaded down her back to twist around her legs. She also had a cut along one cheek that bled profusely down her flesh. Perhaps it was the cause of the shout that had triggered Fox into discarding their plan of approach. The other woman, Shadow Light, adjusted her grip on the crystal dagger held against Aurelia's neck.

Owaen squinted. With his keen Elven eyesight, he could see it was a shard of some dark green mineral, almost the same colour as his irises. He experienced a dull flash of memory. He'd seen its like before. But where?

Above them, the small woman threw back her head and laughed. Her bright eyes flashed with dark delight.

"My beautiful Skye, too afraid to come alone," she crooned down to them. Her eyes flashed and the dagger point scratched Aurelia's neck deep enough to bleed. Aurelia winced and Rhydian, who could clearly see well enough what was going on far above them, swore. Shadow Light continued. "You were such a good little youngling. What went wrong?"

"Wrong?" Fox hissed. "*Wrong*? What was ever *right*? You farmed me like a fucking pig for magic-"

"I did that for your own good!" Shadow sneered. "For the good of dragonkind! We shouldn't need to abase ourselves to the lesser races-"

"You bloody, scaly-"

"Don't interrupt me, you flea," Shadow snapped over Owaen's snarled insult. "This is your fault too-"

"Can you hear yourself, Shadow?" Fox shouted over them both. "You really have no shame, do you? All those lives, taken, stolen, and you still don't give a damn?"

"The only lives I give a damn about are the ones in Mionlach, when you ripped the dragons apart and *reveled* in it!"

Fox was breathing heavily, and despite the cold air plummeting lower in temperature still, Owaen could see a faint sheen of sweat forming over the back of Fox's neck.

"Why shouldn't I?" Fox yelled. "After what you did while they stood by!"

"And that tattoo," Shadow hissed. "How could you? I'll never forgive you-"

"What in the ever loving fuck are you talking about?" Fox shouted so loud the vast courtyard echoed and rumbled around them. "Forgiveness? Me?" He threw back his head and laughed, mad and full of rage. "You clearly haven't learnt anything at all, and the gods only know you've had the time to think about it! I made you give me that tattoo to think about what *you* caused! What you did to me, to the Elves, to this *entire fucking city.*"

Fox inhaled deeply, and Owaen's heart ached for the fury and pain that hummed between them along the thread they shared within.

"You cried like a little bitch when you marked my skin," Fox went on, "and by the invisible gods that have never helped me once, if you mark one more piece of Aurelia's flesh I will *rip* your heart out and your face off, so your tears have nowhere to go but spill out of your lidless eyes without end!"

Shadow Light blinked at Fox's outburst. Then laughed.

As Fox breathed through his nose in frustration, Owaen realised Aurelia's gaze had fallen to him. Her green eyes widened, and she flicked her gaze to the ruined tower that cut through the sky above and beside them. Owaen followed her gaze, seeing nothing but another small cascade of faint dust and grit loosen from the roof terrace, dropping away like dirty rain. He looked back at Aurelia, but her eyes were shut tight now. Shadow Light had shoved her to the very edge of the domed roof. There was only a narrow section to balance on that would be unsafe at the best of times.

"Not here," Fox bit out. "Let her go, and I'll go with you instead."

Owaen jerked his head down to face Fox. "What? No-"

"I'll go with you," Fox hissed, ignoring Owaen. "Just let Aurelia go without," Fox gritted his teeth, clearly affected by the sight of Aurelia's bloody face and neck, "further harm."

"Are you out of your gods damned mind?" Owaen hissed back.

He realised he was still holding onto the reins of his horse, hard enough that the leather bit into his palm. He shoved them away, taking a step towards Fox. A dry rattle came from the unstable tower. Owaen bit his lip. That would be *just fantastic*, if the whole thing came down upon them now. The back of his neck prickled, but he focused his gaze on Fox. Rhydian had edged forward slowly, his hands clasped over his chest, to stand by Fox's side.

"Shadow Light," Fox said with determination, either dismissing or unaware of Rhydian's approach. "Let her go. I'm here. Isn't that what you wanted?"

With a brittle laugh, the small woman licked her lips. "Fine. I-" she paused.

It was hard to see exactly what Shadow was doing, but yellow eyes widened and her nostrils flared. She appeared to be scenting the air.

Owaen did the same and could only scent the frost and the vines that twisted around the stone blocks of the city, life that was growing, pulling it apart slowly, millimetre-by-millimetre, year-by-year. For a moment, the only sound was the cold air shifting through the courtyard and the faint coo of a pigeon inside a collapsed public hall off to their right.

"Oh my gods," Shadow breathed, peering over the edge, eyes bouncing around between the three of them below. "You brought it *here*?"

Confused, Fox took an unsteady step back, his hands in his hair. "What?"

"The other shard," Shadow insisted as dark hunger washed over his feminine face. Aurelia stilled, her own eyes falling to Rhydian. She bit around her gag, attempting to mumble something at Rhydian.

It sounded like *take it away*.

Teeth bared, eyes filling with wild excitement, Shadow Light smiled. Not at Fox, not at Owaen. But at Rhydian.

"Where is it?" the small woman demanded. She licked her lips.

"What?" Rhydian mumbled, his eyes on Aurelia.

Aurelia was trying to shake her head without pressing onto the dagger at her skin. Shadow Light yanked her by the hair, pulling her head back at a painful- looking angle. Owaen dropped his gaze to the young king and recognised the expression on the man for what it was. Understanding. Rhydian clutched his chest tighter. When Owaen glanced up, Aurelia closed her eyes in defeat.

"*Where is it?*" Shadow screeched after a quick glance at the tower, her gaze darting back to Rhydian. "Show me! *Now!*"

"What are you talking-" Fox began. Shadow Light was so close to the edge now, Owaen could sense the fear from the young king like a sour tang on the air.

"*The other shard!*"

"What are you talking about?" Fox repeated. "What-"

"This." Rhydian stepped forward. "Jessikah, Shadow Light, means this."

Owaen watched without comprehension as Rhydian reached into his travel stained shirt and withdrew a metal chain. He slid it over his head and held it up. Dangling from its length was a single piece of crystal, small as a little finger, dark green like the dagger that was still threateningly pressed against Aurelia's neck.

Fox stared at it dumbly.

"Why that?" he snapped. "That's just a piece of barely charged vivianite." His gaze swung up to Shadow. Shadow was staring with open greed down at the tiny shard. Rhydian's breathing was hitched, his gaze firmly on Aurelia, who was staring at him sadly.

"Give it to me," Shadow hissed, with another furtive glance at the tower above them before staring wildly down at the tiny green pendant swinging from Rhydian's chain. "Take Aurelia back. Just give that to *me.*"

"Why do you need that? It's nothing," Fox insisted, moving to stand closer to Rhydian and grabbing the young king's wrist. "I'm offering to go with you," he snapped. "Just let Aurelia go, you evil prick."

Shadow Light's gaze barely made it to Fox before fixating on the shard once more.

"Perhaps we can both get what we want," Shadow Light muttered. He raised his voice. "To you it feels like nothing, yes? Well, to me, along with this," Shadow indicated the crystal dagger under Aurelia's ear with a cursory glance, "it is much, *much* more. Throw it up here, little king."

"Promise me Aurelia will be ok," Rhydian called up, yanking his wrist from Fox's grip. Fox stared numbly while Rhydian wound the chain around the tiny shard with shaking fingers.

"Throw it up here *now!*" Shadow Light called down, and pushed Aurelia to the edge, so that her boots were slipping on the softened, green copper guttering. Aurelia was shaking her head desperately. Owaen's hand tightened on the hilt of his sword.

"Promise me-"

"*Throw it!*"

With a grunt, Rhydian drew back his arm and threw the shard. His enhanced, magical bloodline was clear in the strength and accuracy of his aim.

Owaen watched it sparkle in the wan light, the chain loosening behind it like the tail of a tiny, metallic comet streaking upwards. It reminded him of when Owaen had first met Skye as she descended from above. She had arrived on the back of the black dragon that taunted them now, almost at this spot, disguised as an Elven woman with green hair and adorned with sparkling gems that caught the sun in an ethereal, iridescent display of colours.

There was no joy in Owaen's heart now. The single, shining jewel was caught by a tiny hand. Shadow's other hand stabbed the dagger into Aurelia from behind, and a swift kick knocked her over the edge of the roof.

And the world had slowed, changed.

Even the colour. The daylight changed from golden warm to blue and cool, like the sun had set and a full moon had risen. The temperature dropped and Owaen watched the sweat on the back of Fox's neck crystallise into frost as he *moved*.

For ages to come, Owaen's dreams would be filled with the sound of Fox's body breaking, with the speed he moved with a wild, wordless roar. Owaen was glad he didn't see what came after, what Fox had done to himself in order to get to where Aurelia was plummeting.

At the crisp sound of bones breaking and cartilage cracking, Owaen heard the dull rush of air shifting high overhead, something that he had heard only a few times before. The sound was one of transformation, of matter rearranging. Along with the dull hum came the sound of the earth trembling below, as a deceptively soft looking black mist formed along the ruined domed roof.

So Owaen moved as well, accompanied by the sounds of Fox's bones coming apart. He spun and raced into the council chambers, into the unknown and towards shadows, chasing the darkest one of all.

53

Fox

Year 367

The City of the Seers

"Aurelia," a voice choked out. "A-alive?"

"Yes," Rhydian replied hoarsely, "but I'm not sure if you are."

Underneath wild golden brown hair, Rhydian's gaze was filled with fear as he blinked his wet eyes over Fox.

Fox tried to move. He couldn't. His body didn't work. There was an unmoving, warm weight against him. Aurelia's limp form pressed him down into the cobbles and she smelled very faintly of flowers, something acidic, but mostly sweat and dirt. A thick, luxurious cloak was draped over them both. If Fox could have moved his arms to wrap them around her, he would have.

The king was on his knees beside Fox, his hands held out before him as he trembled, unsure of how he could help. That made two of them. Fox could take the pain he was in. He'd been in far, far worse after all. But it still hurt.

A *lot*.

Fox's mind was full of traumatic sensations as his tortured body tried to work. The more he tried to fight it, the more everything hurt. One painful feeling stood out the most. Shame. Aurelia was likely going to be fine. But it was Fox's fault they were here. He clenched his eyes, closing them to the cold, golden sky above.

"I forgot," Fox croaked. Rhydian leant closer, his brow furrowed.

"What?"

"The plan... I'm s-sorry."

"Fox, you idiot, Aurelia is okay. She's unconscious, but she's alive..." Rhydian's breathless voice cracked. "I just don't know what to do for *you*."

Neither did Fox. He blinked away the haze of agony.

"Owaen?"

Rhydian took a shaky breath, and shook his head, eyes darting between whatever was left of Fox and Aurelia.

"What?" Fox hissed in pain as he tried to sit up. His body flopped with a wet, painful jerk instead.

"He's gone," Rhydian explained hurriedly over Fox's curse of frustration. "There was a... black mist and Jessikah, um, Shadow, disappeared through a gap in the dome. Owaen ran off... he headed down the side of the building."

The warm weight, strangely soothing to Fox's chilled, agonised flesh, shifted over him.

"Aurelia?" Rhydian cried, grabbing some part of her that Fox couldn't lift his head to see.

A soft moan hummed against his ruined chest.

"Aurelia," Rhydian murmured, "I've got you. You're going to be okay."

"O-off," Fox croaked. Rhydian understood straight away.

With a soft grunt from the king, the agonising and calming weight was dragged across Fox's chest. His eyes shut tight of their own accord against the jarring pain. Then, all at once, Aurelia's weight and the warmth of the cloak was gone. A faint sob came from his right; Fox couldn't tell if it was Aurelia or the king.

"Fox," Rhydian said quietly. Fox opened his eyes at the catch in the king's voice.

Against the agony in his spine, Fox turned his head to where Rhydian had gathered Aurelia to his chest. Something popped in Fox's neck, this time the pain followed by a sharp splintering jerks as his bones started to shift, knitting together. He closed his eyes once more, sending his frigid power out to his limbs. It was a fight to breathe as the jagged pieces of his bones grated against each other, skin stretching and vessels tightening inside his tortured flesh.

"Fox," Rhydian repeated, his voice still low, desperate.

Fox tried to move, and his body obeyed him this time. Mostly.

He managed to roll to his side, swallowing his agonised scream as red and white hot pain lanced along every cursed nerve ending in his body. Rhydian shifted away as much as he could whilst Fox bit his lower lip hard enough that it gushed blood. He turned himself over to lie face down. He counted to three. And then pushed himself up to his knees.

Panting, with his palms on the cobbles below, slick with his dark red blood, Fox raised his head. Rhydian had one hand pressed to the gaping stab wound in Aurelia's shoulder. But his gaze was fixed intently on Fox, eyes still wide, mouth hanging open. Fox followed his gaze down.

"Ah," Fox murmured. He placed a bloody palm on the bone sticking through his thigh. The red and white splintered end was protruding outwards about two centimetres. "That's n-not ideal."

Fox raised his head to stare at Rhydian while he sent magic down to his leg, placing a bloody, freezing hand over the tip of the bone. With a quick jerk, Fox shoved it back through his torn flesh with a sickening, grating snap. Rhydian held Fox's gaze without breaking away. Fox groaned, and Rhydian bit his lip, his dirty face paling. The king's hand pressed tighter to Aurelia's wound, surely causing her pain, but she barely stirred.

"Where?" Fox hissed flatly, blood splattering from his torn lip.

He shuffled forward on his knees, the soft wet sounds of his body readjusting the only sound besides the soft scurry of white flakes that fell from the grey sky above. Fox glanced up. It was snowing amongst the wisps of bitter ash, but only over the courtyard. It would have been a wonder if he'd had the interest to care.

"That way," Rhydian said, his free hand pointing to a wide street that led alongside the council chambers.

Fox nodded once.

Inhaling deeply, he reached out to place his broken hand on top of Rhydian's, directly over Aurelia's bleeding wound. Rhydian tried to pull away, but Fox's icy, agonised fingers held his fast. Fox closed his eyes, breathing deeply through his own pain, sensing Aurelia's beneath his and Rhydian's hand, willing her flesh to mend, focusing his magic in a way he'd never done before.

Fox was used to manipulating energy that was dead in a way, like making a crystal window for a room in the caves of Lolihud, out of nothing but the dust. But flesh? Fox hadn't wanted to heal the owl back in the forest for Aurelia. Not because he wanted it to die, but because he was afraid. He'd ripped flesh apart, scales and blood torn to ribbons, but now, as he mended his own strange flesh back together, he sent the same tentative magic flow into Aurelia. This time calling on Rhydian's as well.

Imagining a separate, glowing body that existed in the same place as his own physical body helped him concentrate. Slowly, wondrously, Aurelia's bleeding wound staunched, her flesh growing and mending together. As he imagined himself a being of light, he saw the same for her within his mind. It was like a skeleton of light inside her, pulsing with the flow he sent her way. Fox knew she would also need time to recover, as the energy from her own body was being rearranged to mend itself with the aid of his. She would need rest. For him, there was still work to finish.

As if to make the point, a taunting roar welled up from deep within the building next to them, and a piece of the gutter crashed to the ground nearby. His heart stuttered in his chest. There was no time to wait for more breaks to mend.

Bracing himself, Fox withdrew his freezing hand from Rhydian's and Aurelia's reddened skin. This time, he couldn't contain his grunt of pain as he willed himself to stand, swaying more than a little. But on examining Aurelia, her eyes closed in peace, not pain, Fox took a moment to feel pleased with himself. Pleased that he had caught Aurelia instead of that fucking nuisance of a purple dragon, and without slicing her up with claws while he was at it. In fact, Fox had done the opposite.

That's how you catch someone, Flare, you self-serving scaly shit.

At your own expense.

Not theirs.

"Get her away," Fox coughed out, smiling to show Rhydian it was going to be okay. Rhydian grimaced up at him, but eventually he nodded, blue eyes full of both fear and gratitude.

More roars shook the council chamber. The acidic stink of dragon was stronger now. Of course, Owaen had raced inside to try to take care of Shadow by himself.

"You stupid Elf," Fox hissed, stumbling towards the frost and ash that coated the cracked stones beneath his boots.

As more of his bones shifted into place inside, each movement as agonising as the breaking had been, a thought had Fox laugh out loud. More fresh blood leaked from his lips.

Owaen might be stupidly trying to fight a full sized dragon on his own, but Fox hardly felt any smarter, considering his current condition. If Fox needed any more proof that having a dragon sized opinion of himself was laughingly futile, the broken bones mending inside of him were proof enough. But he was growing stronger with each painful thud of his heart, and each step towards finishing what he should have long ago.

"You dumb dragon," Fox muttered to himself, blinking through the pain that fogged his vision, as he quickened his lurch into a run, towards the council chambers and the violent chaos within.

54

Owaen

Year 367

The City of the Seers

"**I** can smell you, filthy Elf."

The deep voice taunted Owaen from somewhere to his right, amongst the gloom of the abandoned chamber. Owaen ignored it.

He continued his silent hunt, creeping around blocks of fallen masonry, some pieces bigger than him, fallen from the dome and arches far above. His brother's ostentatious sword was in one hand, the hilt a comfort and a curse, his other hand trailing along the cool stone at his side. Over the stink of the dragon, Owaen could also smell the ash that covered everything. Outside it was fused to the stones by light and rain, inside it was dry in patches. Soft puffs shifted under his heavy boots as he stalked his prey deeper inside.

On a whim, he paused and held soot-stained fingertips to his nose. He grimaced. The ash was mixed with pigeon shit, and carried a faint reptilian miasma like the dragon he was tracking, but older, stale. Shaking his head at the evidence of Fox's chaos in the north from years before, Owaen continued on, grim faced and determined.

The voice came again, closer.

"You dare think you have a claim to her? She'll *never* be yours, Elf."

Owaen almost snarled aloud that Skye had a claim on *him*, but caught himself in time with a silent chuckle. He refused to be lured into giving his position away. There was too much riding on this. He just hoped he had the strength to get it done by himself. Owaen owed it to Fox, no matter how much Fox protested that Owaen could not take this evil creature down. Fox's ego had blinded him before. Owaen licked the ash off his lips. He squashed down the small voice inside that cautioned him about his own blind arrogance.

"Nothing to say, dirty Elf?"

There was a shifting of rubble from the innermost chamber, the cavernous circular space surrounded by a ring of thick, carved columns, and inside of the columns had stood a circumference of once living trees.

"I'm going to crush you," Shadow Light crooned. "And then I'm going to finish what I started, when you stuck your filthy Elven nose into what you had no right to before. Skye is *mine*. Her magic, endless, pure, until you tainted it."

Only half listening to the taunting mutter, Owaen glanced up. There was a gap far above, the break in the dome large enough for him to see the main tower with its awkward lean. The barest hint of a shadow, possibly another shitting pigeon, shifted faintly on the rooftop terrace, only just visible between breaks in the balcony wall that surrounded it. Lowering his gaze, Owaen moved on, stepping quickly from a stone column to the dried husk of a dead tree. It pained him to be so close to something that was once a living part of this sacred place. So much had happened here, good and bad, in a place that had been built to foster relations between species. Instead, the city had become a symbol of the way each race thought that the others were lesser.

Sensing a large shape in the gloom to his far right, Owaen stepped left, continuing to skirt the edge of the centre chamber. The giant open space, with its ring of soaring dead trees, was intersected by columns of pale light shining through the wrecked roof, catching the disturbed dust in the air, allowing him to track the movement of-

A giant, black head of oily looking scales snapped at him viciously from the shadows.

With a startled curse, Owaen ducked behind the closest dead and blackened tree. A frustrated roar followed him. The stink of ozone and acid became so overpowering that Owaen gagged, and his hair shifted with static in the wind of the dragon's frantic scrabbling and pushing against the trees. There was a mass of jumbled rubble preventing Shadow from reaching Owaen directly, but a sword-sharp claw sawed through the pile. Snarls and stinking hot breath accompanied the desperate, snarling jabs.

Fuck.

Owaen darted further along the ring of trees. The columns whisked past on his left, the dead forest on his right, curving around the chamber. He rushed through patches of daylight that shone down like ash filled columns of grey sunshine as his passage, and the snapping dragon following close behind him, kicked up the dust that had lain still for years. He was desperately looking for more fallen stones that were low enough for him to scramble onto.

He needed height.

Sheathing his sword while he was running around a curve, and dodging an approaching dragon, was no easy feat. But as soon as Owaen saw a low-hanging branch over a tumble of blocks, he climbed them like a goat, leaping up with a grunt. Yellow eyes, large, furious and tinted an odd green, flashed underneath him. One of his boots actually bounced off the black, scaled snout that lunged after him. Owaen pulled himself up. He was grateful that the columns were too close to the sprawling trees for Shadow Light to take flight. There was space enough within the centre of the vast room, but on the edge in the ring of trees there was not. As Owaen panted and climbed, his muscles straining, the room became cloudier and thicker with disturbed dust and ash.

Nearly slipping, he swore. Shadow Light disappeared beneath him for a moment, only to reappear a moment later on the far side of the tree. This time not in a lunge for Owaen, but ramming the tree he was in. The tree shuddered with a loud boom. Owaen nearly lost his grip. Large cracks rang out amongst the sound of Shadow's enraged roar. Owaen cursed again and climbed higher. He had a vague plan, and prayed that this time, this one went in the way he intended.

Claws hissed through the air as he pushed himself along a thick branch, exposing him to the centre of the room. He spared a quick glance for the immense circular council table that took up the centre of the room. It was a mass of different coloured wood; the pattern arranged in sacred geometry that he didn't understand.

But for now, he didn't need to understand anything except how important it was to prove himself and extinguish this shadow once and for all. And to do that, he needed height, his brother's sword, and courage. He did have some magic, most of his family had, but there was little use for it here. What would manipulating the light achieve? What would being able to reshape the structure of a crystal achieve? What he needed most was something deeper, more primal.

"Are you a ferret? A filthy, stinking rat?" roared the dragon below as he rammed the tree again.

With a grunt, Owaen jumped clear just as the tree came splintering down, crashing into the chamber with a cascade of creaks, groans, and pops. Owaen landed in the next tree, splinters of dead wood tearing at his hands. He pushed the pain away and climbed higher still, pulling himself up with slippery, reddened hands. His boots struggled to find purchase.

As the dragon shouldered its way through rubble and climbed over the fallen tree towards Owaen, there was a chilling moment when he realised there were no more branches above that would support his weight. This would have to do. The dead branches were too fragile. His bloodied hands were a liability for holding on with any chance of a solid grip. There wasn't any fancy way to do what he intended, which suited Owaen just fine. He steadied himself as best he could and drew his brother's sword.

"Are you an insect?" leered the creature below as he tore at Owaen's tree with desperate claws, wings stiff and standing out backwards behind him to avoid the sharp spikes of fractured wood.

Owaen edged as close as he dared to the end of the branch he was barely balanced upon, bitter ash and copper blood coating his mouth, until he was right above the rippling spines of Shadow Light's neck. He sighed, hoping his bones didn't smash as badly as Fox had broken his.

No.

Don't think of that now.

But he did need the dragon to move slightly and point those spikes away. He tightened his grip on the sword, the ruby barely visible under the black soot that dulled its shine.

"Hey fucker!"

Shadow looked up, delaying his next launch against the tree, his mad yellow-green eyes wide with malice in his oily black scaled face. He snapped his jaws once with a loud snap, before opening them wide to hiss at the ash-covered blonde Elf wobbling in the tree above him.

"You are an unclean, polluted-"

"Nah. Want to know what really I am?" Owaen taunted in return, his own teeth bared and stained red. He was barely aware of a deep hum from the earth below as the tree around him shuddered. Shadow Light didn't hear or feel it, either.

Reptilian eyes narrowed, black nostrils flaring with rage. Owaen smiled.

"I'm your *death*."

With Skye's name on his bloody lips, Owaen wrapped both hands on the sword hilt. And then leapt into the air.

It was a majestic drop, full of glory, down towards the dragon. Owaen had the brief wish for someone to see it.

Shadow Light blinked, surprise on his scaled face, watching Owaen drop towards him with a sword longer than his teeth or claws. The black dragon had time to roar a challenge as Owaen descended, sword at the ready, and his blonde hair flying behind him. He landed with a thud on Shadow Light's snout and plunged his sword down.

Owaen's satisfaction at landing on his target was short-lived.

There was a jarring, metallic crack.

And his brother's prized sword broke in two.

The dragon and Owaen blinked at each other as the broken blade fell away. The shocked silence was broken by a ringing thud below, followed by a metallic echo.

Very slowly, Shadow Light's gaze rose from marking the blade's failed descent. Very, very slowly, the large yellow eyes focused inwards and came to rest on Owaen.

He was still straddling the dragon's snout like a horse. His boots were centimetres away from the wicked teeth. He was still holding the broken hilt in a sooty hand. Beneath the black filth that marred its surface, the beautiful ruby shone innocently. Feeling the hot breath of the dragon on his calves grow stronger, Owaen tore his incredulous gaze from the useless hilt. The yellow eyes in front of him narrowed.

And beneath Owaen's legs, he could *feel* the dragon smile.

"Oh fuck, Skye," Owaen hissed as Shadow's eyes, eyes as large as his head, brightened with dark delight and anticipation, "I'm sor-"

One of Shadow's forelegs, with its razor tipped claws, reared up from Owaen's left, clearly intending to swipe him down like a cat with a mouse. Owaen refused to shut his eyes. But the deadly claws never made it.

Something else moved, this time from his right. It was a blur, moving fast, dark and silent.

It was a man, his hair ink dark, eyes fully black.

Fox arrived in a noiseless rush of cold air, slamming with brutal force into the full sized black dragon.

But he didn't stop at making contact.

He kept going.

Into the dragon.

And the silence of Fox's arrival was shattered by the cataclysmic wreck of a violent impact and implosion. The noise reached Owaen before the realisation dawned on what had happened. There was a violent jerk beneath Owaen, a vicious ripping and seemingly endless wet gurgle followed by a loud, ear-splitting snap, followed by another snap, and then another louder than the first two combined. Yellow dragon eyes directly in front of Owaen's face widened in shock.

Then fury.

Then pain.

The sound of something large, alive and wet being torn apart was something Owaen would never forget. He let go of the useless hilt, throwing himself sideways off Shadow Light's scales. He landed amongst the lower, thicker branches of the tree behind him, lucky to not impale himself on the ripped open trunk.

The sounds in front of him kept going. They were grotesque, savage and infinitely satisfying.

Owaen hung onto a branch with both arms wrapped around it, while the dragon thrashed before him, a large, gaping, and bloody wound on his side. Shadow Light staggered back, the light in his wicked yellow eyes fading as Owaen watched, claws scrabbling at the cavernous hole in his torso. Scales hung in tattered ribbons and red, glistening meat was pierced with the splinters of long arched bones.

Ribs, Owaen realised, trying not to vomit. Fox had broken apart Shadow Light's ribs to get to his target within.

A muted roar of triumph came from inside the wound. It was followed by another jerk of the shocked dragon. A chunk of red meat, the size of a sheep, was hurled outwards with such violence from inside that it landed on the tree right below Owaen's boots. It didn't slip down. It became impaled on a snapped off branch. As Owaen stared at it, the wild pumping of the bloody, meaty mass stuttered and slowed. And stilled.

It was a dragon heart.

A very newly dead one.

But the dragon it came from was still, unbelievably, alive. But whatever grim power flooded his scaled veins was burning up, the bright yellow reptile eyes dimming.

Cold chills broke out over Owaen's trembling flesh at the sight of the heart impaled on the tree beneath him. It appeared presented to the chamber around them like a swollen, grisly offering, a bloody and hard-won prize. Its owner stumbled away, the crimson carnage of his chest gaping open for all to see.

Owaen couldn't help it. He vomited.

After he was done, he was vaguely aware of Shadow Light falling backwards. His fall was more of a slow topple, and the black dragon landed with a heavy thud, wings snapping as he came to rest. His limbs twitched amongst the broken trees and clouds of ash. The great black tail lashed and twitched as if on its own. The dragon was trying to speak, his brain and lungs not quite caught up to the fact there was no longer blood coming their way. His black snout was pointed to the sky, gasping at the leaning tower through the ruined roof above.

"You l-lying-"

There was a movement in the red pulp below, a figure emerging from the wound, covered in gore, slick with dragon blood.

But Owaen kept his eyes on the dying dragon's face. He simply could not look away; wanting to savour the moment he had hoped for, for so long. Even though it had not gone to any plan he could ever have imagined. This death wasn't by his hand and as sickening as it was, Owaen was desperate to savour it.

"You-" there came a choking gasp as the dragon arched his neck, eyes fixed on the tower, "you l-lying l-little shi-"

With a great shudder, the enormous black dragon went still.

Shadow Light was dead.

The sound of someone lazily clearing their throat and spitting broke the stillness.

As the ash danced through the beams of wan daylight that dissected the ruined chamber, Owaen held on to his branch and simply breathed. He gagged and tried to breathe through his mouth instead. The stink of dragon and the rich, metallic scent of blood were like an extra layer of filth coating his exposed flesh.

It was strange, Owaen thought as he tried not to be sick again. The sword in question, Caspian's sword, was now in two pieces in almost the same spot it had all begun.

Owaen glanced to his left, towards an area barely visible through the wreckage. It had been there, in the outside walkway, that encircled the round chamber. It was there that Lyyda had died. A servant in the City of the Seers, Lyyda had rushed to hand Owaen his sword. A sword that wasn't allowed to be in here due to ancient tradition, but the threat on that fateful day had been enough that an oath bound servant had rushed in to deliver it. That servant was the first innocent to die here, struck down by an Elven council member. In turn, events had been unleashed that had led them all down their respective chaotic paths.

Owaen swallowed, thinking of the dark-haired woman who had brought him what she shouldn't have, to a place she shouldn't have been.

I'm sorry Lyyda, that it took so long to avenge you too.

A wet cough, perhaps a quiet laugh, and someone spitting again came from below. Unable to hold it in, Owaen vomited against the tree once more.

Along with the smell of freshly dead dragon and the sound of what was likely Fox spitting out bits of the same creature, Owaen let his guts go with all the force of a man who had eaten a suspicious pie from a back street pub.

When he was done, he unclenched his hands from the branch very carefully. He was shaking less, his stomach was mostly emptied but his heart was still beating in leaps and bounds. He wiped his mouth, took a breath, and started the climb down. As he half-slid, half-climbed down, he was disgusted by the sensation of oily blood on the dead tree beneath his hands. He did not look at the heart.

Eventually, Owaen's boots touched the red mess on the council chamber floor. He kept one hand on the tree. Fox was upright, panting hard, covered head to boot in dark red blood. Glittering eyes blinked at him, filled with a fierce glint. Red stained teeth appeared.

Fox was smiling.

Closing his eyes to the sight, cursing his still sensitive stomach, Owaen breathed in and out carefully through his mouth. Thankfully, Fox gave him a moment.

"You..." Owaen mumbled, "you..." His voice drifted off. He wasn't sure what he wanted to say. Silence greeted him, and his eyes opened slowly.

It was hard to tell with the thick layer of shining red that covered him, but Fox was looking pleased with himself. He was staring at his hands. They were cupped, palms facing up. Taking a breath, Owaen let go of the tree and stepped forward, just one step, as if testing his balance. His heart rate was not quite back to normal; his head was still trying to come to terms with what his once sweet, laughing Skye had done. What she, as a man on a mission, had done was something that Owaen never wished to experience again in his life. Boots steadying beneath him, he took another step.

"So. That was," Owaen cleared his throat. "Uh, that was unexpected."

Fox glanced up. Owaen was careful to keep still under the force of the black and gold eyes fixated on him. Fox licked his lips and Owaen's stomach lurched. One red stained eyebrow rose.

"But necessary."

"Mm-hm," Owaen croaked, wary of the dark light still gleaming in Fox's eyes.

The pink tip of Fox's tongue appeared between his teeth. "I know I should have done that sooner." He glanced back down at his hands.

"This is not your fault, Skye."

Owaen watched a muscle twitch along Fox's bloody jaw.

"I let it go too far," Fox said, his voice a soft breath.

Owaen took another step, his boot making a squelching noise as something hard crunched under his heel. He tried to ignore it. "This is not your fault."

He was close enough now to see into Fox's cupped hands. They were covered in blood, but the dagger and two small pieces of crystal, their bloody chains hanging between Fox's fingers, were recognisable for their jagged shapes.

"I don't understand," Fox murmured. He glanced back up to Owaen, his mouth now a thin line. The mad light in his eyes was fading, much to Owaen's relief. "What were these to him? They're just another type of quartz that resonates well with magic."

"Perhaps we can address it another time?" Owaen reached out slowly and covered Fox's bloody hands with his own. Thick dragon blood was already congealing over the coolness of Fox's chilled flesh. "I think I need a wash."

Fox threw back his head and laughed, the lightness of the sound at odds with his macabre appearance. He met Owaen's scowl with a smirk.

"You do look like shit, my love," Fox murmured, a different gleam entering his gaze.

"Well," Owaen murmured. He swallowed. "I think you've never looked more beautiful."

Wide eyed, Fox stared at him, speechless.

"However, you need a bath," Owaen continued and released Fox's hands. As soon as he did, though, Owaen pulled Fox against his chest. Blood, guts and all.

With a gentle sigh, Fox leaned into him, clasping the shards of crystal between them with bloody hands. Owaen closed his eyes. It was a gesture to acknowledge his elated relief, yes, but also to avoid the chunks of crimson coloured gore stuck in Fox's hair. Owaen cleared his throat and told his stomach to calm the fuck down.

"Thank you," Fox breathed against him.

"You're welcome." Owaen sighed, his eyes opening. He avoided looking at the red and black mess behind Fox. "Thank you, too."

"You're welcome," Fox said quietly.

"Can you," Owaen said, but hesitated. He chose his next words with care. "Can you move on from this, do you think?"

Fox pulled away a fraction to stare at Owaen, his gaze calculating. Owaen slid his hands up Fox's arms, over his ruined, bloody clothes, to reach up and tug on his sticky strands of wild hair.

"Skye?" Owaen urged. He shifted his boots away from the red puddle expanding in their direction.

"I'm going to try," Fox said eventually.

"Good." Owaen nodded. "Good. That's all I ask. I'm glad to hear it." He tipped his chin at the violently ripped apart corpse. "Care to do the honours?"

"It would be my pleasure."

Fox continued to stare at Owaen, his breathing hitching only once and the gold in his eyes darkening a fraction. Behind them, with a dull *whump*, the dragon started to smoke, then burn. As black coils of stinking smoke rose towards the ruined roof, it quickly got uncomfortably hot where they were standing.

Fox smiled, a gentle curve of his lips. His gaze dropped to Owaen's mouth. With a regretful sigh, Owaen shook his head.

"No," he said very clearly.

Fox's eyebrows shot up, some of the blood on his face cracking as it dried.

"You are covered in pieces of someone that was breathing a mere moment ago, and I have just vomited," Owaen snapped. He released Fox and stepped away, his hands up before him. "Nope. *Nope.*" His stomach heaved. "If I don't get out of here, I'm going to do it again."

A smirk appeared under the sticky red mess on Fox's face. He shrugged as his fingers curled around the bloody items in his hands.

"Besides, we need to go help Aurelia and Rhydian," Owaen mumbled, wiping his face with a grimace. He looked around for the broken pieces of his brother's sword. "And-"

"They're fine," Fox interrupted, his gaze still on Owaen's mouth. "Aurelia is recovering. Rhydian was fine. He'll find us if he needs. I liked your suggestion. I *really* want a bath. Now."

Owaen sighed deeply. He nodded, knowing there was no use. Fox bit his blood stained lower lip, his gaze calculating. The shining black of his eyes appeared deep, endless. With a slow smile, Fox stepped closer.

"Carry me?"

The daylight faded as fast as the light of satisfaction brightened in Fox's eyes.

Owaen was indeed carrying him, bridal style, towards a series of waterways that Owaen prayed were still there. Their need for a wash was dire. But Fox had refused to set one bloody boot into the old compound that had housed the dragons on their visits to the city.

As Owaen steadfastly ignored the metallic sweet smell of dragon blood that was now almost all over him as badly as Fox, Owaen had time to think. He didn't want to. He wanted to stare into the black and gold eyes that didn't leave his face once as Owaen walked them deeper into the silent city.

"Your body," Owaen began. "Your bones-"

Fox reached up to run a cool finger along Owaen's jaw.

"It hurt. I'm better," he said it as a matter of fact. "Earlier, I panicked when I heard Aurelia shout. I was more careful when I came to find you. Keep walking."

"Skye-"

"Keep walking."

"What?" Owaen spluttered. "What do you think I'm doing-"

Fox slid his hand over Owaen's mouth, fingers pressing his lips together to silence him. Owaen quickly shook his head at the bloody hand so close to his nose and mumbled *nope*. Smugly, Fox dragged his hand away, down Owaen's chest.

"Its just a little bit of blood," Fox murmured and poked Owaen once hard over his heart. "Aurelia deals with it every time the moon rises. Don't be scared, lover."

Not touching that comment at all, Owaen kept walking. The sky above was almost black, the Skye in his arms aglow with mischief and wonder. Owaen arranged his thoughts once more and tried again; hoping the man in his arms would stop interrupting.

"I didn't know you could move like that."

Fox gave Owaen's face a lazy look of appraisal before he tipped his head back, eyes closed. But he made no comment.

"You were desperate, not concentrating, and your magic led the way," Owaen continued. "You are an amazing creature, my love. "

Fox nodded, eyes still closed. He sighed dramatically.

"I am, aren't I?"

They had come to the courtyard Owaen had prayed was still intact. It was, sort of. The yard was barely a tenth of the size of the great courtyard in the heart of the city, enclosed by four walls. It had only two arched openings in the crumbling stone for access. There was a circular pool in the centre, only a metre or so deep and about four metres across. Thankfully, it was almost full of water. Four shallow channels of running water flowed in under the four walls through prettily carved stone grates. The channels were fed from an underground river and the canals seemed to be working from the way the water bubbled into the pool. The water circulated in the pool and was fed out in overflow grates around the pool. Owaen hoped wherever the water overflowed to wasn't going to be adversely affected by the gore that was about to flow that way.

Overhead, the golden sky was mostly clear and a few stars had appeared in the dusk. A faint mist of ash and smoke hung in the air. There was also the faint musky aroma of heirloom roses somewhere. After a quick search with his Elven eyesight, Owaen easily spotted the last bloom. It was struggling to stay open despite the frost that was slowly reclaiming the quiet yard. He had a fleeting thought to pick the single pink bloom for Fox, but he dismissed it. Even if Fox let Owaen put it behind his ear, the last blooming rose in this lonely place had surely earned its place amongst the dying buds around it.

Owaen paused at the archway. Fox opened his eyes.

"Wash me," he said.

"Ha. Tell me something first," Owaen began and squatted low until Fox's boots made contact with the cracked stone. Owaen was strong, but it still cost him a loud grunt. Fox was a grown man in this form, after all. Owaen didn't understand magic, power or how energy worked, or how a dragon was contained in there somehow. He didn't need to.

"Owaen," Fox sighed, pulling off a boot with one hand, the other on Owaen's chest for support. "Right now?"

"Just tell me," Owaen said, his hand clasping Fox's over his heart. "Why keep Shadow so gods be damned close all this time? I still don't get it. Please. Help me understand."

Fox was silent as he pulled off his other boot. He gathered them up and threw them into the closest of the four channels of clear water. They landed with a gentle splash. Fox turned back to him, and Owaen watched him think carefully about what he was going to say. They were not quite the same height, but Fox was tall enough to Owaen that Owaen could see clearly as Fox licked his lips again. Owaen rolled his eyes in disgust.

"If you needed a reminder of what not to be," Fox murmured, smirking at Owaen's expression, "where else would you keep your demons, except right by your side?" Fox reached into his soiled pants and carefully set the dagger and two pendants on the ground. They would need a rinse as well.

Bracing himself, Owaen stepped forward and rested his hands on Fox's shoulders, his forehead pressing into the cool flesh of Fox's brow.

"You don't need to do that anymore."

"Mm."

"No more shadows. All you need to do is to be *you*. In doing that, you cast light."

"Owaen."

"Yes?"

"You say some wonderful things."

"Thank you."

"But I want you to shut the fuck up now."

Throwing back his head, Owaen laughed and quickly scooped Fox up over his shoulder. He was delighted at the startled, very un-dragon-like squeak it earned him. Owaen stepped quickly to the pool while Fox struggled and hopped carefully over the low wall. He sank them both down into the water. Both his laugh and Fox's sound of protest were cut off quickly at the bracing cold. He was careful to sit down first, landing heavily, sliding Fox down into his lap.

Owaen's bruised arse was worth it though, and he quickly scooped up the now waist high water to fling it at Fox's sticky, red face. Fox spluttered in front of him, flinging damp hair from his face with hands that were mostly clean of blood and remnants of dragon flesh. His glittering eyes were wide and glossy in the dim light of the cool evening, glaring at Owaen. Except they also contained something that Owaen hoped echoed the joy that was bubbling deep within himself.

Owaen winked, and before Fox could speak, he pushed Fox backwards, dunking him under the surface.

Fox emerged a moment later, coughing, yet laughing like Owaen had never heard before. The sound caught in his chest and expanded to fill his heart with a golden light. Owaen had a wild romantic thought that the sound might cause the dead roses around them to bloom again. He didn't look to check; he was busy avoiding the reprise attack launched at him, as Fox pushed him under in turn. The sounds of their combined laughter was likely loud enough to echo through the otherwise silent city to be heard by Rhydian, and Aurelia if she was awake too, but Owaen didn't care. They had earned this.

Eventually, their playful wrestling turned to something else, and before long, Owaen sat back in the pool. His uneasy stomach had settled down as the red tinge to the water cleared. There was a mess of discarded items on the ground behind the wall, weapons belts, the sad hilt of the broken sword and their clothes, all needing a deeper wash, but they were forgotten for now. The thought of their clothes discarded together made Owaen happy in a way that was simple and yet meant so much.

Even when Owaen had cupped the crystal clear water in his hands, to let it run over Fox's back, his tattoo the same riot of deadly shapes and colours, Owaen had wondered at the feeling of peace descending upon him. There were more layers to Fox's story yet to be told. As the red rivulets ran down Fox's lithe yet strong form, Owaen called on the gods to enable Owaen to be there to help wash away the rest of Fox's rage as well.

Gods, please grant me the abilities I need to aid in the healing that this beautiful creature so desperately deserves.

Please.

There would always be a stain. But perhaps it would fade to something softer, not hot, charged and bloody.

Kneeling in the water behind Fox, Owaen had traced the lines of the heart wrenching design across Fox's shoulders with a trembling thumb.

"Tell me?" Owaen whispered.

"No," Fox murmured, head bowed, chin lowered to rest on his chest.

"You will, though?"

Fox exhaled, his breath a quiet sigh. "One day." Fox raised his head, turning to meet Owaen's gaze. "Kiss me."

So he did.

Their lips met in a lazy caress, slow and heated, without urgency but full of promise. Fox had sat up and wrapped his arms around Owaen, his cool fingers twining into the slick strands of Owaen's hair.

And now, Owaen was seated in the water with Fox in his lap, cool fingers tracing Owaen's face, light and reverent while the water barely rippled around them. Only the occasional shift of Owaen's legs, spread out before him, sent the glossy surface of the pool rippling into shattered lights, reflections of the cold, white stars above. Owaen rested his head back against the stone, eyes closed, a faint smile on his lips.

"What?" Fox asked, blinking water out of his long, dark lashes. His skin was back to its normal pale sheen, the last of the gore washed away.

Instead of answering, Owaen reached out, brushing the wet ends of Fox's black hair away from his cool cheeks, first one and then the other. Fox turned his head lazily to kiss each of Owaen's palms.

It was fully dark now, and Owaen didn't want to speak. He didn't want to break the silent spell that enclosed them here. It was a quiet refuge after so much blood, rage, and chaos. Dropping his hands from Fox's cheeks, Owaen sat back and rested his head against the polished stone of the curved wall, letting the cool water lap against him. Even after years of no caretaker, the stone here was smooth and not as uncomfortable against his back as he might have expected. The heavy weight in his lap likely helped his feeling of contentment. Cool lips brushed Owaen's.

"It's easy," Owaen murmured, "when it's just you and me."

"It's hard," Fox teased against his mouth.

"I hope so," Owaen said dryly.

"No." Fox paused. "I mean well, *yes*. But..."

Eyes still closed, Owaen lost his senses for a moment at the feel of Fox pressing against him. "But?"

Cool hands reached for Owaen's face, and he opened his eyes. Fox was right there, his glittering gaze looking back and forth between Owaen's eyes.

"Letting you in is hard," Fox murmured, eyes wide and serious.

Owaen caught himself, making sure his brain knew which name Fox needed to hear, right here and right now. It *was* hard.

"Fox."

"Owaen."

"It's a choice that you've already made."

"What do you mean?"

Owaen reached up to cup Fox's hands. He kissed their twined fingers next to his cheeks with tender, chaste presses of his damp lips.

"You're here, you're doing it."

"What?"

"By being here," Owaen shifted underneath Fox and Fox's eyelids fluttered. "Right here, you're letting me in. We have plenty of time to see just how far."

Fox pulled back so he could stare down at where their bodies were straining against each other.

"Okay," was the whispered response.

"Besides," Owaen said lightly, "maybe for now, right now," he shifted again, "it will be me letting you in, instead, hm?"

There were some adjustments to make, and some preparation required, but in the end, the wait was worth it. The water rippled, and the courtyard filled with the sound of their intimacy, the gentle sighs of two strange creatures coming together. Both their bodies were hard and heavy, and fit together as they should in every way possible. As the cool air caressed their exposed, flushed skin, both of them breathed in such a way that it was almost laughter. Until Fox paused above Owaen, his eyes wild. Sensing a moment of seriousness, Owaen hid his groan of frustration.

"I'm sorry you ever got caught up in dragonish greed," Fox panted, serious again.

Silently, Owaen gathered him to his heaving chest, biting back the pleasure of his release and held on to the man who was close to tears above him.

"I can feel your heart beating for me," Fox said, cool, swollen lips moving over Owaen's neck. "The best heart I have ever known, the one I locked away-"

"Hush, lover. It's okay. I'm okay, you're okay."

"Was I as bad as *him*? To try to keep a pure heart *untainted*?"

On his back, half shoved against the stone wall of the pool, Owaen tugged on Fox's hair until they were eye to eye, the water rippling around their waists.

"Don't," Owaen murmured, landing a lazy kiss on Fox's wet mouth. "Don't think of that."

"But-" Fox said, breathless, as Owaen moved his lips to Fox's ear. "I am sorry, I am, I really-"

Impatient, ready, Owaen slid his hands to Fox's hips and moved him for them both. Their combined gasps pleased Owaen, and he was sure there were stars behind his eyelids as well as in the dark honeyed glow far above them.

"I dreamt of you, I dreamt of this," Owaen sighed, staring at the dark golden sky, Fox's outline lighter somehow than the stars above them in the blackness, shifting in bright sparks on the surface of the water.

"This?" Fox snickered, gesturing between them. "*Exactly* this?"

He moved of his own accord this time. Owaen gasped louder than the wild laugh above him, hands white knuckled on Fox's hips.

"No," Owaen smiled. "Or yes? Oh, *yes*... It really doesn't matter. *Oh*."

As the quiet sounds of the night stirred around them, the occasional flap of bat wings overhead and the lonely call of an owl, the time passed. Thankfully, the air was now only faintly tainted by smoke, ash and burning dragon flesh. Fox tangled his limbs tighter around Owaen, and Owaen closed his eyes, breathing the salt and wild scent of cool skin against his open mouth, sounds of pleasure escaped him unhindered. He was faintly aware of the tremors again; the stone vibrating with a gentle pulse in time with the one he loved above him. Their relieved cries of mutual pleasure filled them up, the soft sounds like the scattered dust rising for a moment, before settling once more.

Afterwards, the night was dark, and the pair of them were still, content.

Fox was still wrapped around Owaen, and Owaen was tracing the lines of Fox's face, the usual hard lines softened by his pleasure. Owaen was grateful that they were here by themselves. In their troubled past, their moments alone together had been rare. When they had first come together, there had only been stolen moments as their peers, conceited Elves and suspicious dragons, had watched them closely.

Owaen had been a type of outcast already, more in touch with the everyday person than the lofty Elves with their high opinion of themselves. The dragons had watched over their jewel, Skye, in the guise of a young, and slightly rebellious, Elven woman. She had tried so hard to break away from the dragons that she had arrived at the City of the Seers in a different form. Owaen knew that Skye felt that this was required so she could finally come to her own conclusions, on what power meant, and what responsibility meant as well. What *connection* had meant.

"Your heat consumes me. It melts the skin off my bones," Fox mumbled, breathless. "Your eyes are full of a green fire that *burns*."

"Only for you, my love."

They had met, and their attraction had been instant. Fox nuzzled Owaen's collarbone with cool lips, and Owaen traced the line of Fox's neck with warm fingertips. Owaen remembered Skye had once admitted there had been some kind of predestination about it all. Perhaps that was true. But Owaen honestly didn't care for destiny. They had met. Things had certainly gone wrong, *very* wrong, and things had happened that he wished had not, for both of them. But they had found each other. And after a not so accidental separation, they were together once more. As the tremors faded from the earth below, Owaen kissed the top of Fox's damp head. His grin was a combination of wonder and smugness.

"So. The earth really moved for you, huh?"

Owaen could practically feel Fox roll his eyes against Owaen's sweat slicked chest. In answer, Fox sat up, pulling away. He wiped his damp, black hair out of his face with an arrogant movement that had Owaen stirring beneath him again.

"What do you mean?" Fox asked with a slight frown. "The tremors?"

"You don't know, do you?" Owaen asked gently.

"Know what?"

Owaen pursed his lips. Perhaps now wasn't the time. He shrugged and glanced down, eyebrows raised suggestively. He sat back and crossed his arms behind his head. Fox's golden black eyes glittered like the radiant, star covered sky above.

"Hello again, my love," Fox said, smiling.

55

Fox

Year 367

The City of the Seers

Fox winced as Rhydian coughed again.

"It's not your turn to die, kingling," Fox joked.

"Too soon, Fox," Rhydian said after another cough, "too soon." The young king stared at him, eyes narrowed in accusation. "In any case, it's *your* earlier bonfire of scales that's clogging my lungs."

Settling back onto a block of stone, Fox shrugged, feeling smug. What could he say to that? Who knew that the carcass of a dragon stunk of awful things as it smouldered?

Oh, that's right, Fox mused silently, *I do.*

He inhaled deeply and loudly. Rhydian pointedly ignored the obnoxious gesture.

They were camped in an overgrown garden off of the main courtyard. The garden was another unkempt space that was next to the dragon compound where Fox refused to enter. But the water feature here, another shallow pool, was untainted by any stray chunks of gore. Fox was still slightly damp, and more than satisfied. Owaen was off poking around and Rhydian was sitting beside Fox. Aurelia was still asleep in the king's arms. The pair of them hadn't yet made it for a wash, and they certainly needed it. But Rhydian was adamant that Aurelia could sleep as long as she needed before Rhydian helped her with her needs. Aurelia was dirty, her hair a mess, and there were dark circles under her eyes.

She was out like a torch shoved into a bucket of cold water. But despite her exhaustion, there was a weary calm on Aurelia's face. Her forehead was smooth and her breathing even.

Fox understood. The right pair of arms was a potent healing balm for the heart than the greatest medicine or magic.

It must have been the middle of the night, but none of them besides Aurelia were ready for sleep. Certainly Fox was far too wide-awake to give in to unconsciousness just yet. Despite the limp, sated wonder of his flesh, his mind was spinning slowly with all sorts of memories, ideas, and sensations. Most of them were linked to the occasional scent of ash and smoke that blew his way as the cool night breeze changed around them.

The bitter tang of the air sent Fox's thoughts back to Mionlach, where he had caused so much devastation that the remnants of his rage still rained down to this day. Fox was adamant that Owaen wasn't ready to hear what had happened. It wasn't just about Shadow Light and the dragon's betraying their care of their young queen. It was about family, about the origins of magic and how ruthless you needed to be in order to wield it, hold it and live with yourself afterwards. Owaen would likely never forgive himself once he knew the full story. After Owaen's brave if ridiculous plummet from a dead tree onto a violent dragon, Fox had promised himself Owaen would never need to know.

Fox was keenly aware that he was selfish enough to hold those revelations within him in a kind of penance. Which he would gladly bear for them both. Especially after all the chaos Fox's actions, or lack of earlier action relating to Shadow Light, had caused. Idly, his hand brushed over the crystal dagger and the two pendants.

The dagger was a wicked-looking shard of crystal, and the strange sheared off tip could be lined up to fit the two smaller crystal pendants. It was a dagger that had been used to disrupt a curse, with some success. And then it had been used to kill a prince with less. Along with that, the two pendants had been charged with some tiny spark of magic to enable Aurelia and Rhydian's mother to communicate over long distances. Fox frowned, biting his bottom lip and tasting the minerals on his skin from the abandoned pool. He was worried that he couldn't understand why Shadow had been keen to take them for himself. One of his fingertips traced one of the golden chains with a languid caress. He was hoping to sense something. Anything. All he could feel were objects that felt neither cool nor warm, with no spark of anything at all.

Sighing, Fox rested his head back on the block of stone they were settled against, a warm fire crackling away near his feet. Surely there was time enough to wonder about the mysteries yet to be solved? He stared up at the dark shape of the tallest tower that loomed above the main courtyard back in the centre of the city. He shook his head. For now, he had his friends here. And Owaen. Whatever label they would put upon each other, it would never be fully correct.

Maybe 'friend' would do?

Fox's snort had Rhydian raise an eyebrow at him. Fox brushed it off with a causal wave of a pale hand. Owaen would never accept that title. Fox smirked at the night sky, full of twinkling stars that he both loved and abhorred. The lofty points of light were cold, distant, and admired for how they looked, not for how they acted, how they felt, or how they viewed the world below.

His gaze roamed around, taking in the derelict walls of pale polished stone. The top of the vast forest that surrounded the city was visible. Even with the meadows of strange wildflowers that bloomed amongst the grass, the canopy was a dark line that attracted the eye wherever you could see over the buildings and the crumbling wall beyond. He'd hated that their journey to find Aurelia had led them here, and he'd hated that Owaen had had to see this place the way it was now. Not like the thriving city that Owaen had loved and been so proud of, like his family's cabin, a little southeast of the city. Fox shifted uncomfortably and bit his lip. It was likely Owaen would like to see it.

Could Fox really hold back with what Owaen likely deserved to know? Fox had ripped out the heart of his tormenter, a delicious experience that he'd held off for so long that the actual doing of it seemed unreal. But Fox hadn't done it just for himself. He'd done it for the innocent Elves, including Elven children, funnelled into that gods forsaken cave, for the sake of magic and power. He'd done it for Owaen.

Magic.

Fox's top lip curled.

Why the fuck was it so important to everyone?

Wasn't love infinitely better?

Fox smoothed his face into his normal mask of cool. It was a familiar way of existing. But one that Owaen's love would likely melt for him. Fox's offer of a dragon heart at Owaen's feet was more than just a symbol of Fox's revenge. It was an offer of love too, brutal as it was. Fox had no issue with it. He'd torn out Shadow Light's heart, gifting it to Owaen, the absolute opposite of Fox's enemy in every way. Owaen was an arrogant Elf, but he was also a champion of the innocent, and he was obstinately adamant he was going to love Fox in whatever form Fox chose to appear.

Am I Skye?

Am I Fox?

Who did he want to be?

Fox stared blankly out at the world around him, not seeing it. What he saw was a small fox in the woods across a bubbling creek, a dead rabbit hanging from its little jaws. It was likely taking the carcass home to its mate, and Fox didn't need to think too hard about who he'd rather be.

Unable to help another sigh slip from his lips, still slightly swollen thanks to Owaen's scorching attention, Fox rubbed the back of his neck. His fingers brushed over the very tip of the ink that marked his skin. But if he was Fox, who was that now, exactly? Without his shadow by his side? A daily reminder of what not to become? Was he right to feel empty? What would fill the hollows inside him where bitter, raging flames had burned amongst the ever-present cold?

As if sensing the direction his thoughts were descending to, Rhydian stirred beside him, his shoulder bumping Fox's slightly in companionable proximity. Aurelia, facing away from Fox, didn't stir, her deep breathing slow and even. The king's voice was soft.

"You're thinking so loud that you're going to wake Aurelia."

Fox snorted again, staring at the weak flames licking across the chunks of dead vines. His feet were bare. Rhydian was still wearing his boots, the worn leather toughened by his trials and covered in mud and soot. Fox poked Rhydian's boot with his big toe.

"Ha."

"You seem quite calm," Rhydian murmured. He cleared his throat, a teasing gleam in his eyes. "Do you think the sun is finally coming out of your shadows?"

"Shut up."

"Well-"

"No, kingling. That's too sappy, even for you." Fox shivered in mock disgust, his voice teasing. "Leave the mush for Owaen. Ugh."

Rhydian laughed in the dark beside him quietly. "You're still mean."

"I still don't care."

"But-"

"Hush."

Rhydian huffed beside him. Taking the sting out of his words, Fox reached an arm up and over Rhydian's head, resting it along his shoulders to pull the young king close, all the while trying not to unsettle Aurelia. Fox pressed a kiss to Rhydian's cheek as he reached across to stroke Aurelia's hair, once, before his long fingers caught on something.

"You might be right, though," Fox murmured eventually, picking out twigs and a piece of stone from Aurelia's gnarled, dark strands. "But don't tell anyone."

A throat cleared from the gloom in the corner of the quiet little garden.

Rhydian jumped. Fox smirked, knowing full well Owaen had returned.

"What did he say to you?" Owaen murmured to Rhydian as he headed over.

Fox scoffed at him.

Owaen stepped into the low, orange glow of their fire and dropped some more dried out branches to their pile of fuel. They were from the multitude of vines that were reclaiming the city. Like Fox, Owaen was still damp. His cheeks flushed, his brows relaxed under his semi dried hair. The blonde strands normally dried straight, but as Fox's hands had been threaded through them for a very, very long time, they were drying in bizarre shapes from the side of his head. Fox hadn't mentioned it. He liked Owaen looking scruffy. He'd never admit it, though.

"Just tell Fox to behave," Owaen continued, the dark green of his eyes hooded in the night but clearly full of mischief. "He likes that."

While Fox spluttered, Rhydian snorted, attempting to muffle the sound in his arms. Aurelia sighed and nestled further into Rhydian's embrace. Instead of returning to sleep, her breathing turned into a jaw-cracking yawn. There was some manoeuvring, but she turned herself in Rhydian's arms, still on his lap, her knees now against Fox's thighs. Owaen sat down on Fox's other side, hands busy, full of their weapons belts and a rag torn from somewhere. It looked like he was going to give them a wipe down. Wishing him luck with that, Fox turned his attention back to Aurelia.

Dull green eyes blinked at Fox slowly. Unsure of his reception, Fox reached over to grab one of her hands. He kissed her fingertips carefully.

"Hello," he murmured.

"Hello," she answered, her voice thick with sleep. "My head... ugh. My ears are ringing. Can I keep sleeping?"

"Mm. As long as you want," Fox replied, folding her hand back to her chest.

Something in his face must have given his apprehension away.

"This wasn't your fault," Aurelia whispered, wincing. Fox fought the urge to look away.

"You don't know the entire story. It was." A muscle tensed in his jaw and he worked to relax. "All of it. Shadow Light, even Chase. I'm sorry. None of this should have happened. I.. I got ahead of myself and lost in what happened to me, none of which had anything to do with you. If I had been any less selfish, perhaps the queen would never have…" Fox ran out of things to say, the direction of his thoughts lost under Aurelia's calm gaze.

"This wasn't your fault," Aurelia repeated, her voice hoarse. Rhydian handed her a dented flask to sip from.

"Aurelia-"

"Fox. Be quiet." She had another sip before handing the flask back. Grimacing, she shifted, clearly in some pain. "Rhydian told me enough, about Jessikah, about Chase as well, for me to know it wasn't your fault."

"What? He did?" Fox withdrew his arm from Rhydian's shoulder and sat up. "When?"

Rhydian cleared his throat, his cheeks slightly pink. "When you were… um."

"Bathing?" Owaen said, smugly. Fox refused to look around. The satisfied smirk in the blonde Elf's voice was clear enough. With his arms around Aurelia, Rhydian fumbled with the flask as he popped the cork in, before dropping it behind her.

"Sure," Aurelia said with a tired smile. Despite their dull sheen, her eyes took on the same gleam as Rhydian's earlier. "When you two were *bathing*."

Fox relaxed back into a slouch, arms crossed over his chest. The fire crackling beyond his feet suddenly became very interesting. There were a couple more sniggers from Aurelia until the silence fell thick and cool again. Fox had never felt any shame for any part of himself or his interests. But it was slightly disconcerting having the only three people he had ever kissed here all together, and all thinking about the fact he may have been too vocal not long before.

After a moment, he shrugged. He didn't care. It was amusing. Sort of. He dropped his hands to his lap while Aurelia yawned and nudged Fox with her knee.

"I meant it, though. And I heard what Rhydian said. The nickname Shadow Man won't suit you anymore." She coughed. "I understand now why you hated it so much."

Fox refused to look at her. "Do you," he snapped grouchily.

"Yes." Ignoring his tone, she yawned yet again, her voice thick with sleep. "I guess we need a new one."

Fox could see Rhydian tugging her hair in warning, but Aurelia's lips curved into a sly smile as her eyes closed. Her voice was faint.

"How about-"

"Aurelia," Fox hissed. "Stop it right now."

"-Sunshine Man?"

Fox's eyes widened in horror while next to him Rhydian buried his face in Aurelia's hair, attempting to hide his laugh.

"Hmm, no?" Aurelia's voice was barely a whisper. "Rainbow Dragon?"

Dropping his face into his hands, Fox groaned. Owaen was laughing openly.

"I like her," Owaen said when he could speak. "She's funny."

"I hate you all," Fox snapped, pulling the remains of his tattered, damp cloak around his shoulders.

Beside him, Aurelia attempted to laugh, but she ended up wheezing instead. Fox was quick to get on his knees, huff forgotten, his cool hand on her forehead as her eyelids fluttered while she tried to settle. He wasn't able to do more than send some coolness into the cells that waged a low fever in her blood, but it seemed to be enough. Her eyes closed and her face relaxed. He steadfastly ignored the gentle tremor beneath them in the stones of the city while he worked. When he was done, Aurelia was out like an extinguished flame once more. Fox sat back down, this time to be welcomed by Owaen's open arms.

"You need to rest too," Owaen said against Fox's hair. "And tomorrow we can talk about *that*."

"About what?" Fox mumbled as he burrowed into the peace that wrapped around him in the form of two strong, warm, and steady arms.

"The fact that every time you use your power, the earth gets a hard on."

Fox's eyes snapped open. He couldn't think of a single thing to say.

"Huh." Rhydian's voice was thoughtful and amused. "You're right."

"We'll travel to my parents' cabin," Owaen went on. Fox stilled against him.

"They had some interesting notes on geology, crystals and magic that I never quite got my head around. This would be a good reason to try to make sense of them."

Fox reached up to pat Owaen's neck.

"Later," Fox said, keeping his voice even. "Back to Aneirin first."

After that, it was quiet.

Three of them slept deeply while the fourth watched the flames burn until the flames were gone and the fire a tumbled pile of dying embers. Fox watched until the embers fell to ash, the only warmth left in the arms wrapped firmly around him.

With eyes glittering under the midnight sky, Fox wondered how steady those same arms would stay. Once Owaen realised that his parents weren't the great Elves he thought they'd been.

56

Aurelia

Year 367

The City of the Seers

Aurelia and her best friend Bindy had been teenagers when they had first discovered glow wort. It was a mildly intoxicating and often hallucinogenic fungus. Purple spores could be harvested and made into a paste with honey or butter, to be consumed in small chunks that left you giggling, seeing colours and hearing words. Sometimes the effects wore off with no adverse hangover. Other times your head felt like it was on inside out, backwards and upside down.

Like how her head felt now.

When she woke to the grey dawn, the light speared her eyes and soft, frozen flakes of snow irritated her face.

"Shit," she mumbled, her voice sounding weird in her head. Her ears were still ringing and sounds were muffled. The arms around her shifted.

"Aurelia?"

"No."

"No?"

"Just... no. Ow."

Fox's dry laugh irritated her ears as much as the cool snowflakes made her skin itch as they melted. Cool lips pressed against her forehead and part of the weird hangover faded.

But not all. She tried to sit up but cried out at the pull of tender, swollen flesh behind her shoulder. The arms around her shoulders tightened, settling her cloak closer to her clammy skin.

"Please don't move yet," Fox murmured. Further coolness spread through her face and body, the pain fading to a dull throb. He pulled away. "Better?"

"Maybe. I don't know." She yawned and tried to focus her gaze. "Everything hurts. It's hard to think."

They were camped in what looked like had once been a lovely courtyard garden. It was large enough to hold twenty horses with ease. There were shrubs dried to husks in various designs amongst the low walls. She could see the carved and polished pale stone beneath the twisted wood and patches of pale green moss. The scent of flowers was on the cool morning breeze and the day was still. The low clouds above reminded her of Lolihud. The thought had her heart squeeze in her chest.

Did the Elves of the caves, those left behind and not able to march into Aneirin, did they know yet all that had happened? What of the Elves already in Aneirin? Were they overcoming the lies they had been fed in order to heal alongside the humans, in spite of... well, *everything*?

She released a long, slow breath, meeting the eyes of the tall blonde Elf across the cheerfully crackling fire. His deep green eyes crackled with a faint sheen that only magic could endow.

"Good morning, sweetheart," the stranger said with a warm smile.

"Good morning."

"That's Owaen," Fox murmured. "He's mine."

"Okay then." Aurelia cleared her throat. She appraised the brightness of his emerald gaze. "You're an Elf?"

He nodded. "I'm Fox's Elf."

Fox's laugh was a gentle hum against her side. Green eyes crinkled at the corners as Owaen winked. Aurelia shook her head, trying not to be too obvious with her wince at the movement. Sensing her discomfort somehow, Fox pulled away. Black and gold eyes glittered close to hers, cool and appraising. Pressing her face to his chest, she smiled, the golden topaz pendant on his chain pressing against her cheek. She hardly saw it, but he was wearing it over his ruined shirt. Drawing back a little way, Aurelia patted his cheek while he brushed long strands of hair from her face in return.

"I'll be fine," she said.

"I'm glad." Fox pulled her back with a hand on the back of her head.

"But I need to get up and pee."

Fox pulled away and looked down at her, one eyebrow raised.

"I'm glad to hear that as well," he said. "After checking on the horses that are hobbled in some meadow or another, Rhydian is likely taking care of his own needs. But I am sure *he* will be more than happy to help you with that when he returns."

Aurelia narrowed her eyes at him. "Hm."

They were quiet for a moment and Owaen looked away, a small smile still playing across his handsome face. The Elf was idly rotating the hilt of a sword in his hands. The gold hilt was beautifully worked, but she was sad to see that its blade was broken clean off a few centimetres past the cross guard. Aurelia watched the metal flashing in the grey light as it turned. As a flash of light caught her sore eyes, she turned into Fox's chest, realising he was wearing what had once been a white shirt. She'd never seen him in anything but black before. Her new nickname for him came back to her in a rush, and she bit her lip to stop a mad laugh escape from her dry lips.

"Fox."

"Aurelia."

"You're a dragon."

"Yup."

Her mind was still sluggish, and Aurelia digested this information slowly. While mulling it over, boot steps approached. Rhydian appeared at one of the archways across the paved yard.

"He's also been a woman!" Rhydian called cheerfully as he headed over. He had a single blue flower in his hand. He looked... adorable. His voice was too loud for her tender ears. But Aurelia was more fixated on what he'd said.

What?

Owaen looked up at her gasp, nodded once, before dropping his gaze to his hands, fiddling with the broken hilt. Snow continued to fall, the white flakes becoming lost in the pale strands of his hair. Something tugged at her sluggish mind, but in the light of what she had just learned, it fell away. Aurelia pulled the purple cloak up to her chin, grateful for its lush warmth, but also its coverage. Her cheeks may have turned pink. She certainly had things to discuss with Fox, like being fucking *spied* on, but this? She needed longer to process it.

If Fox, or Skye, had ever been a woman, that certainly explained *some* things.

But not others.

For some reason, that made her grin through the throbbing pain in her head.

"Do you remember, Fox? I always wanted my own dragon."

"Yes." Fox paused, eyes twinkling. "You certainly had this one."

Aurelia's wide eyes met his, and for a moment, there was silence. It was soon broken. Both of them burst into fits of uncontrolled laughter at the same time. Aurelia's gasping chortle was weaker than Fox's, but the hilarity was clearly shared. Rhydian looked back and forth between them for a moment, eyes narrowed. Eventually, he shook his head and sat down, the flower still in his hand. Owaen was frowning, his mouth a thin line. He opened his mouth to speak, thought better of it, and shook his head.

"Wait," Fox gasped, snorting as he tried to speak. "Get up."

"What?" Rhydian looked up from examining his travel-stained cloak.

He was frowning at one of the torn and frayed corners with confusion.

Aurelia pushed the cloak away and held out weak arms. "My turn to pee."

Rhydian jumped up immediately to assist her, the flower thrown at Fox.

Fox laughed again.

How much longer could she sleep? Aurelia was fully prepared to find out.

Back against Rhydian's chest, Aurelia woke again, the throbbing in her head marginally less, the ringing in her ears almost gone. She could have kept sleeping, and she knew she needed to. But after catching some of her foul tasting hair in her mouth, her priorities changed. She absentmindedly rubbed the callouses on her fingers together, wishing for her favourite soap that not only smelt wonderful, helped soothe her irritated skin after weapons practice.

Lolihud crossed her mind again. Simple things, like archery practice. Growing up in the caves with parents who treated her fondly when they weren't off mining rare crystals, for dragons who no longer came. So much would need to change. So much had already changed.

After setting out on a mission to save her people, she had met a prince who had somehow saved her in turn. There was so much she didn't know about him, and yet he had met her at each new challenge with a calm innocence that was like nothing she had ever known. Was the peace she felt to be with him really love? Or was it a mutual understanding, with their histories full of lies and layers of betrayal, of the people who looked to their leaders for protection and the truth? Power seemed to attract greed, or was it the other way around? Rhydian certainly balked at the mention of his being a king, and hadn't really seemed that excited when Aurelia remembered Fox saying that Aneirin needed attending to.

Her mouth watered at the scent of meat cooking, a brace of rabbits caught earlier by Owaen. But she stayed where she was, working through the thoughts in her mind, still moving slowly and sluggishly.

But Rhydian was just a young man who had helped her; using his own hands to help with what he thought was a sprained ankle when they had first met. He was a king, yes, but he was also clearly torn between care of his people, and care of her, one of the Elves. And while he had opened his castle to the Elves immediately on the battle coming to its epic conclusion, there was a hesitancy in his attitude toward rectifying his parents' shameful past.

Her heart twisted painfully at the thought of him returning there, to face what was a united front of two races, united in their confusion that the king had left. Aurelia settled into his arms and tried to turn off her wild thoughts, her body still worn out with the course of the past few days and then some. She needed to eat more of the rabbit and get her strength back up.

Rhydian's lips touched her ear, his voice low. "Are you okay?"

"I will be," Aurelia sighed, too weary to twist around to glare at him. "I've said that a thousand-"

"No... not like that. I mean..."

Aurelia couldn't help it. She yawned. "Like what?" she murmured after she could talk again.

"When Jessikah took you, I mean when Shadow Light took you. Did he," Rhydian paused, his voice still quiet and his tone uncertain. "Did he... hurt you?"

Aurelia was half asleep, but as her body readied itself for more rest, she realised what Rhydian had been trying to ascertain. She pressed her face to his warm chest.

"Oh," Aurelia murmured, "I see. No. She... he didn't."

"You'd tell me though? You'd let me help you, if you needed? There's no shame in that."

Still wishing for a bath, Aurelia's eyes closed against her will. She said a prayer to the gods for the gentle heart that beat against her cheek. She needed to wake up and tell him how she felt for him, but first, just a nap. Perhaps next time she woke, her brain would start to feel normal. As she drifted off, warm hands pulled up the cloak around her shoulders, settling her against the steady beat of love against her cheek.

"Aurelia?" Rhydian murmured. "Who's cloak is this?"

But sleep had already claimed her.

Aurelia awoke again hours later.

Her head was clearer. But there was another ache that needed to be seen to as soon as she woke. Her mouth was dry, but not from lack of water.

Overhead, the sun was high, with low clouds thinning out. The snow had stopped before it had a chance to pile. Now there was wet slush in the corners of the garden and the sound of drops from dead wood onto cold stone filled their rough camp with liquid music. Owaen was gone to check on the horses, Fox murmured to her sleepy query. After she had taken care of her body's needs, Rhydian was helping her with breakfast. It was hard to keep her food down, as her stomach was in knots. She had fallen asleep with three words on her tongue and had woken up with the same words ready to spill.

Gods, how did people stand this?

Glancing up from the haunch of rabbit in her greasy hand, Aurelia realised Fox was watching her with an odd expression on his face. Mouth full, she mouthed *what* at him.

He raised a dark brow, tilting his head while continuing to examine her. His eyes darted to Rhydian and then back to her. She had the distinct feeling her cheeks had turned pink. Fox had been holding the pieces of green crystals in his hands, but he lowered them carefully to his lap, his gaze continuing to flick between her and Rhydian.

Unable to stand it, Aurelia let the rabbit meat go limp in her hands, her eyes wide. After swallowing, she mouthed at him again.

Go away.

Right now.

Fox stared at her some more and slowly shook his head. He was trying not to smile.

"Aurelia? Aren't you hungry?" Rhydian murmured.

"N-no." Gods, her voice was barely a squeak. Fox bit his lip, holding back his laugh.

You are a bastard.

Fox nodded his agreement and stayed where he was. He made a *'go on'* motion with one hand. Aurelia's breathing hitched. She was about to launch her food at him when a hand appeared in front of her, holding a small yellowish lump of something.

"It's not the soap that you use," Rhydian said, shyly. "But I brought some with me. I kept some in my boot for you, so it might-"

"I love you, Rhydian," Aurelia blurted, glaring at Fox.

There was a moment's silence. Aurelia could tell Rhydian was pleased without turning to face him; his smile was like a new sun beside her. Across from them, Fox was miming an ecstatic cheer. Aurelia launched the half chewed rabbit haunch at him after all. Fox's muffled *ouch* was satisfying. Turning towards Rhydian's brilliant smile, Aurelia could finally breathe, soaking up his joy. His strange blue ringed eyes twinkled, and he looked like he'd been handed something he'd always wanted.

He was beautiful.

"I love you," she repeated, clearer and firmer, her eyes stuck to his while he held the soap out in offering. There was still a dull throb in her head. Her thoughts were sluggish, but the ache in her heart was gone. Rhydian continued to beam at her as Owaen appeared from the greenery, brushing something off his arm. He looked up and glanced at the three of them. His eyes narrowed.

"What did I miss?"

Fox reached up to grab Owaen's hand, tugging the tall Elf down to sit beside him. Aurelia buried her face in Rhydian's chest.

"Rhydian," Fox said warmly, "was just about to take Aurelia for a *bath*."

Despite Fox's teasing, the thought of intimacy in this place was unappealing, to say the least. There would be plenty of time, later, as Rhydian himself had said, kissing her forehead. For now, Aurelia was content to let the heaviness in her body be soothed by the gentle sensation of Rhydian carefully washing her hair.

He moved around her, kneeling in the shallow hot water still bubbling up from the cracks where she had bathed before. She wasn't sure quite what had happened, but after days of rarely eating and being stabbed and thrown off a height *again*, Aurelia almost felt like her old self. She was still experiencing the odd headache that came from nowhere and faded fast, but she was healing.

Hot water cascaded down her neck as Rhydian used his flask to rinse out her hair. They were both naked because he'd rinsed their clothes. Despite his earlier statement that there would be time later, as he moved with calm efficiency beside her, she could see he was clearly interested in taking things further. But when she reached for him with the stirring of faint interest, he swatted her hand away.

"No. I am going to wash you. Then you will rest."

His tone had wavered at the end, but Aurelia had hidden her smile. She settled down, crouched on the hot stones while he made sure she smelt, looked and felt more like herself than ever.

"I love you," Aurelia murmured, testing it out.

Rhydian's hands paused over her shoulders. He squeezed her gently.

"Say it again, please."

With a soft laugh, Aurelia dropped her forehead to her bent knees. She wasn't as fine as she was making out to be. It was clear the young man by her side was well aware of that, by how attentive he was being. And also because he was just that thoughtful of others. Aurelia smiled, eyes closed.

"I love you, Rhydian."

"I love you too, Aurelia." Warm water rushed down her bare, clean skin once more and she sighed. There was still a tender spot on her back, but she ignored it. Rhydian had been through worse at her hand, and she didn't want him to worry.

"Do you know why?" she murmured, lazily.

A soft kiss was planted in her wet hair.

"For what you show me, not what you say." Aurelia chewed on her lip to hide her soft sigh of pleasure as more water was lovingly poured over her. "But..."

"But?" He kept his hands moving this time, but his tone was hesitant.

"But we need to learn more about each other. I mean ... you're a king. Yet I don't even know what your favourite weapon is," she joked, trying to make light of what she needed to say.

Rhydian put the flask down. Aurelia tilted her head, resting her cheek on her knees to open her eyes and admire him as he moved. He sat down beside her, mirroring her pose, cheek resting on his bent knees to face her.

"Can you forget I'm king?"

"Forget?"

"Um, well," he mumbled, his voice faint. He closed his eyes, and she waited. He didn't elaborate further; he merely cleared his throat instead. "As for my favourite weapon?" His eyes narrowed. "Is that important?"

Aurelia nodded, her wet hair squelching between her cheek and her bare knees.

"I think so. The little things are as important as the big things that brought us together, like…"

Rhydian bit his lip. "Like my parents, a war and a couple of angry dragons?"

"Yes," Aurelia said gently, watching his face relax, understanding what she was trying to say. He reached out to cup the back of her head, smiling even if it looked a little sad.

"You're right."

"So?" Aurelia sat up and stretched, wincing at the discomfort in her back. His eyes followed the drops of water running down her damp skin, but he stayed seated next to her, gentleman that he was.

"So what?" he said, brows coming together.

"What is it? Your favourite weapon?"

His heated glance dropped down to his lap.

Ignoring the pain in her head and back, with her hand trembling only a little, Aurelia cupped a handful of water and splashed him in the face.

This time, when Aurelia woke later in the afternoon that same day, her hair was still damp, but her mind was clear. Blinking rapidly across their crackling fire at the wild garden with its quiet dignity, something followed her to consciousness.

Aurelia sat up with a jolt, eyes wide.

Fox had the crystals spread around him, muttering to himself.

"What the fuck are these? Why would Shadow Light need these?"

"Magic users are weird," offered Owaen, who was sprawled next to Fox on his back, one booted foot resting on the opposite knee. His eyes were closed and his hands were crossed behind his head. The sparkling golden topaz pendant that she had seen on Fox earlier was now resting on Owaen's chest. The gold chain was a metallic glint amongst the wrinkles in his shirt.

Aurelia blinked at it, before landing her gaze on Fox.

"Flare!" Aurelia hissed, startling him.

Frowning, Fox gestured at the dagger and the pendants. "What? Were these Flare's?"

Aurelia shook her head, squinting back at the crystals.

"No! I mean, maybe? He told the queen that they were vivianite. But that's not what I meant." It was hard to breathe again as the events of the last few days rushed back. Three faces stared at her while she tried to get her words in order.

"Ow, shit," Aurelia hissed, as a dull slice of pain lit her skull from within. She gripped the purple cloak tightly until the pain faded. Her face screwed up as she tried to work out the images rushing back to her. "He was so weird."

"What's wrong?"

She waved Rhydian's hand away. Owaen pushed himself up, staring at her with concern. His long blonde hair was tousled on top, and she could see for the first time that the sides had been cut short.

"All magic users are weird, especially dragons," Fox muttered. "And not to be trusted." He sat up and glanced around, his voice raised in a wild call. "So I am going to hunt you all down and *take it back.*"

Owaen reached up to grab Fox's arm, but Fox was staring angrily at where Aurelia was rubbing her forehead, some of the old fury back in his gaze.

"I'm going to wipe it all out," Fox continued to call out, seemingly for the hell of it. "I'm going to do what they tried to make me do. I'm going to take it all back and the rest of you are going to fucking deal with it!"

Silence followed his ringing yell. All three of the others stared at him. A flock of birds flew overhead in a scatter of squeaky wings.

"What?" Fox asked, eyes wide with feigned innocent.

"You know," Rhydian hedged, while Owaen shook his head, his mouth a thin line, "my parents probably said something like that to each other before they, oh, you know, went *mad.*"

"Shut up, both of you," Aurelia snapped. She waved a corner of the purple cloak at them. "Flare?" she said again, looking at each of them. "Where did he go?"

"Go?" Rhydian reached out to touch her forehead, but she knocked his hand away with an impatient gesture.

"Flare was here!" she insisted, trying to get them to understand. "Where did he *go*? And the man that was with him?"

"What man, Aurelia?" Fox said slowly, his brow furrowed. His eyes were narrowed, the odd gleam like a sharp blade back in full force deep within the black and gold depths.

"Flare was here with a *man*. He was tall, blonde." Aurelia closed her eyes and tried to speak in a way that made sense, while explaining all that had happened. "Before you arrived here, as they split up, Jessikah, Shadow, he was arguing with them. Something about a map, and the green dagger. When Jessikah realised Rhydian had bought the shard here, the one his mother had given me, I knew it was something that Jessikah wanted desperately, but shouldn't have."

"You tried to stop me from handing it over," Rhydian offered.

"Yes. I don't think the man wanted to gag me, but once he was gone with Flare, Jessikah made me gag myself with my bound hands, then tightened it. I could have fought her, maybe. But the man, Flare was scared of him. He had the opportunity to hurt me, but he didn't. He was peculiar. There was something off about him."

Fox was up on his knees now, holding up the dagger so it caught the weak afternoon light. "Did they say why they needed these?"

"No," Aurelia. "They were arguing, but I didn't understand." She paused and fingered the rich velvet material of the cloak. "This was his."

Owaen was staring at it with disgust, the sword hilt back in his hand as he toyed with it absentmindedly. One thumb caressed the red gem on its pommel. Fox tilted his head sideways and examined her cloak with narrowed eyes.

"He gave you his cloak?" he asked.

Silently, Aurelia nodded. She was aware of the oddness of that.

"Rhydian," she said and tried to think. "Do you remember that blonde man that rode out of the castle when your father came back?"

"Yes."

"I think it was him. His figure, his moonlight, pale hair, it was the same. And..." She looked at Owaen, wondering how to choose her next words.

"And? What else, Aurelia?" Rhydian asked softly, rubbing a hand over her back in slow circles. "Take a breath, don't rush."

"Um." She cleared her throat, inhaling the bitter smoke from the fire as the smoke drifted her way. "Well."

"Well?" Fox urged.

"He, ah, now that I think of it, he looked like," Aurelia took a breath and blinked at the blonde Elf across the fire. "You."

Owaen looked confused. He indicated himself with the hilt. "Me?"

Beside her, Rhydian sighed disgustedly. "Attractive?"

Not quite knowing how to answer that Aurelia shrugged. "But cleaner, not as dusty. And Flare was afraid of him," she murmured, rubbing her forehead again with calloused fingers. Gods, she needed a drink.

"For fuck's sake," Fox snapped. "Flare was afraid of his own shadow." He paused. "No joke intended," he added darkly.

"Really," Aurelia said, sitting up straighter, swatting Rhydian's hand away. "You could be brothers."

The useless hilt dropped to the cold flagstones. Only the soft crackle of the fire filled the silence as the metallic ring faded away. There was also a faint rattle of stones far off and above them, like a small pebble coming loose from the tower that was visible over the garden wall. Owaen shook his head slowly, mouth open. After a moment, he closed it.

"Owaen's brother is long dead, Aurelia," Rhydian murmured.

Silently, Owaen nodded. But he looked pale.

Fox turned to face him. "Owaen?"

"My brother," Owaen began, but stopped. He took a deep breath. "My twin died long ago. We weren't identical, but we looked very similar. But even if he hadn't died, he wasn't fully Elven, so couldn't live this long. He didn't have magic." Owaen shifted uncomfortably. "Um. At least not to begin with."

"Truly, Owaen," Aurelia said, "he looked like a leaner version of you. I didn't realise at first. My head, it's been hard to think..."

Rhydian got to his feet. He dropped a hand to Aurelia's hair, as if needing to protect her from whatever hellish revelation this was.

"But your bother had magic later?" Rhydian asked, his blue eyes troubled.

Owaen closed his eyes, his expression pained.

"Owaen?" Rhydian urged, his tone firm.

"Um." Owaen wiped a hand through his hair. "Yes. He was the oldest only by a few moments. But our father knew that my brother had no magic and I was supposed to protect him. That wasn't good enough for my brother. He worked out a way to siphon, uh, to absorb magic from others, and wield it for himself."

Aurelia watched as a muscle in Fox's jaw twitched. Fox's voice was flinty when he spoke.

"Oh, *did* he now? And this Owaen lookalike just happened to be buddies with the dragon, whose end game was the same with me?" Fox looked at Owaen, then back to Aurelia. "Just who the fuck was this person?"

Without a sound, Owaen got up with a fluid grace that Aurelia envied. What she didn't envy was the shocked expression on his face as he stepped away, clearly needing some space. After a moment, Fox muttered 'fuck that', pushed himself up and followed to a corner of the yard where the stones were mostly intact, the thick vines, even the dead ones, holding them up.

Owaen's hands were in his hair and Fox was gesturing wildly at him. Both of them were speaking with hushed, whispered hisses and the weird echoes made it impossible to tell exactly what it was they were arguing about. Obviously, it was about the likelihood that a dead brother was not so dead after all. What confused Aurelia was the faint look of dread she had seen on Fox's face as he hurried after the trembling Elven man.

What else did Fox know? That perhaps Owaen didn't?

After a few minutes of heated exchange, Owaen stormed back to the fire.

His expression was grim. "Tell me about his eyes."

Aurelia's heart stuttered. "Oh shit."

The expression on Owaen's face was all she needed. They stared at each other in shocked understanding.

"What about his eyes?" Rhydian interrupted their silent exchange.

Owaen let her answer for them both, his face now white under his tanned skin, his face dangerously expressionless. Fox remained silent; he stood next to Owaen with his arms crossed over his chest, scowling.

"Blue," Aurelia whispered, hesitating. Owaen nodded at her to go on, his jaw working silently. "But each one was different. Not like Rhydian's. His have a ring of blue over a different blue. This man had one dark blue eye, the other light blue, and they shone like..."

Owaen closed his eyes, his chin dropping to his chest. He finished her sentence with a poetic description that was absolutely correct.

"Like liquid silver catching the light."

"Owaen," Fox said, grabbing Owaen's arm.

"Shit." Owaen shook it off and turned away from them to stare up at the sky. "My gods... Shit, shit, *shit*."

Aurelia struggled to push herself up, and only reluctantly accepted Rhydian's help to rise. He kept his arm around her as Owaen turned to face them, his face a mask of pain. He stepped forward, his large hands moving to grab hers with a surprisingly gentle grip.

"I know your head hurts," Owaen whispered. "But can you remember his name?"

Aurelia nodded. She hadn't thought to offer it at first, because after meeting so many creatures with different faces, what was a name?

She licked dry lips. "Caspian."

"Oh fuck," Owaen hissed, dropping her hands. "Gods *damn* him! This can't be a coincidence that he's here now. Fuck! Caspian, what the fuck are you up to?"

Rhydian pulled her towards him as she sobbed once at the naked longing on Owaen's face, not realising she was close to tears at all. Fox was standing alone, his hands now clenched by his hips, expression blank, eyes dark and glittering. Aurelia shrugged off Rhydian's grip. This time it was her taking Owaen's hands instead.

"He said something else," she murmured.

Owaen looked up at her, his dark green eyes wide, hardly seeming to see her.

"What else?" Fox demanded.

"Another name. He kept repeating it when he thought I wasn't listening. A woman's name."

Owaen's eyes met hers, horror dawning. He shook his head.

No, he mouthed, pleading with her silently. For what, she didn't understand. How could he know what she was about to say? He shook off her grip.

"Um." She really needed a drink. Wine, water, mead, it didn't matter what. "M-Morgan."

With a low moan, Owaen dropped his face to his hands. His shuddering breath might have been a heaving sob. At the sound, Fox finally moved and rested his hands upon Owaen's trembling shoulders. His earlier blank expression was replaced with alarm.

"Owaen?"

Fox slid his hands down Owaen's arms to glide around his broad chest, holding him close. Face still buried, Owaen sank back into his embrace.

"How bad is this?" Fox's voice was calm. "That your brother is alive and friendly with Shadow Light? And flapping about with Flare?"

"You don't get it," Owaen muttered, his hands falling away. He was staring at the garden with glassy eyes. "My brother... oh my gods... my *brother.*"

Fox pressed his face to Owaen's neck from behind, waiting. All of them were waiting for Owaen to explain it. Yes, to find your long dead sibling was alive would be a shock. But it was clear here that there was much, much more to it than that.

"By himself, Caspian was," Owaen took a shuddering breath, "he was potently volatile."

Owaen turned his faraway stare to Aurelia. She stepped back into Rhydian's embrace unconsciously, remembering the fierce calm *otherness* of Caspian's bossiness with Flare and Shadow Light. Owaen continued, speaking as if just to her.

"But if Morgan is involved? Gods help us." Owaen shook his head, green eyes boring into Aurelia's. "If Morgan has anything to do with this, Caspian will be absolutely fucking unhinged."

57

Rhydian

Year 367

The City of the Seers

R hydian cursed as he limped back towards their new camp, his bruised right foot aching.

Blackthorn had been so relieved to see his human again that he'd stepped on Rhydian's boot in excitement. The two horses from Aneirin were hobbled in the meadows around the dilapidated city. When Rhydian had greeted the horse the evening before; Blackthorn had forgotten that he was a serious warhorse and whinnied like a young foal. The horse had known something serious was afoot, considering the magical method of their journey from Aneirin to the cave.

Seeing the animal's innocent joy at having Rhydian nearby had warmed his heart. The burden of his crown pulled heavily at him from the south, but he had his beloved horse to share a laugh with. He also had a beautiful woman, to whom Rhydian was making his way back across the meadow. His fingertips grazed the bobbing heads of fragrant flowers he couldn't name as he walked, lost in thought. Morning mist drifted in white wisps around the city walls, but the meadow was crisp, clear, and open.

After the devastating news of the evening before, the solemn group had opted to sleep out in the meadows with the flowers and the fresher air. Inside the walls, the bitter stink of burnt dragon still tainted the silence, and despite the lack of protection around them,

Rhydian had slept better than he had in a very, very long time. There were no dreams to disturb his sleep, just the gentle scent of blossoms and the occasional brush of Aurelia's hair against his face.

A gentle fire hissed from within a circular depression dug into the rich soil, amongst a small clearing of now trampled blossoms. Aurelia was sitting with her knees bent, arms crossed around them whilst watching him approach with wide, green eyes. Their verdant shade was a sharp contrast to the dark purple cloak around her shoulders. Despite its origin, it had been necessary to hold on to, as the night temperature this far north was bitterly cold, the days not much better.

Rhydian flashed Aurelia a shy smile as he sat down. Wordlessly she reached for him, grasping one of his hands, his fingertips stained yellow from pollen. He liked the feel of her calloused fingertips, not just for the strange sensation on his skin. He admired what they stood for, that she had trained hard to be a champion, if a misguided one, of her people.

As he settled against her, his gaze wandered over the unmoving pile of cloaks across the fire. It was likely that the other two were awake, as both Aurelia and Rhydian had been up for a while seeing to their morning needs. But Owaen and Fox ignored the dawn to stay hidden from the others, wrapped in their cloaks and each other. Rhydian was worried, mainly for Fox. Owaen's solid presence had been exactly what Fox had needed, both for his dormant power to rise once more, and to calm the rage in his heart. But the news of this Caspian person had shattered Owaen's calm arrogance.

Rhydian shuffled closer to Aurelia so that their shoulders touched, unsure about the day ahead. For now, he was happy to listen to soft morning birdcalls. After the sun rose a little higher, Aurelia cleared her throat.

"Do you think," Aurelia asked quietly, "Fox would kneel for Owaen?"

Surprised by her line of thought, Rhydian glanced at her for a moment before turning his gaze to the two figures across the fire, still refusing to face the day. Rhydian took a breath before he answered, his voice also pitched low.

"I don't think I can answer that either way, and still feel like I could sleep safely at night." Rhydian hesitated, aware that the pile of cloaks shifted minutely. "Does it matter who kneels for who?" he muttered, eventually.

"I think it does." Aurelia turned to face him, eyes full of something he couldn't name. "You're a king, Rhydian."

"Apparently."

"You are." Aurelia squeezed his hand. "But you knelt for me during the battle."

Because I asked you to kill my father.

Instead of saying the words that hummed on his tongue, Rhydian returned her squeeze.

"Always," he said, solemnly. "For you, Aurelia? After what you did for your people and for me? Always."

Aurelia seemed to understand what he was trying to say.

"I love you too," she murmured, bringing their joined hands to her lips.

They were quiet for a while, listening to the insects buzz loudly as the sun rose higher. A bright red dragonfly buzzed past them. The sight tugged at Rhydian's memory and he smiled. He gently pulled his hand from Aurelia's, sliding it into his shirt. His fingers were icy, and he hissed as he fumbled around, but found what he was looking for.

Aurelia's smile was as heartbreaking as it was beautiful as he held up the garnet, holding it by the chain. Her green eyes shimmered as she watched it swing back and forth, dark red, opaque and flashing with veins of what looked like silver or gold. Unable to speak, she blinked rapidly and nodded when he gestured to her neck. After it was settled where it belonged, under her long hair, she pressed her face into his chest. He held her close while she sniffled into his shirt.

Rhydian kissed Aurelia's mostly clean hair, smiling over her head at Blackthorn, who had wandered closer.

Satisfied, the horse lowered his nose to the meadow and continued to graze, carelessly thinking that all was right in the world once more.

The morning mist had burned away by the time Owaen and Fox emerged from their tattered cocoon.

The sun was high; the insects were out in annoyingly loud swarms. The air was cool and fragrant, and Rhydian didn't want to leave. It wasn't the same as his soft, green grass covered meadows of home, forever scarred by a hopeless battle. Even so, he wanted to stay here, amongst the flowers, despite the chaos that awaited him at Aneirin, and the threat of a volatile maniac on the back of a sneaky, purple dragon. He wanted to spend time with

Blackthorn, but there was a sinking feeling in his guts about what the day might actually bring.

Owaen was sitting quietly by the fire, staring at the flames. His jaw was clenched and there were dark circles under his dark green eyes. His clothing was fairly clean, but if Rhydian looked hard enough, faint brownish spots were visible. Owaen's eyes lifted from the fire and met Rhydian's without a word. The blonde Elf's gaze was appraisingly cool in a way that Rhydian was well aware he could never hope to match. Rhydian looked away first, although the hilt in Owaen's hands, with its single uncut ruby, winked occasionally in the corner of his vision as Owaen toyed with it almost obsessively. Now that Fox and Owaen were awake, Rhydian almost wished they were still asleep. The tension in the air was thick enough to slice with the inch of blade that was poking out of the broken weapon in Owaen's white-knuckled hands.

Owaen offered Rhydian's battered flask to Fox, who shook his head. Owaen took a sip for himself, watching as Fox wrapped the three pieces of green crystal in a scrap of fabric. The fabric he was using looked suspiciously like the missing corner of the cloak Rhydian was wearing, but Rhydian made no comment. He was more concerned with the wicked-looking dagger as it disappeared into the soiled folds.

"Fox," Rhydian murmured, unable to stand the tension any longer.

Fox didn't look up from his solemn task, but he tilted his head to show he'd heard. His black hair was a mess, his skin was pale and his mouth was set in a thin line.

"Be a good dragon and do something safe, something responsible, with those."

Owaen choked on his mouthful of water. Fox's hands stilled. Rhydian could feel Aurelia turn to stare at him, but he was focused on the dangerous glint in Fox's mesmerising eyes.

"Excuse me." Fox gave Rhydian a look. "What the fuck did you just say?"

"Oh, sorry." Rhydian grinned. "*Please.*"

After a moment, Fox barked out a startled laugh. Aurelia shook her head; Owaen rolled his eyes and Rhydian's bowels unclenched. With a raised eyebrow, Fox went back to securing his small bundle with a strap of leather thong. Rhydian narrowed his eyes. The thong looked familiar too.

"Safe?" Fox muttered. "Responsible? Are you sure you've met a dragon, kingling?"

Passing the bundle to Owaen, Fox sat back and appraised Rhydian calmly.

"Hm." Rhydian cracked his neck and thought about it. There wasn't a right answer to that question. He changed the subject. "For what it's worth, Owaen, please know that Aneirin will offer its aid to help in... whatever you have to do with..." his voice faded.

Talking about Owaen's brother was still as volatile as its subject matter, if Owaen's expression was anything to go by. Owaen opened his mouth to reply, but then closed it quickly and simply nodded. Fox rose to his feet beside him, and stretched, eyes closed as he faced the sky. Aurelia got up and did the same, smiling ruefully at Fox, who was muttering under his breath. Something about *what part of being a dragon was responsible*, if Rhydian heard correctly.

"I've seen you stand up for things you believe in, Fox. That's responsible," Aurelia said as she stretched, stomping and bending her knees.

Fox refused to look at her, but he opened his eyes, the gold flecks bright as the sun beat down coolly from above.

"So was that you being responsible, Fox the man, or Skye the dragon?" Aurelia pushed.

Fox moved towards her with a small smile, and automatically she held out her arms. He stepped into her embrace and pressed his face into her hair. His voice was muffled, but Rhydian could follow the conversation. He was close enough to see the gold glint in Fox's eyes as he stared at Rhydian over Aurelia's shoulder.

"This is not my original form." The black and gold slits disappeared for a moment but stayed fixed on Rhydian when it appeared again. "But I am still a dragon." A lone crow passed overhead with a macabre call, but Rhydian couldn't look away from Fox's stare. Aurelia pulled back to stare at Fox, tugging on the dark hair gathered in feathered spikes over his forehead.

"You need to share more than that. You know everything about me. It's time you shared in return. I know you watched me from Lolihud." Fox's eyes widened. She went on, unperturbed by his intense stare. "It wasn't just when we were in Aneirin that you watched the prince. Before that, I know you watched me with Rhydian."

While Rhydian pondered what the hells she was talking about, Fox seemed to be sorting through various things to say as he examined Aurelia's face.

"I am not sorry," he said, evidently settling for arrogant honesty.

"I know," Aurelia sighed. "But I wanted to do this."

She punched him on the arm quite hard. It didn't affect him at all and he appeared quite unmoved, as if his shrug were any sign of how he felt about her discovery. Smirking, Fox spared a glance to a slightly confused Rhydian. With a soft laugh, Fox turned, kicking dirt upon their fire, extinguishing the embers with both earth and squashed flowers. As the sharp scent of smouldering grass and blossoms rose from the smothered fire, Owaen fiddled with the things he'd stuffed into his shirt.

"I still deserve more information than that," Aurelia groused, and to Rhydian's surprise, Fox nodded. A pale hand scratched idly at the back of his head while he kicked at the ring of stones and ash.

"When I went to Mionlach and did what I felt was necessary to the dragons, I found out some things about magic. I'm not sure about what I learned. I need time to figure it out." Fox brushed his hair out of his face, looking anywhere but Owaen.

Aurelia wasn't done. She was clearly feeling better and Rhydian was happy enough to let her dig for more information.

"About what? How much time have you already had?" Aurelia crossed her arms over her chest, so like Fox that Rhydian had to hide his smile. "How much time do you need? I know this must have happened before you came to Lolihud. So you've had *ages*."

Owaen stopped what he was doing, one blonde eyebrow raised. Fox cleared his throat and waved a hand in front of himself with a shrug. Owaen's eyes narrowed into thin lines. Rhydian watched the tension between the pair rise again, well aware there was more to both sides of this conversation.

"Oh, you know," Fox said, his voice brittle. "I learned about my origins, dragon things. Things like..." he hesitated, one of his hands clenching.

"Things like what?" Aurelia pressed, looking Fox up and down, her tone accusing.

Fox turned away from Owaen, his eyes unfocused. "Things."

"*What* things?" Aurelia snapped.

"Fine, fine." Fox licked his lips. "Things like... um. The fact that Flare is not in his original form. But as a dragon, I was in mine."

"Wait, wait, wait. That was *you*," Rhydian breathed, Fox's admission sparking something in Rhydian's memory. All three pairs of eyes focused on him but he went on, lost to that horrible day in the cave, when Fox was dying and a green-haired statue of crystal had been standing alone in the blue glow. "That crystal woman in the cave, that was you, when you first met Owaen. It was, wasn't it?"

Not waiting to hear what Fox would answer, Owaen stalked off into the flowers, the sun breaking through the clouds highlighting his broad shoulders. Rhydian watched him go, the Elf running his hands through his hair. He stopped not far away with his back to them and appeared to be staring at the trees beyond the meadow. The forest was a thick, green wall around them, solid and fathomless, waiting for them to enter once more. Owaen stared at the trees, his back straight and unflinching.

It gave Rhydian chills, thinking that this man had attacked a dragon with just a sword to avenge the one he loved. Touching his unmarked throat, he wondered at that. He'd died for Aurelia. But was that the same? All he did was let go. But Owaen had run after his enemy, towards certain violence.

Fox's soft voice interrupted the thoughts shifting uncomfortably in Rhydian's head. "Yes."

Something deep and filled with longing shifted inside Rhydian, shifted in sympathy at the sadness in his voice.

"Yes," Fox repeated. He looked across the brief span of bobbing flowers between him and Owaen's back. It was obvious that the Elf could hear them. "That was my disguise when I first met Owaen. I think he made that statue in the cave when he woke occasionally..." he hesitated, but Owaen refused to turn around.

Rhydian shifted in his boots, unwilling to break the silence this time.

Eventually, Fox continued. "When I knew I was coming here, I didn't want to arrive here as a dragon. I wanted to hear what others thought of dragons without realising they were talking to one." For a moment Fox looked crushingly sad, but his face hardened so quickly Rhydian wondered if he'd imagined what he'd seen.

Turning to Owaen, Fox raised his voice, sounding more like his unruffled self, "Why did you let my statue shatter when I touched it?"

Owaen shifted slightly to face the city. His faraway gaze examined the decrepit walls, the leaning tower, the top of the great soaring dome of the council chamber still visible, his hands clenched at his sides. "Because I hoped I was finally awake. That I didn't need it to keep me company anymore."

Fox stared at Owaen, mouth slightly open before his jaw hinged tightly shut. He inhaled deeply through his nose. Aurelia was staring at Fox, clearly still willing to push Fox further. Rhydian grabbed her hand in warning, but she shook it off.

"Wait," she said. "What-"

"No." Fox shook his head, his eyes more black than gold. His voice was icy. "Not now. I need to find Flare. He's the only dragon left. He's responsible for so much of this crap. I'm going to find him, strip him of his magic and turn him back like the others." His eyes narrowed. "Just as Owaen and I planned to do to all magic users long ago."

This earned him a grimly amused snort from Owaen.

"That's not *quite* what we talked about. And you know it."

Fox ignored the emerald eyes burning in his direction. "I also need," his gaze softened for a moment as Fox stared at his pale hands, "to find Caspian."

The loud exhale from Owaen was all Rhydian needed to hear to know just what Owaen might have been feeling about that.

Head hanging, the blonde Elf turned from the city and crossed the riot of bobbing fragrant flowers back to Fox. Fox wordlessly put one arm around Owaen's waist, and gathered Owaen's hand to his chest. They touched foreheads for a moment. Rhydian turned away, examining Aurelia as she dusted off her dark clothes. Her expression was thoughtful. Shivering a little, Rhydian gathered her into a hug, pulling the purple cloak around them both. She was muttering to herself.

"Flare, whatever you are, you are a coward. I hope you're as scared as you've ever been," she murmured against his chest. After a frustrated sigh, she relaxed. Her arms wrapped around Rhydian's waist and she breathed deeply against him.

He closed his eyes. Aurelia felt warm, soft, and hard all at once. Despite everything, she felt safe.

Rhydian was content to stay quiet like that forever, amongst the fragrant blooms and lost to the rest of the world, separate. But Owaen's low voice broke the spell, and the reality of the day returned.

"Are you ready for this?" This was directed at Fox, who nodded, smiling faintly.

"Ready for what?" Rhydian asked, lifting his head from Aurelia's hair. She turned in his arms to face the others.

Fox pointed to himself. "I'm your ride home."

"*Yes!*" Aurelia whooped, at the same time as Rhydian shouted, "NO!"

His guts turning to water, Aurelia smacked Rhydian in the chest.

"Rhydian! That's a great honour he's offering us," she exclaimed, dancing with excitement against him. Behind her, Fox was biting his lower lip, trying not to smile. He was failing miserably. Rhydian would have scowled if his face hadn't gone numb.

"If it's decided then, and we definitely don't need the horses, I'll let them go," Owaen interrupted with a tired grimace. He looked apologetically at Rhydian. "They should be fine. There's grass and water here, and Fox and I will return to bring them home. We'll take the time to plan ahead, *plans* that we will stick to," he added darkly as he walked off.

Aurelia was bouncing on the balls of her feet, one hand over her mouth. Fox was clearly pleased by her reaction, his eyes a sparkling gold. Clearing his throat, Rhydian shook his head, running a trembling hand through his tousled hair.

"Of course that's um, great, but I mean," Rhydian stumbled over his words, desperate to think of anything besides being off the ground again. "My horses…"

"Come on, Rhydian," Aurelia laughed, not fooled. "I'll keep you safe."

Gathering her close, Rhydian pitched his voice as low as it could go and still be audible. "I think we should keep you on the ground, after what has happened to you, twice, since we've met, right?"

She cupped his chin. "Fox will keep both of us safe."

Rhydian glanced past her. Fox raised an eyebrow. "Can't we travel like before, like we did to Owaen's cave, with the horses?"

"No," Fox said with a firm shake of his head. Blackness consumed his eyes.

"Why not?"

"Because I don't want to," Fox snapped, his smile gone. "Don't you trust me?"

Trapped, Rhydian swore under his breath, and did the only thing he could think of. He buried his face back into Aurelia's hair and tried not to examine the genuine possibility that he would disgrace himself in front of two courageous Elves, and a dangerously fierce dragon. Laughing at him softly, Aurelia squeezed him tight, rocking him mockingly like a babe. When she stopped, he was only half grateful. He knew why she had halted her teasing movements. The hairs on his neck had risen at the same time as Aurelia had stilled, her breath catching in her chest between them.

Coldness rippled behind him and the surrounding flowers tilted away before springing back in a sweetly scented breeze. The blossoms danced wildly as the dust settled, a barely visible soft verdant mist blowing away with the unnatural rush of air. As Aurelia drew away from Rhydian, her hands released him, and his own breath caught at the sight of her face. Aurelia's expression was one of joy, of wonder; there were glossy tears in her clear green eyes. To Rhydian, she had never looked so beautiful. It was obvious what he needed to turn around and witness close up, but it was hard to tear his gaze from her face. That was until an enormous, chilled shadow loomed over them. A loud, frigid and mineral scented breath of air blew through his hair from above.

As his heart sped up, Rhydian slowly turned around.

He was met with a large, shiny golden eye right next to his own.

Leaning down, the immense emerald green and gold dragon exhaled over him again, this time directly into Rhydian's face. As his hair lifted off his forehead for a moment, sharp teeth as long as his arms were exposed in a dangerous twist of finely scaled reptilian lips. It seemed to be the dragon equivalent of a smile. Or by the wicked glint in the golden eye, perhaps it was a smirk. The colossal head tilted for a moment, its golden green crown of spikes catching the light. The dragon eventually spoke with a low rumble, sharp white teeth on full display.

"Kiss me, kingling."

Rhydian closed his eyes and shook his head. Directly in front of him, a deep laugh rumbled. The low voice spoke again, words that Rhydian could feel in his bones.

"Come on," the dragon purred. "Kiss me *again*."

Over Aurelia's startled laugh, Owaen's voice was curt. "What?"

The dragon laughed again and something large, impossibly smooth and cold nudged Rhydian's chest very, very gently.

Rhydian tried to remember how to breathe. It was harder than it should have been. After Aurelia thumped him hard on his back, his breath came back in a rush. At the same time, he remembered being on Flare's spiked back, with nothing but the wind and clouds beneath him. He dug his boots into the earth, trying to convince himself what was about to happen wasn't really going to. That was worse than breathing. He failed and broke out into a chilling sweat.

There was only one way he could think of to distract himself. He leaned forward until his warm lips touched cold, shiny scales. Softening his lips, he planted a chaste kiss on the dragon. Aurelia squeezed his hand, and he opened his eyes at last. The dragon pulled its head up and away, looking so pleased with itself that Rhydian had to laugh.

"Are you still Fox?" Rhydian asked, his voice surprisingly steady.

"Always," the dragon grinned, flashing them a mouth full of sharp teeth.

In the distance, Owaen was ignoring them, taking the horse's bridles off. Rhydian was aware how much he would worry about them and tried to put on a brave face for Blackthorn. Owaen caught his gaze once, scowling, but kept on with his task without comment.

All of a sudden, it seemed too much for Aurelia. Unable to contain herself any longer, she rushed forward and wrapped her arms around one of the great, clawed forelegs a short distance away. Pressed her face to Fox's leg, she peppered his scales with kisses. Above them, Fox's happy, deep sigh was strangely intimate for his great size. The dragon lowered its large golden scaled nose and twisted its neck to nudge her affectionately.

After a moment, she turned to meet his beautiful, fully golden stare.

"I wish you could have flown us into Aneirin. I can't believe you hid this from me."

"Mmm," the dragon rumbled. "But you had to sneak in the back door, little thing, and we didn't want to alert the king-" the dragon paused, throwing a sheepish look Rhydian's way.

Noticing Rhydian's dark look, Aurelia smacked the leg she was wrapped around, hard. "Hush. At Lolihud, can you imagine, Fox? What we might have gotten up to?"

Instead of answering, Fox licked the top of her head, catching her long hair on his tongue and causing Aurelia to screech loudly. But she was smiling hugely, her eyes glossy. Too soon the pair of them turned to face Rhydian, and Owaen was back, his expression expectant. Rhydian straightened his shoulders. He spared another glance to Blackthorn, whose ears were back as he eyed the dragon with more suspicion than fear. The other horse was hiding behind the black warhorse and shivering.

"Excuse me," Rhydian murmured, needing a moment, and headed to the two animals. He hid his shaking hands in his cloak and wandered around the dragon and the two Elves, grateful that the flowers when crushed, released a gentle fragrance that lifted his spirits enough that he wouldn't cry.

"Are you jealous, Blackthorn? Good." Fox called behind him, his deep voice full of mirth. "You should be."

58

Flare

If Flare had ever wanted to see what it looked like for a grown man to have a silent tantrum, the time was now. As he watched the raging yet soundless meltdown in front of him, Flare simply could not look away.

The little dragon was perched in the shadows of the cracked balustrade at the top of the leaning tower. His wings twitched at the pageant of impotent violence taking place before him. Not quite realising it, Flare was repeating Aurelia's name over and over. His tiny purple eyes were wide, fixed on the blonde man across from him on the terrace.

The day before, or was it two days? Flare had been lost in grief, confusion, and fear. They had been on the tower for a long time, frozen with indecision.

When they had first parted ways with Shadow Light, staying out of sight was the first part of Caspian's plan. Flare had been unable to look when Shadow Light had dragged Aurelia into the council chamber, but her eyes had left scorch marks on his dull scales. Caspian had yanked Flare out of the air, while he squeaked in a most un-dragon-like manner. Caspian had then taken the cracked steps of the once beautiful tower far too fast than was reasonably safe, climbing with barely contained excitement if his bright, strange eyes and flushed cheeks were anything to go by.

Once they had emerged onto the roof terrace, the frigid wind whipped around them and blowing Caspian's hair into upright, wavelike shapes. Below his boots, the paving had been cracked, the whimsical and elegant patterns now jagged and sinister. A hardy looking weed was growing in the cracked paving, a single yellow flower blooming amongst the dilapidated terrace.

The tough little plant had likely sprouted from a seed dropped from some bird passing through. Since Flare had no great bulk in his tiny form to keep warm, when Caspian had let Flare go, the little dragon had landed on a crumbled stone bench to try to soak up the weak sun only a little way from the flower. Caspian had slid down nearby, discarding his leather satchel, moving to where he could see the great courtyard, the council chamber roof and, as he exclaimed under his breath with disgust, down into the abandoned chamber itself with that 'fucking gods awful round table'.

Then they had waited.

And waited.

And waited some more.

The yellow sun arched lazily overhead behind the grey clouds across the sky. Caspian was thoroughly put out when he had to relieve himself in the stairwell. He came back with a piece of pale stone that he was idly tumbling in his shapely fingers, his jewelled rings flashing. His scowl softened as he toed one of the loose pavers with his boot as he sat back down. But as he settled the sword at his hip, furious yelling erupted from below.

Caspian had casually peered up and over the edge of the crumbling tower balustrade. His grin was wide, delighted, and full of anticipation. He started to hum a nonsense rhyme that he seemed to make up on the spot.

"Magic, magic everywhere,

But not enough for me.

Magic, magic, hmmm... *oh what luck,*

I've got you now, Skye, come on, let's-"

With a strange, strangled sort of noise, Caspian stopped humming. His whole demeanour changed, and he even appeared to stop breathing. Flare, on his perch on the stone bench where he was refusing to watch whatever awful thing was about to unfold down in the vast plaza, examined Caspian closely.

"Oh," Caspian said eventually, in a very different tone of voice than moments before. He slumped back down behind the wall and turned to Flare.

Caspian blinked once, very, very slowly, as if his eyelids were refusing to drag down and back up over his metallic, piercing blue eyes. The breeze lifted his blonde hair across his face, but even then Caspian didn't move.

The dragon stared in fascination as several expressions warred for dominance on Caspian's cruel and admittedly beautiful face. Eventually, an eerie kind of blankness won, his strange silver-blue eyes wide, staring blankly at nothing.

Without warning, the stone that Caspian had been fiddling with in his hands burst into a little cloud of dust.

"Oh," said Caspian again.

Eyeing the frozen man warily, Flare had hopped off the bench and crawled his way to the edge of the terrace. He ignored a strange tingle under his claws from the tiles as he passed. Peering his snout over the edge, Flare saw immediately what had shut Caspian up so efficiently.

Not a what.

A *who*.

"Owaen," Flare breathed, astonished.

As soon as the name left his lips, Flare realised his mistake. Unable to help it, he turned. Caspian was glaring at him. His odd eyes, each different to the other, were full of such fury that Flare had a moment to think 'oh shit'. His eyes narrowed into silvery, luminous blue slits. Caspian's jaw clenched so hard that Flare assumed the man's teeth might follow the way of the exploded little stone, which was now a fine powder that covered one of Caspian's white-knuckled hands.

With one eye on the inevitable eruption of wrath beside him, Flare only caught some of the important details of the tense scene below. There was a furious argument, Fox's enraged yelling and then the tone changed, as Jessikah demanded something of the king. All the while, Owaen, whom Caspian had been certain was locked away, stood back from it all, watching from Rhydian's large black horse.

The king had thrown something small and green to Shadow Light with a mighty swing, and Flare and Caspian both had recognised the scent of what it was. Before he had time tc wonder how Rhydian had brought it here, let alone carry it without Fox confiscating it. Aurelia had been thrown off the roof. Flare jolted forward even as he knew there was no way in all the hells he would be quick enough, but Caspian's frigid hand caught him by the tail, his other hand wrapping around his snout.

Flare needn't have worried, though. Fox moved, with magic or without, Flare wasn't sure. There was no disruptive metallic scent to the air, no haze that sometimes accompanied a burst of power. Accompanied only by the sound of bones shattering, the snaps clear all the way to their hidden perch at the top of the tower, Fox *moved*. And Aurelia landed upon him with a dull thud. As Flare's heart stuttered, he realised she had survived. Fox, a shattered thing on the ground beneath her, was still.

Even Caspian jerked at that.

"Damn," he muttered, releasing Flare's snout. Flare's tail was left frozen with revulsion inside Caspian's other twitching hand.

Shadow Light didn't wait to see what followed. He ducked inside a gap in the domed roof, Flare clearly able to scent the magic in the other dragon's blood shifting, rearranging a new body. Something Flare was sure Shadow Light hadn't been able to do, and he knew without a doubt that the pendant he'd collected from the king was the very same Aurelia had travelled to Aneirin with. It had come to the queen from Flare as part of the dagger originally, after all. He didn't know all of its properties; only that it was seemingly unlimited in its transformative potential.

An oily black mist followed the disappearance of the little form of Jessikah, really Shadow Light, and Flare's own magic begged him to grow to full size in turn, sensing Shadow Light's transformation on the other side of the ruined dome roof. But he was still deathly afraid of Caspian, who could simply end Flare if he chose. Flare wasn't sure how, but Caspian knew enough of his parents' secrets that it seemed a likely bet, and like always, Flare chose to bet on survival instead. Which meant staying where he was.

When Flare glanced back at the courtyard floor, Owaen had disappeared. Fox was moving, albeit slowly, and Aurelia was in Rhydian's arms. Caspian's hand twitched on Flare's tail. Flare bit back a moan of disgust.

Movement caught their eye from inside the council chamber, through the gaps in the roof, this time towards the far edge. There were enough holes and gaps in the dome that tantalising glimpses of the action within were visible, highlighted by the weak beams of light that made it down inside. Not all of the confrontation could be seen clearly, but there was a flash of a small blonde head dashing behind the dead remains of the giant trees.

There was loud roaring, rumbling and taunting, but soon a dark and fast moving blur streaked into the chaos, actually *into* the black dragon. After a horrible wet, crunching series of gruesome and echoing violence, there was silence.

As Flare gagged, Caspian's hand jerked cruelly at Flare's tail once more. A hot jolt of some dark power twisted its way inside him, along his tail and up his spine, before Caspian released him. Flare groaned in distress at the scene far below, and the fact that he could feel a coil of something subtle and magical joining him to Caspian yet again.

"F-fuck me," Caspian, his eyes filled with a wild light, murmured haltingly, as if unable to help himself, "that was *incredible.*"

While Flare digested the horror of what had likely happened to himself from Caspian's hot jolt, and also to Shadow Light below, eventually Owaen staggered out of the building. He was carrying a completely blood coated figure in his arms. The smirk amidst the gore was unmistakable. Fox was holding the broken hilt of a sword, its single red ruby barely catching the light, as it was partially covered with the same dark gore that covered Fox.

Caspian gasped and froze again at the sight.

Or perhaps he had exclaimed over Fox's, no, *Skye's*, dreamy expression. At this height, it was hard to see, but Fox looked well pleased with himself.

After checking on Aurelia, who was gathered in the clearly relieved young king's arms, Flare had seen enough, and slunk back over the roof edge to hop back onto the old bench. He risked a glance at Caspian. The man's nostrils were flared, his dusty face pinched. Caspian withdrew from the edge after staring wordlessly into the empty dome for a long, long while as the stink of burning dragon flesh rose with acrid black smoke. Eventually, Caspian shuffled back to sit on the tiles next to Flare's bench. The man's right eyelid started to twitch.

As Flare's tail flicked back and forth to bring back some feeling into its nearly strangled length, he watched as an eerie calm settled over Caspian, replacing the earlier shock.

Eyes wide and unblinking, Caspian stared at Flare.

"I did not plan for this," he said, his voice a furious whisper, "for *him.*" He was looking at Flare oddly as if he was daring the little dragon to disagree. Flare blinked cautiously, not taking his gaze off the man for a second.

Moving as if in a dream, Caspian curled his hand into a fist and lifted it to his mouth. Twisting it a little, he bit the fleshy part of his palm, quite hard. The bright rush of red blood from the corner of his white mouth was a shock on his white face. Apart from a single twitch of his eyelid again, there was no other reaction. Eventually he swallowed;

dropping his bleeding hand to his lap, blood leaking into his lap. Caspian either didn't realise or care, tilting his head to the sky, eyes narrowed in accusation.

"When I joked on the road about a family reunion," he hissed, "I did not mean this fucking disaster of a synchronicity."

They sat in silence for a while, as Caspian's breathing became both faster and shallower. His fingertips fidgeted on the elaborate sword hilt at his hip. By the time the sun had moved lower through the grey afternoon sky, the tower creaking occasionally, Caspian's breathing was irregular and his cheeks were flushed. His fist was still curled in his lap, the blood drying to a crescent moon pattern in the shape of his even teeth. The man had settled into an unearthly calm.

Avoiding Caspian's stare, Flare shifted his gaze to the lone yellow flower. He watched impassively as an approaching wasp hovered nearby until a bloody hand snapped past Flare's vision. The hand ripped the flower from its roots. Caspian held up the flower as if for the wasp to see. As the insect buzzed around his fist, he crushed the petals into paste. The wasp flew off with a loud buzzing chirp.

And then Flare had a front row view of how Caspian's unearthly calm morphed into shock, before descending into icy, barely restrained rage.

Flare watched the two grey birds fly off with squeaky wings before his gaze dropped to the man falling apart before him.

His eyes were ablaze, and his fists pummeled the air with unhinged jerks and punches. His normally shiny boot heels thumped at the dirty tiles beneath him, long legs pumping and kicking while the wind carried his silent screams of rage away. The sheathed sword at his hip started scraping and tapping with his violent movements and the fact that Caspian had to stop punching the air with both hands, to silence the sword with one, only enraged him further.

He was clearly at a loss about what to do. Unable to make a sound, for the sake of the appearance of his brother in the ruined city below, Caspian's furious expression was a mask of such wrath that Flare could only gape. Caspian's normally cool face was a twisted, flushed mass of dusty smudges and sweating skin, his teeth gnashing.

While Caspian made absolutely no sound, Flare could read every single bitten off word, and read the venom in which it was mouthed.

Fuck.

Fuck, fuck, fuck.

His brother's name featured as well.

Fuck you, Owaen.

Why? Why now, Owaen?

FUUUUUUUUUUCK!

Flare thought it was over until, gaining a second wind, Caspian descended into further apoplexy. His blonde hair was wild, stuck up out from his head as he tugged on it roughly, his face contorted with the restrained impotence of his rage.

MINE!

SKYE IS MINE!

FUUUUUUUUUUCK-

It went on for some time.

The next day, Caspian licked his cracked lips.

"I'm hungry," he complained, quietly. He rubbed his forehead underneath the strange grey streak in his blonde hair. "I've remembered something, too. That fucking *map*."

As they listened to the echoing murmurs down in the city, Flare raised his head momentarily to stare at Caspian for a moment. There wasn't anything to say.

Flare tucked his head back into his wings to dream of crystals, fresh, potent and juicy, waiting for him to devour them all.

Just like the ones that he had enjoyed in Aneirin's now abandoned temple.

They were stuck in their waiting game, that only one side was aware that they were playing for longer than they expected. Fox and his companions stayed for a while, apparently needing the time to recover and regroup after what they had all been through.

Flare didn't blame them.

But, finally, when the golden green dragon took off into the sun, with three tiny figures on her shining spiked back, Caspian took a deep breath and pushed himself up with a groan. He moved to the centre of the sloped terrace where some of the tiles were more chipped than others, brushing his wild hair off his face with a trembling hand. After staring at the tiles for a moment, he gave Flare a look. The intense spike of energy along Flare's tail pulsed.

"Fetch the blade of my sword."

"But-"

"What I meant to say, Flare," Caspian licked his dry lips, rubbing his forehead under the grey streak in his hair as if it pained him, "was go fetch my sword or I will personally make sure that Aurelia falls again, this time without a dragon for a fucking cushion."

When Flare returned with the broken blade from the bloody, charged mess in the council chamber that would haunt his dreams forever, it was Caspian's left eye that twitched. But after wrapping a scrap of leather from his satchel around the palm of his hand, Caspian yanked it roughly from Flare's claws.

"What are you going to do with that?" Flare mumbled, his stomach roiling at the soot and blood that covered him.

"I lost the arrow," Caspian muttered, as if that made any sense at all.

With that said, Caspian knelt and started clearing away dirt from around the centre tile. He was muttering to himself. Flare realised he was repeating what Fox had called out to the silent city when he assumed none was there to hear.

"What was it? Oh. That's right." Caspian tried to imitate the arrogant tones of Fox's voice. "*I'm going to wipe it all out,*" Caspian muttered. "*I'm going to take it back…*'Ugh. Don't forget '*magic users are weird*'. What is wrong with her? Magic is a fucking blessing."

"Is it worth this, though?" Flare hedged. "Do you really need it?"

The ruined tip of the sword blade paused as Caspian froze. "*You*, of all creatures, ask *me* that?"

After a patronizing chuckle, Caspian leaned in closer to Flare. The dragon could see the white flakes of his cracked lips. They looked like the snowflakes that had fallen while they waited, as if they hadn't been able to melt in contact with Caspian's icy rage.

"Flare. If you ever speak to me so stupidly again, I shall bite off your magical little tongue. I shall choke it down my tight throat, like the most proficient whore in all of Aneirin attempting to deep throat a massive-"

"Yes! Argh! I get it! I'm *sorry*."

Caspian bent back to his task and muttered some more.

"I'm just sure *you* would love to give your magic back. But I won't. Ever."

Flare spent some time perched on the stone balustrade, unwilling to risk flying off for water or sustenance, the fierce spike of Caspian's power coiled around Flare's tail like a tiny leash. He could see the tiny speck of the two horses browsing in the meadows, idly wondering if it was safe for them to be out here alone. Knowing Rhydian a little, it was likely the new king would send someone back for them if Fox somehow didn't arrange that beforehand.

While Caspian scraped away behind him, a low mist formed across the flowers. The giant trees of the forest loomed out of the white like green sentinels, visible all the way around the city over the wall past the riot of ever-blooming flowers. Glancing down, he noticed that the great map that formed the main pattern of the great courtyard was cracked through most of its finely made features, the scope of its design even encompassing Baile Mara, the old city on the sea, that predated the City of the Seers.

"Ow, fuck. Not yet, not now."

Cringing, Flare turned to face the digging going on behind him, his wings twitching erratically. At first, he was unable to make out what was wrong. Then he realised there was a chaotic network of new cracks spreading out from where Caspian was working; a new one appeared as he stared. Flare ruffled his wings, and Caspian looked up, squinting at him.

"Don't even think about it. If I go, you go with me."

He didn't elaborate. Flare didn't need him to. The hot splice of magic that Caspian had bestowed upon Flare jerked maliciously along the dragon's spine. If Caspian plunged to his death here, as attractive as that sounded, it was likely Flare wouldn't survive. The tiny dragon leapt off the balustrade and landed with a smooth glide near the perilous excavation.

"Caspian."

"What."

"Um. What exactly are you doing?"

Caspian tapped the ruined sword blade to the cracking tiles. "Digging."

"*Caspian.*"

"Oh." Two different coloured blue eyes blinked innocently at Flare. The effect was spoilt by their wickedly metallic gleam. "Didn't I tell you what we headed to this city for, before we met our lovely friends on that lonely road?"

"N-no?"

A beatific smile spread across Caspian's face, his cheek marred by smudges of fine dust and blood. "We came back for the egg."

The silence that followed was sliced by the renewed scraping of the blade along the edges of the central tile. About a foot by a foot, it was almost dislodged from its neighbours. As Flare stared dumbfounded, his gaze bouncing wildly from Caspian's tight smile to the digging before him, another crack shot past them, all the way to the edge of the roof.

"That's not ideal," Caspian murmured. He put the sword down, and the tower rumbled when he nudged the cracks with his heel.

"Caspian."

Caspian twisted around, as if looking for some alternative to what he was doing. His pale brows were drawn together in a worried frown. "I wonder…"

"Caspian."

"Mmm?" he answered absentmindedly as he wiped his hands on his ruined pants, adjusting the flashy golden sword at his hip, his gaze fixed on the loosened tile.

"Caspian!"

At Flare's frantic tone, Caspian finally looked up. His expression was suspiciously calm, but the twinkle in his silver-blue eyes told Flare all he needed to know.

"Yes, my shiny little jewel?"

"Egg?" Flare stared at him. "Wh-what egg?"

"Oh, you sweet little thing," Caspian drawled as he pulled his discarded satchel close to his hip. He slipped the strap over his shoulder and smiled winningly at Flare. "Skye's unhatched twin, of course. Now be a dear and come over here. I need you close by when this whole shit stack falls apart."

"Wait, *what*?" Flare squeaked.

Without waiting for Flare to gather his thoughts, Caspian reached across, yanked Flare off the ground, and deposited the dragon without ceremony onto his shoulder.

"So," Caspian said, as he rubbed his filthy hands together. "You caught Aurelia when she was pushed off a tower, right? You caught her in midair?"

"Y-yes?"

"That's settled then. Do it for me."

"What! *Wait*! When?" Flare screeched, the pigeons overhead scrambling off their nest once again.

"Right now, sweetness!" Caspian laughed and yanked the loose tile free.

It all happened rather quickly.

Amidst the cracking, chaos and dust that followed, Flare caught sight of a sparkling green shape, the same material as the crystal dagger and matching pendants. There was little time to digest what he was seeing, though, or to think about what Caspian had shared.

Because the terrace, along with the entire tower, collapsed.

It felt and sounded like the entire world came apart around them. The ear-splitting violence of a building disintegrating, a building that had stood for hundreds of years, was immense. Blocks of stone became boulders; the boulders became pebbles, and the pebbles shattered into glittering particles of dust.

If the sparkling, shimmering dragon had looked behind at that moment, it might have seen what was left of the tower. It might have seen a single dirty brown cloud, rising and expanding on the forested horizon above a ruined city, a fitting symbol for one volatile man's quest to get what he wanted, at any cost. The magnificent gold and emerald dragon might have seen it all, and turned swiftly back to investigate.

It didn't.

EPILOGUE

The Hollow

"A hollow is formed when a branch or large offshoot dies, falling away from the parent tree. A void can sometimes form, weathered into a snug nesting space, where new life is nurtured. But a hollow may also form a gaping wound, where no creature dares to dwell."

Taken from 'Plant Lore for the Continent of Beinacoilia' by Hypatia Carter, commissioned for the Library of Seers.

Added underneath in an expressive scrawl:

'My dear wife, I wonder about the forest and our boys. I think the trees talk amongst themselves. Will the forest look after them, after what we did?

x Illarion'

Owaen

Year 367
Owaen's family cottage
A short ride from the City of the Seers

From the far side of the little cottage came the soft snort of contented horses. The thick trees and flowering shrubs of the ever-present forest were crowded close by, but thankfully there was enough cleared ground around the small building. It allowed the afternoon sun to make its dappled way down to the soft grass, making for a perfect spot to laze about and feel content.

Which Owaen was not.

The air was cool and fresh, and Owaen was numb. He squinted down at the dusty blanket under his chin that smelled faintly of dried rosemary. His arse was bared to the blue sky above, his ankles crossed, feet dangling above his calves. He was numb and restless, and trying hard to be grateful for the peaceful moment. What he had right now, without thinking too far ahead, was a fleeting but welcome blessing. There was a lot to think about, especially certain people.

Or, more accurately, a certain person.

Which he really, *really* didn't want to do.

Owaen was aware that returning to his family's three-roomed cottage might leave him with more riddles than answers. Fox and Owaen had been here a night and less than a day, and potentially it was still too early to judge how effective sorting through his mother's notes might be. There were odd shelves and bookcases all over the house, not just her study. Cobwebs filled the space along with dusty notes that he'd never really been inclined to read before. Along with an odd array of collected paraphernalia from her travels over the years, the little cottage was bursting with the unknown.

Things that, maybe, were better left that way.

Fox had watched Owaen carefully as they had moved quietly through the cobwebs, but said nothing. Fox knew that Owaen wanted answers, but had declined to offer any suggestions on how to find anything of particular relevance to the questions they both had.

For himself, it was still in question if Owaen could handle what they found.

On the day before, they had flown for hours to reach Aneirin by the afternoon. Owaen had a suspicion that Fox was taking his time for Rhydian's sake. Amongst the glittering spikes, the king had planted himself firmly between Owaen and Aurelia. The young king hadn't moved once.

Owaen smirked affectionately. Rhydian's face had been a hilarious shade of green when they stopped to stretch their legs alongside a river. The colossal, golden green dragon had splashed the young king with his spiked tail. Rhydian had acknowledged his wet clothes with a pained expression, but no comment.

Their eventual arrival in the king's homeland had been to a mixed reception, which seemed unsurprising. The city's last interaction with a dragon hadn't been welcome, apparently.

After circling above to alert the castle to their arrival, Fox had landed gracefully in a corner of the large forecourt, arching his brilliant green neck primly while humans and Elves raced around first in fear, before getting a hold of themselves and standing to gawk. Owaen hadn't wanted to stay long. He hadn't wanted to stay or speak with any Elves. It was too soon. He had refused the king's generous offer to stay. So, after a still green-faced Rhydian had hugged a large man with a bushy beard and a leather apron, the young king had run inside the sprawling, tower-topped castle, and Owaen had felt a pang of loss for the city they had left behind that morning. A few servants came out soon enough, along with the king, now pink cheeked and teary-eyed, all of them carrying sacks of food, blankets and clothes.

Aurelia hadn't cried, but she hadn't let go of Fox's leg until Owaen was settled in between his spikes with the supplies. Fox had climbed delicately to the castle wall to get clear of the city dwellers below before a magnificent leap into the sky. Fox had flown most of the afternoon and into the night, stopping twice so Owaen could relieve himself against various trees while Fox pretended not to peer over his shoulder.

They had arrived back in the north during the night after a full day of flying, Fox soaring in the cold air and Owaen wrapped in both their cloaks. Owaen had gone to the meadows of the City of the Seers to fetch the two suspicious horses, Fox soaring overhead. When they had finally come to the cabin, Fox, as a man once more, had refused to put on any clothes at all for the walk back to the cabin, despite the chill. Owaen, leading and not riding the horses, waved for Fox to walk ahead of him with feigned reluctance. The black haired figure had smiled at him, his bare feet barely making a sound on the frost covered old road.

Seeing the cabin emerge from the shadows had sparked a deep ache within Owaen. He hadn't spent a lot of time here, before the City of the Seers was rocked by disaster in the shape of a black dragon.

The horses were secured in the barely standing hut joined to the back of the cottage with water and oats, the old scatter of wicker bee hives now piles of sticks and moss nearby. Owaen dropped their supplies at the old wooden door while Fox bent down and tugged off Owaen's boots for him. Biting back a smile, Owaen let Fox take care of him, until he realised what Fox was doing. Fox had already reached into one of the sacks and pulled out the bundle of green crystals. The pendants on their chains went over Fox's pale neck. And the dagger-

"My boot?" Owaen had asked doubtfully.

"Yes," Fox had replied primly. "They stink," he had added, as if that explained such an unlikely hiding place for a potentially lethal, magical object.

After shoving open the stubborn door, they moved around inside the cottage, lighting candles that still smelled of rich beeswax. Both of them had been solemn and quiet for that. Except their pensive mood hadn't lasted long. They were finally alone after a shitty few days. It had been too much to resist continuing with silent glances. Fox had looked at Owaen, Owaen had leered at him in return, and soon enough Owaen's clothes were off and they went to work reacquainting themselves with each other on just about every flat surface in the cabin. Except for his mother's study.

Later, as the cobwebs and dust settled inside, they had bathed their sweat and bruises in the fresh creek at the back of the cottage. Despite the occasional ache that had Owaen wincing each time he sat down, now the gentle morning was *almost* perfect.

The knowledge that someone had appeared from his past that Owaen had never, ever thought to see again was just too much.

Because *he* was dead.

Owaen's hand curled into a fist, a wrinkled section of blanket squeezed within.

Except *he* wasn't dead, was he?

He had yet to say his brother's name out loud.

There was a hollow inside his chest where the knowledge of his brother's survival weighed painful and heavy. It wasn't just the fact that Caspian was alive and Owaen hadn't known. It was that Caspian must have been aware that Owaen was in the city with Fox, but had actively *avoided* him.

Owaen glared at the blanket's edge, where it rippled along the long grass that cushioned them. Had Caspian known where Owaen was, when Owaen dreamt in the darkness of a cave full of quartz, bones and evil memories?

Unable to help it, Owaen's glare was soon directed at Fox. Fox ignored him, but his lips twitched, aware of the dark glance focused his way.

"Are you still mad about those hideous garden ornaments?" Fox murmured. "I hated them before, and time did not improve them."

Fox was sitting cross-legged next to Owaen, eyes closed and his face tilted to the gentle sun. One of his beautiful hands was supporting his weight on the blanket behind him, while the other played idly with the two green shards of crystal resting on his bare chest. Fox had apparently felt the heat of Owaen's glare. A thin slit of glittering black appeared as Fox opened one eye to peer down at Owaen, a slight smile on his fine lips.

"No," Owaen snapped.

Unable to help it, Owaen's gaze shifted from Fox to examine the cruelly scattered pile of little gnomes. Even after years of neglect, they had, until recently, been almost perfectly aligned along the garden path. Fox had 'accidentally' kicked *all* of them over this morning on emerging to join Owaen outside. Fox had gasped dramatically, clutching his chest and murmuring his condolences as he flopped down on the blanket.

All the while biting back a mocking smile.

Admittedly, the fucking gnomes *were* hideous, but that wasn't the point. Owaen's father had collected them for his mother, and that meant something. Well, Hypatia had expressed her disgust of them loudly and quite often, but still. Even if time hadn't improved them, nor the moss and algae and faded paint added any character, it was still rude. Owaen pursed his lips.

As for how much time had passed and not improved the gnomes, Owaen still wasn't brave enough to ask. After seeing the one he loved, completely covered in reeking, steaming blood, thankfully not his own, Owaen had been taken back to the darkest days of his life. Maybe he understood a little more of how Skye had felt, when she had shut Owaen away, for however long it had been, to keep him safe.

"Safe," Owaen muttered, dropping his forehead to rest upon his folded arms.

Beside him, Fox mumbled something about being responsible. Maybe their thoughts were in alignment after all. Fox's deep sigh was long and drawn out.

Calming the scowl on his face, Owaen turned to rest his cheek on his arms so he could examine Fox. The pale sun was dappled here, so far from the tops of the looming canopy above. The patterns made attractive shapes on Fox's smooth white skin, vastly different from the way he had appeared as the green-haired Elf that Owaen had come to love. Owaen shifted, reaching out to trace the lean muscles of Fox's side. His pale lips curled upwards at Owaen's feather light touch.

"You have nice lips," Owaen said quietly.

"Yours are still puffy," Fox teased, his eyes opening to thin slits once more. Ignoring the dig, Owaen reached over, brushing his fingertips over the two green pendants. They felt strange, tingling. He let them go and dropped his hand to rest on Fox's thigh. Owaen yawned lazily, pleased with the way Fox's eyes opened to watch Owaen stretch his neck.

With his cheek resting on his folded arms, Owaen jutted his chin at the little green crystals. "They feel cold to the touch. Like your skin."

Fox screwed his nose up, squinting at the sky. "They don't feel like that to me. They feel warm, or neutral perhaps." He sounded mildly concerned.

"We'll figure it out," Owaen assured him. He hoped.

The cottage, with its endless piles of notes on the natural world, crystals, magic and geology, had to contain some answers to at least some of their troubles. Ignoring the biggest trouble of all, a tall, blonde pillar of trouble, Owaen's eyes drifted shut as the cool breeze and the dappled sun lulled him into a doze.

The peace didn't last long.

Owaen opened his eyes. A loud buzzing was coming from the grass beside their blanket.

He pushed himself half up and blew his hair from his face. Owaen searched the garden in front of them a moment before he saw them. A giant black and orange winged insect was determinedly dragging a frantic brown spider through the stalks of the long grass.

"What in the actual fuck is happening there?" Fox hissed beside him. Owaen smothered his grin. "I want to simultaneously vomit and cheer. I'm just not sure which one I'm rooting for. *Ugh*. Get them away."

"That, my brave dragon, is a spider hornet," Owaen explained with a straight face, "with its lunch, a weak excuse for a huntsman spider."

Fox made a series of loud gagging noises. Owaen's eyes narrowed.

"Let them pass," Owaen warned, eyeing Fox, who was impossibly paler than usual, "they're just doing what insects do. Keeping the forest healthy."

Fox bit his lip. He refused to look at Owaen. "Hmm."

Laughing, Owaen dropped his head to the blanket, settling back down. After a moment, a soft rush of cold air tingled along his neck. The buzzing from the grass nearby ceased. Owaen whipped his head up as the faint tang of ozone reached his nose. The grappling insects were nowhere to be seen.

"Fox!" Owaen barked sharply.

Fox was reclining back with both hands on the blanket behind him, legs out straight, baring his chest to the sky. His eyes were closed. Innocent contentment radiated from him.

"*Fox*. Where. Did. They. Go?"

"Oh, Owaen," Fox sighed airily. "I'm sure they're off living happily ever after."

Scowling, Owaen reached over and pinched Fox's hip, hard. Fox laughed, deep and unconcerned, lazily swatting Owaen's hand away. Cursing, Owaen waved his fingers to shake off the sting. Fox was stronger than he looked, after all.

"Rhydian was right," Owaen groused. He was pleased with how quickly Fox's eyes snapped open at that. He eyed Owaen intently, his glittering gaze chilled.

"About what?" Fox's tone was clipped.

"He was right, in that you can be quite mean."

Fox pushed himself to sit up, crossing his legs, resting his hands on his knees.

When he spoke again, his voice was serious and had lost some of its chill.

"I'm trying to be nice, too."

Something shifted between them. Owaen pushed himself up to sit with his legs out, gathered Fox to him, pulling Fox over his lap and against his chest. He inhaled the cool, mineral musk of Fox's hair.

"Beautiful creature," Owaen murmured, and planted a kiss on Fox's brow. "You're healing," another kiss, "not healed. I am the same... healing."

With a shapely toe, Fox poked at the grass beyond the fabric of their blanket where the bugs had been.

"We might never be. *I* might never be."

Craning his head a little, Owaen pressed his sun-warmed cheek against the cool flesh of Fox's, resting it there. "All we can do is try."

It was Fox who broke the quiet peace this time.

They were stretched out on the blanket, wrapped around each other. A cool hand brushed messy blonde hair from his face, the fingers travelling down his neck, lingering on the golden chain around Owaen's neck.

"Owaen."

"Mm."

"We've had quite the day here, getting to know each other again."

Owaen's jaw tensed, knowing what was coming. He waited for it, the 'but' at the end of Fox's quiet statement unspoken, but hanging in the air for one of them to pluck out if they were brave enough. Owaen pressed his face into the cool flesh of Fox's chest.

"Let's talk now," Fox murmured as his gentle hand idly toyed with the ends of Owaen's hair. "You know we have to."

Owaen mumbled a string of curses into the darkness and refused to open his eyes.

"What was that, little Elf?"

"I said," Owaen mumbled, "about what?"

A cool finger poked Owaen's shoulder. "Owaen."

Without looking, Owaen twisted and grabbed the finger; bring it to his lips for a chaste kiss.

He wasn't ready to talk about this.

What could he possibly say?

Really, if Caspian was behind any of this, what in the world could Owaen do about it? This was his brother. The older twin. But in Owaen's mind, Caspian was his little brother, not because he was weak. But because he was born to a family full of potent magic, with none of his own, and strange eyes that their mother might have been able to fix. But had chosen not to. The boy had stubbornly distinguished himself in other ways, his volatile temper being one of them.

Caspian's uniqueness, their mother called it his *affliction*, had shaped the angry little boy's life. It was possibly still guiding Caspian's life choices to this day. Was it possible that Caspian had something to do with Shadow Light, and with what happened to Skye? Owaen swallowed back his moan, unable to voice such things.

Such things were unspeakable.

Such things should have been unthinkable.

But Caspian was alive, and out doing what he did best, or worst, and things were likely to get fucked up in the very near future.

Especially if Morgan was involved.

Finally, lifting his head away from Fox's soothing embrace, Owaen tried to say something, anything. But he could only stare wordlessly at Fox's beautiful eyes; the face was different, but the once innocent soul was still the same. Bright, fierce and full of challenge. Fox raised a fine, dark eyebrow and waited, the gold glittering across the glossy black of his captivating eyes.

"The library in the City of the Seers," Owaen murmured instead of speaking his brother's name, "what came of it? Is it gone?"

Fox sighed, his gaze softening at the pain on Owaen's face. "It might as well be, my love."

"Fuck." Owaen sighed. "Fuck Shadow Light. That stupid fuck."

"Mm." Fox rubbed slow circles on Owaen's back. "Hush. Tell me of your brother," Fox paused. "Please."

"Cas..." Owaen cleared his throat with a dry cough. "Caspian was born without magic, but he found the use of it later. He spent his early years trying to live up to... my gifts. When he finally got what he wanted, he was so triumphant about it, except that he hid it from our parents." His brother had sworn Owaen to secrecy. Owaen hadn't liked it, but agreed. There was a scar on his arm somewhere to seal the pact. Not from a knife, from a flame. That reminded him of something.

"I think he burned down a library once."

"He sounds like a delight," Fox said dryly. "I can't wait to meet him."

Owaen grunted in response, turning things over in his mind.

"Caspian looked like me, although he was far more pretty, and wickedly skilled with a sword."

Fox snorted and Owaen spared a moment's thought for the broken sword, his brother's prize passion.

After Morgan, that was.

"My brother was as smart as a seer," Owaen went on, "but as unpredictable as one of those red firecrackers they throw into crowds at Samhain."

Fox looked at him blankly. "A firecracker? What the fuck is that?"

Owaen grimaced.

"I mean Caspian was explosive, like if you threw an oil lantern into a pile of dry hay. Or into a wall of old parchment." He wondered if the stash under the old couch inside was still any good, or more of a fire hazard.

"I see," Fox said pensively. "Wonderful."

Owaen remembered the smoke billowing up from the library along the cliffs, the shouts and wailing of the city below. Accompanied by the memory of the bitter ash on salty air, an uncomfortable thought followed.

"Do you know, I think it was the first time I'd seen him so..." his voice drifted off. Had Owaen been so blind to Caspian's malevolence?

"So?"

"So *happy*."

Running his hand over Owaen's back, Fox was silent for a moment.

"After a childhood of trying to live up to you, it's conceivable that your brother felt like he finally had something to rejoice in for himself."

"I just told you my brother burned down a fucking *library* and that's your response? It was okay to *rejoice*?"

Fox's laugh was cruel. "I don't have the pleasure of knowing your brother yet, but I know that I rejoiced when the dragons wept, and their homeland burned. Which adds to what we need to talk about. I need to find Flare as well. My rage is burning for that scaly purple shit. We should get on with that-"

"Lets leave rage out of it for now," Owaen interrupted darkly, "and use our brains to think. Your rage blinded you-"

"My rage?" Fox interrupted in turn, his voice cold. "Let's talk about rage. Especially *your* rage."

"M-mine?"

"Yes," Fox snapped. "Keep that in mind when you take a look at what's left of your precious city's library, Owaen."

"Ah, fuck." Owaen dropped his face back to Fox's chest. "I'm not- ugh. I don't know how to deal with this."

"I've got a few ideas already," Fox murmured, his voice coiling around Owaen's spine like ice. Owaen shook his head.

"No. We are not using *any* of your ideas. Absolutely not."

Fox smiled innocently.

"My brother, Caspian," Owaen continued, his eyes narrowing at Fox, "Well, I tried to be there for him. But he was just so different. I tried to treat him the same as everyone else."

Fox made a soothing noise. Taking a steadying breath, Owaen lifted his head, keeping his face close to Fox's. He needed to see Fox's reaction as Owaen chose his next words very carefully.

"Our mother and father, they didn't try as hard as I did."

Fox's nostrils flared, but he remained silent. He nodded at Owaen to continue. Owaen's next breath seemed harder to take than the one before it. He cleared his throat, eyes darting back and forth between Fox's glittering eyes. Owaen battled to keep his voice as even as he could.

"Tell me about magic, Fox. Tell me about the dragons, about what you did to them."

Gold and black eyes narrowed, glimmering with unknowable depths. Fox shook his head. Owaen licked his lips, words forming as his mind shied away from them. He took a breath and forged on.

"Does any of it," Owaen murmured, watching Fox closely, "have to do with my parents?"

Fox's expression didn't change. But his already pale face went whiter, and the gold in his eyes shimmered brighter for just a moment. That was all the confirmation Owaen needed.

Owaen closed his eyes, attempting to shut out the sight and unwelcome thoughts of what he had long suspected about his parents.

About his brother.

The after image of Fox's brilliant black and gold eyes shimmered behind Owaen's closed lids. And as much as Owaen tried to hold them there, the image changed, slowly morphing into eyes of different blues, reflecting the light like mercury.

Against his will, as if even Owaen's imagination couldn't contain Caspian and all that he was, one of the strange, silvery blue eyes winked.

Shit.

Rhydian

Year 367

Aneirin Castle

*B**lood Binds All.*

It had been written on the wall above a fan of daggers. It had been written deep within the mountainside castle, below his place at the top of his tower. Blood Binds All. Words left in the somber shadows of an abandoned chamber.

But did it? Or was it fear that held things together, people following what they knew for the sake of staying safe? Maybe all of it was nonsense. Maybe it was love that bound them all. And if it didn't, then it should.

A hand reached from behind him, startling him for a moment. That is, until the soft scent of flowers filled his senses, accompanied by Aurelia's reverent touch. Her hand slid up Rhydian's chest to cup his throat with a soft caress.

"I know Flare saved you from that dagger, from the choice I made," Aurelia murmured into his shoulder, sounding faintly bitter. Her fingers danced over his sensitive flesh, her short nails and callouses rasping over his faint stubble. Her voice hardened. "I know the fact that I spilled your blood with your consent broke apart your father's curse. It needed to happen. But I can't forgive him. He simply stood by when Shadow Light bound my hands, and when Caspian gagged me. I hope Flare knows Fox is coming for him. I hope he can't sleep for nightmares." Aurelia paused, her voice quiet. "Nightmares about the broken dreams he has concocted for both of us, with his scaly, cowardly heart."

Silence followed her words. They stood together for a while, Aurelia's hand resting warmly over his throat.

Rhydian tilted his head back, giving her more access. After a light squeeze, a gesture he instinctively took as one full of regret, she pressed a firm kiss between his shoulder blades. Her hand slid down to his waist and Rhydian captured it with his, bring them up to press them both to his heart. Aurelia's words were at the forefront of his mind. Of cowardice and broken dreams. What could he say? What words would do against an honest statement like that?

They had arrived back in Aneirin the afternoon before, back to where it had all begun to unravel. As they stood on the top of his tower, their breath misted before him as he stared out across the terraced city, the farmlands and the scarred meadows of the battlefield. The brisk wind started to pick up, and Aurelia's hair flicked around them both. With an inaudible sigh, she nestled closer against his back.

Rhydian stared at the forest stretching endlessly north, where Fox had returned with Owaen. To where Blackthorn was most likely snorting his displeasure at being abandoned in a strange place, to be handled by two strangers.

Rhydian's free hand tightened on the stone balustrade, the black arrow pressed between his palm and the gritty surface. He was still wondering how it had come to be at the steaming baths in the ruined city. Rhydian hadn't known why the arrow was there in that place, so he had kept it. It had likely been discarded there by Owaen's brother. Caspian seemed to be behind at least some of the chaos that had fallen upon them. He had shown Aurelia the arrow when they had made it to his chamber last night. She had paled, and asked him promptly to burn it.

But for what it symbolised, along with all the memories bound to its deadly tip, Rhydian had found that he couldn't. The weight and shape of it in his hands reminded him of seeing a beautiful woman with long, dark hair emerge from the forest across a lonely river, while he gawked like a farmer. The arrow reminded him of his father, and a choice that Rhydian had made. He had humbled himself by asking Aurelia for help with something that he knew he couldn't do alone.

Was it murder and therefore wrong? Or was it justice and therefore right? Was all the betrayal that littered his parent's choices an excuse for what he had done?

Rhydian swallowed past the unease in his throat. Magic could do so much harm, and a very tiny part of him could see where the curse over Aneirin had been made to keep the population in a safe kind of isolation. But magic could do so much good as well.

Big things, little things. When he had marvelled at Aurelia's clear, beautiful skin, she had laughed at him. She used some of the little magic she had to take care of useless things sometimes, matters of vanity being one of them.

"What is it like?" he had asked her the night before.

"What?"

"To use magic?"

Aurelia shrugged. "For me, it is a matter of concentrating on the sparks that float around my body. For Fox, I think magic is another matter entirely."

He inhaled against her now, scenting the soothing aroma of strange flowers in her hair. At the top of the tower, the wind lifted the long strands around his face as he tried to find whatever sense of calm was available to him for the moment at least.

Because right now, the arrow also reminded him of washing long dark hair in an abandoned city, when Rhydian and Aurelia had been alone for just a little while. Nothing intimate had passed between them, other than simple touching and trembling embraces.

Rhydian's cheeks flushed at the memory of Aurelia's bare skin so close to his in the water, the shallow liquid hiding nothing. Aurelia had been worn out, yes, but unashamed. Rhydian's shyness had amused her. Hopefully, last night after they had returned to Aneirin, had made up for it.

After his stomach had settled down.

"Don't ever leave," Rhydian whispered as Aurelia moved above him.

She stilled, brushing hair from her face as his hands trembled upon her thighs. Her clear green eyes were wide, her cheeks flushed as she stared down at him. She looked somewhere between well pleasured, frustrated and confused.

"Why would I leave?" she breathed, leaning down to bite his bottom lip.

"Because," he gasped against her mouth as she started to move once more. "You just… *ah*. You might."

Rhydian thought of the caves in the south full of Elves, Aurelia's home. He thought of her falling into a white mist. He thought of her falling in a ruined city to the sound of bones breaking, as her oldest friend broke himself apart to catch her. Rhydian's heart chilled at the memory, and Aurelia's eyes softened at the expression that crossed his face.

"Don't be daft, Rhydian. I'm not going anywhere, not now. Not yet."

"But-"

Aurelia covered his mouth with her hand at first, before replacing it with her lips. Rhydian wanted to ask her what she meant, but his words were soon forgotten. His words were shuffled to the back of his mind as his body reacted to hers as she moved above, against, and around him with love and heat.

The sounds of their mutual pleasure filled his room until late into the night, both of them recovering from their shared release. There was no fire in the fireplace; they hadn't made it that far.

Rolling over and pulling their blankets up to their chins, Aurelia had slid her hand beneath the thick fabric, her touch warm on his chest. As his heartbeat beneath her palm, Aurelia had looked him straight in the eye.

"However, just to be clear, I don't want to be a queen."

Rhydian had nodded, unable to speak right then. He had closed his eyes. Her words eased something within him, something that was bound up behind his heart, hidden chambers full of fears.

Her words eased him because now that they were back in his kingdom, he was completely certain that he didn't want to be a king.

Especially if his family weren't even truly royal at all.

Now he was on his tower in the cold light of morning, the once comforting noise of the ward below bustling with chaos, and the city glittering beyond like a collar around his neck. His gaze dropped from the arrow in his fist to the sight of Aurelia's bare feet.

"Aurelia, I love your feet, but it's bloody freezing out here. Why didn't you put on boots, or socks at least?"

Aurelia huffed a laugh into his back, her breath cool against him and tasting of apples. She flexed one of her feet for him to inspect.

"I stubbed my toe on something under your bed when I was looking for my pants," she murmured. "And it bloody hurt. I didn't want to put boots on straight away."

"Oh." He noticed one of her big toes looked red. "What was it?"

Aurelia's voice became teasing.

"A little toy knight made of scraps and sticks." She snickered. "With a rather large-"

"Sword!" Rhydian interrupted hastily. "It's a *sword*."

"Mm?" Aurelia pressed closer. "Really?"

"I made it when I was little," he said defensively as she laughed quietly against him. "I liked the stories of knights and brave battles."

Rhydian pulled Aurelia to his side, his free hand rubbing his chest. His heart was beating a little faster than was usual, and he wondered if Aurelia had noticed. Her palm was still pressed close. It had been beating strangely since they arrived back last night.

Thinking of battles and bravery had him bite his lip. Battles were not anything like he had expected. He hoped to never see one again. Between armies or creatures of magic. The dark glances from some of his folk and the Elves when he'd passed through the castle yesterday had been enough of a test of his bravery.

"Lady Hywel used to tell me about bravery," he murmured. "About dark places. She spoke of the weapons we chose to take there, where only courageous kings dared to tread."

Aurelia kissed his cheek softly, her touch a comfort and her floral scent filling his senses, grounding him. He leaned into her while he continued quietly.

"I used to think she meant a physical place."

"She didn't?" Her palm rubbed over his heart as if sensing how his thoughts turned to painful things, like dragons, like Dawn of Fire, betrayed in the forest by the two who had sworn to help her.

"Now that I think of her stories as an adult, I feel like she might have meant something else, about my family in particular. About the weapons we used. I don't know."

"Speaking of weapons, I need a new sword." Rhydian kissed the top of Aurelia's hair at her words, grateful for her change of subject. "My old one was taken away by Jessikah...ugh. Fuck, that's annoying. I mean Shadow Light."

Trying to shake off his heavy mood, Rhydian replied with a light-hearted tone.

"I know of an old armoury-"

"Ha! No thanks." Aurelia tugged on his shirt. "But I'll take a new one if you have it. Um." She paused. "There's something else."

"What?"

"I think Caspian took your father's sword."

Rhydian waited for the blow to his family's pride to come.

It didn't.

"Huh. I guess I should be angry. Except I'm more confused about why that means less to me than it should."

"Apart from the loss of a fine blade," Aurelia's tone was dry. "I can think of some valid reasons why it doesn't bother you."

Neither of them mentioned the fact that if Caspian had taken the king's sword, he had likely left the dick and balls all over his father's forehead too. Rhydian exhaled in a long, slow sigh, watching his breath mist away in the frigid air.

For a while they stood together silently, breathing together and inhaling the rich aromas from below. Smoke, horse dung and the occasional whiff of cooking food. Rhydian was grateful to be back in a way, and safe enough. Flare was off somewhere with a mad magic user, but for now; the calm peace of the day was something he could enjoy. Until he went downstairs and faced the tension between the Elves and humans who had recently been bitter enemies.

He couldn't blame them at all. They had every right to feel as they did. But leaving them at such a time hadn't been a wise decision in their eyes, even if it hadn't been a choice for him. Aurelia had been taken. Rhydian had to follow.

Aurelia let go of his chest to rub her thumb over her lips.

"I wish I had some glow wort." Her beautiful features distorted into a grimace. "I think both of us could use a drink. To drink until we're sick."

"Again," Rhydian muttered under his breath.

"Don't be ashamed. You waited until you were away from his scales."

Rhydian shook his head. "Don't say *scales*. Ugh. Too soon."

There was no way that he wasn't grateful. His arms were only still slightly tender from dragging Fox up a mountain, but his legs and back were sore. Sitting so long in an awkward position on a dragon wasn't as comfortable as horse riding. But worst of all, he had vomited during their last rest break. Watching the brilliant gilded green dragon take to the air again had been sad, but also a relief. The lone blonde Elf on Fox's back had waved once, and then they were gone to the clouds. Rhydian had been breathless with wonder along with nausea at the sight, and sincerely hoped that he would never be airborne again.

In the courtyard below, Wyll was hurrying across the cobbles with Merion towards the gates. Wyll's hastily spoken words were too faint to hear, but his hiss of frustration was not. Rhydian peered down at them, struck by something.

"Merion isn't wearing his apron. Huh. I've never seen him without it. He looks mad too."

Aurelia followed his gaze. "You can see his expression from up here as well I can?" She paused. "You *do* have magic in your blood. You're right, he looks pissed."

Rhydian nodded slowly, wondering how much magic had been a part of his life without him being aware of it. The curse was obvious, but... it was quite far down, and he could see everyone's faces clear enough if he concentrated. Maybe it was time to go in. He'd meant to go in before Aurelia tracked him down. It seemed bad luck to be at the top of a tall building with her, considering all that had had happened.

"Merion was furious when you came back without Blackthorn," said Aurelia, interrupting his thoughts. Her tone was thoughtful.

"I know. And Wyll. Everyone is angry with me about something, humans and Elves. I don't want to be their king."

Silence followed his last statement. He hadn't meant to blurt it out quite like that. But Aurelia didn't seem surprised.

"I know." She cleared her throat. "This is going to sound incredibly selfish, but fuck it. When I met you in the forest, before it was fully certain who you were, I preferred it like that between us. Before all of this."

A dark tendril of resentment circled across his heart. Rhydian tapped the arrow against the balcony stone. "Me too."

Aurelia pressed against him. Her tone was thoughtful when she spoke again.

"Do you believe in destiny, Rhydian? In how we met as we did, but are here together now, despite all the lies... the deceit and betrayal? Your father, the leader of my people..."

Rhydian took a moment to absorb her words. But it seemed simple.

What destiny would be so cruel to allow both their peoples to be led by lies?

"No." He thought of two young people in the forest, plunging a spear into a dying dragon, making their own cruel way in the world. "There's no such thing as destiny."

Lost in thoughts of her own, Aurelia gazed distantly at the horizon of trees that ringed them across the valley of Aneirin, the rusty red mountains behind the castle at their back. Rhydian was happy to watch her, content that she was here. Until a frown marred her forehead. She turned to meet his stare, her green eyes troubled.

"Do you believe Fox, that he didn't kill the dragons?"

The question required some more thought than he'd given it, but the image of Fox's startling, violent and unforgettable tattoo was still clear in his mind. Fox had said he hadn't. But- Rhydian answered as honestly as he could.

"I don't know." He inhaled the cold air, scenting that the night was likely to bring frost. "When I found him in the forest, Fox said the dragons would have wished he'd killed them." Rhydian closed his eyes, trying to recall the words. "He said they were cruel, arrogant, lusting after power." He opened his eyes, searching Aurelia's troubled green gaze for answers. "What could you do to a dragon that would make them wish they were dead?"

Aurelia shook her head. Her dark hair was blowing across her eyes and she batted it away impatiently.

"I-" she started to speak, but she stiffened against him. She turned to face the north.

"Aurelia?"

She shook her head; eyes widening the more he stared. Rhydian was

fascinated by her change of expression until it slipped from shock, and then into horror.

Her mouth formed an *O*.

"Aurelia, please, what's wrong?"

"Oh my gods," she breathed, blinking rapidly.

"What is it?" Rhydian could feel his strange heartbeat intensify, and the arrow nearly slipped out of his hand as his palms started to sweat. He slipped it into his cloak.

"Rhydian, Fox was telling the *truth*."

"What? How do you know? He's held back so much from both of us. I don't know what-"

"He admitted Flare is not in his original form, but that when Fox was a dragon, Fox was in his. I can't explain that part, but for Flare?" Aurelia shook her head. "*'I'm going to find him and strip him of his magic, turn him back like the others',* he said."

Rhydian had no idea what she was talking about.

"Rhydian! Fox didn't *kill* the dragons. He turned them *back*."

"He what?" Rhydian still didn't get it. Aurelia turned to face him, her green eyes wide. She swallowed hard.

"He turned them back into what they were *before*," she said, pulling him towards her by his shirt with both hands.

"Aurelia! Before what?"

As if realising she was about to rip the material in her fists, she let go of his shirt abruptly and stepped back. "Before they were dragons."

The freezing wind had nothing to do with the ice that slid down Rhydian's spine.

"What are you saying?" he whispered. "What do you mean?"

Aurelia covered her mouth with her hands, speaking through them as if it was better to hold them back. She stared at him.

"You're part Elven, not fully human from what your parents did, right? You have dragon magic in your blood. We both do, which means we're just humans with magic, after all." Her hands dropped away, and she laughed coldly. "And *dragons*! Dragons are another step up, full of more magic than any of us. Don't you get it?"

He shook his head, sensing he really didn't want to get it, while Aurelia touched their chests, one hand over her heart, the other over his.

"Like Fox said, he's going to find Flare and *turn him back*, like he did the others." Aurelia was breathing rapidly, her cheeks flushed. "The other dragons that he turned back into..." she took a breath, "into *us*."

They stared at each other, alarmed and shocked, the wind gusting around them now.

"The dragons were once... Elves?"

Eyes wide, Aurelia nodded.

Well, shit.

In the forest, Fox had said the Elves came from humans, so the dragons were once...?

"Oh." Suddenly it was hard to think, or to breathe. "W-we should go back inside," was all Rhydian could manage.

Aurelia nodded numbly, letting Rhydian lead her to the door. He ushered her inside first, then closed the door behind them, shutting out the noise and chill of the wind. It was silent there, apart from their loud breaths. They paused at the landing at the top of the stairs, a few torches flickering silently, the bitter tang of soot on the air.

He rubbed his chest, thinking of Dawn of Fire and her bones left to be overgrown by the trees and the moss in the forest that he loved. Had she been something else, someone else, before his parents had found her, and taken her magic, and her life? What other secrets were the giant trees reclaiming?

His heart was beating wildly and seemed to pulse with more than just blood. As if the magic that Aurelia had mentioned running through his veins was waiting in dormant expectation, waiting for its chance to rise.

Alarmed, they stared at each other in the dancing glow of the orange flames.

He hoped Fox and Owaen had reached their cottage, and that there were answers there. Answers that Owaen would know what to do with before Fox made any decisions for all of them. Fox was no longer carrying a shadow on the outside, but like the rest of them, there were layers of scars deep within that had yet to heal.

They would need to face the coming storm, already circling them like the deadly whirlpool past the decimated meadow. It would be a storm created from the chain of events that his mother and father had left in their futile quest for power. He could only hope his courage was stronger than his fear of facing the aftermath. Anger simmered deep within him at the idea. Shame and guilt circled his heart like the whirlpool, magic like a dark shadow that left him breathless. He felt helpless. He had no framework to follow in order to climb out of the depths his parents had left him in.

Rhydian did the only thing he could in the light of what they had discovered. Straightening his shoulders, Rhydian took one of Aurelia's hands, and led her down the spiralling stairs, to what warmth and peace he could offer.

For now.

Cas

Year 367

The Forest

*M**organ raised her head, green eyes filled with desire, but also bewilderment.*

"This is wrong," she murmured, wiping her mouth on his bare thigh while he caught his breath.

"It doesn't feel wrong to me," he'd teased. "Why?"

Her shrewd gaze looked him over, studying him with narrowed eyes. For a moment, she looked sad.

"Did you know that you taste like the honeycomb from your dad's prized beehives?"

Well, that was unexpected. His hands had slid through her hair, fingers wrapping around the shining red strands. He smiled and bit his bottom lip.

"You're welcome. Now keep going."

With a start, Cas came to in a rush of wind and whirling thoughts.

He glanced down, half expecting to see Morgan's red hair in his lap. Instead, he saw the purple sheen of dragon spines between his thighs. And his hand, coated in fresh, bright red blood.

Shaking, Cas held it up in front of his face, staring numbly at the little finger that was pointing off at an impossible angle. It appeared to be hanging by a single flap of torn skin, a single splinter of bone, and a dented gold ring. The ring was set with a sparkling, faceted amethyst. Cas wondered if he should swallow the gemstone for old time's sake, and at that point he realised he just might be in shock. As he watched the little appendage wobble with the movement of the dragon beneath him, a dull throb started in his hand. It quickly grew worse. It didn't matter, though.

He just had to keep going.

Cas blinked and tried to get a hold of himself. Spitting out stone dust and blood, he looked around, noticing the fact that he was on Flare's back at the same time that they were flying high across a wide, clear river. The golden sky had a smoky yellow cast to it that painted the forest below in unpleasant sickly tones. He nearly ran his ruined hand through his hair before he thought better of it. His other arm was tucked into his chest, his precious treasure tight against his wildly beating heart. Tightening the grip of his thighs to Flare, Cas wondered if he'd made any lewd jokes to the dragon about riding without holding on before he'd passed out.

Maybe he could have planned the retrieval of the egg with more panache.

Covered in dust and bleary-eyed, he stared down at his hand; the pain rearing its head, the little finger hanging still attached in much the same way Cas was clinging to Flare. Refusing to be beaten. He tucked the egg into his chest more tightly.

The egg.

Cas knew for a fact it was the only other dragon egg in existence. Besides, the green shards that were left from Skye's own hatching. Cas would have liked to put the egg in his satchel, but with his current condition he was unwilling to move an inch. Maybe not until they landed, wherever that would be. He hadn't decided.

Aneirin? He thought idly of the racist fools that lived there, of Wyll and the anarchy Cas hoped to spread. Yes, he needed to get the map that he'd finally remembered in that fucking library. But he wanted violence, too. For no reason other than that it would please him to destroy the home of the man that had taken advantage of Cas at his weakest. It had been a fool's bargain, yes. And despite the old king's magic coming to him in the end, Cas wanted the king's home broken open, like the black dragon that was now a smoking, sticky pile of ash and shattered bones.

His forehead ached at the thought. His hand was truly afire now with pain, but the idea of pressing it to his head was agony. He needed to heal it, yes, but he also needed to be on the ground for that. And to land, they needed distance from the city first.

Would it be too dangerous to take Flare to the quarry town Baile Fuar? That was where the stones of the City of the Seers had come from, somewhere his brother had often gone. His hand curled into a fist before he could stop it.

Cas yelped at the pain, fury seething like hot syrup through his blood. His pulse was indeed racing, and he was on edge. No wonder he'd been fantasizing about Morgan's mouth wrapped around his-

"Caspian! You're awake! Are y-you okay?"

Cas gripped Flare's spike tighter at the dragon's frantic interruption.

"I'm just fucking fantastic, Flare," he spat vehemently.

The pain in his hand was getting unbearable, and the fury with his brother was just as bad. As he glared at the offending, flapping digit, he wondered if he could just cut it off. Sever it in the same way that he'd like to cut off Owaen's arrogant fucking head if they had the misfortune to meet each other again.

Because if they did, Caspian would be more prepared. He just had no idea how.

Admittedly, it had been very convenient that Owaen had been locked away years ago, leaving Cas to roam free and search for his heart's desire. He had thought he'd found it, the egg, and the knowledge that Skye was the key. The two together would unlock all of his wildest dreams, which had always been out of reach.

And now fucking Owaen had appeared with Skye, and Cas' dream was further over the horizon than ever. Cas' eyes narrowed as he stared down at the glittering green edge of the egg, just visible inside the folds of his ruined shirt. He needed new clothes. Especially another fucking cloak. At least he wouldn't have to pick Shadow Light or Flare over the other any more. Even flush with the king's magic, Cas hadn't been fully confident he could have ended Shadow Light, even in the form of a tiny woman. He might have unleashed some she-demon from the deepest hells for all he knew.

He tried taking deep breaths, allowing the cold air to cool his rage slightly, until he remembered all over again just how much of a mess he was in. Mentally, emotionally and physically. He was disgusted with the state of himself, hating the chaos he was in and the filth all over him. It reminded him of the farm and behaving like the unhinged beast everyone thought he was, for the sake of a taste of magic. Was it too much to ask to never be that helpless again? To not have to rely on others simply to survive?

His parents' conceited faces flashed across his mind, and a crooked smile broke through his grimace. After everything he'd done, there was nothing worse left to do, in order to claim what was rightfully his by birth. He'd almost been there until Owaen had appeared like the golden child from stories about destiny and justice and all that crap. If Cas had control of himself, he might have been able to swan out there and act like the big brother that he was... except Owaen had never let him be that, had he? On their father's orders, too. Owaen was used to prancing around like a peacock and treating Cas like a broken little sparrow.

No, not again.

Never again.

Fuck that.

Unable to contain himself, Cas threw back his head and screamed his curses to the wind. It had been *torture* to hold them back in the city whilst the others had been taking their leisurely fucking time.

"Fuckity fuck fuck *fuuuuck*!"

Ahead of him, Flare moaned fearfully into the wind. Disgusted with the dragon for no reason at all, Cas eyed the row of spikes along Flare's neck. He spared a wild moment to wonder at how many he'd need to slice off in order to stop the dragon from fucking whining.

His hand jerked at the thought and the movement hurt so badly he was afraid he was going to pass out. To comfort himself, Cas hugged the egg tighter, its cold, rough surface irritating against the old scars and new bruises across his skin.

"You're mine," he muttered to the egg as his skin itched.

Although he hated them, he could have healed the scars at multiple points when he had been flush with magic at various times throughout his life. Except it seemed fitting to keep them, a delightful reminder of the first time he'd woken up naked in Morgan's bed. His parents hadn't been there to help him, but Morgan had. Swollen and sore, a young Cas had woken up with his fist clenched around the one bee that hadn't died. He'd worn the scars proudly for her, along with the others that Morgan had added later.

"Why are you so perfect everywhere, Caspian?"

Cas laughed. "I'd love to say I was born perfect. But I was born missing a vital ingredient, so I can't."

Morgan's voice had been mocking. "Magic isn't everything, you beast."

"Puh. What do you know? Magic is everything to me. Along with you."

"Why me?"

"Why not?"

"That's not an answer, Caspian."

Cas had shrugged, smiling, hands on his hips while he posed, standing over Morgan where she lay on the soft grass.

"Caspian, stop that. You look ridiculous."

His smile widened until he was leering at her like a drunken whore.

"Fuck you, Caspian."

He'd shown her a new pose while biting his bottom lip. "Yes, please."

Blinking numbly, Caspian drifted awake again. He was swaying. His hand was a bundle of white-hot agony. He was also aroused.

"What the fuck... *now*?" he grumbled.

Even for him, there was just no way that could have happened right now.

Probably.

Flare's wing beats had changed, and he realised they were flying lower, closer to the endless sea of trees, their different greens wavering across his watering eyesight. It looked like they were burning, but with shadows, not flames. It seemed fitting that he was delirious and thinking of the forest burning across the entire fucking continent. He was interested in how bright things burned, along with how much pleasure he could partake in while getting what he wanted.

"I want it," Cas hissed.

Flare's scales rippled beneath him. "W-what?"

Shouting to the wind and blinking away the tears of pain in his eyes, Cas laughed, more than just a hint of hysteria to his voice.

"I want it!"

"What do you want?!" Flare was flying more erratically now, his voice a plea.

Cas closed his eyes, enjoying the bracing wind as it loosened some of the grit and dust out of his hair, wondering if Morgan had seen this in her dreams. She sometimes saw things that happened later.

Had she seen this?

His brother turning up here and now, had she seen the joke of it coming together, in which Cas' was the unwilling punch line?

Starting to black out again with pain, Cas grabbed his crotch and squeezed himself hard with his broken hand, the pleasure and the pain mixing, hot and cold sensations racing through his frayed nerves and snapping him awake.

"I want more!" he cried.

"More w-what?"

Cas threw back his head and crowed. "All of it! Everything!"

I'll see you soon, Skye, your destiny is waiting.

He hugged the egg closer, the sentient crystal pressed to his heart, to his scars.

Your destiny is right here.

I'll see you soon too, Morgan, my wonderful Morgan.

"You wanted Owaen to take care of me, father?" he yelled to the grey sky.

"Well, fuck you both! It's *my* turn to take care of *him* once and for all."

Flare was muttering under his breath, a deep rumble on the wind.

"Speak up, dragon!"

"I-I don't understand," Flare whined. "I...I just want..."

"What?" Cas urged loudly, as he fought to calm himself down, the agony pulsing in his hand, the pain making him wild. "What is it that *you* want, my giant, sparkling berry?"

The dragon shuddered beneath Cas in great ripples along his purple scales.

"Oh... I want..." Flare said, almost apologetically. Cas leaned forward as much as he dared to catch the words. Flare raised his voice. "I'm *hungry*."

Cas sat back. He blinked slowly. Well, why not? One had to feed and water their horse, didn't they?

How did one keep a hungry dragon satisfied amidst this mess? A dragon that was still a liability, with how futilely Cas had tried to bind them to each other? As if the answer sprang from his subconscious, the image of a dark tunnel from long ago bloomed within his mind. The place was situated within a steep, black mountain, where the tunnel had led to a cave. After Shadow Light had destroyed the City of the Seers and disappeared at the same time as Skye had, Cas' hand had touched that tunnel wall. And he had sensed his brother sealed inside. Cas had sensed both Owaen and the slow, magnetic pulse of rich, potent quartz.

As his hand throbbed on the rock, so had the crystals beyond the sealed wall.

Hmmm.

If Owaen was free, so was his resting place.

His choked laugh became a mad cackle. Black spots and strange shapes danced across his vision from the agony in his throbbing hand as he gave his groin another squeeze. He smiled as Flare's scales rippled with unease beneath him.

"So you're hungry, Flare Shining One?" he sang above the wind.

Cas licked his dry lips, tasting mischief amongst the blood and dust.

"Let's go *eat*."

The Nightfall Series
continues...

Keep turning for an exclusive preview of Book Three

Shop The Nightfall Series
and sign up to The Nightfall Newsletter:

www.lorentuxford.com

Nightfall in the Forest of Destiny

The Watcher
Year 361
Aneirin City

"Fuck the Elves."

"Yeah! Fuck 'em."

"They bewitched our king!"

"That bloody bitch! Have you seen how she looks at us with those strange, bright eyes?"

"Aye! All of them! With their unblemished skin, looking like they've never worked an honest day in their lives, filled with dark spells and curses as they are."

"Here, here…"

"Elven scum!"

"Animals!"

"Now we can't meet in the holy temple of our own city, now that it's being used to house their bloody elder council! How insulting is that?"

"At least there's ale here-"

"That's not the point, idiot!"

"Oi. Keep your bony elbow off me, mate. That hurt, my wound is still bleeding-"

"Well, don't be daft then."

"The Elves came to wipe us out, and yet we are expected to welcome them with open arms?"

"Too right!"

"We need to wipe them out instead."

"It's only fair… and our new king wants us to be fair, doesn't he?"

Riotous laughs and slurred catcalls erupted from both men and women. As the noise settled, a single, low voice spoke with quiet determination.

"So we deal with them."

Thoughtful silence filled the room beyond the inn's back wall, laughs fading to assertive murmurs. After a moment, a throaty belch joined the thrum. The wooden screech of chair legs scraping along the stone floor set the Watcher's ears into a flinch. A young woman called out, her voice laced with scorn.

"We *will* deal with those pretty fuckers. Permanently."

Laughter and jeers resumed, louder, as tin mugs clinked.

"Here, here!"

"Permanently!"

"We kill them all!"

"Yes!"

"Exactly." Satisfaction laced the low voice of the man who had spoken earlier.

Wyll's voice.

The Watcher's hands clenched.

"I think, ladies and lads," Wyll continued, as the private back room of the inn filled with quiet expectation, "that is exactly what we must do."

Ear pressed resolutely to the outside back wall of The Wet Oak, a middle-class inn of good repute, the Watcher bit their bottom lip. The rear alley, exposed to the chill air rolling down the jagged red slopes of the mountain range above the city, meant their legs were cramping, face numb. A cloak was pulled up high about their neck, but as night fell, the temperature followed. With no clouds obscuring the sky, bright stars blazed crisp and clear after the day's icy rain. It stank of stale wine and fresh piss amongst the mossy cobbles and dank puddles. Yet the Watcher stayed put, crouched in the same position for some time.

Occasionally, hearty aromas floated past from both familiar and foreign foods cooking nearby. The Watcher's mouth watered, yet they didn't move. They had come for one purpose, one that hadn't panned out. But they stayed as slurs and curses had risen in pitch and fervour, aimed at the foreigners residing in Aneirin.

The Elves.

The Watcher was both fascinated by and furious with them. Heart thumping with sickening irregularity, they slumped against the damp wood at their side.

With only the occasional cat hissing from a roof nearby, it was still here, at odds with the heated exchanges beyond the wall. The atmosphere had turned from drunkenly bitter to sober and serious, the slurs darker, meaner. Now, after one voice cursed another for making a drunken pass at the server bringing more ale, the voices hushed.

A door closed with a dull thump that the Watcher felt through the wood and plaster against their icy cheek. Voices cheered again, mugs clinking as a fresh toast was made.

"To the fucking Elves!"

Riotous laughter reverberated through the wood and plaster. Someone hiccupped with coarse abandon. The scornful girl said something that the Watcher didn't quite catch. Wyll must not have either.

"The king?" he queried, voice clear above the din.

A clank of what may have been a tankard slamming onto the table shut down all other conversations. The Watcher held their breath, sour aromas thick in their chilled nose.

"Yes." The girl raised her voice, her tone dripping with resentment. "What of the king, and his misled, sympathetic heart?"

Malicious undertones seeped through the thin cracks between wooden planks. These finally died down as a throat was cleared.

"The king?" Wyll mused with careful consideration amongst the expectant hush. "Hmmm, what shall we do?"

Nightfall in the Forest of Destiny
Book 3 of The Nightfall Series
Buy Now: www.lorentuxford.com

The Continent of Beinacoilia

Aneirin: Human Kingdom of Beinacoilia, built into the side of red mountains. Farmlands follow the curve of the valley, surrounded by forest. The trees in the south are many times the size of those found elsewhere.

Baile Fuar: Began as an open-cut quarry, supplying stone to the City of the Seers. The town is in three parts, along the rim, on the quarry floor, and tunnelled into the bedrock. The townsfolk are a mixture of races and are generally suspicious of outsiders. It features multiple hot springs.

Baile Mara: The City on the Sea, east of Aneirin. The city and its surrounding beaches comprise black volcanic rock. To those who live inland, the city is thought to be completely lost beneath the waves, after a fatal cataclysm in the mid 200s.

Lolihud: A series of vast caves in southern Beinacoilia, where most Elves live. Burrowed under the icy mountain ranges, the Elves mine crystals and rare minerals for the Dragons, who have all but disappeared. Magic amongst the Elves is fading. The name 'Lolihud' is derived from the old language, roughly translating to 'magic candy'.

Mionlach: Where the Dragons preferred to dwell, in the northern part of Beinacoilia. It is the warmest location on the continent due to volcanic activity.

The City of the Seers: Built to house scholars and record their works. Dragons were active in the design and construction, hence its impressive scale. This city was the meeting place of the Council, consisting of Humans, Elves and Dragons. In ruins since the early 300s, the first foundations were laid in the year 0, and left alone for many decades.

Acknowledgements

Thank you to The Order of Oodies. These adventures would not have made it to the page without your unwavering kindness, inspiration, humour, love, encouragement and help. Thank you all for everything, including your sharp eyes and grammar guardianship.

Biggest sis, thank you for your help along with my crowd of little phalluses. The details really are exquisite. Middle sis, thank you for keeping my spirits up. You really did. Thank you also to my mum. I wouldn't have made it this far without your support.

Thank you to all who took me seriously all those years ago, even when making me laugh, beloved friends and family in every time and place.

Thank you to all the great authors that have come before me, for all the stories that you share. I hope to live up to the glorious paths you forged for the rest of us to wander with quartz dust in our eyes.

To all who listened to me talk about crystal penises and cowardly dragons, thank you.

x

Loren

About the Author

After making her own books as a small child, Loren decided it was time to share her stories with the world, much to the delight of her dark sense of humour. With multiple books published, the capricious dialogue of Loren's chatty imagination is finally settling down... sort of.

Born in Australia, Loren enjoys writing, stargazing, birdwatching, strong coffee, wild places, overgrown cemeteries, reading and daydreaming.

www.lorentuxford.com